Murray, Edmund P.
The peregrine spy.

$24.95

| DATE | | | |
|---|---|---|---|
| | | | |
| | | | |
| | | | |
| | | | |
| | | | |
| | | | |
| | | | |
| | | | |
| | | | |
| | | | |
| | | | |
| | | | |
| | | | |

BAKER & TAYLOR

# THE PEREGRINE SPY

# THE
# PEREGRINE SPY

## EDMUND P. MURRAY

THOMAS DUNNE BOOKS ≋ ST. MARTIN'S PRESS
NEW YORK

THOMAS DUNNE BOOKS.
An imprint of St. Martin's Press.

www.stmartins.com

Library of Congress Cataloging-in-Publication Data

Murray, Edmund P.
    The peregrine spy / Ed Murray.—1st ed.
        p. cm.
    ISBN 0-312-30367-X
    1. Intelligence officers—Fiction.    2. Americans—Iran—Fiction.    3. Iran—
Fiction.    I. Title.
    PS3563.U766P47  2004
    813'.54—dc22

                                                                          2003058542

First Edition: April 2004

10   9   8   7   6   5   4   3   2   1

*To*
*Patrick C. Murray*
*and*
*Marie-Françoise Murray*

## ACKNOWLEDGMENTS

Experience and imagination inform *The Peregrine Spy* as a novel. As a chronicle of Iran's Islamic Revolution of 1978–79 and of the machinations of the American and Russian intelligence communities during that upheaval, however, research plays a major role. Like the novel's main character, Frank Sullivan, I have never been much good at bureaucratic detail. I am therefore particularly indebted for information on the operational details and inner workings of such organizations as the Central Intelligence Agency, the National Security Council, the U.S. Department of State, and the Soviet KGB to a wide range of authors, including Vladimir Kuzichkin, Philip Agee, Victor Marchetti and John D. Marks, David Wise, William H. Sullivan, Edward Shirley, Milt Bearden, Ronald Kessler, Tom Margold, James A. Bill, and Gary Sick. I have been scrupulous in using only operational details previously written about in other easily available publications. Other writers about this period in Iran's history whom I have relied on include Ken Follett, Elaine Sciolino, Manucher and Roxane Farmanfarmaian, Ervand Abramian, Betty Mahmoody with William Hoffler, Baqer Moin, Robin Woodsworth Carlsen, Amir Taher, Philip Hiro, Shaul Bakhash, Sandra Mackey, Diane Johnson, and Robin Wright. Rick Roberts's unpublished memoir on living with acromegaly helped build the character of Vasily Lermontov. I owe a heavy debt to many Iranians who did their best to educate me about their complex country, its history and its religious conflicts. I also relied heavily on various services of the New York City Library system, including its microfilm archives of *The New York Times, The Washington Post, The Wall Street Journal,* and other periodicals.

Many hands helped shape the manuscript at various stages of its evolution, including Carl Brandt, Patrick C. Murray, William C. Long, Andy Armstrong, Joel Foulon, Paul Henze, and especially Peter Wolverton and John Parsley at Thomas Dunne Books/St. Martin's Press, and the book's very fine copy editor, India Cooper.

# PART I

Caspian
Sea

ARMENIA
AZERBAIJAN
TURKEY
SYRIA
TURKMENISTAN
UZBEKISTAN

★Tehran

AFGHANISTAN

IRAQ

IRAN

KUWAIT

SAUDI ARABIA

Persian Gulf

BAHRAIN
QATAR

U.A.E. OMAN

PAKISTAN

Gulf of Oman

Arabian
Sea

# TEHRAN, IRAN

## 1978

0 Miles    1    2

0 Kilometers    2    3

TARASHT

Shayad Square ■

Mehrabad
Airport

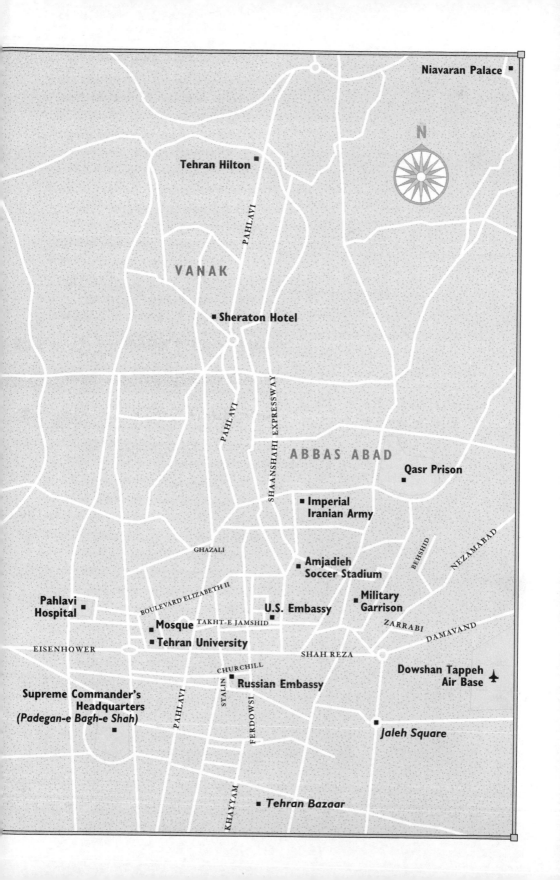

Niavaran Palace ▪

**N**

Tehran Hilton ▪

PAHLAVI

VANAK

▪ Sheraton Hotel

PAHLAVI

SHAANSHAHI EXPRESSWAY

ABBAS ABAD

Qasr Prison ▪

▪ Imperial
Iranian Army

GHAZALI

▪ Amjadieh
Soccer Stadium

BEHSHID

NEZAMABAD

Pahlavi
Hospital ▪

BOULEVARD ELIZABETH II

▪ U.S. Embassy

Military
Garrison ▪

▪ Mosque    TAKHT-E JAMSHID

ZARRABI

DAMAVAND

EISENHOWER

▪ Tehran University

SHAH REZA

CHURCHILL

Dowshan Tappeh
Air Base ✈

PAHLAVI

STALIN

▪ Russian Embassy

FERDOWSI

Supreme Commander's
Headquarters
*(Padegan-e Bagh-e Shah)* ▪

▪ *Jaleh Square*

KHAYYAM

▪ *Tehran Bazaar*

# CHAPTER ONE

NOVEMBER 1, 1978

S ully, have I got a surprise for you."

"I love surprises," said Frank.

Frank Sullivan remembered the first time he'd shaken hands with Dan Nitzke. Clammy. That slick, sticky grip had worked its way into his memory: the touch, the feel of the way the agency had manipulated his life over the past dozen years. He corrected himself. *The way I let the agency manipulate my life.* He glanced at the hands now twisting the steering wheel of the car Dan drove. *I know how that wheel feels,* he thought.

Frank had expected to spend a few relaxed days in Washington, finding an apartment, settling into the job that was waiting for him, and getting a new driver's license. Then he'd fly back to New York, pick up his son, and head off for a weekend at the apartment he lived in now, across the river in Weehawken. As promised, Dan Nitzke had met him at the Eastern shuttle baggage chute.

"Got much luggage?"

"Sort of. Two suitcases, a garment bag. I like to travel light, but I figured I'm going to be living here."

"Yeah," said Dan, looking away at the first of the suitcases tumbling out of the chute and onto the conveyor belt. "You'll be living here." His clear blue eyes peered out over his black-rimmed glasses as he glanced back at Frank. "Once this other thing's over."

Frank said nothing. He studied the honest blue eyes that watched him over the thick plastic rims. He remembered the days—and the long nights—when those eyes had been red-rimmed and rheumy and a meeting with Dan meant keeping a bottle of J. W. Dant bourbon shuttling between them across the Nitzkes' dining room table. Since then, Dan had found his way back to sobriety. The eyes were clear now, but the rosacea that pocked his nose and cheeks remained. Frank watched him as they picked their way through the tiny, packed parking lot at National Airport. Dan looked away again. "I'll lay it out for you in the car. Boy, are you gonna be surprised. We got a lot to do today."

Today, thought Frank. November 1, 1978. I better remember the date. This is going to be one of those days my life changed. Again.

They sped through the Virginia suburbs. Dan talked nonstop, obliquely, with the radio turned high to country music and used car commercials. "We could've got you a license right there in Arlington, but it's always mobbed, so I figured I'd run you down to Fairfield 'cause it's still pretty much country down there and there's never any wait, you'll be in and out in an hour, and then I have to get you to the Triple A to get an international license and then, guess what, over to the Pentagon."

"The Pentagon?"

"Well, it's Pentagon because all the host-country people you'll be working with are military, but before that we have to get you to a barbershop. Hair's got to be shorter and that beard has to come off because—I mean, it might be different if it's the navy, maybe you could at least keep the mustache, but Gus Simpson was in the marines, but the closest military counterpart is a navy commander so we decided Gus gets to be navy, you know Gus, so . . ."

"We never met," yelled Frank.

"No foolin'?" Dan's torrent stopped, but only for a moment. A few years ago he would have said, "No shit?"

"What the hell is this all about?"

Dan drove now with just his right hand on the wheel, twisting a thin strand of hair with his left. Though Dan could handle the written word with clarity and precision, Frank had learned with experience to follow his rambling conversations by waiting patiently for signposts. "Well, the third guy, you don't know him, but he has an army background, so that leaves you with the air force officer rank parallel to your grade, which will make you a major, but the air force likes its men clean shaven, and all that has to happen today because you're on the Pan Am 110 flight out of Kennedy tonight."

Frank reached over, touched the hand Dan had on the wheel, and waited for him to stop. "I go along with the haircut and the beard before I even know what the deal is, right? So then you've got me hooked and . . ."

"Sully, you're great. Like I always say about you, you're like the old fire horse. You hear that fire bell and you start salivating, ready to get right back in harness."

Too true, thought Frank. Too damn true. A crackling alert to a shooting or a fire over his police radio when he'd started his newspaper career as a reporter. Or another agency call to a dangerous job in a distant place. And he was gone. Determined to do the job and do it right. His own writing put aside. The woman he lived with, the son he neglected, forgotten. It had happened in the past. He did not want it to happen again. But he'd heard the fire bell.

"You were never here," Jackie had said, often, after they split. He knew he'd lost her because of the agency, and he'd vowed he would never inflict himself, or the agency, on a woman again. At least not for more than a night or a weekend or a month. My excuse for screwing around, he called it in cynical moments. Or my fear of getting hurt. Again. Or hurting someone else.

Dan's monologue sped on. "I also gotta drop you off near the embassy so you can get your visa. It's all arranged, but you have to go to the embassy on your own, and you'll need your air force travel orders and Pan Am tickets first. I'll pick you up same corner where I drop you forty-five minutes later. I'll swing by every fifteen minutes. You know that drill."

"You've thought of everything," said Frank, guessing that Dan wanted him to ask what embassy he intended to drop him off at. Frank, suspecting he knew the answer, didn't ask.

"Yeah, well, we had to. Besides, Sully, they really need you on this. Guys like you and Gus. Guys with real news media experience. And Third World experience. There's not much of that expertise left inside. The idea comes straight out of the National Security Council, and I've gotta believe your old buddy Pete Howard had a hand in it. NSC and the agency've been working on this a long time, and then it all kind of jelled in a hurry."

"And you thought I'd go for it."

"We sure as hell hoped so. I know how bad we need you, and some of the bureaucrats we have, they're suspicious of a guy like you because you've never been one of them. In fact, that's going to be a problem because the other guy on the team, I call him Archie because his name is Bunker, Frederick J. Bunker, he's a Mormon, real straitlaced and a real good bureaucrat, but he doesn't know squat about media or much about the field. You'll get along fine with Gus, but it's Archie Bunker you'll have to worry about. You figure out where it is?"

"I don't think I want to know."

"Yeah, but I know you read the goddamn *Post* and the *Times* and the *Wall Street Journal* every friggin' day, so I know you've been reading what's going on, so I bet you figured it out, right? So tell me what you think."

Friggin', thought Frank. Another new word.

Dan turned and watched him and laughed nervously over the loud twang of a Johnny Cash song as Frank spoke the two syllables.

"Iran."

"Hey, I couldn't even hear what you said, I was laughing so hard, but I read your lips, and I knew you'd figure it out."

Frank shook his head and began chanting, "Hell, no. I won't go. Hell, no. I won't . . ."

Wrapped up in his own reactions, he'd forgotten how Dan had been shamed by his oldest son. He had been a draft resister during the last stages of the Vietnam War.

"The hell you won't, boy." Dan's lips had tightened. He had both hands on the wheel, and his knuckles turned white.

"Sorry about . . ."

"Forget it," said Dan. "How come you let your license run out?"

"Living in Weehawken's like living in Manhattan. I don't need a car, so I let the license slide."

"But your passport's okay?"

"Yeah. I may not need a car, but I never know when you folks might give me another chance to jump on an airplane. So I keep the passport up-to-date. But Dan, this time I'm not going."

"Well, think about that a minute. Since you signed on again, you know what that contract's like. It's like a landlord's lease. Unless you want to try to break the contract, and that's not possible, they can send you anywhere they want. Besides, you got a great job waiting for when you get back, and some of us have figured out how we can qualify everything you've ever done so ten years or so down the road you qualify for a pension."

"Dan, that's nice. I appreciate it, but I don't ever figure to collect any pension anywhere."

"But all you got do is hang in there with the new job once you're back and it's yours for life. You may not care about pensions and security now, but, I mean, you aren't twenty-one anymore. By the time your kid gets into college and talkin' about grad school, you may be damn glad to have that two-thirds pension check coming in every month."

"It's the kid I'm thinking about, Jake. He's ready to move down here and live with me. Start junior high down here."

"The new job fits in perfect with that."

"I want the job," said Frank, "but I want it now, not maybe someday when I maybe come back from Iran."

"Oh, you'll come back okay. It's not that dangerous over there. Besides, there's somethin' else you should know about it,"

"Wrong," said Frank. "Whatever it is, I don't want to know about it."

"There's somebody you know over there," said Dan.

"There's probably a lot of people I know over there. Half the reporters in the world are over there, and since by now I must know half the reporters in the world, there's a fair chance there may be a fair number of people I know over there."

"Funny you should say that. 'Cause this guy's supposed to be a journalist. For Tass."

Frank stared at the highway ahead. He said nothing.

"I suppose you can guess?" said Dan.

Yeah, I guess I can guess, thought Frank. Vassily Lermontov. He had begun to grind his teeth and made the effort to stop.

"I mean, there's not much chance of you running into him," said Dan. "You'll be locked up with I-ranian military types all day, and there isn't much of a diplomatic cocktail circuit over there anymore, and from what I know of his m.o., your old Soviet buddy'll be running around with the usual cast of left-wing students, but I thought I better let you know he's over there, because I guess he hasn't been too happy with you ever since what happened to him in Ethiopia."

"No, and he wasn't too happy with what he saw going down in Angola, but we did have some interesting conversations in Rome. And Beirut."

"I heard he tried to set you up in Beirut," said Dan.

"Somebody did. Somebody took a couple of shots at me. Lermontov swore it had nothing to do with him."

Two flimsy cars, thought Frank. And a handgun firing three rounds that shattered a headlight. Not a real effort to kill him. A message, perhaps. But who from? After Ethiopia, Lermontov might have motive enough to kill him. Frank, working closely with Ethiopian journalists Lermontov tried hard to recruit, fed incriminating evidence to Pete Howard, then his chief of station. Pete alerted the director general of Haile Selassie's personal security agency. Lermontov and five others had been expelled. But in Beirut, where Frank had tried to unravel the assassination of the American ambassador, Lermontov had no cause to send him a message. He wondered, then and now, if someone in his own agency might have, a warning not to come too close to finding out who stood behind the murder of the ambassador, whose opposition to the war in Vietnam had earned him many enemies.

"What can I tell you?" he said aloud. "Actually, Lermontov and I get along pretty well. All things considered."

"He tried to recruit you, huh?"

"I reported it."

"Hey, I know you reported it, Sully."

"And we tried to recruit each other."

"Don't get so touchy."

"I've got a right to get touchy. Your CI grunts put me through a lot of shit because of Lermontov."

"They aren't my CI grunts. Besides, Counter Intelligence, they're supposed to be paranoid, right? And the way you and Lermontov keep flirting with each other, they may think you're in love with him."

"No. Gray-eyed Russians with short blond hair and thick wrists aren't exactly my type."

Especially when they maybe try to kill me. He wondered if he would ever know. But above all, he knew he wanted another round with Lermontov. He suspected that before the day was over he would be a clean-shaven major in—he couldn't believe it—the U.S. Air Force.

"You must feel like that first time," said Dan. "Remember?"

"I remember," said Frank. He'd been the assistant director of public relations at the AFL-CIO, at least in name, but since he'd drafted his first speech for George Meany he had moved increasingly into the president's orbit, often working with foreign trade union delegations, getting involved with the old man's pet projects like the American Institute for Free Labor Development and the African Labor Institute. It had been exciting at first, but the dead weight of the AFL-CIO bureaucracy and its marble mausoleum on Sixteenth Street soon began to weary him. Like many ex-newspapermen, he still read the industry's trade journal, *Editor and Publisher,* every week, starting at the back with the Help Wanted ads. That's where it had begun, with a blind ad in the back of the *E&P* issue of February 12, 1964, that read, "Experienced journalist with some teaching experience and an interest in Africa wanted for a two-year contract. Good salary and many benefits." He and Jackie had been married less than a year. They discussed it and decided Frank should give it a try.

Frank soon received a call from Patricia Rhoden, president of World Wide Communications. It was only years later that he discovered that someone else—Gus Simpson—got the job they originally had considered him for. Over a year later, World Wide called Frank again about another job, the job that took him to Ethiopia. It was another year before it finally happened. By then, at Pat Rhoden's suggestion, he had become active in the Washington branch of the American Friends of Ethiopia, and at one of their functions he met Dan Nitzke. Dan had introduced himself as a State Department foreign service officer who had just spent two years in Ethiopia. He was friendly, outgoing, brimming over with knowledge and advice about Ethiopia, unfazed when Ethiopians politely corrected him, and, by the end of a long evening, usually quite drunk.

Frank began getting calls, from the accountant in New York who did his taxes, from his former bosses at various newspapers, from his mother, from the literary agent who'd been trying without much success to sell his short stories. FBI agents had been around asking questions about him.

"Are you in some kind of trouble?" his mother asked.

Pat Rhoden called to ask him how quickly he could wrap up his work at the AFL-CIO and leave for Ethiopia.

"Well, I'll have to talk to Mr. Meany."

"He's wired. No problem," said Pat in her brisk way.

Frank held the phone away from his ear and stared at the receiver. Who are these people? he wondered. He heard Pat's voice. "Are you there?"

"Right here," he said into the mouthpiece.

"You'll need about ten days' briefing here at our office in New York. We have you booked out on the twenty-first. You know about the airline strike. Pan Am's the only American carrier into Europe, but Juan's a good friend of ours."

Juan? Who the hell is Juan? wondered Frank.

Pat must have read his mind. "Juan Trippe, you know, the president of Pan Am, so that's been worked out. Then it will be Ethiopian Airlines into Addis." She hammered out details and schedules, the car that would pick up Frank and Jackie at the airport, the apartment that would be waiting for them in New York. "Oh, you and your wife, Jackie, should both resign your jobs as soon as possible. Decide what belongings you'll want shipped over, what you want put in storage. We'll take care of all the arrangements."

It all moved rapidly, according to plan.

On his second day in WWC's headquarters overlooking the library lions on Fifth Avenue, Frank went into Pat Rhoden's office and was startled to see Dan Nitzke bounding up out of an overstuffed easy chair to greet him. "Hi, I bet you're surprised to see me. And boy, have I got a surprise for you."


"This is Fairfield coming up now," said Dan. "We'll be at Motor Vehicle in five minutes."

"I feel like I've been shanghaied," said Frank. "Again."

"That day in New York?"

"That day in New York."

"You should have seen the look on your face when I told you I didn't really work for the State Department."

"I can imagine."

"Boy, were you surprised."

"Yeah," said Frank. "You surprised me, all right." And I surprised myself, he thought.

They raced through the day, pretty much the way Dan had outlined it. There had been a wild, improvisational quality to it all that Frank enjoyed. The professionalism of the Pentagon cover unit impressed him. They were in and out in fifteen minutes with air force documents, including airline tickets and travel papers that identified him as Major Francis J. Sullivan. The photo on his ID card looked just like his unfamiliar, clean-shaven self.

"Without that beard, you look like a leprechaun," said Dan.

"I want my beard," said Frank.

"When you retire from the air force, you can grow a beard."

"How long before I get to retire from the air force?"

Dan shrugged. "Don't ask me. After the war, I guess."

Their footsteps echoed down the Pentagon's endless, rubber-tiled corridors as they left the cover unit. Frank studied his documents. "True name," he said.

"What did you expect? We don't have time for all that other mumbo-jumbo."

"We never do."

"What's the diff? You've never been blown."

Their whirlwind day included an hour at Langley with two Near East Division types he'd never met before and a quick pass at the polygraph, including what Frank by now considered a routine rehash of his years of contacts in many countries with Vassily Lermontov.

"Flying colors," said the technician, who looked painfully young to Frank.

It was Frank's first time in the headquarters building. All his previous contact had been filtered through the agency proprietary World Wide Communications, the firm that recruited him. The awesome structure, with its multiple rings of security, intrigued him. When he thought of all the odd, messy threads dangling from the edges of his life, he wondered why he had ever been recruited or how he had gotten through the security checks. But he admitted to himself that he'd been surprised by the sophistication of an intelligence agency that had a place for characters like himself—or even Dan Nitzke.

"Will there be contact with the Shah?" he asked the Near East team.

"Absolutely not," said one old Near East hand, who'd identified himself as Joe. They sat on hard-backed chairs around a bare metal table with a top of highly polished fake wood.

Frank shrugged. "I asked because I spent some time with him when he was on a state visit in Ethiopia in the sixties."

"Details," said Joe.

"I was writing speeches for Haile Selassie in those days," said Frank. "At some reception, he introduced me to the Shah. We got along. No big deal. We talked about jazz, weight lifting. When the Emperor came back from that twenty-fifth-hundred anniversary bash at Persepolis, he told me the Shah asked about me, said I should have come along. I wished I had. I heard it was quite a party."

"Keep talking," said Joe. He had close-cropped hair, a ruddy face, thick wrists, and slender hands. "But forget the party you didn't go to. I want to hear about the Shah in Ethiopia."

"He asked me to draft his farewell remarks. It pissed some of his people off, but he used what I wrote. We worked out together a couple of times. He was in pretty good shape in those days."

"He's a dead man now," said Joe. "Absolutely no contact. You'll be useless to us if the people you're working with get the idea you have a pipeline to the Shah. How much you know about what's goin' on over there?"

"I read the papers," said Frank.

"Well, not a lot gets in the papers," said Joe. "Shame you haven't got time to do some reading in on the intel. What we've got over there is a situation."

"We and the Brits have been propping this Shah up on his Peacock Throne ever since 1941," said Jack, another of the Near Easternites. "World War II. His father was pro-Hitler, and you have to remember that besides all that oil Iran has a long border with the Soviets."

"And back then," said Joe, "God help us, the Sovs were our allies."

"So we and the Brits kicked the father out and put the son on the throne."

"And we had to do it all over again in 1953," said Joe, "when the Shah's lefty prime minister, guy named Mosaddeq, tried to nationalize the oil industry. The Shah hit the panic button, ran off to Rome, ready to abdicate. The agency managed to stir up enough trouble to get rid of Mosaddeq and bring the Shah back."

"And we've propped him up ever since," said Jack. "Till now."

"Now we've come full circle," said Joe. "This guy has lost control. He tries to be tough, but he worries too much about, you know, world opinion. Whatever that is."

"The papers make it sound like he's been pretty ruthless," said Frank.

"Fact is, we've had a pretty good run with him," said Jack. "I mean, he may be a mean son of a bitch, but for almost forty years he's been our son of a bitch, know what I mean?"

"Up until lately," said Joe. "I mean he's still ours, but lately the son of a bitch hasn't been mean . . . I mean, strong enough. No matter what all these civil rights crybabies and liberal newspapers say about what a nasty bastard he is, fact is he isn't nasty enough. What we need is a military takeover that will ease out this guy and put his son on the throne."

"Just like we and the Brits did in 1941," said Jack.

"It's that," said Joe, "or we get a Commie takeover like already's happened next door in Afghanistan,"

"What about this holy man I've been reading about?" asked Frank.

"He can't amount to much," said Joe. "Hasn't even been in the country in a dozen years or so. He'd been holed up in Iraq a long time, but the Shah managed to get the Iraqis to kick him out. So now he's even further outta the picture, up in Paris."

"He may have some following in Iran," said Jack, "but the real trouble comes from the left."

"The problem is," said Dan, "we don't get much real intel these days except what *Savak* tells us, and *Savak* pretty much tells us what they think we want to hear."

"*Savak* has some of the best interrogators in the world," said Joe.

"Torturers, you mean," said Dan.

"Interrogators who get results," countered Joe. "And another thing . . ."

"We need some new eyes and ears on the ground," said Dan, interrupting again. "That's why we're sending these jokers over in the first place, am I right?"

"Is that why we're sending them over?" said Jack.

"We're sending them over because Pete Howard got another bee in his bonnet," said Joe, looking directly at Frank. "Now he's a big shot over at Brzezinski's National Security Council, he's more high and mighty than ever."

"He's a good friend of mine," said Frank.

"So I heard," said Joe.

Frank fought down his anger and tried to concentrate on what the two Near East Division men had to say. Covert Action approved the idea. Even the ambassador approved the idea.

"But we won't hold that against you," said Jack.

"How long?" asked Frank.

"How long what?" said Joe.

"How long will we be over there?"

Joe and Jack looked at each other. Neither showed any expression.

"As long as it takes," said Joe. "Just show these military types how to win the hearts and minds. You Covert Action types are all alike. Propaganda, that's your racket, isn't it?"

"Sometimes," said Frank. Sometimes, he thought to himself, it's intelligence.

"Covert Action does involve a bit more than propaganda," said Dan.

The two Near East men exchanged another glance. "Just be a fly on the wall," said Joe. "And keep your mouth shut."

"Just show the flag," said Jack. "And don't stir up any trouble."

"Another thing," said Joe. "You've got a limited mandate. Stay away from this KGB thug, this Lermontov. Soviet Division concurs fully with that stipulation."

Frank nodded, not quite sure what all this meant.

"No cowboy stuff, right?" added Joe.

Frank nodded again.

"Ergo," said Jack, "no weapons authorized."

"Speak swiftly," said Dan, "but don't carry a big stick."

"Don't pay any attention to him," said Jack. "When you get over there, pay attention to Bunker. He'll give you your marching orders."

"I hear he's a good man," said Frank.

"Damn good," said Jack. His eyes locked on Frank's. "Trained him myself."

"Balls," said Joe. "Fred Bunker never recruited a dink in his life."

"Don't start," said Jack. "Fred Bunker's one of the best bureaucrats in the business."

"Oh, I'll give him that," said Joe. He stood abruptly and reached across the table to shake Frank's hand. "Good luck over there. You'll need it."

They rode the elevator to Dean Lomax's office on the seventh floor. As head of Covert Action, Dean occupied a spacious office close to the director's. Frank's old mentor, Pete Howard, was there to greet him.

He had first met Pete Howard a dozen years before in Ethiopia when Pete took over as chief of station. Frank's cover job as an adviser to the Ethiopian Ministry of Information put him in close touch with the nation's news media, all of which were government controlled. His close relations with the minister of information, a favorite of the Emperor's, had led to several speechwriting assignments for Haile Selassie and an increasingly important role within his government.

Pete, currently on loan from the agency to the National Security Council, continued to monitor and influence Frank's career. As usual, he wasted little time in small talk.

"I suspect our friends in Near East/South Asia told you stay to away from the Shah."

"They sure did," answered Frank.

"'Course, you'll have to live with that."

"At least with the letter of that," said Dean.

"By all means stay away from the Shah," said Pete. "But if the Shah seeks you out, you can't very well turn your back on the emperor of a friendly nation, can you?"

"Somebody will have to say it's okay."

"Frank's right about that," said Dean.

"Yes," said Pete, "but in the fullness of time these things have a way of working themselves out. The Shah seems to know quite a lot about what goes on in his country. His ambassador here in Washington is very active, knows everyone."

"Nothing much we can do about it if word does get back to the Shah," said Dean. "Word that you're in Tehran, I mean."

"You established such a good rapport with him during the brief time he was in Ethiopia, if the Shah remembers you and seeks you out, as I suspect he will, it would be a terrible waste not to take advantage of what could be a real intelligence-gathering opportunity."

Frank studied Pete closely as he spoke. He won't say it out loud, thought Frank, but I think he just told me to forget what the goons in Near East Division had to say. *Just show the flag and be a fly on the wall.*

"This is a Covert Action assignment," said Dean, "and what we expect of you may not be quite the same as what Near East wants. The station in Tehran already provides the intelligence Near East wants."

Frank felt like a motorist, adrift in strange territory, afraid to sound dumb but needing a road map and directions. "I'm lost," he confessed. "You have to remember I've always worked outside. I'd heard about Covert Action because I knew you two guys, but I never knew what Covert Action was all about."

"And that's the way it should have been," said Pete. "As an agent, you had no need to know about our inner workings, but you're in the process of becoming something more than an agent. You might say we're bringing you in from the cold. We don't have time to explain everything to you now, but let's try some quick points of reference."

"Try to think of it this way," said Dean. "In terms of geography. Covert Action is global. It involves everything from clandestine propaganda operations to special forces military operations anywhere in the world. But always under-cover, always set up in a way that the U.S. government can deny, at least plausibly deny involvement."

"Near East is quite different," said Pete. "Pretty much regional, Egypt, Israel, and that part of the world the British used to describe as east of Suez. Soviet Division is something else again. Regional, yes. All of the Soviet Union, yes, but also with a stake in the recruiting of hard targets, Soviet intelligence and military officers, diplomats, academics, scientists, agents of influence, in short, important Soviets, wherever they may be, anywhere in the world."

"Including Tehran?" said Frank.

"Including Tehran," answered Pete.

"And including your friend Lermontov," said Dean.

"I know Lermontov," said Frank. "He's not my friend."

"You do go a long way back," said Pete, "and that's part of the problem. You work for Covert Action, reporting to Dean. And you've known Lermontov a long time. But right now Lermontov operates in the Near East Division's terri-tory. And Soviet Division considers him one of their hard targets. So both want you to stay away."

"And you have to remember, this is the Central Intelligence Agency," said Dean. "Intelligence gathering is central to all our divisions, Near East, Soviet, Covert Action. And in terms of Iran, we have some problems with our intelligence."

"Petty much throughout the intelligence community," said Pete, "people believe a Communist takeover of Iran is a distinct possibility. A military coup is seen as the only way to prevent the country from becoming another Soviet satellite. And what we keep looking for, and I have to include the National Security Council in this, we keep looking for field intelligence that supports this idea."

"I think it's fair to say," noted Dean, "that NSC depends on the agency. It has no resources of its own on the ground in places like Iran."

"If there's going to be a military coup in Iran," said Pete, "it's going to be hatched out of the building you'll be working in. Supreme Commander's Head-quarters. You'll meet daily with a committee of midlevel military officers. The top brass have offices in that same compound."

"It won't be easy," said Dean. "And you may have problems with your chief of station. Someone you know from your assignment in Rome."

"Rocky Novak," said Pete.

"Oh, yes," said Frank. "We know each other."

"But you worked out your problems before," said Pete. "I'm sure you can again."

"I'm glad you're sure," said Frank.

"And of course there's that other opportunity," said Pete. "I'm sure you were told to avoid your old friend Vassily Lermontov at all costs."

"That, too," said Frank.

"Of course, targeting Soviets in Tehran is Near East's turf. But you and Lermontov have been locking horns for so long it would be a shame not to give you another crack at him."

"But if I do see him I'll start hearing the same old story about how he's recruited me."

"Best way to put that nonsense to bed would be for you to recruit Lermon-tov, wouldn't it?"

"You think I can?" asked Frank.

"I don't think you should miss a chance to try," said Pete. "Tehran's a very small town, at least the foreign community in Tehran. I don't see how you could not run into each other."

"The Sovs have a pretty wide intel apparat in Tehran," said Dean. "Lermon-tov sees you on an airline passenger manifest or a visa list, you know he'll come looking for you."

"You shouldn't go looking for him, of course."

"No, 'course not," said Frank.

"Remember," added Pete, looking at the ceiling, avoiding Frank's eyes, "officially, you have to follow Near East's instructions. It's their turf. And your station chief over there, Rocky, is an old Soviet Division hand, which makes Lermontov of special interest to him." Pete lowered his eyes and looked directly at Frank. "But you work in Covert Action, responsible to Dean here."

"We realize all this is new to you," said Dean. "All these layers of command."

"Turf," said Pete, smiling.

"In the past you've always been the outsider, practically a free-lancer," said Dean. "But now that we're bringing you inside, you'll have to find ways to work within the parameters the rest of us live with."

"Turf," said Pete again, not smiling. "Frank, let me be blunt about this. When I heard that Lermontov was stationed in Tehran, I decided to push hard for you to get this assignment."

"You were already on my short list," said Dean. "You and Gus Simpson are among the few people we had available with extensive mass media experience in Third World countries."

"But no matter what anyone else may tell you, no matter anything else I may tell you, Lermontov was the deciding factor in your getting this assignment. Yes, using the mass media to improve the image of the Iranian government and the military is an important component."

"Intelligence gathering with your military counterparts, and possibly with the Shah, just as important," said Dean.

"But Lermontov is your one real mission," said Pete. "Your hidden agenda, if you like."

"Hidden," said Dean, "because you can't seek him out."

"After all," said Pete, "you were told not to. And of course you have to accept that."

"I accept that," Frank had said. But he promised himself he would not be a fly on the wall.

# CHAPTER TWO

The lumbering jet circled the cloud-shrouded mystery. An act of faith told him a city huddled down there, like a veiled woman at prayer, but below he could see only other planes etching long, looping ellipses through the dismal, unwelcoming sky. He counted six through shifting gray layers. Clouds. Mist. He suspected smoke. Planes appeared and disappeared. For nearly an hour, their plane had dipped and climbed among them, banking like a falcon, seeking, not finding a place to strike. A memory of a World War II movie flickered—grainy black and white. Or had it been a newsreel? Bombers stacked up and circling, one by one descending, a bomb bay opening, and wobbling sticks dropping toward shadowy targets suddenly visible below the clouds.

He'd caught the flight, Pam Am 110, the evening before, November 1, 1978, out of JFK. He twisted against his seat belt but could see no sign of the male flight attendants, who had been surly and uncommunicative since they boarded at Fiumicino Airport in Rome. Below, he saw each plane in its isolation, each part of a pattern, but alone. He thought of the hunting peregrine, wings folded tight to its dappled body, yellow talons striking. Alone. Returning to its nest overlooking the pigeon-thick park, the falcon would circle, leave food for the nestlings, and leave. No matter where he worked or at what. As a reporter, a speechwriter, a spy. No matter how he lived or with whom. With a woman he loved. With his son, alone.

He had called Jackie from National Airport, collect. She was abrupt. He told her what he could. She said, "Oh," frequently, in a flat tone. Sometimes, seeing Jake on weekends, he felt like an uncle. When he spoke to Jackie, he felt like an ex-husband.

"Can I speak to Jake?"

"I'll put him on. Have a nice trip."

See you next fall. Fall of the next Shah. Frank felt like a fool, a betrayer, a deserter.

"Hi, Dad."

He told Jake he couldn't tell him much.

"I understand, Dad." Jake, at eleven, was already getting too mannish for Jackie to handle. "Will I still come to live with you in . . ." Jake had learned to be discreet. "When you get back?"

"Bet," said Frank. "Soon as I get back and get settled in and find you a school."

"That's cool," said Jake. He laughed, nervously. "Well, good luck over there."

"Keep the faith," said Frank.

That was their sign-off. "I will," said Jake. Frank waited for the click of the phone and then hung up. He missed his son—and feared for the promise that they would be living together again. The promise hadn't been broken, but he feared it might be in danger.


He'd flown over the Atlantic, across Europe, and deep into the Middle East, wondering what lay ahead. He stared at the empty plastic cup on the tray in front of him. Whatever comes, he told himself, I have to do this. He knew that the intelligence he could glean from his military counterparts, and the Shah, would be a vital part of the job, but he saw intelligence gathering as a cover for the task that really mattered: recruiting Lermontov. He realized he would be going against the directions given him by Near East Division and instead taking his guidance from Pete Howard. Again. Metamorphosing from a lazy fly on the wall to a hungry, circling falcon. He felt thirsty but did not order a drink. The thirst was for the job. He crumpled the empty plastic cup and stuffed it into one of the seat-back pockets. He pushed the tray up and locked it in place.

He knew he'd been hooked and resented the disappointment he had caused Jake. Again. He wondered when, if ever, they would begin the life both had looked forward to. Father and son. School. Trying to be a friend, role model, and teacher to an adolescent who often mystified him. Holding down a job that would seem like a regular job with a suburban office to go to every day. Eventually, a suburban house. What Jackie, if they were still together, would call "a normal life, for a change."

Gus Simpson, who had boarded in Rome, had stretched out across a vacant row of middle aisle seats, securing seat belts above his knees and across his waist. Frank, standing in the aisle, had watched. "Snug as a roach in a hooch," said Gus as he tucked two square white pillows under his head and pulled a gray blanket around his shoulders.

Frank looked down at the trussed-up form of the man he had heard so much about. He sensed the curiosity he felt about Gus must be mutual, but even in the plane's secure, humming cocoon they remained wary, cordial, distant. Frank went back to his seat by the window and picked up the remnants of the previous day's *Washington Post* and *Wall Street Journal*. He again scanned the key stories. Only two in the *Post*. Both on the front page. "Workers Strike Iran's Oil Fields; Army on Guard," read one headline. "Shah of Iran Given Assurance of U.S. Support," said the other. Three of the *Journal*'s inside stories focused on the global impact of the oil strike. The main story warned, "Iranian Oilfield Strife Adds to Doubts About Shah's Ability to Hang On As Ruler." A page-one summary mentioned an "Ayatullah Khomaini" who called for more mass demonstrations near Tehran's bazaar. A newspaper strike had shut down the *Times* and the other New York papers since August. Frank missed them. He considered himself a newspaper junkie and hoped the strike would not diminish the number of New York dailies. He believed no one newspaper, and no single source of intelligence, could ever get complex stories right. The newspapers couldn't even agree on the spelling of Tehran. The *Times,* as he remembered, had it Teheran. It was Tehran in the *Post* and the *Journal*. He wondered if anyone had anything right about the country.

The plane rocked, and a brusque order to prepare for landing signaled a swift, bumpy descent. The clouds thinned; the plane stabilized, and patches of landscape shifted like a cubist collage in and out of focus: snow-smeared mountains sloping down through a desolate tree line; huge houses with brown, sprawling gardens and tin-roofed shanties.

A looming construction crane caught his attention. Pitched at an odd angle, it looked like a giant, distant, wounded bird, a pterodactyl fossilized into steel. A low cloud, swollen by smoke, swallowed it. The plane seemed to accelerate as it descended, suddenly free of the clouds. Frank counted the towers of smoke rising from the city—four, five, six, seven—and wondered what circle of hell waited. In some of the spiraling gray towers he could now see flashes of orange flame. What are we doing here? he said to himself. How did I let this happen to me? Again. He glanced up the aisle and saw Gus's face peering around the seat. His thin hair stood straight up. He fumbled the wires of the eyeglasses over his ears, registered Frank, and said, "This it?"

" 'Fraid so."

"Shit."

The landing flaps came down with a thud. Frank saw the cracked, potted, pale gray tarmac racing up at them. The huge plane bounced, wobbled, bounced again, and screeched along the runway with a fierce deceleration. The intercom crackled, "Please remain seated with your seat belts securely fastened while the captain taxis to a full stop at the . . . terminal. Thank you." The plane swung in a semicircle and stopped.

Here I am again, he thought. A job to do. And I want to get it done.

Armored personnel carriers, two orange fire trucks, and a white ambulance with the Red Crescent cruised by. His eyes followed an open jeep with a uniformed driver and a mustached man in civilian clothes standing with one hand on a mounted machine gun. Frank wondered if the man in mufti might be an agent of *Savak,* the Shah's secret police. The jeep sped under the plane's wing. A phalanx of uniformed soldiers with assault rifles approached on the run. Peering down with his nose pressed to the glass, Frank watched green helmets disappear under the fuselage. The passengers sat for twenty minutes in silence before the plane taxied forward. He had expected something grander, but the terminal that edged into the window frame from the right appeared ramshackle. Pale, peeling green and white paint on a wood-frame building with boarded-up windows. He saw two lines of soldiers with M-14s propped on their hips, forming a corridor that led to a wide doorway. He noticed the sign above it that said in English WELCOME TO TEHRAN.

Maybe that's how the newspapers should spell it, he thought.


Dan Nitzke had told Frank "how bad the agency needs you." Then, once he was in Iran, the assignment had begun with two days off, Thursday and Friday, the Islamic weekend. Embassy offices functioned both days, but Tom Troy, who headed the agency base at the Iranian Dowshan Tappeh air force facility, told them Rocky Novak, their embassy-based chief of station, wouldn't see them until Saturday.

"If that makes you guys feel like outcasts, get used to it," said Troy. "This is a base station, on Iranian air force territory. Lemme show ya the map."

The Sahab Geographic and Drafting Institute map of Tehran, thumbtacked to the whitewashed plasterboard wall behind Troy's gunmetal desk, showed a confused maze of streets, relieved at its northeast end by a long, irregular rectangle of white. "That's Dowshan Tappeh," said Troy. "Pretty fair-sized air force base, specially for bein' in the heart of town. Iranian flyboys tell us that's the way the Shah wanted it. If it ever gets attacked by Iraq or somebody, there'll be lots of civilian casualties in the neighborhoods right around it for the bleedin'-heart media cameras."

"I remember them well from Vietnam," said Gus.

"Like that," said Troy. "Big as it is, you can see these two major runways, but big as it is the U.S. of A., which has got a couple of hundred air force advisers here, real air force, plus us, gets sequestered in this little corner over here. Locked gates between us and them and security checks every time our air force guys gotta go over there, which is pretty fuckin' often since everything the Iranians got to fly is made in America and the Iranians never will learn to handle it on their own."

Frank was used to hearing Americans complain about their host-country counterparts, but while they had Troy's attention, he had other questions about Tehran.

"Where's our other work location?" he asked. "Supreme Commander's Headquarters."

"Over here," said Troy, pointing to a large hexagon with several buildings sketched in. "Again, right in the heart of town."

"And the embassy?" asked Gus.

"Right here, a lot closer to Supreme Commander's than we are here. Like I said, you guys are outcasts."

Though he and Gus had worked together in Vietnam, Troy seemed brusque and distracted as he introduced them to the office they would share with others on his staff. He turned them over to Stan Rushmore, a gruff, heavy-set New Yorker. Evening had set in as Rushmore turned over the keys to the Fiat Millecento that would be theirs for the duration of their stay. "Which may not be long," muttered Rushmore. Driving a Chevy Nova that looked huge compared to their Fiat, Rushmore led them to the house they would occupy. Frank followed, making mental notes on their short route to reinforce the hand-drawn map Tom Troy had given them. Rushmore pulled up at the curb in front of one of a series of identical houses. He climbed out of his Nova long enough to point to one of them and drove off.

"I get the feeling," said Gus, "no one's real anxious to have us here."

"Somehow," said Frank, "I get the same feeling."

They noticed the broken lock on the wrought-iron fence at the foot of the stone steps of the house they would occupy. "Wouldn't make much difference, would it?" said Gus. "Locked or not, that gate wouldn't keep out much."

Brick and poured concrete gave the house a solid appearance. Dark metal shades covered the ground-floor windows. In the damp, thickening twilight, the house stood like a blind sentinel, second from the corner in a row of five buildings, identical except for the varying colors of their front doors. The numeral 39, painted in black in stylized pseudo-Arabic script, stood slightly off center on the concrete arch over their dark green door. Lidless, empty plastic garbage cans were on their sides to the left of the steps, gaping at the street, rocking in the breeze that picked up as darkness gathered around them.

"Oh, well." Frank struggled up the steps with his bags. He fished in his coat pocket for a set of the keys Rushmore had given them, turned the dead bolt, then noticed what appeared to be three bullet holes in the center of the door. He caught Gus's eye and nodded toward the door. Gus leaned forward and grunted.

"Probably a traditional Persian symbol of welcome," said Frank.

"Nice tight cluster," said Gus.

What am I doing here? thought Frank.

He found the key for the lower lock and undid it. The heavy cedar door swung open on a shadowed hallway. He groped for a light switch, found it, flicked it, then flicked it two more times. The hallway stayed dark.

"Not to worry. Like a good Boy Scout, Father Gus came prepared." Gus dropped his bags in the hallway, unzipped an outside pocket on one, and came up with a flashlight.

"Better close the door first," said Frank.

"Good paranoid thinking."

Gus pushed the door shut, then flicked on his flashlight. They found the kitchen, tried the light switch without success, then discovered three candleholders on the chrome-topped table. Gus lit the candies, then, hat and coat still on, picked up the sheet of paper under one of the candles.

"'Welcome to your new home,'" read Gus, slumping into a chair. Frank watched from the kitchen door. "'Rent on this unit paid by base command and cleared with appropriate USG agencies for official personnel occupying premises. Owner lives in the corner house, number 35. You need have no contact with him. Report all problems to base command.' That's Troy, I guess," said Gus without looking up, "'Expect occasional power outages. Do not overstock the refrigerator as power outages are frequent. And redundant. Servants service premises, including dishes and laundry Saturday and Wednesday. Leave individual laundry in individual rooms. Do your own shopping at official U.S. Military Post Exchange. The attached map shows PX location and local restaurants, none of which are recommended. You will find some basics in the cupboard over the sink. Sincerely, Base Command.'"

"Welcome to your new home," said Frank. "I better put the car away."

Two teenagers, eyeing the car from across the street, walked quickly away when they saw Frank coming down the steps. Following Rushmore's instructions, he backed the car down the steep drive into the basement garage. He closed and padlocked the overhead door, surveyed the empty street, and climbed the stairs to the bullet-pocked entrance to his new home.

"Grab a candle," said Gus, "Let's take a look around."

They discovered a spacious, sparsely furnished living room adjacent to the kitchen. Its three front windows were covered with the same heavy metal that lined the inside of the front door.

"Nice view," said Frank.

They found a windowless bedroom behind the living room and behind that a utility room with boiler, hot water heater, washer, dryer, and ironing board. Rectangles where two windows and a back door might have been had been sealed up with concrete. They headed back toward the front of the house, and suddenly the lights came on.

"I guess that's a power in-age," said Gus.

They held on to their candles and glanced at each other. The lights faded off.

"Outage," said Frank.

Upstairs, cupping flickering candles, they found four open doors off the hallway. The first led to a bathroom with a frosted but unsealed window. The back bedroom had two curtained windows looking out over a narrow alley and the shuttered back windows of another row of houses.

"With a little help from a rope, that could be our back door," said Gus.

They found a middle bedroom without windows, an echo of its companion downstairs. The front bedroom featured a matching cherry dressing table, chest of drawers, four-poster bed, and wardrobe closet. The bed was made, thick with blankets and topped with a patchwork quilt.

"Nice room," said Frank. With his coat still on, he'd only begun to notice that the house was without heat.

"You can have it," said Gus, nodding over his candle at the three windows that looked out over the street. "I'll take the cul-de-sac down the hall."

The lights came back on, "That may be a sign," said Frank. He studied the room again, glanced at his candle, waited. He set the candle down on the dresser, waited another moment, then blew it out. The lights stayed on. "That is a sign," said Frank, "I'll take the room."

He headed downstairs for his luggage. He and Gus shuttled up and down, maneuvering a bag at a time on the narrow stairway.

"There's some cans of chicken soup in that kitchen cupboard," said Gus as he struggled to the top of the stairs.


The steaming ceramic bowls and the cold Formica tabletop conspired to form beaded webs of moisture. Frank stirred his soup, letting the steam spiral up to his nostrils. He could detect no smell. He tried a spoonful. Lukewarm and tasteless. Probably good for a cold, he thought.

"We have to find a better way," said Gus.

"To eat?"

"Please, Lord," said Gus, raising his pale, watery eyes over the wire rims of his glasses. Frank guessed that under better circumstances those eyes would be hazel.

"I promise we will," said Frank. "I'm a good cook."

From what he knew of Gus's past, Frank guessed him to be in his mid-fifties. He peered at Frank over the wire-rimmed glasses balanced on the tip of his nose.

"How much warning did you have about this?"

"None," said Frank. "I got off a plane in Washington, yesterday I think it was, expecting to go to work down that way. Instead, the old buddy who met me at the airport said, 'Boy, have I got a surprise for you.'"

"Yesterday?"

Frank nodded. "I think yesterday," He told Gus of the hyperkinetic hours he'd spent in and around Washington.

"Word I got in Rome," said Gus, "was you'd been briefed at Langley and would fill me in on whatever it is we're supposed to be doing over here. At least until Archie Bunker got on the scene."

"Do people really call him Archie?"

"Well, not to his face. Fred Bunker's his rightful name, and he's really not an Archie Bunker type, but he's the kind of good gray bureaucrat that old field farts like me find it hard to take seriously."

Dan Nitzke's description had been about the same. "Not much field experience, and for a guy in Covert Action he doesn't seem to know anything about news media, but, God help you, he's going to be head of your team."

That made no sense to Frank, but it seemed consistent with the rest of their assignment. None of it made much sense.

"Let me break it down to you as best I can, the way I got it from Dan Nitzke and a couple of guys in Near East. The idea seemed to originate in the National Security Council. I'd have to guess Pete Howard had a hand in it."

"Your rabbi," mumbled Gus.

"People say so," shrugged Frank. "I got the idea the Near East guys didn't much like Pete, or me and other Covert Action types."

"A lot of people resent Pete," said Gus, "because he's so good at what he does. And maybe a tad arrogant about it. You can also figure the Near East guys don't like having to handle an assignment from the National Security Council, which they see as a branch of the White House."

"What's wrong with being a branch of the White House?" asked Frank.

"You might be foolish enough to think State, the CIA, the National Security Council, the FBI, the White House, and so on were all on the same side. And the enemy is the Soviet Union and all its Eastern Europe satellites and Communist China. But that would be wrong. Our first and primary enemy is all those other bureaucracies we have to compete with for attention and budget. Plus, within the agency, you and I report to Dean Lomax, Covert Action, right?"

"Right," said Frank. "I guess."

"Covert Action has its own turf to protect, and the enemy at the gates is all the other divisions, Near East, Soviet, Eastern Europe, Africa, Far East, and on and on. Not to mention other shops like Counter Intelligence you don't even want to know about. Competition in house is even worse 'cause it involves career advancement, promotions, pensions, paychecks, all that really important stuff. It's only when we're done kickin' ass with all those other outfits that we can pay some attention to the Soviets."

"I've got a terrible feeling you're right," said Frank.

"Yeah, I'm right about all that," said Gus. "But I still don't have much of an idea what the job is. And why the hell we got elected."

"Okay," said Frank. "You know the Shah has a world of troubles on his hands. Protests. Shootings. Talk of torture. Demonstrations, not just here but Washington, New York, Paris, London. Just about any place that's got Iranian students. The agency and, I guess, NSC believe the Russians pull the strings."

"What about this holy man?"

"Khomeini, or whatever his name is?"

Gus nodded.

Frank had seen only a few brief references to the man identified as Ayatullah Khomaini by the *Journal* and Ayatollah Khomeini by the *Washington Post*. How important can he be, Frank wondered, if our leading papers aren't sure how to spell his name?

"I don't know," he said. "I get the feeling both State and Langley think the real problem is the Soviets."

"Sounds like World War III," said Gus.

"Maybe not quite."

"Yeah, it is." Frank had barely touched his soup. Gus had finished his. "You may as well hear it now. My favorite after-dinner topic. Simpson's theory of World War III. It's all the border wars and mad bombers, all the tribal shootups and head bashings that go on all the time all over the world. That's your World War III, my friend, and it doesn't matter whether we or the Russkies get involved or not. Fact, unless we think, usually by mistake, that our own national interest is involved, we won't get involved, and unless some worldwide television cameras stumble into it the rest of the world won't even much know it's goin' on and sure as hell won't give a damn."

Frank's soup had turned cold. He thought of warming it up but knew it would still be tasteless. "I wish we had some booze."

"Capital idea," said Gus. "The gentlemen retire to the drawing room for brandy and cigars."

"And discuss world affairs. Including the Gus Simpson World War III Protocol."

"Right," said Gus. "I wish I could drink to that. You know, your old friend Pete Howard for years has been trying to convince our frozen-stiff cold warriors that nationalism has become more important and more of a threat than Communism. The old-school types think World War III will happen between us and the Commies, like their version of what went on in Vietnam. To the Viets, they fought a war for national independence, independence from the French, the Chinese, and then, of course, from us. But we didn't want to hear that. For us it was a proxy war, just like Korea, us against the Soviets and Chinese Communists with the locals caught in the middle."

"Still doesn't sound like a world war," said Frank.

"Not if you just look at Vietnam. But this world war goes on everywhere, from Northern Ireland to South Africa, from the Philippines to Central America, India and Pakistan, Afars and Issas, Hutus and Tutsis, Jews and Arabs in the Middle East, Arabs and Christians in the Sudan, all the time all over the fuckin' world."

"What about here?"

"Sure, here. I mean, I just got off the boat, but I got a hunch what the Iranians want is to run their own country. By now they must be gettin' pretty tired of the game of nations bein' played on their lawn. They had the Russians and the Brits tearin' up their pea patch for more than a century, and the last thirty years or so they got our boots muddyin' up the carpet. But I got a hunch our friends in Near East Division didn't have much to say about that."

"Not hardly," said Frank. "Our side just wants the military to take over the country and use the Iranian news media to wage a, you know, 'win the hearts and minds of the people' campaign."

"Like we did in Vietnam," said Gus.

"I didn't say it was a good idea," said Frank. "I just said that was the idea. The Shah sent word to the military to set up a joint committee. The acronym, God help us, is Jayface. The Joint Armed Forces Ad Hoc Committee on Enlightenment."

"God help us is right," said Gus. "What's Jayface supposed to do?"

"Learn how to use the news media to enlighten the people about the wonderful role of the armed forces in preserving the nation."

"And killing its troublemakers?"

"Maybe not too heavy on that," said Frank. "Maybe we could cook up some worthwhile civic action programs. Publicize that."

Saying it out loud made him feel uneasy. Gus peered skeptically at him over the rims of his glasses.

"As for why you and me, I guess we're among the few guys still around the agency with real news media experience and who know how things work in Third World countries."

"More like how things don't work," said Gus.

"Maybe more like that," said Frank. "Anyway, the ambassador bought into the idea and sold it to the Shah. Seems the Shah had started to wonder if the Americans are still on his side. Jimmy Carter keeps talking about human rights and repression in Iran, and the Shah thinks this just encourages the opposition."

"I guess it might," said Gus.

"So maybe our real mission is to show the Shah that the U.S.A. wants to do what it can to help. The final word from one of the Near East guys was something like 'just show the flag and don't stir up any trouble.'"

"Wish I'd known," said Gus. "I would've brought a flag."

Frank wondered how much else he should tell Gus. About all that Pete Howard had said. About the Shah. And about what Pete had called "your one real mission," Vassily Lermontov—"your hidden agenda," Pete had added. Frank took that as a warning to keep it hidden.

"Anyway," he said, "after the Near East guys got done telling me what not to do, Dan took me up to Dean Lomax's office."

"Don't tell me," said Gus. "Lemme guess. Pete Howard was there."

"Yeah," said Frank. "He was."

"What words of wisdom did they have for you?"

"Well, enough to convince me to take the assignment."

"You had reservations?"

"Didn't you?"

"Well, yes, I did. And my wife wasn't too happy about me flying off into somebody else's civil war. Again. But I guess my curiosity got the better of me."

"I can relate to that," said Frank. "And Pete and Dean Lomax think the job has some real intelligence potential."

"With our friends in Jayface?"

"That, plus the fact that our Jayface meetings will be at Supreme Commander's Headquarters, where all the top military brass hang out. If there's a chance of a military takeover, that could be the place to find out about it."

"Makes sense."

"Maybe," said Frank. "But the guys in Near East told me they had all that covered. That this was just a goofy idea cooked up by NSC that nobody likes except the ambassador."

"Anyway," said Gus, "I'm glad the ambassador's on our side."

"Yeah, but problem is, our chief of station doesn't think much of the idea. Or of me."

"Rocky Novak?" Frank nodded. "What's he got against you?

"Long story, but we had a run-in a couple of years ago in Rome."

"On that books-to-Russia deal?"

"You know about it?"

"I inherited it," said Gus. "Couple years after you fired half the people involved."

Pete Howard, then still with the agency, and Dean Lomax had been part of what they called a board of directors with oversight of a proprietary company that openly produced Russian-language books, everything from Bibles to Dostoevsky to Solzhenitsyn, and covertly smuggled them into the Soviet Union. With offices in New York and throughout Europe, the operation, particularly in its Rome office, also became deeply involved with Russian refugees during the great exodus of the early 1970s. Sensing problems with the organization, the board recruited Frank to do an efficiency study and make recommendations for changes. Frank uncovered far more problems than the board had ever imagined, including an American agent in charge of the office in Rome who had become deeply involved with the Soviets.

"Rocky was gone by the time I got to Rome," said Gus, "but word was one guy you got rid of was a big favorite with Rocky."

"I didn't fire anybody," said Frank.

"But some people got fired," said Gus.

"Yeah, well, some people got fired. Some offices got shut down. Some people got shifted around. Some quit."

"All because of a report you wrote."

"No," said Frank. "All because they'd been fucking up. The guy Rocky was so high on even tried to defect. Good chance the Russians had been playing him for some time." When Lermontov arrived, he took over the development of Rocky's prize agent, a bearded, long-haired American who happened to look like Frank. He smiled at the memory. Lermontov had tried to recruit them both. Frank had wondered if he could tell them apart.

"Word I got was Rocky even blamed you for driving his boy over to the Soviets. And he dearly loved that book project because it gave him access to so many Soviet targets."

"Not that they ever recruited anybody worth a damn," said Frank.

"You expect more trouble from Rocky?"

"Yeah." Frank nodded and looked up at Gus. "I guess I have to."

"So why did you take the job?"

"Good question." Don't lie, he cautioned himself, but he knew he would hold back the truth About Lermontov. About the Shah. About himself. He stared into the bowl of unappetizing soup. "I guess I got tired of being an outsider."

"Meaning?"

"I guess I started out like you. Hired by a body shop. Working on contract. Starting pretty high up on the ladder, GS-14, without going through all the training and low-level assignments most everyone else goes through."

"And being resented for it," said Gus.

"Except I guess you went inside."

"Long ago," said Gus. "I got tired of being out in the cold."

"Yeah, I got tired of that and I got tired of being what amounts to a temp. I guess I wanted a steady job."

"But that job you went down to Washington for, I know a little bit about that job. If you took that, so I heard, they'd have brought you inside."

"That's the idea."

"Be careful what you wish for," said Gus. "I got my wish, and working inside turns out . . . what's the old cliché? The grass is always greener . . . someplace or other. But the deal I heard was they'd have brought you inside and qualified all your contract years for a pension."

"Yeah. That was the idea."

"But you didn't have to come over here to get all that."

"Well, no." Don't lie, he told himself. Just a stretch. "But Dan Nitzke made it sound like if I didn't take this assignment they might have to take another look at the job in Washington."

"That bastard," said Gus. "Look, that job was yours. I heard it a couple of months ago. Straight from Dean Lomax. They felt you deserved it. Kind of a reward for all the stuff you pulled off all these years. Besides, they knew you'd be damn good at it."

"How come you know so much about this?"

"Well," said Gus, pushing away his empty soup bowl, "I was up for that job."

"Oh, shit. I didn't know."

"Hey, it's okay. 'Sides, I'm already qualified for a pension."

"I was afraid, if I didn't take the deal in Iran, all that might go down the tubes."

"Might've," said Gus. "But I don't think so." He turned the soup bowl in his hands, studying it, like a fortune-teller with half a crystal ball.


They found little to do on Friday. After a breakfast of strong instant coffee, they drove over to Dowshan Tappeh. Tom Troy's offices were all but deserted. A young man in air force military police uniform sat by the phone on Troy's desk, reading a battered paperback.

"Colonel Troy's over at admin, meeting with regular air force types. Something they go through every Friday."

"He leave any word for us?" asked Gus. "Simpson and Sullivan?"

"Just if you came by to let you know there'll be an Iranian military driver here eight in the morning to take you wherever you're goin' tomorrow morning."

"Good," said Gus. "We should be well rested by then."

"Know any place we can do some food shopping?" asked Frank.

"Not today. It's Friday. Most everything's closed. Holy day."

Fasting and abstinence, thought Frank. He and Gus retreated to their dismal quarters and told each other war stories about hard times on other Third World assignments.

# CHAPTER THREE

Frank woke, tense and sweating under the heavy blankets, vaguely aware of a troubled dream. He had no idea where he was and thought for a moment he was a child, an infant. He wondered where his son was. Jake? He pushed the covers off, sat up abruptly and called out, "Jake?"

He stared at the three curtained windows and remembered. Tehran. He'd set his alarm for six, but the clock on the dresser showed seven. He heard the thud of knuckles on his door.

"You awake?"

"Uh-huh," mumbled Frank. "Sorta, yeah."

"We're late."

Frank rolled out of bed and opened the door. Gus, in a robe, looked as bleary-eyed as Frank felt.

"What time we supposed to meet that driver?"

"Eight o'clock," said Gus.

"Let's move," said Frank. "We'll make it."

He'd showered in lukewarm water, shaved, and dressed and was checking the knot in his tie at his dressing table mirror when he heard glass shattering behind him and metal skittering across the floor. He turned in time to see the grenade roll under the bed. He bolted from the room, hit the hallway floor, and turned a somersault that brought him to Gus's feet. Gus peered down at him over the rims of his glasses, pivoted, hurled himself back into his own room, stumbled, and thudded to the floor. Frank cringed, thinking the grenade had gone off. He could hear Gus's muttered curses.

"Shit, piss, fuck . . . what happened?"

"A grenade," said Frank.

"Through the window?"

"Yeah."

"You sure it wasn't a rock?"

"It looked like a grenade."

"A grenade would've gone off by now."

"It rolled under the bed."

Gus grunted. Frank could hear him struggling to his feet.

"Even under the bed, if it's a grenade it would've gone off by now."

Frank heard footsteps and looked up just far enough to see Gus's shoes coming into the hall.

"What I suggest we do is we get out of here and tell our friends about it and let them send some bomb squad types over here and check it out."

"Okay." Frank warily pushed himself up.

"And if I've got any broken kneecaps," said Gus, "I'm going to sue."

Tom Troy wasn't in, and a square-shouldered young corporal named Cantwell had told them Colonel Troy would have some paperwork to go through when they returned to the base in the afternoon. Frank and Gus exchanged a glance, shrugged, and, following Cantwell, carried their briefcases out to the bulletproof Chevy Nova that waited for them. Cantwell, in the uniform of the air force military police, cautioned them about the *jube*.

"Leastways, that's what the I-ranians call it," he said pointing to a guttered, frozen-over stream that ran along the side of the road where their car waited. Its exhaust had melted a hole in the ice. "Open sewer to me," said Cantwell. "Got 'em all over the city. Looks frozen over, right? But some places that ice is real thin. You step on it and it cracks, no tellin' what you might step into."

"We'll be careful," said Gus.

A tall, heavy-set Iranian stood by the car. His round, weathered face wore a tired half smile.

"This is your Iranian military driver," said Cantwell. "He's authorized to shuttle you between here and Supreme Commander's, where you meet with your Iranian counterparts. Sergeant, this is Commander Simpson and Major Sullivan."

"Sergeant Ali Zarakesh, at your service." He snapped to attention, but his civilian outfit belied the military posture. He wore a brown leather jacket over an open-throated shirt faded to an uncertain gray. Gus and Frank casually returned his formal salute.

Ali had warmed the car's interior against the biting cold that had turned morning dew into hoarfrost. Steam covered the windows. "Don't wipe," said Ali, as he circled a gray rag over the windshield in front of him. "The driver has to see out. No one has to see in."

Frank and Gus each wore dark stocking caps pulled low over their foreheads and winter parkas over their suits and ties. I wish I'd kept my beard, thought Frank.

Traffic was light. Only patches of overnight snow remained on streets that shimmered in the morning sun. Frank sat up front with Ali, asking about the route they followed.

"We drive west but not too far," said Ali. "Not as far as the university, and a little south but not so far south as the bazaar."

"And not past the Grand Mosque," said Gus.

"Not past any mosque," said Ali.

"Good," said Gus.

From the occasional street sign Frank could make out through the veil of steam on the windows, he realized how often Tehran streets changed their names. The bilingual street signs impressed him. He had grown used to African cities, where street signs were rare and people knew the names of only a few main thoroughfares.

"Look, this one's called Roosevelt," he noted as Ali turned onto another broad street. "In Addis, the main drag was Churchill Road."

"We have a Churchill Road here, too," said Ali. "And another called Eisenhower. But I don't know for how long."

"The Shah must be a great admirer of America," said Gus.

"Our pilots fly your F-4s," said Ali. "Our soldiers shoot at students with your M-14s."

Ali drove so rapidly and his turns were so abrupt that Frank soon became confused.

"Where are we?"

"Not far from your embassy. But burning tires block so many streets . . ."

For no reason Frank could see, Ali swung the car around in the narrow street, tilted two wheels up on the sidewalk, and sped back in the opposite direction.

They passed a vacant, muddy expanse littered with the prefabricated ruins of an abandoned construction site. A giant building crane, pitched at a precarious angle, slipped even further on its muddy base as he watched. Through the fogged windows, the image reminded him of the crane he'd seen through clouds and smoke as their plane descended into Tehran.

As Frank watched, the tottering crane seemed to bounce, then caught itself and held, like a skeletal version of the leaning tower of Pisa.

"What was happening there?" asked Frank.

"That one? Military barracks. And fancy apartments for officers with families. Stopped now. Like everything. All over Tehran, cranes like that stand useless. The Shah wanted to lift up the whole country. No more."

Frank made mental notes but had trouble following Ali's route. "I need a map," he said to Ali.

"More than a map," said Ali. "To know Tehran you need a hundred years.

Only the martyrs know Tehran, and for them it's too late." Ali made a sudden turn to his right. "And you need a nose," he continued. "To tell you what trouble or traffic comes soon and which way to change. And three eyes. Right, left, and rear view to see where you've been and who's behind you."

Gus turned and peered through the steamy rear window. With an index finger, he wiped a tiny patch clear. "Like the big black job behind us?"

Ali nodded. "Paykan. Persian copy of Russian car. *Savak* always use those when they want you to know they're with you. Otherwise, they use blue Mercedes."

"It's nice to know we're worth so much attention."

"Oh, Americans always get attention here. It must be a very big country. So rich."

Frank listened as Gus carried the conversation, impressed by the casual questions that began to develop a portrait and, beyond the portrait, the outlines of a landscape.

"You're an army man?"

"Seventeen years, sir. I used to drive a tank, a Sherman tank. But now I have trouble with my kidney. So now for you I drive this American tank." He patted the dashboard. "A good car."

"I noticed you're not in uniform," said Gus.

"Commander Simpson?" said Ali, glancing at Gus in the rearview mirror. "Yes."

Ali turned to Frank. "And Major Sullivan?"

"That's me," said Frank.

"Uniforms are not very popular here these days."

"We can appreciate that," said Gus.

"Thank you, sir. I try to be careful. I have too many children otherwise."

"How many?" asked Gus.

"Six, sir."

"That's not so many."

"May I ask how many, sir, you have?"

"Oh, six less than you," said Gus. "But we've learned to live with that."

"It is God's will."

"*Inshallah*," said Gus. He fell silent, staring at the steamed-up window beside him. Frank sensed that Gus and his wife might not quite have learned to live with that.

"Are your children with you?" he asked Ali.

"My oldest, seventeen, is in the army. Stationed in Isfahan. I worry about him. It is a very religious city there."

"Troubles?" said Gus.

"Not so much as here. But I worry about my son, about soldiers in a holy city like Isfahan. Many there support Khomeini and hate the Shah."

"How 'bout your other children?"

"Well, they are in the north. I sent them with their mother to my family near Rasht. We have some olive trees up there, land I bought for my parents."

Frank resolved to get himself a street map, even if it meant photocopying section by section the map on Tom Troy's wall. He knew the day would come when he would have to negotiate the city without Ali's help. Ahead, he spotted a long tangle of motionless cars. He expected Ali to make one of his sudden cuts into a side street. Ali continued straight ahead, edging to his left.

"Traffic jam?" asked Frank, wondering how a tie-up could have developed when there were so few trucks or cars on the streets.

"Not traffic jam," said Ali. "Benzene line." Ali now drove on the wrong side of a broad, two-way street. The few vehicles coming in the opposite direction kept to the far right.

The veil of steam on the windows had thinned and, refracted through streams of moisture, Frank could see the long cluster of double- and triple-parked vehicles. Drivers stood in groups, stomping their feet and flapping their arms to keep warm. From his newspaper reading Frank knew that Iran, despite its vast supplies of oil, suffered gasoline and fuel shortages because strikes and sabotage had hit the refineries as part of the growing rebellion against the Shah's government. The jumbled knot of cars curved up a street to their right. He couldn't spot the end of the haphazard line or the filling station it targeted.

"Peaceful," said Ali. "But people will get killed on that line, get into fights and get killed, when it starts to move. Persians don't know how to queue."

Frank squinted through the steam-streaked window, troubled by the thought of even a few Iranians killing each other on filling station lines in the middle of a revolution that saw Iranians killing each other by the hundreds.

"The same for cooking oil," said Ali. "Men will kill for benzene, and women will cut and scratch and claw, and yes, even kill for cooking oil."

Ali turned to the right onto another broad avenue. On their left chain-link fences, topped by concertina wire, partly obscured a vast complex of two- and three-storied buildings of poured concrete. Armored personnel carriers and jeeps with mounted machine guns patrolled both sides of the fence. Two tanks stood sentinel outside what appeared to be the main gate.

For the first time that morning they encountered heavy traffic moving fast in both directions. Ali drove ahead another half mile and swung into a traffic circle with scattered vehicles that swirled like angry bees. Ali accelerated where Frank would have slowed, cut right where Frank would have eased left.

"Remind me never to drive in this town," said Gus from his back seat. Frank made a mental note to drive like a New York cab driver.

Ali snapped the Nova to the right coming out of the circle. He crowded the curb, slowed, and began tapping his horn as he approached the main gate. He edged the Nova into the narrow alley created by the two tanks. He rolled his window down, stuck his head out, and waved toward a kiosk.

A young soldier with a corporal's inverted chevrons stepped out, one hand holding a clipboard, the other on the handle of a holstered .45. A half dozen other soldiers with automatic weapons stepped out from behind the kiosk. They kept their weapons at hip level but trained on the car. Gus sank low in the back seat.

Ali spoke to the corporal, who appeared to recognize him. As the corporal relaxed, Ali tugged what Frank guessed were his own military ID papers from the thick rubber band that secured them to his windshield visor. Ali spoke slowly in Farsi, glancing at Frank and Gus, as the soldier checked and returned his papers. The soldier studied his clipboard. From Ali's jumble of Farsi, Frank heard him enunciate, "Soo-li-van. Siimp-sohn."

The soldier nodded and peered through the window at Frank and Gus, who had removed his cap and sat upright. The soldier waved them through; the gates parted wider, and Ali drove ahead.

He picked his way toward the largest of the buildings, a multisided structure shaped like a gerrymandered voting district. They pulled up parallel to an outside staircase where a trim, coatless man of about Frank's age stood waiting. From his brief exposure at Dowshan Tappeh Frank recognized the blue uniform as Iranian Air Force. Ali killed the ignition, tugged at the emergency brake, said, "Wait me," and eased his bulk from the car.

Gus wiped the window on his right with his glove and studied the staircase.

"That's what I thought. Those stairs don't go anywhere," he announced.

"Looks to me like they go up," said Frank.

"Yeah. They go up to the second floor, but there's no door up there."

Ali opened Frank's door. "No one is here but the major. He will take you upstairs."

"Up those stairs?" called Gus from the back seat.

"No. No one understands those stairs. Up stairs inside."

They clambered out of the car. The slim, dark-eyed Iranian Air Force officer saluted with a motion that managed to combine crisp, military respect and an open curiosity.

"Major Anwar Amini," he said. "Welcome."

Frank moved toward him, hand extended, saying, "Frank, ah, Major Francis Sullivan. U.S. Air Force." They studied each other intently as they shook hands. "And this," said Frank, "is Lieutenant Commander Gus Simpson, U.S. Naval Reserve."

He realized how stiff and formal he sounded. Gus lightened the tone.

"Call me Gus," he said, shaking Major Amini's hand and grasping him by the elbow.

"Anwar," said the major.

"Glad to meet you, Anwar," said Gus.

"Anwar," echoed Frank.

"I will be part of the interservice committee working with you," said the major.

"Jayface?" said Gus.

"I'm afraid so." Anwar smiled. "Our bureau is just upstairs. Please. Will you follow? The sergeant will be waiting for you when you are finished."

"Thanks for the ride," said Gus.

Ali grinned, saluting in mufti.


They followed Major Amini, who ushered them in through glass doors, then up a broad marble stairway under an unlit crystal chandelier. Frank's first impression of luxury quickly faded. Bare concrete floors, plasterboard walls, and weak fluorescent lights greeted them on the second story. The walls seemed to ooze a damp chill. Frank sensed an odor like cabbage that had been cooking too long. He noticed a coat rack of metal pipes with a few wire hangers, a single military overcoat, and, on the rack above, an air force officer's cap.

As they crossed toward an open-doored conference room, the fluorescent lights went out. They entered a spacious but windowless rectangular room.

"The others will just be coming," said the major. "Let me take your coats." They shed their parkas. Anwar carried them to the hallway coat rack.

"Can I get you some tea?" he asked as he returned. "Cold drinks?"

Frank's stomach rumbled. "Tea," he said.

"Tea," echoed Gus.

"Maybe some rolls," ventured Frank.

The major pressed a green button on the wall. Frank's mind veered from the button to speculation about how the room was bugged and by whom. He barely heard Anwar's question.

"Do you have an agenda for today's meeting?"

Frank looked blankly to Gus.

"Well, ah, no," said Gus. "We thought today should be more of an exploratory, ah, get-acquainted, exploratory session. Tomorrow . . ." Frank admired the sincerity of his frown. "Tomorrow we'll have an agenda."

Fuckin'-A we will, thought Frank. He realized again how ill prepared they were for their hastily conceived mission—and the hidden agenda Pete Howard had given him.

"I'd like to hear your thoughts," said Frank. "I mean, while we're waiting for the others. Your thoughts on the situation. The situation and what we might do."

Anwar smiled. His eyes were watchful, alert. "You have seen the situation. Today is especially bad. Riots. Marches." His hands spread outward. "I have no idea what we should do."

"Between us, we'll think of something," said Gus. All three smiled.

"Yes, sir." A short, very dark young man with a drooping black mustache stood in the doorway. He wore a white waiter's jacket over chino slacks, white socks, and plastic slippers. *"Chay,"* said Anwar. Frank guessed *chay* must be a variation on *chi,* the standard Middle Eastern word for tea, but the rest of their conversation was lost on him.

"No rolls," said Anwar, "but there will be our *barbari* bread with *chelakebab* for lunch. If the *barbari* is ready before lunch, he says he will bring. But I doubt."

"Tea will be fine," said Frank.

"Good morning." There was no mistaking the general: two stars on each shoulder. A round, unwrinkled, well-fed man, he wore a uniform that fit and flattered him so well Frank suspected it had been custom made. A widow's peak was his only apparent concession to age. His olive complexion and Vaseline-slicked black hair would have enabled him to pass as a native in Rome. Frank guessed his office must be in the building, for he showed no signs of having just entered from the cold. Anwar saluted, casually. The general merely nodded.

"I am General Dariush Merid," he said looking from Gus to Frank. "At your service, gentlemen. Let us be seated. The others are here and will join us just now."

General Merid marched the length of the table to take the high-backed wooden chair at its head. Gus and Frank followed, taking the metal chairs to the general's right. Anwar left one chair vacant and sat on the general's left.

"Well," said Merid. "Welcome." Something shy slowed the unfolding of his smile. He shifted his weight and tried a brighter smile. "Was your trip comfortable?"

"Very comfortable," said Gus.

Frank was grateful that Gus sat closer to the general. The general's lob of a question had thrown him. He never could have volleyed a reply as quickly as Gus had. Instead, Frank's mind spun through the whole absurd sequence of his landing in Washington and, totally unprepared, flying back through JFK and Rome to Tehran.

"Comfortable," Frank managed to say at last. "But troubling."

The general, who appeared uneasy with small talk, hadn't been prepared for "troubling." He studied Frank evenly. Only the whitening tips of his pudgy fingers, gripping the edge of the table, betrayed his tension.

"Ah, what kind of trouble?"

"Just at the end," said Frank. "As we circled the city. So many fires. So much smoke."

"Ah," said the general, with only the hint of a smile. "More smoke than fire. Burning tires. Some minor arson. Student pranks. Leftist troublemakers."

"Frankly, sir, it looked like more than that . . ."

General Merid raised a hand. "Do you agree?" he asked, turning to Gus.

"I was asleep," said Gus.

"Ah, a man after my own heart. I always like to nap when I fly. That way I arrive refreshed. Ready for anything, even after a long flight."

"Do you travel much?" asked Gus.

"I used to. In the early 1960s, in fact, I was our embassy's military attaché in Washington. Then, four years in Rome. I loved Rome."

"That's where I've been based the past two years," said Gus.

Building, slowly building, thought Frank. He watched Gus play the general.

"Wonderful city," Gus continued. "Since I retired from the navy, my wife and I feel quite settled there. Some consulting work. Department of Defense. Nothing I can talk much about. You know."

"Of course," said General Merid.

Though he was not much of a tennis player himself, it occurred to Frank that he and Gus might make a good doubles team. Gus moved well where Frank stumbled. Frank drove hard where Gus lay back. As Gus learned more about the general by asking more about Rome, Frank glanced at Anwar. The young major smiled and looked away.

The dark waiter with the white jacket returned with their tea. Two men of military bearing followed him into the room. One, in civilian clothes, bore what Frank thought of as classic Middle Eastern features: swarthy complexion; hooked nose and high cheekbones framing piercing eyes that were as jet black as his hair; of medium height but with tensed muscles that tested the limits of his inexpensive gray suit. The other, in the uniform of an army major, was younger and fair, with a bounce to his step as he led the way into the room.

He bypassed the others and went straight to General Merid, who stood to greet him. They saluted, shook hands, and embraced.

"*Daheejon,*" said the major.

"My son," said General Merid in English. "This is Major Nazih, Hossein Nazih, my nephew, my protégé, you might say."

Behind their backs, Anwar rolled his eyes toward the ceiling. Like Frank and Gus, following the general's lead, he had stood to greet the new arrivals. He turned to shake hands with the beak-nosed man in civilian clothes.

Frank noticed Gus studying their waiter, who seemed to linger longer than necessary. At a reproving glance from Anwar, the waiter, moving slowly, left the room.

"How has it been, uncle?" said Major Nazih.

"Tiring," said the general. "Very tiring."

"You should not take these things so seriously. We will soon have it all under control." He turned to the others. "Gentlemen. You must forgive us." His words had the tone of an order rather than an apology. "But I haven't seen my uncle for a week now. Pressing matters at the palace."

"My nephew is very close to His Imperial Majesty," General Merid said softly to Gus.

"Oh? How is the Shah holding up these days?" asked Gus.

"Ah, are you the Sullivan one? Francis Sullivan?"

"No," said Gus. "I'm the Simpson one." He nodded toward Frank. "That's the Sullivan."

"Ah, I must have a word with you," said the major, with a lingering glance at Frank. *"A plus tard."* He moved to the chair just to the right of General Merid. "May I take this chair, Uncle?"

"Of course," said the general. "Please."

Until his own name had been mentioned, Frank had taken more interest in the beak-nosed man in the gray suit. Now he realized the man's piercing black eyes studied him, perhaps wondering why Major Nazih had singled him out. He perched behind the metal chair to Anwar's left, bent slightly forward, his hands cleaving to the chair back like talons on a tree branch. The coal-black eyes held steady on Frank, who noticed, for the first time, the small, dark, egg-shaped bump high on his forehead.

"Well, now that we are all here," said the general, taking his seat and folding his hands on the table, "perhaps we can begin."

The man in the gray suit was the last to sit, taking the chair opposite Frank. Frank, uncomfortable, looked away. The dark eyes went on studying him.

"Perhaps we should all introduce ourselves," said the general. "Each one telling a little bit about himself. Let's begin with you, Commander Simpson."

The freshman icebreaker, thought Frank. Again, he was glad Gus sat closer to the general.

"Lieutenant Commander Gus Simpson. U.S. Navy retired." Frank's peripheral vision told him the dark-eyed man had at last shifted his gaze as Gus continued. "Second lieutenant in World War II. Background as a Marine Corps public information officer. Military attaché, Athens, London. Briefing officer in Saigon. Pentagon spokesman. Currently on a DOD consulting contract, posted in Rome. Till they asked me to come over here and meet General Merid."

"Very good," said the general, beaming.

Very good, Frank agreed. Gus had kept his lies close to the truth.

"And now you, Major Sullivan."

"Frank Sullivan. Air force. Before that, a few years as a newspaperman, reporter. Like Commander Simpson, background as a public information officer, civic and community service programs, adviser to military public information officers in several African countries."

"What were you doing in Ethiopia?" said the youthful Major Nazih.

Frank hadn't expected trouble so soon. He felt the burning dark eyes swing back to him.

"That was a bit different. I was involved with the IEG military, but the Ethiopians asked to have me detached to work with their Ministry of Information."

"And with their Imperial Majesty, so I understand."

Frank studied the young major, who had come to their meeting directly from the palace. No contact with the palace and the Shah, he'd been told. Absolutely no contact.

"Well, yes," said Frank, forcing a smile. "When an emperor makes a request, it's hard to turn him down. Haile Selassie liked the way I wrote. So I started doing some speeches for him, policy statements, things like that."

"You just about ran the country, so they tell me."

"Nothing like that," said Frank. "I was just a fast man at the typewriter was all."

"My uncle, ah, not General Merid, my uncle at the palace, he has liaison with your embassy. He has informed the Shah of your presence. The Shah remembers you well. He is fond of you."

"I'm honored," said Frank. "And surprised. We only spoke a few times."

"And poor Haile Selassie. He did not end well, did he?" said the major.

"No," said Frank. "They said he died in his sleep."

"But we know someone helped with a pillow over his face, don't we?" said Nazih.

"I heard that's what happened."

"And Ethiopia suffers badly without him. But I suppose all that happened after you left?"

"Three years after," said Frank.

Major Nazih studied him. Frank, tired of being stared at, stared back. He detected a languid, feminine fluttering of the major's dark eyelashes.

"Perhaps we'll have to keep you here forever," said the major, turning his long lashess toward the general. "We wouldn't want the Shah to suffer Haile Selassie's fate, would we?"


A beep sounded from General Merid's wrist. He checked his watch.

"Ah, four o'clock. I must be going. An important meeting." The general stood, scraping his chair on the concrete floor. Five chairs echoed the sound. "Shall we adjourn?" said the general. "And at zero eight hundred hours, precisely, tomorrow we will meet again. And Mr. Sullivan will have an agenda for us, am I correct?"

"Correct," said Frank. He checked his Timex, which tended to run fast. Five after four. The dark-eyed man, who had introduced himself as Captain Munair Irfani of the Iranian Navy, and Nazih followed the general. Major Anwar Amini of the air force lingered while Frank and Gus struggled into their parkas.

"You must be fatigued," said Anwar.

"I know I should be polite and lie about it," said Frank.

He had fought hard to keep awake, stifling yawns and pinching himself after the heavy lunch they'd eaten at their conference room table. The over-cooked lamb on soggy rice with cabbage and unleavened bread and sweet tea rebelled in his stomach. He'd ventured into the bathroom after lunch and found it consisted of several holes in the concrete floor, a pitcher of water next to each. Frank, tightening his sphincter, urinated down one of the holes and vowed to stuff a pocket with toilet paper for tomorrow.

He'd noticed Gus nodding off several times during their afternoon session as the general droned on about the importance of getting the armed forces involved in civic action programs with the population, particularly in the rural areas, which he referred to, often, as "the real Iran."

Anwar escorted them down the wide marble staircase under the graceful, unlit chandelier, which Frank now realized had the shape of a crown. Anwar held open the glass doors, and they walked into the bracing air.

"Tell me something," said Gus. "Our waiter. Does he speak English?"

"Hamid? As a matter of fact," said Anwar, "he does. Why do you ask?"

"He seemed to pay attention to the conversation. And we weren't speaking Persian."

"You are very observant," said Anwar. "Yes, he speaks English and he spies on us. At least for *Savak*."

"At least for *Savak*? Does he work for anyone else?" said Gus.

"Ask him," said Anwar.

The room's got to be bugged, thought Frank. A waiter who might eavesdrop on their meetings did not seem much of a threat. He looked up at the stone stairway that led to a blank wall.

"Does anyone know about that stairway?" he asked.

Anwar looked up, shaking his head. "No one knows." He looked out beyond the thousand eyes of the chain-link fence at the city beyond. Four funnels of smoke bracketed the gray sky into nearly symmetrical quadrants. "No one knows," Anwar repeated.

Their Chevy edged away from a cluster of parked military vehicles and eased toward them. Anwar continued to study the funnels of smoke that drifted across the sky.

"Almost like tornadoes, aren't they? When I was stationed in Texas, taking courses with your air force, the same base where they now have the Crown Prince, I saw a tornado. Very impressive. Two months ago we had even more smoke signals to watch. It started with *Ayd-e Fetr,* the end of *Ramadan*."

"The month of fasting?" said Gus.

"Yes," said Anwar. "It fell, I believe, on your 4 September. Just two months ago, isn't it? The breaking of the fast. It started fairly peaceful that day. Demonstrations at the university, the bazaar. And from all over the city people marched on Shahyad Square, the huge monument you must have seen on your drive in from the airport."

"I remember it," said Frank.

"Peaceful that day, but over the next three days the demonstrations grew. New demands, new slogans attacked the Shah more openly. Then, on 7 September, he declared martial law. The next day there were many confrontations—casualties at the university, but the worst was at Jaleh Square, near Dowshan Tappeh, where you have your office. Hundreds were killed, mostly secondary school students who staged a sit-down demonstration. The soldiers fired on them, on schoolchildren in the open square. Hundreds they killed. Black Friday, the people call it, and since then we have been at war."

"Who's winning?" said Frank.

Anwar shrugged. "Watch the smoke signals," he said. "Perhaps they can tell you."


Frank, sitting up front, had persuaded Ali to let him lower the window. He wanted to think, to follow the route Ali took back to Dowshan Tappeh, to study the streets for any hint they might convey about what was happening. He worried about his confrontation with Major Nazih. The others, including Gus, had heard him reveal Frank's previous contact with the Shah.

He hadn't told Gus about that. Or about Lermontov. Or the conflicting directives he'd been given about both by Near East Division and Pete Howard. He'd followed the agency's basic rule about compartmentalization. Even people working on the same team shared information only on a need-to-know basis. Gus didn't need to know about his previous dealings with the Shah and Lermontov, but now Gus had heard about the Shah from Nazih.

He felt guilty about not telling his new partner but hoped Gus would understand. The more Frank thought about Nazih's revelation, the more it worried him. Nazih's words could compromise him with any of the Jayface members who might have contacts with the opposition. He remembered how guarded the Iranians had been as General Merid led them through their introductions. Major Nazih had revealed more about himself—and perhaps about the general—than he'd intended. The others had offered little more than name, rank, and branch of service. When they were done, Frank had counted to himself, sure they were missing someone. He reviewed the scene in his mind, remembering how he had turned to the general.

"Weren't we supposed to have someone else? A colonel from the . . ."

The general had cut him off. "No, no colonel . . . ah, the colonel won't be able to work with us. Other pressing duties."

"I see." In this case not even a name, thought Frank. "No replacement?"

"No," said General Merid. "His branch has . . . pressing duties."

"Oh, that's right," said Gus. "A chicken colonel from the Imperial Guard."

"A what?" said General Merid.

"Chicken colonel. You must have heard that expression."

"No, no," said the general, laughing. "Tell me. What does it mean? Chicken colonel."

"It's the insignia, at least in the U.S. military. A colonel's insignia is a silver eagle. The joke is that a colonel's insignia isn't a real eagle, just a chicken."

By now General Merid was laughing so hard his eyes teared. "Chicken colonel. I can hardly wait till I see him to make fun. Colonel Chicken."

"It's a good name for him," sniffed Major Nazih. "He won't be missed. He's a zero only good for keeping his nose up *Savak*'s ass."

Frank had glanced around the table. If the Imperial Guard chicken colonel wouldn't be reporting their meetings to *Savak*, he wondered who would. He wondered about the general. Had *Savak* briefed him on the American passion for civic action programs? Perhaps Nazih, his irreverence adopted as cover for a clever agent. Or Major Amini, Anwar, the friendliest of the crew? Why was he so friendly—and cautious?

Frank shivered. He'd been so wrapped up in thinking about their meeting, he'd forgotten that he sat next to Ali, heading back to their office at Dowshan Tappeh. The air cutting through the car's partially open window had turned chillier.

Behind him, Gus snored, a light, wheezing sound. Frank studied the all but empty streets. They told him nothing. He rolled up the window.


"You got trouble," barked Troy as they entered his office. "Novak wants to see you, and there's a mob burning tires outside the embassy gates."

"Nice," said Gus. "Between a Rocky and a hot place."

"Here, I drew you a map," said Troy. "There's a back way in. They say that's quiet. But you might be better off if the mob gets you. Novak's got a bug up his ass about something. I just got off the fucking scramble phone, and my ears are still ringing." He handed the map to Frank. "Take the Fiat. The Chevy's bullet-proof, but it looks too fuckin' American. Now get goin'."

"Both of us?" asked Frank.

"Well, he just wants to see you. But nobody goes anywhere alone in this town these days. I can't spare an escort, so Gus, you'll have to go with him. Which might be a good thing. Facin' a pissed-off Rocky, it might be a good thing to have a genuine knife fighter along."

"Knife fighter?" Frank couldn't picture Gus wielding a knife in anger.

"Oh, yeah," said Troy. "Fact, last time I saw this guy he took out a couple of VCs that tried to off us in a blow-job bar in Saigon." Frank studied Gus with new eyes.

"Ancient history," said Gus. "We've got a more recent problem to tell you about."

"Just what I need. Another problem."

"Frank here got an air mail special delivered through his bedroom window this morning."

"You got what?"

"It looked a like a grenade," said Frank. "It rolled under the bed, and we decided to get out of there without trying to get a better look."

"Couldn't be too serious if it didn't go off before you got outta there. I'll have one of my guys break out his bomb squad gear and check it out."

" 'Preciate it," said Gus.

"Why the fuck couldn't Rocky keep you guys down in his own shop?" said Troy. "And outta my hair."

"You already told us," said Gus. "Because Rocky wants to have as little to do with us as possible, since he doesn't want us here in the first damn place."

"Yeah, you got that right," said Troy. "Look, before you run outta here, some housekeeping, real quick." He handed each a manila envelope. "Residency permit, pass to Dowshan Tappeh, pass to Supreme Commander's Headquarters. This says you received them and won't lose them on pain of death. Sign here," he said.

They signed the forms.

"Good," said Troy. "That makes you official. Now, turn around and get the fuck outta here. Mr. Novak is waiting."


Frank caught a glimpse of spiraling smoke beyond the soccer field as he cut off Roosevelt. Gus sank lower in the seat next to him. Both had their stocking caps down to their eyebrows. Frank eased the Fiat left into another street barely wider than the car. He braked by a metal gate with a low brick guardhouse behind it. A marine in dress uniform stepped out.

"Can I help you, gentlemen?"

Frank pulled off the stocking cap. "Mr. Novak is expecting us."


Though they had clashed in Rome, Frank respected Rocky Novak as a no-nonsense professional. He knew no one told jokes in Novak's presence about the fact that he wore a hearing aid. Rocky ruled his domain in Tehran from a large basement office with an oversize oak desk, but the bare concrete walls and sparse furnishings contrasted sharply to the elegant suite Novak had occupied under his cover title as chief political officer at the embassy on Via Veneto.

Here, a worn vinyl couch stretched against one wall; two filing cabinets with security bars and combination locks lined the opposite wall; a safe stood behind the desk, and an IBM Selectric sat on a typing table to Novak's right. Frank half expected to see a polygraph and other tools of the interrogator's trade.

"Come in and sit down," called Novak from behind his formidable desk. "You, too, Simpson, since you're here. I've got some shit to get through. Then I'll get to you." Rocky worked his way through a stack of cables, reading quickly, sorting them into two piles. "Sullivan, what the fuck am I gonna do with you?" He kept his head buried in the cables.

Frank made no effort to reply. He knew Novak turned his hearing aid off when he concentrated on clearing paperwork. Gus caught his eye. Frank shook his head and raised a finger to his lips. He also knew Novak sometimes tricked the unwary by leaving the hearing aid on.

Gus fidgeted on the edge of the stiff couch. Frank sat back, watching Novak skim through his cables, thinking again about the agency's flakiness—sending him out barely briefed and with no reading-in time, traveling with air force ID but in true name, unfamiliar with the country, ignorant of the language, his identity and his Ethiopian background already known to God only knows how many Iranians. Novak initialed the last of his cables. He picked up a stack in each hand and placed them in the safe. He removed the ribbon from his IBM typewriter and put the ribbon in the safe. He slammed the safe, twisted the combination lock, and adjusted his hearing aid. "I can't preach security to everybody else if I don't plug up my own asshole, right?"

Frank and Gus said nothing but nodded agreement in Novak's direction.

"So they've got you back in again," said Novak, glaring at Frank. "Are more heads going to roll?"

He turned a knob clockwise on the battery of his old-fashioned hearing aid. Frank tried to remember if that meant up or down.

"I've got a hunch heads will roll," said Frank. "But it's got nothing to do with me."

"That's true. And nothing you're going to do will stop it. Simpson?"

"That's me," said Gus.

"Glad to meet you. If I had my way you'd both be outta here on the next plane."

"I must admit," said Gus, "I like Rome better."

"Well, we're here now. God help us. I had that little demonstration out front arranged special to make you feel welcome, and you bastards had the nerve to sneak in the back way."

"I'm glad to hear you have students on the payroll," said Gus.

"They aren't students. Some young thugs *Savak* hired for me."

"I'm beginning to think you're serious," said Frank.

"You know me, Sullivan. I'm always serious, and I seriously the fuck wish you guys weren't here. All right, Sullivan. Time for you and me to take a walk. Simpson, wait here. I won't keep this bozo long. Let's go, Sully."

Frank knew they were headed for the bubble, which meant Novak had heavy matters on his mind. Frank followed him upstairs, past the bulletproofed marine in his small office behind thick glass. The marine took nothing for granted. He waited for Novak to hold out the ID badge on his lapel and studied the photo against Rocky's impatient face. His eyes cut to the visitor's ID badge that hung from the chain around Frank's neck. He had just signed Frank in a few minutes ago, but he politely insisted on taking a close look at the number on the badge and checking it against the list in his ledger. He asked Frank his name, then asked again to see photo ID. At last a buzzer sounded, and Novak led them up a broad, carpeted staircase to the embassy's second floor.

"Good man," muttered Novak. "Some of these assholes, if they've seen you once they wave you through."

They walked past the ambassador's office with its State Department seal on heavy oak doors to another barred stairway with a digital security lock. Novak punched in the code and led Frank up a narrower stairway. Frank guessed the door ahead led to the communications room. Novak turned to their left and led Frank across a wide corridor to the bubble, a strange chamber that looked like a plastic beehive laid on its side. The transparent door, walls, ceiling, and floor; the glass chairs; and the glass-topped tables made it difficult to conceal a listening device. Rocky's index finger tapped a final series of digits, and he pulled open the door.

Totally transparent, it looked so insubstantial Frank expected it to sway when he stepped inside, but the bubble was solid. He knew agency security officers swept its chairs and tables daily for bugs. Access was limited to the chief of station and anyone he wanted to talk to in absolute privacy. The bubble and the communications room, which handled all embassy communications but was staffed solely by CIA employees responsible to the chief of station, were the real measures of power in the embassy.

"Information is power," Novak had told him under the bubble in Rome. "The ambassador has fancier rugs and drapes, but I control the information."

Frank could hear and feel the whoosh of air as Novak pulled the clear plastic door shut behind them. "Sit your ass down," said Novak. They pulled up chairs opposite each other at a small round table. A longer glass conference table stretched out behind Novak's back. He adjusted his hearing aid and said, "Talk."

"About?"

"You know what the fuck I want you to talk about."

"About the major?"

"Talk, for chrissake."

"How did you hear so fast?" Frank hesitated. He knew Novak well enough to realize he might be fishing, staging even the anger he'd expressed over the scramble phone to Troy. He regretted mentioning the major.

"Well, I thought he was gay was all."

Novak scowled. "Who the fuck you thought was gay?"

"Major . . . I forget," said Frank. "Whatever his name is."

"Nazih?"

At least we've got the right major, thought Frank. "I . . . I'm not sure," he said, "Something like that. I've got it in my notes."

"Don't fuck with me, Sullivan. He came from the palace. He knew about Ethiopia."

"Oh. Okay," said Frank. "Now I know what you mean." He recounted Major Nazih's questions about Ethiopia. "He seemed to think I was a lot more important there than I was."

"Keep talking," said Novak.

Frank knew that Novak, as a matter of operational policy, maintained a steady level of intimidating anger but that his anger was up a notch above normal when he made the effort to pronounce the final *g* on his gerunds, particularly on his obscene gerunds.

"Quit . . . fucking . . . stalling."

"So I'm stalling. I'm trying to be sure I don't forget anything."

"Talk to me, Sullivan."

"He said the Shah remembered me."

"In front of the others?"

"Yes."

"That's just great. What else?"

"He said the Shah had been told about my being here by another of his uncles. An uncle at the palace. I'm not quite sure what kind of uncle he means."

"Uncle, cousin, whatever. Some kind of fucking relative. Like that Jayface general."

"Nazih may be his nephew," said Frank, "but he's also the general's squeeze."

"What?"

"His squeeze. That's what I was trying to tell you. His popsie."

"Popsie?"

"As in Popsicle. You know what a Popsicle looks like, right? Fruit flavored, right? Visualize it. Eating a Popsicle."

"All right, enough. I got the picture. How do you know?"

"Well, they made it fairly clear. Nothing flaming, I mean. Just apparent. Eye contact that . . . well, lingers. Intonation. Merid's whole manner changed as soon as the major waltzed in. Called him 'my son,' 'my colleague.'" Frank's voice went up half an octave, followed by his eyebrows. "'My protégé, in a manner of speaking.'"

"I wonder about you, Sullivan. Your imitation's too good."

"Well, I passed my last poly a day or so ago. There was also some eye rolling behind their backs by the other guys."

"And they're both in the army?" said Novak.

"Hey, it's a noble tradition. Remember your ancient Greeks? All those warriors in short skirts? You were in Athens, right? During the coup. Didn't some of those colonels have their little lieutenants?"

"Maybe we can use this," said Novak. "What else?"

"That's about it. Except the last thing he said about it was what worried me the most." He expected Novak to respond. Novak stared at him and said nothing. "Don't you want me to keep talking?"

"Yeah, but I got a hunch I'm not gonna wanna hear what I'm gonna hear."

"Well, the last thing he said, he talked about what happened after I left Ethiopia. The coup and all that. He said maybe they might have to keep me here forever. So what happened to Haile Selassie wouldn't happen to the Shah."

Novak nodded. "I knew I didn't wanna hear it. Look, Langley sent me a cable on what you did with the Shah in Ethiopia. Spent some private time with him. Got some good reporting, but don't get any ideas about seeing him while you're here. The ambassador meets with the Shah. And from this shop the chief of station, and only the chief of station, meets with the Shah. Do you fucking understand me?"

"I understand," said Frank.

"Any questions?"

Yeah, a couple of hundred, thought Frank, remembering Pete Howard's instructions to take advantage of any opportunity to meet with the Shah.

"No," he said. "But there is something else. The guy from the Imperial Guard, the Shah's bodyguard squad, right? He wasn't there."

"And?"

"General Merid said he won't be there. Ah, pressing other duties, right?"

"Keep talkin'." Novak's anger seemed to have ebbed. Frank hoped the worst was over.

"Well, Nazih gave us the idea the colonel from the Imperial Guard was tight with *Savak*."

"And?"

"Well," said Frank, "he wasn't there."

"And?"

"So you got a call from someone, right?"

Novak said nothing. His expression didn't change.

"So we can figure the room is bugged, at least by *Savak*. Maybe the military. Not by us because if you had an agent with access to bug the place you wouldn't need me and Gus and Bunker coming over here."

"I fucking *don't* need you and Gus and Bunker coming over here. You got a great imagination, Sullivan. You shoulda been a writer, a novelist. This is fucking fascinating. Keep talking," he snapped.

Frank wished he hadn't brought up the Imperial Guard and *Savak*.

"So what my imagination tells me is that *Savak* has our meetings wired or someone else in our little nest is wired to *Savak*. But who?"

"Gee, Sullivan, I wish I could tell ya. I really do."

"Okay," said Frank. "Okay." But he knew it wasn't okay. As a spy, he expected others would spy on him. But he hadn't expected that his chief of station would have Iranian assets spying on him.

"Look, Frank. I'll level with you. You did a helluva job with the book club operation when you were in Rome. You screwed up one of my guys who worked with it, but maybe he had it comin'. I read everything in your 201 file before you got t' Rome. All great shit. I read the update, in a hurry, before they threw you over here. More great shit. You've always been a little flaky, but that's not your real problem. Your real problem is you get too involved. You got too fuckin' involved in Ethiopia. You got too fuckin' involved in Rome. Maybe gettin' involved is a good thing, sometimes. Like in Ethiopia. But not here. You shouldn't even be here, much less gettin' too involved. Got it?"

"Got it."

"As long as you're here, just walk through it, okay? I'll be honest with you. Once Bunker's in place, I'm gonna ask NE to pull you outta here."

I'm not here because of Near East, thought Frank. I'm here because of Covert Action. He said nothing. He didn't want to give Novak a better idea of what strings to pull. He wanted to stay and get the job done.

After a long pause that he hoped looked thoughtful, Frank nodded and said, "Okay." Then he asked, "How come?"

"You know how come. Now that all the shitfaces on Jayface think you've got a pipeline to the Shah, they won't be telling you squat about what's really on their minds."

"Maybe it could work the other way around. Maybe some of them might figure I could be the only way they could get a message to the Shah. Not a whole lot of junior officers have access to the commander in chief."

"Yeah, I thought of that," said Novak. "But mostly it makes you look like a palace fink. If Bunker was here I'd ship you out on the next plane, but that's the other good news I got today."

Frank smiled. "Talk to me."

"Delayed," said Novak. "Ten days. High-level briefings. Our pissant President wants a new National Intelligence Estimate with more military input. They're working up a presidential finding, and they want Bunker up to speed on the requirements before he comes out here. So you're gonna have to sweat it best you can, at least until Bunker gets here. But stay outta trouble. Don't get too involved, and stay the fuck away from the palace."

"I haven't been invited," said Frank.

"Keep it that way. Stick to the misfits they'll have you locked up with at Jayface. God knows what you'll find to talk about all day, since they won't know squat about what's going on, and for chrissake don't stir up any trouble."

Show the flag, thought Frank. And be a fly on the wall.

"And don't get mixed up with anyone else at the Supreme Commander's, because we do have a few assets up there, though God knows they aren't worth much. Stay away from the embassy as much as possible, and let the rest of us do what we're supposed to do. Got that?"

"Got it," said Frank.

"And Sullivan, you've already been told what else to stay away from, right?"

"Right," said Frank. Here comes Lermontov, he thought.

"I don't know how blunt the Near East or South Asia or whatever the fuck they call that division these days laid it out, but I'm going to be very fucking blunt. For as long as it takes to get you shipped outta here, you're gonna keep a very low profile. This town is crawling with journalists from all over the world who think they smell a civil war or some fucking disaster, and you and Simpson both have the good fortune to know a lot of journalists from all over the world, and the last fucking thing I need is to have any of them run into you and start asking around about what the fuck you're doing here. To make it worse, one of the so-called journalists is that Lermontov thug who's supposed to work for Tass. You two go back a long way together, right?"

"Yeah, we do."

"All the way to Ethiopia where you got his ass PNG'd, right?"

"Right."

"And he's had a major league hard-on for you ever since, right?"

"No big deal," said Frank. "Just he's showed up a few places where I had an assignment."

"Like Rome," said Rocky. "Where he tried to recruit one of my assets. Like Beirut, where he tried to get you killed."

Frank shrugged. "A lot of people got shot at in Beirut in those days, including our ambassador, and no one ever figured out who set that one up either."

"Let me make this very fucking clear, Sullivan. You are to have no contact, I repeat, no fucking contact with this fucking Lermontov thug. Is that clear?"

"Clear," said Frank. And clearly the opposite, he thought, of what Pete Howard had told him to do.

A tense, gray-haired secretary looked up from her desk as Frank followed Rocky into the ambassador's outer office. Gus, already escorted upstairs by one of Rocky's case officers, waited for them.

"He's expecting you," said the secretary, arcing her eyebrows from Novak to an imposing set of metal-covered doors.

Novak looked at his two charges and muttered, "Don't mention it to the ambassador. What I said about the demonstration. I was just jokin'."

Ambassador Cornelius O'Connor stood with his back to them, staring out through the ceiling-high rear windows overlooking lawns and pines and sycamore trees that stretched toward his residence and the rear gates of the embassy. Another emperor, thought Frank. But not master of all he surveys. The demonstration at the front gates was only a murmur that the ambassador couldn't see from his spacious office. Frank could recognize the sound of a chant leader's voice over a bull horn and a rhythmic crowd response that sounded like "uh-uh." He could smell burning rubber, and from television news clips he'd watched he could imagine the scene. He tried to focus his attention on the small hands clasped behind the ambassador's back.

"Mr. Ambassador." O'Connor continued to stare out the rear windows. Novak fiddled with the knob on his hearing aid and tried again. "Your Excellency."

"I hear you, Rocky. But God, this depresses me." The ambassador turned to face them. The white hair, neatly cut, framed a ruddy, almost unlined face. If the hair had been dark, O'Connor would have looked very young, thought Frank, and very innocent. He was relatively short, not more than five-eight, Frank guessed. Like many short men, he tended to stand at his fullest height, legs and spine straight, chin slightly lifted. He walked around the desk, glanced at their badges, and extended a tiny hand, first to Gus, then to Frank. "Simpson . . . Sullivan. Welcome aboard."

He motioned to a circle of plush chairs and a sofa that surrounded a low table of ornate teak. Frank and Gus sank into deep cushions on either end of the sofa. O'Connor settled into a stiff leather chair facing the sofa and the huge windows behind it. Frank noticed he sat ramrod straight, his delicate hands firmly propped on his knees. Novak eased himself into the remaining chair.

"The other one?"

"Fred Bunker. Not here yet," said Novak. "Not till sometime next week.

He's scheduled in on Scandinavian Air from Paris. As of tomorrow, they'll be the only ones still flying in."

"No more Pan Am flights?"

"No more," said Novak.

"Well, that's to be expected, I suppose." O'Connor turned, first to Gus, then to Frank, then to a point somewhere just over their heads in the infinity beyond the sofa. "I'm glad to have you here, gentlemen, because to tell you the truth all this has caught us pretty much by surprise."

"Mr. Ambassador . . ."

O'Connor cut Novak off with a raised hand.

"Yes, yes, I know you told us trouble was coming, and it's here, but there's more out there than the usual bunch of radical students and Communists and left-wing guerrillas. There are people out there we don't know about and *Savak* either doesn't know about or isn't telling us about. Merchants, even some of the military, conservative, religious people—we don't know much about them or why they're out there."

"*Savak* keeps us pretty well wired into the turban men," said Rocky.

"Oh, yes," said the ambassador. "God knows we talk to *Savak*. We talk to the Shah, his advisers, the top military, and we talk to the Israelis, who always seem to know more about what's going on than we do."

"What does the Shah say?" asked Gus.

O'Connor glanced at Rocky. Rocky acted as though he hadn't heard.

"I get the feeling . . ." The ambassador hesitated. "I talk to the Shah just about every other day. He talks and talks, but I get the feeling, he wants . . . something."

"We know what he wants," said Rocky. "He wants to run."

"We've been told that," said O'Connor.

"A source close to the highest level," said Novak.

"I know, Rocky, I know you're doing a good job with what you've got to work with, but you've only been here a few months. And the embassy's resources have been cut to the bone. In 1960 the ambassador here had twenty-three political officers. Today I have eight. And we need to reach out beyond the Iranian assets we've got who tell us the Shah is in perfect health but afraid and our only enemy is *Tudeh* and the Soviets."

"We know the Soviets created, pay for, and run the *Tudeh* party," said Novak. "And we damn well know the *Tudeh* party has its hands into all those Muslim groups."

"We know because that's what *Savak* tells us, and sometimes I think what *Savak* tells us is what they think we want to hear."

"Don't sell *Savak* short."

"Barbarians," said the ambassador. "And we get blamed for creating them."

"They didn't get the heavy stuff from us. Israeli intelligence taught 'em that stuff. And Mossad still has a tight in with *Savak*."

"You're right," said the ambassador. He turned to Frank and Gus. "The Israelis don't even have an embassy here. No diplomatic recognition. Just a mission. But Mossad appears to be very active and well informed."

"I don't know," said Rocky. "They seem to make too much of this religious business."

"And that's not what Washington wants to hear, is it?" said the ambassador. "Washington's requirements keep asking for confirmation that the Soviets and the *Tudeh* party they run here are responsible for everything. Somehow I'm not quite convinced this Khomeini character is a Soviet asset, but then we don't know a hell of a lot about who the hell or what the hell Khomeini is."

"He's being used," said Novak.

"Maybe he is," said O'Connor, "but I've been here two years . . ." He looked down at his hands, clasped and unclasped them. "Well, nearly two years, and I've never seen anything like this." He glanced from Gus to Frank, but, as he continued to speak, sitting stiffly in his stiff leather chair, he again looked over their heads. "The Shah himself approved this project of yours. He thinks the military can play a role in winning the loyalty of the people. Whether it's too late for that or not, I don't know. Your contacts at Jayface have the advantage of being younger officers. The only one I know is General Merid, the army man. At least one, the navy captain, is said to be quite religious. Are you a Catholic, Sullivan?"

"Lapsed."

"Good. You may be more understanding than a holier-than-thou."

"He means me," said Novak. "Ever since we got a white man for Pope last month, he's been on my case."

"White man?" said Frank.

"Yeah. First time we had a white man for Pope since we had all those French Popes back in the fourteenth century."

"What about all those Italians?" said Gus.

"Hey, don't tell me you consider Italians white?"

"You know you don't mean that," said the ambassador.

"Hell I don't."

Frank knew Novak was a product of New York, from somewhere in the far reaches of the Bronx. He'd been one of the rare Polish Catholics at DeWitt Clinton High School at a time when most students were Jewish, and he'd gone on to Fordham and Georgetown. Despite a doctorate in Slavic studies and many years working in Europe, though, the rough Bronx edges had not worn off.

"Rocky just likes to shock people," said the ambassador. "But it won't hurt in this situation to have some understanding of the religious impulse. There's more than politics involved here. At least politics in the usual cold war terms."

Novak looked pained. "At least with a good Polish Pope we've got someone who understands Communists. And the cold war."

The ambassador ignored him. "I'm glad you've started meeting with your counterparts at Jayface. There's no need for you to just hang around until Bunker arrives."

"I still wonder about that, sir . . ."

O'Connor waved Novak off with a pale hand.

"I know you wanted to wait till the whole team was here, but we need to see what we can find out about this mess from some new sources as soon as we can, don't you agree?"

"I don't think we'll find out much from these bozos in the first damn place," said Novak.

Frank rubbed the bridge of his nose with the fingertips of both hands to cover his smile. Evidently the ambassador had already won a round against Rocky. Frank had become accustomed to tension between the agency's chiefs of station and the ambassadors they worked with. He'd learned the same problem existed between the KGB's *rezidents* and the ambassadors at Soviet embassies. Some natural instinct had always managed to keep him out of the line of fire.


The bitter smell of burning tires pinched their nostrils as they walked across the lawns and under the sheltering pine trees and towering sycamores that stretched from the embassy to the iron back gate. Spirals of black smoke curled into the gray sky beyond the leafless top branches of the sycamores. An uneasy hush had replaced the shouts of the demonstrators.

"Sounds like all's quiet on the embassy front," said Gus.

"Maybe they heard we're heading for the back gate," said Frank.

"Do you think your buddy Novak really arranged all that?"

"No, not really. Not at his own embassy." He glanced back over his shoulder and up through the branches of the sycamores. One spiral of black smoke made him think of a Midwest twister looking for a place to settle. "At least, I don't think so."

Two marine guards stood at the gate. One studied the papers pushed through the bars of the gate by an excited Iranian in his twenties. Others pressed behind him, keeping up a low, unintelligible murmur and waving clutched papers above their heads.

The other marine stood apart, studying the narrow street beyond the gate and the windows of the apartments that watched the back of the embassy like rectangular dark gray eyes. The second marine, whose dress greens bore the stripes of a corporal, turned and saluted as they approached.

"Your car's waiting for you, sir. Right behind that shed."

"Thanks," said Frank. "But what's going on at the gate?"

"Host-country nationals, sir. Waiting for the consulate to reopen."

"For visas?" said Gus.

"Sir, yes, sir, but it would be better, sir, if they didn't get too good a look at you gentlemen. They might get too curious, if you follow my meaning, sir."

He was the perfect marine, thought Frank. Tall, fair, solidly built, square shouldered, and square jawed. He might have marched right out of a recruiting poster. Well trained, absurdly young, but aware of his responsibility and capable of exercising authority. Or at least trying to.

"You mean all those folks want to get away to the country of the Great Satan?" said Gus.

"Sir, it wouldn't surprise me if some of the same crew who were out at the front fuckin' gates a few minutes ago shouting 'Kill the Americans' bop-assed around the block and are waiting out here now, begging for a U.S. visa, sir."

"It wouldn't surprise me," echoed Gus.

"But I would appreciate it, sir, if you would sequester behind that shed where your car is until you're ready to leave. Out of sight, out of mind, if you know what I mean, sir, and we don't want these I-ranians getting any ideas about you comin' out that gate."

"I think we better get the car." Frank realized the marine was getting nervous, and polite young men with guns worried him when they got nervous. The corporal escorted them to the car.

"Give me three minutes, sir. Get your engine nice and warm. Then drive around the shed nice and easy, and we'll swing the gates open for you. After that, you're on your own."

Frank made a mistake. While the engine warmed, he lowered his window. And forgot it.

The gates swung open. Frank drove through in second gear, turning to his right as he exited. A bony but strong hand thrust suddenly through the window and grabbed his left wrist.

"Please, sir, take me with you to American." Frank braked, and a circle of Iranians began to close around the car. "I am very America. My English is excellent. I can work well very hard."

Frank tried to pull his arm away, but the Iranian, short and slightly built, held him with intense, pleading dark eyes and bony fingers in a viselike grip. He worked his head and shoulders into the car, breathing hard in Frank's face.

"I'm not going to America," said Frank.

"Where are you going, sir? What is your destination now? Where do you stay in Tehran?"

Frank tried again to pull away. "Our assignment has been changed," he yelled into the ear of the man who held his wrist. "We're going to Ethiopia. A very poor country in Africa where many people are dying of leprosy." He saw the intense eyes falter, and the grip on his arm eased. "But I'm used to lepers. I've worked with lepers in Africa before." He pulled his arm free, and the Iranian drew back, mouth agape, staring at Frank.

Frank began to ease the small Fiat through the crowd. Young men in dark trousers and heavy sweaters and jackets still pressed close, flanked by women in long black coats and chadors on one side of the street and middle-aged men with black mustaches in parkas or somber coats on the other. The crowd backed off, encouraged by a few young men who stretched out their arms, gently moving people away to make a path for the car. Frank studied the face of one college-age man who helped to part the crowd. He expected to see anger and hate but instead sensed sadness and something deeper that he couldn't name. It lay in the eyes, dark, quizzical, bewildered.

"We betrayed them," said Gus. "And I don't want to be here when they really get mad."


"So far," said Frank, "I got a hand grenade through the window, a message from the palace that freaked out Rocky, and an Iranian wannabe-American who nearly pulled my arm off."

"Sounds like a pretty good day," said Troy, rocking back in his chair, laughing.

"Despite all that," said Gus, "we would like to file some cables."

Troy swiveled toward Gus. "Do you really have to?"

Gus glanced at Frank, and Frank answered for both of them. "Yeah. Yeah, we do. We need traces on our Jayface friends, especially the little army major with buddies at the palace, and to see if there's any derogatories, especially on the guy from the air force, because if there's not he might be worth going after, but also just on g.p.'s it might not be a bad idea to let our friends back in Virginia know that we put in a dishonest day's work for our honest day's pay."

"Okay, okay. I get the message," said Troy. "You can use the IBM in Rushmore's office. Don't take your time. I'm gonna have to stay and baby-sit you two, starting with opening Rushmore's safe and getting you the typewriter ribbon, and sometime tonight I wanna get home to dinner."

"Ah, about that hand grenade?" said Gus.

"A dud," said Troy. "No way it could explode. Just a message. The window's fixed, and tomorrow we ought to be able to get some plates put in up there."

Just a message, thought Frank. Like the shots that got my headlights in Beirut. And it's only the beginning. He could sense more trouble coming. From the streets. From the Shah. Perhaps from Lermontov. And, for sure, from Rocky.

# CHAPTER FOUR

I'm going to need help with cables," said Frank. "I've only worked inside once, but right now I've forgotten most of what I learned. And I don't even know the cryptonym for Iran."

"SD," said Gus. "Don't sweat it. I'll be your secretary. Immediate Flash, NOFORN?"

"Why Immediate Flash?" said Frank. "This stuff isn't that important."

"That's why," said Gus. "Immediate Flash makes it sound important. We don't want anybody in Langley to get the idea this is some bullshit assignment."

"Okay," said Frank. He shrugged. Maybe someday I'll get to understand bureaucrats. Immediate Flash meant the highest transmission priority. The cable would be in Langley within seconds of being sent from the embassy. He had to struggle a moment for NOFORN. No Foreign Distribution. Which meant only American clients of the agency would see it.

Gus popped in one of the ribbons Troy had given them and placed a type-face ball in the IBM Selectric typewriter. "We're KUSTAFF," said Gus as he banged out a request for any available backgrounds on their Jayface counterparts. "Peregrine, that's you, right?"

"How'd you know my cryp?" Frank had not learned his own cryptonym until he first worked inside a station in Lusaka.

"Hey, I've read some traffic on you over these many years. You've been Peregrine ever since Ethiopia."

It bothered Frank to learn that he'd carried the same cryptonym ever since his first assignment in Ethiopia. It also bothered him that he'd become so fascinated with the falcon some anonymous code clerk had named him for.

Gus muttered as he typed. *Traces and any derogatories requested on:*

*a. SDHERALD-1 two-star general; attaché ODYOKE early 1960s, four years RI late 1960s.*

All the jargon he'd learned of rubrics and parameters began pouring back into Frank's memory as he watched Gus work the bureaucratic formulas. Frank guessed SDHERALD meant the Iranian Army. General Merid had told them he'd been a military attaché in Washington, which would account for ODYOKE, and he remembered RI from his own days in Rome.

    *b. SDHERALD-2 major, attached palace, nephew SDHERALD-1.*

    *c. SDWAVE-1 captain.*

    *d. SDTRIB-1 major, trained Reese AFB du.*

    *e. SDELECT-1 col., contact with SDEAGLE-1.*

Gus pulled the cable from the typewriter and gave it to Frank to read while he switched ribbons. TRIB with its reference to Reese had to be the air force; WAVE, no problem, the navy; ELECT must be the missing chicken colonel from the Imperial Bodyguard. EAGLE, he knew stood for *Savak*. He remembered "du" as date unknown.

The second cable matched names with the limited descriptions given in the first. The communications room at the embassy would encrypt and send the two cables at staggered times, minimizing the risk that, even if they were decoded, an interceptor could match up content with names.

    *a. Dariush Merid*

    *b. Hossein Nazih*

    *c. Munair Irfani*

    *d. Anwar Amini*

    *e. lnu, fnu*

Last name unknown, first name unknown, thought Frank. "If we put that in, they're going to come back wanting us to get his name."

"Not to worry," said Gus. "The station will know it and fill it in. That's why they pay Rocky and his guys the big bucks."

"I'm glad you told me," said Frank. "Now we better do one on the word from the palace."

" 'Fraid so," said Gus. He again switched ribbons. "I'll do the headings. I don't know the crypt for palace. The station will. You can write this one."

*Ident d., an untested source of unknown reliability,* Frank began and tersely reported what Nazih had said about the Shah's recollections of him from Ethiopia.

"That should stir up a shit storm," said Gus as he read Frank's cable.

"I know. But they're going to hear it soon anyway, so they may as well hear it from me. How 'bout one more on our no show?" Frank did a final cable informing headquarters that one of their counterparts, Identity E, the colonel from the Imperial Bodyguard whom the ambassador had identified as close to *Savak*, would not participate in their meetings.

"That should do it," said Gus.

"That should do it, except for an agenda for our Jayface friends tomorrow."

"Troy'll kill us."

"I'll be quick," said Frank. "Why don't you go talk cables to him, and I'll bat it out."

While Gus carried their cables down the hall, Frank went to work. He headed his paper simply AGENDA with the next day's date, 5 NOVEMBER 78. He labeled his first section CIVIC ACTION. He outlined programs the military might undertake in both urban and rural areas. He called on what he knew about similar programs in countries from Ethiopia to Southeast Asia, plus a few ideas like benzene distribution and sewage systems he thought might have particular local appeal. He had just typed SECTION 2: IMAGE ENHANCEMENT and was halfway through the one-page agenda he planned when he heard a door open behind him. He turned and saw a bearded mountain of a man in a hooded parka, blue jeans, and black cowboy boots filling the doorway.

"Oh?" said the giant. "And who might you be?"

"I might be an air force major here on temporary assignment."

"Ah." Frank thought the giant might have ventured a smile, but it was hard to be sure through the vast beard. "You must be Sullivan. Or Simpson."

"I'm the Sullivan," said Frank. "The Simpson is down the hall with Colonel Troy."

"Bill Steele," said the big man. He entered the room and eased the door shut behind him. "I'm the security officer for the branch."

"Frank Sullivan." He stood and reached out a hand. Steele's handshake was gentle.

"I checked out that house of yours today. There are a couple of things I'll take care of tomorrow to tighten up the place best as we can. The electricity needs work, and the plumbing, and we'll get some steel window screens upstairs. I put some more candles in for tonight—and matches. And a couple of flashlights and extra batteries on the kitchen table. Oh, and I turned the heat on. Should've done that before you got here."

"Not to worry," said Frank. "Are you—air force security?"

"I report to Colonel Troy."

"Okay. I wish I'd known I could've gotten away with a beard. I shaved mine off before I . . ."

"Trust me," said Steele. "I didn't have this when I came over. The boss doesn't mind, and over here it helps. Especially dealing with Iranians. Which I do a lot of." He nodded at the typewriter. "You going to be at that long?"

"Another fifteen, maybe twenty minutes. I also need to hit the copier for a minute."

"The copier?"

"Yeah," said Frank. "It's an agenda for a meeting with our counterparts. They asked for it, so I'll need copies."

"Well, you better talk to the colonel. Let him read it before you make copies. We're as bad as the Soviets about copiers. We only got one, and it's locked up in a storeroom. He and I have the only keys. I hope the damn thing's working."

"Me, too. I figure there's no carbon paper, and I don't want to type this thing five times."

"Russians do it," said Steele. "They want copies of material the Soviets don't like, they type till their fingers wear out. Call it . . ."

"*Samizdat?*" said Frank.

"Somethin' like that."

With their tasks finished, Steele suggested that Frank and Gus stop at the *chelakebab* stand opposite the main gates of the air force base. Troy had already left, hurrying home to dinner. Steele had helped Frank run his agenda through the copier, and they were in Stan Rushmore's office, putting typewriter ribbons in separate safes, stuffing stray pieces of paper into burn bags, and locking up.

"Now tell me about this chili-kebab," said Gus. "I heard that can be a pretty dangerous place to do your shopping these days."

"Not that I know of," said Steele.

"Tom . . . Colonel Troy, I mean, while we were chewing the fat just a couple of minutes ago, he told me an air force guy got his throat slit at that chili-kebab place."

"Different place," said Steele. "We shut that one down. Besides, the guy was drunk, which is not a good idea these days, and making a scene about wanting a woman, which is a very bad idea these days. Things have changed a lot since these folks started getting excited about Khomeini."

"Folks back in the States don't seem to have heard much about him," said Frank.

"They will," said Steele. "The Iranians think he walks on water."

"You seem to know a lot about the locals," said Gus.

"Not a lot," said Steele. "None of us do. But I deal with the Iranians more than most. Which reminds me. Your servants were in today, but with you having eight o'clock meetings downtown and that being about the time they get to the house, you're gonna have a communications problem."

"Housekeeping," said Gus.

"Biggest part of my job," said Steele. "There's no real food at the house. I put in some basics. Canned goods, salt and pepper."

"Toilet paper?" asked Gus.

"Yeah, lots of toilet paper. Take some to your meetings with the Iranians."

"Will do," said Gus. "But tell me. I've been lots of places where you take a dump by squatting over a hole in the floor and there's no toilet paper so you bring your own. But in the crapper at Supreme Commander's they had something new. What's with the pitcher of water?"

"They tell me it's in the Koran. Feed your mouth with your right hand. Clean your asshole with the left."

"Okay," said Gus. "But no towels, no paper? You can shake your hand dry, but no matter how good you are at wiggling your ass, and I bet our chubby little general is pretty good at that, there's no way you can shake your ass dry before you pull your pants back up."

"Maybe they're smart as we are," said Steele. "Maybe they bring their own paper."

"Okay," said Gus. "But it smells pretty bad. Can't they do somethin' about that?"

"You're lucky it's winter," said Steele. "Smells a lot worse in summer even though they usually hose it down every day."

Frank decided he liked this giant who paid attention to the locals, took care of details, and worried about security.

"I'll talk to the servants in the morning," continued Steele. "But leave a note and some money if you want them to get you anything on the local market. It's a husband-and-wife team. The husband speaks English but can't read it. The wife doesn't do much talking, but she can read English and she can understand. Fresh milk, eggs, things like that. Leave a note."

"Yogurt?" said Frank.

"Yogurt?" echoed Gus.

"Something I learned," said Frank. "In a new country, try to get some of the local yogurt. Healthy bacteria in yogurt gets your stomach used to handling local bacteria in the food, water, leafy veggies, stuff like that."

Steele smiled. "I do that myself. Leave a note and some money. Tomorrow afternoon I'll take you to the Post Exchange. There are two. The commissary at the embassy where you can get booze, cameras, cigarettes, clothes, but not much in the way of food. You can take care of that on your own when you're down there. I'll get you started at the military PX near the base. No booze, but real American meat and potatoes, frozen, canned, dried, powdered, whatever. Some fresh vegetables and fish flown in, but don't count on it. The housewives will beat you to it every time."

"Are you married, Bill?" asked Gus.

"Yeah, but I can't volunteer my wife to help you out. I sent her and the kids back home. Far as I'm concerned, it's too hairy around here for families."

"You don't recommend Iran?"

"I like Iran," said Steele. "I've been here two years." He looked at the maps on the walls of the office where Rushmore had his desk. Like the maps in Troy's office, they were pierced with pins. "Every place you see a pin, we've had a problem. Somebody killed, beaten up, mugged, house broken into, car set on fire, some damn thing. I like Iran, but I don't recommend it anymore."

They found the *chelakebab* shop without difficulty and parked opposite it on the dark street called Farahnaz. The hand-printed sign above the door was in Farsi, and the windows were steamed over, but Steele had described it well. A bell tinkled as Frank opened the door, and two young Americans turned from the steam table and its mix of odors. They might have been twins, thought Frank at first glance. Tall, slim, ruddy complexions, and regular features. Both wore dark blue parkas and black wool caps pulled low over their foreheads. Frank noticed one difference. Long, light brown hair curled below the back rim of the cap worn by the young man nearer the door.

"Evening," said Gus.

"Evening, sir," said the long-haired American.

"Cold out there," said his partner.

"Yes, it is." Gus looked over the steam table and glanced at the two Iranians behind it. "What do you recommend?"

"Well, you could have lamb and rice, or maybe some rice and lamb," said the American with no visible hair. Frank now noticed he had brown eyes and stood shorter than his blue-eyed friend.

"Sounds like what we had for lunch," said Frank.

The blue-eyed American reached out his hand. "Todd Waldbaum," he said.

"Frank Sullivan. And this is my father. His name is Gus Simpson."

They exchanged laughs and handshakes. The brown-eyed American said his name was Dwight Claiborne.

"There is a cafeteria at the base, but this is actually better," said Todd. "There's also a pretty good market right next door. Has a lot of American stuff, but this time of evening it's closed."

"I got a hunch," said Dwight, "a lotta what they sell comes out the commissary back door."

"Wouldn't surprise me," said Gus.

"Saw you guys coming out of Colonel Troy's office." said Todd. "We're air force guards. Regular air force."

"Gotcha," said Gus.

Dwight took two brown paper bags of food from one of the Iranians. Both countermen wore stained white uniforms. One was tall, very thin, and bearded. The other was short and stocky and wore a drooping mustache and a sullen expression. Todd dug into his pockets for a handful of rials.

"How did you fellows get here?" said Gus. "I didn't see a car."

"We just walked over," said Todd. "We're still on duty."

"This is like our lunch," said Dwight. "You should pardon the expression."

"Are you parked out there?" asked Todd.

"Uh-huh," answered Frank and Gus together.

"Tell you what," said Todd. "We'll wait outside. Keep an eye on your car."

" 'Preciate that," said Gus.

The bell tinkled, and a cold blast of wind hit them as the young guards left.

"I like those young men," said Gus. "Something tells me it might be a good idea to get to know some of these air force guards. They must have weapons."

Frank had tried for spinach and learned the Farsi word for no is *"nah,"* as in *"nah spin'ch."* The taller counterman had tilted a huge pot in Frank's direction, revealing overcooked cabbage.

*"Kalam."*

Frank had learned another word, and he ordered *kalam* to go with their rice and lamb. "I'm trying to balance our diet."

"Lots of luck," grunted Gus.

Frank tried for yogurt, but there was *nah* yogurt.

Outside, Todd and Dwight stood by the blue Fiat.

"I take it it's not a good idea to park on the street," said Gus.

"It's a very bad idea, sir," said Dwight. "About the best thing could happen, someone would steal it or slash your tires or put sugar in your gas tank. But you'd be real surprised how fast a raghead can hook up a bomb to your ignition while you're in a place with steamed-up windows."

"And it's always a good idea to look in your back seat before you get behind the wheel," said Todd. "By the way, if you want to get some wine to wash this stuff down with, believe it or not there's still a liquor store around the corner."

"Maybe the last one in Tay-fuckin'-ran," said Dwight.


Frank and Gus had just settled into their candlelit dinner at their Formica-topped kitchen table when the lights suddenly came on.

"And the Lord said, 'Let there be electricity once in a while.' "

*"Inshallah,"* said Frank and blew out the candles.

The lights briefly flickered, then glowed.

"It must be a sign," said Gus. He had opened one of the bottles of a South African Riesling of "guaranteed excellence" they had bought at the dark and nearly barren liquor store they found not far from the *chelakebab* parlor. Todd and Dwight had described the drawn blinds on the windows and the poster-size portrait of Khomeini on the door. A smaller color photo of the Ayatollah had been tacked to the empty shelves behind the counter. The owner confessed his love for "that man," even though his business would be finished when Khomeini came.

"And you think he will come?" said Gus.

"He will come," said the man. "He is here."

"He can't be good for business," said Gus.

"No. Not good for business. Even now, so many foreigners have gone. And Persians, they still buy, but . . . I must confess, gentlemen, in this country to make an honest living these days you have to be a crook. And I can't cheat Persians the way I can cheat foreigners."

"I wonder how much he cheated us," said Gus as he sipped the wine.

"Probably not as much as he could have," said Frank. "Anyway, God is good. We have light, wine, even food."

"Sort of food." Gus ignored the overcooked cabbage, finished chewing a chunk of lamb, and tested a forkful of rice. "You know, until I got here, I thought this was all about the Tudeh party, Russian troops massing on the border, socialist students, and Communist guerrillas. Now I think it's about bad food and benzene lines and the old man with the long white beard."

"I had a talk with Steele about the PX. He'll take us tomorrow. That may help," said Frank.

"It won't make the man with the white beard go away. And, according to a public opinion poll of one liquor store owner, the problem isn't Russia. The problem is the enigma wrapped in a tall black turban."

"We should ask our friends at the Supreme Commander's about this Khomeini."

"Dollars to doughnuts, or rials to soggy rice, we'll get the standard *Savak*-embassy line."

"Maybe not from all of them," said Frank.

"You will as long as they're all together. And I don't think the general would take too kindly to us trying to go one-on-one."

"The general's going to get bored—and careless."

"Maybe," said Gus. "But I have to admit, right now I am more interested in getting to the PX. Besides, I remember you saying you're a pretty good cook."

"My son likes my cooking. Least he says so."

"How old is he?"

"Eleven."

"That's old enough to speak his mind."

"That job in Washington, we're supposed to start livin' together down there." Frank couldn't hold back a grin.

"Sounds like you're lookin' forward to that."

"I am," said Frank. "But I know it's an awesome responsibility."

"Life in the Washington 'burbs won't be as bad as life here," said Gus. "Just concentrate on good home cookin'. You cook. I'll wash the dishes. When Bunker gets here, we'll let him dry. We'll manage the perfect ménage." He poured each of them another glass of the Riesling. "Now that we finished the lamb, young Mister Sullivan, I've got a bone to pick."

"Oh?"

"From what our little friend Major Nazih had to say this morning, seems like there might've been a few things you didn't tell me about your briefing at Langley."

"Yeah, I guess."

"Like about the Shah," said Gus. "Is there anything else you haven't told me?"

"Probably."

"When the old need-to-know bugaboo butts heads with keepin' your workin' buddy in the dark, I don't know about you, but I vote for turnin' on the light. Like havin' that flashlight in my suitcase, remember? I don't like workin' in the dark."

"I hear you," said Frank. "Tell you the truth, by the time those guys in Near East got done with me, I was ready to turn this damn job down. No contact with the Shah who could be a gold mine of intel. No contact with anybody beyond Jayface. And then it got worse."

"You gonna tell Papa Gus, or not?"

Frank proceeded to tell Gus more about Vassily Lermontov than he needed to know.

"Now that you told me all that," said Gus, "I kind of wish you hadn't told me."

"If he does show up," said Frank, "maybe you will need to know."

"No contact," said Gus. "Remember?"

"Yeah, but Near East also told me no contact with the Shah. Rocky said it again up in the bubble, but after listening to Nazih this morning I wonder how long that's going to last."

"I dunno," said Gus. "You may have a pretty good rabbi in Pete Howard, but in his own domain the chief of station is king. And if Rocky says, 'Tick,' you better not tock."

"No contact with Lermontov. A guy I've been involved with for ten years or more. Just show the flag and don't stir up any trouble. It didn't sound like a job worth doing, but when I started to let Dean Lomax know how I felt . . ."

"And Pete Howard?"

"Yeah, Pete was there, but what bothers me, I'm sitting there in Dean's office, not wanting to go to Iran, and I let it happen to me."

"You sound like Joan," said Gus. "Talking about me. You must've noticed. At the airport in Rome. That's why she was so pissed. She likes to remind me I wound up in Vietnam same way I wound up in the marines."

"How's that?" asked Frank, puzzled.

"Lettin' other people decide things for me. Most people in the Marine Corps got there because they enlisted. Me, I got drafted."

"I thought the marines never needed the draft to fill their quota."

"What can I tell you? They must've had a bad week. And I wasn't exactly what you'd call prime gyrene material. I was a dumpy little thing. Kids used to call me Wimpy Simpson. I not only got drafted, I drew a drill instructor who decided he'd make a marine out of me if it killed both of us. Damn near did. But I'll tell you what. About halfway through I saw a way for Wimpy to eat the can of spinach and turn into Popeye. I went through hell to become a marine, but I did it. I even got to be a hand-to-hand instructor at Parris Island. Even did that for the agency for a while down at the farm. But for what? I mean, I like a knife fight as much as the next guy, but how often can you use that stuff? Knowing how to write a good cable, now, that you can use."

"Today at least, I had a pretty good drill instructor."

"Don't count on it. You're gonna have to learn to open your own can of spinach. Other part you don't know," said Gus, "you went to Ethiopia on a two-year contract, right?" Frank nodded. "Same deal I had in Zambia," said Gus. "Except when my two years were up the deal was over. You wound up staying in Ethiopia, what, six, seven years?"

"Like that."

"When my two years were up, the agency asked to me go to Vietnam. And I went along with it, which really pissed Joan off. If you had stayed in Ethiopia only two years, you would've got the same offer—and had a shot at all the fun, all the pussy, and all the promotions that went with it." Gus paused, reading Frank carefully. "And you prob'ly would've let it happen."

"That's what bothers me," said Frank. "I let things happen." Gus uncorked another bottle of Riesling. Frank tipped his glass for the pour, then let it sit. "Locked in."

"If you feel locked in, you can always just quit and get out," said Gus. "No matter what they say in the spy books, it's really not like the Mafia."

Frank nodded but went on as though Gus's words hadn't penetrated. "The bind I'm in now, the other part I didn't tell you, no matter what Rocky says, or what Near East says, Pete wants me to take a crack at Lermontov."

"Ever think," said Gus, "maybe without Lermontov there is no Frank Sullivan, or at least no Peregrine? Ever give that a maybe? Like he's Pete Howard's real reason for sending you here."

"Yeah," said Frank. "And it's a scary thought. That is what Pete wants."

"What do you want?" said Gus.

"All of it. My son. The job in Washington. Lermontov. The Shah. And I want myself. I want to quit letting things happen to me."

"That's a lot," said Gus. "But tell you what. You wanna work inside, you're gonna have to join the team and forget this self of yours. You aren't the Lone Ranger anymore. And I ain't Tonto."

Frank nodded, staring at the Riesling. Maybe Gus was right. He needed Lermontov to validate his own career within the agency, to complete it. To put to rest, as Pete Howard had said, all suspicions that Lermontov might have turned him into a KGB mole. But he didn't want to let it happen. He wanted to make it happen.

# CHAPTER FIVE

ave you heard the news?"

General Merid stood at the head of the table, bouncing on his toes, a smile curved and sharp as a scimitar stretching his round cheeks. Frank and Gus barely had entered the room.

"News?" said Gus, struggling out of his parka.

"The Shah plans to announce tomorrow the formation of a military government. Headed by General Nazeri of the Imperial Guard. Do you realize what this will mean for us?"

"Ah, no, I don't," said Gus.

"It means our work becomes central. It means the military is now the government, and a military program to win the hearts and minds of the people becomes a government program. Our friend Hossein Kasravi, the chicken colonel who has not been with us these days because of his pressing duties, will now be deputy prime minister. We will have total support for our work."

"Say, that is good news. Mind if I hang up my coat? I want to take some notes on this."

Frank stretched out his hand to the general. "Congratulations. You must be very pleased."

"It is a great moment for our country. And for our committee."

"The new government has also banned all newspapers," said Anwar, catching Frank's eye. "From now on you'll have to listen for the garbage man."

"Why the garbage man?"

"They are our country's real news carriers," said Anwar. He was younger and trimmer than the general, and his blue air force major's uniform was worn more casually than the general's crisp khakis, but the lines of his face reflected more thought and care than did the general's unwrinkled brow. "The *ashkhalees*, as we call them, gossip with all the servants and housewives putting out their garbage, even the servants of our leaders. Then they gossip with each other, so among them they have the news of the whole town, and they carry it with them on their rounds, and the servants and the housewives relay it to the men who run, or at least think they run, the house. And the country. I'm sure that's how even the Shah gets his news, although he may not know it. What his ministers' servants get from the garbage men, his ministers pass on to the Shah."

"You must have heard them," said Nazih, the fair young army major. "They come round yelling, *'Ashkhalee, ashkhalee, ashkhalee.'* And the women come out of their houses with their garbage and their gossip."

"I have heard them," said Frank. "Usually before I'm awake."

"As long as we have garbage men," said Nazih, gazing at Frank, "we don't need newspapers."

Frank's agenda had made a big hit with their counterparts at Jayface. It provided a format for talk about civic action programs Iran could have put into effect a decade before but would be impossible to attempt now in a nation at war with itself. No one mentioned the impossibility. Gus talked about the success of such programs in other countries. Frank argued for a major propaganda offensive behind the civic action program, a daily newspaper in Farsi and possibly in Arabic in the south, armed forces television, and, most important of all, radio broadcasts.

"That's true," said Anwar. "Not many people have television yet, but everyone has radio." He paused, jabbing an index finger at the agenda. "And many, many, many have cassette recorders."

"Cassettes?" said Frank. "That's interesting." He began taking notes. "Maybe we could do something with that."

"Hah," said General Merid. It was a comment rather than a laugh.

"The Imam is already a master of that," said Munair Irfani, the navy's representative, whose dark eyes, as usual, fixed on Frank. He spoke gently. "Ayatollah Khomeini and his people."

"Tell me about that," said Frank, trying not to stare at the blood-flecked knot on Munair's forehead.

"Well, even when he was in Iraq, before our government convinced the Iraqis to banish him . . . but the others know all that." Munair paused. The general had managed to catch his eye. "I don't want to take up everyone's time with all that. Perhaps you and I could talk some other time."

"Sure," said Frank. "We could do that."

He wondered if they ever would. He tried to pay attention as General Merid launched a monologue about a course in military civic action programs he had taken at Fort Myer while assigned as an attaché in Washington.

"Maximization of the civilian infrastructure in third party nations can proffer a solidifying basis for the coherent reorganization of military units in productive operational activities, not only in peacetime, but also at times of civil stress . . ."

Frank suspected the general had pulled one of his textbooks off the shelf the night before. Still, the general's fascination with civic action could give them the chance to conduct meetings with a semblance of purpose, even if there was no hope of putting the ideas into practice.

Meanwhile, far more important to Frank were the hints they were beginning to get from their counterparts that they might have information worth pursuing: Khomeini's use of cassettes; a comment the general had made about the "big men upstairs who people think will stage a coup." He believed he and Gus, with patience, could soon learn more.

During the tea break, Major Nazih guided Frank up the hallway, away from the others. "Is there a chance," said Nazih, "your driver could be alerted for a possible assignment this afternoon?"

"He's Iranian Army," said Frank. "He should be responsive to a request from you."

"But he is assigned to you. There is a possibility, only a possibility, mind, His Imperial Majesty may be able to see you this afternoon."

"Wow. That's short notice. I have no clearance from my embassy, or from Washington."

"I do apologize for the short notice. But as I'm sure you understand, His Imperial Majesty faces enormous pressure these days. Enormous demands on his time. And, after your work with Haile Selassie, I'm sure you're used to the ways of emperors."

Frank turned away, embarrassed by Nazih's fluttering lashes. "I'll have to discuss it with my embassy," he said.

"I'm sure with your authority you can make the necessary arrangements."

What the hell does he mean by that? wondered Frank. "I'm afraid I have far less authority than you imagine."

"I do, I confess to you, have a very strong imagination. It's a uniquely Persian attribute. Meanwhile, just in case, you might alert your driver."

"I'll go try to find our driver now," said Frank.

"Do tell him it's just an alert. I won't know for sure till midday. After our meeting."

"What time shall I tell him?" asked Frank.

"I . . . I really don't know. Not yet, I mean. I'll know by midday."

Frank didn't bother getting his parka. He spotted Ali as soon as he stepped into the cold air, standing at attention like a soldier disguised as a civilian by the car that he'd parked in an area close to the building where parking was prohibited. Frank crossed to him quickly.

"Ali, is it possible you might be able to drive me to a meeting, a part of town I really don't know, this afternoon?"

"Yes, sir."

"I'm not sure what time, and I may have someone else with me."

"Sir?"

"Yes?"

"I am not supposed to tell you, sir, and please do not tell anyone I told you, but Major Nazih already alerted me."

"Good. I was hoping he might have. Then you know when and where to pick us up?"

"Yes, sir. Fourteen-thirty hours. By the guardhouse at Dowshan Tappeh."

"Correct. Thank you, Ali."

What a piece of work this Nazih is, thought Frank. The outside stairway that led to a blank wall on the second floor distracted him. He studied the white-washed stone where it stopped. Maybe a door opened there, once upon a time, since bricked over. But he could detect no outline, no shadow of where a door might have been.

Shortly after noon, their dark waiter with the drooping mustache entered the room. He went directly to Nazih and whispered in his ear. Nazih nodded, glancing at Frank. The Jayface meeting concluded just before one.

Nazih helped Frank into his parka. "Good news," he said. "We're confirmed for three-thirty."

Strange, thought Frank. That a waiter should bring the news to Nazih. Then he remembered that the waiter worked for *Savak*.

"Could you have your driver meet us?" asked Nazih. "Say, at two-thirty by the guardhouse at Dowshan Tappeh?"

"We can meet at two-thirty," said Frank. "And I'll let you know what my embassy says."

"They will agree," said Nazih. "I can assure you. *Tout à l'heure,* Major Sullivan."


Anwar joined him at the foot of the stairs. Cold air rushed in as Major Nazih left.

"You have such interesting friends," said Anwar. "I take it you see the Shah this afternoon."

"I think I was the last to know," said Frank.

"Beware," said Anwar smiling. "What play was it . . . the ides of March? Of course. *Julius Caesar.* Shakespeare is popular among us, you know. All those kings and queens and courtiers, full of intrigue and so much like our own royal court today. We can identify with all that, probably much better than Americans."

"Well, Kennedy gave us a taste of Camelot."

"Perhaps. But not like here. The Russians could also understand. Caesar. The Czar. The Shah. All the same man. His Imperial Tyranny. 'Beware the ides of March.' Here we might say beware the tenth of *Moharram, Ashura*. Only a few weeks away. Do you know about it?"

"A bit," said Frank. In fact, he knew nothing, but he suspected he was about to learn.

"It honors the martyrdom of Hossein, son of Ali, the first Imam, and his seventy-two companions, all killed in a battle on the plains of Karbala in the month of *Moharram,* nearly thirteen hundred years ago. And then, more than eleven hundred years ago, the Twelfth Imam disappeared. He was only an infant. We still await his return, the way the Jews still await the Messiah, the Messiah you Christians think was Christ. Some among us think the Twelfth Imam will return when Imam Khomeini's plane sets down out of the sky from Paris." Without pausing, Anwar looked away and said, "But that's mere history. You're more interested in news, isn't it?"

"Both," said Frank.

"There will be news, more arrests. Soon. Including Karim Sanjabi. You know who he is?"

"Head of the opposition?"

Anwar nodded. "He has gone to Paris to meet with Khomeini. When he returns he will be arrested, with others, including another National Front leader, Mahdi Bazargan."

"Won't the National Front object?"

"Yes, but not too loudly. Sanjabi's arrest will make it possible for others to move up, especially with Bazargan also out of the way. Opposition fronts are always divided, aren't they? I don't refer to Iran, of course, but divided opposition helps to keep tyrants in power."

"How do you know these things?"

"Friends. No. Not friends. Sources. You might ask His Imperial Majesty about it."

"I don't think so," said Frank. "I think it's going to be just, you know, just a courtesy call."

Frank drove the Fiat to the embassy for a hastily called meeting in the ambassador's office. Along the way, he briefed Gus on what Nazih had arranged.

"It's not just that I don't like this guy," said Gus. "I flat out don't trust him. He worries me."

"He's cooking up something," said Frank. "So far I don't see anything to do but go along."

"What he's cooking up may be you," said Gus.

"Should I have said I'm too busy to meet with the King of Kings?"

"Maybe just that you're not qualified to meet with him," said Rocky.

"It really is terribly abrupt notice," said the ambassador, folding his delicate hands on the glass table in the plastic bubble. "But my overnight cables include one saying that, at the request of the National Security Council, Mr. Sullivan here should be prepared to accept an invitation to pay a courtesy call on His Imperial Majesty. Did you receive something similar, Rocky?"

"I received something." said Rocky, glaring briefly at Frank. "Something that flat-out contradicts an earlier cable I got saying, again, absolutely no contact."

"Well, we can't ignore the National Security Council, now, can we?" said the ambassador.

Nazih knew, thought Frank. How the hell could he know?

"Mr. Ambassador, sir. Rocky. I have to tell you. This Nazih character, he seemed to know the meet had been approved."

"Who the fuck told him?" said Rocky.

"How the fuck would I know?" answered Frank. He turned to the ambassador, whose ruddy complexion had turned a shade more florid. "Sorry, sir. But I told Nazih I would have to check with my embassy, and he said, 'They will agree.' Something like 'I assure you, they will agree.'"

"Doesn't mean he knew," said Rocky.

"Sounds like he knew," said Gus, earning a cold glance from Rocky.

"He knew, and it worries me," said Frank. "How did he know? And how can we do what we're supposed to if a guy like Nazih knows all about us and what we're up to before we do?"

Frank remembered what Pete Howard had said about the Shah's ambassador, who seemed to know everyone in Washington. He thought about the rivalries back home, Near East Division versus Soviet, both opposing Covert Action and all hostile to the National Security Council. Nazih's words and the NSC cable approving a meeting between Frank and the Shah made him suspect that somewhere there must be a leak, and he wondered how much of a threat that leak might be.

"Seems to me this Nazih character may just be blowin' smoke," said Rocky.

I wonder, thought Frank.

"Be that as it may," said the ambassador, "I believe we have no choice but to have Sullivan go through with it."

"There's desk jockeys back at Langley Near East Division'll have a shit fit," said Rocky.

"I believe if we all just view this as little more than a Sunday afternoon courtesy visit . . ." The ambassador let his sentence trail off.

"That's how I see it," said Frank.

"I guess I'm not feeling too fucking courteous," said Rocky. "I also don't like you taking an Iranian Army driver up there."

"I should have preferred an embassy driver myself," said the ambassador. "Proper protocol."

"Major Nazih had already made the arrangement," said Frank. "Without telling me."

"Like I said, you aren't qualified for this. You let an Iranian Army faggot outmaneuver you."

"What's this?" said the ambassador.

"Long story," said Rocky. "Look, Sullivan, we got no fuckin' choice. Get in your car with Gus here and get back to Dowshan Tappeh. You meet your driver and Nazih and go make nice with the Shah. Don't stir up any trouble. Then get your ass back here and let me know what happened."

"It'll make a nice story for that son of yours," said Gus, "how you hobnobbed with the Shah of Iran, but I worry about what Nazih might have waiting for you up there."

"I'll tell you all about it," said Frank. "Right after I get to tell Rocky."

"You may be in for a long day," said Gus. "Don't worry about the Jayface session. I'll bang out a cable on that—and keep a candle in the window for you."

Nazih sat up front with Ali. Frank slouched low in the back. The falling temperature had rimed the light snow that had fallen in the city. As they ascended into the Elborz Hills under a now sparkling blue sky, Frank noticed that the accumulated snow far exceeded what had fallen in the lower parts of Tehran. The highway itself had been cleared except for a light and, Frank guessed, recent dusting. Ali followed a series of twists and turns, punctuated by an increasing military presence as the iron gates of the palace came into view. Through the gates and banks of tall plane trees, Frank could see a vast, square, drab white building.

"That's the palace?" he asked.

"That's the palace," answered Nazih.

A semicircle of guards with bazookas formed behind the gate as Ali pulled up. Soldiers with casually held automatic weapons lined the car on both sides. Ali rolled down his window. Nazih leaned across the seat and beckoned to a guard with officer's bars on his greatcoat. Nazih showed no identification, but the officer spoke into a crackling walkie-talkie. Frank noticed the video camera perched on top of the guardhouse aimed their way. He saw no signal, but evidently the officer standing by their car did. With a wave of his hand, he ordered the gates open. Ali eased the Chevy through. He stopped, put the car in neutral, and pulled on the hand brake.

"We must alight now," said Nazih, in a bored tone. "For security." He launched himself out of the car. With a grunt, Ali swung himself out of the driver's seat. Frank followed their lead. Soldiers with metal detectors sounded every inch of Frank and Ali, checking keys, spare change, belt buckles, and, from Frank, even a pen with a metal clasp. Nazih endured a much more cursory check. As the car started up the drive, Frank noticed two Chieftain tanks sited on knolls to either side of the drive. The cannon protruding from the turrets loomed threateningly, but their size and frozen aspect convinced him the tanks were museum pieces, meant to impress rather than attack.

Then the turrets moved. The cannon lowered, aimed straight at the car.

"Whoa," said Frank.

"Not to worry," said Nazih. "That's just to let us know they can, if they have to."

"I feel like the groom at a shotgun wedding," said Frank.

"What a charming expression," said Nazih. "Perhaps that's just what you are."

As they approached closer to the palace, Ali swung off to the right onto a narrower road. "We're not going to the palace?" said Frank.

"Not there," said Nazih.

They climbed toward a smaller and handsomer building with high arched windows and a steeply sloping roof. It commanded a slope marked by the winter-bleak shell of formal gardens.

"We're going here," said Nazih. "Here His Imperial Majesty has his offices." He pointed and said something to Ali in Farsi.

Ali answered in English, "Yes, Major." He eased the Chevrolet into a marked parking area.

Frank checked his watch. Three-fifteen. Fifteen minutes early.

"Some of us who spend some time in these precincts call this the 'small palace' or the 'real palace,' even the 'Russian palace.' Have you spent any time in Russia?"

"None," said Frank.

"I'm surprised. You should. I don't know if there's a Russian word for château, but if there is, particularly a provincial château, I think it describes this building."

"I take it you have been to Russia?" said Frank.

Nazih ignored the question. "When your ambassador comes to visit His Imperial Majesty, which these days is quite often, he usually sees him over lunch in the main palace. Important, of course, but His Majesty has asked to meet you in his offices. In the subtleties of court culture, that indicates you are of a lesser stature than the ambassador. But, if you consider the distinction between dining room table and office, you rank perhaps as someone to be met with in a more businesslike setting. Do you follow me?"

"You are not easy to follow," said Frank.

"I do not intend to be, but I count on you to follow me."

"Then I guess I'll follow you."

"A word, or two, before we enter. I've already told your driver you may be here for quite a while. However long it takes, he and I will wait to return you to your office. You and I will, of course, wait on His Majesty's imperial pleasure. In an outer office. The guards who patrol the palace area will recognize your car's American manufacture and armor plating. The ambassador's car is similar, but a Chrysler rather than a—how do you say it?—a Chevy, but they will know enough to ask their superiors before challenging your driver. There will be no problem."

"Thank you," said Ali.

*"Ghabel na-dareh,"* said Nazih. "Your driver insists on speaking to me in English."

"Perhaps," said Frank, "in deference to my ignorance of Farsi."

"Clearly. Once we are inside, though I appreciate the American spirit of independence, I must ask you to put yourself totally in my hands. At least until your meeting with His Imperial Majesty begins, at which point you may rest assured I will leave you. That is what he wishes."

Nazih spoke to Ali again in Farsi, and Ali answered, "Yes, major." Ali swiveled out of the car and opened the rear door. Frank followed Nazih.

The blue-tiled halls echoed their footsteps. A seated guard in a uniform Frank now recognized as that of the Imperial Bodyguard nodded wordlessly to Nazih and cocked his head toward a door off to their right. Nazih opened the door and gestured to Frank. They entered a small room with a few chairs against the wall and the bust of an imperious-looking man in military regalia.

"The father?" asked Frank.

"The father. Reza Shah Pahlavi. Founder of the dynasty. Let us be seated and wait."

They sat and waited, facing a door opposite the one they had entered. Nazih made no attempt at conversation, convincing Frank the room had been bugged. Sooner than Frank expected, the door he faced opened. The tall, slender, white-haired but youthful-looking man who entered wore a formal gray morning coat and said, in impeccable English, "Major Nazih and, I presume, Major Sullivan, will you kindly come with me?"

Nazih stood and with a gesture let Frank know he need no longer follow him. The white-haired man who had greeted them led the way into a vast and exquisitely furnished room, but Frank at first noticed little but the figure of the Shah. He stood in the center of the room, facing the door. He seemed much shrunken from the last time Frank had seen him, perhaps a decade before in Addis Ababa. Frank bowed.

"Your Imperial Majesty."

The Shah smiled, cracking his lips but showing no teeth. Not at all the smile Frank remembered.

"Shall we call you Major Sullivan? Or may we again call you Frank?"

"Frank sounds good to me." He took a step closer. The Shah extended his hand. Frank remembered how shy he was of being touched, except when they put on boxing gloves and sparred. The Shah nodded. Frank reached out. Damp, cool, the Shah's fingers barely brushed Frank's palm.

Frank quickly surveyed the room. There were three doors, arranged, he suspected, so visitors could be shuttled in and out without encountering each other. A huge map covered one wall. There were beveled mirrors in gilt frames, three phones, two gold-plated and one sky blue, gold cigarette boxes studded with jewels but no ashtrays or lighters, an oak desk, and a table and chairs in a style Frank guessed to be Louis XIV. Video surveillance cameras peeked out from behind the paneling of at least two walls. Frank could hear them creak when they turned. He suspected their visibility was intentional.

"We shall never forgive our great, deceased friend, the Conquering Lion of Judah, for not bringing you to Persepolis."

"I've heard it was a great celebration."

"You would have enjoyed. A much better time to have seen Iran than these recent days you have been here."

"I'm deeply honored to have this opportunity to see you."

"May we be seated?" said the Shah. He lowered himself into a tall, straight-backed oak chair behind a bare oak table. "Major Nazih, thank you."

"Your Imperial Majesty." Bowing, Nazih backed out the door held open for him by the Shah's majordomo, who followed Nazih out, shutting the door so softly Frank barely heard it.

He sat across from the Shah in an identical oak chair. The Shah's appearance shocked him. When they'd first met in Addis Ababa, the slender, broad-shouldered Shah moved like an athlete and exuded robust health. Even at five-eight, he had towered over the diminutive Haile Selassie. Despite their lack of height, Frank recognized in each a presence that made him every inch an emperor. But now, slumped in his chair, the Shah seemed a faint shadow of the man Frank had met in Ethiopia. He wore a gray business suit that drooped off his shoulders, a blue shirt, and a paisley tie. Heavy lids veiled the flashing dark eyes Frank remembered.

"How many years has it been since we met?"

"Just about ten years, sir."

"A decade does not seem so long, but these are strange times," said the Shah. "What brings you to Iran?"

"To work with your military, the Supreme Commander's military, on ways to improve relations with the people."

"Not unlike the work you did in Ethiopia."

"Very similar."

"But ten years ago, in Ethiopia, you were not a major in the United States Air Force."

"It's more or less . . . an honorary title."

"We understand. When you were in Ethiopia, did Haile Selassie know your honorary title?"

"Different circumstances, sir. There my primary work was with the Ethiopian journalists, the mass media. My work with the military was secondary."

"Did you know Ato Nebiyah?"

"Ato Nebiyah?" The question had surprised him.

"Head of the emperor's personal intelligence unit."

"Ah . . . yes. We had common friends."

"He greatly admired you. He said to us once he couldn't understand why the Americans didn't recruit you, since you knew Ethiopia better than most Ethiopians. He said he urged his friend, the head of CIA there, to recruit you. Is that how it happened?"

"Sir, I was in Ethiopia a long time. I guess I might have overlapped with at least two, maybe three, CIA station chiefs."

The Shah smiled. "You've become quite *diplomatique*. How long will you be here?"

"I have no idea."

"If someone asked me that question . . ." The Shah again smiled, faintly. "I might express the same answer."

"What are your plans?"

"That's one reason we asked you to come. Perhaps you can help us to plan. Perhaps you can help us to understand what the Americans expect."

"But there are others far more qualified than I. Ambassador O'Connor . . ."

"Yes, but we no longer know if we can trust Mr. O'Connor. He has become, may we say, mixed in his feelings and in his counsel."

The Shah paused, giving Frank an opportunity to comment. Frank said nothing, waiting for the Shah to continue.

"We suspect your work with our military may not be very meaningful. We suspect you could do work more meaningful. Haile Selassie said something interesting to us once. About you. What impressed us was his feeling for you. He said he could trust you. We remember his words. 'The Americans have sent us a good spy this time. He is useful.' Could you also be useful to us?"

"I would like to be. But I'm not sure how."

"We shall guide you."

"I would be honored by your guidance."

The Shah's eyes studied his hands, folded on the desk. He looked up at

Frank. "Ten years. So many changes in those years. Haile Selassie gone.
Nkrumah gone. De Gaulle and Pompidou. Ho Chi Minh and Mao. Both gone.
Chou En-lai. Chiang Kai-shek. Khrushchev. Nasser. Ben-Gurion. Gone. Johnson. Eisenhower. All gone." He seemed to remember every ruler who had died
over the past ten years. "And our own dear friend, Assadollah Alam." He looked
up at Frank and smiled faintly. The eyes seemed dead.

Who was Assadollah Alam? Frank wondered.

"And soon," said the Shah, "we shall be gone."

"I hope not, sir. You're still a young man."

"Fifty-nine. Just a month . . . three weeks ago. It is not so old, is it?"

"No, Your Imperial Majesty."

"But who knows what can be eating away inside even the best of us? Perhaps our enemies are right, about all the evil they say we've done. Our doctors
also think they know."

"What do they say?"

"Doctors. We can not tell if their diagnosis is medical or political. Everyone
wants us to leave. For our health. For a rest. Even your ambassador. When we
asked him his advice, whether we should leave, he looked at his watch, Can you
imagine such a thing? Do you know him?"

"We've met. Only since I've been here."

"But you are very good at—how is it the Americans say it? Ah, sizing people
up. How do you size up your ambassador?"

"He seems like a good man," said Frank. "But in a very tough job."

"Do you think his job is to undermine our rule?"

"Not at all, sir."

"Do you know the British allow this evil holy man to broadcast his attacks
on our government over BBC?"

"Yes, sir."

"My French doctor says we have cancer, but this *akhund* Khomeini is the real
cancer that eats away at us. And the French give him refuge, and the British give
him their radio."

"As do the Russians," said Frank. "From Baku, Pretending to be Iranians."

"Americans are always quick to tell us what the Russians are up to. Like the
CIA man here. Novak. We're sure he is good at his job, but he seems to care only
about the Soviet Russians. Not at all about Iran." He paused, and Frank realized
he was again being given an opportunity to respond.

"I guess," Frank fumbled for words. "I mean, with the long border between
Iran and Russia, he must be concerned about both."

"You spar with us," said the Shah. "As you did, but with gloves on, in
Ethiopia. Of course, Iran has a long Russian border and a long history of playing
the Russians off against the British, the British off against the Russians. And for

a while we thought the Americans had rescued us from both. But we tell you the British and the Americans are in this together. They come here together. Your ambassador and the British. Who can I trust?"

"Yourself above all, sir."

"Yes. Above all."

Frank thought of the man he had boxed with ten years before. He had done little each two-minute round but block the Shah's sharp jabs, his own punches pulled short, glancing off a glove or an elbow. Three rounds had been their limit after a session of weight lifting. The Shah had been strong at both bench presses and deep knee bends. It came as no surprise when he learned the Shah took pride in his abilities as a swimmer and skier. But his exercise regimen had not saved him.

The windows behind him looked out over the frozen gardens and, through the sparkling clear sky beyond, at the city below.

"You can see all of Tehran," said Frank, looking over the Shah's sagging shoulder.

"Yes. And all of its troubles." The Shah glanced to his left. "And from over there you can see all of the world and Iran's place in the world." Frank twisted in his chair to follow the Shah's eyes to a far wall dominated by a huge illuminated map. "Let us show you."

The Shah pushed against the arms of his chair as he rose. He walked slowly to the map, a Mercator projection that positioned Iran at the center of the globe. "You're used to seeing these with Greenwich Mean or the United States at the center. But this map used to hang in your embassy, back in the days when your ambassador was Douglas MacArthur the Second."

"The general's son?"

"No. You would think so, from the name. But Douglas MacArthur the Second was the general's nephew. On the other hand, the general's own son is named after the general's brother, Arthur MacArthur the Third. Very strange, these MacArthurs. Though we of course greatly admired General MacArthur. And his nephew. They were true statesmen. Men who understood the danger of Communism and the threat the Russians pose to the freedom of all us. Don't you agree?"

"To a degree," said Frank. "Yes." He had thought of his own son. Jake. Named for his mother. Some people might find that strange.

"Look here," said the Shah, hands clasped behind his back as though tied, eyes again locked on his map. "See how central Iran is. MacArthur, Ambassador MacArthur, used to lecture visitors to his office, particularly American congressmen and cabinet officers, on the vital importance of Iran to the free world. Linchpin of CENTO. The dominant military power in the Gulf. Allied with Turkey and Pakistan, also secular nations with non-Arab Islamic populations. Strong ethnic and political ties to Afghanistan. Friendly toward Israel. Buffer between Soviet Russia and its expansionist ambitions. A vital supplier of oil to America, Great Britain, Japan, yes, even Israel."

The Shah squared his shoulders. He'd come alive, and Frank did not want to take him away from his map.

"When was Ambassador MacArthur here?"

"I hate to say." The Shah continued to study his map. "Ten years ago."

Wrong question, thought Frank.

"The late 1960s, early '70s. He was our most successful lobbyist for more American military aid. Far better than our own ambassadors in Washington. A man named Farland came after, briefly. He was followed by another great ambassador, in 1973, Richard Helms. He understood this map."

"I met Mr. Helms," said Frank. "Just once. In the American embassy in London."

"I knew him well," said the Shah. "He'd been the CIA station chief here, long before he became director. He and his wife were very happy to be here when he returned as ambassador. Your Congress had given him a very bad time. Some nonsense about Chile. He had to resign as CIA director. But he loved Iran. He understood us. And we respected him. We wish we could say the same of your current leaders. Frankly, we worry about this Carter. After Helms left, your President Jimmy didn't even bother to send us a new ambassador for six months. Then this O'Connor person came. He'd been here barely a year when he left for a three-month vacation. Your president and your ambassador, how can they pretend to care about Iran?"

Good question, thought Frank. He remembered the ambassador's complaint about the cut in embassy political officers from twenty to six. Maybe Washington had lost interest in Iran.

"With you to guide him, the ambassador should be able to follow events, Your Majesty."

"I think he is still on vacation. Like your President, who tries to be friendly, but we would have been much happier if President Ford had won the election. Carter came here, you know, for New Year's, this year. Said some nice things. He referred to Iran as an island of stability in a troubled region and said this was a great tribute to us. A few weeks before, just about this time last year, the Empress and I visited the Carters in Washington. He greeted us with television cameras in his Rose Garden while your police fired tear gas at brawling students who staged a demonstration against us in the street. We were nearly blinded. And on television for everyone in America, in the world, to see. That evening, more kind words and Sarah Vaughan and Dizzy Gillespie to entertain us. By the way, I still have that Sarah Vaughan album you gave me. A farewell present when we left Ethiopia. We appreciated that it wasn't new, that it must have come from your own collection."

"It did," said Frank.

"We thank you again for it. Do you know this Jimmy Carter person?"

"No, sir. I've never met President Carter."

"You are fortunate. What do we have from him now? All this human rights talk, self-determination, cutting the sale of arms. He doesn't understand the real world. This Carter seems too much like Kennedy. Do they really think, all these liberals, intellectuals, professors from Harvard and students from everywhere, do they really think that if this holy man from hell succeeds in destroying our government it will mean the dawn of a new age of enlightenment, with human rights and democracy for all? I assure you it will not. These unwashed *mullahs* will install a repressive Islamic government, fanatics who will do their best to lead our people back to the Middle Ages. But your president seems to listen only to these naive fools."

"I understand President Carter's national security adviser . . ."

"Ah, yes," the Shah cut him off. "Brzezinski. He's Polish. Poles understand the Russians. We would like one day to show him our map. He would understand. He is close to our ambassador in Washington. But we wonder how much your President listens to him."

"How did you come by the map?" asked Frank, hoping to deflect the Shah's anger.

"A farewell gift from Ambassador MacArthur, He wasn't sure his successor would make proper use of it. He knew we would. Before he left, he had it installed here. 'Keep up the good work,' he said."

"And I'm sure you do."

"We try. But these days, I must confess, the view out that window concerns me more than my wonderful map." He nodded toward the windows but did not look their way. "When I look down those hills, I see what is happening to our country today. I see our future. And I shudder."

Frank struggled to find words that would do more than comfort. "Perhaps," he said, "paying attention to both would be good. The map and the window."

"Yes," said the Shah, still staring at the map. "That would be good." He turned to Frank. The eyes showed some of the old intensity. "Do you think we should leave? Abdicate?"

"No, sir. I definitely do not. But that's a very personal, gut reaction."

"We admire your guts," said the Shah, smiling. "Even the Empress thinks we should go."

"How is Her Imperial Majesty?"

"Very well. She is the rock we lean on. Shall we sit?"

He went to the chair behind his desk. Frank went to the chair opposite.

The Shah nodded, sighed. "It can be tiring. We must meet again. Speak to . . . your ambassador. Who . . . to whomever you must speak. His Imperial Majesty

Haile Selassie, he told us he first met you when he had to make a statement about the Panama Canal. Some crisis about American rule over the Canal Zone. He wanted a statement that would reflect his role as a leader of the Non-Aligned Nations but also would not offend his American sponsors. He had asked an Ethiopian journalist, educated in America, to draft a statement, but the journalist recommended bringing you to discuss and draft the statement. Is that accurate?"

"I'm amazed, sir. That you should know all that."

"The Emperor and I were very close. We admired him greatly. We understand he approved the statement you drafted, that you wrote for him often after that, advised him, traveled with him, but not to Persepolis."

"I regret not having traveled to Persepolis."

"Can it be arranged for you to work with us as you did with him?"

"I would be honored. It might be more effective if it were you who discussed it with the ambassador."

"I understand. Is there a mechanism that might make this possible?"

"You might want to discuss the possibility with Major Nazih."

"Major Nazih?"

"Yes, Your Imperial Majesty. I realize our work with the military may not be very productive—very meaningful. But it does provide a context for my being here."

"I have already approved your . . . what is it called?"

"Jayface."

"Horrible name." His features puckered as though he'd just bitten into a spoiled fish. "Can you invent something for those people to do? Something that would depend on you to guide them. I will approve whatever it is on the condition that you remain."

"I understand, sir. I will think of something. May I get word to you through Major Nazih?"

"Perhaps. For a time. Major Nazih is a very bright, knowledgeable young man. With many contacts. Including the Russians. He keeps us in touch with what matters in their embassy here."

The Russian Embassy? That bastard, thought Frank. "I'm glad he's well thought of."

"We will expect to hear from you. Perhaps through your ambassador." The Shah looked at his watch. "Forgive us. We are like your ambassador, telling you it is time for you to abdicate."

Frank stood. "Thank you, Your Imperial Majesty, for granting me this time."

"Wait." The Shah picked up the blue phone. He spoke into it in Farsi, listened, spoke again, and hung up. "Don't go far. We have another visitor. We will ask you to join us in a few minutes."

Now what? thought Frank.

Cross-legged, one foot swinging in apparent irritation, Major Nazih sat in the anteroom. "I don't mind being helpful, but this is taking much longer than I expected."

Their wait proved short. The door behind them opened, and the majordomo entered.

"Major Sullivan. His Imperial Majesty would like you to rejoin him."

Frank glanced at Nazih, who looked at him blankly and shook his head. Frank shrugged and followed the majordomo into the Shah's office.

The Shah, hands folded before him, sat behind his desk. At his elbow stood Vassily Lermontov.

"We meet again."

The hairs on the back of Frank's neck tingled. He knew that in this setting the Russian did not pose a threat, but Lermontov seemed to command the room. His position at the Shah's elbow conveyed a sense of ownership.

"We understand you two know each other," said the Shah.

"We do indeed," said Lermontov.

"Mr. Lermontov has impressed us with his knowledge of your role in Ethiopia. And since," said the Shah.

"He's impressed me, too," said Frank. "Hello, Vassily."

"Ça va, Frank?"

"Ça va bien," said Frank, shrugging one shoulder.

"We have only agreed to this," said the Shah, "because of Major Nazih's assurance of why Mr. Lermontov wants to meet with you. If we learn the reason behind this is other than what we have been told, Major Nazih, as he knows, will suffer severely."

"And you," said Lermontov, "will have another persona-non-grata scalp to add to your collection."

In agency parlance, the term meant something quite different—recruiting Soviets, not getting them PNG'd. Frank looked from Lermontov to the Shah and said, "I'm not much of a scalp hunter."

"Of course," said Lermontov. "But when opportunities fall your way, what can you do? I have no resentment for what happened in Ethiopia."

"You've told me that several times," said Frank, "but you keep bringing it up."

"And you keep bringing up what happened to you, or almost happened to you, in Beirut, though I have assured you I had nothing to do with that."

"We will leave you gentlemen to your mutual hostilities. As we would leave Russia and the United States to theirs, if we could. But geography imposes certain obligations. Propinquity is not necessarily a blessing. Nor is economic dependence. So we must deal with you both. And now, gentlemen, we are going to do something we have never done before, for anyone. We are going to leave this office to you. For your discussions. We shall do so because this map, which we have discoursed upon with each of you, will be here to remind you of what is at stake here in Iran."

"And we realize Your Imperial Majesty will be listening," said Lermontov.

"We shall not. You might want to discuss that question with members of my intelligence staff. Several of whom are known to Major Nazih. And perhaps to you. They monitor our work. We do not monitor theirs. And now, if you will, excuse us."

The Shah pushed himself up from his desk and made his slow, stiff way toward the door. Frank and Lermontov bowed, and the Shah left them.

"Well, no need to stand on formality. Is there?" said Lermontov.

Frank gestured to the oak chair behind the desk. "Will you take the Shah's chair?"

"No. I have no notion of replacing the Shah." He moved around the desk with the grace that had always surprised Frank in so big a man. He took a chair at the far end, turning it to face Frank. They kept their eyes on each other as they sat.

"You seem to have a big influence over him."

"Not at all. I do, however, over Major Nazih. He works for me."

Frank nodded toward the ceiling.

Lermontov shrugged. "His Imperial Majesty is aware. Nazih also reports to His Majesty's private intelligence branch, to J2 and *Savak*. That I know of. Perhaps he also works for Mossad . . . and for you."

"No. No, he doesn't work for me," said Frank. He wondered how much Lermontov knew about Jayface. Everything, he guessed, but he decided to volunteer nothing.

"Please do not think I was sent here because of you," said Lermontov. "I had been here nearly a year before I learned you were coming."

"When did you know?"

"Just a few days before you arrived."

"That's impressive," said Frank.

"We are, after all, a professional organization," said Lermontov.

"Really?" Frank said it with a smile. He hadn't found out himself till the day before his arrival. He wondered if the Russians had someone inside the agency who knew before he did, and if it had been Lermontov who funneled that information to Nazih. He thought about Gus and the need to know and about keeping your buddy in the dark. He thought about security and Counter Intelligence. If Nazih's apparent knowledge had originated from a KGB agent within the agency, the threat would be far more serious than he'd thought. And he wondered, How in the hell am I going to handle this?

"Moscow instructed me to attempt again to explore your interest in getting to know us better."

Here we go again, thought Frank. "That could be dangerous," he said aloud.

"But I thought you capitalists believed in risk. And rewards?"

"We've played this game before," said Frank. "It gets stale, mate."

"Ah, very clever. Stalemate. I see you haven't lost your sense of humor."

"Neither have you, if you think I want to get to know the KGB better."

"I didn't say the KGB. I said 'us.' The Russians. Not KGB or Soviets. They're the past. The Russians are the future. You should get to know Russians better."

"And how could I do that?"

"For a start, you should visit Russia someday. I could be your guide."

"That might give some people back in the States the idea that I'm not very loyal."

"It's the game we play, isn't it?" said Lermontov. "We demand absolute loyalty of our people, and then we train them to undermine the loyalty of our recruiting targets."

"Am I a recruiting target?" asked Frank.

"Of course," answered Lermontov.

Can the Shah be part of this? wondered Frank. Setting me up for a pitch?

"There is much I could teach you about Russia. And, if you take the risk, the rewards could add up to a tidy little nest egg, enough for you to retire and write all those books you want to write."

Frank thought of all the times he had fantasized about somehow making enough money to do just that. Selling a book to the movies. Winning the Irish Sweepstakes. He wondered if Lermontov could be serious.

"You amaze me," he said. "You know we're on video." And he wondered if the video could read his mind. "Or did you sabotage the camera?"

"Not at all. In fact, I can have a copy made for you."

"You do have some influence here."

"Some." Lermontov spread his broad hands on his bulky knees. "Some, but not enough."

Frank looked at his wrists and wondered, Can a grown man's wrists possibly get bigger?

"The world is changing," said Lermontov. "The Soviet Union is changing. I am changing. Have you noticed?"

"You seem . . . less at ease than usual."

"For sure. Anything else, physically?"

"Have you gained weight?"

"Some, but that's not why I look bigger. I look bigger because I've gotten bigger."

"I noticed your wrists."

"Yes. And my jaw and my skull and my clavicle, my sternum, my ribs, my pelvis, my knees, my ankles, of course my spinal column. All my bones have grown. It is called acromegaly, caused by a hyperactive pituitary. I am breaking out of my skin. I do not exaggerate, my friend."

Friend? Frank wondered.

"To an extent the tendons and muscles around the bones react, and they also grow, but the bones grow more. I remind myself of the Soviet Union. I have grown beyond my capacity. Soon, without help, I will break apart. Collapse. Perhaps I exaggerate, but not much."

"What can your doctors do about . . ." Frank hadn't grasped the word. ". . . about it?"

"My doctors. My Soviet doctors broke my jaw last year. Brutally. And reset it. Clumsily. My jaw had grown so much I couldn't get my upper molars to bite down on the lower. They call it malocclusion. I can't chew my food. So my doctors broke my jaw."

"You're the one who needs to take a risk," said Frank.

"What are you saying?"

"You know what I'm saying. You need a change. A change of doctors."

"Believe me," said Lermontov, "the KGB provides the best the Soviet Union has to offer."

"I'm sure," said Frank. "But perhaps you should visit New York. Or Washington."

"If you got to know us better," said Lermontov, "if we worked together, that might be possible. When you return to America, perhaps I could be assigned there, to maintain contact."

"I see."

"At Columbia Presbyterian Hospital in New York," said Lermontov, "there is a Dr. Hyman Roth, perhaps the world's leading endocrinologist. Without doubt, the most outstanding expert on acromegaly. Can you guess how I know about him?"

"Your UN mission?"

"No. My own efforts when you took your wife back to the States for plastic surgery after your auto accident in Ethiopia. You went to Columbia Presbyterian because the world's leading expert on black scar tissue was there."

"Correct," said Frank.

"Most plastic surgeons, of course, don't know how to deal with keloids. Why should they? Most Negroes can't afford plastic surgery. From what we learned, the agency spared no expense in supplementing your insurance. I was glad. Jackie's a very beautiful woman, and her surgeon, Dr. Weinstein, did a wonderful job."

"I'm impressed, but what does this have to do with you?"

"In finding out all I could about Dr. Weinstein, in hope that might yield something I could use in my . . . dealings with you, I discovered that his closest friend was Doctor Hyman Roth."

"The endocrinologist."

"Yes, I do need a change in scenery," said Lermontov. "I've made some explorations of medical care elsewhere. Britain. Canada. But for the care I need nothing compares with Columbia Presbyterian and Dr. Roth. Besides, I think you owe me this."

"I do?"

"I have been very successful in my career. Except for you. And acromegaly. The acromegaly worried my not very bright superiors. As it got worse, my career began to stall. I haven't had a promotion in five years."

Frank studied him, saying nothing.

"And you," said Lermontov. "My other disease. What happened to me in Ethiopia because of you was not such a great disgrace. It did me no good, but I had been aggressive and got caught. Others also got caught, however. I was blamed for getting the others caught. That created more of a problem. But my real problem has been all the other times when we have been in the same place at the same time and I have been able to report no progress on recruiting you. That has made some of my superiors suspect you have already recruited me."

That sounds familiar, thought Frank. He thought of some of the Counter Intelligence spooks and other bureaucrats in the agency who mistrusted him. He suspected that Pete Howard was right. The only way he could prove that Lermontov hadn't recruited him would be to recruit Lermontov. They had circled each other too long. Their marathon dance might make anyone suspicious. He inhaled deeply, slowly, and decided to make the leap.

"Maybe that's our solution. You don't recruit me. I recruit you."

Lermontov smiled. Frank shivered.

"That way the KGB could kill me, more quickly than acromegaly," said Lermontov.

"Risks. Rewards," said Frank.

"You do want to get me killed," said Lermontov.

"No, but if you could get yourself assigned to your UN mission, or your embassy in Washington, so you could seek medical treatment there . . ."

"Emergency treatment."

"Exactly." An emergency, maybe for both of us, thought Frank. "Perhaps I could help."

"No," said Lermontov. "If I allowed you to help, it might appear suspicious."

"Whatever the risks, you need a change," said Frank. "A change of doctors."

Lermontov shook his massive head.

THE PEREGRINE SPY 91

"I know it would be difficult," said Frank.

"Difficult, yes," said Lermontov. "The people who monitor you, like the people who nursemaid me, must have wondered about us. Why haven't I recruited you? my nursemaids wonder. Why haven't you recruited me? your people must think. The only way either of us can redeem himself, perhaps, is through the other. And so we trail each other around the world."

"We do?"

"So it seems," said Lermontov. "Ethiopia, of course, was not planned. And Lusaka was not planned, at least not by us. But I was sent to Beirut because of you. And to Rome. Even to our UN mission in New York. We did not meet, but I did see you several times. From a distance. We decided nothing could be done there. We thought you might be a waste of time, which was a relief to me because I was again being criticized for not having recruited you."

And I was sent here by Pete Howard, thought Frank, because of you. They looked at each other and smiled. Anyone watching might think we were lovers. Why not? thought Frank. We understand each other better than most lovers do.

"Two spies in the same leaky boat," said Lermontov. "Would that be an apt expression?"

Too apt, thought Frank. "You know," he said, "even if you did want a change of scenery, a change of doctors, my people would say you would be much more valuable . . ."

"I know. We all want an agent in place. But if I did agree to this, for me there may not be a place much longer. I have tried to give you some hints in the past that the Soviet Union is not the great colossus you Americans think it us. And not every KGB agent is ten feet tall."

"You come close," said Frank.

"Goliath, not a KGB agent, of course, but they say Goliath stood ten feet tall. A Soviet neurologist, one of my doctors, believes Goliath had acromegaly. It not only made him big and slow but also caused his skull to press against an optic nerve and damaged his vision. So the big, slow-moving giant perhaps never saw little David sneaking up on him with his slingshot and stones. Very proud of his materialist explanation of the Bible story, this doctor of mine. He told me about his theory just before they broke my jaw."

"I hope you aren't going blind."

"Perhaps I am. Like Goliath, I have acromegaly. The Soviet Union has megalomania. Both ailments can affect vision. They can make us seem bigger, but not more powerful. And neither of us can survive without change."

"If it could happen at all, it would take time," said Frank.

"Time is something I don't have much of."

"How much?"

"It depends on what kills me first. If I do not get proper care soon, this disease may kill me within a year or two. If I talk to you, the KGB could come down on me anytime. In which case my execution would come—quickly. The collapse of the Soviet Union, I give that five, perhaps ten years. I think we are having a contest, the Soviet Union and Vassily Lermontov, which of us shall break apart first. With proper medical treatment, I may outlast the Soviet Union."

"You're not serious."

"I am very serious. The situation is even more serious. You see what already has happened in Afghanistan. We supported a coup last April to get the government we wanted because we see what will happen here. Khomeini will take over in a matter of weeks, and he does not love the atheistic, Communist Satan on his northern border. We need Afghanistan in our camp as a counterbalance, but the situation there remains unstable. The strings on our puppets are very loose. I have worked on that problem. Dari, the Afghanis' major language, is virtually the same as Farsi. Which I know. There is much I could tell your people. Four of our republics border Iran and Afghanistan. All are Islamic, and all will be influenced by what happens here and in Afghanistan. Among them they provide more than half the rank-and-file troops in our military. You can tell your people now that within a year the Soviet Union will invade Afghanistan, and that will be, not the beginning of the end, but the end of the end. You can tell your people Lermontov told you that, and they will laugh at you, and in a year you can remind them. Despite the optimistic reports the CIA makes every year on the strength of the Soviet economy and military, both are falling apart. Those CIA reports are very useful, by the way, for both of us. They help our morale, and they help the CIA to get its annual budget increases. I could tell your people much. I could bring documents."

"I'm sure," said Frank. "But if you defect, what about your family?"

"I have no family. My father, a hero of the Soviet Union, got himself killed at Stalingrad. My mother died soon after. And my wife, she left me as this . . . got worse. She said I frightened her. We never had children. My superiors don't like sending people overseas who don't have family ties back home, but because of my rank and my record of being overseas so often, my superiors won't worry that I might defect. Still, you must find a way to get me to America."

A pleading tone in Lermontov's voice reminded Frank of the young Iranian whose bony fingers had gripped his wrist as he tried to drive out of the embassy's back gate. He's too big to whine, thought Frank. He wondered if Lermontov had read his mind. The big man straightened in his chair. His voice took on a tone of basso authority.

"But I must know soon that I can count on you. I can stay in place for a time, but I do not have much time, and the risk I take now may make that time shorter." He looked at the watch secured to his thick wrist by a leather band, then raised his hard gray eyes to meet Frank's. "Somewhere a clock ticks, just like the clocks in all those nuclear-war and end-of-the-world spy movies. Except we don't know where to find this clock. We don't even know for sure who set it, some dying emperor, some holy man in a white beard and black turban, maybe some bureaucrat in Washington or Moscow. We can't shut it off, and we don't know how much longer that clock gives us. But we know it ticks, and we know our time will be up soon. Any delay could be fatal. To our plan. For sure to me. Perhaps to you."

"You're not shittin' me?" said Rocky.

"I shit you not," said Frank.

"He wants to defect?"

"He's willing. Like I said, his first step was to try to recruit me. So he gets to go to the States to handle me. But when I tossed the pitch back to him, yeah, he went for it."

"He understands this isn't a joy ride to Disneyland? That we'll want him to stay in place?"

"We went through all that." They sat across the glass-topped table, alone in the bubble. Frank summed up all Lermontov had told him about the time pressures, the threat of acromegaly, the threat of exposure.

"Three fuckin' days," said Rocky. "You got here three fuckin' days ago. He didn't waste much time findin' you, did he?"

"That's what worries me. He knew I was coming. If they've got somebody back home . . ."

Rocky shook his head. "More likely somebody here. The Shah knew you were coming. So his people knew. No tellin' how many. That doesn't worry me. What worries me is why your buddy is in so much of a hurry."

"I don't know if he's more worried about the KGB catching him or having his bones explode on him," said Frank. He downplayed Lermontov's views on the collapse of the Soviet Union, knowing Rocky would be skeptical, but he did outline Lermontov's knowledge of Soviet intentions in Afghanistan.

"This shit is dynamite. What's the next step?"

"He's willing to be debriefed about KGB structure and operations, Soviet operations here and in Afghanistan, past, present, and future, the Soviet economy and military, Soviet Third World operations, which is his specialty, and KGB United Nations ops, which he had one tour on. But he wants me to handle him. Says he won't trust anyone else till we show that we'll help him." Rocky fiddled with his hearing aid, and Frank wondered if he'd been tuned out. He tried anyway. "We go back a long way."

Rocky nodded. "Yeah. Yeah, you do."

Frank knew he'd been heard. He watched as Rocky opened his hands and studied them. He's cooking, thought Frank. But what?

"Look," Rocky began, still studying his hands. "I know I've given you a hard time on some things since you got here. You think you got a job t' do with these Jayface fuckers, okay. Talk to them. But leave Lermontov to me."

Frank hesitated, sensing trouble. He knew Lermontov would never agree to working with Rocky, but he also knew he could not challenge the authority of a chief of station.

Rocky glared. "You having a problem with your hearing aid? I said I handle Lermontov."

"I heard you," said Frank. "I have no problem with that. But Lermontov might."

"He's mine," said Rocky. "It's gonna be up to me to solve any problems he might have."

Frank knew he had to find a way to stay involved. "What about the Shah?" he said.

"What about the Shah? You got nothing new."

"Cancer. He admitted he has cancer."

"Any details?"

"Not yet."

"Not yet don't cut it. You got nothing new on the Shah. You had clearance for one meeting. You had your meeting. You're done with the Shah."

"Well, the Shah, he set up the next meet with Lermontov. He volunteered a room down the hall from his offices."

"Fuckin' amazes me," said Rocky. "His Imperial High Hat must have cancer of the brain. Either that or the KGB recruited'm. Why in the hell would he go to all this trouble to set you up with a Soviet thug?"

"He's got his own agenda," said Frank. "He wants me to come up with an idea that will mean I have to stay on here as an adviser."

"For the Jayfacers or for him?"

"Both. Overt Jayface and covert him."

"I got a hunch his agenda may include you gettin' him to the States."

Frank remembered what the Shah had said about his own medical problems. "You may be right. He doesn't seem to trust his French doctors much."

"How tight is he with this Lermontov?"

"Not very, I don't think. He made it pretty clear he doesn't trust the Russians. 'Course, he also made it pretty clear he doesn't much trust us, or the Brits, these days."

"Who does he trust?"

Frank shook his head. "Maybe not even himself. He seems very alone."

"He trust you?"

"He seems to."

"Tell you the truth, I don't give a fuck about the Shah. You're the one likes fartin' around with emperors. I've recruited my share of Soviets, but never a KGB-er with a background like this Lermontov. So you can go on suckin' up to the Shah if you want, but Lermontov's mine."

I wish you luck, thought Frank. He realized Rocky's concession on the Shah had extended his lease in Tehran—and might give him a chance to rescue Lermontov's defection.

"When's your next meet with the thug?"

"I worked it out with Lermontov for two days from now, at the palace same time."

"That's awful fuckin' quick."

"I told you he's in a hurry."

"That may be good for us. We can count on gettin' a shit pot full of debriefin' requirements pourin' in from NE and Soviet Division. They'll be wantin' t' send some of their scalp hunters over t' get in on the act."

"That sounds like trouble," said Frank.

"You got that right. Big trouble if they get here and start fucking things up, but they can't come over without my approval. I can't flat out turn them down, but you'd be amazed about how slow I can fucking get about not answering cables I don't wanna answer. I don't like the idea of your thug settin' the pace, tryin' t' rush us. But in this case two days is good. It doesn't give those idiots back home time enough t' fuck things up."

He paused. Frank knew he had more to say, "Look, Sully, this business with Lermontov looks good. And we got no choice but to run with it. But anything that looks this good has got to have some land mines along the way. If I was to let you handle it, you'd be in way over your head. A deal like this, you got to watch your ass with everything from jealous types in Soviet Division and NE to paranoid types in Counter Intelligence. But most of all you got to watch your ass with this Lermontov. He worries me. He may be runnin' some game we haven't figured out yet. Don't ever assume a walk-in walks in on the level."

"I hear you," said Frank, "And believe me, he worries me, too."

"Good," said Rocky. "Better I pick it up."

Only then, almost as an afterthought, did Rocky turn his attention back to Frank's meeting with the Shah. Frank knew that Rocky, as an old Soviet hand, would be far more interested in Lermontov. He considered it a symptom of the agency disease, CIA-itis, an inability to see anything but the Soviet giant on the horizon. Lermontov worries me, he thought, but so do old Soviet hands.

"So what else can we do for this Shah of yours?" said Rocky.

"Any chance we can get him the same thing Lermontov wants, a visa to America?"

"Gettin' the Shah to America will be even harder than gettin' Lermontov there."

"We've got to get Lermontov to America."

"That I can work on," said Rocky. "Kissinger, David Rockefeller, Jimmy Carter, Brzezinski, those guys. Gettin' the Shah to America, that's their job."

"What's my job?"

"You? You got it easy. Since you're so hot to trot with the Shah, do a cable on that. I'll do the Lermontov cable. You established contact, turned it over to me, chief of station, Russian speaker, and experienced Soviet Division man. Makes all the fuckin' sense in the world, right?"

Wrong, thought Frank, but he kept the thought to himself and said, "Right."

"That's the only cable I need. Forget the other shit. We tell the folks back home what your buddy said about the collapse of the Soviet Union, they'll laugh in our face. We got other people workin' on Afghanistan. They don't need your help."

Frank's stomach tightened, and he could feel the anger flaring under his skin. Through clenched teeth he managed to say, "You're the boss."

"I know," replied Rocky. "We only got two days. I'll have a safe house set up by tomorrow. Exclusive for Lermontov. You can give him the location when you meet up at the palace. Don't tell him I'll be there. You can surprise him."

"I don't mind surprising him," said Frank. "I just don't want to lose him."

"Yeah, well, just remember. He's not yours to lose. He's mine." Their eyes locked. Neither looked away.


He could not sleep. When he closed his eyes, images of Lermontov filled a giant screen. When he opened his eyes and stared at the metal plates Bill Steele had installed, memories of Lermontov crashed through like the grenade that shattered his window the day before. The grenade had not exploded, but he remembered Rocky's words. Anything that looks this good has got to have some land mines along the way. He thought of Lermontov as a land mine, a grenade that hadn't gone off. Yet. And he remembered the day they'd gone hunting in Ethiopia. It had been Tesfaye's idea.

Tesfaye Tessema, editor of the English-language daily, the *Ethiopian Herald,* and Frank's closest counterpart, was friendly with Lermontov. Friendly but, as far as Frank knew, not an agent.

"He must hate you," Tesfaye had once said.

"Why should he hate me?"

"He's never said so, but he must. Students and journalists are part of his job. He does quite well with the students, but among the journalists I don't think so well. Except with a few, perhaps on some of the Amharic papers, including our good friend who accused us."

An anonymous report submitted to the assistant minister of information in charge of the print media had accused Tesfaye "and his American friend" of stealing millions in advertising revenue. The ministry's meager advertising revenue never approached a million, and no one of authority in the ministry had taken the report seriously.

"I know that made Vassily mad," said Tesfaye, smiling. "He let me know that he wrote it and our journalist friend who works for him merely translated it into Amharic and turned it in."

"But why would Lermontov bother?" asked Frank.

"Just to make people more suspicious of you. He knew such nonsense couldn't hurt me, but many people like to believe the worst of you Americans."

"Tell your friend Lermontov I appreciate his interest."

"He is interested in you," said Tesfaye. "He tells me he would like to get to know you. He's always trying to recruit me, and I think he figures he can't because of you."

"Does he think I've recruited you?"

"No, and that makes him even more intrigued. How can you have so much influence without ever trying to recruit anyone? You should get to know him."

"You should pursue this possibility," Pete Howard had said. "Get to know him. See what you can find out."

"What worries me," said Frank, "is what Lermontov may have found out. About the case we're building against him. And his crew."

Frank had determined that all of the Russians based in Ethiopia with press credentials—correspondents of Tass, the Novosti Press Agency, Soviet television and foreign-language radio outlets, and various newspapers with the exception of *Pravda*—all reported to Lermontov, who was also accredited to Tass. Ethiopian security forces granted a degree of latitude to foreign intelligence agencies, but then the Russians went too far. Frank learned through Tesfaye that Lermontov himself had begun cultivating a multilingual foreign-born journalist who also served as a translator for the Ministry of Information and occasionally for the Emperor. Frank relayed the information to Pete Howard. Within a week Tesfaye invited Frank to join him on a hunting trip with Lermontov.

Again, Pete Howard encouraged him. "Just make sure Tesfaye watches your back."

Frank remembered Lermontov's weapon of choice. He'd brought along an array of hunting rifles wrapped in a tarpaulin, but his favorite looked like a cannon mounted on a shoulder stock.

"It's a PTRS semiautomatic, developed as an antitank rifle during the war," said a cheerful Lermontov after they'd unloaded their Land Rover and set up camp in a wooded area in the Awash Valley. "This fires a round roughly twice the caliber of an AK-47. Look at the size of the bore."

Frank stared down the huge barrel, and Lermontov showed him a handful of huge shells. Somehow it seemed fitting that a man as big as Lermontov should carry such an oversize weapon.

"I could shoot you in the buttocks with this, and it would kill you. We'll be going for wild boar, and if I do shoot one, I don't want to have to try to shoot him twice."

And I didn't want to be between that cannon and a wild boar, Frank remembered, wide awake and staring at the metal-covered windows beyond the foot of his bed. Then he closed his eyes and, as though in slow motion, saw the huge, tusked boar charging out of the bush. He heard the roar of Lermontov's massive rifle behind him. He wondered if he had really felt the rush of wind as the huge bullet sped past his right ear. He knew he had seen the boar stumble forward and fall in a quivering heap not more than a yard away from his feet. He still wondered whether Lermontov had tried to kill him or had saved his life. Two weeks later, the Ethiopian government expelled Lermontov and five other Russians for conduct inconsistent with their status as accredited journalists.

Beirut, he thought. No, I don't think you tried to have me killed in Beirut. But Ethiopia. I still don't know. He could hear the bullet whistling past his ear in the Ethiopian bush. He could hear the bullet striking his car, metal against metal on a street in Beirut. He thought of the watch on Lermontov's wrist and remembered his words about time running out on the Soviet Union; about time tightening the grip acromegaly had on him. He heard an echo of the casual remark of their driver, Ali Zarakesh, that the streets named Churchill and Roosevelt might not have those names for long; the warning of the air force major, Anwar Amini, to watch the funnels of smoke in the sky over Tehran. Through the night, Frank sensed time running out. Somewhere a clock ticked, a time bomb, but he had no idea how soon it would go off. "Watch the smoke signals," Anwar had said. "Perhaps they can tell you."

# CHAPTER SIX

The white-haired majordomo took their coats. "Major Sullivan, you will be meeting today first with His Imperial Majesty's guest. The same gentleman you spoke with last week, in a room I will take you to. His Imperial Majesty may take some time for you after that meeting. Major Nazih, you may wait just here."

Two Imperial Guard enlisted men, with Uzi submachine guns cradled in their arms, stood before the doors to the Shah's private offices.

"Major Sullivan, kindly follow me," said the majordomo, and Frank followed down a long, narrow hallway. At the far end, his white-haired guide, again in a gray morning coat, knocked at a door and, without waiting for a reply, opened it and bowed Frank in.

Lermontov stood with his back to the door, thick hands folded behind him, gazing through French doors toward the snow-gilded slopes and the distant city now invisible in the afternoon glare. He crossed the room and reached out to Frank with an enormous paw.

"It's good to see you again, old friend." Though Lermontov's hand swallowed Frank's, his grip had become far gentler than Frank remembered from earlier days. Frank glanced at his hand, then caught Lermontov's eye.

"Ah, yes," said the big man, releasing Frank's hand. "I don't squeeze as hard as I used to, right? I have to be careful these days. If I forget, now that I've gotten bigger, I can crush somebody's fingers. Besides, I don't have anything to prove anymore."

"Did you ever?"

"When you first met me, I was a very junior officer. Very insecure. I had to show everyone how tough I was."

"You had me convinced."

"Good. I must admit we did not think you were so tough, but you had begun to intrigue us. One of the Ethiopian journalists who worked for us told me you had said that you did not believe Communism was America's enemy. When I reported that, Moscow became very interested in you."

"As a target?" asked Frank.

"Well, at least as someone worth keeping an eye on. Someone with interesting ideas."

"I might have been misquoted."

"Perhaps," said Lermontov. "But in the years since, I've come to realize what you said, or what my Ethiopian friend attributed to you, was very accurate. Communism isn't your enemy. Russia is. China will be. Both may join the capitalist camp—and still be your enemy. We may shout about economic systems and human rights and forms of government, but we fight about national interests."

"Ideology is dead?"

"No," said Lermontov. "Ideology isn't dead. It never existed, except as a cover for national ambition and, for some, to disguise personal interest. Do you think Stalin cared a rat's ass about ideology?"

"You've picked up some interesting American slang," said Frank.

"We get a monthly update."

"Are you serious?"

"I am always serious," said Lermontov. "You know that."

He sounds like Rocky, thought Frank.

"But we discuss ideology," said Lermontov. "Not slang. Stalin wanted to expand Soviet imperialism and, above all, to keep all power in his own hands. He cared about Communism about as much as the Shah cares about his White Revolution."

"From what I've read," said Frank, "the Shah seems pretty proud of his White Revolution."

"He should be proud," said Lermontov. "The Americans love him for it. It makes him look like a benign, progressive ruler. He cares about it for the same reason he cares about his Imperial Bodyguard, about Savak and the torture rooms in Evin prison. They all help to keep him in power."

"Don't you feel a bit . . . nervous? Talking about the Shah like that? Here?"

"You mean because this room is bugged?"

Frank nodded.

"I'm beyond that," said Lermontov. "In fact, in my own meetings with the Shah I've become quite open. I think it helped convince him of my sincerity, including my sincerity about wanting to talk to you. The Shah is very shrewd in handling people. That also helps keep him in power."

"It can't just be about power."

"Power is what he craves," said Lermontov.

Frank reacted slowly. He could feel his skin tighten. Lermontov had hit a chord. He could feel himself begin to change, but he resisted the change.

"The Shah's a good man," said Frank. He added to himself, Who maybe went wrong.

"A good man. Keep repeating it. Maybe you'll convince yourself."

"I am convinced. And convinced the world isn't as corrupt as you make it sound."

"Not corrupt," said Lermontov. "Not necessarily corrupt. But, of necessity, determined to fight for our own interests."

"What about here?" asked Frank.

"Here? Simple. You want Iran. We want Iran."

"Not us. The Iranians. What are they fighting for?"

"Also simple. They want Iran. The Iran that emerges from this will identify its national interest with Islam. A way of protecting itself from the Great Satans of the West and the godless atheists to the north."

Frank nodded. The bastard might be right. Lermontov, and perhaps Russia, might be ready to join the capitalist camp. Lermontov had called him "old friend." Perhaps. But Frank still thought of his friend as an enemy.

"Maybe we're wrong to call it nationalism," said Lermontov.

"Tribalism?" offered Frank.

"We reserve that for Africans. We don't much use it for ourselves. Perhaps we should. Like your Irish tribes in Northern Ireland. Or look at this neighborhood. The Kurds say they fight for a nation, but different factions, different clans, spend more time fighting each other than they do the Turks, the Iraqis, the Iranians. And among our beloved comrades in Afghanistan, you take the party labels off and all you have are the same old tribes who've been fighting each other for centuries—and will for centuries more."

"Friend of mine says World War III has already started," said Frank, remembering Gus's words. "All these little wars, like this one, add up to the World War III we'll be fighting for the next thousand years."

"Smart friend. Pete Howard?"

"No," said Frank, "another friend." He wondered how much Lermontov knew about Pete.

"I'm impressed. Another intelligent one. You, Pete Howard, and someone else. I didn't think America had so many."

"Wait till you spend some time in America. You may change your mind."

"You forget. I've been there. I went to school there."

"That was a long time ago," said Frank.

"You're right. I need a refresher course."

They sat facing each other in armchairs across a low, wood-topped coffee table, their backs to the French doors glazed by sun and frost. The cameras in the Shah's office had been relatively easy to detect, but here Frank could see no hint of hidden video. He was sure Lermontov's more practiced eye had also scanned the room. An ornate porcelain vase with artificial blue flowers stood between them.

"Shall we move the flowers?"

"No," said Frank. "I like blue flowers. Even if they are artificial." He placed a note Rocky had approved on the table with a photocopied section of the map of Tehran in Troy's office. Lermontov studied them.

Frank wanted to keep talking and sound as natural as he could without saying anything to distract Lermontov from the map, on which a small street in the north end of the town's foreign ghetto had been circled in red, and the typed sheet, which gave the address of the safe house, instructions for reaching it, and reassuring words.

*Never before used as safe house. Fully detached building. Never had American tenant. Previous have been French and German.*

"We really shouldn't continue to impose on the Shah's hospitality," said Frank. "The hotels aren't busy these days. Perhaps we could book a room at the Sheraton or the Hyatt."

"Good idea," said Lermontov, who went on reading.

*Two-car garage under building. Flash car lights when you arrive. I will open garage doors from inside, close them behind your car. Stairs lead from garage up into house. Security guy I trust making it tight. Can we make it Friday evening, 7:30? I'll be there half hour before you. Any problem, try again 7:30 Saturday evening.*

"I prefer the Sheraton," said Lermontov. "I've used it before. Can you book a room?"

"Sure," said Frank, making a mental note to book a room and have Gus occupy it.

He handed Lermontov a note that read, "My chief of station wants to meet you."

Lermontov crumpled it in his giant paw and shook his head.

"Let's make it Friday night," he said. "At the Sheraton."

He left the paper ball on the table, folded the other papers Frank had given him, neatly and quietly, and put them in an inside jacket pocket.

"Friday at the Sheraton. Perhaps we can have dinner."

"Good idea," said Frank. "I'll arrange room service."

He picked up the paper Lermontov had crumpled and stuffed it into a pants pocket. He tore a sheet of paper from his notebook and printed out another message.

*'Please act surprised.'*

Lermontov glanced at the paper and pushed it back across the table toward Frank.

They chatted for half an hour, about acromegaly, Afghanistan, Islam, and the uneasy peace that prevailed in Tehran. Frank thought of the uneasy peace that prevailed between him and Lermontov. He may be playing a game we haven't figured out yet, he thought. The echo of Rocky's words bounced off the walls of his mind.

I trust no one. Not even myself, thought Frank. Much less an officer of the

KGB. He and Lermontov had danced often; still Frank could not tell who led and who followed. They again confirmed their spoken plan to meet at the Sheraton and headed down the hall together.

In the reception area the two armed guards stood where they had, before the doors to the Shah's suite of offices. One of them spoke abruptly in Farsi.

*"Be neshin-id."*

"They ask us," said Lermontov, "tell us, rather, to take a seat."

"Perhaps we should."

They sat in straight-backed chairs that flanked the outside doors, facing the guards. Frank saw no sign of Nazih and wondered if the Shah had summoned him into his office. The guards stiffened as the door between them opened.

"Ah, gentlemen," said their elegantly clad host, "you have completed your business. Major Sullivan, His Imperial Majesty would like to have a word with you. If you kindly can wait just here, he will summon you shortly."

"Thank you," said Frank, standing.

"Please. No need to stand." He turned to Lermontov. "Shall I notify your driver that you are ready?"

"Please," said Lermontov.


Frank endured a thirty-minute wait seated in the straight-backed chair with nothing to look at but two stone-faced members of the Imperial Guard, each with a submachine gun tucked into the crook of his arm. Deadly silence seemed the only other occupant of the building. Frank looked from one guard to the other. They stared at a spot beyond him and above his head, but he knew that if he moved, they would notice. He heard a faint click. The guards shifted their attention: one to Frank; the other to the inner door that opened. The tall, thick-chested man in the doorway wore the blue uniform of an officer in the Imperial Bodyguard. The silver eagles on his shoulders identified him as a full colonel. His bearing identified him as a man of authority.

"Major Sullivan?"

"Yes, sir." Frank stood.

"I must apologize for your long wait. As you know, these are difficult times. His Imperial Majesty would like to see you for a few minutes."

What happened to the man in the morning suit? Frank wondered. Have the Imperial Guards pulled off a coup? And where the hell is Nazih?

The colonel spoke to the guards in Farsi and beckoned to Frank to follow him. "This way."

The Shah, hands clasped behind his back, stood before his illuminated map, his face masked by oversize sunglasses. "Ah, yes, Major Sullivan. May I introduce you to our new deputy prime minister, Colonel Hossein Kasravi."

Frank recognized the name of their missing chicken colonel. Clearly, being deputy prime minister carried more clout than being a member of the Jayface team. He stuck his hand out, and the slightly flustered colonel shook it.

"General Merid has spoken highly of you," said Frank. "But I never thought I would have the chance to meet with you."

Kasravi and the Shah exchanged a glance. The Shah shrugged.

"Ah, yes. General Merid," said Kasravi. "I must have a talk with him, soon."

Although a general outranked a colonel, Frank had the impression that in the real world the general would defer to the deputy prime minister.

"Ah, one thing more," added Kasravi. "Major Nazih will not be returning with you to Tehran. The way will be cleared at the gates for you and your car. Your driver has been instructed. On future visits, the way will be cleared for you and your driver. Please use the same car."

"What's happened with Major Nazih?"

"He has been detained," said Kasravi. "A . . . pressing commitment. I will leave you with His Imperial Majesty."

The Shah nodded. Kasravi bowed, once, twice, three times as he backed out the door.

Detained. Commitment. Interesting word choices, thought Frank. He wondered about the majordomo.

He had sat with the Shah for nearly an hour after Kasravi had left them. The Shah wanted to talk, but his conversation rambled in a way Frank could barely follow.

"It is so difficult to know whom to trust these days. To confide in. Take advice from. The Empress, of course. And my sister. But not Assadollah Alam. He died, you know. There was no one closer, more trusted. His death was another betrayal. I have been so alone. He had been our prime minister and then for many years our minister of court until he died last year. Cancer. I know it isn't contagious, but we were so close. Cancer killed him, and now it kills me."

"What do your doctors say about treatment?" He had asked the same question at their first meeting. Again, the Shah's answer was vague, more political than medical.

"That I should go to France, perhaps Switzerland, for treatment. But neither the French nor the Swiss are very good at security. And now the king of the mullahs, this Khomeini, has been given sanctuary in France. I can only imagine what the mullahs would subject me to in France if I went there for treatment, and now I find betrayal in my own house. This Russian who wants you to get him medical treatment in America. Give him asylum and get him out of our country. I do not like him. He insults our government and then thinks we respect him for being so honest. We do not want trouble with the Russians or I would send your Lermontov back to Moscow today. You won't be seeing Major Nazih at your meetings."

"What's happened?" asked Frank, wondering about the abrupt leap from Lermontov to Nazih.

"Major Nazih has been detained. We will need another means to contact you. Can we rely on your ambassador?"

"Of course," said Frank. "But why has the major been detained?" As soon as the words escaped, he realized the Shah might consider the question rude.

"In our own house. Our own court." His tone had sharpened. "He had been playing too many games in too many different directions, including the game he tried to play with you."

"What game was that, Your Imperial Majesty?"

"He tried to put you in a bad light with us. Apparently at the urging of this Russian, who has his own games to play. But it is not important. Others far more important will soon be arrested. What does the arrest of someone as small as your Major Nazih matter? Besides, it has a strategic value. It sends a message to the Russians. And it isolates this Lermontov. That should help you."

"I hope . . . I hope I haven't contributed to the major's problem."

"Rubbish. Others have also been detained."

His voice began to fade. He removed his dark glasses and turned to face Frank. His eyes looked sunken.

"What must I do to contain this cancer? Lance it? Spill more blood? What would you do?"

I would get the hell out of here, thought Frank. "Perhaps a new government," he said. "With a role for the popular but moderate religious leaders."

"Do you think that might work?" the Shah asked.

The question stunned Frank. "You would know far better than I," he said.

The Shah turned in his chair and looked for a moment toward the sun-glazed window behind him. Frank knew he could see nothing beyond the glare of the snow.

"We wonder. Perhaps a vacation. We might discuss your idea with our prime minister . . ." The Shah hesitated, seeming to have lost his thought. Frank offered a name.

"General Azhari."

"Yes. We can trust General Azhari. The Immortals. We can trust the Immortals. Admiral Hayati thinks we should take a vacation at a naval base in the south and let the Immortals and the soldiers put down this rebellion."

"Will you take his advice?"

"We see blood on the snow. When we look behind us and the sun sets and strikes the hills, that is what we see. We see blood on the snow. A strange treatment for cancer, isn't it?" His shoulders hunched. The turtle shrank into his shell.

From the sound of the laboring motor, Frank knew that Ali kept the car in low gear as they descended the Elborz Hills from the palace toward the city. Snow that had melted under the midday sun now had begun to freeze over as the evening cooled. He hoped Ali would not ask what had happened to Major Nazih, but soon discovered that Ali knew more than he did.

"Major Nazih left in a blue Mercedes," he volunteered. "With three men in black leather overcoats. Others also left in a *Savak* van that followed the Mercedes."

"Do you know the man with the white hair? Wears a formal suit with tails?"

Ali nodded. "He is one of two or three deputy ministers of the court. Since the death of Assadolah Alam, there has been no minister. I do not know his name. He left, with others, in the *Savak* van. One of the Imperial Guards, a nephew of mine, said the rumor makers say they were all involved with the Russians in some way."

And Lermontov survives, thought Frank. How? Why?

"Major Sullivan, sir."

"Yes?"

"This makes me worried." The car skidded on an icy patch, but Ali accelerated out of the spin. "Am I also in trouble?"

"No." He started to say, "Not as far as I know," but held back. He managed a smile. "And I don't think I'm in trouble either."

"Good," said Ali. "Are you a family man, sir?"

"Yes, and I know you must be worried about your family." Jake. Jackie. For the first time in days, he thought about his family.

"Yes," Ali agreed. "I must worry about my family."

"I'll do my best to keep us both out of trouble."

I have to, thought Frank. For Jake.

"Thank you, sir. I will also do my best."

The arrests forced Frank to drive from Dowshan Tappeh to a bubble meeting with Rocky.

"And you better have Gus ride shotgun," Tom Troy had advised.

Since Gus had challenged the need-to-know wall between them, Frank had agreed they would work better together by keeping each other informed. He outlined all that had happened at the palace and confessed that he worried, despite himself, about Nazih; worried what General Merid's reaction would be; worried about the gracious majordomo and what role he might have played in whatever web Nazih had spun. He even wondered if Lermontov had somehow found a way to arrange the arrests as a means of making his position with the Soviets seem in jeopardy.


Rocky, as Frank had suspected, had heard about the arrests from *Savak*'s Eagle-1. But *Savak* had provided few details, only that those arrested had been in contact with Noureddin Kianouri and other exiled leaders of the *Tudeh* party.

They left Gus behind in Rocky's office and climbed to the bubble.

"So maybe your KGB buddy's out of the loop," said Rocky. "Maybe the Sovs have given up on Kianouri and the *Tudeh*."

"But the other day Lermontov flat out told me Nazih works for him."

"Well, if the Shah's intelligence branch didn't already know it, they must have been listening when Lermontov told you about it."

"So?"

"So maybe the Shah wants to do us—or you—a favor. Maybe he figures it's better for us to let Lermontov hang around here rather than PNG him back to Moscow where you and I can't get at him. I've got a sit-down meet with Eagle-1 tomorrow. I'll get more then. We're on for the day after tomorrow with Lermontov?"

Frank nodded. "Meeting's set for Friday, seven-thirty, the safe house."

"You think he'll show?"

"I think he'll show."


Frank, in an office next to Rocky's, began his cable drafting with a brief report on his meeting with Lermontov. Begging Gus to bear with him, he spent over an hour drafting a carefully nuanced narrative of his conversation with the Shah. He drew no conclusions, but Rocky did.

"It sounds like he's lost it and he knows it."

Frank kept his cables on meeting Colonel Kasravi and on the apparent arrests by *Savak* brief, almost telegraphic. Rocky added a station comment confirming the arrests and citing his own earlier cable based on information from Eagle-1.

"I don't think anyone's ever met this Kasravi character before," said Rocky. "The ambassador sure hasn't, and none of the military attachés know him. You realize he could give you a pipeline into the prime minister's office?"

"We'll see what happens," said Frank.

"Gus tell you what he's got goin'?"

Frank looked his way.

"Haven't had a chance," said Gus.

"Your buddy oughta know about it," said Rocky.

" 'Course," said Gus. "Just haven't had the chance. It's our waiter, this Hamid character I asked Anwar about. Seems he's also the waiter for the big brass, the generals up on the third floor."

"Seems he speaks English," said Rocky. "Gus got the full name, date and place of birth, the usual, and we asked for traces. Nothin' on him, so I told Gus to go ahead and pitch him."

"Sounds good," said Frank. "He go for it?"

"Haven't had a chance to get him alone since I got the go-ahead," said Gus. "Been meanin' to tell you about it, but you've been pretty busy. Up at the palace and all."

"Yeah," said Frank, "I guess. We do have some time in the evening, though, don't we?"

"Anyway," said Gus, "till we find out if he goes for it or not, there won't be much to tell."

"If it works out," said Rocky, "with one of you talkin' to Kasravi and the other with a snitch who listens to the generals, looks like maybe I won't be able t' get rid of you two bastards."


General Merid, nervous when he arrived for their meeting the next day, became even more agitated when an Imperial Bodyguard corporal interrupted to announce that Colonel Kasravi wanted to see Major Sullivan in his third-floor office at nine hundred hours.

"Why . . . why does he want to see you?"

"I have no idea," said Frank. "I didn't even know he had an office upstairs."

The general tugged at the hem of his jacket. Tension furrowed his usually smooth forehead. "I see. Then he will want me to attend the meeting as well. To escort you."

"Yes, sir. I'm sure you're right."

"Yes. At zero nine hundred hours. Well, that still gives us an hour. Shall we begin our own meeting? Our own discussions?"

No one mentioned the absence of Major Nazih. General Merid eased into his chair and looked from one American to the other. Frank tried to imagine how he would feel if someone close to him, his son, perhaps, had been picked up for some unknown reason. Jake, disappeared into the black hole of a secretive juvenile detention system. He shuddered. Please be okay, he prayed. The silence around the table weighed like a damp shroud. Gus did his best to stir up interest in civic action programs he'd been involved with in Vietnam.

"Vietnam?" said Munair. "Wasn't that a disaster for your country?"

As they started their climb to the third floor, Frank said softly to General Merid, "As I'm sure you know, yesterday . . . yesterday Major Nazih and I did not return from the palace together."

"What can you tell me?"

"Only what our driver saw. Major Nazih left in a blue Mercedes with three other men. And other members, members, he thought, of the Imperial Court also left in a van."

"Under *Savak* control," said the general.

"Do you have any idea why?"

"No. But Colonel Kasravi can enlighten us. He has excellent contacts."


Colonel Kasravi, however, had other plans for his meeting. "Thank you, general, for showing Major Sullivan the way," he said moments after they entered his tiny, sparsely furnished office. "I will see he gets back to your meeting as quickly as possible. Perhaps you and I can meet here this afternoon. Let us say thirteen hundred hours?"

"But Colonel Kasravi, sir . . ."

"Thirteen hundred hours," Kasravi repeated.

Frank felt the general's embarrassment and looked away. He sensed more steel in Colonel Kasravi than General Merid and Major Nazih had indicated when they had joked about the chicken colonel. Perhaps that had been one of Nazih's mistakes.

"Yes, colonel. Thirteen hundred hours." Frank heard General Merid open the door behind him. Kasravi did not even give General Merid time to close it before addressing Frank.

"Thank you for being prompt. Please be seated."

"Yes, Your Excellency."

"Please. I'm only a deputy prime minister. You don't have to *salam-ta* me."

Frank nodded and took a seat across the small, gunmetal desk that Kasravi sat behind. A single file folder sat open on the desk. Kasravi glanced at its contents and closed it.

Frank took his tape recorder from a jacket pocket and asked, "Will this be okay?"

"Yes. In fact, it will be a good idea. I have certain information to convey to you, and it is important that you report it accurately."

Frank nodded, pressed the play and record buttons, and opened up the notebook he'd also brought with him.

"I've been instructed to inform you in the matter of Major Nazih," said the colonel. "The information I am about to give you may be conveyed to your government. But it may not be conveyed to any of your counterparts on Jayface, including the general, or to any other Iranians or any foreign nationals or uncleared Americans. Is that clear?"

"Yes, sir," said Frank. NOFORN, he thought, anticipating his cable heading.

"Major Nazih, along with several members of the Imperial Court, all, I might add, or nearly all, members of a tight little Qazvini Mafia, have been detained."

Frank circled "Qzn Mfa" on his notepad, wondering what that meant.

"They had conspired with elements of the *Tudeh* party to undermine the Imperial Government of Iran, to establish links to renegade mullahs and to smuggle the leader of the *Tudeh* party back into the country by boat from Baku across the Caspian with plans to land on a beach near the city of Rasht. We have this morning informed the Russian Embassy of our knowledge and displeasure concerning this plot. We plan no retaliation or public announcement, but we have told the Russians we expect them to refrain from any similar activities, particularly as it may concern support of certain renegade mullahs. His Imperial Majesty's private security branch initiated this action with the assistance of military intelligence. *Savak* had no involvement except for taking the detainees into custody. In fact, J2, our military intelligence, has detained certain members of *Savak* who themselves have been involved in this conspiracy. We believe your embassy has no prior knowledge of what we have done. The primary Soviet agent in this plot is Vassily Lermontov, whom, of course, you know."

"Of course. Is he under surveillance?"

"Of course," said Kasravi. "So are you. But, at His Imperial Majesty's specific instructions, in deference to you, your KGB friend will not be expelled."

"But why, why in deference to me?"

"That is all I have been instructed to say."

"Yes, sir. But may I . . . may I ask one other question? What's a . . ." He glanced quickly at his notepad. "A Qazvini Mafia?"

"I have no instructions on that." For a moment, the steel melted and the colonel smiled. "But you might consult a map."


They wrote their cables in Stan Rushmore's office at Dowshan Tappeh. Frank covered his meeting with Kasravi; Gus handled the Jayface meeting.

"And one more on Hamid," said Gus. "He went for it. Cash on the barrelhead. American dollars."

"Good," said Frank. "Hope he's productive."

"He may be," said Gus. "But look, I'm sorry I didn't tell you right up front. Guess I was still pissed at you keepin' me in the dark about Lermontov."

"You made your point," said Frank. "You didn't have to rub it in."

Frank's Timex, which tended to run fast, read seven-thirty-five when the flash of car lights from the street sent him scuttling down the steps to the garage. He heaved the doors up and stepped aside as a white Peugeot eased its way in alongside the blue Fiat. Frank tugged on the rope that lowered the doors, slipped the padlock through the hasp, and clicked it shut.

"I hope I'm not late," said Lermontov, as he squeezed his huge frame out of the Peugeot 504. In his bulky overcoat and lamb's-wool cap he looked even more overwhelming than usual.

"You're right on time," said Frank. He led the way upstairs. Despite his bulk, Lermontov mounted the stairs so quietly that Frank had to glance over his shoulder to make sure the Russian had followed him. Frank bypassed the closed kitchen door and turned into the large front room.

"Looks like a nice place," said Lermontov.

"Yes, and I suspect I owe it all to you."

"Me?"

"Well, yes. The station must have felt you rated special treatment. This is a whole lot nicer, and bigger, than the house they gave us to live in."

"I know. Is this the room that's bugged?"

"Far as I know, the whole house is bugged."

"I doubt. You had no instructions to confine our conversations to this room?"

"No."

"Interesting. Do you mind if I look around?"

"Help yourself."

Lermontov put his worn soft-leather briefcase on the large walnut-stained dining room table and dropped his coat and cap onto a chair. He opened the briefcase, dug into it, and extracted a black plastic device with a red bulb at one end. He ran it over the table top, then around the sides, also checking as he went with his fingers.

"There's something here, but nothing happens. That bulb should be flashing." An opaque vase with blue plastic flowers stood on the table. "Does that look familiar?"

"Yes," said Frank, remembering the similar arrangement in the room assigned to them outside the Shah's offices.

"The Americans sell the Iranians their leftovers. Everything from fighter jets to bugs." He circled the vase with his scanning device. The red bulb remained dark. Like a housewife testing fruit at a market, he squeezed each flower. "This one," he said. "Feel it."

Frank touched the soft plastic and could feel metal. Lermontov circled the room, checking the radiant-heat floor vents, examining the mantel over the fake fireplace, tapping the walls. "Something here, but nothing happens. Have you used the phone?"

Frank shook his head, and Lermontov picked up the black phone on a book-stand next to a blue Naugahyde armchair. "Dead, but in Tehran that isn't unusual. We're lucky the lights are on." He unscrewed the mouthpiece. "There's another. Very amusing. Because the electric power here is so unreliable, all the listening devices must be battery operated. It appears the bugs are more or less permanent installations, but your technicians forgot to activate them."

Batteries not included, thought Frank. He'd encountered such agency incompetence before, but he would not admit that to Lermontov.

"Maybe your scanning device hasn't been activated."

"No. I do not leave such things to technicians. I tested it before I left the embassy. You must inform your *rezident*—chief of station, I mean. He should have someone shot."

"He may," said Frank.

"It's the same man, isn't it? Who was in Rome when you tried to clean up that stupid book operation?"

"Would you like to meet him?"

"I would rather die," said Lermontov. He handed Frank an envelope, pointing to three neatly printed words. *'Read later alone.'* Frank put the envelope in his inside jacket pocket.

"He'd like to meet you," said Frank.

Lermontov glared at him. His massive right fist clenched, and his features hardened. "Is he here?"

"Let me get him." Frank moved toward the kitchen, opened the door, and nodded. Rocky pushed himself up from the table and followed Frank into the front room. Lermontov was stuffing his black scanning device back into his leather briefcase.

"Mr. Novak, I presume."

Rocky responded in Russian.

"Your accent is quite good," said Lermontov. "Your recruiting techniques, like your listening devices, quite poor."

Rocky touched his hearing aid. "What devices?"

"Your technicians forgot to activate your eavesdropping devices. No batteries."

"Fuck me," said Rocky with real anger.

"They did," said Lermontov. He turned to Frank. "And you, my good friend, fucked me. You betrayed me, you bastard. And sentenced me to death." He secured the straps on his briefcase and shrugged into his heavy coat. "I will need you, or at least your key, to open the garage door." He scooped up his hat, turned his back, and moved toward the door.

"Wait," said Rocky. "You want Frank to handle you?"

Lermontov stopped. He turned to face them. His broad shoulders filled the doorway. "I want no one to handle me. I would work with someone I can trust. Not with this bastard who betrayed me. And certainly not with you." He angled his shoulders to get through the door. His steps thudded heavily on the stairs.

"Gimme the fucking key," snapped Rocky. Frank tossed it to him, and Rocky followed Lermontov down to the garage. Frank stood at the top of the stairs and could hear Rocky speaking evenly in Russian.

"Open the door, please," Lermontov responded with an edge in his voice.

Frank heard the garage door ratcheting up and the roar of the Peugeot turning over. Now what? he wondered.

Rocky summoned a car from the embassy by cranking up his walkie-talkie and uttering a single word: "Now." He and Frank waited, facing each other across the walnut-stained top of the dinning room table.

"You set that up?"

"How could I set that up?" said Frank.

"You want to handle him, right? So you set it up he walks out 'cause I'm here."

"You said he's yours."

"Doesn't look that way, does it?"

"No," said Frank. "It doesn't look that way."

"You holdin' out on me?"

Frank thought of the envelope Lermontov had given him. He nodded and reached into his jacket pocket. He glanced at the envelope and handed it to Rocky.

"It says you're supposed to read it alone."

"I feel pretty alone," said Frank.

Rocky ripped open the envelope, unfolded the single sheet, and read. "Says, 'I will contact you.' He's playin' us."

"He's been playing us," said Frank. "It started with Nazih."

"Shit, he's been playing you for years, you dumb fuck." Rocky leaned back in his chair, studying Frank. "Think we can get him back?"

Frank shrugged. "He says he'll contact us."

"Uh-uh. He says he'll contact you."

Frank sensed the resentment in Rocky's words. "I wonder how," he said. "There's no Nazih. I doubt the Shah."

"He'll find a way," said Rocky. "He knew enough to prepare this note in advance."

"He might've suspected something."

"Fuck yes," said Rocky. "He's a good spy. Good spy always suspects something. You brung nothing but trouble since you got here, Sullivan. Brought, not brung. You bring out the street in me."

"What now?" said Frank quickly. "We just wait?"

"All we can do. Except get a cable off. Tell the home front this thing blew up in our face. Only problem, since we blew it, Near East and fucking Soviet Division have even more of a reason to send over some pooh-bahs to sit on us. Show the field idiots how it should be done. And I thought I was lookin' at a promotion." He drummed the table with his stubby fingers. "Even a medal."

He'll blame me for that, thought Frank. Rocky caught his eye.

"And it'll give all the good folks back home who don't much like you anyway even more of a reason to pull your ass outta here."

I knew that was coming, thought Frank. For years he had wondered if Lermontov could be recruited. Then, in an unlikely setting, Lermontov had seized the initiative. Frank knew he had not made it happen. Lermontov had made it happen. But now Rocky, proud chief of station and vain Soviet Division veteran, had undone all that. His blundering had propelled their target out of their safe house and into the Russian Embassy's sanctuary in Iran. Despite Lermontov's three-word note, Frank believed any effort to recruit him would now prove difficult. He envisioned the watch strapped to Lermontov's massive wrist and could hear the ticking of a clock, time running out. If it were going to happen, Frank knew he would have to make it happen. And soon.

"Look," he said. "If we do get another crack at him, I've got an idea."

# PART II

# CHAPTER SEVEN

For nearly a month, Frank would wait, worry, wonder, and work at what he considered his day job with Jayface. Lermontov sent signals, most notably through what Frank would have considered an unlikely source, the British ambassador. The final signal came from an even more unlikely source, Hamid, the waiter recruited by Gus.

He realized he'd focused so hard on his Russian target, he lost sight of Iran. Gus brought him back down to earth.

"Forget about your friend from that cold country up north. You read his note. He'll contact you. When he's ready. Time for us to get back to work."

"You're right," said Frank. Time to get back to work, but he feared time was running out.

"So we didn't recruit Lermontov. But we did sign up Hamid," said Gus.

"Not 'we,'" said Frank. "You signed up Hamid. I have to admit, I didn't see the potential."

"Sometimes a dinky little hit to the opposite field is worth more than swingin' for the fences and comin' up short."

"You missed your calling," said Frank. "You should've been a hitting coach."

"You could use one," said Gus, peering at Frank over the wire rims of his glasses. "You want some of that Russian poison you drink?"

"It's Swedish," said Frank.

"Absolutely," said Gus.

Frank had discovered that both he and Gus did not believe in ice cubes. Gus kept his Dewar's in the refrigerator. Frank kept his Absolut in the freezer, where they also kept their glasses. Gus poured them each two fingers.

"*Salut.*"

"*Salut,*" echoed Frank. "We better be careful. Tomorrow may be Sunday in Christendom, but it's just another workday here."

"Sunday," said Gus. "I want to be home. Home in Rome with Joan."

"You really love that lady, don't you?"

"Damned if I don't. And I wanna be home."

"I know how you feel," said Frank.

Gus pushed himself away from the sink and sat down opposite Frank at the table. "No. No, I don't think you do. It's not like I love that lady like I did, well, maybe like I did before I went to Nam. But Joan and I, to tell you the truth, ol' buddy, we don't give very much of a hump about humpin' anymore. We haven't done much of what's called making love in five, six years. Part of it's knowin' at this stage we aren't gonna have any kids. Not at her . . . our age. We did a lot, I mean a lot, of humpin' when I first got back from Vietnam, but when we were goin' at it I kept seeing one or another or all of those lovely little Vietnamese hookers who'll suck your cock better or fuck you better or even cook for you better than any woman in the world, and then I knew sex with Joan would never be as good, and I started to love her even more than ever I did, and I swear to God, I want to be home."

Sleep eluded him as he thought of the sad story of Gus's happy marriage. He thought of his brief encounter with Gus and Joan at the airport in Rome, en route to Tehran. Through descriptions they had been given, he and Gus recognized each other in the uncrowded boarding area. Years before, the same body shop had hired each for agency assignments in different parts of Africa. Now, for the first time, they met. They nodded, and Frank walked over to Gus and the woman who stood by him.

"We must be on the same flight," said Frank.

"I guess." Gus looked older than Frank had expected, more ravaged by the life of the field man. The slender woman with him wore no makeup and made no effort to hide her anger or her tears.

"Glad to meet you, Mrs. Simpson," said Frank.

"Sorry," said Gus. "Frank Sullivan, my wife, Joan."

She glanced at him coldly and with a firm, dry grip shook the hand he offered. She looked at her husband and said, "You shouldn't be doing this." Only then did she drop Frank's hand.

"I'll be back before you know it."

"They shouldn't even be asking."

Frank guessed her to be a decade younger than Gus, still attractive, but showing her years in the hard, tight lines of her mouth and the spiked crow's feet branching from her cold, gray eyes.

"Good to meet you," said Frank. Again, she ignored him. He nodded toward Gus. "See you on board." He walked away, leaving them to their private war.

In Tehran the weather turned colder, and the war continued. As he and Gus picked their way across the ice-spangled walk to the waiting Nova, Frank noticed the exhaust had melted a hole in the frozen-over *jube*.

"All peaceful?" asked Gus as he climbed into what had become his usual seat in the back.

"Peaceful, yes," said Ali, "Peaceful, but not peace. Bad news in Isfahan." Ali started to move the big Nova forward, slowly. "Students, religious students, some armed, yesterday they attack Bell Helicopter. The army drove the students back. Many were killed."

Frank remembered Ali's oldest son was in the army and based in Isfahan. "And your son?"

"Shot."

Gus leaned forward. "Bad?"

"He was my oldest. Only seventeen, but he was my oldest."

Seventeen, thought Frank. His own son, Jake, was only eleven, and New York's mean streets at their worst couldn't compare with a nation at war with itself. But if something did happen, I couldn't protect him, he thought. Half a world away.

Gus pulled off his stocking cap. His sparse hair stood on end. "Will you go down there?" he asked.

The car rolled past the guardhouse, and Ali turned left, heading toward Supreme Commander's Headquarters.

Ali shook his head. "My wife has already gone. I cannot. I am on duty here."


Their morning Jayface sessions had developed their own rhythm. At their Saturday meeting they reviewed and amended the latest installment of Frank's civic action proposal. This one dealt with military involvement in the distribution of cooking oil. The plan called for military action to curtail the strikes that had severely limited production.

"That you can count on," said General Merid, making eye contact with Frank. "I have it on good authority." He fell silent. His eyes lost their focus, as though some element of doubt had taken hold. His olive skin and smooth features seemed paler and more clouded. He straightened his shoulders and resumed with a more confident but hollow tone. "The oil workers will allow enough production of both cooking oil and benzene to meet domestic demand and pay for essential imports. A million barrels a day."

"Really?" said Gus. "When do you think that will start happening?"

"Within four or five days," said the general. "You can count on it."

Frank's tape recorder spun, but he also took notes, heading the page 11/11/78. What we used to call Armistice Day back home, he thought, but no armistice here. The revolution had slowed but not stopped. That morning, Anwar told him, the government had arrested several leaders of the major opposition parties, including Karim Sanjabi and Mahdi Bazargan.

"Just like you told me a week ago," said Frank.

"Your embassy should be pleased that you were a week ahead with the news."

"Yes. They should be," said Frank. But he had his doubts.

He wanted to find a way to get someone to listen. With Jayface as their sole base of operations, he had begun to fear they might run out of time, but the partial resumption of oil production offered some hope. At Gus's suggestion, Frank planned to delay completing the civic action proposal until Fred Bunker arrived and had a chance to review and approve it.

"He's a bureaucrat to the bone," Gus had said. "And if he thinks you tried to slip in a finished product to the locals before he got here, he'll work on finding ways to crucify you—slowly—till the day he dies."

With a mixture of appreciation and resentment, Frank realized, again, how much he had to learn from Gus. They now expected Bunker to arrive on the fifteenth, just four days away. The civic action proposal could wait.

"We should have our proposal ready for you within a week," said Gus. "Maybe just about the time oil production starts up."

"That would be most excellent," said the general, nodding and bouncing the tip of a sharpened pencil on the tabletop. "The deputy prime minister is most anxious to have a look at it."

Frank had hoped for an even more lethargic pace. He feared that once they presented a finished proposal to General Merid, the military government might review it and reject it, which would leave Jayface—and its American advisers—with little reason to go on functioning. He knew he needed Jayface to provide the cover for what he considered his real but forbidden missions in Iran: intelligence gathering with the Shah and recruiting Lermontov.


Gus sat at the typewriter in Stan Rushmore's office, drafting a cable on the day's Jayface meeting. He pecked with two fingers, but faster than Frank could type with ten. Frank realized how much he'd come to rely on Gus's pragmatic gift. From the mechanics of cable drafting to dealing with various levels of Iranian and American bureaucracy, Gus had become his on-the-ground guide.

"You promised your King of All Kings some ideas for Jayface that would lock you in as a long-term adviser."

"I wish I hadn't."

"But you did. And it's a bum idea to make promises to an emperor and not deliver."

"I've been thinking about it," said Frank.

"Good."

"But I haven't thought of anything."

"Not good. And I've got a hunch our chicken colonel will get on your case about it."

"You're probably right."

"Look, I've got one for you. Remember back at that meeting when you came up with an agenda that was heavy on all that civic action stuff the general liked so much?"

"I remember having trouble staying awake when he went off on the 'real' Iran."

"I might have nodded a time or two myself, but one of your ideas was a propaganda effort to support the civic action."

"None of which can happen."

"Right. But now we've got a different situation. We've got a military government. And no newspapers."

"So why not a general interest newspaper published by the military?"

"You got it," said Gus. "With an American adviser with credentials just like yours."

"Or yours," said Frank.

"Not me," said Gus. "I just want to go home. But I got a hunch you have reasons for wantin' to stay. And remember, it's a lot easier to start a newspaper than it is to build a sewer system."

"I like it," said Frank. He'd become the de facto publisher of the daily English-language newspaper in Ethiopia and had enjoyed the experience, and he had thrived in all the newspaper jobs he'd held in the States. "I wouldn't mind being a newspaperman again," he said, and went to work drafting a newspaper proposal. "But to tell you the truth, I don't see much of a future here for either of us."

"I don't see much of a future here for anybody," said Gus. "Americans or Iranians. At least this gives us a way to keep a foot in the door. If there's still a door to keep our foot in."

Frank hoped there might still be a door. Gus's newspaper idea might buy us some time with the Shah, he thought. And he wanted time to try to bring Lermontov back in. He tried to think as the KGB man must think and sensed that the big man would not contact him soon. Let the Americans worry. Let them think they may have lost their chance to recruit a high-level KGB officer. He resented playing the Russian's game. He remembered how, as a young teenager, he had given up trying to play pool after being humiliated too often by older boys who could split a rack, call their shots, and run the table. The game Lermontov played now left Frank with that same helpless feeling, watching, with nothing he could do but wait while the Soviet dictated the play.

Frank knew Lermontov would guess he had showed his note to Rocky.

Lermontov wanted the Americans to know he still might cross over—but let them sweat and wonder what they would have to do to draw him back in. Frank wondered what it would take and knew only that he needed time.

"How 'bout you edit this one?" said Gus, handing Frank his cable on the Jayface meeting. "I've got one more to do. From Hamid. Including some stuff may interest you. Seems what he does for *Savak* at Supreme Commander's is only his day job. His night job is for J2. And guess where?"

Frank shrugged.

"Military intelligence, right? He spies on our buddy Anwar, the air force major. He cooks and runs the kitchen for Anwar's family."

"Busy man."

"That he is," said Gus. "And guess what? He tells me Anwar and his wife want to get outta here and get to the States. Wife's got relatives there."

"Interesting," said Frank. "I wonder who else Hamid works for."

"If I find out, I'll let you know," said Gus. "You and Anwar seem to have hit it off. I'm puttin' in the cable that if we try to recruit him, you should be the one to pitch him."

Frank nodded.

"Give you somethin' to do," said Gus. "While you're waitin' to hear from Moscow."

Their Sunday Jayface meeting began with a long discussion of their idea for setting up a daily newspaper published and distributed by the military. Frank described the newspaper effort as a possible forerunner to a military broadcasting system with a mix of news, entertainment, and educational programming. It included a role for an adviser with a background in Western private sector and Third World governmental mass media.

"Oh, I like that idea," said General Merid. "The suggestion for an adviser. Perhaps that's a role you could fill yourself, Major Sullivan."

"Well, we have a long way to go before we have to think about that," said Frank.

"But we must press ahead," said the general. "How soon can we have your ideas in writing?"

You can have them now, thought Frank. But he remembered Gus's warning about Bunker.

"Well, so far it's just an idea. We'll need some time to work it up."

"This is all very urgent," said the general. "Especially with a military government in place. Gentlemen, I would like to make a suggestion. Commander

Simpson and you, Major Sullivan . . ." Still unused to his fictitious title, it took Frank a moment to realize he was Major Sullivan and another moment to focus on General Merid's words. "You will have so much to do," said the general. "So I suggest we continue to meet every morning but allow our American friends to spend their afternoons drafting the various proposals I will present to the deputy prime minister. You can work here if you wish."

"Ah, it might be best if we worked at our office at Dowshan Tappeh," said Gus, frowning over his glasses to underline his sincerity. "We have access there to equipment and background materials we may need. We can even cable for anything we don't have here."

"Yes," said the general, "I'm sure your offices are better equipped than what we have."

"General, I have another suggestion, if I may," said Frank.

"Of course. Of course."

"In view of what's happened—the new government—and the impact that's going to have on the nature and, ah, the urgency, of our work, I'd like to have your permission to take notes and prepare minutes, which we could review and amend at the next meeting."

"Excellent idea. Excellent." The general had begun again to bounce, ever so slightly, on his toes. "Excellent idea."

As the general's high subsided, his expression saddened. Even the civic action projects failed to engage him. Frank guessed that the general's mind drifted to fears about the fate of Major Nazih. The other Iranians had hurried off after General Merid again called a four o'clock halt to their discussion. Anwar lingered.

"You seem tired," he said.

"To be honest," said Frank, "I haven't been sleeping well. Back home I'm used to burning up nervous energy by working out. I jog almost every day, and I have a set of weights."

"You should use the gym at Dowshan Tappeh," said Anwar.

"Is it okay for Americans?" he asked.

"Of course," said Anwar. "The base is Iranian, but Americans at Dowshan Tappeh have full access. In fact, it would be a good way for you to meet some of the *homafaran*."

"*Homafar?* You've got to, please, pardon my ignorance. But what's a *homafar?*"

Anwar's dark eyes studied Frank, not with the intensity of the navy's Captain Irfani, but with a questioning, skeptical curiosity. Without speaking, he asked, I wonder how much I can tell you? They stood at the head of the marble stairway with its crowning, unlit chandelier, waiting for Gus, who had gone in search of Ali and their car.

"I have so much to learn. About *homafaran,* Islam, even about the gym at Dowshan Tappeh."

"You will find everything," said Anwar. "With patience. Sometimes Americans barge in, in big groups, and try to take over everything—the weights, the boxing bags, the running track, and especially the basketball courts. But if you are patient and do not go with a group that tries to take over all the equipment, you will find everything."

Frank nodded. "I understand."

"Perhaps we can meet, at Dowshan Tappeh, this evening. Say around six. In the cafeteria. I will show you around the gym. Perhaps introduce you to some friends."

"That would be good," said Frank.

"There will be news," said Anwar. Frank sensed that Anwar was testing him. "Within a few days. Now that you're going into the *ashkhalee* business, you should be interested in news."

*"Ashkhalee?"*

"The garbage man. Our main source of news. We told you about them. You are interested in news, aren't you."

"Sure," said Frank, trying to sound casual.

"Within a day or so General Nasseri, who headed *Savak* for many years, will be arrested. And others, including Amir Abbas Hoveida, the former prime minister, and Dariush Houmayun. They say he wrote an article that appeared in *Ittelat* attacking Ayatollah Khomeini last January."

Nasseri, Hoveida, Dariush Houmayun. Nasseri, Hoveida, Dariush Houmayun. Frank kept repeating the names to himself as Anwar added other details.

Others will be arrested, the Shah had said, far more important than this Major Nazih.

"But why would the Shah arrest his own people?"

"He throws some bones to the National Front, to Khomeini," said Anwar. "The National Front it may appease, but not Khomeini. It will only increase his blood lust for more."

Frank suspected there would be more cables to write. Anwar touched his elbow as a group of Iranian Army officers, chattering loudly, entered through the ground floor doors. Frank and Anwar started down the wide stairway. The army men fell silent, glancing at Frank, as they passed.

Frank and Anwar stood at the foot of the stairway that led nowhere, their breath frosting the air as they waited for Gus and their car. Frank remembered Hamid's alert to Gus: Anwar and his family want to get to America. He decided to push a bit harder.

"We've heard reports, our embassy has heard reports that the generals are planning a coup, an actual takeover that would replace the Shah with his son and a regency council."

Anwar smiled. "The generals may talk," he said, "but they do not plan. They discuss and decide against. They know generals can't make a coup by themselves. They talk to each other. They talk to the American generals or the American Embassy about a coup. But they can't make a coup without soldiers. Without the pilots and *homafaran*."

"There must be some support for the Shah," said Frank.

"*Javadan,* the Imperial Guard, they can count on. They can count on *Savak*. Not even the police. You must realize, the soldiers are simple, uneducated young men. They are as religious as the people they come from. They go to the same mosques. They listen to the same religious leaders. They listen to Khomeini. When they fire at demonstrators, they fire at their own people. Khomeini tells the people to let the soldiers kill them. To be a martyr for Allah is sacred, and Khomeini knows the soldiers will not go on killing their own people. The soldiers may make a coup for Khomeini, but not for their generals or the Crown Prince. You must watch Khomeini. The opposition parties, the militant groups, *Mojahedin, Feda'iyan,* the student factions, all divided. But Khomeini unites all opposition."

"I understand," said Frank.

"Do you?" His dark, inquisitive eyes again studied Frank.

"No, I guess I don't." Frank felt betrayed by his own ignorance. *Mojahedin, Feda'iyan*—he had never heard of the groups Anwar had mentioned. He wondered if he would meet other Iranians as willing as Anwar to educate him.

"What do you know," he asked, "about a Qazvini Mafia?"

Anwar smiled. "What have you heard?"

"Just someone mentioned it," said Frank, not wanting to let Anwar know it had been Colonel Kasravi. "Someone who just smiled when I asked about it. Said I should look at a map."

"And did you?"

"I found a town called Qazvin, northwest of here, maybe a hundred and fifty kilometers."

"That's it. Home of your famous friend, Major Nazih."

"I didn't know he was so famous."

"He is now," said Anwar. "Along with all his friends from the palace who were arrested with him. All from Qazvin, so they say, which is famous for the lusts of its men for each other. Of course, people from Qazvin say the real homosexuals all come from Isfahan, and the Isfahanis say Tehran is the real capital city of queers. What it all adds up to is that somewhere in Iran there must be a few."

"General Merid?"

"He is also from Qazvin," said Anwar with an echo of Colonel Kasravi's knowing smile.

"Will he be arrested?"

"I doubt," said Anwar. "He is from Qazvin but not, I think, part of his nephew's Mafia." The bulletproof Nova pulled up beside them. "I will tell you more this evening," said Anwar.

"This evening," said Frank.


Frank sat in the American cafeteria at Dowshan Tappeh, stirring with a plastic spoon the black, unsweetened coffee in his plastic cup, checking his watch, checking the doors, wondering if Anwar would keep their appointment. Frank sniffed at his plastic coffee. It had no smell. He sipped it. It was burning hot but had no taste.

"The food is terrible here." The voice behind him startled Frank. "But I enjoy the apple pie." Anwar slid a tray onto the table and sat opposite Frank. "I haven't had really good apple pie since I left Texas."

"You should come over to our place for dinner some evening. I make a real good apple pie." It was a lie. Frank seldom baked, but he knew he could manage to make a decent apple pie. He'd tried a couple of times for Jake. The first proved a watery disaster. Jake was polite. The next had been better, at least on the second day, warmed over and served with ice cream.

Recruiting and seduction seemed to parody each other, he thought. Offer a sweet, tell a white lie. Get your target to come to your place.

"I had them heat it up," said Anwar, already wolfing down the dried-out slice before him. "It helps a bit. Besides, I wanted to talk to you for a minute."

"I didn't see you come in."

"Good. I noticed you watching the doors. I came in through the kitchen. My father's sister works back there."

"You're full of surprises."

"Good. I don't want to be obvious. I also wanted to check with my aunt to make sure my cousin, her son, didn't change his mind."

"Cousin?"

"He's a *homafar.* And a bodybuilder. And, I suspect, *Mojahedin.*"

Frank did not want to jump on this last revelation. "You were going to tell me about the *homafaran.*" He would ask about his cousin's ties to the *Mojahedin* later.

"Was I?" said Anwar, scraping his pie plate, "Yes. You should learn. A class apart. A rank apart. NCOs but higher in rank than a master sergeant. Only in the air force. The name comes from the *homa,* a mythical bird of ancient Persia. Not a peacock, like the Shah. You should not—this is important—you should not let the *homafaran* know you meet with the Shah."

"Why not?"

"To them, the Shah represents all the evil, all the corruption, that tears apart our country."

"Are they right?"

"It goes deeper than one man. But yes, the Shah is at the heart of the corruption."

"Does it bother you that I meet with him?"

Anwar shrugged. "Does it not bother you?"

"Perhaps it should," said Frank. "But when we meet, when I talk to him, it's hard to imagine him being . . ."

"A killer?"

"It's hard to imagine."

"A tyrant? A thief? I know you have to meet with him. You have your job to do. You must learn what you can from him. From us all. I understand. But do not let the *homafaran* know you sit at the feet of the Shah. Remember, they are also *Mojahedin*. Men of the left. They will be the key."

"To what?"

"To everything." Anwar curved his hands around a steaming cup of tea. Frank suspected that, like the coffee, its greatest asset was its warmth. "They are highly respected. For their skill. For their training. They are of the people, but they are the key to the world of modern technology that can lead Iran out of the dark ages. They tend to be secular, and yet they are committed to Khomeini."

"That sounds like a contradiction," said Frank.

"Uniquely Persian. I, too, love Khomeini. Yet, when he comes, I will have to go."

"Why?"

"Because his idea of Islam will take us back in time, shut us away from the West, and we need the West. I love him because he is pure of heart and he will drive out all that has made our country corrupt. But when the Shah falls, the *Mojahedin* may be our best hope against the new tyranny. We could have a just Islamic government, with leaders like Shariat-Madari and Ayatollah Taleqani. But religious leaders like Shariat-Madari may not survive the new tyranny. The *Mojahedin* may not survive."

"Because of Khomeini?" asked Frank.

"Yes," said Anwar. "Because of Khomeini."

"And yet you admire him."

"Uniquely Persian," said Anwar. "I am Persian. I am Muslim. And even I am devout, not as devout as our friend from the navy, but devout."

"Munair Irfani. He seems, well . . . strange. Tell me about him."

"Name, you know. Rank, captain. I don't know his serial number. Why call him strange?"

"That bump on his forehead. And the way he stares at me. I thought I'd read somewhere Iranians are very shy about making eye contact."

"Most Iranians, yes. But in the military we are trained to look directly at our superior officers. To establish trust. And of course to do exactly what they tell us. To establish discipline. But I must admit, even for a military man, Munair does stare at you . . . hard." He finished the last mouthful of apple pie. "Truly taste-less. Munair tries to figure you out. He doesn't understand why you're here."

"If he figures it out, ask him to tell me."

"You mean you don't know?"

"Not really. I get the feeling there's so much we don't know about Iran. That's one reason, I guess, why we're here."

"That would be a very good reason. America needs to know more about Iran. Munair wonders if maybe that's why you're here. And he wonders if you can be trusted. So does my cousin, the *homafar*."

"And . . . ?"

"I told him I don't know but that I had decided to trust you. My cousin wonders if you are CIA."

Frank sensed trouble. "What did you tell him?"

Anwar shrugged. "He hopes you are CIA. For reasons he will tell you, if he begins to trust."

I can guess his reasons, thought Frank. He wants to defect and get a ticket to the U.S.A.

"Sounds interesting," he said. "What about Munair?"

"Munair wonders if an American can be trusted to understand Islam. He is truly devout. That's why he has that bump on his forehead. He prays very hard, not just bowing to Mecca but bringing his head to the tiles of the mosque floor when he kneels and bows to Mecca. So hard, so often, he's raised that bump. He wonders if someone from the West can understand how much our religion means to us. And how much we love Ayatollah Khomeini."

"You don't have a bump on your forehead," said Frank.

"I told you I am not so devout. I love Ayatollah Khomeini because my country needs him, but I am a man of the modern world."

Frank thought of the demonstrators screaming, "Death to America," at the embassy gates and of the possibility that some then circled the compound to wait at the back gate in hopes of being admitted to the consulate to apply for an American visa. Like Anwar, uniquely Persian.

"It seems to me Iran will need men like you here. And your cousin. Espe-cially if Khomeini comes, to help keep Iran in the modern world."

"Iran will need men of the modern world," said Anwar. "But Khomeini will destroy such men. If I am lucky, perhaps I will be able to go before he comes."

If you're lucky, thought Frank, and if you find some American like me to help you.


The gym smelled like a gym. Sweat and wintergreen and unwashed towels and rancid gym clothes and dust rising from the floor as a heavy barbell crashed, slipping from the wet palms of an overweight lifter who had just completed a series of military presses. The smell of sweat-stained leather bounced off the heavy bag thudded by a chiseled young man in shorts and sneakers. Frank had begun to wonder about the absence of smells in Tehran. Perhaps it was the cold, dry winter air. The stench from the holes in the floor that passed for a bathroom at Supreme Commander's Headquarters stood out as one exception, and he was sure that in summer the *jubes* must be redolent of the odors of Iran, but now the gutters were frozen over most of the time. Even the smells of the *chelakebab* shop had seemed washed out by steam, but the gym smelled like a gym.

Only a handful of Iranians occupied the gym. No Americans. "That is my cousin, beating up the leather man," said Anwar.

"Not a man," said the boxer, who worked the heavy bag bare-handed. "Only a bag."

Two men thwacked a medicine ball off each other's bellies at close range. Another, deep in concentration, worked four Indian clubs in an intricate routine. The lifter walked off the strain of his last set of presses.

"These are all *homafaran*," said Anwar. His cousin gave the heavy bag a reprieve. Frank noticed the bleeding, callused knuckles. "They are also all *Moja-hedin*." Anwar spoke softly. "They think I don't know that, but I do."

"You know nothing, cousin." He turned to Frank and extended his hand. "Welcome, American." His tone made the greeting sound like *Welcome, Satan*. He stood taller than Frank had realized when he first saw him, bent with such intensity into punishing the heavy bag. Frank guessed him to be six-three, unusual for an Iranian, probably a light heavyweight, with the powerful, sloping shoulders of a boxer and the fine-cut muscular definition of a dedicated body-builder. "My name is also Anwar Amini, but you can call me Anwar the Taller." He smiled and glanced at his cousin. "He is called in the family Anwar the Smarter."

"And I am called Frank Sullivan. An American with a lot to learn—about *homafaran* and Persia and Islam and Ayatollah Khomeini—and other things."

It was only as the others stopped exercising, except for the man with the Indian clubs, that Frank noticed the small cassette player on a bench against a far wall playing what Frank took to be popular Iranian music, a female vocalist backed by strings.

"My cousin also tells me you also want to work out."

"If that's possible."

"Of course. American air forces are allowed. This is a good time. Not crowded, as you see. And we are often here." He hesitated, studying Frank with an intensity matching that of the navy man at Jayfacc. "Other times you can also come, but be careful. Others, enlisted men, even *homafaran* who are not—not like us—might be unfriendly. Be careful."

"I will."

Anwar the Taller turned his back on Frank and crossed the floor to the cassette player. He popped out the tape that had been playing and selected another from a neatly piled stack on the bench. He turned the volume up as the voice of a *muezzin* began the high-pitched wailing of the traditional call to prayer. There was a pause. All the Iranians, except the man still intent on his twirling Indian clubs, stood with folded hands, waiting.

A new voice, equally high pitched, but different, began to speak. The tone shrilled from the tiny cassette player, both strident and strangely flat. Anwar the Taller caught Frank's eye and glanced toward the cassette with a nod that told Frank this was the voice of Ayatollah Khomeini. Anwar again turned up the volume and approached Frank.

"Even those of us who are of a secular mind recognize his greatness."

"The tape," said Frank. "It came from Paris?"

Anwar smiled. "No, not this tape. It is only a copy of what came from Paris. You must understand. These days the Ayatollah's tapes come from everywhere. The original of this may have been telephoned by the Ayatollah from his base in Neauphle-le-Château and read into someone's tape recorder right here in Tehran. But the quality of telephone transmission from France is not great. So a cassette recorded there may have come here on a flight from Paris, with a pilot, a steward, someone. But in Mashhad they come through Afghanistan. In Abadan they come through Kuwait. In Bandar Abbas they come across the Gulf, across the Shatt al Arab to Ahwaz. In Tabriz they come from Van in Turkey or even from Baku in Soviet Azerbaijan. Even from Baghdad they come across the Zagros Mountains to Kermanshah and Hamadan and Qom. The people can listen to the BBC, and, yes, they make tapes of Khomeini's interviews on BBC, and they make copies of those and copies of those copies. The tapes come from everywhere. They come from heaven. *Allah-o akbar.*"

"*Allah-o akbar,*" echoed the other *homafaran*.

Frank had set his cassette deck on their kitchen table and played the tape Anwar the Taller had given him.

"He doesn't turn me on," said Gus.

"He turns Iranians on."

"Well, Hitler turned the Germans on, but there was a difference. I don't speak German any more than I do Persian, but you hear those old broadcasts of Hitler or see those old movies, you get what it was that got to people. This . . . this just sounds like a squeaky, cranky old man."

"Maybe that's what he is," said Frank. "But Iranians listen and do what he tells them."

"Which is?"

"One thing he tells them on here is to take his tapes and make copies and spread them around and make copies of the copies."

"Did they give you a translation?"

"No, but I taped Anwar, the other Anwar, while he was talking to me. He said this isn't a new tape, but he wanted me to hear this so we could see how Khomeini gives the marching orders to the *mullahs* and how what he says to do gets done. Someplace on here he talks about the burning down of that movie house in the south . . . in Abadan when all those people were killed. He talks about the protests two days after that. Says they happened yesterday. We can check the date of the fire, add three, and have a probable date for Khomeini's tape."

"Looks like you're gonna have some heavy cable-writing duty."

"I already did. A start anyway. Since I was at the base, I checked out our office. Bill Steele was on duty, and he set me up. I drafted as much as I could."

"I'm impressed. All this and you cook, too. Will you marry me?"

"I don't think so. But I will fix up something to eat. And I guess anyway we better get into the office early. I'll need you to check over what I drafted before we arrange to get the tape down to the embassy. Oh, he said we shouldn't get the tape translated at the embassy."

"He who?"

"Anwar the Taller, the *homafar*. He said there are leaks, locals who work in the embassy but who love Khomeini."

"The ambassador will shit."

Frank woke the next morning to the cries of the *ashkhalee* man and the rattling garbage cans. I-cash-clothes. I-cash-clothes. I-cash-clothes. He had been dreaming, and part of his dream had been the tall man with a long black beard and black hat and long black coat who made his rounds through the courtyards and alleys of the Brooklyn apartments and tenements Frank had grown up in. It had taken Frank many childhood years to translate the sounds that echoed up the narrow courtyard as *oy-gesh-close*. He thought the words might be Yiddish, but there were no Jews he knew well enough to ask. Though the neighborhood was mixed, the neighbors did not mix. Jews, Italians, Irish, Poles, Germans all walked the same streets, but seldom in each other's company. The I-cash-clothes man bought used clothes and, at least with the Jewish housewives, exchanged neighborhood gossip.

*Ashkhalee* and I-cash-clothes. Who needs newspapers? He thought of his own summers, spent first as a paper stabber, then driving a thick-tired Toro garbage hauler on the beach at Riis Park and quarter-ton garbage trucks to the dump opposite Floyd Bennett Field, and he realized he must have dreamt about that, too, and he thought how every job he'd ever held for very long had been the same job, the same dream. Always the plough and the stars. Finding stuff and one way or another delivering it somewhere else. I-cash-clothes and the rattling of trolley cars on Nostrand Avenue. Reporter. Novelist. Spy. Always looking for a story to tell. Always struggling for the words to tell it. Not a dream, he thought. It's my life. *Ashkhalee* and the rattling of garbage cans.

# CHAPTER EIGHT

Sullivan, you're a fuckin' pisser. You been here not even a couple of weeks and you stirred up more shit than a barrel of monkeys could in a couple of years."

Frank read Rocky as being in a good mood. He waved Gus and Frank to two metal chairs that flanked his desk and went on talking.

"You really spooked the ambassador about the embassy havin' leaks. Leaks," repeated Rocky. "Hah. He damn near pissed his pants."

"I thought you'd like that one," said Frank, hoping Rocky would file the cable he'd drafted.

"And this one, about the Qazvini queer Mafia. It may not be important, but the folks back home'll get their little vicarious jollies off. I'll file it, but all this other stuff from this Anwar Two." Rocky glanced at the papers on his desk. "The fuckin' *Tudeh* party doesn't amount to squat. All the Russians do is put this Khomeini character on Radio Baku. The *Mojahedin* and these *homafaran* are the key. The generals couldn't stage a coup if their flabby asses depended on it. What you're askin' me to file contradicts everything the embassy and the station have been filing about the Soviets and their *Tudeh* party and the military for months, make that years. I can't do it, Sullivan. I won't."

Frank said nothing. He exchanged a glance with Gus, looked back at Rocky, and shrugged, remembering other cables Rocky had told him to forget about. Lermontov's reporting on Afghanistan, the weaknesses of the Soviet Union, all that the Shah had told him. He had expected trouble from Rocky. Again, it stared him in the face.

Rocky studied him, then nodded. "Look, I know how you feel. But we can't contradict ourselves without . . . It needs . . . more support. Okay, tell me . . . We know all about the *Mojahedin. Savak* files a ton on them every fuckin' day. But who are these homofurs?"

"*Homa,*" said Frank. "With an *a* at the end. *Homafar.* I don't know what the '*far*' is about, but the *homa* is a mythical Persian bird, a symbol for the air force."

"We never heard of them before. If there's a bunch of them at Dowshan Tappeh, how come Troy never filed anything on them?"

"Maybe," said Gus, "there was never anything to file on them before."

"What is it about you, Sullivan? You get here and the walls start to talk." Rocky's tone had turned sharper. "Right now, before we go any further, we have to assess this fucking *homafar*'s reliability."

"Traces come back?" asked Frank.

"SDTRIB-2." Rocky riffled through the cables on his desk. "Air force *homafar*. Not much on him. Took some technical training in the states, U.S. Air Force, someplace in Texas, I forget where." He pushed the cables aside. "No derogatories."

"Well, I can keep talking to him. See how what he says pans out. Is he right about what's on the tapes?"

"Who knows? We got a Farsi speaker checkin' the tapes. But your other little buddy was right about that other stuff. Believe it or not, *Savak* arrested their old boss, General Nasseri, who was Eagle-fucking-1 until five, six months ago. Along with Hoveida, who was prime minister until last year, and the guy who wrote the nasty story about Khomeini in one of the Farsi papers. Oh, and they also banned all the newspapers, just like you said they would. So SDTRIB-1, Anwar the major, looks pretty good. SDTRIB-2, Anwar the *homafar*, I dunno."

"It's SDTRIB-1 who gave me the stuff on the coup probability."

"I know. In that case it's not so much the source. It's the contradiction. The ambassador'll say the same fuckin' thing. He wants to see us again soon as he gets here with his Brit buddy from havin' lunch with the Shah."

"*With* his Brit buddy?" said Gus.

"Don't ask me," said Rocky. He glanced at Frank. "More shit your buddy Sullivan stirred up. Why the hell does the fuckin' British ambassador wanna' have a meet with you?"

"No idea," said Frank. "But something tells me it can't be good."

"Maybe it's that last name of yours," said Gus. "Maybe he thinks you're IRA."

Let's hope it's nothing worse, thought Frank.

One of the phones on Rocky's desk buzzed.

"His nibs." Rocky picked it up. "Yes, sir. You made good time getting back . . . Sullivan's here. We'll be right up." He replaced the phone. "Whatever it is, Gus, it's just Sullivan. Wait here. Let's go, Sully. We're on."


The ambassador sat with another man on the couch in his office. Both rose.

"Rocky, I'm sure you know His Excellency, Ambassador Oliver Hempstone."

"Good to see you, Mr. Novak," said Hempstone. He did not extend his hand across the glass-topped coffee table that separated them. Rocky nodded and said nothing.

"And this is the man you wanted to meet, Frank Sullivan."

"Yes, well, shall we get to it?" Hempstone stood a full head taller than Ambassador O'Connor; as pale as O'Connor was ruddy, he was slender with angular features and hair several shades lighter than his gray, snugly tailored pin-striped suit. His appearance made Frank think of a furled umbrella with a carved head for a handle.

The four men stood awkwardly till O'Connor motioned to the two chairs across the coffee table and said, "Let's be seated. This may take some time."

"Yes," said Hempstone as he unfolded himself into his spot on the couch. "As a matter of fact, Mr. Sullivan, Mr. Novak, this is a bit awkward. We've been approached, point of fact, I myself was approached at a lunchtime farewell gathering for our chargé d'affaires. Approached, Mr. Sullivan, by a gentleman whom I understand you know."

"Let me guess," said Rocky. "A gentleman named Vassily Lermontov, representing the Soviet news agency Tass, who wanted to interview you on the availability in Great Britain of medical treatment for a certain disorder of the pituitary system."

"Quite so," said Hempstone. His smile seemed to relax him. "And quite good. How did you know?"

"I know my target," said Rocky.

"He confided that he had been in touch with Mr. Sullivan and had met you, but . . ."

"He and Sullivan go back a long way," said Rocky.

"Yes, but he indicated that you, you collectively, you Americans did not seem to appreciate the gravity of his situation."

"Oh, we appreciate it," said Rocky. "But I didn't realize he was shopping himself around."

There goes Lermontov, thought Frank, studying Hempstone, who avoided his look.

"Where's my buddy Gerry Mosley stand on this?" asked Rocky.

"Yes, well, I naturally discussed Mr. Lermontov's approach to me with Mr. Mosley. He informed me he'd been cultivating Mr. Lermontov for some time. Without my knowledge, I might add. He said his effort sounded like a go." Hempstone turned from Rocky to Frank. "Until you, Mr. Sullivan, suddenly arrived. Mr. Lermontov, from that point until his recent approach to me, became . . . difficult to contact. When he did speak to me, he seemed to indicate a certain . . . reluctance to work with our intelligence."

Frank spoke for the first time. "Does the Shah know about this?"

"I'm afraid so. Yes," said Hempstone.

"That's just dandy," said Rocky. "What is it you Brits say? Sticky wicket?"

"Much worse, I'm afraid. My Canadian counterpart tells me your Russian friend has also spoken to him."

"He sounds desperate," said O'Connor.

"He sounds like a time bomb," said Rocky. "Tick plus Tock. Waiting to go off."

"The question is," said Hempstone, "what shall we, we collectively, do about him?"

"Lemme talk to Mosley," said Rocky. "We get along pretty good."

"I hesitate to advocate that," said Hempstone. "For one, we have this Lermontov's reluctance to involve our intelligence community."

"Fuck, I mean, screw his reluctance," said Rocky.

"For another, special relationship with the U.S. and all that, I'm afraid Gerry Mosley has a rather traditional view of British interests in this part of the world, especially vis-à-vis the Russians. To him it's still the Great Game."

"That sounds a bit nineteenth century," said O'Connor.

"Quite. And you lot are mere upstarts in his view."

"Mosley understands Commies," said Rocky, "and we do get along pretty good. I'll talk to him. We'll work it out."

"Gerald might like nothing better, but I'm afraid it's already gone beyond that. I've recommended to Her Majesty's Government that we pursue this matter."

"What's that mean?"

"It means, well, that I suggest you leave Comrade Lermontov to us."

"Why the hell should we do that?"

"Rocky . . ." O'Connor raised a hand.

Rocky ignored him. "Why the hell should we lay off?"

"Well, for one, we have a bit more experience in this area. But perhaps the most compelling reason is that this appears to be what Mr. Lermontov wants," said Hempstone.

"Great," said Rocky. "So we let the KGB set our agenda."

"I suspect that at this stage of his evolution, Mr. Lermontov and the KGB are perhaps not identical."

"I wish I could speak British the way you do," said Rocky. "Maybe I could convince myself up is down. Fact is . . . Never mind. Lermontov is a legitimate American target."

"According to your legitimate target himself, he has changed his mind and now seeks British protection."

"Bullshit. He's just playing you limey bastards to get a better deal from us."

"Rocky, really. There's no need to be offensive."

"Yeah, there is. I've been offended."

Frank watched the three men go at each other, glad, for a change, to be a fly on the wall. For a moment, he wished Mosley were with them. And Lermontov and his ambassador. Let the great egos clash. All he wanted was to find a way to bring Lermontov to America.

Rocky took a deep breath. He glanced at Frank, then turned to Hempstone. "Sorry, Your Excellency. I get carried away sometimes. What's Her Majesty's Government say about your recommendation?"

"That we pursue Lermontov's request? For asylum and medical treatment?"

"Yes, sir."

"Well . . ."

"Well," what a wonderful word, Frank said to himself. It gives you time to think. He noticed that the British diplomat used it often.

"Well," repeated Hempstone, "it's a delicate matter. A response may take some time." He turned to Frank. "This Lermontov seems an interesting chap. I do hope to get to know him better."

I wish you luck, thought Frank. Bad luck. He studied Hempstone's eyes. They were a cold gray, halfway between the dark gray of his suit and the light gray of his hair.

As they left the ambassador's office, Rocky poked an index finger upward. Frank followed him up the narrow metal stairs to the bubble.

"This stinks," said Rocky as he slumped into a chair.

Frank sat beside him. "What do we do?"

"We? I dunno what the fuck *we* do. I talk to Mosley."

"What do you say?"

"I dunno. Yet. The ambassador's right. Mosley is kinda nineteenth century, handlebar mustache, likes to quote Kipling. Spent a lot of years in Kenya, great white hunter type. Kept tryin' to get me to go on a hunt with him when I first got here. I'm a city boy. Never catch me dead on anybody's fuckin' safari."

Frank wondered if Mosley and Lermontov had gone hunting together.

"Trouble is," added Rocky, "even if the Brits come back and tell Hempstone to lay off your KGB buddy, Mosley's liable to go after Lermontov on his own anyway."

"Lermontov's spooked as it is," said Frank. "All we need is . . ."

"Yeah, I know," said Rocky. "All we need is another fucking gung-ho idiot like me fucking up the deal."

You said it, thought Frank. I didn't.

"Mosley's a hard-ass motherfucker," said Rocky, "but if Lermontov doesn't wanna deal with MI6, maybe we still got a shot. What I gotta do is con Mosley into gettin' into a pissin' match with his ambassador over who gets to sign up Lermontov."

Great, thought Frank. We're not the only ones who would fuck up a KGB recruitment by fighting over the credit. "Okay," he said, "Meantime, what do I do?"

"I dunno. Lermontov said he'd contact you. But I wonder if we have much time to wait. If your reporting is worth any fucking thing, this tape you got, once Khomeini gets here, you got, who knows, maybe a couple of days t' bring Lermontov in."

"Maybe a couple of weeks," said Frank.

"Maybe a couple of hours if the Sovs find out he's tryin' t' peddle himself t' us and the Brits and pull his hard ass outta here."

"So we can't just wait for Lermontov to contact me."

"No," said Rocky. "I can try to convince Mosley his ambassador's gonna get the credit for baggin' Lermontov. And maybe get Mosley to send a cable sayin' let the Americans deal with the crazy Russian and his medical problems. And I try to find a way to shut the Canadian door. See what Langley can feed us negative about endocrinology up there, and in the U.K."

Frank knew Rocky liked to pretend he had trouble with multi-syllabic words, but, when he wasn't thinking about it, he had no trouble with "endocrinology."

"His nibs is gonna be pissed I got a little rough with his Hempstone buddy, but these Brits piss me off. They think they still own the world."

"Our cousins," said Frank.

"Yeah, well, some people back at Langley like to talk about our cousins, but remember your Bible stories. Cain and Abel. Jacob and Esau. Those guys were brothers. If brothers can fuck over each other that bad, just think about how much shit cousins can lay on each other."

Rocky cracked his knuckles, something Frank had never seen him do before.

"You think I fucked up," said Rocky. "With Lermontov. Maybe I did. But the way he's shoppin' himself around, makes me think we're better off without him."

No, thought Frank. We can't give this up.

"What you told Hempstone makes sense to me," he said. "Lermontov's play-ing the Brits to get a better, or maybe a quicker, deal from us."

Rocky sat with his hands folded so tightly the knuckles turned white. He nodded. "Maybe you're right. Let's play it out. I'll take a shot at Mosley and talk to his nibs again. You wait."

"I don't like waiting," said Frank.

"Me neither." Rocky glanced at his watch. "Hate to say it. We got another meet with his nibs. Five minutes. Different topic. More shit you stirred up."

He picked up the phone on the glass-topped table. "Guy in my office. Gus Simpson. Take him up to his nibs's office." He hung up gently.


The ambassador sat with another man on the couch in his office. He didn't rise. "Please, come in. And pardon us. Chuck's been a bit under the weather."

The man struggled to his feet. Rocky moved quickly to grab him by the elbow. "No need to stand, Chuck."

"It's okay." He managed to reach out and shake hands, first with Gus, then with Frank.

"Chuck Belinsky."

Frank and Gus introduced themselves without benefit of their fictitious ranks. Belinsky slumped back onto the couch. Frank detected a familiar pallor in his skin and yellow rings around his blue-gray eyes.

"Chuck's recovering from a nasty bout of hepatitis. In fact, he should be evacuated, but he insists on staying," said the ambassador.

"Nothing all that serious, guys," said Belinsky. "And I thought it would be a good idea to have someone who speaks a little Farsi around."

"Chuck's been our consul in Tabriz, right, Rocky?" Rocky turned his head away. "But we, ah, we managed to get him transferred down here," continued the ambassador. "When things got a bit hairy up there. We didn't have anyone . . . like him around. I did take your advice, gentlemen, about not having that tape you acquired translated by . . . ah . . . by indigenous staff, but Chuck's been listening to it. And, well, I must admit Chuck loves Persia and its culture, but I don't think he's been co-opted by the Islamic Revolution."

"Or the Commies," said Rocky.

"In any event," said the ambassador, "he believes it is indeed Khomeini. He's been listening to the Great Ayatollah just about every day on Radio Baku. And lately a lot on BBC."

"If it isn't him, it's a great imitation, and he isn't easy to imitate," said Belinsky. Frank's attention shifted from the ruddy complexion of the ambassador to Belinsky's jaundiced features. Pouches of flesh hung under his eyes, his chin, even his lower lip. His suit jacket hung loosely off his shoulders. Still, Frank could sense a fuller, rosier Belinsky before hepatitis had struck.

"Between us," said the ambassador, "we can confirm that much of what that tape says should be done has been done."

Frank had trouble focusing on the conversation. The British pursuit of Lermontov troubled him, and so did Belinsky's appearance. He looks worse than the Shah, thought Frank. The more he studied Belinsky, the more Belinsky avoided Frank's eyes. They all knew Belinsky had hepatitis. Frank wondered what else Belinsky might be trying to hide. He forced himself to concentrate on Belinsky's words.

"Those fourteen points, for example, on August thirty-first, I heard Ayatollah Shariat-Madari, a moderate in some respects, at a public meeting in Tabriz, it's his hometown, calling for action on the fourteen measures Khomeini cites on the cassette. The same fourteen points. Word for word."

"And we had a report from Mashhad, way off to the east near the border with Afghanistan, that on the very same day an Ayatollah Shirazi made an almost identical speech," said the ambassador.

"In short," said Belinsky, "your cassette looks authentic. And important. Good job, guys."

"Thank you," said Frank.

"Can you get more?" asked Belinsky.

"We can try."

"See if you can get some that go back in time, to support the authentication. I understand Khomeini started making tapes from his exile in Iraq as far back as 1967, but I've never been able to get hold of any. And this massive reproduction business must be quite new." Belinsky paused and looked from the ambassador to Rocky. "I'm sure," he added, "it would be interesting to get some tapes that are as up-to-date as possible."

"We'll do our best," said Frank.

"As for this other material, the impossibility of a military coup, the irrelevance of the Soviets and the *Tudeh* party, the importance of these *homafaran,* the *Mojahedin* and the other groups. I'm afraid Rocky and I believe it doesn't quite hold up. We're afraid both at State and . . ."

"And Langley," said Rocky.

"It would not be taken seriously. It flies in the face of too much . . ."

"Well-verified reporting," said Rocky.

"On the other hand, gentlemen, the arrests of Karim Sanjabi and Mahdi Bazargan confirm your earlier reporting from TRIB-1."

"The leaders of both opposition groups," said Belinsky.

"And both recently met with Khomeini in Paris," said the ambassador.

"Sounds like the Shah's starting to take this holy man seriously," said Gus.

"Very seriously," acknowledged the ambassador. "Your information was good, Sullivan. We may have to upgrade the description of Anwar, Anwar One, that is. Whatever his name is. A source of untested and unproven reliability? He's a bit more than that now, but as for Anwar Two, so far, at least, that's quite another matter."

I understand, thought Frank, but I sure as hell don't like it. Aloud, he said, "I understand."

"Oh, and Sullivan, there's another matter. A bit of a problem. Chuck, Commander Simpson. Would you mind if Mr. Novak and Major Sullivan and I excused ourselves for a few minutes?"

The ambassador ushered Frank and Rocky through the heavy door that led to his outer office. The door thudded gently as he closed it behind them.

"You wanna use the bubble?" said Rocky.

"If you don't mind," said the ambassador.

Frank, Ambassador O'Connor, and Rocky settled themselves around the small round table in the bug-proof bubble. Rocky adjusted his hearing aid, and the ambassador cleared his throat. His ruddy complexion seemed even more flushed than usual, setting off his white hair and clear blue eyes. Frank wondered if climbing the steep stairs or uneasiness about what he had to say caused the rosy glow.

"I always feel uncomfortable in here," said the ambassador. "This bubble of yours, Rocky, it makes me feel like I'm in some kind of strange spaceship. Being abducted by aliens."

Rocky sat immobile, hands clasped on the table, saying nothing, staring at the ambassador. Frank could imagine him with his hearing aid replaced by antennae, truly an alien abducting all who ventured into his bubble.

"It's . . . it's the Shah, Sullivan. As you might have guessed."

Frank nodded. Rocky toyed with his hearing aid. The ambassador again cleared his throat.

"He's been informed, apparently by someone who monitors Jayface, about your idea for a military newspaper with Western advisers with appropriate backgrounds."

"And?" said Rocky.

"Well, the Shah wanted me to know he would approve it if Frank here becomes the adviser."

"All this in front of the British ambassador?"

"Yes, Rocky. I'm afraid so."

"What else?"

"Well, he, the Shah, said he wants to see Sullivan. ASAP. Asked me to arrange it."

"And?" said Rocky.

"I felt I had no choice. Not when the request comes direct from the Shah himself."

"It kinda puts Sullivan here up the creek with a leaky paddle."

"I said I would have to clear it with Washington."

"Washington?" said Rocky.

"I'll ask State to negotiate it with Langley. They can't turn down a request like this from His Imperial Majesty."

"The hell they can't." Rocky had clenched his fists, and Frank could sense him choking down an expletive.

"I told him approval might take a few days."

Great, thought Frank. If I get to stay, I may get another crack at Lermontov.

"How 'bout we tell him Sullivan was suddenly reassigned to Washington? Get him outta here on a MAAG flight tonight."

"I'm afraid that would not be a very good idea at all. In addition to ruffling the Shah's feathers, to be quite honest about it, in the short time he's been here, in my view, Sullivan's proved a very good asset. Getting access to Khomeini's tapes . . . He's located right in the heart of the military establishment, and in addition, there is this other matter. Your Russian target. I do not want to be embroiled in this matter, but Sullivan seems very much involved."

"The Russian is my problem. Chief of station, right? As for Sullivan, most of his intel sucks. You said yourself it contradicts just about everything we've been reporting. And if he goes, we'll still be located right in the heart of the military establishment. Sullivan goes. Simpson stays, and he's already recruited a waiter who's in and out of the top brass's offices all day. Plus, in a few days Bunker will be here. What's the diff if we bounce Sullivan?"

"Do I have any say in this?" asked Frank.

"No," answered Rocky.

"He should have some say," the ambassador countered. "There's even a chance—on a personal basis—the Shah may be more forthcoming with Sullivan about some things than with me. Or with you."

"Like what? He levels with me, and I thought you were pretty tight with him."

"He consults with me almost daily." The ambassador, even seated, kept his spine erect to maximize his height. "He seeks my advice. But something like his health, for example. It's very difficult for me to broach that with him. When I try, he evades me. Sullivan, on a personal basis, might have better luck."

"I could try," said Frank.

"Yeah," snapped Rocky. "You could try."

Frank had begun to share the ambassador's queasy feelings about being wrapped in the bubble with Rocky buzzing like an angry queen bee in a tight little hive.

"I feel compelled," said the ambassador, "to report the gist of my conversation with the Shah."

"Feel compelled to your heart's content. I'll get my own cable off to Langley."

To Frank's surprise, they agreed to wait till Washington and Langley responded to their cables. If the idea for a military newspaper adviser won approval, the ambassador would inform the Shah. Even then, Frank should wait for another invitation direct from the Shah. Frank kept waiting for the ambassador or Rocky to mention the British interest in Lermontov. Neither did. He suspected that Lermontov was a problem the ambassador hoped would go away, and he wondered if Rocky had given up.


As they finished dinner in their kitchen that night, Gus, pouring them each another glass of wine, suggested they should get to know Belinsky.

"He's an interesting character. Knows—and loves—this country. Something a bit strange about him, though."

Frank nodded. "I thought so, too." Something beyond the pallor and the jaundiced eyes.

"Maybe that's another reason we should get to know him better," said Gus. "I had quite a talk with him while you were upstairs. He speaks the language. Likes the people. Knows the territory, the culture. Not your average State Department dummy. He's convinced what we're in the middle of is a Muslim revolution against Western culture. Not just liquor and casinos and dirty movies, but little things, like women wearing lipstick and not covering their hair. Men wearing suits and shirts with ties. Rock and roll and even Iranian love songs influenced by American pop. A whole laundry list of Western stuff that the Iranians, not just the mule-headed mullahs but a lot of the average Alis and Hosseins, think has undermined Iranian traditions."

"Did you ask him how come everyone else thinks it's just a Communist plot?"

"Matter of fact, I did. He said that's what most of us think because that's what we're used to thinking. It sounds like his reporting from here pretty much gets ignored. So did his analysis when he was stateside."

"That sounds familiar."

"And maybe explains why he got shuffled off to a backwater like Tabriz."

"Maybe Rocky could find a spot for me up there."

"He would if he could, but there's still a chance your Russian buddy may show up. And no matter what he says, Rocky knows he may need you for that."

Frank wondered what, if anything, he should tell Gus about the meeting with the British ambassador. He decided to take the conversation in a different direction. "Rocky's not a bad sort. He's just doing his job the way he sees fit."

"And he's damn good at it. If you wanted to grow up to be a chief of station, you could do worse than to study Rocky in action. But you gotta remember, types like Rocky, who've come up from inside as regular case officers, don't feel quite right about oddballs like you and me who were recruited from outside, started out as GS-14s and got interesting assignments from the jump."

"I don't think that's Rocky's problem."

"Maybe not," said Gus, "but Rocky's pretty solid old-school anti-Soviet." He went on talking as he carried their dinner plates and wine glasses to the sink and poured them each a drink from their chilled stash of Scotch and vodka. He left the bottles on the table. "It's the way they were all brought up. Pete Howard isn't that much different, but for him history didn't begin with Mr. Lenin in 1917 and geography doesn't end with the Berlin Wall. Our bread-and-butter cold warriors talk about Soviet hegemony, and Pete talks about Russian imperialism." Gus paused for a long swallow of Scotch. "And on the job it's Pete who puts people like you and me in places like Zambia and Ethiopia. He doesn't target us just on the resident Soviets, either. He wants to know about everything. One reason we know so damn little about this place is that you can bet until this shit started to hit the fan a couple of months ago about ninety percent or more of the station's effort went strictly to the Soviets and most of the rest went to the two-bit local Communist party, *Tudeh* or whatever it is."

"*Tudeh* it is," said Frank.

"I don't usually get wound up like this. What got me started?"

"Rocky. We were talking about Rocky."

"Rocky." Gus nodded and refilled his glass. Frank left his untouched. "You can't expect a guy like Rocky to be too happy with your reporting. It undermines everything he's believed in and fought for all his life. The Soviet menace, with maybe a little bit of Red China menace thrown in, is all that threatens the free world. What the Vietnamese are about, or the Koreans, or the Persians or the Arabs, doesn't matter. They're just tools of, in their wonderful terminology, they're all just tools of the Sovs and the ChiComs. Guys like you or me or this guy Belinsky might say, hey, let's listen to the Viets or the Persians for a minute. They may have something important to tell us. To the old guard, talk like that's subversive."

"Maybe you're right," said Frank.

"No maybe about it."

Frank took a sip of vodka and thought about unsent cables. "So what do I do? Forget what Anwar tells me about a coup? Forget what the *homafaran* tell me? Ignore what I get from the Shah?"

"What you do is have another drink," said Gus, pouring more Scotch. Frank put a hand over his own glass and shook his head. "And if . . . I've got an idea. If Rocky keeps putting your cables on hold, which he will, how 'bout you put that novelist skill of yours to work and do an atmospherics. You ever do an atmospherics?"

"You forget. I'm that outside guy who doesn't much get to write cables."

"Let me 'splain you. An atmospherics . . ." Gus paused, sipped his Scotch, and went on. "Okay. An atmospherics is a cable that gives a picture of, well, the atmosphere around a critical situation. Like the war we're in the middle of. The weather, the attitudes of the man in the street, the feelings in the air, paranoia, fear, confidence, whatever. The background, the feel of the situation. Not the hard intelligence. But . . . but, if you're clever about it, you can maybe sneak in more hard intelligence than, well, than might get cleared by the station in a flat-out intelligence report."

Frank took a very small sip of vodka.

"Pete Howard'll love it," added Gus. "Oh. And long. An atmospherics should be long. Maybe twenty pages. You don't send immediate flash. Maybe immediate or even just priority. But it goes cable. It gets read. And chances are, if it's well written, it gets well read."

Frank cupped his vodka glass in both hands and peered at Gus.

"You wanna give it a shot?"

Frank nodded. "Let's give it a shot."

Gus drained his glass. "See? I always get my best ideas when I'm half in the bag."

Frank wondered. He walked his vodka glass to the sink and dumped it.

# CHAPTER NINE

Frank and Gus followed a marine guard up the final flight of stairs to the bubble. Through the plastic, Frank saw a ghostly figure seated at the head of the table. The door gaped open, like a surprised mouth.

"Unusual," said the marine. "Mr. Novak left the door open. Guess he wants you gentlemen to go right in. If you would, please close the door after you."

"Thank you, son." Gus turned to Frank. "Why don't you go first? In case he's packing a nine millimeter."

Rocky had summoned them to the embassy within minutes of their return to Dowshan Tappeh from their morning Jayface meeting. "He's pissed again," Tom Troy had told them.

Frank took a deep breath and led the way. Gus gently closed the door behind them, creating a whoosh of air, a partial vacuum, and an audible click. Frank shivered. He felt as though the bubble had mummified him.

"Nice going, Mr. Sullivan."

Frank read the anger in Rocky's tone. "What'd I do?" he asked.

"Sit down. Both 'a yiz."

Frank and Gus exchanged a look. They picked out chairs next to each other, halfway down the table from Rocky.

"You listen. I'll read." Rocky picked up a sheet of paper from the glass tabletop and glanced at it. "At the recommendation of the National Security Council, no fucking less, Sullivan, you're approved for an assignment of indefinite duration as an adviser to a military newspaper and with unlimited access to the Shah. Cable doesn't say so, but it looks like your old rabbi, Pete Howard, took you under his wing again. I can smell his armpit."

"Why Pete Howard?"

"He's on loan to NSC, right? At the request of Zbigniew fucking Brzezinski, no less, right?"

Frank glanced at Gus. "What about my partner?"

"Is his name KUPEREGRINE? The cable anoints you as emissary to the

Shah. For an indefinite fucking duration. Some fucking body, and I gotta believe Pete Howard, read the ambassador's cable and decided it'd be a good idea for you to meet with the Shah. Which means nobody paid attention to my cable."

None of this is my doing, thought Frank, but he knew that did not matter in Rocky's mind.

"Since KUPEREGRINE is not cleared with host country," said Rocky, crumpling the cable, "the chief of station is pre-fucking-cluded from notifying the Shah. Everybody knows you're agency, but since you're not officially declared, you can't officially have anything to do with me. So the ambassador can let the Shah know, but your chief of station can't let the Shah know. Nice going, Sullivan."

"Don't put this on me," said Frank. "I had nothing to do with it."

"If I didn't know better, I'd say you found some fucking way to fucking back-channel me. You know what it means t' back-channel me? It means stick it up my ass. Cable says we're authorized to inform the Shah that approval comes from a very high level. Ambassador wants to stretch that to the highest level. Like it comes from one head of state to another. He thinks the Shah'll like that. Meanwhile, you can bet his nibs is gloating his rosy ass off. Not saying anything. Just gloating. He wanted you to meet with the Shah. He got what he wanted. He wanted this fucking Jayface operation. Our beloved ambassador got what he wanted. He thinks you oughta stay here. He's getting what he wants. And he ices me out. Simpson, this shit is about Sullivan. What the fuck are you doing here?"

"I've been wondering that since the day I got off the plane."

"Oh, yeah," said Rocky. "I know why I wanted you here. Whatever happens next, it affects both 'a yiz. It also affects Bunker, who finally gets here tomorrow. I knew I shoulda kept you assholes under wraps till Bunker shows up. Now we got fucking Sullivan here gets to meet with the Shah on a steady basis. No matter what, it compromises your deal with the Jayfacers. I spelled this out to Sullivan whenever the fuck it was last week after your first Jayface meeting when Nazih the faggot in front of God and everybody said the Shah wanted to meet with your asshole sidekick, Sullivan here. What compromises Sullivan rubs off on you."

"I don't have any problem with that," said Gus. "I think it'll do us some good. Having a partner who meets with the Shah will give us a leg up with our Iranian buddies."

"You guys must read the same fairy tales. That's what your fucking buddy, Sullivan, said."

"He's not a dumb guy," said Gus.

"You got balls, Simpson. I'll say that for ya."

"Thank you for noticing," said Gus.

"Fuck you. The whole world knows you got balls. Except maybe Sullivan, here. The outsider. You know what this ex-marine pulled off on Guadalcanal?"

"I heard about the Purple Heart. Not the details."

"Fuck the fucking Purple Heart," said Rocky. "Anybody stubbed his toe in combat coulda got a Purple Hard-on. Simpson here came away with a whole chest full, Medal of Honor on down."

"On up," said Gus. "The tin plate in the top of my head's the only decoration I remember for sure. And I wish I could forget that."

Frank wondered how many brain cells of memory Gus had washed away with Scotch.

"Damn thing still hurts when the weather turns cold," said Gus. "And goes off whenever I walk through one of those airport security cages."

"Way I heard it," said Rocky, "a Jap machine-gun nest mowed down a whole slew of our friend's jar-head buddies. Medics couldn't get in t' pull out the wounded. Quiet li'l Gus here managed t' get up the fuckin' hill and took out the fuckin' machine-gun nest by himself with half his scalp flappin' in the wind by the time he got there. How the hell did you do it, Simpson?"

"Quickly."

Frank and Rocky both laughed, and Frank suspected Gus had worked that response before to deflect words that embarrassed him.

"Otherwise they'd have got the rest of my scalp."

"Quickly, Sullivan. That's how Simpson did it. Quickly. And without a rabbi."

Frank had never heard Rocky talk at such length about someone else's heroism. He knew Rocky had to have a reason behind it. There it was. The kicker was in the rabbi.

"This outfit could use more Simpsons. Guys who get the job done. Quickly. No bullshit. Guys who were gung ho marines before they became GS whatevers."

Rocky had begun to take himself so seriously that Frank expected a chorus of "Semper Fidelis," but Gus again diverted the rhetoric.

"We didn't know from gung ho. I think somebody made that up later on."

Rocky tried again. "It true what Tom Troy tells me about the way you handle a knife?"

"Not really," said Gus. "Those who can, do. I taught."

"You still handy with a blade?"

"I'll never know. At my age there's no way I'll ever try to stick anything that might stick back. Long time ago I figured out GS bureaucrats have a longer life expectancy than gut stabbers."

"Backstabbers do better," said Rocky, poking at the cable he'd crumpled.

Frank winced.

"That fucking cable comes from Near East Division. You can tell they're not too fucking happy about taking orders from the National Security Council, so they say requirements follow."

He shifted his focus to Frank, apparently ready to get back to business.

"Sullivan, since you don't know how the bureaucracy works, I'll tell you what that means. It means the division is gonna cook up a laundry list of questions you're supposed t' get answers to from the Shah. More questions than you could possibly ask, and the kinda questions the Shah won't wanna answer any damn way. Near East managed to delay the whole deal till they get full details on how the newspaper operation's gonna work and till Bunker gets here to bird-dog the laundry list. So your friend Pete Howard may have set you up for a nice friendly walk with the Shah, but Near East will set you up to come out of it looking like you stepped into a pile 'a cow shit."

Rocky smiled. Frank guessed that for a change Near East had done something that made him feel better.

Frank drove. Gus talked.

"Take a look at it from Rocky's point of view. He doesn't want us here in the first place. He takes a dim view of this Jayface idea. Maybe, maybe not, Jayface is another brainstorm of Pete Howard's. Plus the ambassador likes it. Chief of station by definition never likes anything the ambassador likes. Even worse, from what I know, in times past the Shah and the agency's chief of station always got on real tight. All the way back twenty-five years ago, Kermit Roosevelt. Then Dick Helms. Rocky doesn't rank in that old boys' league. The Shah meets with the ambassador more than he does with Rocky, and then you come along."

"Me?" said Frank.

"Yeah, you. All of a sudden, you get to meet with the Shah. And Rocky doesn't even get to set it up. The ambassador can tell the Shah. But, like he said, your chief of station is out of the loop. You can't expect him to love your ass."

Back at their Dowshan Tappeh Air Force Base offices, they settled in at Stan Rushmore's typewriter, drafting a routine cable on their morning Jayface meeting. Tom Troy joined them, pulling up a metal chair and straddling it.

"You guys'll have this place to yourselves for a while. I hadda send Rushmore down to Isfahan. Be there a while. Shit hit the fan pretty good down there."

"So we heard," said Frank, thinking of Ali's son. He did not want to talk about it.

With the nosiness of the good spy, Troy had ignored his lack of a need-to-know and took a keen interest in Frank's cultivation of an Iranian Air Force major.

"Sounds like your Anwar's recruiting himself," said Troy.

"Could be," said Frank.

"Plus, Gus's waiter friend says Anwar and his old lady want to get out of here and off to the good ol' U.S. of A."

"Do you have to read our cables?" said Gus.

"Can't resist. You guys write so well. 'Sides, you're gettin' air force stuff we never got."

Frank's meetings with the *homafaran* also intrigued Troy. "Working at Dowshan Tappeh you get to meet a few, but they're pretty stand-offish. They don't even mix much with the pilots or other Iranian Air Force types. You may have something."

"We'll see," said Frank. Bad enough I've got Rocky, he thought. Now Troy thinks we're poaching on his turf. For a moment at least, he wanted to forget his problems, to enjoy his small triumph with the newspaper. He wanted the Shah. He wanted Lermontov. He didn't want to fight with his own people.

He realized there was nothing more he could do but wait for the Shah to summon him to a meeting. Wait, and pray, for Lermontov to resurface. See what he could do for Anwar. Follow Gus's advice to keep on gathering all the intelligence he could and trying, as best he could, to report it.

Gus and Troy, as they often did, had begun to talk about Vietnam. "I loved that country." said Troy. "Damn shame we lost it."

"It was never ours," said Gus.

"Damn shame. Personally, I wouldn't give a rat's ass if we lost this place tomorrow, except for the oil." He thought a moment, studying the map over Rushmore's desk. "And maybe the rugs." Frank labored at the typewriter, then heard Troy, breaking out of a reverie, say, "Sunset and syndrome. Ever since Vietnam. It's what? Five years ago we pulled out? Shit. Ever since then we've been afraid to balls-out fight another war. Sunset for our side. We lost the country, but we'll live with the syndrome forever. Otherwise, we could be flying in advisers here and maybe even some combats to help the Shah wipe out these reds and ragheads."

"I'd drink to that," said Gus. "If we had something to drink."

"Never on the job," said Troy. "At least not anymore."

I could use a drink, thought Frank, but not now. He preferred his vodka straight, without politics, but he knew he lived and worked among people with strong and patriotic political ideals. For the most part, he shared those ideals, but he was grateful that most of the men and women he'd worked with overseas had been brighter, more dedicated, and distinctly more liberal than he had anticipated his colleagues would be.

Even now, for all his problems with Rocky, he felt lucky. Everything else had gone well. Their unseen servants again had packed their refrigerator with virtually all the items on the list they had left, including fresh spinach and locally cultured yogurt. They found the laundry they had left washed, ironed, and neatly folded on the kitchen table along with an envelope with their change and a note listing the requested items that turned out to be unavailable. The care and feeding of spies. He wished he had it so good at home.

The feeling of well-being passed quickly. He bent low over the typewriter, ignoring the war stories shared by Gus and Troy, writing about Jayface, worrying about Rocky, and wondering what new problems the arriving Fred Bunker would introduce into their lives.

Alone in the gym that evening, he pounded his frustrations into the heavy bag. First Rocky. Then Jayface. For sure Near East Division. No contact, they'd told him. Absolutely no contact. He felt surrounded by invisible specters with whom he could have no contact.

Lermontov, unseen in dark alleyways, a disappearing shadow in thick, early morning fog. *I fled him down the nights and down the days, down the labyrinthine ways of my own mind.* He had no tapes for his hands, no Everlast gloves, only the padded-for-warmth leather mittens he wore every day. His knuckles bled into them, but he hammered away at the bag as though it were an enemy in the ring. He buckled the leather with a left hook and set it dancing with a right cross. He heard the door open behind him. He crackled the bag with a succession of jabs, glancing over his right shoulder only long enough to capture the image of a heavy-set man in a khaki uniform. He thudded a left hook off the final jab and stopped at the sound of a loud grunt behind him. He turned and focused on a beefy Iranian in a rumpled uniform he took to be army rather than air force. A sergeant's chevrons decorated one sleeve.

"*Amrikazi?*" said the sergeant. His belly sagged over a thick belt that secured the holster on his hip. His right hand went to the butt of an old U.S. Army Colt .45.

"*Baleh,*" answered Frank.

He had no idea what the sergeant's next words meant, but he did not translate them as friendly.

"*Inglissi mi-danid?*" tried Frank.

"*Nah.*" He spat the syllable out, hand still on the butt of his gun.

No English, thought Frank. He heard voices, footsteps in the hallway. "Me, Farsi . . . *kami,*" he said loudly. He looked beyond the sergeant to see the head and shoulders of Anwar the Taller.

"How are you, Major Sullivan?"

"Good," said Frank. "It's good, very good, to see you."

"Any problem?" Without waiting for Frank to reply, Anwar spoke to the sergeant. "*Be-bakh-shid*" was all Frank caught.

The sergeant stepped aside. Anwar and the other *homafaran* filed into the gym. The sergeant nodded and spoke the same greeting to each of the homafaran—"Be-farma-id too"—then jutted his chin in Frank's direction and looked back at the homafaran.

Anwar supplied the answer. Frank could pick out only the English cognates ... Amrika ... Air Force Polis.

As he listened to Anwar, the sergeant stood squarely in front of Frank, left hand on his hip, the other on the handle of his holstered .45. Despite his fat, Frank sensed the power in his sloping shoulders and the menace in his tiny black eyes. Frank studied his short, thick neck, wondering if he could find a vulnerable spot. He suspected not.

The sergeant's only reply to Anwar's monologue was the phrase Frank could now identify as maag bargh Amrika. The sergeant backed toward the door, eyes still on Frank. He turned and walked from the room, leaving the door ajar behind him.

"That was rude of him," said the man who exercised with the Indian clubs. He hadn't yet begun his routine. He crossed to the door and closed it. "He should not have stared at you that way."

"Plus maag bargh Amrika," said Frank.

"You know the meaning?" said Anwar.

Frank nodded, "Death to America." His throat was tight. "What's his problem?" he asked.

Anwar looked at the door the sergeant had exited through. "He is a very devout man. Military police. Army, not air force. They are responsible for the security of the facilities that are apart from the airfield. The cafeteria, the gym, the offices, the gates. They are not very good at their job, and they resent the air force personnel because we get better pay, better accommodations, better food, better everything. Of course, they resent you Americans much more. This sergeant, he is very devout but very angry. Be careful from him."

"What's his name?" said Frank.

Anwar hesitated for a moment. "Abdollah Abbas. But do not make trouble for him."

Frank shook his head. "I just want to take your advice." All that, and death to America, thought Frank. "I just want to avoid him."

"It would be good to avoid him."

Another for my list, thought Frank. Lermontov. The Shah. Sergeant Abdollah Abbas.

"But you can relax now," said Anwar. "Go back to your workout. Come, I will give you a good workout." Anwar braced himself against the heavy bag and wrapped his arms around it. "Come, attack."

Instinct told Frank to beg off. "No thanks. That's enough for me."

"Come. I want to see how hard you can hit."

Frank knew he faced a test, not just of how hard he could hit, but of how much trust he would put in his gym mates. "Okay." He tried a tentative jab. With Anwar securing it, the bag had virtually no give. He tried another jab and a hard right and picked up the rhythm of his routine. The whole weight of his body went into every punch, even his short, quick jabs. He circled in, changing directions, knees always bent, sometimes flat-footed, sometimes up on his toes, his legs and butt snapping into each punch. The *homafaran* echoed his grunts with monosyllabic words of approval—good, yes, good punch. Sweat poured off him, staining his gray sweatshirt. He began to tire. His pace slowed, and he finished with a left hook that buckled the bag.

Anwar grunted. "You hit hard."

"Not as hard as you," said Frank.

"I'm bigger," said Anwar.

Bigger. Stronger. Younger. Faster and every bit as mean, thought Frank. He knew he would have to offer to hold the bag for Anwar. He hoped Anwar would decline. But Anwar spoke first.

"Come," he said. "Will you hold the bag for me?"

I must trust this man, thought Frank. Or he'll never trust me.

"Sure." Frank took off his gloves and tossed them on the bench.

"Your hands are all blood," said the youngest of the *homafaran*.

"They'll be okay," said Frank. He bent his knees, gingerly wrapped his arms around the bag, and braced himself against it.

"You better hold tighter than that," said Anwar.

"Right," said Frank. He tightened his arms. Anwar, as Frank had done, began with two jabs, then picked up the pace and power of his punches. Frank's peripheral vision caught the blur of a right hook coming his way. He blinked, flinched, and felt the impact of the hook smashing into the bag an inch from his forehead. He knew he had to trust Anwar's accuracy. He hoped he could trust his intentions.

Frank sensed that as Iranians, admirers of martyrs and given to flagellation, the *homafaran* would wonder at this strange, middle-aged American who would draw his own blood in pursuit of a ritual they also enjoyed. A hard right thudded into the center of the bag, stinging Frank's midsection. He managed to regain his breath but thought, This is going to be hell.

Hell paid dividends. Since Frank had begun working out on the heavy bag with Anwar the Taller, a new level of trust had begun to develop.

Anwar demonstrated the exhaustive knowledge of a determined lecturer. Frank considered his education in the sectarian differences among guerrilla groups opposed to the Shah the price he paid for a steady supply of Ayatollah Khomeini's tapes and information about opposition within the military.

Frank had struggled through a series of bench presses, starting with seven repetitions at 135 pounds, working up in weight and down in repetitions to a single grunt with 200. Anwar, who had spotted for him, then slid under the bar, executed ten reps with the 200, and added two 45-pound iron plates for his next set of ten.

"You heard, I know from my cousin that Sanjabi and Barzagan have been sent to prison." Anwar had the ability to continue his lectures while hefting what to Frank seemed an incredible poundage of iron. "What you don't know is how crowded our prisons have become. Our prisons, especially Qasar, have grown so crowded that to make room for the Sanjabis and Bazargans, they have to let out *Mojahedin*. And even . . ." He finished his set and let the bar clang down on the support racks over the bench. "Most important of all, even Ayatollah Taleqani."

"I'm sorry," said Frank. "You know I don't know much. Who is Ayatollah Taleqani?"

Anwar the Taller sat up. Pumped from the heavy bench presses, his sharply etched chest and shoulder muscles quivered. "You see, Anwar the Smarter may be very smart, but he can't tell you everything."

All the *homafaran* spoke English, but only Anwar spoke at length. The others seemed content to confirm, mostly with nods and monosyllables, what Anwar said.

"We are like your Black Muslims in America. Your Malcolm X people and the people who killed Malcolm X. The Muslim *Mojahedin* are very strong in prison, especially in Qasar, where they have jailed Ayatollah Taleqani many times for maybe fifteen years or more off and on. Now, Taleqani again has been released. They released many *Mojahedin* early last year and now, many more are being released to make room for the *Savak*s like General Nasseri who are going to Qasar."

A chorus of laughter and "that's right" and "yes" rose from the other *homafaran*. Even the man with the Indian clubs managed a grunt.

"We have America to thank for this," said Anwar.

"America?"

"Your civil rights people. Amnesty International. President Carter. They have been complaining about political suppression in Iran, about *Savak,* about torture. The Shah loves his F-14s and F-16s, the AWAC surveillance planes, and all the other wonderful things he gets from the Americans. So do we. It's our job to take care of them, and we love our work."

The club wielder grunted, and the heavy-set weight lifter struck his chest with the flat of his hand.

"So the Shah wants to keep the Americans happy. He put the jailers in jail and put *Mojahedin* on the street. And Ayatollah Taleqani has already opened an office. He is talking to young people."

"Why was he in jail?"

"Ah, he has always opposed the Shah. Since the days of Mossadeq. Since the days of the White Revolution when the Shah said women should not wear chador, land should be taken from the aristocracy and the clergy and given to the peasants, *bazaari* should go to jail for charging prices that were too high, all things that sound good to foreigners and our own Westernized elite but do not sound so good to most Persians. As much as Khomeini, Ayatollah Taleqani has opposed the Shah, but he is not like Khomeini. He is not so . . . Well, he understands the people. He is not a *Mojahedin*. He argues with us, but he understands why we are still Marxist even though we accept Islam and why we will support Khomeini and the revolution when it comes but also why, once the Shah is done and Islamic Revolution rules, they will attack us. *Mojahedin* and *Feda'iyan* may fight each other. We will defeat the Shah. We will defeat the Americans and Russians if we have to. But then there will be another civil war, and I do not know who will win that one."

The others were silent. With a flourish, the man with the Indian clubs finished his routine. He tucked the clubs under his arms and bowed to Frank.

"Now you will understand," he said.

"That is why we need you, Major Sullivan," said Anwar.

"Me?"

"Yes. You see, the *Mojahedin* have been looking for an American we can talk to. Your embassy doesn't talk to us. Your CIA talks only to *Savak*. When my cousin started telling me about you, I listened. I asked our leaders if I could talk to you. They said I could try, within limits. Sound you out. Even I asked my cousin if I could trust you."

"What did he say?"

"He said I would have to find out." His shrug reminded Frank of Anwar the Smarter. "Anyway, I have to trust you. You see, the Muslim *Mojahedin* have been active. The Americans should know that now we will be more active. We will make a difference. The Islamic *Mojahedin* will make a difference. *Homa-faran* will make a difference. The military will make a difference. Not the generals, the soldiers. The people will make a difference, but the people are not trained. The people are not disciplined." His eyes locked on Frank's. "We are."

The next evening they worked in more exercise than usual. The beefy Sergeant Abbas looked in and spoke briefly, hand on his .45. He stared at Frank, turned, and left, again leaving the door ajar. The *homafar* working out with Indian clubs was close enough that he was able to reach out with his right leg and kick the door shut, without missing a beat of his routine.

Anwar handed Frank a cassette tape. "It's the same as the one just here." He pressed the play button on the cassette recorder on the bench against the wall. The by now familiar, high-pitched voice of Khomeini shrieked out at high volume.

"When your people translate it, they will hear the first plans for *Tasu'a* and *Ashura,* the holy days of *Moharram*. My cousin has told you about that, isn't it?"

"He has," said Frank. "*Moharram* isn't far off, right?"

"I have looked," said the man with the clubs. "This year, your two December is our one *Moharram*."

"And the holy days come on the ninth and tenth of *Moharram*," said Anwar. "The Imam calls for great peaceful demonstrations, in all the cities, in the countryside. Everywhere. But above all, here in Tehran. Millions will march."

"Won't the military try to stop it?"

Anwar smiled. "If the military try to prevent, it could be worse than Jaleh Square, but I do not believe the soldiers will open fire."

"Why do you think the soldiers won't shoot?"

"Because the Imam tells them not to. They, too, will hear this tape in the mosques. Their brothers and sisters, their fathers and mothers, will hear it, and they will tell the soldiers not to harm the people. Khomeini tells the people not to attack the soldiers. He tells the people to let the soldiers shoot at them, kill them. He says if enough of you become martyrs the soldiers who kill you will turn against their masters. He tells the people to carry flowers and give them to the soldiers. He tells the people to have young girls in chadors to carry flowers and put flowers in the barrels of the guns the soldiers carry and for young men to put flowers in the gun barrels of the tanks."

"Will the *Mojahedin* be involved?"

"Not as *Mojahedin*. Not as *homafaran*. But some of us, we will hear this tape, and we may be there. Not as *Mojahedin,* but as followers of the Imam."

Frank noticed that, for the first time, Anwar had begun referring to Khomeini not as Khomeini or even as the Ayatollah but by the more reverent title of Imam. The door opened. The sergeant again looked in on them. He nodded at Anwar, glanced toward the recorder still relaying the word of the Imam, and said in English, "Good." He looked at Frank. He stood with his arms at his side, not touching the .45. He nodded back toward the recorder, then again at Frank, and said, "Good." He turned and left, shutting the door behind him.

"Sergeant Abbas approves," said Frank.

"Perhaps," said Anwar.

# CHAPTER TEN

Khomeini's raspy, high-pitched voice sliced out at them, far too loud in the hushed confines of the bubble. Frank, who had driven straight from Dowshan Tappeh to the embassy, eased the volume.

"This is incredible," said Belinsky. "This is *jihad*. Holy war. What they've been waiting for to fire up their people."

Frank listened, grateful that Belinsky's reading supported what Anwar the Taller had told him, but still wondering why Belinsky avoided his inquisitive eyes.

"I thought the military government meant an end to this stuff," said Rocky.

"It has been quiet," said the ambassador.

"*Moharram* will be quiet," said Belinsky. "Peaceful but powerful. Because that's the way Khomeini wants it."

"I have to tell you," said Frank, putting aside his concerns about Belinsky, "tonight, when he played this for me, my gym buddy, Anwar Two, well, he's always sounded skeptical about Khomeini. But tonight, as he listened to this, he had fire in his eyes. Called him the Imam."

"I can understand," said Belinsky. "Martyrdom. Flowers in the gun barrels. At one point he says you don't have to shoot the soldiers in the breast. Touch them in their hearts. He had me about ready to take to the streets."

"If he gets his way," said Frank, "he'll have all Iran taking to the streets."

"Balls," said Rocky. "You guys are listening to one squeaky-voice preacher and forgetting that the Shah has a forty-thousand-man military in back of a military government. No way they're gonna let this unholy holy man take over the streets."

"I hope you're right," said the ambassador.

"I'll talk to Eagle-1 about it," said Rocky. "See what *Savak* thinks. See what the *Tudeh* party is up to. I don't suppose your *homafar* pal had anything to say about that."

Frank shrugged. "You know. Far as he's concerned, they don't exist."

"Yeah, well, we know better." He caught Frank's eye and nodded. "Don't we?"

In the presence of the ambassador and Belinsky, Frank knew, Rocky wouldn't mention Lermontov, but the Russian was on both their minds. *I will contact you,* Lermontov wrote. But when? And what are the British up to?

As Gus had predicted, Rocky refused to transmit Frank's cable on the release of key *Mojahedin* and Ayatollah Taleqani from prison. Rocky dismissed Taleqani as just another holy man and said *Savak* had already reported on the release of the *Mojahedin*.

"Kinda like bangin' your head against a wall," said Gus.

"A fucking Rocky wall," said Frank.

That afternoon, tense and quiet, Frank continued drafting his atmospherics cable in the office they shared with the absent Stan Rushmore. They had decided Gus should undertake some domestic errands, including a run to the commissary. Frank's fingers danced on the keyboard of Rushmore's IBM, choreographing images that would build an atmosphere of a Tehran at war with itself.

The giant, teetering construction crane they had seen in the muddy field near the soccer stadium became a symbol of all the abandoned projects undertaken by the Shah. They passed it often in the limited compass of their travels through the city. Surrounded by the prefabricated shells of what had been intended as military housing, it still managed to stand, sucked ever deeper in mud, tilting more precariously, like the fossil of a trapped raptor incapable of recognizing that it had already become extinct. He'd seen many cranes like it in all parts of the city, as many as half a dozen to a site, though none in such danger of collapse, looming like abandoned sentinels over fields of lost battles, shells of buildings and windows without glass staring blankly over cluttered, fenced-in lots, speaking mutely of a stalled economy.

He sketched a portrait of a military that, except for the Imperial Guard, seemed alienated from its role as protector of the Shah, its Supreme Commander. He described their Jayface meetings in detail and all he had been told there, as well as his meetings with the *homafaran* in the gym and all he had learned of Khomeini's use of cassette tapes and of the inroads made by the *Mojahedin*. He kept his narrative descriptive, emphasizing the smells of the gym, Khomeini's high-pitched voice, and the way the Ayatollah's photo showed up in odd places, like their still-functioning neighborhood liquor store; he told how drivers of the city's orange jitney taxis had photos of the Shah pasted to one windshield visor and of Khomeini taped to the other, with the Shah flipped down if they were passing a military roadblock and the Shah turned up out of sight and Khomeini made visible when close to the university, the bazaar, or one of Tehran's many mosques.

Only in asides made by one of the contacts in the sweaty gym or the chilly meeting room at Supreme Commander's Headquarters did he quote anything about the *Tudeh* party's limited role or the clerical leadership's strong hostility toward the atheistic Russians. He noted that no one displayed photos of Stalin or Brezhnev or Noureddin Kianouri, the exiled head of the *Tudeh* party. Then he wondered if that might be a stroke too much. By late afternoon, when Gus returned, Frank guessed he was halfway through.

Frank kept working while Gus read what he'd done. "This is great," said Gus when he'd caught up. "We'll make an intelligence officer, or at least a bureaucrat, out of you yet. It needs some editing, but you're on your way."

"Edit away," said Frank. "I appreciate a good editor."

"Okay." Gus looked at his watch. "What's your schedule?"

"Shit." Frank pushed himself back from the typewriter. "I should do some work on our civic action program. And I need to get over to the gym by six. I need to see my workout buddies."

"How 'bout I work on editing this a while. You put in about an hour on civic action, then head for the gym. I'll pick up where you leave off on the civic action stuff. When you're done in the gym, come back here and pick me up. We'll be good boys and put everything in the safe and go home and get some chow."

"Sounds good to me," said Frank.

"And get ready for Mr. Bunker."

"Oh. I forgot about that," said Frank.


Frank had just finished moving his belongings into the back, windowless bedroom.

"Good," said Gus. He leaned against the doorjamb, arms folded across his chest. "It's smaller, there's no view and no air, but I'll sleep better knowing you're not in the grenade room."

Frank started hanging the clothes he'd dumped on the bed in a wardrobe closet. "I don't much like moving a couple of weeks after I moved in."

"You know, you might be right," said Gus. "It might have been smarter to let Bunker get here, see how much nicer that front room is, and pull rank to take it away from you."

"An hour ago you told me I should move in here before Bunker shows up."

"You're as bad as Joan," said Gus. "She says every time I make my mind up I always change my mind. Like I did about retiring."

A loud buzzer cut through the air, and both men jumped.

"What was that?" said Frank.

The buzzer sounded again. Gus had disappeared; his muffled voice crept into the room from the dark hallway. "I think it's the doorbell."

"I didn't even know we had a doorbell," said Frank.

Gus peered at him around the doorjamb. "Well, we haven't had many callers."

"Yeah, I know. And the last guy threw pebbles at the window." The buzzer sounded again.

"Bunker," said Gus. "If we hadn't left the lights on, we could pretend we're not home. Don't worry. You'll love him and his uptight Mormon soul. A real stand-up guy and an outstanding paper pusher."

Frank remembered Dan Nitzke's description: a straitlaced Mormon and a real good bureaucrat. Their descriptions didn't help. He didn't know much about the ways of bureaucrats, and he realized he understood as little about Mormons as he did about Muslims.

A rattling sound climbed the stairs. "Sounds like the ghost in *Christmas Carol*," said Gus.

"Let's go see." Frank edged past Gus and went to the front bedroom. He knelt and looked out onto the street under the blind he had lowered to within two inches of the window frame. He stood, walked past Gus, and led the way down the stairs. "Stan Rushmore's out there," he said. "Standing in the street next to his Chevy."

The door rattled again as Frank hurried down the stairs. "Hold your water." The rattling stopped. "Who's there?"

"Fred Bunker. Open up, for God's sake."

Frank unlatched the door. He stepped back and said, "It's open."

"Why hasn't that lock on the gate been fixed?"

Bunker was tall, taller than Frank had imagined. As he stepped into the hallway, carrying a brown leather attaché case, Frank guessed six-two or three. He looked solidly built, and gray eyes glared out from behind steel-rimmed glasses. Early thirties, over 200, close-cropped, curly brown hair. A tan wash-dry poplin suit that was too light for the climate, with a lined London Fog coat draped over his arm. Frank took it all in very quickly. He could tell he was going to have to pay very close attention to this bureaucrat named Bunker.

"We haven't done much about the bullet holes, either," said Frank.

"What bullet holes?" Though he was only a few inches taller than Frank, Bunker had a way of lowering his head to look down at his listener through his steel rims when he spoke.

Frank moved past him to the open doorway. He waved at the bulky figure standing by the big car just beyond the pale circle that fell from a street lamp. "Thanks, Rush."

Frank looked at the luggage at the foot of the stairs. In the half light he counted four large suitcases, two garment bags, two small bags, another, larger attaché case, and what looked like a portable typewriter case.

"You must be planning on a four-year tour."

"Four weeks should do," said Bunker.

"Come on," said Frank. "I'll give you a hand with that. The bullet holes can wait."

With Gus's help, he moved Bunker's luggage into the front bedroom upstairs. While Bunker unpacked, Frank cooked a supper of grilled lamb, boiled spinach, and rice. He cooked without salt but made up for it with pepper, garlic, and herbs. With the rice he'd used a generous amount of saffron, which had become so expensive in the States he'd quit buying it. He'd selected his spices from open barrels at a market still operating opposite the air base, shopping with his sense of smell.

Frank retailed his shopping story to Bunker over dinner. He was proud of his cooking and enjoyed Gus's grunts of appreciation.

"Not bad. All things considered. Not bad."

"We'll shop at the commissary tomorrow," said Bunker. "This is all well and good, but there's no point of having a commissary if you don't take advantage of it."

"I'll clear the dishes," said Gus. He made no move to clear the dishes but lit a cigarette instead. "Cigarette, Fred?"

"I don't smoke," said Bunker.

"Neither does Frank. Joan keeps telling me I should quit. And I do. But no matter how often I quit, she never seems satisfied. Did you ever smoke, Fred? It's a filthy habit, like drinking. As I remember, you don't drink, either, do you?"

"I enjoy a good wine with dinner," said Bunker.

"I'm glad to hear that," said Gus, who had been downing even more than usual through dinner and beyond.

Bunker cleared his throat. "This is probably a good time to work out our basic parameters." Bunker spoke a language Frank barely understood. "I know both of you were dispatched here unexpectedly and without the chance to do the reading-in I've been implementing over the past ten days. As head of the KUSTAFF team, it's my responsibility to brief you—briefly . . ." He allowed a fleeting smile. Even when sitting at the kitchen table, he managed to peer down at them. Frank watched the reflections in his steel-rimmed glasses of the bare ceiling bulb dancing, changing shapes, shifting angles. "I've been through the presidential finding, the latest NIE, a recent Forty Committee paper, a DDO memo under the rubric 'Coup Considerations,' the latest country survey, skimmed the State Department Area Handbook and all the recent cable traffic and internal memoranda. As head of the KUSTAFF team—I said that, didn't I?"

"Yes," said Gus and Frank, in unison. Gus poured himself another glass of wine.

"Before we go any further, gentlemen, could we synchronize our watches? I was all right up to Paris. A six-hour time difference, Washington-Paris. But when we got here, the flight attendants announced the local time as two and a half hours later than Paris. I made the adjustment, even though I couldn't believe it. I now have local time eight-forty-seven. Is that correct?"

"That's what I have," said Frank, lying slightly. As usual, his Timex ran five minutes fast.

Gus stared intently at his watch. "Correct," he said. He took his glasses off and squinted at the crystal again, "Absolutely correct."

"Every other place in the world, time zones are a civilized sixty minutes apart. Only in this godforsaken place have I ever heard of an extra half hour difference."

"Not quite," said Frank.

"Not at all," said Gus. "It's a big world. All kinds of variations. Some of the islands in the Pacific. Parts of Australia, India, Sri Lanka. They're all thirty-minute jobs."

"Even Newfoundland," said Frank. "Right up there in Canada."

"Nepal's even stranger," said Gus. "When it's noon Greenwich Mean Time it's five forty-five in Kathmandu."

"Kathmandu," sniffed Bunker, looking as though he'd smelled something unpleasant. "Which reminds me. What's our schedule with the ragheads?"

Frank and Gus looked at each other. Gus shrugged. Frank shrugged.

"Ah, what ragheads?" said Frank.

"You know what I mean. Jayface."

"Oh," said Gus. "Those ragheads. Well, here in this strange time zone, Thursday and Friday are the weekend. Islam, you know. But lately our general has had us meeting on Thursday, which is tomorrow, but not on Friday, the heavy-duty holy day."

"Tomorrow I can't make it. I have to sit in with Tom Troy early morning, then the ambassador at ten, lunch with Roger Novak and the ambassador, and then your presence will be required in the ambassador's office at two for a meeting involving all . . . five of us."

"Sounds like a full day," said Frank.

"And a full house," added Gus.

"Then, what about Jayface?" asked Bunker.

"We've been working on a civic action proposal," said Frank. "You may have read about in the traffic."

"Yes, indeed. I'd meant to ask about that."

"Well, it's ready for you to look at. We haven't shown it to anyone else. Not even Rocky. Not even in rough draft. But our general . . ."

"SDHERALD-1."

"Correct," said Gus.

"He's getting kind of antsy, so soon as you get a chance, we'd like you to give it a read."

"Roger that," said Bunker.

"Part of it," said Frank, "I guess the most important part of it, is Gus's idea for the military to publish a general interest newspaper."

"And Near East wants more details on how that will work," said Bunker.

"I've tried to get a meeting with Kasravi, Colonel Kasravi, the deputy prime minister, on it, but these days he's got a revolution to take care, of so I guess it may take a while."

"Keep after him," said Bunker. "We can't afford to be polite about this business."

"I'll keep after him," said Frank.

"There's the other thing," said Gus.

"Right," said Frank.

"What other thing?"

"Well, you have to remember, I'm not a case officer, just an agent."

"I understand. A career agent."

Frank smiled. He had never heard the term before. "I don't think so. More like an occasional agent. Kind of in and out, and at the moment back in. But I've never worked inside. Gus has more or less had to teach me how to write cables, and he introduced me to the idea of an atmsopherics cable about Iran."

"Great idea," said Bunker. "Have you sent it?"

"Hell, no," said Gus. "We wanted you to see it first."

"Good," said Bunker. "When do we meet with Jayface?"

"Saturday morning at eight," said Gus.

"You mean we have to meet with them on the weekend?"

"No," said Gus. "The weekend is Thursday-Friday."

"Absurd," said Bunker. "Thursday and Friday for a weekend. Half-hour time zone. Why can't they be like the rest of the world?"

"Fred, you haven't been stationed much overseas, have you?"

"I certainly have. Paris, Bonn, London. Relatively . . . brief tours, it's true. In fact, I have been—primarily—a bit of a headquarters man."

"That's kind of what I remembered," said Gus.

Frank noticed the way Bunker had detoured back to reality. Primarily a headquarters man. The truth must matter to this guy even if his language sounded phony.

"In any event, as I was saying, as head of the KUSTAFF team, I've been privy to new NE Division requirements which place heavy emphasis on plans for a military coup that might retain or replace the current government and arrange for the departure, perhaps temporarily, of the Shah."

"He'll be thrilled," said Gus.

"What's that supposed to mean?" said Bunker.

"That the Shah will be thrilled to hear we plan to kick him out."

"We do not plan to have him kicked out. Our job is to ascertain the intentions of the Iranian military in that regard. I mean in regard to his abdication in favor of his son as regent, with a council of elders, if you will, to guide the Crown Prince until he reaches his majority."

"Did you memorize all that?" asked Gus.

"Yes," said Bunker, again with absolute honesty. "As you'll see, when you read the traffic, it falls within the parameters of our requirements as defined by NE Division and the NSC. With our operational center right in the headquarters of the Joint Chiefs of Staff . . ."

"Whoa," said Frank. "We don't meet at the headquarters of the Joint Chiefs of Staff. Far as I know, there's no such thing in Iran. Place we meet is called Supreme Commander's Headquarters."

"And the Shah is the one and only Supreme Commander," added Gus.

"Yes," said Bunker, nodding. "You're correct, of course. That was a slip on my part. Sorry. I must have been thinking of the American paragon."

"Do you mean paradigm?" said Frank.

"He means Pentagon," said Gus, grinning. He paused for a long draw from his wine glass. "But you know something?" He paused again for a shorter sip. "Somehow I don' think the Supreme Commander is plannin' a coup to get himself kicked out." Frank noticed Gus had begun to slur. He hoped he could find a way soon to bring their evening to a close, but Bunker plowed on.

"It falls within the parameters of our task to ascertain what the military may plan along the lines of a coup, irregardless of the Shah's personal preferences."

Frank studied him as the strange sentences poured from his thin-lipped mouth, like a synthetic language echoing from a robot's hidden sound system. Frank hoped his gestures or expression might give some hint of what it all meant, but Bunker's manner was as opaque as his language. His lips barely moved when he spoke. The light reflecting off his glasses obscured his eyes. Frank glanced at Gus, wondering if he was sober enough now to be able to translate it all later. Bunker fell silent, but only for a moment.

"Which reminds me. Sullivan . . . Frank. You don't mind if I call you Frank, do you?"

"'Course not."

"Good. There'll be cable traffic coming on this overnight, but as head of . . . I wanted to be the first to let you know, verbally, that your status as an adviser to the Shah on a continuing basis has been well received at a very high level."

"Rocky will love that," said Gus.

"I should think so. Having someone from his shop meeting with the Shah on a personal basis puts quite a feather in his cap."

"He may not see it that way," said Frank. "I mean, I don't know, but he may have a notion that a chief of state should be talking to the chief of station, not to some low-level agent."

"Oh, I doubt that Rocky's that petty," said Bunker. "In fact, the cable traffic won't reflect this, but Pete Howard, who I understand goes back a long way with you, took the initiative to get Brzezinski himself involved in the ultimate decision process. I met with Pete and Zbig two days ago after it had all been cleared through division, where there was some . . . understandable . . . reluctance to formalize. Whatever reluctance NE, or Rocky, may has to fade when the President's national security adviser says it's a go."

"I guess," said Frank. He could not imagine Rocky fading.

"The division did evince some concern at the abruptness of your meeting, before division even had time to forward its requirements. But at your next meeting," said Bunker, "as you'll see when you peruse the overnight traffic, you will have some rather taxing requirements."

I know what that means, thought Frank. It means those fuckers in Near East Division who don't want me meeting with the Shah have come up with an impossible basket of things I won't be able to get the Shah to tell me about and they'll be able to say we told you so.

"I understand," he said. It also occurred to him that so far at least Bunker had said nothing about Lermontov. He guessed that Bunker would restrict any message on that topic to Rocky.

"In addition, there's a very strong feeling in NE that this SDTRIB-1, the apparently very forthcoming air force major, should be recruited. Made witting. Given tasks. Paid. Small amounts to begin with. Nothing too demanding at first, but made an agent in place who soon can be given very hard requirements involving the GOI military. Particularly since the major's cook has already told Gus the family wants to get to America. There's a separate cable coming overnight laying all this out because, naturally, I couldn't carry any classified documents with me. It will stipulate that, as the more experienced case officer, Gus Simpson should undertake the recruitment."

"Wait a minute, Archie."

"What did you call me?" Bunker didn't stand, but even seated he seemed to swell up to his full six-foot-three and glower down at Gus.

Frank tried to interrupt. "Actually, I'm not a case officer at all. Just an agent."

Gus managed to look genuinely puzzled. "Frederick? Did I call you Frederick? Sometimes I get a little formal when I'm drunk. I shoulda said Fred."

"That's not what you called me." His face crimsoned. He stood.

Frank looked up at him. Wow, he thought. He really is tall.

"We'll continue this conversation at another time," said Bunker. Suddenly, the color drained from his face and he glared at Gus. "Don't ever call me that again." He turned, stalked from the room, and pounded up the stairs.

"Hey, okay, Fred," yelled Gus. "What's he so pissed for? 'Cause I called him Frederick?"

Their Jayface meeting began brusquely. "Major Sullivan, please," said the general. "What is happening with our civic action proposal?"

Frank glanced at Gus. Ever so slightly, Gus nodded.

"Very soon," said Frank. "A new member of our team has just joined us."

"Head of our team, actually," said Gus.

"He has meetings at the embassy today. We'll be introducing him to you all on Saturday. Ah, since he is head of our team, we need him to review the proposal, make any changes he recommends."

"And how long will that take?" asked the general.

"Saturday morning," said Frank. "We expect Saturday morning, Sunday latest."

"Very well," said the general. "Shall we get down to the business of our meeting?" It was a command, not a question. "Do you have anything for us today, Major Sullivan? As opposed to, perhaps, Sunday."

"Yes, sir. We do," said Frank, ignoring the sharp tone. It had been more than a week since Nazih's arrest. He could understand the general's edginess. "It's a revision of our first draft on an armed forces newspaper, including the suggestions you and the others made previously."

"Very good. I've been looking forward to this. We need to present this as soon as possible to Colonel Kasravi. Do you have copies for all?"

"Yes, sir. I do." And yeah, he thought, we sure do want to meet with Kasravi about it. And give you a chance to ask him about your little nephew.


Frank had persuaded Gus to handle Bunker's shopping list. They had only two hours between their Jayface meeting and their scheduled appearance at the embassy, but Frank wanted to finish up the civic action proposal and his atmospherics cable. He found that Stan Rushmore had staked out a claim to his own office.

"Welcome home," Frank said on entering. "Long time no see."

"Yeah, I know," said Rushmore, swiveling around in his desk chair. "I suppose you got an urgent need for the typewriter."

"Tell you the truth, I've got some stuff to do, but it's not much and it can probably wait. How've you been?"

"Well," said Rushmore, with a big man's sigh that was half grunt, "there have been better decades."

"How was Isfahan?"

"You know about that?"

"Our driver," said Frank. "His son got killed down there. With the army. Tom mentioned you'd gone down."

"Yeah. Sorry about your driver."

"Bad down there?"

"Could be worse, I guess. Look, I'm as gung ho an American as anybody, but that Bell Helicopter operation down there . . . They were askin' for it."

Frank figured it was better not to ask more questions. Rushmore seemed to want to talk. Frank didn't want to pressure him into silence.

"Thing is, most of those Bell guys are chopper jocks who served in Vietnam. Which is fine, except they brought Saigon with them. Couple of dozen absolutely gorgeous but pretty outrageous-lookin' Viet hookers. Miniskirts, high heels, tight jeans, hot pants, net stockings."

"No chadors?"

"Not hardly. At least one of 'em, I'm pretty sure, must be a transvestite. They got a gamblin' casino. Pot. Opium. Smack. And all this in Isfahan. It's one of the holy cities, know what I mean? A blue-domed mosque about every block, more turban men than you can count. Not a good mix. And you know chopper jocks, they aren't exactly the discreet kind. Only a matter 'a time before some local shit hit the helicopter fan."

"What happens now?"

"We gotta get 'em outta there, but that ain't so easy. The Iranian oil cartel and the military say they need 'em to keep their chopper fleets flyin'. My job was mostly to try and put the fear of God in them to keep their heads down for a change and hope this blows over. But between you'n me, it's gonna blow but it ain't gonna blow over." He paused, shook his head, and stared at the back of his thick-fingered hands. "You really wanna get to the typewriter a while?"

"I wouldn't mind."

"Okay. Lemme get my ribbon out. What're you workin' on?"

Frank hesitated to say, but he believed in sharing with people he trusted. "Couple of things. A civic action program for our counterparts, which will never get off the ground, and an atmospherics cable. For myself, I guess."

"You havin' trouble getting some of your intel filed?"

"Like that," said Frank.

"An atmospherics is a good idea. I didn't know you were so savvy."

"Gus's idea."

"Figures. Sometimes you need a few gray hairs to figure out how to get the job done, despite the job."

"That sounds like a cop talking," said Frank.

"Ex-cop and still a cop," said Rushmore. "Air force police, remember? It's my day job. Then I get to work on my other job."

"Sounds familiar."

"Yeah. It's about what we all do. Though I sometimes wonder why."

I know why, thought Frank. At least for me. I will contact you. Tomorrow would make it a week. He guessed the general had heard nothing more about Nazih. And *I sure as hell haven't heard from Lermontov.* He wondered if the British ambassador had.


Gus had already stashed Bunker's commissary order in their refrigerator when he picked up Frank at Rushmore's cubbyhole. His shopping foray had been a success. "A few substitutes," he said, "and more frozen steaks and lamb chops than he'll ever be able to eat, which means we may get some, and pancake mix and powdered milk and powdered eggs, and we can get him some real eggs on the local if he wants. If he doesn't mind paying for it, I don't mind buying it."

Frank took over the driving as they left Dowshan Tappeh for the embassy.

"He does kind of overdo," said Frank as they pulled through the gates and onto Farahnaz.

"Like his luggage . . . and his language," said Gus.

"Do they have a course in that?"

"What?"

"The way he talks."

"I dunno," said Gus. "I'm like you. I got recruited sideways. Taught hand-to-hand down at the farm but never took Junior Officer Training."

"But you've worked inside a long time."

"God rest my soul, that I have. Archie is typical of a breed. You've met mostly the opposite. A guy like Pete Howard. Almost always overseas. Does whatever he can to avoid Langley. Then there's the guys who do whatever they can to avoid overseas, unless it's maybe Paris or London. Archie Bunker is typical of that breed."

"You oughta quit calling him Archie."

The nature of the city's traffic had changed. In the absence of protests, burning buildings, and roadblocks of smoking tires, the careening craziness of Tehrani drivers had become more like peacetime Beirut or high-noon Mexico City. Frank, grateful for their Fiat's stick shift, adjusted to the pace, slicing right to left, in and out of clogged, zigzagging lanes.

"You oughta be a taxi driver."

"I was," said Frank. "In New York." He hated to think of all the jobs he'd tried so he could concentrate on the next novel or short story or poem. And yet, he'd always wound up trying to find the best way to do the job, as Rushmore had said, despite the job.


When Frank and Gus arrived at the ambassador's office, they found Rocky and Bunker listening to the ambassador, muttering on the phone. He slammed the receiver down.

"It never ceases to amaze me, in our highly technological age, the ways that technology—sometimes—works. And often does not work."

"You get through?" asked Rocky.

"Of course not." He turned to the new arrivals. "Welcome, gentlemen. Grab some chairs. All I wanted to do was put in a call to the British Embassy, a few blocks away. Couldn't be done. But if I wanted to call Paris and talk to the Great Ayatollah . . . Well, we all know something about Paris. It can take a year or more for an ordinary Parisian to get a telephone, and even then half the time you can never get through to anyone. Phone service here is much, I mean very much, worse. Most of the time. But Khomeini can get off a plane from Baghdad, land in Paris, and an hour later be on the phone to Tehran, Qom, Isfahan, or wherever else he wants."

"*Allah-o akbar,*" ventured Gus.

"Allah has nothing to do with it," said Rocky. "God isn't on this holy man's side, but the Soviet Embassy and the KGB *residenza* in Paris sure as hell are. Khomeini had an operation going there with some of his Americanized front men, Yazdi, Ghotzbadeh, a bunch of 'em. He walked into an operation with phones, fax machines, cassette recorders, whatever, as soon as he got off the plane, and guess how all that got in place."

"Not divine intervention, I'm sure," said the ambassador. Frank noticed he looked well rested, his cheeks ruddier, the bags under his eyes less pronounced.

Bunker had been quiet. Frank guessed he'd had time enough to deliver the jargon-weighted messages he'd conveyed from Langley, Foggy Bottom, and the Executive Office Building.

"Well," said the ambassador, "on to the business at hand. There are quite a few topics. I've made some notes."

The ambassador impressed Frank with his ability to take charge without flaunting his authority. He brought Frank and Gus up-to-date on the meeting that had been going on before their arrival in a manner that wasted a minimum of Rocky's and Bunker's time. He described the overnight cable traffic tasking the team to provide details of plans being made for a military coup and providing a long list of questions for Frank to pursue with the Shah.

"I want you to read the cables before you leave here. I must confess to you the intelligence requirements you are asked to place on the Shah are rather—extensive. There is no way you could ever handle them all in a month of meetings."

"All I can do," said Frank, "is listen to what he has to say."

"Agreed," said the ambassador. "The British ambassador and I meet with the man almost daily. He's quite upset, by the way, about Khomeini on the BBC. He believes it's a sign the British government is plotting to overthrow him."

"He may be right," said Rocky.

"Be that as it may, in the nature of things I should be the one to pursue most of the requirements laid on Sullivan, and Frank, I intend to convey that in my own response to the cable."

"That's good," said Rocky, "but what we really need t' do ASAP is t' get Fred here into the loop and find out what the fuck is goin' on with the top military."

Frank and Gus looked at each other and shrugged. Their unplanned dumb show, Frank realized, might only serve to show how dumb they were. They looked at Rocky, the ambassador, Bunker. Fred cleared his throat.

"There's a strong feeling back at Langley, and at the highest level of the National Security Council, that the Iranian Joint Chiefs of, er, I mean, the highest levels of the Iranian military are planning a coup which would depose the Shah and install the Crown Prince as regent."

"I thought the Crown Prince was in Texas," said Gus.

"He is," said Bunker. "But he could be returned soon enough."

"Has anyone asked him about it?" said Gus. He looked to Frank for help, but Frank had decided to say nothing. "Or his father?"

"That's not germane," said Bunker.

"Look, you two," said Rocky, shifting his glare from Gus to Frank. "They're plotting a military takeover right in that building where you guys sit around all day. You got their waiter signed up, and you mean to tell me you can't find out a fucking thing about their plans for a coup?"

"We'll find out about it," said Bunker.

Maybe we'll find out about it, thought Frank. If they have any plans for a coup.

"I'm glad you're on board," said Rocky. "Sullivan, you also got this pissant air force major feeding you all kinds of noise, and you haven't even made a move to recruit him. At a minimum, you should have him and the general taking some money, begging for visas, doing little illegal favors like getting some not-too-difficult-to-get documents."

"I concur," said Bunker, looking down at Frank through his steel-rimmed glasses. "I grant that the team has done a good job on the previously accessed cables I've read, but, barring any precluding factors I'm not aware of, serious recruitment, beyond one servant, appears a nonstarter."

Precluding factors, thought Frank. Definitely a nonstarter. He sensed something unsaid, hanging in the atmosphere, but he couldn't figure what. For another hour, they worked over the operational approach Frank, Gus, and Bunker should follow in the days ahead. They were winding down when the ambassador called for a break. Bunker asked directions to the men's room, and Rocky called Frank aside. They stood by the window that looked out over the sycamores and pines.

"Bunker tells me you're working on a fucking atmospherics cable, and that sounds like you found a way to go behind my back on reporting some of this shit you've been wanting to report."

"You're the boss," said Frank. "I don't want to go over you or around you. I just want to do the best job I can."

"Maybe you do," said Rocky. "Look, Bunker's real upset." Frank detected the hint of a smile. "Troy drove him down here. Bein' nice to the new big man in town, right? Passin' the time 'a day, Troy told him about the dud grenade that got tossed in your window."

Frank nodded. So that's what's wrong.

"That's the room you gave Bunker, right?"

"It's the best room in the house," said Frank. "I was still in it till yesterday. But we figured, he's the head of the team . . ."

"Well, he's upset. Thinks you're settin' him up t' get fragged."

What a lovely idea, thought Frank, "Is that why he was so quiet today?"

"Well, that and the ambassador kind of lit into him about all the dumb requirements."

"That can't be his fault," said Frank.

"No, but he was here. Hammer the messenger, right? What about our other business?"

Frank didn't have to ask. He knew Rocky meant Lermontov. "No word," he said.

"That Cossack fucker. He's letting us stew in our own borscht."

Frank nodded, appreciating the mix of Rocky's metaphors and sure that he was right. "How 'bout the Brits?" he asked.

"No word. I ask the ambassador couple 'a times a day if he's heard anything from his buddy Hempstone. Nothin'. I put in a couple calls t' Mosley. Asked Eagle-1 t' pull his sleeve. Nothin'. Meantime, Soviet Div's havin' a shit fit. Bunker's the wrong guy to send over t' tell me about it. Keep our little plan between you and me. Don't tell Bunker shit."

"I won't," said Frank. "But it's not going to matter if we don't get to our target, or if the British wrap him up first." He had an idea, but he knew the risk he'd be taking if he spelled it out to Rocky.

"Least I know he's still in town," said Rocky. "*Savak* says he's working the students pretty hard, farting around with his *Tudeh* party."

Frank decided to take the plunge. He inhaled sharply and began, "Look. What happens if we—if you get off a cable? Ask the folks back home to try to get the Brits to back off."

Rocky studied him. "The folks back home?"

"Yeah. Near East. Soviet Division."

"National Security Council?"

"That might be a good idea," said Frank. "I guess Brzezinski has the clout."

"And your friend Pete Howard?"

Frank's throat tightened. He nodded.

"Tell me," said Rocky, "what did your friend Pete Howard tell you to do about Lermontov?"

"Follow the briefing I got from Near East. Stay away from him."

"How 'bout if Lermontov got in touch with you?"

Frank had feared that Rocky would back him into a corner. Lie, he told himself, but as close to the truth as you can.

"Guess he kind of left that up to me."

"Kind of, huh?"

Frank looked away just as the ambassador reentered the room.

Rocky followed his glance. "We should be in the bubble for this. But fuck it. I'll send the cable. Eyes only Brzezinski. That may keep it away from the cowboys at Langley, but you can bet Pete Howard'll see it. And push Brzezinski to get on with the Brits. Good idea." He punched Frank on the arm, a short punch but hard enough to sting. "You reel in that KGB bastard and keep me in the loop on it, I don't give a shit if you do get Bunker fragged."


To Frank's surprise, Bunker wanted to get in some work. "Look, do you have copies of that material at the house? The civic action proposal and the atmospherics cable?"

"Ah, no," lied Frank, as he eased the Fiat through the embassy gates.

"Regulations, you know," said Gus.

"Well, all that's going to change," said Bunker. "I'm cleared to take certain levels of nonclassified documents to work on at home. I do it all the time at Langley. It makes no sense not to do it here. I've requisitioned a typewriter and a false-bottom desk for the house. They'll be in place tomorrow. Tonight we'll have to go by the office and pick up copies. I want to put in some work, and I don't want to sit around that office. I could use a glass of wine."

Frank began to wish he hadn't lied about the copies he and Gus had been working on at the house, copies that he'd tucked into a T-shirt in the middle of the T-shirts in the middle drawer of the chest of drawers in his new room. Which reminded him.

"Ah, Fred?"

"Uh-huh?"

"I'd been meaning to ask. Are you okay in the room you're in?"

"Well, as a matter of fact . . . Tom Troy said that was your room before I got here."

"Yeah, it was. But it's the nicest room in the place, and Gus and I figured that as head of the team . . ."

"Nonsense. I mean, I appreciate that, but if you'd gotten comfortable in that room . . ."

"Well, yeah, I kinda liked it," said Frank. "Kinda got used to it."

"Let's skip the fact that I'm head of the KUSTAFF team. I don't want to push you out of your room."

"Okay. We can switch whenever you want."

"Tonight," said Bunker.


"This is very good," said Bunker.

To cover Frank's lie, they'd detoured by the office at Dowshan Tappeh and picked up copies of the atmospherics cable and civic action program. After snacking on leftovers, Bunker had decided to work on the atmospherics cable first. He'd downed a half-full water glass of wine before he'd begun work, poured another, and then barely touched it. Frank noticed he read like an editor, not a censor, crossing out very little, using quick, incisive strokes to make what Frank hoped were minor changes.

"I hate passive verbs," said Bunker.

"Funny," said Frank. "So do Gus and I. We thought we got most of 'em."

"You missed a few." The pen flicked, and Frank could sense the excision of the "was" from "was thought" or the "is" from "is believed." "And I don't like this business about nobody displaying photos of Stalin or Brezhnev or this *Tudeh* party guy. It stands out like a sore thumb. What you don't see. Everything else is what you do see, smell, hear." The pen made a long, scratching sound.

"I have to admit," said Frank, "I wondered about that. I guess I was trying to make a point."

"Sometimes when we try to make a point, we raise our voices," said Bunker, "and lose points." He shook his head. "This is very difficult. This material about the generals not having rank-and-file support for a coup. But if that's what the source said, I think it should stay in."

Frank and Gus made a pretense of checking over the civic action proposal, but both were too fascinated by the way Bunker worked to pay much attention to their own chore. All three ignored the wine glasses now beaded with moisture that spread onto the Formica-topped table.

The lights went out.

"Shit," said Bunker, slamming down his pen.

"Flashlights and candles at the ready," said Gus as he moved into a drill he and Frank had perfected. In less than a minute, they had four candles flickering around the table and two high-powered flashlights standing on end, beamed toward the ceiling.

"Creates a nice atmosphere, don't you think, for reading an atmospherics cable?" said Gus.

"Not for me," said Bunker. "I need new glasses as it is. In this light . . ."

Frank peered at his watch. "Like I thought. Couple minutes after nine. Anwar told me the electrical workers cut the power every night at nine when the government's news program comes on. Strikers at the television stations shut down two of the three channels. But when the news programs, which Anwar says are mostly propaganda, come on, the electrical workers turn the power off."

"Is that in your cable?" asked Bunker.

"No."

"It should be. From what I've seen so far, I won't be changing much. I'd like to get this off tomorrow, but I want you want to add that bit about television. It fits in well with what you wrote about Khomeini's cassettes becoming the only mass media that matters. That's brilliant, and new. You'll be the first to report that."

"We tried to report it a while ago," said Gus, "but there was some skepticism downtown."

"I see. I think with my imprimatur the station will transmit this one. Tomorrow's Friday. Second day of the Islamic weekend, right?"

"Right," chorused Gus and Frank.

"We'll have time to finalize your cable, get it off, maybe finalize that civic action package."

Hard-charging, thought Frank. He'd begun to like the guy.


They set up shop in Rushmore's office before eight, and Frank made his additions to the atmospherics cable. Gus retyped it while Frank and Bunker worked on the civic action proposal. Both documents went into the noon delivery to the embassy with a covering memo from Bunker.

"I have to hand it to you," said Gus. "You give good memo—and good editing."

"I'm a good bureaucrat. It's about knowing how to get things done within the system."

How different, thought Frank, from Rushmore's credo of getting the job done despite the job.

"You did a fine job on that atmospherics cable," said Bunker, slipping off his glasses and rubbing the bridge of his nose. "On the other hand, the civic action proposal, it's filler, isn't it?"

"A way of keeping our foot in the door," said Gus. "General Merid is hot for it, and to tell you the truth, without it we wouldn't have much to talk about."

"It's not very imaginative, or even up-to-date on current civic action thinking."

"We figured we had an audience of one," said Gus. "General Merid. He had some civic action training in the States. We wanted to play to what he'd memorized. No surprises."

"Maybe I can embellish a bit, verbally. Just to keep the ball bouncing."

Mormons can enjoy a glass of wine at dinner, thought Frank. Mormons can say "shit" when the lights go out. Mormons can embellish. Welcome to the club. All religions are one. Then why are we always killing each other?

# CHAPTER ELEVEN

A h," said General Merid, "Chicken Colonel Bunker, I presume?" He laughed at his own joke. Frank and Gus smiled. Bunker did not.

"Not quite," said Bunker. "Just a light colonel. Lieutenant colonel."

"Yes," said the general. He glanced at Gus.

Gus turned to Bunker. "Ah, Fred, the general and I had a little joke about chicken colonels."

"Shall we get down to business?" Bunker launched a replay of the name, rank, and background routine they had run through at their first Saturday meeting two weeks before, only this time Frank and Gus were on the sidelines. Bunker detailed his fictitious rise through the ranks of the army after ROTC at Brigham Young University. Frank wondered if he had stayed in the military long enough to advance beyond lieutenant, but Bunker obviously had worked hard on developing his military legend. Too hard. Eyes glazed as he droned on. He plowed into his peroration, coming down hard on civic action experience in Laos, and, Frank thought, segued rather well into introducing their proposal.

"Ah, yes," said General Merid. "This is the moment we've been waiting for."

"We have copies for each of you," said Bunker, reaching into the battered oversize brief case Frank had provided. "I realize you've all been through this in draft form, but if you'll just glance at the executive summary up front you'll see we've newly prioritized key items, development of water supply and sewage systems, efficient distribution of gasoline and cooking oil, creation of an armed forces newspaper and broadcast network . . ."

Frank noticed the beak-nosed navy man staring at Bunker. He turned to Frank with a puzzled expression, then fixed his dark eyes again on Bunker.

During their midmorning tea break, Bunker announced that at the end of their meeting he would like to spend five minutes privately with each of them discussing their military backgrounds in more detail. The navy man, Munair Irfani, called Frank aside, turned his back to the others, and said softly, "Who is this person?"

"Well, he kind of told us, at length, didn't he?" said Frank.

"Do we need him?"

"Definitely. He's head of our team."

"Why are you here? It makes no sense. But at least you and the other gentleman try to understand. This one . . ."

"Give him some time," said Frank.

"There is no time," said Munair. Up close, the eyes pierced even more intently. The garlic on his breath intensified the aura that his stark features and dark stare created at a distance. Frank noticed that dried blood flecked the bump on his forehead. "Have you looked around Tehran?"

"Not much," said Frank. "Except from the air, coming in."

"What did you see?"

"A city in flames."

"Not even," said Munair. "You saw a city in smoke, embers, a funeral pyre. It has hardly begun, but it is already over. You are senseless here."

"That's why we're here," said Frank. "Because we have been senseless here. No ears. No eyes. No sense of what's really going on. We need ears and eyes."

"That is true," said Munair. "And we might have helped you to see. But not this . . . light colonel." He returned to his place at the table.

Anchors aweigh, thought Frank. I guess we just lost the navy.

Anwar also took him aside. "Are they replacing you?"

Frank shook his head.

"Then why have they sent another?"

Frank shrugged.

"Do not take him near my cousin and the other *homafaran*."

General Merid managed only to raise his eyebrows in Frank's direction as Bunker loomed over him in a far corner after the meeting ended.


"I thought that was a fairly shipshape meeting." Bunker sat up front with Ali, half turning to talk over his shoulder to Frank and Gus.

"Quite shipshape," said Gus.

"Yes," added Frank. Their colleagues' reactions to Bunker worried him. Except for Munair, they had been polite but very guarded.

"Can we delay lunch for a bit?" said Bunker. "I want to get off a detailed Field Information Report on everything that went down. Particularly my conversation at the end with General Merid. He was very forthcoming about my request to . . ."

"That's great," interrupted Gus. "Tell us about that. After you finish your FIR."

"Oh, yes," said Bunker, glancing at Ali, who kept his eyes fixed on the traffic.

———

"Don't you trust our driver?" asked Bunker, once Frank had closed the door behind them in the quiet confines of Rushmore's office.

"I don't trust anyone," said Gus.

"That sounds fairly paranoid."

"For a spy," answered Gus, "paranoia is reality. Other than that, I like Ali. He just lost a son in a dustup down in Isfahan. I feel for him. I might trust him with my life, but I don't trust anybody, not even myself, with information he doesn't need to know."

"Sound operational procedure," said Bunker. "I stand corrected."

"Don't stand corrected," said Gus. "Sit down and write your cable."


Frank went to work peeling and slicing apples after Gus and Bunker had gone to bed. He'd shopped the local market, glad to find both nutmeg and cinnamon. He'd cheated with a prepared crust mix picked up at the commissary. An old-fashioned round glass milk bottle from a local shop served as his flour-coated rolling pin. It had been so long since he'd done any baking, he wanted to try a practice pie before preparing another for Anwar. The oven warmed the kitchen, and he sat close to it, sipping coffee, thinking, wondering about Lermontov, about the military's plans for a coup, about his problems with Rocky, and about the pressure from Langley to recruit Anwar. He recognized the padding of Gus's feet on the stairs and looked up.

"What the hell are you doing?"

"Thinking."

"Do your thought patterns always smell this good?" Gus stood in the doorway, bleary-eyed without his glasses, his sparse hair standing on end, a robe loosely tied over his pajamas.

"I finally decided to try that apple pie I've been threatening to bake," said Frank.

"At this hour?"

"Well, if it comes out a disaster, I figured I could chuck it and no one would ever know."

"Doesn't smell like a disaster."

They stayed up, waiting for the pie to finish baking, waiting for it to cool.

"It's for Anwar," said Frank. "He told me he loved real American apple pie. I figured you could offer it to him. Not this one. If this comes out okay, I'll bake another one for him."

"Why me?" said Gus. "You're the baker. Why not you?"

"'Cause headquarters said you should pick up the recruiting, remember?"

"I remember, but if I was Anwar I might think it was kinda strange. He talks to you about apple pie, and I show up with pie and a pitch to recruit him."

"I've got a hunch you'll do better with apple pie than with trying to pay him."

"Is this your own private philosophy of recruiting?"

"I guess," said Frank.

"How many folks have you recruited that way?"

"A few. Not many."

"I bet not many. I hope you don't mind if I try apple pie—and some cash."

"Let's try the pie first," said Frank.

Frank served the first runny, still-steaming slice to Gus. "We should've let it cool more."

For a moment he forgot about Anwar and thought again about Lermontov, wondering if, during his time in the States, he'd developed a taste for apple pie. He thought about the British ambassador and MI6. About Rocky's cable to Brzezinski. He cut a slice of pie for himself. How long do we have to let it cool?

That evening, in the American cafeteria at Dowshan Tappeh, Anwar joined him.

"So, what is this great surprise you whispered to me about?"

"Well, I don't have it with me. It's too good for here. But I do have a real apple pie for you. I wondered if maybe I could invite you for dinner, maybe tomorrow night."

"You? And me? With Gus and Light Colonel Bunker?"

"Well, I'm working on the seating arrangements."

"May I invite you instead to my home? My wife would like to meet you."

"Just me?"

Anwar nodded.

"How about Gus?"

"Please. Just you and the apple pie."

"When?"

"As you suggested. Tomorrow evening."

"You're sure tomorrow will be all right with your wife?" asked Frank.

"Of course. If I say it. She's not an American wife."

I should have known better, thought Frank.

"Let us meet here," said Anwar. "Same time. I will drive you and bring you back."

Bunker had been busy. An Iranian crew working under Bill Steele's direction had moved an IBM Selectric with a swivel chair and typing table and a cedarwood chest of drawers with a false bottom into the house. The typing setup graced the downstairs front room. The chest went into Bunker's back room upstairs. Frank noticed that an impressive radio sat on top of it.

"Shortwave?" he asked.

"Shortwave," Fred answered. "Surprised you didn't bring one over."

"Well, I came over kind of sudden," said Frank, who had never owned a shortwave radio.

Bunker had requisitioned himself a Browning nine millimeter with a spare magazine and a box of shells. He stashed the Browning in the false bottom of the chest along with copies of their civic action program.

"Sorry I wasn't able to requisition weapons for you. I made the request through Bill Steele since all that's under his purview as the substation's chief of security. But word came back that it's been quite a while since you were checked out on the Browning, Gus, and Frank, they say you were never checked out."

"Just as well," said Gus. "There's nobody I particularly want to shoot anyway."

Frank just nodded. He'd had a Browning in Zambia, and he'd picked up another on his trek into Angola and had several weapons in Ethiopia, but he had not obtained them through regular channels. He did not want to explain all that to Bunker. But Bunker's bureaucratic skills in getting things done again impressed him.

Bunker's anticipation of the changes requested by their Jayface counterparts in the civic action program proved accurate—not extensive but enough to require a complete retyping of the first section they had worked over the previous afternoon. It would be a breeze for a professional agency secretary, but as tensions increased, all the secretaries had left for home.

"I suggest we ask the Iranians for secretarial help on this," said Bunker.

"Good thinking," said Gus.

"After all, it's not exactly classified material," added Bunker.

"Very good thinking," said Frank. Otherwise, I'd be the one retyping the crap.

Bill Steele had brought a heavy load of mail from the embassy. The take included two letters and a package for Gus, a letter from Jackie and even one from Jake for Frank, and a letter for Bunker that his wife must have mailed before he left. Gus and Fred tore into their mail, retreating to opposite corners of the room. Frank wanted to wait till evening when he was alone in his room to read his letters. He'd already squared his plans for having dinner at Anwar's home with Gus and Bunker. It had been sticky. Gus had the assignment of recruiting Anwar, but Anwar had invited only Frank. Frank had tried to make light of it.

"What can I tell you? He said he only wanted me and my apple pie."

"It makes sense," said Bunker. "You've had the entree. If it's going to work, you'll have to be the one to take it to the next level. Once he bites, you can turn it over to Gus to close."

"Makes sense," said Gus, his back still turned. He said nothing more.


Anwar lived in a neighborhood new to Frank yet not far from Frank and Gus's house off Damavand. Their street was just north of the sprawling air base. Anwar lived on the south side of Dowshan Tappeh, off a street that bore the same name as the neighborhood, Niru-ye-Haval.

"We could live in military housing, but my wife prefers being close to her family. They are Baha'i and very wealthy. We have a separate house but in a compound that is all her family."

"I hope you like your in-laws."

"I do."

Though their drive was a short one, Anwar had taken the precaution of dressing in civilian clothes. Even in this neighborhood, Frank suspected, a man in military uniform with a foreign passenger might attract hostile curiosity.

"But you're not a Baha'i, are you?" said Frank.

"Oh, no. I'm a reasonably devout Twelver Shi'ite. Not as devout as our friend Munair, but devout."

"No knots on your forehead?"

"Correct." He smiled, more relaxed than Frank had seen him. "That is . . . uniquely Munair."

"I read that the National Front leader, Mahdi Bazargan, also has a bump like that."

"True, he does. Like Munair, he sees no contradiction between being a devout nationalist and devout Muslim."

"Some of the foreign journalists say Bazargan may be Khomeini's prime minister."

"Perhaps. Perhaps there may be many prime ministers in the next few months. But there will be only one ruler."

"Khomeini?"

"Why is it so hard for you Americans to see that?"

"Because we never heard of him until a few months ago."

"You are so blind," said Anwar.

"You are so right," answered Frank.

"You know you lost Munair."

"Lost him? How?"

"You've noticed how he studies you. When I told him I had decided to trust you, he seemed to accept that," said Anwar. "Until Colonel Bunker arrived."

"Oh."

"Admiral Hayati, Kazem Hayati, who is in charge of the navy, instructed Munair to cultivate you. They are very close, but now Munair doesn't think you can be trusted."

"How can we change his mind?"

"We? You talk as though you've recruited me."

"You've been helpful."

"Not that helpful. You've put Munair in a difficult position. He cannot disobey his admiral, but his belief in Islam makes it difficult for him to trust Americans."

"I guess I can understand that," said Frank.

"Good," said Anwar. "And perhaps I can help you with Munair."

The gated compound reminded Frank of similar enclosures in Ethiopia. Anwar dimmed his lights as a guard peered through a small window in the metal gate. In a moment the gate swung open. Anwar pulled past an opulent main house and off to the right where three more modest dwellings clustered around a lopsided shed that served as a garage. Anwar ignored the garage. He parked alongside the farthest of the houses and led the way inside.

"Mina. We're here."

Nothing could have prepared Frank for Mina. Tiny, beaming, miniskirted, booted, wearing a cashmere sweater, she bounced down the hallway.

"Oh I'm so glad so glad so glad Anwar finally brought you. We never see anyone the least interesting these days and Anwar's told me so much about you and you sound so interesting and I'm so glad he finally brought you. Hi. I'm Mina."

"And I'm . . . breathless. How do you do?"

"Frank Sullivan. I know who you are. You aren't breathless. Come in. Come in."

"I have a gift. Something for dessert. I know Anwar's looking forward to it."

She peeked under the tin foil. "A pie. Apple pie?"

"It's been in my refrigerator. It will taste better if you can warm it up a bit."

"You baked it yourself?" Mina asked. She didn't wait for an answer. "Anwar's always, always asking me to get cook to bake an apple pie, but cook hasn't the faintest. I'll be right back. Anwar, take his coat." Pie in hand, she retreated up the hallway.

"She's quite mad," said Anwar. "And I must admit, though a man shouldn't say such things about his wife, I love her very much."

"Congratulations. And of course you should say such things about your wife."

"Thank you."

He hung Frank's parka in a wardrobe closet and led the way into a sparsely furnished but comfortable dining room. The house proved more spacious than it looked from the outside—a long hallway and wide staircase, high ceilings and hardwood floors. A settled, flickering fireplace warmed what might otherwise have seemed a chill elegance.

"We have some very fine Russian vodka and some even finer Iranian caviar."

"Two of my favorite commodities in all this world. But I must admit I haven't had any caviar since we came to Iran."

"Like many things, it is hard to come by these days."

"Poof," said Mina, coming back into the room. "My family has it stored by the case. Since you brought us apple pie, we'll send you home with a couple of pounds."

"Mina. We have a tin. Not pounds."

"I'll run across later and fetch some from auntie's pantry. But not now." She pronounced "auntie" as most Americans would, "antie." At other moments, her accent had sounded British.

"How do you like your vodka?"

"Well, if I'm going to be having it with caviar, just plain would be fine."

"You sound like a Russian," said Anwar.

"No, but I learned how to drink vodka with caviar from a Russian."

"Was she very beautiful?" asked Mina, spooning caviar onto a salad plate.

"Mina, you're being rude."

"I'm not rude. Just inquisitive."

"He was very big," said Frank, "and not at all beautiful."

"No matter what people say, Iranian caviar goes very well with *barbari*."

Mina Non Sequitur, thought Frank. And nonstop. He had already discovered the flat Iranian bread that tasted wonderful fresh from the oven but tended to stale quickly. The piece he broke off felt warm and soft. He used it as a spoon to scoop up a heavy portion of caviar. The combination of tastes melted the tensions that had stiffened his neck and shoulders.

"Wash it down," said Anwar, handing him a water glass half full. He raised his own glass. *"Na zdarovye."*

"Now who sounds like a Russian?"

"They are our neighbors, after all."

They sipped their Stolichnaya and settled themselves in straight-backed chairs semicircling a compact glass coffee table.

Anwar glanced at his wife, smiling. It seemed he couldn't look her way without smiling. "Mina doesn't drink."

"I'm surprised you do."

"We're at home," said Anwar.

"We were more at home in America," said Mina.

"That's true. Mina is American, you know."

"No," said Frank. "I didn't know."

"Born and mostly bred." Her eyes, huge, almond shaped and hued, danced to the leaping rhythms of the fire. "My parents live in Los Angeles."

"I thought," Frank hesitated, "I thought the house next door . . ."

"Oh, it's my father's house, but Ameh Nasserine, my father's sister, and her terrible tribe occupy it."

"We met in Texas," said Anwar. "I was in training and Mina was at university. Her father was not too happy about it all, especially about my bringing his daughter back to Iran."

"The Baha'i—my family is Baha'i—have always been persecuted in Iran."

"Not under the Shah," said Anwar.

"Yes, under the Shah. The Shah himself has been good to many Baha'i, but what he does hasn't changed what others do."

"You're right," said Anwar, nodding solemnly, then smiling.

"I know so little," said Frank.

"We can change that," said Mina. "You can come every night for the next month and I'll give you the standard lecture course, Baha'i 101, and you'll learn . . ."

"Mina," said Anwar, laughing. "Major Sullivan may have a few other things to do."

"Oh, I know, but it's been so long since another man noticed me, since another man's been able to notice me." She turned to Frank. "It's been months since I've been able to go out of the house without a great coat down to my shoe tops and a chador to cover my hair and my hands and most of my face except maybe one eye to try to see where I'm going. Don't misunderstand me." She reached out and touched Frank's knee. "Anwar is a wonderful husband. A woman couldn't ask for a better man, more affectionate, more attentive. And he's wonderful in bed."

"Mina, please."

"But once in a while it is rather nice to be noticed by someone other than your husband. Just noticed. I'm not talking about any mad affair. Just noticed. Please come more often."

I am breathless, thought Frank. He smiled and began to understand Anwar's reflexive grin whenever he looked Mina's way. "I'd love to," he managed to say, "but Anwar's right. There are some other things I have to be doing."

"Oh you men." She must know her pout is charming, thought Frank. "You're all alike. Like Anwar with his air force and his meetings and his great concern about the Shi'ite revolution. Poof."

She popped up from her chair, turned, and headed for the hallway. She didn't flounce, but, sure they were watching her exit, she did twitch her tiny, well-rounded butt.

Mina was not gone long. Frank heard her boot heels tapping toward them on the hardwood hallway floor. The sound reassured him. Tapping. Not stomping. If she'd been angry, her anger had melted, and the smile she turned on them as she entered the room made both men respond with schoolboy grins.

"Dinner isn't served just yet," she said, settling into her chair, "but it will be soon. Even cook seems to realize this is a special occasion. Please have some more caviar and please come see us again. Soon."

Frank, more than content with vodka and caviar, followed Mina's polite lead and with a teaspoon dropped a modest black mound onto the no longer warm but still fresh *barberi*. Then he did it again. He could wait all night for dinner.

"I couldn't spare you Mina, of course," said Anwar, "But at least we spared you the children."

"Oh, wow," said Frank, swallowing a mouthful of caviar too quickly. "You needn't have. How old are they?"

"Four and six," said Mina. "I could go fetch them."

"Mina, please. We have things to discuss it would be better for the children not to hear."

"Please," said Frank. "I'd like to meet your children. I have a son of my own, eleven now, and I miss him very much."

"Then you're married," said Mina.

"No. Separated. Divorced," said Frank.

"Why Major Sullivan," said Mina. "You're blushing."

"It . . . it must be the fire," said Frank.

"I'll fetch the children." And she was gone.


An uncomfortable silence eddied between Frank and Anwar. They toyed with caviar and vodka, and Frank wondered if Anwar felt as awkward as he did. Neither had ever spoken of their children before.

Mina seemed to have been gone only a moment. Frank looked up to see her framed in the doorway, a hand on the shoulder of each child. A lovely family portrait, but troubling. He glanced at Anwar, who should be in the picture.

"Our son is Anwar. Another Anwar," said Mina. "I understand you know Anwar the Taller. Anwar our son was born in America. Our daughter, we call her Mina Two, was born here."

Frank looked to Anwar, then back to Mina and the children. He hadn't realized how much Anwar and his wife looked alike. The same spare frame and sharp features, almond eyes and olive complexions framed by neatly cropped dark hair. Seeing the children brought it home.

"I'm the older," said young Anwar, bowing very formally. Mina curtsied.

"You're a very beautiful family," he said to Anwar.

"Thank you," said Mina.

"Are you in the air force?" asked her daughter.

"No," said Frank. "I mean, yes. But the American Air Force. Not the Iranian Air Force like your father."

"Do you have children?"

She's as inquisitive as her mother, thought Frank, glancing and smiling at Mina.

"Yes. I have a son. He's eleven."

"That's older," said young Anwar.

"Why didn't you bring him to dinner?"

"Oh, he's way off in America."

"Silly. No one brings their children to Tehran these days," said the solemn Anwar. "It isn't safe."

"Can you take us to America?" asked his sister.

The children lingered. The four-year-old Mina settled on Frank's lap while her brother, still standing, grilled him about America.

"I was born there, you know, but I don't remember it much."

"Perhaps one day soon," said his mother, "you may get to live there again, and meet Major Sullivan's son."

"Will your son think I'm too young to play with?"

"No. No," said Frank. "I think you'll get along just fine."

"What is your son's name?"

"Jake," said Frank. "His name is Jake."


"You're wonderful with children," said Mina, coming back into the room. It had taken some insistence on Anwar's part to get her to take the children upstairs. "Your son must miss you."

"I'm afraid he doesn't get to spend much time with me." He glanced at Anwar. "I guess men are out of the picture too often."

"Of course," said Mina. "You leave civilization to women. Such barbarians."

"We aren't all that bad," said Anwar.

"Poof. If it weren't for women, there'd be no society, no culture. Not even families. Just war and religion. Especially here. At least in America our children would have a better chance to grow up civilized. But I worry about Mina. She was born here. Does that make her an Iranian?"

"It may," said Frank. "But she has an American mother. That makes her an American. You should run it through the embassy. Get her an American passport."

"I've already done that," said Mina.

I should have known, thought Frank.

"Then you won't have any problem," said Mina. "Getting us all to America?"

I'm being played, thought Frank. He smiled. And I'm enjoying it.

"Anwar told me you've lived in many countries. So I had cook prepare some specially Persian things. He wanted to cook American, but he followed my orders. I hope you don't mind?"

"I can always cook American for myself," said Frank, but his expectations sank when Hamid entered the room. Frank thought of the invariably sodden *chelakebab* and stale snacks he served at Supreme Commander's Headquarters.

"You recognize him?" said Anwar.

Frank nodded.

"Don't worry. He does what he has to do at work. Hamid cannot read or write, but he speaks and cooks in several languages. Isn't that so?"

Hamid nodded and began serving. They remained semicircled around the coffee table, ignoring the large oval dining room table behind them. Hamid set out individual plates of salad greens decorated with radishes cut like roses and miniature carrots spread like a fan, separate bowls of yogurt, and a tray they shared containing mint, leeks, basil, and other herbs Frank could not identify. To Frank's regret, Hamid removed the caviar, but only as far as the dinning room table, which he used as a serving stand.

Still silent, Hamid left them.

"I hope you enjoy," said Mina.

"I am. It all looks much better than what Hamid serves us at work."

"Yes, Hamid," said Anwar. "I notice your friend Commander Simpson talks to him."

"Maybe he's trying to negotiate something better for lunch," said Frank.

"You should warn Commander Simpson to be cautious with Hamid," said Anwar.

"Really?"

"As I told you and Commander Simpson, Hamid reports to *Savak*. He watches over us all during the day, because we are military officers, and, since Mina's family are Baha'i, he watches us in the evening, but not for *Savak*. In the evening he works for J2, military intelligence. I understand Mossad and the GRU have also tried to recruit him. I'm surprised you haven't."

"I had no idea," said Frank. "What are his languages?"

"Farsi, Arabic, French, English, of course, and, interestingly enough, Russian."

"Oh?" Frank wondered if Gus knew that Hamid spoke Russian.

"He also speaks Kurdish," said Mina. "I've heard him with some of the other servants."

"He's an Azari," said Anwar. "Originally from a poor area somewhere between Baku in Soviet Azerbaijan and Tabriz."

"Maybe you're right," said Frank, smiling. "Maybe we should recruit him." He watched as Anwar and Mina glanced at each other.

"You could do better," said Mina.

Hamid returned. He placed a huge tray on the table behind them. He cleared the salad and served plates of green rice, laced with mint, basil, onions, and leeks from a steaming earthenware pot. He added to each plate slabs of fried chicken and onions, then placed on their crowded table two bowls of a stewlike sauce, which Mina identified as *khoreshe*. Both involved lamb, one with eggplant and tomatoes; the other with tomatoes, onions, and what Frank took to be chickpeas.

"It has pleased me," said Hamid, bowing, "to have prepared for you in the Persian style this humble meal. Enjoy, with God's blessing."

"*Inshallah,*" said Anwar.

"*Inshallah,*" echoed Mina.

"Thank you," said Frank.

They ate with just their hands and the thin, pancakelike bread to wrap their food.

"I hate to tell you," said Mina, "but there's more. A saffron rice that's very special. Hamid will be very disappointed if we don't gorge ourselves on it."

"Save some room for the apple pie," said Frank.

"I will," said Anwar.

Hamid, possibly calling on his knowledge of Kurdistan, made coffee in the Turkish style, but, at Frank's request, his came without sugar. Hamid had warmed the apple pie.

When Hamid had left them, Anwar said, "This is wonderful." He took another forkful. "You really do know how to corrupt a man, don't you?"

"It's a great American tradition."

"Khomeini is right. You are the Great Satan."

"Official America doesn't believe in God or Khomeini," said Frank. "All we worry about is the Soviets."

"Don't you know anything about the history of this part of the world?" said Mina sharply. "Long before Soviets, Russia has always wanted this part of the world. It doesn't matter if they call themselves Soviets or czarists. Iran, Afghanistan, a gateway to the subcontinent, warm-water seaports, all the way back, at least to . . ." Her flash of anger had taken him by surprise. ". . . to Catherine the Great."

"Catherine the Great Satan," said Frank.

"Exactly," said Anwar. "And it's a great pity, the way we have turned against America."

"It's true," said Mina. "You were loved here, more than any other foreigners. For a while."

"You will think we are fickle," said Anwar. "But after World War II, when the Russians occupied us in the north, you forced them out, and you forced the British in the south to give up their control of our oil. You freed us from the two colonial powers who had fought over us for more than a hundred years, and, for a time at least, you were loved for it."

"What happened?"

"1953," said Mina.

Frank nodded. He knew enough of Iran's history to recognize the date of the coup that toppled the government of Mohammed Mosaddeq, the prime minister who had attempted to nationalize Iran's oil industry.

"Do you know the name of the street you follow most of the way when you go to the palace?" asked Anwar.

"Pahlavi?"

"That is its name just now. And you know what that name signifies?"

"The Shah," said Frank. "The Shah's family name."

"The name the Shah's father chose when he made himself Shah. Till then, he had been Reza Khan. Pahlavi was an ancient Iranian language. Before Farsi. Before Persia. Before Islam. Reza Khan made people stop calling our country Persia. He wanted to go back to Aryan times and said we must be called Iran. He was much influenced by Ataturk, who back then had turned Turkey into the secular state it is today. Reza Khan gave freedom to women and tried to forbid them to wear the chador. He wanted men to give up their prayer caps and wear fedoras like a European. Can you imagine a man like Munair wearing a fedora?"

"No," said Frank. He couldn't suppress a grin. "I guess I can't."

"As I told you before, that's why he has that knot on his forehead. From touching his head to the tiles of the mosque when he prays to Mecca. He couldn't do that wearing a hat with a brim."

"Today, no one wears fedoras," said Mina. "Not even Americans. But here women have to wear the chador or be stoned. The Shah's father did away with that fifty years ago."

"But it wasn't just about funny hats and chadors," said Anwar. "Reza Khan was also much impressed by what he considered his Aryan brothers, the Germans, because the Germans fought our enemies, the British and the Russians. That's why England and Russia invaded us in 1941 and replaced Reza Khan with his son, who has been Shah ever since."

"What Anwar means to be telling you," said Mina, sharply, "is that the street, Pahlavi, used to be called Mosaddeq."

"You must forgive me," said Anwar. "Sometimes I get carried away by our history."

"Major Sullivan, Great Satan," said Mina, suddenly very soft and feminine again. "Can you take us to America?"

"Me?"

"No, I was asking Mohammed Mosaddeq." Again, anger flashed, but now only in her eyes. Her voice remained gentle.

"Why do you want to go to America?"

"So I can be a woman." She said it softly, eyes on her plate. She raised her eyes to his. "So I can be me. Without a *chador*."

"Anwar?"

"I don't want to be a woman. Or wear a fedora. But I would like to be myself."

"You can't here?"

"No." They said it together.

"Where would you go? What would you do?"

"I have friends in Texas," said Anwar. "Mina has relatives, her parents and many relatives, in Los Angeles."

"No," said Mina. "We should go to Washington. Texas is too much like— not enough like Paris or London or Rome or New York. And Los Angeles, I don't want to be surrounded by my family. Anwar can be a consultant in Washington. Washington needs people like him who understand the Iranian military and speak Farsi. And me, little Mina, I want to go to Washington and work for CIA."

"Say what?"

"You heard what I said. I'm an American, so I could work for CIA. And America needs people like me and Anwar."

"That's true," said Frank, "but I'm not sure America knows that. And I have a hunch Iran needs people like you and Anwar even more than America does."

"I don't care," said Mina. Her thin features contracted, lips not pouting but pursed; her sparkling eyes darkled and narrowed. "I want to be American, and I want to be beautiful. And I want everyone to know it."

"You are," said Anwar. "You are already American and very beautiful."

And you must be a very tough woman to live with, thought Frank.

"No," said Mina. "Not here. I am too hard, too harsh. Too harassed." It was another of her odd inflections. She pronounced it "hair-assed." "Too shrouded. In America I could be happy." Her eyes melted toward Anwar. "In America I always could be beautiful for you."

Frank saw that Anwar was tiring. He wanted to get home, but he also hoped to outlast the indefatigable Mina. He did not. But finally, Anwar sent Mina off to bed. "Wait up for me," he said, "I want to have a word alone with Frank."

Mina obeyed. She might be American, but, as Anwar said, she was not an American wife.

"Speak to Hamid before you leave," said Mina. "He has some caviar for you to take home. Good night."

They watched her leave, and Anwar closed the double doors that led to the hallway. He went to a stereo system and put on, to Frank's amazement, a Billie Holiday tape. "I'm pullin' through and it's because of you . . ."

Anwar sat so close to Frank at the coffee table that their knees touched. "I have tried to help you as much as I can. Can you help us?"

"You should talk to my friend Gus. He has more knowledge of these things than I do."

"Can he help us?"

"I don't know. You've been so helpful to us here that, to tell you the truth, the Americans might do more to help you if you stayed here."

"Help us how?"

"Arrangements can be made."

"The only arrangement that could help us is an arrangement that would get us to America, help us to find a way there. Earn a living. Get our children into school."

"Other arrangements can be made."

"Here? What arrangements? Money? My wife's family is extremely wealthy and more generous than your friends are likely to be. Prestige? What can you do to further the career of a military officer under the Shah when the Ayatollah rules?"

"Will you talk to Gus?"

"Of course. I talk to Gus every day. I like him. But I want to talk to you, and Mina and I want to go to America."

"To tell you the truth, so do I. But I have an assignment here."

"I wonder about you," said Anwar. "Munair may be right about you."

"That's another reason why you're so valuable here," said Frank. "Because you're smart enough to wonder."

"I have something for you. Something from Munair."

"Oh?"

Anwar crossed to the stereo system. He waited till Billie Holiday finished the last chorus of "Strange Fruit," then ejected the tape and replaced it with another cassette. The tape sputtered, then Frank recognized the familiar, raspy voice.

"It is very old," said Anwar. "Munair planned to play it for you himself, and explain it, as a test. But you already failed the test. My cousin has played other tapes for you, but not so old."

"Tell me what he says."

"No need." Anwar retrieved a manila envelope that sat on one of the stereo's speakers. "Here. In his painstaking way, Munair translated it for you. You can read later. It dates from 1967, from Iraq, where Khomeini settled after being exiled for opposing the Status of Forces Treaty the Shah signed with the Americans. Do you know about these things?"

"I'm afraid not," said Frank.

"To be truthful, neither did I. Our schools and government do not educate us about such parts of our history, but Khomeini does."

"He sounds very angry," said Frank, nodding toward the voice that trebled from the speakers.

"Yes. He had much to be angry about. Here, for example, he attacks the man who was then premier, Abbas Hoveida, for extorting money from the merchants of the bazaar to help pay for the Shah's coronation on his fortieth birthday."

"The same Hoveida who was arrested last week?"

"The same," said Anwar. "Listen. Here Khomeini attacks what you call the Status of Forces Treaty. Khomeini had been in and out of prison several times for protesting against the Shah and his corrupt government—but it was because of this, his attack on the Americans, that he was exiled for good in 1964, put on a plane for Turkey. A year later he managed to get to Najaf, a Shi'a holy city in Iraq, where he made this tape.

"You must understand how much he hates America. Because of you Americans and that treaty, he has not been allowed in his own country for fourteen years. Listen, here he tells us the Status of Forces Treaty is a document for the enslavement of Iran. Not only American soldiers but their cooks, mechanics, housekeepers, and drivers they bring with them are exempt from the laws of Islam and of our country. He says our country has become a colony of America as it once was a prisoner of the Russians and British."

"So he's got some history with hating us," said Frank.

"Perhaps, but also he hates Israel," said Anwar, "and the Muslim leaders of countries who allow Israel to exist. When the Shah sent him into exile, Kuwait would not accept him, and he was never really welcome in Turkey and Iraq. Here he says the foreigners will not let Egypt, Iran, Iraq, and Turkey unite. But the duty of Muslim leaders is to unite their thoughts and protect their borders. Had they been united it would not be possible for what he calls a bunch of Jewish thieves to steal Palestine while the Islamic countries slept. He calls on the clergy and army to oppose the Shah's government, the corrupt of the earth, he calls them. Listen. Here he says America seeks to exploit Iran, and to do that America will try to destroy Islam because Islam and the Koran stand as barriers in the path of the Great Satan."

Anwar drove him home. "You trust me enough to let me know where you live?"

"You trusted me enough to take me to your home, right? So, sure, I trust you."

"You shouldn't. Persians love intrigue, conspiracies. We like to play with words. To gossip. To invent stories. It's an old saying among us. You should never trust a Persian. Even me."

"But if I can't trust the man who tells me not to trust Persians, perhaps that means I should trust Persians."

Anwar laughed. "You would make a good Persian. You like to play with words. Perhaps you should never trust yourself."

"Ethiopians have that same saying about themselves."

"It is perhaps a Third World disease. But Hamid, whether he is Persian, Azari, or Russian, be careful of him. J2 and *Savak* will be told that Commander Simpson has spoken to him."

"I figured that, and it's okay. I figured we're all more or less on the same side."

"More or less," said Anwar. "I'm not sure I trust you as much as I used to."

"Don't. And remember, I am the great corrupter."

"The apple pie man."

The I-cash-clothes apple pie man, thought Frank. Exhaustion had fallen over him. His mind spun, but slower and slower, like a top about to fall. He knew he would not read Jackie's and Jake's letters. He knew midnight had passed and another day would begin at six.

Anwar pulled up at the curb. He looked toward the house. "It seems very modest."

"It is."

"Strange. We always think the Great Satan lives in great splendor."

"The grass is always greener," said Frank. "Think about it. America may be a nice place to visit, but would you really want to live there?"

Alone in the quiet kitchen, he poured himself an Absolut and pried open one of the tins of caviar Mina had bestowed on him. He spooned a taste of the caviar, let it dissolve in his mouth, and tried a sip of the vodka. He'd been looking forward to the indulgence, but the pleasure he sought eluded him. Lermontov intruded. Caviar and vodka. So very Russian, here in Iran. But where was Lermontov? Somewhere here in Iran. He feared that Lermontov had become an obsession for him. He remembered Anwar's toast. *Na zdarovye.* Focus on the day job, he told himself. Your cover. Jayface. Anwar. Something about their evening and, however briefly, spending time with Mina and Anwar's children also troubled him, though, and he could not understand why. Okay, he told himself. They made me think about Jake. But I think about Jake a lot. He thought about four-year-old Mina, perched on his lap. He thought about her brother, standing so stiffly before him, questioning him about America. *Will your son think I'm too young to play with?* They made him think about Jake, but more than that, their presence, physical, touchable, brought Jake home. He thought of the family portrait, physical, palpable, mother and children, framed in the doorway, but the father not there. He stared at the caviar that had no taste and the vodka that had no bite. Where am I? Not in the picture. What am I doing here? Chasing a KGB officer. Neglecting my son. Another absent father. Leaving civilization to women. Anwar's family made him think about Jake and about himself. He had to help Anwar get to America and stay close to his children. He knew it was what he wanted for himself. He realized he couldn't walk away from Lermontov, but at least he could help Anwar and his family.

# CHAPTER TWELVE

The week seemed to have evaporated, leaving only a blurred stain on his memory. Their Jayface meetings had become holding patterns. Like an ominously silent air traffic control tower, Colonel Kasravi sent no word.

Anwar had been resistant to Bunker's idea of pleading a family emergency to get himself a visa. "I have a better idea. Mina and the kids take advantage of their American citizenship and fly back to the States. I have my cousin and some of his *homafar* friends get an F-4 fueled up and primed for takeoff at some point when chaos is even worse than usual, and I take off, flying under the radar screen, over the Zagros, staying south of Tabriz into Turkish air space and head for the American base at Incirlik. The Americans arrange clearance for me. I land and ask for asylum."

"As fantasies go, I like it," said Frank. "Otherwise, it sounds like a good formula for getting yourself killed."

Is everyone I know suicidal? he wondered. He never figured out how serious Anwar had been, but Anwar did agree to drop the idea. Two days later, he said he had talked to Mina and they agreed that it would be a good idea to meet with Frank's friend who knew about consular matters.

Belinsky had completed translations, with commentaries, of both the 1967 tape made by Khomeini while exiled in Iraq and of new tapes dealing with the coming *Ashura* ceremonies that Frank had obtained from Anwar the Taller. They discussed them with Rocky in Belinsky's office, and Frank made a special request.

"Chuck, on one of these tapes, my guy told me, Khomeini talks about not confronting the soldiers. Avoiding violence. Putting flowers in the gun barrels."

"Right?"

"Look, on the tape where he talks about all that, could you get a copy made for me? Cued up to that part?"

"What d'ya want it for?" said Rocky.

"I'm not even sure. Maybe to give me a way to talk to the other Anwar, maybe even to Kasravi, about how they think people will react to that."

Belinsky said he would do it if it was okay with Rocky, and Rocky said okay. Belinsky, however, took much more interest in the 1967 tape.

"Fascinating stuff," he said. "The translation your contact gave you was accurate, and all the checks Langley could run verified the tape as authentic, which makes it important. We know what Khomeini's been doing recently, but until now we've had no idea where he's coming from, whether he really hates us or whether all this 'Great Satan' talk is just rhetoric."

"From what my Iranian buddies tell me, even from the tone of his voice, I've got a hunch he truly hates our ass," said Frank. "From what Anwar said the old man feels we got him kicked out of his own country over that Status of Forces business."

"Good to know that," said Rocky. "The folks back home have sent out queries for embassy reaction to some State Department brainstorm to send someone over to Khomeini wherever he is outside of Paris to try to make some kind of accommodation."

"Makes some sense," said Belinsky. "We have a common enemy. The U.S. opposes the Soviets because they're Communists. Khomeini opposes them because they're atheists."

"It might not hurt to try," said Frank. "But I'd be willing to bet a nickel Khomeini would refuse. And go public and tell the world we begged to meet with him and he said flat out, 'Get thee behind me, Great Satan.'"

Rocky's laugh seemed genuine. "You should write his fuckin' speeches."

"I'd love to," said Frank.

"I'd love to have you write my cables, too. Next best thing, I'm gonna steal some of what you said. The ambassador and I have a meet in the morning to coordinate our responses to these latest brainstorms from back home. I'll go do a cable right now backin' up what you had to say about the tapes. Uncle Sam could come away with lot of rotten egg on his face if he tries to cozy up to a pissed-off holy man and the holy man tells Uncle to go fuck himself."

"I don't think the Ayatollah would do that," said Belinsky.

"I'm willin' t' bet he does a whole lot worse before we're outta this." Rocky left them, and Belinsky turned to Frank.

"You really think Khomeini hates us that much?"

"I try not to think," said Frank. "I'm just a reporter."

"And a very good one. The ambassador let me read some of your cables. Wonderful stuff—not just the quality of the reporting, also the quality of the writing, which helps to get good reporting listened to. I wish I wrote half so well. Could I hire you as a ghost writer?"

"I'd like to tell you I'm too expensive, but you could probably get me for cheap. Like just for some free advice."

"Tell me."

"Well, I have a friend. A couple of friends. Husband and wife."

"Iranian?"

Frank nodded.

"Who want to get to America?"

"Correct."

Belinsky shook his head and sighed. "Tell me about your friends. They should make something like two million, six hundred thousand, two hundred and two on my we-want-American-visas list."

Frank wondered if maybe Belinsky was in the visa-selling business. He dismissed the thought. Belisnky didn't deserve such suspicions. "You're saying I should forget it."

"No," said Belinsky. "Tell me their story. Maybe I'll have an idea. But please don't be disappointed if I tell you it's unlikely. Or hopeless. Half of Iran would leave for America tomorrow if they could, up to and including the royal family."

"I know." How well I know. He noticed that a slight pallor had crept back into Belinsky's cheeks. He tried to check Belinsky's eyes, but Chuck looked away.

Frank told him all he could remember about Anwar and Mina and added Bunker's suggestion about trying to find a route other than that of an official defection.

"He's right," said Belinsky. "I try not to know too much about such matters as defectors, but I suspect Fred's right. Baha'i, you say?"

"She is."

"They truly are a persecuted minority here."

"But she's not the problem. She's an American. Born there. The kids are American citizens. He's the Iranian."

"Would he be willing to do what it takes to pretend he's Baha'i, that he converted in order to marry . . . whatever the wife's name is?"

"I think so."

"Find out. If he is, that could make him a candidate for asylum. The position of the Baha'i will be even worse when the mullahs come to power. And a Baha'i who served in the Shah's military and trained in America and who has an American Baha'i wife will be an even more likely candidate for persecution. If he's willing to do what's necessary to establish all that, I'll talk to them. I'm still a consular officer. I'll see what I can do."

"Think maybe, I mean, I don't want to rush things, but think maybe I could take you by their place tomorrow night? I mean, him showing up at the consular office might not be such a good idea."

"You're right," said Belinsky. "I can make it tomorrow night. Can you pick me up at the Damavand? The hotel across the street. I've got an apartment there."

They quickly worked out the details. Frank wondered if he should tell Rocky.

"Frank," said Chuck, "there's something else I should tell you."

Frank waited, trying to study Belinsky's expression, but Belinsky looked away.

"I know I shouldn't tell you this, but I think I should tell you."

"What is it?" said Frank.

"About your Russian friend."

What the fuck is this? wondered Frank. "What Russian friend?"

"The big one," said Belinsky. "Something I reported to . . . something I reported. My source tells me the students plan a big anti-Shah rally at the university Friday evening, starting about seven. After the prayer meeting. Your friend will be involved."

"Who told you this?" asked Frank.

"A sensitive source," said Belinsky. "I know I'm not supposed to know about your friend, but of course I know about him."

"Of course," said Frank. He wondered if Belinsky was setting him up. And for what. "Rocky know about this?"

"I just thought I should tell you."

"Why?"

"My source said so. He isn't a friend of your Lermontov."

What the fuck is going on, wondered Frank. "Your source is a Russian?"

"Well, not Russian, but Soviet. Georgian, actually."

"You think I should go?"

"No. I wouldn't go near that campus if I were you. You look too American."

"You go there."

"I've had some experience with it. I speak Farsi. I know people, people who know I work in the consulate."

And who know you can hand out student visas, thought Frank.

"You know what I mean," said Belinsky.

"Yeah, I heard what you said. So why's your sensitive source want me to go? So I can get my ass blown away?"

"He didn't say you should go. He just thought I should tell you about it."

Frank decided to try again. "Who'd you say this guy was, told you about Lermontov?"

Belinsky again looked away. Frank had wondered if Chuck reported to Rocky, rather than to the ambassador. Now he felt sure of it. But he couldn't figure what this message about Lermontov meant.

"Mind if I ask Rocky about this?"

"He knows," said Chuck.

"What'd he say?"

"He said you need to talk to your Russian friend. But he can't send you. Said it would get his ass in a sling unless he got an okay in advance from the home office, and he knew the home office would shoot it down."

"But he thinks I should go?"

"He can't say so."

This is just great, thought Frank. "He offer up any ideas how I should get there?"

"Well, I'll be going," said Belinsky.

"So I can go with you?"

"It may be risky," said Belinsky, "but I'm taking a risk going to your air force buddy's house."

"So I owe you one."

"It's about doing each other some good," said Belinsky, lowering his head, "with our sources."

"Okay," said Frank. He realized he'd come down too hard on Belinsky. "I'm a bit paranoid, I guess. And it's not always a virtue. Not even for people in our line of work."

"Thanks, Frank." Belinsky turned to face him. "We can't always tell each other everything, right?"

"Yeah," said Frank, thinking about his problems in telling Gus and Bunker what they needed to know. The thought made him shudder as he wondered about what he needed to tell Rocky about taking Belinsky to Anwar's and what Rocky should have told him about seeking out Lermontov at the university.

He drove Belinsky home, all the way straight across Takht-e Jamshid Street from the gates of the embassy to the door of the Damavand at the opposite curb. Light traffic eased their brief crossing.

"Damavand," said Frank, as he pulled up. "What does it mean?"

"The name of this place? It's the name of a mountain, highest mountain in the Elborz. Believe it or not, when this place was built, it was the tallest building in Tehran, so they named it for the highest mountain. Now, it isn't even half the size of those two ugly monsters on either side. But it has its charms. There's a good restaurant, and the embassy maintains a couple of apartments on the top two floors. For visiting firemen, like me."

"At least it's a nice short commute," said Frank. "Tell me. That street that goes by the air base, Dowshan Tappeh, that's also called Damavand, right?"

"Right. In fact, you stay on that, sixty clicks northeast, you come to the mountain."

"I'd love to go to the mountain," said Frank. "But something tells me not this tour."

"No, maybe not this tour," said Belinsky.

"I guess not," said Frank, looking into his eyes. "Hey, Chuck, as a recovering hepatitis victim—I had a real bad bout when I lived in Ethiopia—can I ask you something?"

"Okay."

"Have you been sticking to your diet?"

"To tell you the truth," said Belinsky, looking away, "I've been a shade—a bit depressed. My wife, she went back to the States. Took the kids. Tabriz got pretty bad long before Tehran, but she . . . she was pretty unhappy anyhow. Said I was married to Iran. Didn't have any time for her or the kids. I did everything I could to keep her here. Maybe more things than I should've. But she finally split anyway. She's filing for divorce, and it's sort of true. I am in love with this place. But now Iran is about to divorce me, too. And I've been . . . a bit depressed."

"How long ago did the hepatitis hit?"

"Three, four months back."

"You know you shouldn't be drinking."

"I know. But I kind of wonder what difference it makes."

Dr. Sullivan, thought Frank. From cancer to acromegaly to hepatitis. If I were God, I'd prescribe a trip to America for all three. To Sloan-Kettering for the Shah. To Columbia Presbyterian for Lermontov. And to the best hospital near wherever his wife lives for Chuck Belinsky. But I'm not God. All three, he realized, and Anwar, play more valuable roles here, agents in place. Agents of the Great Satan. In this hell of a place.

"Look," said Belinsky, "I appreciate your taking the time to talk to me. About the hepatitis and all. And I promise, I'll cut back on drinking."

"Don't," said Frank.

"Don't? You mean I should kill myself?"

"That's what you'll do if you cut down. You need to stop. Cut out alcohol. Cut out salt. Anything fried. Don't cut down. Cut out. You know the drill."

"My doctor gave me two pages of do's and don'ts."

"Maybe he did, but he didn't do a good enough job of scaring you. Drinking just a couple of weeks after hepatitis has kicked the shit out of your liver can turn a death wish into reality."

"I notice you take a drink."

"I had hepatitis ten years ago. You had it, what, ten weeks ago? You're killing yourself."

"I better get going. Parked cars make the soldiers nervous."

"When I look in your eyes and see yellow rings, I get nervous."

"I'll be good," said Belinsky, "I promise. See you tomorrow night."


Rocky scanned Frank's request for a trace on Mina. He grunted. "What's she look like?"

"Short, skinny, pointy nose." He shrugged. It was all true. Sort of. "Seems to run her husband, which could be important. And very bright."

"I see the degrees she claims. Get the parents' names. Location. Anything else you can."

"Will do."

"Sure you can?"

He hesitated and said, "Well, I think so." If they want to get to the States, he thought, I damn well know I can. But he didn't want to tell Rocky about all that. At least not until he had a chance to test Belinsky's advice on Anwar.

Rocky, almost as an afterthought, told Frank his atmospherics cable had been sent. "Bunker kept buggin' me about it, so I sent the fuckin' thing. I gotta admit, it was pretty good."

I wish you could admit you want me to put my ass on the line at the university Friday night, thought Frank. And I wish I could tell you I'm taking Belinsky to Anwar's tomorrow night. But you might have to shoot that idea down, right? We need a new mantra. The need to not know.


Frank had discovered basketball. The Dowshan Tappeh gym included a full-size court, used almost exclusively by the Americans. At six, it tended to be empty. Following a one-man shootaround, leaping after rebounds, taking alternate left- and right-hand lay-ups, dribbling back for his next perimeter shot, he kept up a constant flow of motion. But that evening when he got there, he found Fred Bunker already on the court.

"Hey, Frank. Don't tell me you're a basketball player?"

"Okay. I won't. 'Cause I'm not. For me it's just a way to work up a sweat."

"What about . . ." Fred lowered his voice. "Your gym buddies?"

"I get in there, too. Mind if I take some shots?"

"Come on."

Frank took a bounce pass from Fred and, with his knack for envisioning the ball swish through the bottom of the net, sank a short jump shot.

"All right," yelled Fred.

Frank hustled under the basket, grabbed the ball as it fell from the net, sunk a lay-up with his right hand, again grabbed the ball, put up a left-hand lay-up that rattled the rim and went in, and tossed an outlet pass to Fred, who stood at the top of the key.

"For a guy who doesn't play, that wasn't bad," said Fred. He launched a fadeaway jumper that banged high off the rim. Frank grabbed the rebound and passed it back out. Fred dribbled twice to his right and, with a quick right-hand release, hit his shot.

"See if you can do it again," yelled Frank. Fred took his pass and did it again.

Frank soon realized Fred played at a level far beyond his own high school and playground experience.

"You must've played college ball."

"Brigham Young. Believe it or not . . ." He charged the basket, leapt, hung just under the rim, and popped a two-handed shot in. "I'm not but six-three, but I used to be able to dunk."

"That's impressive."

"Well, not only was I younger and in better shape, but I also had twenty pounds less to get up in the air."

"You look in pretty good shape."

"I'd like to get rid of some of this." With both hands he grabbed the flesh that circled his midsection.

"You should join us in the gym."

"No. I'll leave that to you. You're doing too good a job to add . . ." Again he'd turned his voice lower. "I'll stick to the basketball team."

"Team?"

"Yeah. We have a team. Play in what they call the All-American League. Which I don't think is such a great idea of a name, since a lot of the Iranians here speak English. But it's teams of different units of U.S. Air Force groups, and us."

"Us?"

"We're called the Trojans. As in the people who report to Colonel Troy. The regular air force guys hate us. They don't think a bunch of over-the-hill bureaucrats belong in the same league as real live air force jocks. You can imagine what they call the Trojans. They get especially pissed when we beat their ass." The smell of sweat, Frank noticed, had given Fred's vocabulary a funkier tone.

"Think I could get a game?"

"Frank, I don't know. Most of the guys, we all played college ball. Not too many years ago. And we're mostly a lot bigger than you. You could ask Bill Steele. He's our center, coach, and head honcho. You can shoot; I saw that. But I also noticed that right leg of yours."

"Yeah. That thing. Bane of my existence. I don't have a kneecap in that leg. Bone infection when I was real little. Like two. I was in the hospital so long I had to learn to walk all over again when I finally got out."

"This league might be a little rough. Especially since these regular air force guys hate us."

"When do you play next? Maybe I'll just come out and watch."

Fred took a pass from Frank at the top of the key and dribbled hard toward the basket. Frank stepped in front of him, feet planted, arm upraised.

Fred pulled up. "Hey, you could get killed that way. Never step in front of a guy that way."

"I figured you wouldn't want to get called for the charge," said Frank. Besides, he thought, I've always been suicidal.


The next morning he asked Bill Steele about playing. Bill said what Fred had said but urged him to come out and watch, and Frank said he would. Even though a sudden early winter cold snap with a freezing rain had drizzled into his knee and set him limping, he still wanted to post up inside with the big boys. After a dozen years of coping with Lermontov, he still wanted to play out his role without scalp-hungry honchos like Rocky and the would-be intruders from Near East and Soviet Division telling him what he could—and could not—do. Tracking Lermontov to the university on Friday would help. He knew he couldn't slam dunk, but he wanted to play as best he could, and it hurt to be told he could not play at all.


A nervous frown like a canal of thought twitched between General Merid's gray-flecked eyebrows. The other Iranians seemed abstracted, distant.

Fred, hard-charging as usual, allowed only a few moments for greetings before asking, "What's the good news from the deputy prime minister?"

"He . . . he has not yet given the proposal his full attention. Other . . . pressing duties."

"You have no news?"

"No news," said the general. "Only rumors."

"What rumors?" asked Bunker.

"We will all be shot at sunrise. Yourselves included."

"You're joking."

"Yes," said the general. His smile dissolved the frown, but his eyes retained a sad cast.

"Whew, That's a relief. You had me worried there for a minute," said Bunker. Frank had never before heard anyone in real life say "whew."

"We should all worry," said General Merid. "These are worrisome times."

"Well, we should look on the bright side," countered Bunker. "This delay gives us a chance to review our proposal. Anticipate any possible questions or objections. Prepare cogent responses. Particularly in regard to the newspaper. Considering His Imperial Majesty's interest, that might be the most feasible first step."

Bunker did his best to lead them through a review of the newspaper proposal, raising possible objections, citing potential problems. The others agreed with all the points he raised. No one, except Frank, offered any solutions, and even Frank's efforts were halfhearted. His mind kept jumping to what he might say to Lermontov if he managed to confront Lermontov at the rally following the Friday evening prayer meeting at the university. He rehearsed in his head what he night say and wondered how Lermontov would respond. It proved a long morning.

Gus had again delayed their departure from Supreme Commander's Headquarters for a last-minute trip to the bathroom.

"What did Hamid have to say?" asked Frank when they were back in Rushmore's office.

"How did you know I was talking to Hamid?" said Gus.

"You're going to have to find some place besides the bathroom to meet with him."

"You're right. I'll work out something. But at least I have to give this guy credit for not just telling us what he thinks we want to hear."

"Well, what did he tell you?"

"You aren't going to like it, Fred, but what he said was the big brass upstairs have a good laugh over our civic action ideas."

"Will they shoot it down?"

"That's the good news. At least according to Hamid. He says they won't shoot it down. They know the Shah took some interest in this newspaper idea, so what they talk about doing is just sitting on the whole package and letting it die a natural death."

"Where does that leave us?" asked Bunker.

"I dunno," said Gus. "But I don't think we have to pack right away."


General Merid, rosy cheeked from the cold, arrived uncharacteristically late for the Thursday morning Jayface meeting. A Bodyguard corporal who'd been waiting for him spoke softly in Farsi as he shed his coat. The color drained from the general's chubby face, and his lips tightened. He looked at his watch and motioned to Frank.

He turned his back to the others and in a voice barely above a whisper said, "Colonel Kasravi wants to see you. Alone. In his office at zero nine hundred hours. Sharp."

Frank climbed the stairs five minutes early, then lingered before the colonel's door, which suddenly opened.

"Come in," said Kasravi. He closed the door behind them and motioned Frank to a chair by his table, which stood bare except for a thick loose-leaf binder and an oversize manila envelope sealed with heavy tape. "For today's discussion, please do not use your recorder."

"May I take notes?"

"Yes," said the barrel-chested Kasravi as he sat opposite Frank. Frank fished in his briefcase for his notebook and glanced regretfully at the recorder.

"Your newspaper proposal will be acted on. We've set a target date, 7 January on your calendar. But only if we have firm commitment, not just tentative approval, well in advance from your government of your availability as an adviser for the project on a continuing basis. And of course as an adviser to His Imperial Majesty."

"How far in advance?"

"Not later than 11 *Moharram*. Your 12 December. That will get us beyond the holy days of *Tasu'a* and *Ashura,* which I expect to pass without incident."

"Don't you expect the usual parades, demonstrations?"

"You need not look so worried." Score another for the colonel, thought Frank. He hadn't realized his concern showed so apparently. "We have had recent demonstrations in Qom, Mashhad, other cities, without violence," added Kasravi. "*Inshallah,* we shall again during *Moharram.*"

"*Inshallah.*" Frank wished he could be as optimistic as the colonel. "*Moharram* 11."

"Correct," said Colonel Kasravi. "Your 12 December. And not one day later."

"May I suggest, sir, that we move that deadline up a bit? If we give my government until December 12 to respond, they will take until December 12, which would only leave a little more than two weeks to prepare for publication."

"I leave that up to you. Our publication deadline will remain 7 *Safar,* our Islamic calendar."

"Very good," said Frank, wondering if Kasravi's promotion to deputy prime minister had forged the steel he now displayed. He also wondered what else he could negotiate. "Sir," he tried, "if possible, could we begin preliminary work on the project even sooner, on a tentative basis? Planning for a new publication, recruiting journalists, all that will take time."

"I have thought of all that. We will begin the project with a single newspaper, in English only. We will assign you the staff and facilities of *Kayhan International,* our English-language daily. As you know, the military government shut it down along with the other newspapers when we came to power. It will remain shut down, but you will have the opportunity to take its staff and create a new newspaper. Also its printing and distribution facilities."

"That . . . that sounds great," said Frank.

"It remains to be seen how great it will be. You will have to be very careful with the staff. The editor is a good man, loyal to the Shah and respected by other journalists, but some of the others . . . they include some left-wing riffraff who like to stir up trouble. That's why we want an English-language newspaper you can monitor yourself. We will also assign a senior information officer from the prime minister's office and, of course, someone from *Savak* to work with you."

Oh, well, thought Frank. I've worked with censors before. And survived.

"You said your government would require a more detailed proposal before making a final commitment on your availability. Our operational plan is spelled out in this document, which I have had translated into English for you." He slid the loose-leaf binder across the table to Frank. "Can you convey these details to your government at once?"

"Of course," said Frank. "I'll have to make arrangements at the embassy, but I'm sure they'll get a cable off today and have this material sent immediately by diplomatic pouch."

"Good," said the colonel. "Since I have done all this for you . . ." Kasravi hesitated. He held his hands out before him, palms upward, as though praying, or studying the lines for guidance. "There is another matter, a matter of some delicacy." He touched the sealed envelope that sat before him on the table. "In this envelope . . ." He withdrew his hand. "Admiral Hayati, who heads our Royal Navy, asked Captain Irfani to handle this matter. Munair, Captain Irfani, thought it unwise."

Because he doesn't trust the Americans. Frank wondered what would come next.

"Munair has told me that he asked your Jayface colleague Major Anwar Amini to give you a tape made by Khomeini. He thought it would help you understand the situation we face."

"It proved very helpful."

"Good. But this other matter, it involved material Major Amini is not cleared to handle. Only because Munair, Captain Irfani, is so close to Admiral Hayati . . . You see, it is a proposal, a proposal drafted by Admiral Hayati himself."

"And you want me to have it?"

"No," said Kasravi. "Not I. Admiral Hayati wants you to have it. For a special reason. He wants you to have it because of your special relationship to His Imperial Majesty."

"I'm afraid I don't understand."

"This package contains a document, a thirty-page plan Admiral Hayati presented to the Shah in October. A plan that calls for a military takeover of the government, the withdrawal of the Shah to a naval base in the south until such time as it takes for the military to secure the monarchy. It calls for the arrests of hundreds of corrupt people, plus thousands of revolutionaries and radical clergy."

"What did the Shah say?"

"It is my understanding that he said it would be against the constitution. He said he did not want the blood of his people on his hands just to save the monarchy."

"Then there won't be a coup."

"Perhaps. Admiral Hayati reported to his colleagues that the Shah did not say no to his plan. Only that it must be considered in light of the constitution."

"I still don't understand why Admiral Hayati wants us to have his plan."

"It is our hope, Admiral Hayati's hope, that you will find the opportunity to discuss his plan with His Imperial Majesty."

Frank's paranoia kicked in. "That sounds risky." He glanced at the sealed package as though it contained a bomb.

"Perhaps. But if the Shah knows the Americans have it, he may be forced to act on it."

"I suspect he would want to know how I got it."

"If you tell him, Admiral Hayati, myself, perhaps others, would face grave trouble."

Interesting word choice, thought Frank. Grave trouble. If the Shah finds out, we may all be dead men.

"I suspect," said Frank, "that if the Shah thought the Americans had the plan, he would ask the Americans on a very high level, maybe through the ambassador, for advice on what they think he should do."

"What would the advice be?"

Frank shook his head. Shrugged. Muttered, "No idea."

"I see." Kasravi studied him closely. "If the opportunity should present itself, you must use your own judgment."

"Agreed."

"Unfortunately, we do not have a translation for you, but Admiral Hayati has authorized me to summarize it for you."

Another job for Belinsky, thought Frank.

Kasravi placed his right hand on the sealed package, as though taking an oath on its contents. "The plan calls for the navy to take over the oil fields if the workers resume their strike and to take over the ports. Admiral Hayati would also be responsible for taking over key factories and the electrical grid that supplies the nation. The Imperial Guard would secure Dowshan Tappeh. There is concern about the loyalty of some elements there. Particularly *homafaran*. Here in Tehran, the army will seal off the university, secure the airport, the military ordnance department in Abbas-Abad, the military installations and reservoir near Yusefabad, the radio masts near Qasar Prison."

Frank scribbled furiously in his self-taught Speedwriting, cursing, but understanding, Kasravi's refusal to allow a recording of his words.

"It doesn't say so here," Kasravi continued, "but the prisons will be left unprotected."

"Prisoners will be released?"

"That will be up to the prisoners and their guards. I suspect arrangements will be made."

"I suspect." If possible, in American dollars, thought Frank.

"J2 will work with the Shah's personal intelligence group. *Savak* will have no role."

"Interesting."

"Yes. J2 suspects some *Savak* agents talk to Khomeini's people And others to the Russians."


"Your Colonel Kasravi buddy might want you to get yourself killed," said Rocky. He and Frank hunched over the glass-topped table, alone in the bubble. "Accordin' to the ambassador, the fuckin' Shah already thinks Jimmy Carter and the CIA are plottin' with the mullahs to get him kicked out. Shah finds out we got this coup proposal he'll think for sure we're tryin' t' fuck him. He might think we wrote it."

"In Farsi?"

"We got translators. Look, I put Belinsky on alert. I want to get him up here. Belinsky confirms this stuff is real, I may think about lettin' the Shah know we got it. Understood?"

"Understood," said Frank. He wondered why Rocky would consider changing his mind so abruptly. *Maybe he wants to get me killed.*

Rocky installed Frank in a vacant office close to his. He said he wanted to get Frank's cable about the proposed coup off as soon as possible. His alacrity puzzled Frank. He'd grown used to Rocky's resistance to most of what he wanted to file. Then he realized that what Kasravi had told him fit neatly into the requirements laid down by Langley: details confirming plans for a military coup. Nothing that contradicted previous reporting about the central role of the Soviet Union in Iran's troubles. Even Kasravi's report of possible Soviet infiltration of *Savak* had cheered Rocky. *The secret of good reporting,* thought Frank. *Intelligence that fits policy requirements.*


Rocky confirmed his suspicions. He read Frank's cable quickly, changed nothing, and muttered, "Just what the fuckers want. Now what about this newspaper business?"

Frank, Rocky, Chuck Belinsky, Ambassador O'Connor, Fred, and Gus now crowded the bubble. Frank summarized what Kasravi had told him about the approval of their proposal for the *Armed Forces Times*.

"Near East may not like it," said Rocky, nodding in the direction of Frank and Gus, "but Covert Action will fuckin' love it, and since that's your shop, that's what counts. Lemme see a cable on it before you get outta here. How soon do you want your approval?"

"Can we get it by Monday?" said Frank. "December fifth. That gives us most of a week to get cranking before *Ashura* hits the fan."

"We'll get it done," promised Rocky.

"And it purely will hit the fan," said Belinsky. "I don't know if all of you heard about it, but the government announced this morning, like Frank told us last week, it will ban all demonstrations during *Moharram*. If the government sticks to that, sir," said Belinsky, addressing the ambassador, "I suggest you may want to take extra security precautions to protect the embassy."

"Well, I don't want us to go into a panic mode that might create more panic."

Though they sat around the large rectangular table in Rocky's bubble, the ambassador had already asserted control by calling for a discussion of security problems during *Moharram*. The problems seemed abstract to Frank. He worried more about his own safety and security at the university. Tomorrow, he thought. Seven in the evening. The first of *Moharram*. Not far away. The thought made the security problems the others discussed seem less abstract.

"Sir, I was fortunate enough just a while ago to get through to Ayatollah Shariat-Madari," said Belinsky. "He laughed when I told him about the ban. Said it was absurd that the faithful needed the government's permission to honor the martyrdom of Imam Hossein. 'Let them refuse permits,' he said. 'We have no need for their permits.' He said he would make this his message at the Friday prayer meeting tomorrow. He'll also be on the phone urging other religious leaders around the country to do the same. I asked if this would mean confrontations with the military. He said, *'Inshallah.'*"

God's will gets blamed for a lot these days, thought Frank. He wondered if the same message would be delivered at the prayer meeting at the university. Please, Allah, let there be no confrontation with the military tomorrow.

"Good work, Chuck," said the ambassador. "We'll need you to do a cable on this."

"I've already done a draft, sir. Bu I thought I should wait till after this meeting to finalize."

"Good," said the ambassador. "I'm having lunch with the Shah tomorrow. I'll get a reading from him on how he sees this *Ashura* business. We also have a security expert from Washington just arrived. We can discuss embassy security needs with him tomorrow, after I see the Shah."

"Balls," said Rocky. "I know these Foggy Bottom security creeps. Their only function is to convince everybody everything is fucking hunky-dory and then get out of town before the rest of us get our asses shot off."

Frank said a silent prayer of thanks, grateful that Rocky had aimed his firmly pronounced final *g*'s at someone else.

"I'm with Chuck," continued Rocky. "If he says the shit will fucking hit the fan if the military tries to ban a holy day parade, I say we fucking batten down the hatches. What would happen to New York if the Pope said too many Irishmen get fucking stinko and got the city to ban the St. Patrick's Day drunk fest up Fifth Avenue? The fucking micks would tear up the fucking city, fucking cathedral and all."

"I agree with you about that," said the ambassador, laughing with the others, except, Frank noted, for Rocky. Rocky did not laugh. He glowered.

"Oh, Rocky. And Frank. Another matter," said the ambassador as his own smile faded. "Also tomorrow, after I return from the palace, I'll need to meet with you two privately, in my office. Ambassador Hempstone will be with me. I understand he and his wife will be leaving soon, but evidently he has some news for us."

"Good?" said Rocky. "Bad?"

"I don't know," said the ambassador.

Frank and Rocky sat alone in the bubble.

"What d'ya think?" mumbled Rocky. He'd turned his hearing aid back up.

"I dunno," responded Frank, wishing he and Rocky could talk openly about tomorrow. And Lermontov. "Any word from home?"

"Not yet. But it figures the Brits might've given their ambassador a chance to respond t' whatever they said before givin' our gang a tinkle."

Frank studied him, concluding that Rocky had sent the eyes-only cable to Brzezinski and that Brzezinski or someone high up had acted on it.

"Meantime," said Rocky, "my so-called buddy Gerry Mosley's ducking me. Never happened before. Most times he's the eager buddy-buddy beaver. Not this time. Worries me. Eagle-1 tells me he talked to him. Told him I needed t' meet. Still nothing."

Frank could feel Rocky working up his anger. He didn't know what to say but ventured, "Mosley must want Lermontov bad as we do."

"I don't want Lermontov bad. I want him good. And soon. Very fucking soon."

"You pissed at me?" said Frank.

"Should be. But I'm not."

"Why should you be?" asked Frank.

"I dunno," said Rocky, fishing. "You tell me."

With a good spy's paranoia, Frank wondered if Rocky had gotten word of his plan to take Belinsky to Anwar's home that evening. I should have told Rocky, he thought, or I should have asked Belinsky not to tell the ambassador. He'd done neither.

"You seemed awful pissed when the ambassador talked about meeting with this State Department security expert."

"Yeah, well, that was real. This security creep—he comes out of State, and State's job is to represent the U.S. of fucking A. t' the rest of the world. And to do that and have enough jobs to keep every Foggy Bottom faggot on the payroll, you have to have functioning embassies all over the globe even if it means keeping open embassies like this one where people stand a good goddamn chance of getting their ass shot off. Right here, just for example, back in seventy-one, I was in Rome back then. The ambassador, Douglas fucking MacArthur, damn near got whacked right here. The guy what had that map you so elo-fuckin'-quently wrote about in that atmospherics cable. Friend of mine was here told me about it later. Same story. Embassy had just been briefed by some old boy out of Foggy Bottom about how hunky-dory everything was. MacArthur came outta the feel-good meetin' and was headin' up to see his buddy the King of Kings when he got jumped by a carload of leftist ragheads. Managed to get out of it with his ass intact and got the hell out of Iran for good pretty soon after. Moral: Whenever you hear a State Department security expert say everything is hunky-dory and security is tight as a virgin's vagina, wrap a bulletproof vest around your ass and duck. Besides that, why didn't you tell me about takin' Belinsky to your buddy's tonight?"

Here it comes, thought Frank. " 'Cause I fucked up. I should've told you."

"Yeah, you shoulda, but with everything else you pulled lately I can't get but just so pissed when you pull somethin' new, 'specially when I'm already pissed to the eyeballs about this Foggy Bottomless insecurity expert."

"Sorry," said Frank.

"You do good work, Sullivan. Sometimes. But you didn't have to try this shit with Belinsky and your Iranian buddy behind my backside. I woulda said okay and I still say okay. I mean, I don't mind if you get this Anwar's ass in a sling or get yourself jammed up, but if you get Belinsky jammed up the ambassador will chew my ass out from here to Langley and back again, and that kind of shit I don't need. Belinsky was smart enough to tell the ambassador, which means it would've been smart to let me know about it, because the ambassador told me after tellin' Belinsky t' forget about it. But the ambassador owes me a few, so I convinced him to let Belinsky go through with it. It'll make this Anwar even more helpful for as long as we're all here, and he and his wife might be useful stateside, if any of us get there alive. But the ambassador said he'd have my scalp if anything happened to Belinsky. You got any idea how you're gonna get the two of you there and back?"

"I've got an idea," said Frank.

"That's what you told me about bringin' Lermontov back in. And we still haven't seen his Russian ass."

I'll see his Russian ass tomorrow night, thought Frank. I hope.

Frank's idea for getting Belinsky to Anwar's seemed simple. Bill Steele, driving a nondescript van, picked up Belinsky at the Damavand. Steele took extreme evasive measures and saw no signs of a tail. By the time they drove onto the base at Dowshan Tappeh, Belinsky had edged his way into the back of the van, where he could not be seen from the outside.

Steele parked and went into Tom Troy's office. He emerged five minutes later with two men in the white-helmeted uniforms of the U.S. Air Force Military Police. They joined Steele in the front seat; Frank sat in the middle, Anwar by the door.

They drove through the checkpoints, where Steele was well known, that led onto the Iranian Air Force portion of the base. They exited by a gate on the south side that led into Anwar's Niru-ye Hayal neighborhood. Then Frank's simple idea grew complicated.

He and Anwar had just removed their ill-fitting white helmets when, in a very even voice, Bill Steele said, "Better put those snowballs back on. We got trouble."

"What?" said Frank, as he slipped the helmet back on.

"Company. Looks like military vehicle," said Steele. "Followed us out the base."

"Military intelligence," said Anwar, wincing as he squeezed into the helmet. "For me that could be big trouble."

Steele kept the van moving at a moderate, steady pace through the residential neighborhood.

"We can't let them follow us to my house," said Anwar.

"Maybe the best bet is for me to get out and talk to them," said Steele. "I know most of those guys assigned to the base."

"Unfortunately, so do I," said Anwar.

"Let's just hope they don't get too nosy," said Steele, as he gently braked the rattling van.

"What about me?" called Belinsky from the back.

"Just keep quiet," said Steele. "Real quiet." He pulled the van to the side of the road, put it in neutral, and pulled on the hand brake. "If anybody's a believer, pray." He slid out and walked slowly toward the back of the van.

Without turning, Frank could see the dance of flashlight beams around the van.

"If they look in and recognize me, we're lost," said Anwar.

"Real quiet," said Frank. "Let's just be real quiet."

The murmur of voices outside the van reassured him with its softness. A wave of deep, masculine laughter sounded even better.

Bill Steele climbed back into the driver's seat. "We're okay. I think." He pulled the van back onto the road.

"Are they following?" said Anwar.

Bill studied the rearview mirror suspended from the door.

"Yeah. They are."

"Then we're not okay," said Anwar.

"Oh, Jesus," moaned Belinsky.

"Hold on," said Steele. "They just swung around. Headin' back, looks like."

"Thank God," said Belinsky.

They passed a dark, deserted mosque on their left.

"Praise Allah," said Anwar.

Frank and Anwar again removed their white helmets.

"I gotta go on a ways," said Steele. "Those guys knew I was agency, but they wondered why I had a couple of snowballs with me. I told 'em that was just cover, you work with me. Told 'em we had to go pull one of our guys out of a girlfriend's house where he had too much to drink. They're healthy young men. They could understand that, but they got kind of curious about the girlfriend. Offered to escort us."

"That would have been fun," said Frank.

"No, it would not," said Anwar. "For you Americans it's all a game. For me it would be death." He sat tense, rigid, and as far away from Frank as he could, pressed hard against the door.

"I'm sorry," said Frank. "I didn't mean to be funny." A game, he thought. A Great Game.

"Anyways," said Steele, "I told 'em we had to go way out beyond the football field up ahead, so I think we better do that, just in case they circle around. Then we maybe come back another way."

"I can show you," said Anwar. "But please, say nothing of this in front of my wife. She will be frantic enough that we are late."


"Where have you been?" cried Mina. She threw herself into her husband's arms. "I've been frantic. Frantic."

"Just we had to wait for Mr. Belinsky," said Anwar.

Steele waited in a small pantry room off the kitchen, reading a John le Carré novel. Before the fireplace in the spacious front room, Belinsky outlined his plan in detail and provided drafts of the documents needed to verify Anwar's conversion to Baha'i. Mina said her family, with close financial ties to many elements of the bazaar, could have the documents created, with appropriate dates, seals, and signatures.

"They can do anything," said Mina. "They could even make Anwar an American passport."

"That could be risky," said Belinsky. "Let's just stick to the conversion."

"All this bothers me," said Anwar.

"What's the problem?" said Belinsky.

"It seems too . . . complicated," said Anwar. "There should be a simpler way."

"Like stealing an F-4?" said Frank.

"I don't want to deny my faith," said Anwar. "Or betray my country."

"What about your family?" snapped Mina.

"If you're not sure you want to do this . . ." said Belinsky.

"We must do this," said Mina, cutting him off. She turned to Anwar, not smiling, not pouting. "You know I can't stand it to stay here. Not even with you."

"I know," said Anwar. "I agreed. But so much deceit."

"Deception," offered Belinsky. He said a single word in Farsi, then added, "Think of it as deception. Evasive tactics, like a fighter pilot might make. For your family's sake."

"Anwar, if you don't want to," said Frank, "other arrangements can be made."

"No," said Mina.

"You and the children could go now," said Frank. "Anwar could follow when he feels ready."

"You are the Great Satan," said Anwar. "No. I agreed. I will go with Mina. And our children."

"Good," said Mina. She turned to Frank. "The children wanted to see you. But I thought it best not. With all these . . ." She glanced at Belinsky. "Arrangements."

"Give them my best," said Frank. "I've been thinking about them a lot."

"Good," said Mina. "I hope Anwar has, too."

Wow, thought Frank. This is one tough lady. A kitten to her husband, perhaps, but a she-lion to her cubs.


With Anwar's uniform and helmet stuffed into a duffel bag, Steele retraced their path to Dowshan Tappeh. He dropped off Frank and headed on to the Damavand with Belinsky.

Frank stashed the uniforms he and Anwar had worn in a closet in Rushmore's office. Feeling like the Great Satan that Anwar had called him, he washed himself twice. Appropriate. A whore's bath at the sink. You could stay, Anwar. Send your wife and kids off and you could stay. An agent in place for the Great American Satan. To you Americans it's a game, Anwar had said.

Frank drove home alone, flicked the lights, waited for Gus to open the garage doors and backed the car down the drive. Frank didn't move until Gus checked and rechecked the street.

"No cars," said Gus. "Street's empty."

Frank checked his watch. Midnight had passed. December first, a day short of the first of *Moharram*. Beware the tenth of *Moharram,* Anwar had said weeks before. Soon *Tasu'a* and *Ashura* would be upon them. He thought of the funnels of smoke they had watched, rising from the city. He thought of tornadoes and hoped that Jake was safe at home in New York. He started up the drive, wondering whether Lermontov would actually be at the university that evening. Gus pulled the garage door down behind them. An agent in place, thought Frank. What every spy wants. But all the agents want to go home to the Great Satan, home to America.

Me, too.


Frank's mind had been on Anwar and his escape to America, but the massive shadow of Lermontov soon obscured all other thoughts. Frank stood behind the embassy gates and watched the orange taxi pick up Belinsky at the door of the Damavand Hotel. After a moment the taxi pulled away from the curb, swerved around oncoming traffic, swung a wide U-turn, pulled up by the embassy gates and braked abruptly. Should be an interesting trip, thought Frank. He nodded to the young marine who stood by his side. The marine cracked the gate, and Frank slipped through. He heard the gate clang shut and the chains being pulled taut, feeling as though a last sanctuary had been closed behind him. He climbed into the back of the cab and sat next to Belinsky. The driver leaned on his horn and the accelerator with equal intensity and propelled them into the evening traffic.

"He knows where we're going?"

"Oh, yes," said Belinsky. "He's my regular. I use him all the time. We have a routine for the university. A straight run up Takht-e Jamshid. Not much more than a mile to the back gates. A half hour later he starts circling by the front gates, every fifteen minutes till I come out."

"Suppose you don't come out?"

"I always come out," answered Belinsky. He thought for a moment, then added, "So far."

Frank recognized Pahlavi as they crossed it, then the Meydan-e Kakh traffic circle. "You're sure about my friend?"

"I spoke to my source this afternoon, by phone. He confirmed. Your friend will be there."

Frank nodded toward the silent driver. He'd seen no more than the back of his head, covered by the drawn-close hood of his black wool jacket, and his right gloved hand on the wheel.

"Don't worry," said Belinsky. "He doesn't speak English."

Maybe he doesn't speak English, thought Frank.

The stone paths of the university's spacious quadrangle had been cleared, but snow still covered what Frank took to be flower beds. In its winter aspect, the campus seemed drab. Tall, unornamented brick buildings flanked the nearly deserted quadrangle. Even the mosque seemed stark and plain.

"Pretty dismal, isn't it?" said Belinsky.

"Yeah, it is."

"You should see it in better weather, with a rally going on. They get a hundred thousand and more in here, chanting and screaming. Quite a sight."

"How 'bout when tonight's prayer meeting breaks up?"

"Not so many, I don't think," answered Belinsky. "But enough."

"Let's hope we're out of here by then."

A handful of students clustered around scattered kiosks that appeared to be stacked with pamphlets and newspapers.

"*Mojahedin*," said Belinsky, following Frank's gaze toward the kiosk with the largest crowd. Frank nodded, guessing that his *homafar* friends would be glad to hear that.

"That's the *Tudeh* kiosk," said Belinsky, nodding at a slightly aslant structure across the quadrangle. "Hardly anyone, and no sign of a Russian."

"There he is," said Frank. Lermontov stood in the center of a knot of students at the base of a statue that faced away from them at the far end of the quadrangle. Lermontov gave no sign of recognizing him. Frank, with his dark glasses, a pulled-down stocking cap, and the turned-up collar of his pea coat, was grateful. He didn't want Lermontov to see him too soon. To order his cadre of students to cordon him off. To bolt before Frank could speak to him.

"Nice and slow," he said. "Let me go talk to him." They continued across the quadrangle, heading for the statue that stood by what Frank took to be the main gates.

"That the Shah?" he asked.

"That's him," answered Belinsky. "The students like to say he stands there with his back to the university. They tried to tear it down back a couple of months ago. Must be a pretty tough statue. Big riot. Bunch of students got killed, but the Shah's still there."

So's Lermontov, thought Frank. As he drew within a few feet, he took off his dark glasses. Lermontov, whose lamb's-wool cap reached to the top of the pedestal, looked over the heads of the group around him. He'd been joking with them, smiling. Now, his expression turned to stone.

"You shouldn't be here," he said.

"From now on," answered Frank, "I plan to be wherever you are."

Lermontov turned away, heading across the quadrangle in the direction of the *Tudeh* party kiosk. Frank watched as the big Russian's broad shoulders hunched.

One of the students seemed to recognize Belinsky. He nodded. Belinsky did not respond. The student moved away, following Lermontov. The others straggled after.

"Time to get out of here," said Frank.

"That's all?" said Belinsky.

"You expect me to wrestle with him or something? I rattled his chain. That's all I need. For now. Time to get out of here."

"Just in time," said Belinsky. "The mosque is starting to empty out."

Frank turned in time to see the animated, chanting crowd heading out of the mosque. "What are they chanting?" he asked.

"*Maag bargh Shah*. Death to the Shah," said Belinsky. "And they're heading for his statue."

They circled the statue and, without rushing, moved through the main gates. Their hooded driver stood by his orange taxi. For the first time Frank noticed that the left sleeve of his black jacket hung empty. He held the door open as Frank and Belinsky scrambled into the back seat.

Frank and Rocky sat alone in the bubble. Rocky, hands folded on the glass table-top, said nothing as Frank detailed all that had happened at the university.

"I got no idea what the fuck you're talkin' about," said Rocky when Frank paused. "And this little chitchat never took place, right?"

"Right," said Frank.

"Musta been an unauthorized mission."

"Right," repeated Frank. Except it was a chapter in what Pete Howard had authorized as Frank's hidden agenda.

"So we won't have any traffic on it, right?"

"Yes, sir."

"Don't get smart. But just between us, I can tell ya it was no coincidence the driver showin' up soon as you two come out the gates. Chuck thinks he recruited an unwitting asset all by himself. But that driver's a certified *Savak* thug. I set it up with Eagle-1. Chuck takes a lot of chances, but I do my best to keep his ass covered."

"How'd the driver know we were coming out right then?" asked Frank.

Rocky shrugged. "My guess, some *Savaki* agent there on the campus got in touch by radio. Who knows? Maybe one of the bunch talkin' to Lermontov."

"The driver's got a radio?"

"Constant touch with *Savak*. They keep three cars circlin' wherever the taxi's at. They spot surveillance, they can signal that. He spots trouble, he can call in reinforcements—if he needs them. He packs a Czech M61 machine pistol, not but about ten inches with the stock folded, which is how he carries it. In a shoulder holster. Eagle-1 tells me he's real good with it. He's only got one arm, but he only needs one t' handle the M61."

"I'll sleep better knowing that," said Frank. "And of course he speaks English, right?"

"Don't tell Chuck."

"I won't," said Frank. "He was fine, by the way."

"Glad to hear it. Tell you the truth, Chuck worries me. Eagle-1 says he takes too many fuckin' chances. Not to mention hepatitis. You think you got to Lermontov?"

"I dunno," said Frank. "He doesn't get in touch soon, I'll try to track him down again."

"How?"

"Who's this source of Chuck's?"

"None 'a your fuckin' business," said Rocky.

"I know that. Just he might be able to give us another lead on Lermontov."

"Maybe. We got other sources who can maybe do that. Includin' *Savak*."

"I really don't like doing business with those people."

"Forget that shit," said Rocky. "Those people are us."

Frank dreamt that night of Belinsky's taxi driver, a one-armed, hooded, dark angel of death. As Frank watched, he reached into his jacket and drew out a stunted, metallic machine gun. His hood fell back, and Frank saw his face. The face of the Shah.

# PART III

# CHAPTER THIRTEEN

After one look on his first day, Bunker never again ventured into the bathroom at Supreme Commander's Headquarters. As usual, he excused himself as soon as they returned from their Jayface meeting to Dowshan Tappeh and shed their coats in Stan Rushmore's office.

"Speaking of bathrooms," said Gus, "Hamid . . ."

Frank shook his head. "Are you guys still doing it in bathrooms?"

"I've asked Hamid, but he keeps saying that's the best place. And what the hell, it's not like there were stalls anybody could be hiding in. Anyway, Hamid gave me this." He tugged a sealed, unmarked envelope out of his jacket. "Personal for you. No one else to see it or know I gave it to you. And he doesn't know where he got it from."

Frank carried the unopened envelope with him into the bubble. He hadn't expected to see the two ambassadors sitting side by side next to Rocky. Frank noted the differences between them. Seated, Hempstone did not look particularly taller than O'Connor, but his cold gray eyes, angular features, and pale complexion contrasted sharply with O'Connor's ruddy appearance and open expression. He decided to leave the envelope in his case.

"Sit down, Sully." With a nod, Rocky indicated a chair facing O'Connor and Hempstone. "We just got up here a minute ago, so I don't know much more than you do, except Ambassador Hempstone says he has news for us. Your show, Mr. Ambassador."

"Yes, thank you. I'll get right to it. We've received instructions from . . . from Her Majesty's Government to stand down on this matter involving Mr. Lermontov."

"What's that mean?"

"I hate to admit it, Mr. Novak, but I'm afraid it means that for Great Britain the Great Game is over. Gerald Mosley doesn't like it; matter of fact, neither do I.

But we must be realistic in this. Only you Yanks remain powerful enough to counter Russian influence in this part of the world."

The sun sets again on the Union Jack, thought Frank. Hempstone must have been thinking something similar. Frank thought again of a furled umbrella, but now with its folds wrapped even more tightly.

"It is rather sad, contemplating a shrinking empire. Egypt, Palestine, Suez, Kenya, Ghana, Sierra Leone, Nigeria, so much of Africa."

"Not to mention your American colonies," said Rocky.

Hempstone ignored him. "India, Ceylon, Singapore, Malaysia."

As he listened to the British ambassador's litany of loss, Frank thought of the Shah's requiem for all the world leaders who had died over the past ten years. All the world leaders and his own close friend. Assadollah Alam. "And soon," the Shah had said, "we shall be gone."

"We manage, so far, to hold on to Hong Kong. Gibraltar. Great Britain will survive. Wales. Scotland. We won't give up Northern Ireland. So we may still call ourselves the U.K. A kingdom, yes, but hardly an empire." Hempstone pinched the sharp crease of his gray wool trousers. Frank wondered if all his suits were of a gray several shades darker than his hair. "The Soviet Union, on the other hand, is very much an empire. Even more so than in czarist times. The entire East Bloc. They may soon annex Afghanistan."

Frank remembered what Lermontov had said. Afghanistan would be the end of the end of the Russian Empire. Emperors and empires, crumbling. Caesars, czars, shahs.

"To make matters worse," said Hempstone, "the bloody Russians have taken so many of our own. Philby, Maclean, Burgess, all that lot. It's no wonder Mosley wants to bag one of theirs."

"He agree to back down?" asked Rocky.

"No," said Hempstone, again pinching the crease of his trousers. "Despite instructions from home, including instructions from his own agency, Mr. Mosley continues to pursue your Russian friend. From what he tells me, he's tried several ways to try to contact him, even speaking to someone at *Savak* with whom they both liaise, plus several leftist students and someone with the *Tudeh* party. Far as I know, no response."

"But he keeps tryin'?" said Rocky.

"So I suspect. He will, of course, in time, have to desist. Particularly so since Mr. Lermontov quite apparently does not wish to deal with . . . with our intelligence agencies."

"What about you?" asked Rocky. "You let Lermontov know what Her Majesty's Government said?"

"I have not. Our arrangement was that Mr. Lermontov would contact me."

"How?"

"He did not say."

He's keeping us all on the hook, thought Frank. He remembered the unopened envelope in his briefcase. Or maybe not.

"I gotta believe it's from him," said Frank. He and Rocky were alone in the bubble. He tossed the envelope onto the glass-topped table.

"It's for you, so open the fuckin' thing," said Rocky. "If one of your admirers sent you a letter bomb, let it blow your fuckin' fingers off. Not mine."

Frank took a ballpoint pen from his pocket and gingerly pried the envelope open. He drew out a single sheet of paper. "Tonight. Same time and place. Alone." He handed it to Rocky.

"His writing?"

"Looks like," said Frank. "Maybe my little trip to the university did some good."

"Maybe," said Rocky. "But maybe he's gettin' the idea the Brits don't want him. So maybe he figures he's got no choice but to try us again."

Frank studied him, thinking hard before he spoke. "Rocky, Hempstone just told us they haven't been in touch with Lermontov. He doesn't know the Brits have been told to stand down, and this Mosley is still going after him. So maybe, just maybe, Chuck and I did some good going after our good friend at the university."

"You want a fucking medal? 'Sides, I don't know anything about that. You did anything about that, you did it on your own."

Frank nodded, said nothing.

"So anyway, now we know this waiter Gus recruited, this Hamid, for sure works for Lermontov."

"For sure," said Frank. "But at least he didn't bring us a letter bomb."

"Might as well've been. Soviet Division's been burning up the wires. Mostly about me making arrangements A-SAP for the division chief no less and his fucking deputy to move in here and take over the Lermontov recruit. 'Course, I haven't responded yet. Meanwhile, comes another cable from Near East Division suggesting, at the request of NSC, we give you one more crack at Lermontov. I gotta believe NSC did ask the Brits to back off and got an okay."

I think maybe I made something happen, thought Frank. He suppressed a smile.

"Soviet Division ain't gonna like it," said Rocky, "but far as I'm concerned we got a green light for you to go tonight without me askin' permission. As per suggestion of the National Security Council via Near East Division, KUPEREGRINE met with the KGB motherfucker who's fuckin' us over. Or words to that effect is how I'll cable them soon's you get back here and tell me what the fuck happened."

"Are we clear for me to hit him with my idea?"

"We, as in you and me. Yeah, we're clear. Why not? Nobody else knows about your fuckin' idea. So hit the Russkie over the fuckin' head with it. Hard as you can."

"You bastard," said Lermontov before he'd struggled halfway out of his white Peugeot. He loomed over Frank in the semidark garage and added, "You betrayed me."

Upstairs, he ignored the blue vase. His curiosity about other possible listening devices seemed to have evaporated. "And then, showing up at the university, you not only humiliated me in front of those students, you put us all at risk. Don't you realize you could have gotten us all killed?"

"I had to see you," said Frank. "And it worked. You finally showed up."

"It worked," snarled Lermontov. Frank took a step back, half expecting Lermontov to pounce on him. "Don't you realize, you bastard, for me this is a matter of life or death? I must get to America. Your fucking *resident* and all your other fucking bureaucrats look at me and see promotions, commendations, medals. But look at me. You, you look at me. What you see is a man whose bones ache when he moves. A man whose face cracks with pain when he chews his food. A fool whose brains will explode."

"I warned you he'd be there," said Frank.

They stood on opposite sides of the dining room table, Lermontov still in his heavy coat and lamb's-wool hat. Frank thought the table shook, then realized it was himself.

"I suppose you call that fair play," sneered Lermontov. "You bastards. You play your games, but for me this is not a game."

"I know," said Frank. He remembered Anwar's words when Iranian military intelligence had stopped their van the night before. *For you Americans it's all a game. For me it would be death.*

"That's what bothers me most," said Lermontov. "You know better. And still you play games with me." He tossed his hat across the room, then tugged off his coat and let it fall to the floor. Apparently exhausted, he slumped into a chair and let both hands fall to the table. "You bastard," he repeated, now in a voice so low Frank had to guess at the words.

"I've got some vodka."

"Good."

He'd brought a bottle of his own Absolut along with a tin of Mina's caviar and two spoons.

"It's Iranian," he said, nodding at the caviar.

"I prefer it." Lermontov sampled the caviar.

His jaws did not move, and Frank suspected the giant Russian let the tiny eggs melt in his mouth. The poor bastard can't chew, thought Frank.

"Excellent," said Lermontov. He sipped the vodka. "I am a traitor to my motherland. I prefer this Swedish stuff even to export quality Stolichnaya." He finished the Absolut in a gulp. Frank replenished his vodka. Lermontov drained the glass and held a hand over it. "More, perhaps, later. What response have you had from your people?"

"I'm here," said Frank. "Despite what you've been up to with the Brits."

"You know about that?"

"And the Canadians."

"I needed to see what other avenues might be open for me. After you betrayed me."

"I didn't betray you," said Frank.

"Trying to turn me over to Mr. Novak felt like a betrayal. But the British proved no better. I told the ambassador, Hempstone, I would not deal with MI6. I was very specific, and I told him why."

"Can you tell me?" asked Frank.

"You can guess. British intelligence has been overloaded with traitors. Whole libraries have been written about them. It would be madness to think there are none left—and fatally dangerous for me if one of MI6's current traitors let his Moscow handlers know that one Vassily Lermontov wanted to defect."

"What about . . ." Frank did not know how to phrase it. "My shop?" he tried.

"CIA has its own problems, but I thought I could rely on you to protect me as best you can. Instead, you turned me over to an anti-Soviet relic of the Stalin era."

"I had no choice."

"Exactly," said Lermontov. "Which is why I have to see what other choices I might have."

Frank noticed Lermontov's use of the present tense. "I have to see," not "I had to see."

"And now?" he asked.

"If I had to choose between you and Ambassador Hempstone, that's relatively easy. I know you. And I would choose you. If I had to choose between Gerald Mosley and Roger Novak, a much closer call. But I would have to say Novak."

"Why?"

"Novak is smarter. He waits to hear from me. Mosley pursues me."

"Still?"

"Yes," said Lermontov. "And I allow it. Just in case."

"In case?"

"In case," said Lermontov, "I discover for sure I cannot trust you Americans."

"I'm here," said Frank.

"Yes," said Lermontov. "Despite what happened with your Mr. Novak, you are here."

"That shows interest, great interest," said Frank. "But . . ."

"But your people want an agent in place."

"And you want to defect."

"No," said Lermontov. "I do not want to defect. But I must get to America. Soon." He wrapped his right hand around his left wrist, covering his watch.

Time is running out, thought Frank. For both of us.

"I must get to America," Lermontov repeated. "And be safe there. And get medical treatment there. And . . . my problems have become even more acute with KGB since this Nazih business. Another failure. Another embarrassment."

"You ran him," said Frank. "And you ran him against me."

"No. He worked for me. I paid him. But his little clique of left-wing Qazvini queers ran him. Even now I don't know all the details. Also an embarrassment. Evidently they were tied in with some *Tudeh* party dissidents."

"What did that have to do with me?" asked Frank.

"In common with others, Major Nazih feared your influence with the Shah. Access to the Shah is power. Nazih had access and did not want to see his power diluted by an American spy."

"And now he's gone."

"Despite his many shortcomings," said Lermontov, "he gave us excellent access to the palace. The blame for his loss falls on me, but this time, at least so far, you have saved me."

"I have?"

"Yes. In Ethiopia, based on information you provided, the government expelled me. And others who reported to me. Here, not because of you, but because of Nazih's stupid intrigues, the government would have expelled me. The little fairy tried to play many games—against you, against me. I put my trust in that bastard. But the Shah, who of course is aware, thought it would be helpful to you if I remained, so you and I could discuss my . . . my need to get to America. So now we are even. Once you had me expelled, and now you have kept me from being expelled."

"But you still aren't in America."

"But I am still not in America. And your people don't want me there. If they did, they would have been smart enough not to send your stupid chief of station after me."

"What they want is an agent in place. I have an idea, if you agree to it and can take the risks, it could give them what they want and still get you to America."

"How?" asked Lermontov.

"Recruit me," said Frank.

"What?"

"My idea is for you to recruit me. Here and now. I can start feeding you information useful to you but not damaging to America. I can give you my justification. My disillusionment with the agency. My need for money because I can't save enough to do what I want to do without more money than the agency pays me."

Lermontov studied him. "And what is it you want to do?"

"I've got a son to support. He's smart enough, and public schools in America are bad enough, he deserves private school and, before too many years, college."

"What about that writer's nest egg you want?"

"Yeah, that's real enough," said Frank. "You know about it. I know about it. But I don't think the upper reaches of the KGB will want to finance me to write books, including maybe some books about them."

"Of course not," said Lermontov. "We would only want you as an agent in place."

"Of course," said Frank. "In place and hungry for money right now. I'll stay in place here for as long as I can. The job I go to when all this is over and I get back to the States is a job with the highest-level security clearance and access to intelligence from all over the world. I'll be in that job for the long haul, and I'll need a contact in the States I can trust, and I don't trust any Russian but you. It's up to you to get assigned to Washington, and something tells me you can make that happen. The agency gets what it wants. The Soviets get an agent inside the CIA, run by you. And you get to America, not as a defector, but as an agent in place still within the KGB."

Lermontov studied him, then shook his head.

"I know the risks involved," said Frank. "It means hanging on here for a while, and it means going back to Moscow before you could get reassigned to Washington. And it means the KGB still has control over you, even in Washington."

"You don't know all the risks," said Lermontov. "I doubt this can work."

"It has to work," said Frank.

"You've cleared this with your people?"

"With my chief of station. He doesn't want to try it on Langley unless you go for it."

"I don't like the idea of going back to Moscow," said Lermontov, "or staying within KGB. But I'm willing to take the risks. And I will tell you how serious the risks will be."

"What happens next?" said Rocky, alone with Frank in the bubble. "Think we can bring him in?"

"First, if anything's going to happen, we need quick approval on the scenario. Release on stuff I might have access to here, sanitized as necessary, that I can start to feed him."

"You know this means we're gonna have a shitload of desk jockeys descend on us, all wantin' a piece of the action, wantin' to change your scenario so they can claim it's their scenario."

"All willing to fuck up the recruitment," said Frank.

"Fuckin'-A. All in the greater national interest of promoting their own careers," said Rocky. Just like you did, thought Frank. They exchanged a glance, and Rocky looked away.

Frank recognized Rocky's effort to make peace, but he knew their war continued. "Can we, I guess that means can you, convince the Langley types it's in their interest to give us some room? Let us bring it off and let them take the credit."

"I can try," said Rocky. "You said he gave you some other stuff that might help. What is it?"

"I'm almost afraid to tell you." He reached for his bulky, battered briefcase. "Let me start with the easy stuff. This is a draft, in Russian, of a statement some top advisers to Brezhnev, foreign affairs and military, want him to make. Says the Soviets will move into Azerbaijan, the Iranian part of Azerbaijan. Move in in force if the U.S. doesn't cancel plans to move the Seventh Fleet Carrier Force into the Indian Ocean, close to the Gulf, and send a squadron of F-15s to Saudi Arabia."

"We've got such plans?"

"The Russians seem to think so. Lermontov says their embassy here thinks the statement is a big mistake, that it will freak out leftist Iranians who otherwise support the Soviets, not to mention other Islamic countries. He hopes if the Americans know about it they can use some quiet diplomacy to discourage Brezhnev from coming out with it. 'Course, the Americans have to handle it so it looks like the leak came from Moscow or someone in Washington, not someone in Tehran."

"He gave you this?"

"Yeah."

"You sure that's what it says?"

"Hell, no. I don't read Russian. Rocky, have you got anybody who reads Russian?"

"Yeah, I told you. Me. Belinsky reads it better, but I'm not sure I wanna share this. When's Brezhnev supposed t' make the statement?"

"The *Constellation*—he said the *Constellation*'s the carrier force flagship—is in the Pacific but heading toward Singapore, just around the corner from the Indian Ocean. If the *Constellation* keeps coming in this direction when it leaves Singapore, they want Brezhnev to go public."

"He's already made one statement telling us to stay away."

"And real quick we said we had no intention of intervening. But all this gets a lot more specific. The *Constellation* to the Gulf. F-15s to the Saudis. Russian troops into northern Iran."

"And we react and maybe World War III starts right here," said Rocky.

"Maybe, in a way, it's already started," said Frank.

"Best we can do," said Rocky, "draft the cable quick as you can and pouch this to Langley."

"We better copy it first," said Frank. "In case somebody over there loses it."

"We aren't that incompetent," said Rocky. He looked from the Cyrillic document to Frank. "Maybe you're right. We'll copy it. Sully, I gotta tell you. If Lermontov is playin' us, this could be part of the game. It could be disinformation. It could be usin' us t' affect American policy. When you draft, get those caveats into the cable. But if we are bein' played, our caveatin' won't help but so much. I'm almost afraid to ask what else you got."

"You should be. Lermontov says he knows about a mole."

"Fuck me." Rocky seized the edge of the glass table with both hands.

"He didn't say 'mole.' 'Penetration agent,' he called it. So maybe it is 'fuck us.'"

"No jokes," said Rocky. "This for real?"

"He only knows his code name, and he wouldn't even give me that. He thinks this may be his ticket to get to the States."

"He may be right," said Rocky. "High level, low level?"

"From what he said, sounds pretty low level. Said he knew some of the information the guy had passed on, which could help track him down. But if we don't track him down, Lermontov worries the guy may find out about him."

"And give Lermontov up to whoever the fuck handles him."

"Right," said Frank. "Lermontov says of all the risks he faces, the mole is the most dangerous, and not just to him."

"He's right about that," said Rocky. "Long as we're here, a mole in Langley could put all our asses in a sling."

"But Lermontov said if he could get himself assigned to the embassy in Washington, he'd be in a position to find out more about the penetration."

"Clever fucker. He knows us too well. But I'll tell you what. This mole business could help us. I'll get off a cable to the Holy Ghost himself, eyes only."

Frank knew Rocky meant Henry James, the head of the agency's counter-intelligence operations. Dan Nitzke had worked with him and considered him completely mad. Others shared that opinion, but James wielded enormous power.

"I know the guy," said Rocky. "If Lermontov can give up a mole, that makes recruitin' Lermontov the Holy Ghost's game. If James gets into this, and I guarantee you he will, he'll call off the NE and Soviet Division dogs in a hurry. It becomes his baby, and his way is to take care of business by remote control. And nobody else treads on his turf. They're too worried about what he might know about them. Or could maybe find out or make up. 'Sides, none of those homebodies will have the hots to come over to this armpit of a country at a time where they might face a serious risk of getting their ass shot off. What else have you got on this maybe mole?"

"Not much. Sounds like he's strictly a mercenary. Nothing ideological, which makes some KGB types suspicious. But they've rolled up a couple of operations, East Bloc and Russia."

"Sweet Holy Ghost. He'll love this. How long they been runnin' him?"

"I don't know."

"Find out. Find out all you can. And let Lermontov know this could be his ace in the hole. When's your next meet?"

"Soon's we get some word back from Langley."

"You contact him through this Hamid character?"

Frank hesitated.

"Quit stalling. What's wrong?"

"Another problem. Lermontov's pretty sure military intelligence is about to roll him up."

"Him who? Hamid?"

Frank nodded.

"I thought he fuckin' works for military intelligence."

"He works for lots of people," said Frank. "Lermontov says that's what got him in trouble."

"Just what we need. If they roll up Hamid, what happens to Gus?"

"I asked about that. Lermontov said far as he knows Gus won't be bothered. Unless he doesn't get the message and tries to recruit another J2 agent."

"How come Lermontov knows all this shit about our people and we don't?"

"He likes to say they're a professional organization."

"Unlike us."

"He doesn't say that, but I guess that's the message."

"We better tell Gus real quick," said Rocky.

"Want me to take care of it?" asked Frank.

"No. It's my job. Shit. No Nazih. No Hamid. How the fuck do you set up a meet?"

"He suggested—he said he hadn't been spying on us, but he knows where we live."

"That fucker."

"Our front door's dark green, so he said, if I wanted a meet, put a single chalk mark on the door. That means a meet at the safe house the next night, half hour earlier than the last time."

"How does he signal you if he wants a meet?"

"We haven't worked that out yet, which for now is okay since the ball's in our court. But I sure wish I knew where he lives."

"I'll find out for you," said Rocky.

A four-man military patrol in Shahnaz Square stopped him on his way back from the embassy. His documents appeared to impress the young soldier with corporal's chevrons. He called over one of his men and spoke to him in Farsi.

"After curfew," said the second soldier to Frank.

"Embassy business," said Frank. Around him, he could hear voices shouting into the night. He asked the soldier who had some English, "What are the people saying?"

"*Allah-o akbar,*" said the soldier. "God is great. The Imam has told the people to go to their rooftops and shout. We have a curfew on the streets, but we cannot put a curfew on God."

The voices of the soldiers surrounded Frank, all saying softly, "*Allah-o akbar.*"

"You should watch for the full moon," said the soldier who spoke English. He nodded upward toward a milky section of clouds. "In a few nights, when the moon will be full, you can clearly see the face of the Imam in the moon. All the people say so."

The corporal studied the sky and spoke in Farsi.

"Unless the clouds are too many," said the other soldier.

After determining his destination, they let him pass.

He sat on the edge of his bed, naked except for his Jockey briefs, and said softly, "*Allah-o akbar.*" The usual quiet held in the immediate neighborhood beyond his window, but in the distance he could hear the murmur of soft human sounds. He could not distinguish the words, but he knew that somewhere, not far away, people stood on their rooftops shouting, "*Allah-o akbar.*"

He recalled Anwar's words. Beware the tenth of *Moharram*. *Ashura*. He wanted to sleep, but on recent nights his uneasy rest had been broken by limbs that betrayed him. A cramp in his left thigh had taken him half an hour to shake. He slept again until an arm that flailed across his chest flipped him into sweating wakefulness. He feared another such night but could imagine no defense. He closed his eyes and saw a photograph of himself in the arms of his father in someone's backyard. The date written on the back in his mother's hand, August 1932, told him it was just after his second birthday, eighteen months before his father's suicide. His father had killed himself and left Frank a legacy of suicide. Assadollah Alam had died and left the Shah alone. *He left me, betrayed me*.

He wondered what legacy he would leave his own son, and how much Jackie's sense of betrayal would rub off on Jake. He thought of the slow suicide of his stepfather, steadily drinking himself to death, building a stairway that led to a blank wall. He wanted to talk to his stepfather about World War II days in Iran, but he wondered how much his alcohol-sodden brain remembered of that long-ago time. He longed for sleep, but the thought shocked him awake.

Twin photos montaged. In one he sat on the iron lioness that sentineled the Parkside Avenue entrance to Brooklyn's Prospect Park, her cubs around her. He guessed he was four, the year of his father's suicide. In the other, taken by Jackie, he stood with a hand on the head of the statue while six-year-old Jake straddled the lioness in her new lair at the entrance to the park's zoo. He thought of Mina and her cubs. He thought of absent fathers.

The old photos dissolved into the movie he'd shot in his mind of the planes circling above a Tehran in flames and smoke. He focused on one plane that became a peregrine, diving to strike a pigeon in midair. He wondered if he still flew on the peregrine's dappled wings or if he had become the prey. Had he recruited Lermontov? Or had he become Lermontov's pigeon? He remembered a headline he'd read: "Death Comes to the Peregrine Falcon." Had he become an endangered species, KUPEREGRINE, carrying the code name a cipher clerk had assigned him years before?

The soft voices of the soldiers who had stopped his car echoed in his head— *Allah-o akbar*—followed by another distorted refrain: There is no God but Allah, and Khomeini is his Prophet.


Frank and Rocky climbed the three flights from the basement to the bubble and settled themselves at the glass-topped table. Rocky wasted no time.

"My eyes-only special to the Holy Ghost worked," he said. "Answer back in record time. He's made the whole Lermontov op a Counter Intelligence deal. Froze out Near East and Soviet Division. He'd shut down the whole agency t' find himself a mole. James wants all the details Lermontov's got on the mole t' make sure it's legit. You're gonna have t' memorize the Holy Ghost's requirements and get your guy to respond. So Lermontov isn't a potential defector or even an agent in place anymore. He's elevated to the status of mole spotter."

"Does that mean I can put a chalk mark on my front door?"

"Yeah. You got any chalk?"

"I asked Bill Steele for a piece. He came up with a box."

"Do it during the blackout tonight, if we get one."

"We always do."

"Yeah, but in case we don't, do it as late as you can and make sure there's no lights on behind you. That sets up your first crack at another meet tomorrow night, right?"

"Correct."

"Look, this time give him a note. Tell him to debug the place and talk about it while he's doing it. That'll sound good when his bosses listen to the tape from his wire, because if he's supposed to be recruiting you they'll have him wired. It'll also help him to think you're a pretty smart guy lookin' out for his interest." Frank nodded. "Okay, kiddo. You're on your way. That's the good news as far as our work here goes. The bad news is, when you get back to the States, if your idea works and you do get Lermontov over there, you'll be reporting to Henry fuckin' James himself, and God help you. He's nutty as a fruitcake, and he might fuckin' well convince himself you're a fuckin' mole. You know damn well he's already got your 201 file on his desk and he's wonderin' about that red flag."

"Great," said Frank. "Recruit a KGB officer and get your ass in a sling."

"Don't worry about it," said Rocky, "because there's not much you can do about it, except maybe get James convinced Lermontov's the best damn agent in place he ever had. And you can bet your *tuchis* on it, once James gets ahold of him, Lermontov's his agent. Not yours."


Visions of a red flag on a 201 file teased his imagination as he sped toward Supreme Commander's Headquarters. A letter-size manila folder with his cryptonym, KUPEREGRINE, hand-printed in black and a red tag stapled to it. A dull green legal hanging folder with a red flag attached to a stiff wire next to his pseudonym, typed behind a plastic tab. Dan Nitzke had told him his cryptonym because he thought it was funny to name him for an endangered species. He had never known his pseudonym, but he knew the format: the reliance on weird first and last names with the last name in all uppercase letters, something like Hawthorne J. CHESTERFIELD. Fred Bunker would know, but he did not want to ask Fred a question he might not want to answer, a question from an outsider. As an agent who had always worked beyond the precincts of Langley, he knew he would always be seen as an outsider to headquarters-bred intelligence officers like Fred—even to those like Rocky who had contrived to spend most of their careers overseas. He relished his outsider's status but wondered what the agency looked like from inside. Does a red flag look like a red flag? He hoped he would never know, but he feared having Henry James suspect him of being an infiltrator, a mole, a Soviet agent.

———

Heavy street traffic, complicated by long lines at filling stations, slowed his progress, but as he neared Dowshan Tappeh he realized that for the first time in several days he had time for the gym. Convinced that his lack of exercise contributed to the recent restlessness that deprived him of sleep, he longed for the exhaustion that would follow a hard workout. He'd begun keeping his gym gear in a canvas bag he stashed in the bottom drawer of an underutilized file cabinet in Rushmore's office. He changed quickly and headed for the gym.

As he approached the doors to the basketball court, he could hear the sounds of a game in progress. He looked inside, hoping to see a half-court game that might leave a basket free for him to work at, but the doors opened onto a loud and frantic full-court game. No b-ball for me, he thought. It took a moment before he realized the players included Bill Steele, Fred Bunker, and Corporal Cantwell. Stan Rushmore, belly stretching his T-shirt, waved to him from a bench on the sidelines. Frank sat next to him.

"How we doin'?"

"Up six, which is a miracle considerin' how short-handed we are."

"Who's the little guy?"

"Reggie Manning. Another ex-cop. Outta Chicago. Played college ball for Loyola."

"I haven't seen him around."

"Nah. Usually he's outta town even more than I am. Now we got a shot at winnin' the Dowshan Tappeh tournament, Troy switched some schedules around best he could so Reggie gets to play every game."

Frank watched Manning with envy. Older, shorter, and slighter than Frank, he got to play with the big boys because of superior skill. Both teams battled under the boards, and Manning scrapped as hard as anyone, diving for loose balls, reaching in for a steal, streaking downcourt for an outlet pass from Steele off a rebound. He made the lay-up look easy.

Frank retreated to the gym, where the *homafaran* had already begun their workout. He recognized the reedy voice of Ayatollah Khomeini. Anwar the Taller nodded toward the bench where a cassette tape played. "The Imam," he said. "This tape, he talks about *Tasu'a* and *Ashura*." Frank guessed it was the same tape Munair had sent to him through Anwar the Smarter.

"People will not laugh," said Anwar, "but the Imam can be very comic. Here he mocks the government. He says the people already have permission from Imam Hossein to honor his martyrdom. He says an illegitimate government appointed by the illegitimate Shah cannot make rules against the faith of the people. On behalf of the Islamic government that will soon rule Iran, he gives permission for the people to observe their traditions during *Moharram*. He says he also issues permission for all members of the military government to resign from office and join in the marches. And he gives permission to the armed forces to surrender their weapons to the people."

Frank had not heard the door open but he noticed Anwar's eyes shift. He looked over his shoulder and saw Sergeant Abbas's bulk fill the door frame. The sergeant glanced toward the cassette player and nodded his approval. His right hand rested on the butt of his .45. I don't think he'll surrender his weapon to the people, thought Frank.

"This is near the end," said Anwar. "The Imam urges the people to ignore the nightly curfew, to march on *Tasu'a* and *Ashura* in white robes and chant that God is great."

"*Allah-o akbar,*" shrilled the raspy voice from the cassette. "*Allah-o akbar,*" And the *homafaran* and Sergeant Abbas echoed the cry, "*Allah-o akbar.*"

Frank remained in the gym long after the *homafaran* had left, punishing the heavy bag, punishing himself with heavy weights, wearying himself, wearing himself out. Exhausted, he headed home. He skipped dinner and a shower and fell into a deep sleep. In his dream he marched among the flagellants on *Ashura,* stripped to the waist, beating himself with a leather whip. The whip became heavier and heavier until he saw his arms swing a metal chain against his back.

*Allah-o akbar. Allah-o akbar. Allah-o akbar.*

He woke with a start. He'd forgotten to put a chalk mark on the door. He switched on the bedside lamp and checked his watch. Just a few minutes after midnight. He slipped into a pair of blue jeans and a dark blue sweatshirt and fished a stick of chalk from the box in his briefcase. He put the light out, then padded downstairs. He cracked the door, listened, then peered into the quiet, empty street. He made his mark and bolted the door behind him.

# CHAPTER FOURTEEN

"Colonel Kasravi will be sending for you a bit later," General Merid said to Frank at their morning Jayface meeting.

Apparently no one had yet told General Merid their civic action proposals, with the possible exception of the newspaper, had died. He began an earnest discussion of military involvement in the distribution of benzene and cooking oil. Frank let him go, even contributing what he hoped would pass for thoughtful comments.

His attention picked up when, at tea-break time, a new waiter appeared in place of Hamid. Tall and solidly built with a drooping mustache, he appeared to speak no English. Still, he paid more attention to their conversations than a waiter might need to as he made his way among them with an unchanging, sullen stare.

Frank tried to catch Gus's eye, but Gus looked away. Turning his back to the others, Frank said to Anwar, "What happened to Hamid?" Anwar walked away without speaking.


As the new waiter cleared the remnants of their tea break, a young man with a corporal's stripes on the sleeve of an Imperial Guard uniform entered and spoke to General Merid.

"Ah, Major Sullivan. Could you follow the corporal? Colonel Kasravi wishes to see you."


"Let me come directly to the point," said the colonel as Frank took a chair close to him. "Do you have your tape recorder?"

"Yes, sir."

"Good, The prime minister has asked me to inform you of a major change in policy. On Wednesday, your 6 December, two days from now, close to five hundred political prisoners will be released. The exact figure, at least as of this morning, stood at four hundred and seventy-two, including Karim Sanjabi of the National Front. We will allow religious demonstrations throughout the country on *Tasu'a,* which is next Sunday, and the following day, *Ashura.* Here in Tehran marches through the city will be led by Karim Sanjabi and Ayatollah Taleqani, himself recently released from prison. They have guaranteed the marches will be peaceful, and both know that if the marches turn violent they face a quick return to prison. Ayatollah Khomeini has also called for peaceful demonstrations. We expect peaceful demonstrations. As I stipulated in our previous conversation, you can convey this information to your government but not to any of your counterparts on Jayface, including the general, or to any other Iranians or any foreign nationals or uncleared Americans. Is that clear?"

"Yes, sir. But, sir, may I ask?"

"What is it?"

"Why are you telling me this?"

"Because the prime minister wants the Americans to know it, and your ambassador these days meets only with the Shah. Because the prime minister knows the Shah trusts you, he wants you to be the one who conveys his message to your government. His Imperial Majesty has, of course, approved this approach. Eleven *Moharram,* your 12 December, is only ten days away. We must have your government's unconditional approval of your continuing availability as an adviser by then. The prime minister also wants to be sure your government realizes how valuable you can be as a conveyer of information, in case it becomes clear that your other ideas, including your newspaper, will not be acted on in any foreseeable future."

"I'm sorry to hear that, sir."

Kasravi caught Frank's eye, glanced at the tape recorder, and chopped the air with his open hand. Frank shut the recorder off.

"Thank you," said Kasravi. "On the other matter, you have not, I believe, been granted an audience with His Imperial Majesty since we spoke about that thirty-page document."

"No, sir. I haven't."

"We hope you will have an opportunity soon. Admiral Hayati spoke to me about it again early this morning. He said he would like to meet with you."

Interesting, thought Frank. "I would consider it an honor."

"I would consider it a mistake," said Kasravi. "Such a meeting would compromise the admiral in the eyes of . . . others. I told him, suggested rather, that it would not be a good idea. Your Jayface colleague Munair, Captain Irfani, who is close to the admiral, agrees with me."

"Maybe you're right," said Frank. "Maybe it wouldn't be a good idea, but I would like to meet him."

Rocky had insisted on climbing up to the bubble. Frank wondered why.

"It's not worth much," said Rocky, "but do a cable on what Kasravi told you about Sanjabi and all the rest gettin' outta jail and the stuff on the demonstrations."

"Can I feed it to Lermontov?"

"Negative," said Rocky. "The colonel said no foreign nationals, remember? I don't wanna take a chance somebody may be tryin' to set us up. Your buddy Lermontov was pretty tight with Nazih, remember? Who knows who else he's tight with. You feed him this stuff about Sanjabi gonna get outta jail, and word gets back to Kasravi, your ass is seaweed. And then these guys don't have to worry about you bein' tight with the Shah."

"Okay," said Frank.

"Don't look so down in the chops. You gotta realize the only game in town that counts is Lermontov. It looks like I need you to move that along, but I damn sure don't want you t' do anything t' fuck it up. 'Sides, I got somethin' else for you to feed Lermontov. Somethin' that'll do him and the boys back in Moscow a lot more good than knowin' about Sanjabi."

"Oh?"

"Don't gimme that gloomy 'oh' shit. This is good stuff, about that *Tudeh* party of his. Seems like there's a splinter group. Woke up one mornin' in the middle of this Islamic Revolution. Found out they were in a foxhole and all of a sudden they ain't atheists anymore. Call themselves the Militant Followers of the Imam's Line. *Savak*'s got one of their bozos in with this bunch. He came up with a copy of a report these guys put together on how the godless Soviets plan to take over after the Islamic Revolution brings down the Shah. They plan to send some guys up to wherever it is outside 'a Paris where Khomeini hangs out and brief him on what the Sovs are up to. Tell him who the bad guys are, who the good guys are who he can trust with the *Tudeh* and the Muslim *Mojahedin* and all the other little leftist shits."

"Any chance these were the *Tudeh* bunch tied in with Nazih?"

"I asked Eagle-1 about that. He said he wasn't sure 'cause buildin' the case on Nazih was handled by J2 and the Shah's private spooks. And it figures Lermontov won't know about it because his *Savak* contacts were part of the bunch J2 rolled up when they grabbed Nazih."

Frank shuddered. "What can I give Lermontov?" he asked.

"The whole deal. The report these guys cooked up for Khomeini. The names of all the *Tudeh* creeps involved. The Sovs they work with, names and physical description, which is interesting. So far no mention of Lermontov. No description that sounds like him. Either they know him by another name or, more likely, he uses a cut out. I told Eagle-1 we wanted it all. It gets back to him that Lermontov's got it, I'll convince him Lermontov must have a new Joe in *Savak*. Stuff I'm gonna give you includes a fake cable from me to Langley. Should be enough for Lermontov to convince Moscow he's got a real CIA defector."

"Okay," said Frank. "I just hope it doesn't convince the Holy Ghost that Lermontov's got a real defector."

"I already cleared it with the Holy Ghost. He fuckin' loves it. But what he's really hot for is all you can get outta Lermontov on his penetration agent. So penetrate the shit outta'm."

Frank checked his watch. Seven forty-five. Long past the time Lermontov should have arrived at the safe house. He turned off the light in the front window and sat in the dark. Wondering. Worrying. Had he put up his chalk mark too late? Did Lermontov simply have something else to do that he couldn't get out of? Like a meeting with the British ambassador? Or the MI6 man with the handle-bar mustache? What about the mole? Had Lermontov been rolled up? By whom? By *Savak*? By the Islamic dissidents in the *Tudeh* party? By J2 or who-ever had rolled up Nazih? And if Lermontov's been rolled up, will I be next? He hated questions he couldn't answer. And they kept coming. Was the safe house unsafe and under surveillance? Had he endangered Bunker, who would be rolling down the drive to pick him up in a few minutes? Bunker, who hated to drive in Tehran anyway. He couldn't endanger Bunker. He remembered all the *Savak* material he had in his briefcase. What would happen if he and Bunker got caught with that? He sat in the dark and worried until the flash of lights from dim to bright and back to dim alerted him to Bunker's arrival. He grabbed his guilt-laden briefcase and hurried down the stairs to open the garage door. Fuck the need to know. They had a right to know. He decided to tell Fred and Gus about the contents of the briefcase.

"Look, I've got a problem."

They sat around the kitchen table while Frank wolfed down leftovers from a dinner of veal hollandaise, asparagus, and saffron rice he had prepared the night before.

"'Cause the Russkie didn't show?" asked Gus.

"No," said Frank. "'Cause of what's going to happen when he does show."

"Is it something we need to know?" asked Fred.

"I think so. Not the details, but you do need to know that I'm carrying around some very hot material I'm supposed to feed to Lermontov. If he'd made the meet tonight, I would've given it to him and that'd be that. But I had to lug it from the safe house back here, and I'm worried about what might have happened to Lermontov and am I gonna be next. Tell you the truth, I even worry Lermontov might give me up, try to get me PNG'd."

"Thought he was your buddy," said Gus.

"Be real," said Frank. "He's a KGB officer."

"Where's the material now?" said Bunker.

"Right there. In that big ugly old briefcase."

"Okay," said Fred. "I've got that false-bottom desk upstairs. When the material's in the house, we can stash it there. Tomorrow, I'll get Bill Steele to secure it in one of the safes that stays locked all day, and I'll ask him if he can hook up some kind of secure hiding place in the cars, or at least another briefcase with a false bottom, like mine. That's about all we can do."

"That all sounds pretty good to me," said Gus.

"An operation like this," said Fred, "well, we can't eliminate the risk. But we can limit it. I'm glad you told us."

"So am I," said Frank.

Fred insisted on showing Frank and Gus how to open the false bottom on his desk. Frank had had an identical desk in Lusaka for the Angola account, and he guessed Gus had worked with something similar often.

"I keep this tucked away in a pair of socks that are always in this corner of my sock drawer." Fred drew out a wedge of thin, flexible metal about the size and shape of a tongue depressor. He crouched before the desk and slid the strip of metal into a recess hidden by a decorative swirl of wood. "Right about here." A silent spring released the bottom, which fell into view. Frank saw a single manila folder, the Browning nine millimeter, and a box of cartridges.

Frank stared at the gun. He resented the agency regulations that denied him access to a weapon. Each day, and night, he took far greater risks than Bunker, yet only Bunker had an automatic.

"I wish I had one of those," he said.

"I'm glad I don't have one of those," said Gus.

Fred put Frank's oversize envelope into the drawer and shut it. He had Frank and Gus practice opening and closing the drawer several times.

"That should do it," said Fred. "The magic wand goes back in the sock drawer. Frank, why don't you be the one to open it up before we head out in the morning."

"Okay," said Frank. "And thanks."

"Speaking of thanks," said Gus, "thanks for the heads-up you gave Rocky about Hamid."

"I would've told you myself," said Frank, "but Rocky said he wanted to do it."

"His job," said Gus, "but at least we aren't keeping each other in the dark."

"Let's continue to follow that paradigm," said Bunker.

He hadn't managed to get in any gym time. He knew he needed to spend more time with his *homafar* friends, but he also had to handle his obligations with the Shah, Lermontov, Colonel Kasravi, and Anwar and Mina. In an ideal situation they would have found a way for Fred and Gus to take over some of his contacts, but time seemed limited and the contacts too personal for an easy transition. He'd been accused before of falling in love with his agents. He couldn't buy the idea that he had fallen in love with the Shah or Lermontov or Anwar. Not even with Mina. He'd let some contacts get too close, perhaps. Too personal, yes. He believed he kept a distance, a range of objectivity. But, he thought, maybe I don't.

"New briefcase?"

"Yes," said Frank. He extracted a metal spatula from his shoe, smaller than the one they'd used on Fred's desk, and slid it along a seam in the shiny leather until it caught. A puff of air signaled the release of an inner lining. Frank twirled two combination locks, opened the lid, and pulled out the envelope Rocky had given him.

"We have a report from *Savak* that will interest you," said Frank for the benefit of the wire he assumed Lermontov wore.

Lermontov, who had arrived exactly at seven, had already checked for bugs with his scanner. The red bulb had flashed frequently. "Better late than never. You won't need your tape recorder. From the reactions I'm getting, and previous experience, of course, I would say the vase with the fake blue flowers is the primary receptor. The others are backup in case one of us moves about. Since the vase is the primary receptor, let's make it easy for your technicians. Obviously, they are not very sophisticated. Let's stay close to the vase."

Frank pronounced "vase" with a New Yorker's long *a*. He noted Lermontov used the more correct short *a*.

"Sorry about last night," said Lermontov, "What was it our mutual friend used to say? A pressing commitment. And it was rather short notice."

Frank wondered if Lermontov had heard any word of Nazih since his arrest. He sketched a question on a sheet of his notebook. Lermontov shook his head and wrote, "Nor do I intend to." He studied the typewritten note Frank had given him, asking for verifying details on the mole.

"I anticipated this," he said aloud. He reached into his briefcase and slid a sealed manila envelope across the table. Two words, neatly printed, advised, "Read Later."

"And this report from *Savak*. I see it's in Farsi? I hope I am not mentioned." He seemed unconcerned by the multiple listening devices. "But the least you could have done would have been to prepare a Cyrillic script version."

"I thought your Farsi was pretty good."

"It is," said Lermontov. "But we have people who are much better. I did not expect anything . . . anything like this so soon. We should discuss payment at our next meeting. I will take care of it. Do you know when these fools plan to go to France?"

"Two guys are named in the station's cable, with the dates. They fly to London on party business, meetings with Kianouri and other *Tudeh* exiles. They have a couple of free days and plan to take the boat train to Paris. Supposedly, Khomeini's agreed to meet with them."

"Trust me, they will never see Paris, much less Khomeini. If it's correct, this material has great value. I will request an initial payment of five thousand dollars. Will that be satisfactory?"

It would be wonderful, thought Frank, if I could keep it. "To tell you the truth," he said aloud, "it seems a little low."

"An initial payment. If you can continue to provide material of this quality, assuming, of course, it can be verified, I can arrange higher payments. Tell me, how did you get the cable?"

"I drafted it. Rocky, the chief of station, Roger Novak, likes the way I write. I draft many of his cables. I'm a fast typist, so I typed a second copy for myself. If anyone looks on the IBM tape, they'll see that the cable's been retyped. But no one will. When it's full it just gets burn bagged."

"Amateurs."

"I know. That's another reason I decided to talk to you. Not just the money. I also see how incompetent, how corrupt this agency is."

Lermontov pulled apart the lapels of his suit jacket and smiled. "Don't bother," he said. "Next time I'll wear a wire and you can do your whole script."


"I dunno, Sullivan. You sound awful convincin' when you talk about how incompetent and corrupt the agency is."

"What can I tell you? For a while, I thought I was going to be an actor."

"Speaking of actor, we better script you for the next meeting. Stuff you don't want on the tape you can give each other notes about, like you been doin'. He don't give a shit what's on our tape, but he's gonna need tapes he can give to his people to make you sound like a legit traitor."

"That's an interesting concept."

"Yeah. You can use it for the title of your next book. The legit traitor. Meantime, more from the Holy Ghost. He's got NE puttin' together stuff based on our recent cables they'll massage into shape that you can give it to Lermontov. He also wants more initiative from us on stuff like this *Tudeh* party business. You let Lermontov know we need some verifying details on his mole?"

"He was ready," said Frank. He handed Rocky the "Read Later" envelope.

Rocky tore it open. "Christ. Approximate dates. Exact locations. Czechoslovakia, Hungary, East Germany, Russia. Twelve code names and for about half of them real names. Who they were, what they did. All wrapped up and executed on info from our mole. Fucker's been at it six years."

"Sounds like good stuff," said Frank.

"Yeah. Sounds good. But if we're bein' fucked with, he's just givin' us stuff the Russians know we already got. They may be ready t' give this bastard up anyway. Whoever the fuck he is. Let the Holy Ghost figure it out. Your next meet's when, Friday?"

"Right. We wanted to give him time to come up with my five thousand."

"Tell you what, Sully. If he does come up with five thousand he must've done a hell of a job sellin' you. KGB usually low-ball their new recruits, keep'm hungry and greedy, slowly build'm up. Five big ones is a real high ante for them."

"I should've said it's only a thousand."

"And we split the other four?" said Rocky.

"Something like that," answered Frank. "Anyhow, besides coming up with the money, he wants to see how this *Tudeh* party business shakes down."

"You know those two guys are dead, right?"

"I guess I had a hunch they might get dead, but I thought maybe if I kept my eyes closed nobody could see me."

"What's that supposed to mean?"

"Something kids do when they want to hide and there's no place to hide. Close your eyes, and since you can't see, you think nobody can see you. I don't think I've ever been responsible for somebody getting killed before."

"Come on," said Rocky. "If we didn't give it to Lermontov, Eagle-1 woulda had 'em killed. This way Lermontov gets 'em killed."

"Will he do it himself?"

"No way. They'll hire a couple of locals or maybe even import a couple of hitters from Afghanistan. That language of theirs, Dari, Belinsky tells me, sounds about the same as Farsi, so it's easy enough to bring in a couple of guys who'll fit in real well but can also disappear real quick in case some *Tudeh* types get nosy. It's a cinch *Savak* or the local gendarmes won't give a shit."

Yeah, thought Frank. But I do.


The summons had come during the Jayface tea break. Frank had barely entered the room when Colonel Kasravi asked, "Has your government confirmed your status as a permanent adviser?"

"Permanent?" said Frank. "Permanent sounds like an awfully long time. I believe the phrase we used was 'continuing' or 'continuing basis.' Something like that."

"Correct," said the colonel. "In this world nothing stands as permanent, does it?"

"No, sir. I guess not. But you had set *Moharram* 11 as your deadline."

"That's only four days away," said the colonel. "And you had said you would request a more rapid response."

"And I did. But if nothing comes in today, I would like to use today's meeting, your question to me today, as the basis for another cable, to prod my government for an answer."

"Good," said the colonel. "Please do that. By the way, not that it matters, but I liked the suggestion *Armed Forces Times*. As the name for the newspaper."

Frank had always assumed the Jayface meeting room was bugged, but it hadn't occurred to him Colonel Kasravi's office would be among the listening posts.

"That wasn't your voice, was it?" said the colonel.

"No, sir. That was my colleague, Lieutenant Commander Simpson."

"Pity it will never happen," said Kasravi.

"Yes, sir," said Frank. "It would be a pity if it never happened."

The colonel smiled. "You are persistent, aren't you? Why does this newspaper idea matter so much to you?"

"Sir, I guess I just love newspapers. I got to be editor of the weekly newspaper when I was only twenty in a South Texas town called Alice, and then in Ethiopia running the major daily newspaper was part of my job. When I was growing up in New York, there were something like fourteen daily papers. Now there are only four. I hate to see a newspaper die, especially one that hasn't been born yet."

"I begin to understand," said Kasravi. "The possibility may remain open if we receive word that you have been posted here as an adviser. But I must tell you events are moving rapidly. The release of the political prisoners, which I told you about on Monday, took place as scheduled yesterday. Sanjabi and Ayatollah Taleqani will, as I told you, lead peaceful demonstrations on *Tasu'a* and *Ashura*. We will announce this to the foreign press at zero eight hundred hours tomorrow. BBC and Voice of America will broadcast the news in Farsi. The Russians will broadcast from Baku. They are our mass media these days—Ayatollah Khomeini's tapes and the foreigners."

"Colonel, if I may suggest it, the government should do more of this kind of thing. Inform the foreign press and through them the people of Iran of positive measures the government takes."

"Do you think our people believe the foreign press more than our own news media?"

"Yes, sir. I do."

"You are very bold to say so," said the colonel.

"At least some of the foreign press, sir."

"Like BBC?"

"Well, yes, sir."

Kasravi offered another of his rare smiles. "I would suggest you do not express that view to His Imperial Majesty. You are right, of course. Many Persians, myself included, rely on BBC for news about our country. But His Imperial Majesty believes BBC—and the British government—have become tools of Mr. Khomeini."

No "Imam" for the colonel, thought Frank.

"And in fact," said Kasravi, "we brief the foreign press every day. They rarely transmit the material we give them."

"I might be able to help you with that. I understand the world press. What they consider newsworthy. How the British and the Americans and the French journalists differ from each other. How the Russians differ from everybody. How individual newspapers, say, like the *Wall Street Journal,* the *New York Times,* the *Washington Post,* have different approaches. How BBC differs from the *Morning Telegraph.* How you can hook the interest of one with one story, the interest of another with a different story. What material none of them will take an interest in."

"It all sounds very ambitious, Major Sullivan. For these times. I wish you had arrived here and shared your skills with us a year or two ago. Nevertheless, I will discuss your suggestions with the prime minister. We shall see."

"It could be helpful, sir. To drown out the noise from Neauphle-le-Château."

"We shall see. And now . . ."

Frank interrupted him. "Colonel, I just wondered . . ."

"Yes?"

"Well, Gus, Commander Simpson, also has an extensive background working with the news media. In fact, the name you liked for our newspaper, *Armed Forces Times,* he came up with that idea. I wondered if he could work with me on trying to work out some of these ideas."

"I'm afraid not. Your Commander Simpson tried to recruit a *Savak* agent who also worked for us, military intelligence. You yourself, to the best of our knowledge, have not attempted anything so foolish. We do not want to make an incident over what your friend attempted, but we consider him . . . may I say we consider him in quarantine?"

I should have quit when I was ahead, thought Frank.

Now what? wondered Frank, as he pushed his way through the glass doors of Supreme Commander's Headquarters. He walked out into the parking area, where he saw their driver, Sergeant Ali Zarakesh, and Corporal Cantwell, leaning against a fender of the big, bulletproof Nova. He walked up to them and looked from one to the other.

"I have been instructed to drive you to Niavaran Palace," said Ali with a stern expression.

"And I've been instructed to take your other car back to Dowshan Tap," added Corporal Cantwell with a slight smile. "I also have this for you." He handed Frank an eyes-only envelope.

"Okay," said Frank. "I appreciate that." He stuffed the envelope into a parka pocket, found the keys to the Fiat, and tossed them to Cantwell. "It's all yours."

A much younger majordomo greeted him. "You may have to wait a while. Rather than sit in this drafty hall, there is an office just this way I believe you have used before."

Frank wondered if he would find Lermontov again waiting for him, but the bare room, with its familiar vase of fake blue flowers, proved empty. Frank settled into a chair, ready for a long wait. He nervously fingered the eyes-only envelope, which he had shifted to an inside pocket in his suit jacket. He felt tempted to read it again but knew he had no need. He had scanned it in the car and forgotten nothing.

*The Shah wants to see you. Late this afternoon is all we have, so be prepared to wait. Word comes from his nibs who expects you to break the news about the coup proposal that you understand USG people in Washington have a copy of. What does the Shah think of the various proposals? Also review the status of the armed forces newspaper. The overnights included full and final approval of your role as an adviser on an indefinite basis. Tell the Shah. You can tell the Jayfacers tomorrow. Come back here after your meet.* Again unsigned, and again he knew it had come from Rocky.

He welcomed the wait, even the fact that he had nothing to read. It gave him an opportunity to think, a luxury that had become rare. He worried that in rushing from one contact to the other he would miss a vital beat. Above all, he worried about pinning down Lermontov and finding out more about the mole, but he also worried about neglecting Jake and, yes, Jackie.

When he was finally summoned and followed the young majordomo into the Shah's office, the first thing Frank said was "I don't think I've ever told you about my son, have I?"

The Shah stared at him vacantly, and Frank wanted to bite his tongue.

"I did not even know you had a son," said the King of Kings. He remained slumped in his high-backed chair. He looked even more worn than on Frank's previous visits: his face, a gray reflection of the suit he wore; his features, gaunt; his eyes, hooded.

"Sorry, sir. Just I was thinking about him while I was waiting." Frank fumbled, trying to say something that might make sense. "Like your son, he's in America. A student, but only in the sixth grade. I was thinking of all the things I would have to tell him when I get back home."

"Perhaps we could go together," said the Shah.

"I beg your pardon, sir?"

"When you go back home to America, will you take me with you? I would like to meet this son of yours."

"Would you like to go to America, Your Majesty?"

"Oh, yes. Sloan-Kettering. Johns Hopkins. Columbia Presbyterian. My son is in air force training at Reese, a base near Lubbock in Texas. Perhaps we could exchange visas. He could come here as regent. I could go to America as patient. I'm sure you Americans, like our friends the British, would like to ship me off."

"Please don't include me among any Americans who might want to ship you off. In fact, I have what I hope you'll consider good news. We received approval today from my government of my assignment on an indefinite basis as adviser."

"Indefinite?" said the Shah. "I do not consider 'indefinite' good news. A man in my position would have preferred to have heard something more . . . 'indefinite' sounds . . . very indefinite. Like American support of our rule."

"I'm sure, Your Imperial Majesty, that America's support of your rule is very definite."

"And permanent?"

Oh, shit, thought Frank. How do I get from here to asking what he thinks about a proposal from his military for a coup that would depose him?

"I have to admit, sir, I've never had much faith in the ability of American politicians to stick to any policy. For America, permanent and politics may be a contradiction in terms."

"I agree," said the Shah, straightening in his chair. "Monarchy makes much more sense than political democracy."

"You know how much I admired Haile Selassie," said Frank. "I guess I must have a weakness for monarchs."

"But your government seems to consider monarchy a weakness."

Frank saw his chance.

"I've heard, sir," he said, trying to sound casual, "that somehow the American government has a copy of a proposal developed by your military. A proposal that seems to consider the monarchy somewhat weak, at least at this time."

The Shah's expression darkened. "What do you know of this?"

"My contact at the embassy told me about it. He has his own channels, of course. From what he said, I got the impression that Ambassador O'Connor had not been informed."

"Good. We should prefer to keep it that way. At least for now. Have you read the proposal?"

"No. Just been told some of the highlights."

"Such as?"

"Well, that the plan calls for you to leave Tehran for what I believe is described as a medical leave at a naval base on the gulf."

"They call it a 'vacation,'" said the Shah. His voice put "vacation" quotation marks, punctuated by an uncharacteristic sneer.

"We'd been told you'd been given the proposal and the military waited for your approval."

"Do you have any idea how your government obtained a copy?"

"Sir, my government doesn't normally share its top-level secrets with someone like me."

"Our son-in-law, perhaps. Our ambassador. He's very well connected in America. And in Tehran. Someone in our military must have gotten a copy to him."

"Perhaps," said Frank. "It seems so strange, sir—for your military to give you a plan, to ask your approval, for a coup to depose you."

"It seemed strange to us also," said the Shah, smiling now, but wanly. "How would you have responded, in our place, if your military had given you such a proposal?"

"How have you responded?"

"Our response has been not to respond."

"That seems very wise. Do you think the military, right now, is capable of taking over the country, imposing a new government?"

"*Inshallah.* Or perhaps we should say *Insh-ayatollah.*"

Not God willing, thought Frank. The Ayatollah willing. He had not previously given the Shah credit for such subtle wordplay. Never underestimate an emperor.

"Do you think," Frank asked, "the future depends on the will of Ayatollah Khomeini?"

"Not at all. The future depends on many factors. But this preacher has a following. We will see. The events of *Tasu'a* and *Ashura* may tell us something. For now, we shall wait. We shall see. Then, we shall act."


In the warmth of the American safe house, Lermontov quickly removed his winter greatcoat and lamb's-wool hat. He spread the lapels of his tweed jacket, pointed to his chest, and cupped his huge hands over his ears.

Frank nodded. Okay, he's wired.

"I've been authorized to proceed," said Lermontov. "And, since you are not a very good host, I brought you a present." He unzipped his soft leather briefcase and extracted a one-liter bottle. "Export quality Stolichnaya. It's been in my freezer, so it's nicely chilled. And this—the finest Soviet Beluga. Room temperature. With some biscuits. For you biscuits. I have trouble chewing them. Can you at least provide some glasses and plates? Then we can celebrate."

All my life, thought Frank, I've been looking for a way to sell out. Now I've got it, and it's only a game. Frank handed Lermontov the note he'd prepared.

*Debug the place and talk about it while you're doing it. It will sound good on your tape.*

As Frank went to the kitchen, Lermontov went about systematically dismantling the listening devices he'd previously detected, chattering about how easy it was to detect and neutralize CIA bugs. When Frank returned, Lermontov pointed to the phone, the radiator vents, the vase. He pushed a notebook toward Frank in which he'd written, *Tape recorder?*

They settled at the table, close to the now deaf vase with the fake blue flowers, and toasted each other and enjoyed the caviar and vodka while Frank set his tape recorder in motion.

"You must congratulate me," said Frank. "Word came in the overnight traffic that Langley has okayed my staying here as an adviser."

"Excellent," said Lermontov. "Have you told the Iranians?"

"The Shah, yesterday. The other Iranians, including Kasravi, this morning."

"Good. That makes the timing of this very appropriate." Lermontov pulled a thickly stuffed plain white envelope from his pocket. "Count it, please. Then I will ask you to sign a paper for me."

Twenty-dollar bills. Not new. Frank counted out five stacks of fifty each.

"Five thousand."

"As promised," said Lermontov. "Please sign here." He handed Frank a square of onion-skin paper with Cyrillic script and a stamped seal.

"But I can't read it."

"It says five thousand dollars. You have to learn to trust me."

"I do trust you. I just don't like signing things I can't read."

"A wise principle. But we've moved into a different world now."

"There you go." Frank scrawled his signature across the spot Lermontov indicated.

"Thank you. Now that we've moved into a different world, you will tell your people your effort to recruit me does not look promising. We may meet here once or twice more, then you must tell your people you think the effort should be aborted. We will continue to meet, but at a safe house I will provide. We will rendezvous at locations other than the safe house. I will drive you to our destination. You will be given dark glasses to wear during the ride which will effectively leave you sightless. You will surrender the keys to your car to one of my associates, who will drive your car to another location, where I will drop you off after our meeting. Do you understand these procedures?"

"They sound very well thought out," said Frank, troubled by the way Lermontov had taken over, even to the extent of blinding him.

"It is all for your protection. Including protection from your own people as well as *Savak* or others. Two cars driven by my associates will circle around us at discreet intervals to make sure you and I are not followed. Understood?"

"Understood. But when?"

"Let's meet once more here. Sunday at seven-thirty. Backup Monday, Tuesday."

"Sunday's *Tasu'a,*" said Frank. "Could be a bad day—and night."

"It won't be bad. Khomeini has given instructions the demonstrations must be peaceful. But if it makes you more comfortable, let's make it Monday evening. The *Ashura* demonstration will be over by midafternoon. Unless there's total chaos, the crowds will have gone home."

"Fine," said Frank. "If I need an urgent meet sooner, I'll chalk it on my door. That night. Follow up the next night."

Lermontov did not seem interested, but he nodded.

"What if you need an urgent meet?" asked Frank.

"I won't."

"Never say never. How 'bout you put a chalk mark on your front door?"

Lermontov frowned. "You know where I live?"

"It surprised us. Most Soviets live up in the Zargande complex north of town. But you're on Ghazali Street. We found out."

Lermontov shrugged his massive shoulders. "Not so surprising. I'm declared to *Savak.*"

"You're the *rezident?*"

"I didn't say I'm the *rezident.* I just said that, like the *rezident,* I'm declared as a KGB officer to our Iranian friends. You can look for a chalk mark on my door, if you want, but you won't find one. Understood?"

"Understood."

"Good. The material you provided on the splinter group that plans to defect from *Tudeh* proved most valuable. And useful. Do you have more material for me?"

"Trust me," said Frank. He swung the briefcase Bill Steele had provided up on the table and opened its secret compartment. "Take a look at these."

Lermontov scanned the several documents. "This looks very good, especially this one on your meeting with the Shah. Since Major Nazih's arrest, I have lost my palace access agent. You will remedy that."

"Perhaps not quite," said Frank, "Nazih had daily access to the palace, and not just to the Shah. I see only the Shah and only when he sends for me."

"In the absence of Nazih, how does the Shah contact you?"

"Through the ambassador."

"Your ambassador meets often with the Shah. Can you find out what's said at his meetings?"

"The ambassador wants to hear all about what goes on in my meetings with the Shah, but he isn't very talkative about his own."

*Fake it,* Lermontov wrote hastily on his notebook, then shoved it toward Frank.

"But I can find a way to get access to his cables," said Frank.

"I'm sure you can," said Lermontov. "Do it, please."

Should I salute this bastard, thought Frank, and say "Yes, sir"? He settled for "I'll do it."


"You did real good," said Rocky. He and Frank sat alone in the bubble. "The shit we rehearsed. You did real good on the stuff about you need the money. But also about losin' respect for the agency, about always bein' a kinda half-assed socialist, havin' a black wife and a black kid, about hatin' the way America treats blacks. The Sovs always like it when there's that ideological twist. Yeah, you want money, but you aren't doin' it just for the money. They'll fuckin' love it. Speakin' of money . . . Where the fuck is it?"

"You're sure I can't keep it?"

"Very funny."

Frank pried the white envelope from the briefcase's secret compartment. Twenties spilled across the table.

"Count it," said Rocky.

Frank counted it twice. Each time it added up to $4,980. He peered into the briefcase and found another twenty.

"You're a pisser, Sullivan. Tryin' t' ding me for a twenty."

"It fell out," said Frank. "Do I get a receipt?"

"Sure. What else fell off the back of the truck?"

"This stuff." Frank pulled out three documents in Russian that Lermontov, with a finger raised to his lips, had given him along with a covering summary in English. Rocky flipped through each Russian text, then back to the summary.

"I didn't get a chance to read the English," said Frank. "Just stuck it in the briefcase."

"This is great shit," said Rocky. "Seems as how, after representations by the Americans, Brezhnev has decided not t' make any statements about the *Constellation* and U.S. intervention."

"We didn't get anything from Washington on it?"

"Nope. Somebody back there decided to play need-to-know with us. So we'll come back with 'We don't need to know from Washington. We got the skinny from Moscow.' Sometimes I love this fuckin' job."

Rocky fell silent as he examined the rest of Lermontov's material. When he looked up, he studied Frank, then shook his head.

"These two look even better. If it isn't disinformation. Says the Sovs have pulled back troops from the Azerbaijan frontier as a goodwill gesture to Iran. Then, I guess this one, yeah, says the Sovs are building up their forces on the border with Afghanistan. Shit. Sounds like they've written off Iran to the mullahs but want to flank the holy bastards with their guys in Afghanistan."

"He's giving us intel that's a lot better than what we're giving him," said Frank.

"If this shit is real, your ass is gold. If it isn't, Lermontov may be playin' you. And you can bet, knowin' how paranoid he is, the Holy Ghost's got you pegged as maybe a double agent."

"That's wonderful," said Frank. "Something to come home to."

"Which worries me. I mean, suppose, just suppose this Lermontov guy's tryin' t' set you up."

"How's he going to do that?" said Frank. "He's the one who wants medical treatment in America. I'm not running off to Russia."

"Think about it," said Rocky. "Suppose Lermontov has other plans besides medical treatment. Suppose what he really wants to do is fuck you up. He's maybe still pissed at you gettin' him kicked outta Ethiopia. So maybe he can't get the KGB to go for stickin' an umbrella with a poison tip up your ass, like they did with that poor Bulgarian bastard, or whatever kind of bastard he was. But suppose now he thinks he's got the perfect weapon."

"You lost me," said Frank.

"Henry James," said Rocky. "The Holy fuckin' Ghost. You can bet the farm the KGB knows how the crazy son of a bitch works. Suppose what your good friend Lermontov really wants is t' set you up for a fall. Make it look to James like your KGB buddy's recruited you."

"He couldn't be that devious," said Frank.

"He couldn't?"

"I dunno." Frank studied the palms of his hands. "Maybe he could."

"Don't fall in love with your agent," said Rocky. "Tricky as this thug looks, he might play it both ways. Get to the States for medical treatment and hang you out to dry with the Holy Ghost."

"I hear you."

"Please hear me. And look, when you get back to Langley, if Lermontov convinces his gang he recruited you and he does show up in Washington, talk to James. Tell him you and I talked about this shit. That I didn't want to put all the details in a cable, not even an eyes-only cable to him. James didn't have much t' say on the stuff Lermontov gave you on the mole. But that figures. Who knows where this fuckin' mole might be? He might be somebody works for James. Let James hear it from you before anything maybe does happen. And let him hear it face-t'-face, across his desk. Not in a cable somebody else might get a chance t' read. An ounce of prevention, know what I mean?"

"I'm afraid I do," said Frank.

"By the way," said Rocky, "don't trust James, either."

"Why not?" said Frank. "He wants Lermontov, he has to play straight with me."

"I wish it was that simple, Sully. I really do. I wish James was that simple. But he's crazy, paranoid, brilliant, relentless. He might really believe Lermontov's doubled you, turned you into a KGB fink. He might wanna fuck you over just so he can make Lermontov his exclusive, Henry James–certified defector. There's no tellin' what kinda screwball ideas he might come up with. You gotta play his game. You got no choice. Just don't trust him."

"How 'bout you?" said Frank. "Can I trust you?"

"In this business? Don't trust anybody. Especially me."

You sound like a Persian, thought Frank, Another Third World country heard from. The intelligence community.


He came home to a quiet house. His stomach grumbled, but he felt too exhausted to cook and too depressed to eat. He pulled his Absolut from the freezer. All old spies are paranoid, he thought. Any spy who isn't paranoid doesn't stay alive long enough to grow old. Don't trust James, Rocky said. Can I trust Rocky? Certainly not Lermontov. Rocky had asked him about Beirut. Two flimsy cars and a handgun. A message, perhaps, not a real attempt to kill him. In Ethiopia Lermontov had motive enough to kill him, but in Beirut Lermontov had no need to send him a message. He wondered if that message came from his own people, a warning not to come too close to finding out who stood behind the murder of the ambassador.

"Please, Lord," prayed Frank. "Let me be ever paranoid."

# CHAPTER FIFTEEN

He'd been monitoring the daylong television program for over an hour. The day before, he'd sat with Anwar, Mina, and the children in their front room watching the *Tasu'a* parade. Anwar had explained that the one television channel that continued to operate had limited scope.

"Travelogues. They love travelogues. Especially long, slow-moving Iran Air travelogues of the *haj* to Mecca. Or pilgrimages to Isfahan, Shiraz, Mashhad. Sometimes they just show the flag with military music. No popular music. No movies."

"No soap operas," said Mina. "We used to have some very good soap operas. Not just American soaps like *Dallas,* but our own Iranian soap operas. Everyone loved them."

"Maybe not everyone," said Anwar.

Young Anwar and Mina Two were bored. Frank couldn't blame them. "Long and slow-moving" described the coverage of the *Tasu'a* parade. Single, static cameras were positioned at three spots along the route. The children had been sentenced to straight-backed chairs and silence. With a parent on either side, they stared vacant-eyed at images of flagellants shuffling forward and beating themselves with whips and chains. They took no interest in their father's diligent narration. It's no way to grow up, thought Frank. He thought of the often sadistic cartoons Jake had delighted in. No way to grow up. But he soon started to ignore the children, to forget about Jake and indulge his own fascination with the stark drama that paraded across the flickering screen.

The next day's *Ashura* march, which he watched alone in the living room of the house he shared with Gus and Fred, proved to be a replay of *Tasu'a* but with denser, slower-moving masses and a palpable heightening in the passion of the chain- and whip-wielding marchers. Frank had seen no blood on *Tasu'a,* but among the *Ashura* marchers, particularly the first waves arriving at the final rallying point, Shahyad Square, torn garments and blood-speckled backs spurred the television editors to make sudden cuts to other spots along the line of march.

The camera editor switched back to Jaleh Square. In September troops had fired on crowds gathered at Jaleh Square for a religious rally. "The people call it Black Friday," Mina had said. "The soldiers killed more than four hundred." To Frank, Jaleh Square looked like a big traffic circle, but it was tiny compared to Shahyad Square. Anwar had said Shahyad, with its monument, gardens, flower beds, and fountains, was far bigger than the Place de la Concorde.

Now, for *Ashura,* the tenth day of the month of *Moharram,* the crowds reclaimed both Jaleh and Shahyad and most of Tehran in the name of the father, Ali; the son, Hossein; and the holy spirit of Khomeini. Despite Anwar's foreboding about *Ashura,* despite the bloody backs of the flagellants, the masses obeyed Khomeini's call for a peaceful march. Frank found that evidence of the Ayatollah's power more impressive than any level of violence might have been.

The camera showed the crowds still coming toward Jaleh Square even though tens of thousands had already reached Shahyad, several miles west and north across town. Anwar had told him the *Tasu'a* march took over six hours to pass through the heart of town and involved over a million people. The military expected more than two million today for *Ashura.*

He swung from the television set in the living room to the kitchen, where he stirred the huge pot of chili he'd been brewing and sliced and diced the salad. With any luck, they would live off the combination for two or three days. Gus and Fred, rather than risk cabin fever, had driven the short distance to Tom Troy's office at the air base. Frank welcomed the chance to have the house to himself, but he had begun to imagine that his son, Jake, sat by him. He pointed to the television screen and said, "Look."

Millions of people marching, he said in his mind to Jake. Passionate, peaceful except to their own chain-whipped backs, not kept in check by any visible military or police presence. He thought he might be better off not understanding what the government-paid announcer had to say, because the image was the real message. Millions of people disciplined by the rules laid down by Khomeini, marching to the beat of an Islamic drum. If anybody back in America watches this, and I know no one will, he thought, they would say those Iranian folks look flat-out crazy, beating themselves with whips and chains.

I sit here staring at the tube and see a religious revolution, powerful as any since the days of Moses, Christ, Mohammed, Ali and Hossein. The Protestant Reformation was just that, a reformation. This is revolution, as absolute as the Russian Revolution of 1917 and the Chinese Revolution of the thirties. Those revolutions were about politics and nationalism and the economic system. He tried to explain it to Jake. There's maybe some national pride and economics and cultural pride involved here, but this is about religion, about how people want to worship their God. He imagined Jake saying, "And we just don't get it."

The cameras switched to their second vantage point near a traffic circle just beyond the university where the broad street called Shah Reza changes its name to Eisenhower Boulevard. A quick change created a semblance of movement as the camera swung again to Shahyad Square, built by the Shah at the time of his controversial Persian history bash at Persepolis. The video editor switched to what Frank suspected was a previously taken beauty shot of the Shahyad monument's twin blue-tile towers with their fluted piers and high Gothic arches. "Shahyad," Anwar had said. "It means 'monument to the kings.'" Seeing the thousands of thousands of true believers surrounding it, he knew Shahyad Square would soon have another name. So would the street that ran by the front of the American embassy, Takht-e Jamshid, the Persian name for Persepolis, which gave the Iranians their nickname for the embassy—Fort Persepolis.

He watched and longed to get out among the marchers with his black wool cap pulled low on his forehead, but Anwar and Mina had told him it would be suicide.

"If you went I would have to go with you," said Anwar. "If some madman spotted you and started an attack on you, they would attack me, too. And I do not want to die."

"If either of you go out there tomorrow," said Mina, "I will kill both of you."

The TV editors had switched to a replay of the arrival at Shahyad Square of the open cars that slowly, haltingly had led the march with Ayatollah Taleqani and the opposition party leader, Karim Sanjabi. Armed bodyguards, clearly not military or police, trotted alongside the cars. Several wore the turbans of clergymen. Frank was seeing new faces on *Ashura,* different from those he had seen on *Tasu'a.* Suddenly, he spotted the club-twirling *Mojahedin homafar* he knew from the gym. For a moment he disappeared in the crowd, then the camera caught him again, moving in a high-stepping trot, twirling his G3 automatic rifle, switching it from hand to hand, never losing concentration, his eyes always sweeping the crowd.

I know that man, his mind said to Jake. I know that man.


Frank, as usual, arrived at the safe house half an hour early. He extracted the remains of the Stoli from the freezer and poured himself a short drink. They'd finished the tin of caviar at their Friday meeting. Frank wondered if Lermontov would bring more. He sipped the vodka and began unpacking his false-bottomed briefcase. Tape recorder. Notebook. An envelope with three impressive cables provided by Near East Division. Rocky had speculated that Henry James had indeed convinced them to do better. Frank skimmed the material again. Good, he said to himself. He tried another sip of Lermontov's vodka but found he'd already emptied the glass. The flash of car lights deterred him from his trip to the freezer and sent him instead to the basement garage.

Lermontov surprised him by easing into the garage in a dark blue Paykan. "I'm glad to see it's you," said Frank. "For a minute I thought *Savak* had come to wrap me up."

"For tonight, I am *Savak*," said Lermontov. "I'll explain."

They settled in the living room, and Frank poured them each two fingers of the leftover Stolichnaya. Lermontov shed his lamb's-wool cap, shrugged out of his bulky overcoat, and drained his vodka in a gulp. "I am under surveillance. Thanks to your good friend the late Major Nazih."

Frank registered the "late." "He's been killed?"

"Not yet. Not quite. But tortured in ways guaranteed to amuse *Savak*'s interrogators. A hot poker shoved up his fairy ass, then forced into his mouth. He was willing to talk but barely able to talk by the time they started to ask him questions. He implicated me, of course, but my *Savak* friends knew that. This is the interesting part. They tried to get him to implicate you."

"For what?"

"For recruiting him. And, despite all the torture, he would not."

"I don't get it."

"Maybe he's in love with you. Whatever reason, he protected you."

"But why would anyone want him to finger . . . implicate me?"

"They tell me the order came direct from the prime minister."

"I don't even know the prime minister."

"No, but evidently he also fears your influence with the Shah. He wants to be the one who influences the Shah, and he fears his power may be slipping."

"He does?"

"So I'm told. My friends also told me they've been ordered to keep me under surveillance. They suggested I change cars. I did and took other precautions. I hope you were as careful."

"We were," said Frank. "But where do you get all these cars? I expected to see you driving a Lada, or at least a Volga. But first you show up in a very fancy Peugeot. Now a Paykan."

"Most posts, that would be true," said Lermontov. "But here, because of the two hundred percent import tax, when we sell a used Volga on the open market, we have the extra money to upgrade when we buy a new car. We even have some blue Fiats, just like the one you drive. Even some old taxicabs, BMWs. Toyotas. It gives us the opportunity to avoid looking so obviously Soviet. Even the ambassador, he has an official Chaika, but he prefers to drive his red Mercedes for operational purposes."

Operational, thought Frank. He wondered what operational requirements an ambassador might have. He knew he had been under occasional *Savak* surveillance ever since his arrival, but the new element, Nazih being tortured, troubled him. He did not want to but he could not help trying to imagine the pain, the burning, ruptured anus, the poker-seared tongue. For what possible reason had Nazih refused to accuse him? Never fall in love with your agent, but maybe it's not a bad idea to have your agent fall in love with you. Not that Nazih had been his agent. Frank considered him an enemy, someone not to be trusted. Like Lermontov. Like Rocky. He felt very alone. And he knew that somewhere within the maze that was Langley, a mole might be watching him—and that Henry James might be suspicious of him. He would have to report what Lermontov had told him, but he feared that if he had made an enemy of the prime minister Rocky might have him shipped home.

"You're sure about all this?"

"How can you ever be sure? But it is my instinct always to believe the worst." Lermontov held up his glass. "Is there more of this?"

Frank returned from the kitchen with the remains of the vodka and watched Lermontov's ritual of disconnecting the agency's listening devices.

"Did your people complain about this?"

"Oh, yes," said Frank as he poured the last of the Stoly into Lermontov's glass and flicked on his tape recorder.

"What did you tell them?"

"I denied all knowledge and reminded them that last time around they forgot to include batteries."

"Good." He took a modest swig of the vodka. "Is this the end of this?"

"I was hoping you'd bring more. And caviar."

"Not a chance. You're not a hot recruiting prospect anymore. Just a run-of-the-mill traitor."

"Well, thank you."

"I don't want you to have any illusions."

"I don't."

"Then let's get to work." He finished his vodka. "What do you have for me?"

The new material impressed Lermontov. "Much of it we already know, but what's interesting is that the Americans have been able to get it. It's accurate, and it lets us know we have some security problems, especially with our *Tudeh* party friends. Or some of our sources are not so loyal or exclusive as we thought. Some of this on Kianouri and his wife's family is new even to us. I wish I knew how you got it."

"The rubric, as they call it, where is it?" Frank skimmed through the cable on Kianouri and the *Tudeh* party. "Here . . . 'an established source of known reliability' . . . that usually refers to a friendly security agency."

"Certainty not Stasi."

"Probably Mossad," said Frank.

"These Jews are good," said Lermontov. "Even in East Germany. Even here. All this is good. It will bring you a bonus."

"I could sure use it," said Frank as he skimmed through the material Lermontov had given him. It included a Soviet analysis of the shortcomings of the leftist coup that had taken over in Afghanistan, details on the limited support the Russians would provide to both the *Tudeh* party and the *Feda'iyan Khalq* in Iran, and an assessment of the imminent probability of Khomeini's takeover. Knowing Lermontov wore a wire and would have to share the tape with his colleagues, Frank made no comment, but he pointed to the document on Khomeini and shrugged.

Lermontov smiled. "Have you spoken lately to your friend the former Shah?"

"Former Shah? I wouldn't sell him short so soon. Remember 1953 when Mosaddeq came to power. People thought the Shah was washed up then. He even went into exile. But he came back, and Mosaddeq did a quick fade."

"Like you, I've read about all that, but times change, and you are not Kermit Roosevelt."

"No, I'm sure as hell not Kermit Roosevelt," said Frank, remembering how Roosevelt, a high-level CIA officer, had taken credit for the overthrow of Mosaddeq. "And I haven't seen the Shah in a week or so."

"I would be curious to know his reaction to the marches. Did you watch them?"

"I did."

"I hope you understood what you saw. And I hope the Shah understood. The masses, millions of marchers, acting in absolute obedience to Khomeini, acting in defiance of the former Shah and his useless government. When you see him, please ask your Shah what he thought."

He had not wanted to do it, but he had Bill Steele patch through a call to Rocky, telling him Frank was coming in. They sat in the bubble. Even before Frank turned over the new material Lermontov had given him, he told Rocky what Lermontov had told him about Nazih.

"I was right," said Rocky. "Someone was trying to set you up, but it wasn't Kasravi. It was his fucking boss. Shit, if you got the prime minister that pissed off at you, maybe we better get your Irish ass outta here."

"I knew you'd say that, but think about it. Maybe you were right about Lermontov. Maybe he is trying to set me up. Except instead of using Henry James as his weapon, he's using you."

"Me? What the fuck are you talking about?"

"I've been doing some good things here. Things that hurt the Russians.

Lermontov puts me in a position to have to tell you the prime minister is pissed off at me, pissed off enough to torture a guy to say I recruited him. Maybe he figures he can count on you to have me shipped home."

"He couldn't be that fuckin' devious," said Rocky. "Shit. That's what you said to me about him the other night, isn't it?

"Yeah," said Frank. "It is. Let's give it some time. Maybe I can talk to General Merid tomorrow. See if he knows anything about what happened to his nephew. Or why."

"Okay," said Rocky. "Lermontov offer anything else on the mole?"

"No. Just a note asking if we heard anything from our shop."

"He seem nervous?"

"No. When he's worried, he doesn't act nervous. Uptight, maybe, but not nervous."

"He should be uptight. By now the Holy Ghost has a tight lid on this op, but that first cable would've hit Near East, Soviet Div, Covert Action. My own hunch, based on the agents Lermontov says got rolled up, the mole's somewhere in Soviet Div."

"Wherever he is," said Frank, "he worries me."

"He should," said Rocky, "but for now there's not much we can do about it. You told your Jayface buddies you got the okay on bein' posted here as an adviser?"

Frank nodded. "Jayface. Kasravi. The Shah."

"They all like it?"

"More or less. The Shah didn't like the sound of 'indefinite.'"

"Yeah, well, these days nothin' much is definite. So you may as well stick around. We may all be gettin' shipped outta here pretty soon. Lermontov have anything new to say about the Brits?"

"No."

"He ain't worth much, is he? When's your next meet?"

"Thursday. His place. Daytime. He said he's getting worried about the curfew. He set up the meet out loud, then gave me a note saying to wear a wire. There's a video camera, so I can't just lay my tape recorder on the table."

"Fuckers. They got a guy into orbit before we did. Now they got video cameras in their safe houses before we do."

"Have you got anybody who can handle a wire?"

"'Course I do."

"Batteries included?"

"Fuck you, Sully."

The general sat like a fleshy sphinx at the head of the table, flanked by the Iranian members of the Jayface team. Moist, flickering eyelashes softened the stone mask of his face. His forearms and palms rested on the smooth surface. Frank perceived a black armband on the general's left arm. He looked again but saw no armband. Still, he was left with the sense there should be one.

"You're late," said the general, his eyes shifting to look directly into Frank's.

"Heavy traffic," said Frank. He did not want to ask what was wrong. Still in their coats, the three Americans stood in the doorway.

"I have some unhappy news I must share with you," said the general. "Our colleague Major Hossein Nazih died sometime yesterday. On *Ashura,* the anniversary of the martyrdom of his namesake, Imam Hossein, on the plains of Karbala." The general's words seemed both rehearsed and heartfelt. "Our history has come full circle. My nephew also died a martyr, after suffering horrible tortures, refusing to confess some conspiracy invented by *Savak* that would implicate us."

"Us?"

"Yes, Major Sullivan. Someone, I don't know who, called me from the prison during the night. He told me *Savak* had invented a plot, saying the CIA wanted to take over the mass media and influence the people against the Shah, starting with your idea for a military newspaper. They tried to force Hossein to confess that you had recruited him to act as your spy. He refused."

"Why would he go through torture to protect me?"

The general managed a faint smile. "Not you, Major Sullivan. He died to protect me. If he had implicated you, he would have implicated us all, especially me, as head of . . . our group."

Frank had briefed Gus and Fred about what Lermontov had told him. Lermontov had known about Nazih's interrogation hours before General Merid had received his phone call. Frank wondered if the story told to the general had been concocted as the next step in Lermontov's version of the prime minister's plot or if it represented someone's honest effort to warn the general.

"I have put in a call to the prime minister's office for an appointment. He must get to the bottom of this effort to undermine us and punish those responsible for the murder of Hossein."

How can I stop him? thought Frank. I can't tell him what Lermontov told me. I'm not even sure I believe it.

"If that fails," said the general, "I will take it up with Colonel Kasravi."

Frank hoped neither the prime minister nor Kasravi would see the general.

"In view of what has happened, I have canceled today's meeting. We will convene here tomorrow morning at zero eight hundred hours, precisely. Major Sullivan, could you and I meet privately after the others have left? Your driver can return for you after he drops off Colonel Bunker and Commander Simpson."

"Of course," said Fred, taking command. "And General Merid, as head of our advisory group, may I express our sincere condolences at your loss."

The general nodded. *"Allah-o akbar."*

The Iranians filed out, each stopping to embrace and console the general, each, as he passed, studying Frank, who did his best to appear saddened and otherwise expressionless. He did not have to fake the sadness. No one deserved to die as Nazih had. His refusal to tell the lies *Savak* wanted to force out of him made Frank wonder how badly he had misjudged the man.

"General," said Fred, "would you mind if I had a word with Major Sullivan before we leave?"

"Of course," said the general.

"I'll walk you downstairs," said Frank.

They'd reached the ground floor before Fred spoke, softly. "We'll get off a cable on what the general had to say about Nazih. Anything you want us to get in?"

"No. I may have more when I get back, but you ought to get this off right away."

"NE's liable to shut us down if we've got our titty in a wringer with the PM," said Gus.

"Maybe," said Frank. But not likely, he thought, now that Henry James has his foot in the door. Maybe it's Lermontov's turn to keep me from getting kicked out.


The general stood where they had left him, near the head of the table, alone in the chill, concrete-walled room.

"Come sit by me," said General Merid, nodding at the chair to his right. He eased himself into his own high-back chair. Frank sat beside him.

"I know you were very close," said Frank.

The general gave up the effort to hold back his tears. He made no sound and did not try to wipe away the signs of sorrow that trickled over his puffy cheeks. "You probably guessed, and I know people gossiped about it. He called me Dari."

Dariush, thought Frank. He'd almost forgotten that General Merid had a first name.

"It was our little joke. One of our little jokes. I hope you don't judge us too harshly. Since he was my nephew, it might almost seem like incest. Relations between men are not unheard of in our circle, in our culture." The tears had stopped, and the general's dark, suddenly clear eyes probed Frank's. "I thought you would understand. To lose someone you're close to." Frank nodded but could find no way to express his sympathy. "And to fear what may happen next."

Okay, thought Frank. Let's talk about that. "What do you fear, Dariush?"

"I am not as brave as Hossein. And I do not enjoy pain as he did." A constricted laugh escaped the general's lips. "You'll think we were mad. He used to ask me to whip him. He was not devout, but he used to always march on *Ashura,* flogging himself. This *Ashura,* Hossein found himself flogged more . . . much worse. The *kafers* killed Hossein again. Infidels. Someone truly devout like Captain Irfani would think that a sacrilege, to compare my Hossein with Imam Hossein, but we are all children of the same God." He paused, drumming the fingers of his right hand on the table. "Most of the people taken away from the palace by *Savak* came from our town, Qazvin. I am from Qazvin. They may identify me with the others. Can you talk to His Imperial Majesty?"

"I don't know," said Frank. "It's been a week since he summoned me. I've got a hunch he may have other things on his mind more . . . more urgent than talking to me."

"But this is urgent. It could be the end of us all. The end of me. The end of your work here. I've been honest with you today. I must be honest with you. If they torture me and want me to name you in some plot, I will accuse you. I am not so brave as Hossein."

"I understand." Nazih may have saved my neck, thought Frank, but I may not be so lucky if they try the same godawful game with the trembling general. How do I get out of this?

"And I can't be sure where His Excellency the prime minister, General Azhari, stands," said General Merid. "I have not told the others, but I have tried to contact him on other matters, before this, and he does not return my calls. Colonel Kasravi also does not return my calls. He did send word, through a messenger, that he wants to meet with you upstairs at three this afternoon. I'm to call his office, not him but his office, if you can't make it."

"I'll make it," said Frank. "And, sir, if I should get the chance to meet with His Imperial Majesty, what would you want me to say?"

"Find out—he must know about this. Find out if he will protect me."

"Sir, I hate to say this, but he did not protect Major Nazih."

"Yes, but Hossein had been involved in a plot. The man who called me from Evin prison said Hossein had confessed to being involved with some Russian, a plot to spy on the palace. I have done nothing. No one has recruited me. I spy for no one."

That may not be enough, thought Frank. For either of us. The general's dark eyes pierced his. Frank looked away. He knew the room was bugged. Inefficiently, he hoped. The general might already have said enough to hang them both.

"If you find out the Shah might not protect me, I would know sooner or later they will come for me. And before they do, I can take my own life."

Another suicidal wannabe, thought Frank. No, the Shah won't protect you. Any more than he protected Nazih. Push come to shove, would he protect me?

"I can die like a soldier," said the general. "Not tortured. Not humiliated. I can die like a man."


Ali had managed to get back to the Supreme Commander's Headquarters compound before Frank's talk with General Merid had ended. After the long combination of the Thursday-Friday weekend and the successive days of mourning, *Tasu'a* and *Ashura,* early morning traffic had been heavy and slowed their trip to Supreme Commander's Headquarters, but now the glut of cars and trucks and buses had thinned. Frank decided to have Ali drive him directly to the embassy. He slumped into the passenger's seat beside Ali and pulled his stocking cap low over his forehead.


"Upstairs," said Rocky as Frank entered his office. Frank nodded, and they climbed from the basement to the bubble. Frank unreeled all General Merid had told him.

"Why would he tell you all this?"

"I don't know," said Frank. "Maybe he senses the spoiled priest in me. I can't give absolution, but I can hear confessions. People talk to me. I give good ear."

"You better give good cable. All of it."

"It's going to make NE very nervous."

"Good. The Near East eunuchs are just bystanders now that we've got Lermontov in the picture. Forget NE. Forget Soviet Division. This is a CI op because the madman who heads Counter Intelligence has got everybody convinced any Soviet defector is a potential double agent until Henry James stamps the guy with his personal seal of approval. Oh, he says the stuff Lermontov gave you on the take from what James calls their penetration agent 'indicates some knowledge.' That ain't bad for openers."

"Can I pass that on to Lermontov?"

"Yeah, but in a note. And tear up the note. Any chance Lermontov might have been cornholing the late Major Nazih?"

"I doubt," said Frank.

"James would love to have somethin' like that on the guy. Hey, it's possible. Talk to the general."

"You might be better off," said Frank, "talking to the *Savak* guy who shoved the hot poker up Nazih's butt."

"There's a thought," said Rocky. "Shame you didn't think of that before they killed'm. They'da got him to say it. On tape."

"Maybe not," said Frank. "He managed not to say a lot they wanted to hear."

Rocky's expression hardened. "I'll talk to Eagle-1. You talk to the general."

Frank shrugged. "I'll do it. Meanwhile, the general wants me to talk to the Shah. So does Lermontov."

"What about?"

"The general wants to know if the Shah will save his ass. Lermontov wants to know where the Shah's head is at after *Ashura*. He's convinced the march showed that Khomeini's Islamic Republic has already taken over."

"So's Belinsky," said Rocky. "You gotta read his cable."

"I will, but Belinsky's not the Shah."

Rocky checked his watch. "Look, his nibs got a call from the Shah this morning. He's havin' lunch with him. I can't get him involved in this shit. Recruitin' a KGB officer. Or any of this shit about Nazih and the general. I share a lot with the ambassador, but anything I report direct to Henry James on he's not in the loop. Understood?"

"I understand."

"Okay. What we can do is ask him to let the Shah know you want a meet. I'll tell him you hit some resistance to your newspaper idea. Once you get to the palace, you can ask the Shah whatever the fuck you want. Understood?"

"I got it," said Frank.

"Sit tight," said Rocky. "If his nibs hasn't left, I'll ask him to come up for a minute."

The ambassador had agreed to convey Frank's message to the Shah. After spending over an hour drafting and, with Rocky's help, revising his cable on General Merid, Frank hurried off for his meeting with Colonel Kasravi.

Junior officers scurried through the third-floor hallway, darting in and out of the broad twin doors at the corridor's far end. The door to Colonel Kasravi's office stood open. Frank knocked.

"Come in."

Frank entered and saw the colonel seated at a table piled high with papers.

"Please close the door and take a seat. I'm glad you could come. As you can see, I am very busy, so I will be brief. No doubt you noticed all the coming and going in the hallway. Major Sullivan, I know this puts you in a difficult position, but I must ask you to refrain, for now at least, from reporting what I am about to tell you to your government. Now that your government has approved your status as an adviser to us, we hope to make the fullest possible use of your skills."

"Very good, sir." He hoped it was very good, but Frank wondered where Kasravi was headed.

"You realize, of course, your position, your privileged position as an adviser within the inner circles of our government, a military government in a time of crisis, imposes certain responsibilities."

"I don't quite understand, sir."

"You will. I want to be open with you. You now are one of us, and what has happened can affect your work. But you must promise not to reveal what I am about to tell you to anyone else."

Frank thought of Lermontov asking him to sign a receipt he couldn't read. "Sir, I don't want to make promises I can't keep."

"I understand," said the colonel. "Listen, then. And judge. This morning His Excellency the prime minister, General Azhari, was summoned to the palace. The Shah informed him he wanted to form a new government, a civilian government, within two weeks."

"But why?"

"I do not know," said Kasravi. "But we must face . . . face the prospect of a change in government. As you might expect, the prime minister—his health has been poor recently—he returned from the palace shaken, ashen. His sense of balance seemed . . . unstable. We rushed him to the Imperial Bodyguard medical facility. His doctors diagnosed a mild stroke, and he will be confined to the facility for some days. We have informed His Imperial Majesty."

"How did he react?"

"He instructed us to keep him informed. He has lunch today with your ambassador. He said he did not want to discuss this with Mr. O'Connor."

"What do you want me to do, sir?"

"We do not want to put you in a difficult position, but you said you could be helpful in advising us on how to deal with various foreign media. We would like you to help us in this matter."

"I can agree to that, sir. But at some point I must let my government know what I'm doing."

"I understand. Our problem, we fear letting the world know that at a time of crisis, the head of our military government has had a stroke, however mild. It makes our government look . . . weak."

"Yes," said Frank. "But your problem has other dimensions. Without strong domestic news media, rumor, gossip, and the Ayatollah's tapes become Iran's major means of communication. You mentioned all the comings and goings in the hallway. Evidently quite a few people already know."

The colonel stiffened. "They are all loyal, disciplined officers."

"But not everyone they talk to . . . in their excitement . . . may be discreet. At the Imperial Bodyguard medical facility—doctors, nurses, technicians, clerks, drivers. Gossip and rumors don't have to be composed and printed and distributed like newspapers. They travel with the speed of sound. Within a few hours half of Tehran will have heard some rumor of the prime minister's stroke or heart attack or paralysis or death. Someone may have already called Neauphle-le-Château, and Ayatollah Khomeini may have issued his statement to BBC. The world knows."

"What can we do?"

"Give the world an accurate version of what has happened. Start with BBC. The Voice of America has someone here. *Savak* should be able to let you know what other foreign journalists are here and where they are and how to get to them."

"We have that," said the colonel. "Can you write a statement for us?"

"I can," said Frank. "But first we need you to instruct a doctor at the Body-guard hospital to talk to me, to give me the diagnosis you want him to give, and to agree that our statement can quote him by name and title and military rank, if he has military rank."

"Give me five minutes."

"Take ten minutes and also put whatever mechanism and people you have to work calling an emergency press conference for seventeen hundred hours at the prime minister's office. I suggest you read the statement and handle any questions. I'll brief you on questions the journalists probably will ask."

"Five minutes," said the colonel. He turned and left the room.


Colonel Kasravi approved the statement Frank drafted, with minor changes. "I have already informed His Imperial Majesty of what we want to do. He agreed and asked me to thank you for your help and also to instruct you to come to the palace late tomorrow afternoon. He did not specify, but I would suggest sixteen hundred hours."

"Yes, sir," said Frank. He felt as if he'd been inducted.

"I must again be brief," said the colonel, "And blunt. We monitored your conversation with General Merid. You need not bring the matter up with His Imperial Majesty. General Merid has no significance and faces no trouble. He obtained his rank through favoritism and diplomatic service arranged by a small but influential coterie of homosexuals. I believe your State Department has something similar. Is the expression 'sissies in striped pants?'"

"Something like that," said Frank.

"The call he received from Evin prison was not authorized. We do not care about the general, but we want to know who made that call. Our people, not *Savak*, will question him about that call. Nothing more."

"Is he . . . in detention?"

"Not at all. He will be questioned, perhaps I should say interviewed, about the call. That is all. But I must confess some members of *Savak* did, perhaps, become overzealous in the matter of Major Nazih and your possible involvement with him. His Imperial Majesty's intelligence group became aware of this and informed the Shah. He resolved the matter."

Frank had guessed correctly about the several cables he would have to write, including a report on plans for a civilian government.

"This is one I won't share with the ambassador," Rocky had said. "He can fuck up like a three-legged bull in a china shop. He'd sure as hell ask the Shah about it, and the Shah would sure as hell stir up a hornet's nest tryin' to find out how the ambassador knew about it. I'll flag it with the tightest possible restriction and hope we can keep it the hell away from State."

As he finally headed home, Frank wondered how possible that might be. He knew enough about the infighting within the Washington Beltway to realize the cable would have to go to the President's national security adviser. Brzezinski would demand to know why he'd seen no State Department reporting on the Shah's plans for a civilian government. Then an angry State Department would query Ambassador O'Connor. He wondered if Rocky had found a new way to cause trouble for him.

Rocky acknowledged that Kasravi's decision to have Frank help prepare for the press conference indicated that his problem with the prime minister's office had passed. Now Frank wondered if he wanted that victory. For the first time he wondered if he wanted to stay. He still had a job to do, he told himself, but he'd begun to wonder if the job was worth all the risks he faced. He considered Jayface only his day job, his cover. He'd given up any thought he ever had of trying to save the Shah's ruthless government. Gathering and trying to file what intelligence he could, and above all recruiting Lermontov, seemed all that remained. The task seemed hopeless, though, and he could feel the risks of exposure, arrest, and torture tightening like a noose.

He remembered the stories he'd read about the peregrine falcon, an endangered species; its eggs, weakened by ingested DDT, were too fragile to be hatched. He did not want his shell to crack.

He drove straight to the house, hoping Gus and Fred would have had themselves driven home from Dowshan Tappeh. They had, and despite the late hour they were just finishing up a dinner of leftover chili. Gus dished up a bowl for Frank.

Fred drained his wine glass, caught Frank's eyes and said, "Know something? I need another glass of wine, and I need . . . I need to talk to both of you."

"I'll drink to that," said Gus. He uncorked another bottle of the red while Frank retrieved a beer from the refrigerator.

"I need to talk to both of you," said Bunker again. "As head of our team, I owe it to you, but I have to ask, not a word of what I tell you goes beyond this room. No one else has a need to know."

Frank and Gus looked to each other, then back to Fred. They nodded in unison.

"I've read your cable, Frank, and Belinsky's about *Ashura,* and the ambassador's cable after his lunch with the Shah today. Gus, I know you've seen them. Frank?"

"I read Chuck's and the ambassador's at the embassy this evening. Pretty grim stuff."

"Very," said Fred. "The ambassador in particular. Shocked at how shook up the Shah was by the *Ashura* march. He told the ambassador Khomeini has more power than his prime minister, and this evening, to prove him right, they announced the prime minister had a stroke."

"Grim stuff all right," said Gus, sipping his red. "And . . . ?"

"This war is over," said Fred, "and, frankly, I see no point in continuing to put myself at risk by staying here. Let me tell you what I've done. I've written to my wife. I'll pouch it out of here tomorrow. She has a heart murmur. Nothing serious, but I've asked her to write back to me right away, saying her doctors have decided to hospitalize her. Saying she's scared to death and begging me to come home. I also told her to call Dean Lomax—he's a friend of the family—and ask him to cable me. Soon's I get the cable, I plan to put in for a two-week emergency leave. It's an automatic."

Gus shrugged and said, "Why not just ask for a transfer back to Langley?"

"No. Transfer could take some doing. Emergency leave's an automatic."

"Good thinking," said Gus.

"And, to tell you the truth, two weeks from now I don't think anyone will see any point in sending me back here."

"Why are you telling us all this?" asked Gus.

"I owe it to you. As head of this team, I'm responsible for you. But I think I'll be able to do more good for this operation back in Langley than I can here."

"I don't doubt that."

"Gus, if you want, once I'm back there I can recommend that Covert Action reassign you to Rome. I realize, Frank, you have some things going, particularly with the Soviet. But Gus, I can talk to Dean and get you back to your wife in Rome."

"No, that's okay. I'll sailor on." He saluted. "That's Commander Simpson talking."

"Frank, are you okay with this?"

"No, but I gotta admit . . . my own mind—while I was driving back here tonight—I kept thinking, 'What am I doing here?' What happened to Nazih, the general thinks it could happen to him. Maybe it could happen to any of us.

And yeah, I doubt the Shah can survive. So yeah, I understand how you feel. I feel the same way. I just wish you hadn't told us about it."

"I owe it to you." He pushed himself up from the table, said, "Good night," turned unsteadily, and headed upstairs.

"I don't want to talk about it," said Gus.

"Neither do I," said Frank.


Fred Bunker had been quiet and tense through their Jayface meeting. With Nazih on their minds, the Iranians had little to say. Frank tried to fill up the time reporting on the role he had played in the previous day's press conference. During their tea break, he had walked the hallway with General Merid, assuring him he had nothing to fear from *Savak* or the prime minister.

"They questioned me about the phone call I received from Evin prison. I told them all I could. I did not recognize the voice, and nothing the caller said could help me identify him. I recounted the conversation in great detail. They thanked me. I couldn't believe. They thanked me and said I could go. They would be in touch if they needed me. I couldn't believe."

"You are not a target," said Frank. "I can assure you."

"Colonel Kasravi still does not return my phone calls."

"Don't worry," said Frank. You are not important, he thought. Jayface is not important. Aloud he said, "You are not a target, not a suspect."


His meeting with Kasravi left him feeling better. Kasravi called the press conference "successful . . . thanks to you."

I needed that, thought Frank.

"Just before it started we learned Agence France Presse had filed a story, citing sources in Tehran, saying the prime minister had died of a heart attack two days ago. I used the line you suggested, telling them His Excellency the prime minister, General Azhari, wanted them to know that reports of his death had been greatly exaggerated. They laughed, and from that point on it was easy. As you expected, they did try to ask questions about many other things, especially the health of His Imperial Majesty. I answered them all as we rehearsed—I had been authorized and informed only on the medical condition of the prime minister, I had no knowledge of this, not been informed about that, not been authorized to comment on the other thing. They must think I am very poorly informed. Otherwise, it went quite well."

"Congratulations," said Frank. But he worried about Kasravi. Being so publicly identified with the military government would not win him any friends among the clergymen who seemed so close to taking over.

The Shah told him it had already happened. "I spent some time Sunday watching the *Ashura* marchers, first on television, then over the line of march by helicopter. I have never seen so many people. Millions. Only because this preacher speaks on BBC. He tells our people to be there and to give flowers to the soldiers. My friends the British allow him to use BBC to issue his commands, and our people obey him. My friends the Americans ask me when I plan to leave my country. When will my son return from America to become regent? When will I name a Regency Council or appoint a Council of Experts? Such ideas these people have. Ambassador MacArthur, when he was here, he had a wonderful expression for such people. He said such people whistled in the dark as they walked past the cemetery. My friends the Americans, whistling in the dark as they walk past my cemetery. So far in the dark they can not see that *akhund* Khomeini, that he already rules our country. Yesterday he went on BBC again, calling for a national strike on 17 *Moharram,* a week after *Ashura.* And the people will do it. Cassettes of his message already flood the bazaar. A Council of Experts. Hah. The people heed only one expert, this foul-smelling mullah with a black turban and a blacker heart."

Though his pessimism ran deep, the Shah seemed animated by it. He spoke with more energy; his eyes flashed with more intensity than Frank had seen in recent visits. Color had returned to his cheeks. With his back to the illuminated map that showed Iran at the center of the globe, he stood taller, less shrunken into himself.

"The French ally themselves with these black reactionaries. The British and you Americans abandon me. The Russians wait to pick up our pieces. But we will not disappear for you."

"I'm glad to hear that," said Frank. "Can I help in any way?"

The Shah nodded. "We heard what you did yesterday. Arranging the announcement of the prime minister's stroke. That was good. Perhaps you can help us do more things like that. Improve the way we handle the foreign press. Maybe even the BBC."

"I would be glad to help, sir. And Colonel Kasravi is a good man to work with."

"He has always been loyal," said the Shah.

Loyal, thought Frank. That's what matters. He wondered how much loyalty the Shah could count on. "Should I convey your thoughts on my working with the news media to Colonel Kasravi?"

"No. Better he should hear it directly from us."

Frank had noticed the Shah's inconsistency in his imperial use of the first person plural. He tended to speak of himself as "we" when his confidence and sense of command were strong. He used the singular "I" when he felt more isolated, alone. Since the Shah seemed confident at the moment, Frank decided to risk a question.

"Sir, on the question of dealing with the foreign press, may I ask you something?"

"You may." The Shah changed his posture, clasping his hands behind his back, jutting out his chin, and puffing up his shrunken chest. The Mussolini pose, thought Frank. He inhaled sharply and plunged ahead.

"Sir, it's rumored that efforts are under way to put together a civilian government."

"Who conveyed this rumor to you? This General Merid person?"

"No, sir."

"Good. If it had come from him, we would say ignore it. He is a person of no importance."

"I understand, sir, the question came up at the press conference yesterday. Colonel Kasravi handled it well, saying he had no knowledge of any such initiative."

"Good."

"But if there is any truth to the rumor, it might be wise to head off speculation."

"No. Your ideas are good, but this is not a matter for public comment. We have not confided what we are about to tell you to your ambassador. But we will confide in you, in part as a rebuke to your government. We will not announce publicly at this time, but you may report to your government that Shapour Bakhtiar will head our next government, a civilian government that will take office within a fortnight."

"I will report that, sir."

"And you should give some thought to when and how we should announce this. We want the Americans to know we do not like being abandoned."

"It must be difficult for you," offered Frank. "But it can also be difficult for Americans to understand your government at times. I wonder, for example, about my colleague Major Nazih."

"Your colleague?"

"On the Joint Armed Forces Ad Hoc Committee on Enlightenment, Jay-face."

"Ah, yes. And mixed up, as we recall, with the Russians' *Tudeh* party."

"Yes, sir. I understand he died, was killed in prison."

"Really? It could not have been of much matter. We were not informed."

"It seemed . . ." Frank knew he was stretching his luck, but he wanted to know why Nazih had been tortured and by whose order. "I wonder why his death was necessary."

"We do not know."

"I understand he was tortured."

"You surprise us. We did not think you were so naive as your President. Or is it a disease all Americans suffer? You have no idea what this country requires of its government. To think we can maintain order without a firm hand. To question us as though America had no prisons or executions. No police brutality or . . . What it is called, your third degree?"

"All that's true," said Frank. His perception of the Shah had darkened. This was the man who feared he would see blood on the snow if the military had free rein, who had told Admiral Hayati he did not want the blood of the people on his hands just to save the monarchy. This some man could so easily dismiss the death of Major Nazih.

For the first time, he caught a hint of a sour, acidlike smell from the Shah's ill-fitting gray wool suit. Even in Addis Ababa when they hefted weights and sparred in sweaty gym clothes he had detected nothing like it. The smell of cancer. The stink of a dying empire.

"It is not a simple matter," said the Shah. "Yes, violence and open rebellion demand harsh measures. At times. Your human rights people list our so-called acts of repression, but they forget our acts of mercy. We spared Mosaddeq. We spared Ayatollah Taleqani. We spared even this Khomeini, letting him go into exile rather than prison for fighting our White Revolution."

"I understand," said Frank. I understand, and I know my job is to listen and learn. A reporter. Not judge and jury.

"You know, this same Jimmy person praised our White Revolution, and in truth the White Revolution started with pure intention. Like the waters in our *jube*s. Do you know our *jube*s?"

"Yes," said Frank. "I've seen them."

"So much depends on where you see them. Here, in the foothills of the mountains, they are pure. Designed to provide pure water to the entire city. But as they flow downhill, people corrupt them. Like our White Revolution. Pure at the start. Like the blood in our own veins. Persians can corrupt the purest of intentions. They wash their feet in the *jube*s. They dump night soil in them. What we thought of as a benefit for all became a fresh-water benefit for the elite, corrupted as it flows through us. The source of pure water becomes a sewer, and the people hate us for it. I can feel the *jube*s running through me, through my own arteries, like a . . ."

Like a cancer, thought Frank. He said nothing. He let the Shah's sentence die.


As he reviewed his day with Rocky in the bubble, Frank suggested that only his meeting with the Shah merited a cable. Rocky agreed.

"The ambassador's gonna be pissed the Shah's tellin' you stuff he's not tellin' him, but like the Shah said, that's part of the message. Be sure to get that part in. Get it all in, including the peanut farmer. The stuff about the *jube*-tubes. Straight out. Like a chapter in one of your books. The atmospherics. How he looked. How he sounded."

Though lengthy, the cable unfolded quickly. Frank ended it on a sad note. "The interview over, his anger spent, the Shah, who had seemed animated and confident throughout, shriveled back into his shell. Mussolini had disappeared. Only the shrunken, cancer-ravaged Shah remained."

# CHAPTER SIXTEEN

He stashed sensitive material from his briefcase in the safe, including the spare cassette Chuck Belinsky had made for him, cued to the Khomeini's call for nonviolent revolution. He locked the safe, retrieved his exercise gear from Stan Rushmore's file cabinet, and prepared for a long-neglected assault on the gym. The heavy bag, motionless, hung as alone, as isolated, as the Shah had seemed at the end of their meeting. He had looked forward to a workout, but even more he wanted to meet with the *homafaran*. Where was everybody? He'd been aware of an unusual rumble from beyond the doors that led onto the basketball court. He tried the doors and looked onto a court flanked with tiered benches of spectators, Iranian and American.

His *homafar* gym buddies clustered near the door. Frank and Anwar the Taller exchanged discreet nods. He spotted Bunker, Cantwell, Reggie Manning, Stan Rushmore, and another player he did not know on the court. Bill Steele sat by himself on a courtside bench. Frank joined him.

"How come you aren't in there?"

"Foul trouble," said Steele. He kept his eyes fixed on the game. A scoreboard at the far end of the court showed Visitors 62, Home 68, Minutes, 12:05.

"Who's home?" asked Frank.

"They are. Better record."

"Who's the monster?"

"Brian Brawley. All bad. Played for the Air Force Academy. Big. Good. And a thug."

Brawley, as if demonstrating Steele's description, muscled his way to the basket, leapt with surprising agility for such a big man, and, despite a hard foul by Rushmore, slammed in a basket.

"That's about to make it seventy-one," said Steele. "The son of a bitch also sinks his foul shots. Time for me to get back in there. That's five on Stan. He's out, and I got four."

"Brawley?"

"Not but three."

"Mind if I sit here?"

"Hell, no. Glad you could come out. We need all the support we can get."

Steele trotted onto the court. Stan Rushmore, dripping sweat, shuffled over to the bench.

"I'm gettin' too old for this. How you doin'?"

"Okay," said Frank. "Their big guy looks pretty good."

Brawley swished his foul shot. "Damn good," said Rushmore, "and a mean motherfucker." Brawley turned and raced downcourt before his shot had cleared the net. His teammates trotted behind him. "We can still beat 'em. Watch."

Reggie Manning brought the ball upcourt. No defender turned to face him until he had crossed the halfcourt line, and by then he had passed to Cantwell, cutting rapidly across the court. Each of the Trojans moved well without the ball, and four crisp passes later Bunker, with his steel-rimmed glasses taped to his head, found Manning all alone on the far baseline. Feet and shoulders squared away, knees bent, Manning arced a two-handed set shot that rattled in.

"What the fuck's wrong with you?" one of Brawley's teammates yelled at another. He followed his words with an angry, errant in-bounds pass that Reggie Manning stole and drove to the basket for an uncontested lay-up.

"See what I mean? Five-point game. We're right back in it. Except for Brawley down low, none of these guys play defense. They're all too busy thinkin' about their next shot."

"Reg-gie, Reg-gie, Reg-gie." Frank looked up to see Tom Troy waving a towel and leading a tight cluster of Dowshan Tappeh agency people in a chant.

"Troy's Trojans," said Rushmore. "They call us 'the Scumbags,' but we still got a chance."

"Six guys?"

"Yeah," sighed Rushmore. "Last game of the tournament and that's all we could suit up. They got twelve. And one of them's fuckin' Brawley."

Downcourt, Fred Bunker picked off a ball from behind a casual dribbler. He fired a long pass to a streaking Cantwell, who caught up to it like a wide receiver, leapt toward the basket, sailing with impressive hangtime, and banked in his shot. Brawley called for a time-out.

The clock showed three minutes and forty seconds. Troy's Trojans had clawed their way to an 80–80 tie when Brawley pulled down a rebound only to have it stripped out of his hands by Manning. Brawley lunged at him, trying to grab the ball back. Off balance, both fell, Brawley on top; Manning, right leg twisted under him, was flattened on the bottom.

"Goddamn it." It wasn't a curse but a scream of pain and frustration, and it silenced the crowd. Frank and Rushmore hurried onto the floor. Brawley pushed himself up from the floor. "Sorry, Reggie. Sorry 'bout that."

"Wasn't your fault."

"How bad is it?" said Steele.

"I dunno, but I got a hunch it's bad enough. Help me up. Lemme try it." Steele and Rushmore eased him up. Manning hopped on his left leg and tried straightening the right. "No good," he said. "It's the knee. Feels like a ligament. I've done it before."

"We better get you to the infirmary," said Steele.

"Nah, nah. Just help me over to the bench. The knee can wait till after the game."

"What game? With you and Stan both out we've only got four players."

"So? Play with four. A little extra runnin' around'll be good for you." Hopping on his left foot with the broad shoulders of Steele and Rushmore serving as crutches, he started to the bench when a referee hollered, "You guys got two foul shots coming. Who you want to take 'em?"

"I'll take them," said Manning.

"How the hell can you take them?" said Steele.

"I'm the only decent foul shooter you got. Even on one leg I got a better chance of sinking them than anybody else. Just get me over to the foul line and gimme the ball."

Steele wrapped an arm around him, and Manning hopped to the foul line, planted his left foot, and balanced on the toes of his right The referee handed him the ball.

"You call a reach-in on Brawley?" asked Manning.

"That's right. His fourth. And they're in the penalty, so you shoot two."

"Good." He bent his left knee and straightened it as he released his two-handed shot. It swished in. His second shot rattled around the rim and spun in. As Manning, supported by Steele and Rushmore, hobbled off the court, the spectators, even those cheering for Brawley's team, erupted with applause.

Frank caught Fred Bunker's eye. Fred shrugged. "Ask Bill."

With Manning, clearly in pain, settled on the bench, Frank approached Steele. "Hey, Bill, I know you already said no once, but if you could use a fifth body out there I've got my sneakers on."

The big man smiled. "If I didn't know you're a pretty smart man, I'd think you had more balls than brains."

"There's only a couple of minutes left. How much harm could I do?"

"That's not what I'm worried about. You saw what just happened to Reggie. You're already missing one kneecap. Besides, you're not on the roster."

"Let's talk to the refs. Maybe they'll make an exception. Emergency, right?"

The negotiations took several minutes. Tom Troy joined in and verified that Frank was a bona fide member of his unit. Despite loud objections from one of his teammates, Brawley—who, like Steele, was a player-coach—agreed. "We don't want anybody saying we beat a team with only four players," he said.

The two referees then conferred with the timekeeper, who had become so involved in Manning's injury and one-legged foul shooting that he'd let the clock run down. Steele took advantage of the delay to counsel his team. "We've got just one hope. Brawley's got four fouls. Take it to him every chance we get. If we get him to foul out, we've got a prayer. Get Frank involved if you can."

"We may get you involved," Bunker said to Frank. "Just don't get yourself killed."

The referees and the timekeeper settled on three minutes and thirty seconds. Brawley's team brought the ball upcourt cautiously. Brawley posted up on Steele, backing him closer to the basket, but Bunker doubled up on Brawley. A quick pass to the man Bunker had been covering gave him an open shot. Frank, raised arms flailing, dove in his direction, hoping to distract him. The shot clanged off the rim, but Brawley bulled his way past Steele and tapped in the rebound. Frank glanced at the scoreboard. Tied at 82.

Steele had Frank inbound the ball, then fed it back to him, letting Frank bring it upcourt. Steele set a screen for Bunker, who hooked away from his man, took Frank's pass, and headed for the basket. Brawley, worried about a fifth foul, let him go, content to block out Steele. Bunker's lay-up hit the back rim. Brawley grabbed the rebound and hit the man Frank covered with a quick outlet pass. Frank tried to keep up, but it was no contest. The other man was far too quick, not only for Frank but also for himself. He lost control of the ball; by the time he managed to pick it up, the speedy Cantwell had caught up to him. Forced to pass the ball out, he found Brawley, who outraced Steele and Bunker.

Frank stepped into the big man's path, planted his feet, raised his arms, and read Brawley's startled expression. Brawley did his best to stop, but his momentum carried him into Frank as he got his shot off. Frank heard the referee's whistle just before he hit the floor.

Dazed, Frank looked up to see Steele and Bunker hovering over him. "You know what you just did?" said Steele.

"Yeah. I just got knocked on my ass."

"What you did you just fouled out their ace."

"They called the charge?"

"That they did," said Steele.

"I thought I told you not to get killed," said Bunker.

"I didn't get killed," said Frank. "Just knocked down." Steele pulled him to his feet. Still dazed, Frank went to the foul line. He tried to concentrate on the bottom of the net, but the net spun like a top. Frank blinked. The net stopped spinning, and Frank tried to see the ball swishing through the bottom. His one-handed shot went through. His second shot banged off the back rim, but Bill Steele grabbed the rebound and put it in. The Trojans took a three-point lead.

With Brawley out of the game, his team unraveled. They had no one who could stop Steele inside. Bunker, Cantwell, and the other player, whose name Frank still didn't know, began hitting from the perimeter. Even Frank managed to get off a shot that rattled in and out, and he blocked a pass that Bunker picked up to lead a fast break for another basket. Time ran out.

Final score: Trojans win, 93 to 84.


Frank had wondered about Lermontov's choice of a meeting place. The Amjadieh soccer stadium sat back off Roosevelt, a few blocks from the American Embassy. At 4:30 P.M., even with the short days of the winter solstice closing in, it would still be daylight.

"In that neighborhood," Lermontov had explained, "all the spies and revolutionaries concentrate so hard on your embassy they never notice the football field. The national team practices at that time, so the parking lot will have enough cars that we won't be noticed, but not so many we would have trouble finding a spot. And by that time of day, even in these times, people start to think of other things. Getting off work, evening prayers, their wives, dinner. We will be invisible in plain sight."

Frank decided to pass up a chance to get to the gym; his tailbone still ached from the splattering he'd taken on the basketball court. He left the house early for a trip to the embassy, where one of Rocky's technicians taped a wire to his chest—batteries included. He had given himself more than enough time, but he didn't want to take chances on Tehran traffic or risk getting delayed by a demonstration. He followed Pahlavi and turned right onto Shah Reza. Impelled by curiosity, he made another left and in a few blocks saw the tottering construction crane. He had never been quite sure of its location. He had first caught a glimpse of it as his flight from Rome descended to Mehrabad Airport. Ali drove them on each of the other occasions he'd seen it, except when he saw it in his dreams. Now he had found it on his own and felt a sense of relief. It still had not collapsed. Melting snow had made the abandoned building site even muddier, but the crane had found some purchase in the slime.

He circled the construction and drove through narrow back streets to the north side of the soccer stadium. He found a side entrance and followed Lermontov's instructions to a parking space close to an entrance to the stands. He checked his watch. It wasn't quite four-thirty, but Lermontov's Peugeot already waited. Frank pulled up alongside it. A pale blue Fiat, the mirror image of his own, swung into the vacant spot on the other side. Score another one for Lermontov's used car dealer, thought Frank. He killed his engine, grabbed his briefcase, and, keys in hand, squeezed himself out of the car. A squat, broad-shouldered man in a long black leather overcoat who had craggy Caucasian features and surprisingly gentle green eyes pushed himself out of the passenger's side of the other Fiat. He put his hand out, and Frank dropped the car keys into his puffy palm. They did not speak. Frank turned and walked around his own car and the white Peugeot 504. He let himself in on the passenger's side.

"Welcome, Mr. Sullivan," said Lermontov for the benefit of the wire. "How has your day gone?"

"Easily," said Frank, aware now of his own wire. "For a change. Jayface meeting this morning. Nothing this afternoon." Lermontov handed Frank a sheet of paper printed in his distinctive hand. Frank started to read and kept talking. "Yesterday was different. A very revealing discussion about Nazih with General Merid. And a meeting with the Shah."

Lermontov's note said, *We have a problem. Serious now and likely to become dangerous.* Frank glanced at him. Lermontov kept his eyes fixed on his rearview mirror.

"The Shah's health seems to be getting worse. Much worse," said Frank as he went back to his reading, still chatting about the Shah.

*Under your seat you will find an envelope with important information about my change in scenery plans and medical needs. And about our problem. Do not read it in my presence. Report it to your people and, at our next meeting, you can give me your reactions in writing. Do not misplace this paper.*

"General Merid flat-out confessed he and Nazih were lovers," said Frank, "and that he's scared he may be *Savak*'s next victim." He folded Lermontov's note and put it in his shirt pocket. He wondered how the movement would sound on the nearby wire, and he wondered what serious, maybe dangerous problem they faced. He thought about the sad fate of Major Nazih. "Nazih and General Merid, well, that's a long story. Maybe we should wait till we get to your place."

"Very well. Here are your glasses. The glasses I told you about."

Lermontov started up the Peugeot while Frank slipped on the opaque, wrap-around glasses.

"Wow. I am blind."

"I know," said Lermontov.

Frank tried to count the right turns, the left turns. Lermontov made many of both, following a convoluted route meant both to elude any possible tail and, Frank guessed, to keep him from tracing their journey. What kind of problem? He tried to listen to the sound of the Peugeot struggling uphill but found it difficult to concentrate. He tried to keep track of Lermontov's frequent use of the brakes as an indication they were headed toward a lower part of town, but the Peugeot ran smoothly. As far as Frank could tell they had headed neither up toward the north end of town nor south. A sudden U-turn threw off his count of right and left turns. Lermontov braked and turned to his right, and Frank heard the sound of a garage door being swung open. Lermontov pulled in. The garage seemed to be at street level. Otherwise, Frank had no idea of their route or location. Or of their problem.


The Russians, like Bill Steele, did not go in for frills. "Bare bones" described the interior of the safe house. A card table with two folding chairs stood in the middle of the front room. A naked ceiling bulb cast a circle of light around the table, spotlighting a telephone hooked by a long cord to a far wall. A round stand with an unlit kerosene lamp guarded the doorway that led into the front hall. Framed Air Iran tourist posters graced each wall. They hung well above eye level and masked, Frank suspected, the video cameras. He avoided looking directly at the posters and realized he and Lermontov would avoid any discussion of their problem. Whatever it was.

"You aren't wearing a wire or anything like that, are you, Mr. Sullivan?"

"Of course not."

"Good. I trust you, but nevertheless I will search you. Remove your jacket, please."

Frank draped his jacket over the back of a chair and submitted to a careful pat-down. Lermontov ignored the wire when he tapped it. Frank imagined the technician who would monitor the tape wincing at that and hating him. He hoped the clear substance in the pitcher Lermontov carried in from the kitchen might be Stolichnaya. Lermontov, as though reading his mind, paused in the doorway. He balanced two glasses and a bowl of ice in his other massive hand.

"Just water," he said. "No vodka this time. But I do have something else for you." He set his water service on the card table and drew a thick envelope from his tweed jacket. "As promised, a bonus. We appreciated the quality of the material you brought last time, particularly the report on the Kianouris. Count it, please, and sign the receipt that's in there."

Frank counted out fifty twenty-dollar bills. "Not a lot," he said.

"I like greed," said Lermontov. "One of the more endearing character traits engendered by capitalism. A hungry agent is a productive agent. What do you have for me this evening?"

I have a question for you, thought Frank. What the hell is this problem about? But he knew he could not ask his question. He put his new briefcase on the table. He stared at the package he had slipped out from under his seat in the Peugeot. My answer's in there, he thought, but it will have to wait. He pried open the false bottom and handed over the material Rocky had provided.


Frank shed his wire and tape in Rocky's office and turned it over to the technician. Then, secure in the bubble, he gave Rocky the note he'd tucked into his shirt pocket.

"Problem? What the fuck problem?"

"I guess it's in there."

Rocky tore open Lermontov's neatly wrapped package. He showed Frank the white, letter-size envelope with "Eyes Only" printed in Lermontov's hand. Frank nodded. Rocky unsealed the envelope and unfolded the single sheet of paper inside. He read in silence for a moment, then looked up at Frank.

"We got a problem, all right."

"Does it have a name?"

"Yeah. It's called a penetration agent. And it's alerted Moscow that the American station in Tehran is attempting to recruit a Soviet intelligence officer, identity unknown."

"Shit," said Frank.

"You got it all over ya."

"What else does this guy know? Does he know Lermontov's got a lead on him?"

"Good question. When we got the word from Lermontov on a penetration agent, my cable went eyes only to the Holy Ghost. No indication so far that our mole knows about that. But our first cables on Lermontov as a recruitment target would've gone to Near East and Soviet Division. Which may tell us somethin' about what our penetration agent has penetrated."

"But he doesn't have the identity."

"Separate cable," said Rocky. "Remember, identity doesn't get distributed. Archives only. Counter Intelligence, then limited need-to-know basis."

"What about Covert Action?" asked Frank.

"Yeah. Dean Lomax is your boss, so he'd have seen the cable. Without the identity. And, I gotta believe, your rabbi, Pete Howard."

"Some of those folks would've guessed the identity," said Frank.

"Yeah," said Rocky. "I guess somebody might 'a guessed. But it looks like our mole ain't one 'a them. So far."

"So from now on we talk only to Henry James."

"Startin' right now," said Rocky. "Wait for me. I gotta go eyes-only our Holy Ghost. It's around midnight back home, but they'll red-alert his ass outta bed. Don't go 'way."

With Lermontov's note in hand, Rocky wooshed through the bubble's plastic door. Frank watched his spectral shadow head up the stairs toward the communications room. Frank's right leg twitched. He straightened it, flexed it, but the trembling wouldn't stop. He felt cold, and he felt the urge to pee. Only nerves, he told himself. You don't have to piss. "Don't go 'way," Rocky had said, and he knew he couldn't abandon the bubble and all Lermontov's papers. What now? he wondered. How long will it take for this guy to come up with names that he'll feed to Moscow? Including my name. Still, he realized he had far less to fear than Lermontov. If the hammer comes down . . . He thought of Lermontov. Drugged. Shipped back to Moscow. Disappeared into the cellars of Lubyanka prison. Tried and convicted in secret. Executed. Because I got him jammed up.

Still clutching Lermontov's note, Rocky returned to the bubble sooner than Frank would have thought possible.

"Here. You should read this." He handed Frank Lermontov's note. "Your boy sounds pretty rattled."

Frank scanned the note, which ended, "My life is now in great danger."

"I'm kind of rattled myself," said Frank. "What can we do for him?"

"Dunno. Maybe James'll come up with somethin'. Help your buddy scapegoat somebody else in the *rezidenza*."

My buddy, thought Frank. More likely my enemy. Now more than ever.

"Some kinda black op," said Rocky. "Make it look like somebody else is the bad guy."

"That could get somebody killed."

"Right. Just so long as the somebody isn't Lermontov."

Frank nodded. Anwar had been right. This isn't a game.

"May as well sit and read a while," said Rocky. "In case James does get back to us tonight." They turned their attention to the other hand-printed material in the package Frank had retrieved from Lermontov's Peugeot. Rocky skimmed, nodding his approval. "This guy knows his shit. Hope he knows enough to figure out a way outta the bind we put him in."

"*We* put him in? More like *I* put him in," said Frank. He'd wanted to make things happen. Now he realized making things happen could have consequences.

"Don't get down on yourself. Lermontov's a professional. He knows the game."

Frank shook his head. "It's not a game."

"It ain't basketball," said Rocky. "Yeah, I heard about what you did. Thing we gotta do now is stay on top of our game. This game. Figure out what we can do for Lermontov. Maybe even evacuate him outta here if we have to. Do what we can to put a fuckin' stop to this penetration agent fuckin' us over. Don't go into a guilt funk on me. I need you. Okay?"

"Okay," said Frank. "I'm here."

"Let's get back to what your buddy has for us."

"Good."

"Note says the take he's turning over includes a Soviet analysis of the situation in Iran, predicting a Khomeini takeover and American withdrawal within two months. Also a couple of KGB reports on the Khomeini camp in Paris. They seem to think all the American-educated Iranians he's got up there indicate he's been co-opted by the CIA. That's a laugh. And an update on Soviet intentions in Afghanistan. Nothin' great. When's your next meet?"

"Sunday. Same time. Parking lot at Pahlavi Hospital."

"That's original. The rest is what he wants us to do about his medical problem. Contact Dr. Hyman Roth, Columbia Presbyterian. Jesus, he's translated his medical records into English so you can turn 'em over to the specialist in advance. First installment's here. More to come."

"He sounds pretty anxious."

"Yeah. Well, by now he's got some pretty good reasons t' be anxious."

They spent some time reading Lermontov's medical records, learning more about acromegaly than they ever thought they would want to know. The phone on the glass-topped table rang. Rocky grabbed it. "Yeah . . . Be right up." He slammed it down. "James. Be right back."

The cable he returned with was brief. *Give this matter your highest priority. Submit any and all ideas for operational assistance we may provide on ident a. Also any further indications that may help us identify ident b.*

"Here we go," said Rocky.


On Saturday Frank returned to the gym. More than a week had passed since his last workout. The *homafaran* welcomed him.

"We thought you had given up working out," said Anwar the Taller.

"But we saw what you did on the basketball court," said the youngest of the group.

"You must be Persian in your soul," said the club twirler, his concentration fixed on his task. "If that big American had killed you, if you were a Muslim, you would have gone straight to heaven, a martyr."

Frank smiled. "No, I'm not a martyr, but I saw you in the *Ashura* march."

"Ah, yes. Not I, the *homafar*. I, the *Mojahedin,* guarding Ayatollah Taleqani."

"You watched on television?" said Anwar the Taller.

Frank nodded.

"My cousin told me you wanted him to take you on the march."

Again, Frank nodded.

"You do have a martyr complex."

"No, not me," said Frank.

"You're very quiet," said Anwar.

"Too much on my mind," said Frank, thinking about Lermontov.

"We haven't seen you since before *Ashura*."

"Right," said Frank. "The tape you gave me with the Ayatollah's instructions for the marches turned out to be right on target. Almost like a script for the way it all turned out."

"Exactly," said Anwar. He nodded to the club twirler. "With you in mind, Sa'id made a tape of the resolutions and speeches from Shahyad Square at the end of the march. The quality is not good, but a good Farsi speaker should be able to understand."

"Thank you," said Frank, accepting the cassette from Anwar. "Thank you, Sa'id."

"Yes, sir. You are welcome." The names of the other *homafaran* had never before entered their conversations. Frank wondered if they had reached a new level of trust.

"Seventeen points," said Sa'id as his clubs helixed through the air. "They call for a revolution, for an end to the monarchy, acceptance of the Imam as our country's leader, an Islamic government, justice for the masses, the free return of all political exiles. I don't remember them all, but all are on my tape."

"Thank you," said Frank.

"I've had another tape for you, since the day after *Ashura,*" said Anwar. "The Imam's call for a general strike on Monday. But now that's only two days away."

"I'd still like to be able to play it for my friend at the embassy who speaks Farsi." Frank reached out to take the cassette, but Anwar tightened his grip on it. "You must be careful these days. The Imam tells the people to be peaceful. Here it has been peaceful, so far. But in other cities—Isfahan and Najafabad—troops have fired on the people, killing many. We may see more killing here. Be careful." He released the tape.

The next night, Lermontov dropped him off on a street corner. "My Chechen colleague just pulled your car up behind us." Frank took off the glasses that had kept him sightless. "Pointed north on Ferdowsi, one of our fair city's more elegant byways. All the important embassies, ours, the British, Germans, all the players in the Great Game of nations who sought power in this part of the world have their embassies along Ferdowsi, unlike you newcomers off by yourselves on Takht-e Jamshid."

In the fading afternoon light, Ferdowsi did not look elegant. Bare oak and elm trees echoed the occasional building hollowed out by fire and looters. Frank had in his briefcase handwritten notes from Lermontov that he hoped included new information about the Soviet penetration agent in Langley. He wanted to get away and read them, but Lermontov, seeming strangely relaxed, wanted to play to his wire.

"You may encounter a military checkpoint at Ferdowsi Square, but your identification should get you through. Keep going north. The street changes its name, but it will take you direct to Takht-e Jamshid. Turn right and soon you will see the gates of your lonely embassy."

Frank guessed the big Russian's ironic manner, new to him, targeted whoever would review the take from the wire Lermontov wore. He had used the tone throughout their meeting, imparting an air of condescension appropriate to a spy who would betray his country for an envelope stuffed with twenty-dollar bills. But Frank wondered if the KGB's mole in Langley had made Lermontov the suspected betrayer.

"You may prove very useful to us, if only to show us the weaknesses in American intelligence gathering. The material you gave me tonight makes interesting reading, but it tells me nothing we don't already know. Perhaps the KGB, or another good organization like Mossad, could set up a training program for your people."

"Not a bad idea," said Frank. "I'll mention it to my chief of station."

"I'm sure he'll be amused," said Lermontov. "Au 'voir."

Frank, his briefcase already heavy with the envelopes Lermontov had secured under the passenger's seat, slid out of the Peugeot. He and the burly driver in the black cap and long leather overcoat did a circle dance around the two cars. Frank moved from the passenger's side of the Peugeot to the driver's side of the Fiat. The Chechen made the opposite maneuver. Frank watched the Peugeot pull away and make a right at the first corner. He headed up Ferdowsi past all the other embassies and toward his own.

"Sometimes this guy pisses me off," said Rocky. "A fucking KGB training course."

"Maybe he's right. They're the ones with a penetration agent in our house."

"Any news on that?"

"I gave him our note. He pocketed it." Frank opened Lermontov's package, extracted an eyes-only envelope, and read from the single sheet inside.

*We turn the station upside down each day, spreading fear, suspicion, rumor. Virtually all other work stops. Visitors from Moscow arrive tomorrow.*

"I bet that'll be a fine bunch 'a thugs," said Rocky. "You gotta somehow set up a meet at our safe house where you can talk this out. This passin' little notes back and forth won't cut it."

"He may be afraid to risk it if the Russkies put a tail on him," said Frank.

"Try it," said Rocky. "We gotta find a way outta this before we get all our asses in a sling. Meantime, let's see what else we got." He delved into the material Lermontov had sent. "Here we go. More medical records. And he wants to know if we signed up this Dr. Roth yet. Fucker. We've only been working on it a couple of days. When's your next meet?"

"Tuesday. Same time." He handed Rocky the neatly cutout map section Lermontov had given him. "I park, lock the car, take the keys. They've already made a duplicate set. Another KGB-er picks up my car and drives it off. I walk until another guy, not Lermontov, comes up this street and picks me up in an orange taxi."

"Sounds like your buddy reads too many spy novels."

Rocky took notes as Frank described the Chechen who'd driven his car.

"You get any fix on what part of town the safe house is in?"

"I've been trying." Frank described his efforts to sense without seeing where Lermontov had taken him. "But it may not much matter. He said Tuesday we go to a different safe house."

"Fuck. I don't like the idea of not knowing where you're at, but it's gonna be tough to put a tail on you with this taxicab routine."

"Why bother?" said Frank. "I'm his ticket to America. No way he's going to fuck with me."

"Never assume," said Rocky.

"He also said he wants to stay in close touch. He expects to get recalled to Moscow soon after Khomeini gets here or the Shah leaves, whichever comes first."

A sound erupted from Rocky halfway between a grunt and a laugh. "And who knows which the fuck'll come first. The Great Ayatollah seems to talk outta both sides 'a his beard. Wants the depraved Shah to be tried for his crimes in an Islamic court one minute and wants him kicked outta the country the next. The Shah sounds like he takes it for granted he'll go on a vacation on his yacht in the Gulf till all this blows over and then come back like he did when Mosaddeq lost out. Least that's what he told his nibs at lunch yesterday. You set to see Your Imperial Majesty any time soon?"

"Not that I know of," said Frank. He had a strong sense that time was running out. Khomeini arrives. The Shah leaves. Whichever comes first, it could mean the end of his time in Iran. He wondered where that would leave Lermontov.

"The ambassador has to go back to the palace tomorrow," said Rocky. "Washington sent another laundry list of questions plus a list of folks the Shah should consider for a Council of Experts to run the country. Dumbest list I ever saw. Mostly people who hate each other's balls."

"The ambassador should have an interesting day."

"He's not too keen on the whole idea. Including having to drive up there in the middle of a general strike. No tellin' what kinda shit's likely to break loose. Jesus, Lermontov sure gave you a ton of shit. All in Russian, except for his notes. Here's his list. More stuff on Afghanistan. Stuff on these two characters Ghotzbadeh and Yazdi who front for Khomeini in Paris. Both educated in the States, neither one a cleric. More dumb shit on Khomeini workin' for the CIA. Jesus. An organizational breakdown of their Tehran station. The ambassador's the fuckin' *rezident*. I never heard of that before. *Savak* keeps tellin' us the KGB head honcho is the ambassador's second in command. Langley's gonna love this shit, but we're gonna have a long night."

Late the next evening, soon after his meeting with Lermontov, Frank and Rocky had barely settled into the bubble when Rocky said, "So he had you taxied to his place?"

"How'd you know?"

"After we found out where it's at, I asked *Savak* to put the place under surveillance, just in case. They said they already had it under surveillance, but, since I know they can get careless, I asked them to upgrade the surveil. I had one of our guys check out the *Savak* op every couple of days, just to keep those boogers on their toes. When they saw you goin' in there, they had a shit fit, and one of their guys drove over here to let us know. I'll get a video for you."

"Never mind," said Frank.

"Hey, you can show it to your grandkids. Look what granddaddy did during the war. Here he is, betraying his country to the Soviets."

"Very funny."

"We had you tailed coming out."

"Lermontov said we were being followed."

"He's very good. Shook the tail in a couple of blocks. Where'd he drop you?"

"Soviet Embassy. Front gate. Back off Ferdowsi. Great intersection. Churchill and Stalin. My car was parked there."

"What a prick. You can be sure that's on video, too."

"I can understand you having his house under surveillance and trying to follow us, but why all this bullshit on his part?"

"Because he's one shrewd bastard. All this shows his *rezidenza* that he owns you, which may take some heat off him as the guy the mole is trying to finger. And he's got tapes to prove he owns you to our shop if what he really wants to do is fuck you up with Henry James."

"Playing cat and mouse isn't much fun when you're the mouse."

"Come on," said Rocky with a grin that made Frank uncomfortable. "Let's see the take."

Lermontov had used hand gestures to tell Frank to slip the material under the Peugeot's passenger seat into his briefcase. Now, Rocky riffled through it.

"Good shit," he muttered. "Includin' a bio on his ambassador. A full general in KGB. I'd been wonderin' about him. It's amazin' in a post like this to have a guy of Lermontov's caliber—and rank—second in command. The Shah's right about how central Iran is, maybe not for us but for damn sure to the Soviets. You take Iran and Afghanistan next door, you got maybe two thousand miles of border with the Soviet Union."

Frank nodded. "Lermontov's told me pretty much the same thing."

"Intellectual thugs are my favorite kinda thugs," said Rocky, looking up from Lermontov's material. "I still wish I was . . ." He looked away from Frank and started turning the pages of the day's take. "When's your next meet?"

"Day after tomorrow."

"You give him a note about a meet at our safe house?"

"Yeah. In the car. I labeled it 'Read Now.' He did but just shook his head and gave it back to me."

"He is spooked," said Rocky. "Keep tryin'. Let's see what else he sent us."

Meticulous Lermontov had included several hand-labeled envelopes in the package that Frank had pulled out from under his seat in the Peugeot. One read "Afghanistan"; another, "Tehran"; two said, "Iran," and another said "Next Meeting." Rocky opened it.

"Right on top. What's happening on arrangements for his medical treatment? I think he worries more about that than he does the mole. I hate to tell you this, Sully, but we got a fuckin' fly in the ointment. Not a fly. More like a hornet. When Henry James gets a bee up his ass, watch out."

"Keep talkin'," said Frank, consciously imitating Rocky.

"James sent me an eyes-only cable. Says more or less the Soviets will never okay medical treatment for Lermontov by a doctor not on their Washington embassy's approved list. And if Lermontov wants the best America has to offer, it won't be some sawbones who's a Soviet flunky."

"Don't you think Lermontov would have thought of that?"

"Sure he would've thought of that. What he figures to do, James figured out, once he's in the States he'll want to defect and get the best medical treatment we can arrange for him, and fuck what the Soviets think about it."

"Then James won't have an agent in place. Just another defector."

"Exactly."

"So what's the downside? We get a defector, maybe the highest KGB defector ever."

"The downside is James wants an agent in place for as long as possible. He wants to find his mole. Now he figures Lermontov's maybe playin' us about the latest word from the mole, tryin' t' put pressure on us t' maybe pull Lermontov outta here. So he's not sure, in his own wonderful phrase, we should consummate."

"How do I convey all this to Lermontov?"

"You don't, pending further cogitation and inspiration from the Holy Ghost."

"Am I supposed to know about this?"

"No."

"Suppose I try to draft a response for you? Outline the reason you think we should proceed, even on the assumption Lermontov will want to defect as soon as possible once he gets to the States. But not until we get enough on the mole to nail him."

"Do it," said Rocky. "And you better come with some ideas to keep this mole from bitin' Lermontov's ass. Doesn't look like we're gonna get any help from the Holy Ghost."

"Okay if I talk to Gus about it?"

"Why?"

"Gus is a good idea man," said Frank, thinking of the atmospherics cable. "He knows covert action, black ops."

"What the hell. Try him," said Rocky. "Some-fuckin'-body better come up with an idea."


Ever since *Ashura* the rooftop cries of *Allah-o akbar* sounded louder and closer. After his long nights in the bubble and the communications room with Rocky, Frank could hear them as he turned off Damavand. His neighbors, mostly middle class, many benefiting from the vast American presence, and nearly all, until recently, loyal to the Shah, followed Khomeini's instructions. They shouted God's power from the rooftops in defiance of the curfew.

When he opened the door of the Fiat, the cries seemed to surround him. None yet on this block but closer and louder than the night before. *Allah-o akbar. Allah-o akbar. Allah-o akbar.* Unseen voices in the long, dark night.

A full moon edged out between dark, low-lying clouds. Frank thought of the friendly soldiers who had stopped him a few nights before. He studied the face of the moon but saw no image of Khomeini outlined by its craters. A man in the moon, perhaps, but no beard or turban, no craggy features.

He remembered standing on a Brooklyn street corner one night many years before, when he was about Jake's age, with a classmate who told him that if he looked hard enough at the full moon he would be able to see Monsignor Heinz, pastor of their church, who had recently died. Frank tried, squinting till he saw stars, but the best his eleven-year-old imagination could come up with was the usual man in the moon.

"Can you see him? Can you see him?" asked his friend.

"Yeah. Yeah, I can see him," Frank lied. "Monsignor Heinz, for sure."

He found a note from Gus on the kitchen table. *I cooked and left leftovers in the fridge.* Starving, Frank tore at fried chicken, ate salad by hand, and forked down cold rice. He washed it all down with beer and burped gratefully. He fell quickly into sleep, hearing the mantra *Allah-o akbar, Allah-o akbar* and wondering what the day of the general strike would bring.

# CHAPTER SEVENTEEN

H ave you heard what happened?" asked Anwar during their tea break. "About the strike?"

"Well, yes, the strike appears successful. Almost everything has stopped, just as the Ayatollah wanted. But something more serious has happened. This morning. Have you heard?"

Frank shook his head, surprised to notice that Anwar had traded his blue air force uniform for a tweed jacket, brown slacks, and a tan shirt open at the throat.

"A noncommissioned officer in the Imperial Guards, a sergeant, I heard, walked into the officers' mess hall at breakfast and opened fire with an M-16. They say he managed to get a second clip into his weapon and began firing again, a second clip of thirty rounds before they shot him. They have their own medical facilities right there, so we may never know how many he killed or wounded. But no matter how many, he struck a terrible blow against our country. The *Javadan,* the Immortals, swear to protect the Shah and the country. And if the Immortals have begun to kill each other, we truly have civil war."

"Is that why you're wearing a suit?"

Anwar's hand tugged at the open collar of his shirt. "In a civil war, when Imperial Guards shoot each other, a military uniform may not be a good idea."

"It sounds like only one man who lost control," said Frank. "He knew how and where to do a lot of damage, but it sounds like only one man who went crazy."

"The whole country has gone crazy," said Anwar. "In Hamadan and Kermanshah soldiers give guns to local supporters of Khomeini. In many cities officers cannot control their men, who go over to the local committees set up in Khomeini's name. The oil workers and the civil servants who have been on strike take heart from the general strike. But all this means nothing. A crack in the Immortals could mean everything."

Their meeting had broken up early. Frank was grateful to see Ali and their bulletproof Nova waiting.

"You are early, sir," said Ali as Frank eased into the passenger seat beside him.

"I guess we decided to join the general strike," said Frank as Gus and the subdued Bunker climbed into the back.

"You cannot do that, sir. The military cannot have strikes."

"Relax. Just a joke." Just a joke, but Anwar had switched to civilian clothes. And Ali, an army sergeant, had worn civvies since they'd known him. "Did you hear about a shooting at Imperial Guard headquarters?"

"No, sir. When, sir?"

"Today. Just now."

*"Mojahedin?"*

Interesting reaction, thought Frank. Who would dare attack the Immortals? Leftist Islamic guerrillas. Of course.

"No," said Frank. "I understand an Imperial Guard NCO shot up the officers' mess hall."

"That cannot be," said Ali. "No member of the Imperial Guard would ever do that."

Ali drove them back to Dowshan Tappeh through deserted streets. The cable traffic showed little except reports on the almost total shutdown of economic activity. A message summoned Bunker to the embassy for a meeting with Rocky. Frank took advantage of his absence to tell Gus about the penetration agent's warning to Moscow.

"Jesus," said Gus. "I'm surprised Rocky let you tell me about it. Something like this, especially with Henry James involved, gets held pretty tight."

"I reminded him you've got more experience in this stuff than I do."

"Yeah, but I've also got enough experience to keep my ass out of Henry James's paranoid sights."

"If you can come up with any ideas, we need help," said Frank.

"Hey, you're the guy with the creative energy. All's I know how to do is write cables."

"And use a knife," said Frank. "On this one I need some help from a knife-fighting, cable-writing motherfucker."

"I'll think about it." said Gus. "But if I do come up with anything, don't tell Rocky it was my idea. You can have all the credit. And all the crap that comes with it."


Frank secured his briefcase in Rushmore's file cabinet and changed into his gym clothes. He wondered if the general strike had spread to Dowshan Tappeh. The building seemed quiet; the gym, deserted. He slipped on his leather mittens and shattered the silence, pounding the heavy bag. No one else arrived. He swung into his weight-lifting routine, punctuated by sit-ups and leg raises. Winded, drenched in sweat, with the blood beginning to dry on his knuckles, he called a halt at six-thirty. The *homafaran* never showed up.

Feeling dehydrated, he went to the cafeteria to pick up bottled water. He wished he hadn't. He recognized the broad back of Sergeant Abdollah Abbas. As Frank watched, the sergeant popped open the strap that secured the weapon in his holster. His right hand gripped the butt of his .45. A dozen Americans, maybe fifteen, men and a few women, sat scattered around the cafeteria. A vision of the blood-splattered officers' mess hall at Imperial Guard headquarters flashed through Frank's mind. He backed out the door he'd just entered and headed for Troy's offices. He found Bill Steele sitting with the colonel.

"We've got a problem," said Frank.

"We've got lots of problems," said Troy. "What's your problem?"

"Bill, you remember that Iranian sergeant I asked you about?"

"I thought I told you to stay away from him."

"I do. But he's in the cafeteria."

"Our cafeteria?" said Troy.

"He's in the American cafeteria, counting heads with his hand on the handle of his .45."

"Oh, shit," said Steele, jumping to his feet. "Are your *homafar* buddies in the gym?"

"They didn't show."

"Figures," said Steele. "You know what happened at the Imperial Guard?"

Frank nodded.

"Word's all over the base," said Steele. "The Iranians think the guy's a hero. Iranian Air Force guys. A lot of them joined the general strike. *Homafaran,* pilots. Nothing's flying."

"I wish the fuck we had somebody speaks Farsi," said Troy.

"How 'bout someone who speaks marksman?" said Frank.

"Cantwell," said Steele and Troy together.

"Is he around?"

"I'll find him," said Steele. He hurried from the office.

Frank looked at Troy and suddenly remembered the tape he carried in his briefcase with the reedy voice of Ayatollah Khomeini. "I got another idea," he mumbled.

He thudded down the hallway to Rushmore's office. Someone who speaks Farsi, he thought. Khomeini speaks Farsi. He pulled his briefcase from the bottom drawer of the file cabinet, along with the tape Anwar had given him and Belinsky had cued. Test it, he told himself, not wanting to take the time but taking the time. He checked the footage counter. One hundred and sixty. He played a few seconds of the tape, recognized the high-pitched voice, and turned the volume up to the maximum. He rewound to 150 and headed for the cafeteria.

He had taken less than a minute, but Cantwell already stood by a door opposite the one Frank had entered. Abbas, his hand on the butt of the .45, now stood in the center of the room, drawing stares from nervous Americans.

"What's this I-ranian doing in here?" screeched one of the women. "This here's the Amurrican cafeteria."

Cantwell stood with his left shoulder toward Abbas, his right arm hidden. Frank caught his eye, pointed to the tape recorder, and raised his right palm. He placed the recorder on a table and turned it on. Startled, Abbas looked his way.

"Turn that damned thing off," yelled the same woman. She had thinning gray hair trimmed short and wrinkled, pinched features. For a brief moment, Frank wished that Abbas might draw his gun and get off one true shot before Cantwell killed him.

But Abbas listened. Frank knew the sergeant had heard this tape before. Even the shrill, gray-haired woman sensed that some communication had begun between the beefy Iranian with his hand on his gun and the voice on the tape recorder. She held her tongue as the Ayatollah's message spun on.

Abbas nodded. He took his hand off the .45. He spoke one word. Frank thought he read his lips and wondered if it was the only word Abbas knew in English.

"Good."

He raised both hands and slowly walked toward Frank. The fat sergeant stood within inches of him and said clearly, "Good." He lowered his hands and walked out of the cafeteria.


"What is that thing?" asked Frank.

"A Remington XP-100, sir." Cantwell still held the long-barreled pistol by his right side.

"It looks like it's trying to grow up to be a rifle."

"Kind of the other way around, sir. The mechanics replicate an M600 carbine. It fires a high-intensity cartridge that produces the highest muzzle velocity of any pistol. That and the unusually long barrel make it highly accurate." He hefted it in his hand. "Doesn't weigh but sixty ounces."

"And it doesn't hold but one bullet," said Troy.

"The idea is not to miss, but in that crowd, you never know when some fool might panic and jump up in your line of fire. I like the weapon you used a lot more."

They'd withdrawn to Troy's office. Bill Steele had gone to alert Iranian security officers to the apparent danger posed by Abbas.

"Ayatollah Khomeini," said Frank. "Cued up to a part in one of his speeches where he talks about the need for peaceful tactics. Something like, Do not shoot your enemy in the breast but win his heart. Defeat your enemies not with bullets but with flowers. That kind of thing."

"Steele tells me you had some run-ins with the fat man before," said Troy. Frank told them about his previous encounters with Abbas in the gym, including the evening the sergeant had walked in while Frank and the *homafaran* listened to the same tape.

My buddies said he's very devout, so I hoped he might listen to the holy man's pitch."

"Well, it worked," said Troy. "But I wouldn't count on your buddies bein' your buddies with all this shit that's goin' down now."

"I hear you," said Frank. "But the tape I played in there, I got it from an Iranian."

"Thank God for small favors," said Troy. "I wouldn't've thought it, but turns out you're one fearless son of a bitch."

"Not me," said Frank.

"Yeah, you did good in there," said Troy. "I guess you know your other buddy did himself some good today?"

"You lost me," said Frank. "What other buddy?"

"Bunker. He got himself outta here. Emergency family leave. You know it was comin'?"

"Rocky told me about the headquarters cable."

"Yeah, well, Pan Am's booked solid till Friday, so Rocky okayed use of a non-American carrier. KLM tomorrow afternoon to Rome. Pan Am to Dulles. Bunker's no slouch. Wish my old lady hadn't left me. Could send her back home and have her heart murmur to Dean Lomax."

Gus sat at the kitchen table, sipping red wine. "Our friend is upstairs, packing."

"I heard about it." Frank rescued his vodka and a chilled glass from the freezer.

"Good news travels fast," said Gus as Frank joined him at the table. "I hope he isn't leaving with the thought of being missed. You should've heard him. 'Protocol demands I attend Jayface . . . explain my sudden departure. Don't want them to consider my leaving reflects in any way on the continuing importance . . .' and crap like that there."

"Look at the bright side. After tomorrow morning, you won't have to put up with him."

"Yeah, but I'll have to put up with me, and what I'm really pissed at is me for not bein' smart enough to pull what our friend is pullin' off."

"You could still ask him to talk to Dean Lomax about pulling you out."

"I thought about it," said Gus. "But I signed up for the duration, right? Call it a sense of duty. Or stupidity."

"You aren't stupid," said Frank. "And I've gotta admit, I need you."

"Yeah, well, I have been thinking about Lermontov and finding a way to get him out of his mole trap. So far, I've come up dry, but I'll keep at it."

"I appreciate it," said Frank. "But it seems like a mistake to pass up any chance to get out of here."

Gus shook his head. "You know, if Joan knew about it, she could never forgive me for not doin' just that. But if I did it, I could never forgive myself."


Paranoia reigned at Dowshan Tappeh. Except for half a dozen American air force men and an equal number of Iranian counter workers, no one risked the cafeteria. Frank had not seen the *homafaran* since before the day of the shooting at the Imperial Bodyguard headquarters and his confrontation with Sergeant Abbas. That had been when? Monday. Tension increased yesterday, Thursday, when assassins killed an American adviser to the National Iranian Oil Company and his Iranian counterpart. Bunker had done well to get out, thought Frank. The good bureaucrat. He'd handled it efficiently, even his farewell and departure from Jayface that morning.

Frank, working out alone, tried unsuccessfully to concentrate on his effort to bench press 135 pounds ten times. He needed to meet with Anwar the Smarter. Ask about his cousin. And about his effort to get a visa. Get to see Mina. I'll see Anwar tomorrow morning. Ask if I can come to his house that night. He decided to cut his workout short. Get home early. Shower. Cook. Eat. Sleep. Good plan. Bill Steele caught him in the hallway.

"Rocky wants you."

"Sweet Jesus."

"Not quite. Just the chief of station. Maybe you oughta take a shower."

"No. Let me stink up his bubble. Maybe he won't invite me so often. Hey, you ever hear anything about the fat sergeant?"

"No. Except nobody's seen him. But they expanded the air force security guard that's responsible for the rest of the base. The Iranian Air Force replaced the army military police that had this area."

"Interesting. You do a cable on it?"

"Yeah. Just finished. Fact, I've got that cable, couple of other things I need to get downtown. How 'bout I give you a ride?"

"Deal," said Frank.

Frank welcomed the chance to spend some time with Bill, who gunned his British-made Land Rover with speed, precision, and care.

"This ours?" asked Frank.

"Iranian Air Force. Buddy of mine lets me use it. Better cover than our Novas and better protection than your Fiat if some I-rani idiot runs into you."

With his full beard and hooded parka pulled tight, Steele could pass for a bigger-than-most Iranian.

"Don't mention to Rocky that I mentioned it to you, but I've got a cable Stan Rushmore did on the NIOC American that got killed yesterday. Almost for sure he says the *Mojahedin Khalq* pulled it off and he thinks one of your *homafar* gym buddies pulled a trigger."

"Oh shit. Any name?"

Steele stared straight ahead and, for what to Frank felt like several minutes, said nothing.

"Yeah." Both hands on the wheel, Bill kept his eyes fixed on the road before them. Finally, he said, "Anwar Amini."

Anwar the Taller, thought Frank. No wonder I haven't seen him.


Frank and Bill Steele sat on metal folding chairs while Rocky, behind his impressive oak desk in his concrete basement office, worked his way through the cables Bill had brought.

"Looks like you got another Iranian killed, Sully."

"I did?"

"Looks like you did." The response surprised Frank. Rocky usually turned his hearing aid off when he concentrated on paperwork. "Your jolly fat Sergeant Abbas. You're slippin'. The last one was a major."

"Executed?"

Rocky shrugged. "Just nobody's seen him lately." He initialed the cable. "Good job, Bill. This one can go." He kept his head bent, turning his attention to the next cable. He shook his head and looked up. "Sully, I gotta tell you about this one. Seems like one of your *homofur* buddies may have had a hand in killing those two Iranian oil guys. You seen them lately?"

"Not in about a week."

"I got a hunch you better keep your ass outta that gym. You could be a sitting duck."

"I don't think they'd target me."

"Never ass-ume. Especially when it's your ass." He scrawled his initials across the cable. "Okay. This can go, too. The rest of this shit's for the pouch?"

"Right," said Bill.

"Okay. It can wait for tomorrow. I have a problem with any of it, I'll let you know." Rocky pushed himself away from his desk with a grunt. He swung open the door of his safe and deposited the pouch material. He added the ball and ribbon from his IBM Selectric, shut the safe, and tumbled the lock. "Bubble time, Sully. Don't sweat it, Bill. I'll bring him back pretty quick."


"Don't even bother sittin' down," said Rocky as soon as he'd closed the door of the bubble. He stuck out his hand. "Congratulations."

"What'd I do?" He extended his hand and allowed Rocky to pump it.

"That cable you drafted for me did the trick. That, and a cable Tom Troy sent out about you and that nutty sergeant. Somehow Henry James managed to get ahold of that despite the fact Troy's cable is really none of his fuckin' business. Said you deserved a commendation on that and another on the way you've handled Lermontov. Oh. I almost forgot. That atmospherics cable of yours. Word came back it got a twenty."

"What's a twenty?"

"You really are an outsider, aren't you? A twenty's the highest rating a cable can get. It also got boiled down to a one-pager for an NSC briefing for Carter. James sent me another cable just on that. You Irish prick. You're a fuckin' hero. Never, never in my fuckin' life have I heard the Holy Ghost say that much good about anybody."

"Maybe that should worry me."

"Maybe it should. But for now it looks legit. James says you should apprise— that's the way he talks—you should apprise Identity A of our concern regarding Soviet approval of his medical treatment but of our willingness to accept his defection, if absolutely necessary, once certain prerogatives have been achieved. Like nailin' the fuckin' mole. Your next meet's Sunday, right?"

"Right."

"Good. Apprise him. And good fuckin' luck. Any ideas about what to do about this shit storm our penetration agent stirred up?"

"Sorry. Not yet."

"Sorry is right," said Rocky.


"Thanks for not letting Rocky know I told you about those cables."

"He knew," said Frank.

"What?" For the briefest moment, Bill took his eyes off the road.

"That's why he kept his hearing aid on."

"I don't get it."

"Rocky has good instincts. When he guesses things, he usually gets it right. When he started reading the cables, I've got a hunch because of what they're about he guessed you might've talked to me about them. Usually, when he's reading something important, he shuts off his hearing aid, to keep out distractions. Tonight, he didn't. He wanted to see if we'd say anything that might confirm what he suspected. I don't think we did, but he knew anyway."

"Son of a bitch. He's even smarter than I thought he was."

"Rocky's very smart," said Frank. "I've learned a lot from him." And I've got a hunch, he added to himself, I'll learn even more from the Holy Ghost. God help me.

They drove in silence for several minutes. Bill broke it. "Say, Frank?"

"Yeah?"

"I've got a problem. Maybe you can help me with it."

"I'll help if I can."

"You used to be a reporter, right?"

"In some ways, I still am."

"I've got a problem with reporters. *Wall Street Journal. Washington Post. Newsweek*. Even the BBC. Somehow my name's got out there. And these guys have tracked me down, asking me questions about Dowshan Tappeh, the American presence, the agency's role. This *Journal* guy's real persistent. He even got my home phone. Called me about the NIOC guy, the National Iranian Oil Company guy that got whacked."

"What'd you say?"

"Told him he had the wrong guy. I was just a quartermaster for the air force guards, which is what I'm supposed to be."

"That sounds good."

"Maybe, but I told him that before. He keeps comin' back."

For the second time that evening, Frank asked, "You do a cable on it?"

Bill shook his head. It was a moment before he spoke. "I haven't even told Troy about it. If the agency thinks my cover's blown, they might ship me outta here. And I feel like I got a job to do."

I know that feeling, thought Frank, but I wish it would go away.

"What's the name of the guy on the *Journal?*" he asked.

"He's got a Muslim-sounding name. Which worries me even more."

"Yusef el Baz?"

"You know him?"

"No, but I know his by-line and a bit about him. American born, Egyptian parents. Speaks fluent Arabic, Farsi, couple of other languages. 'Course, somebody could be using his name, pretending to be him, but the real el Baz is legit and real good."

"Persistent fucker."

"Good reporters have to be. Got any idea how he got your name?"

"None."

"Got any enemies?"

"Well, yeah. Don't you?"

"Yeah, I guess so," said Frank.

"There's some Iranian toes I stepped on at the base," said Bill. "Then there's a couple of fuckers in our communications unit at the embassy."

"What's your problem with them?"

"They're fuckups. One in particular. Guy named Teasdale. Likes to shoot his mouth off. I know he does some of his drinking at the Intercontinental. Where the journalists hang out."

"Sounds like a likely candidate," said Frank.

"All that plus lazy, careless, full of himself. And I fuckin' don't put up with him."

"Rocky puts up with him?"

"He doesn't have to. They're scared of Rocky. Me, they figure I'm just some fucker from Douche Bag Tapper."

"From what?"

"Douche Bag Tapper. That's what some of the guys call Dowshan Tappeh."

"Great. No wonder they love us here," said Frank. "Tell you what really worries me."

"I don't think I want to hear this."

"And I don't want to say it, but foreign journalists are here to find all they can about what's going on. The good ones spend as much time as they can talkin' to Iranians. Iranian journalists. The military. The clergy. Students. Any Khomeini followers they can get to talk to them. If your name is out there with the foreign journalists, what really worries me is who else may have heard it."

"Rocky gets that idea, my ass is outta here in a hurry."

"If the wrong Iranians know you're CIA, getting outta here sounds like a good idea."

"I got a job to do here," said Bill.

"Okay. Meantime, any way somebody else could screen your calls?"

"No way," said Bill. "You know my job. I have to be available all the time. Can you imagine somebody picking up my phone and telling Rocky, Mr. Steele will get back to you?"

"No, I can't. All I can say is it sounds like you've been doing the best thing you could do. Stick to the 'Hey, guy, I'm just the quartermaster' routine. Don't hang up on him. Be polite. Pleasant. Never get in a pissing contest with anybody whose boss buys newsprint by the truckload. They always have the last word. And Bill . . ."

"Yeah?"

"I hate to say it, but . . . you ought to tell Rocky. Or maybe have me tell Rocky. He's got good instincts and a good nose. If he finds out some other way, and finds out you kept something this important from him, he'll crucify you."

Frank and Anwar the Smarter had shared a hole in what passed for the bath-room at Supreme Commander's Headquarters, mixing their urine and their con-cerns. They spoke softly and shuffled their feet to avoid the spray that splattered the concrete rim. Frank asked if he could come by Anwar's house. This was not a good time, Anwar said, but could he come to Frank's house? Frank reluctantly told him how to do that. They settled on Monday night, which would be Christ-mas, at eight o'clock.

Lermontov had suggested a brief meeting Sunday evening just in case Moscow suddenly had ordered him home. He said he'd received no new orders.

Frank wondered where they'd stopped when Lermontov dropped him off. "This is Pahlavi," said Lermontov. "Facing south. Your car just pulled up behind us. Drive straight ahead. The next big intersection is Takht-e Jamshid. Turn left. You'll see your embassy in a few blocks."

Frank surrendered his opaque glasses and gave himself a few moments for his eyes to adjust to the early winter evening light. He'd again given Lermontov a note suggesting a meeting at the American safe house. In capital letters, he'd printed out one additional word—*MOLE.*

Lermontov nodded and added to the note: *Tuesday night at 7.*

Frank grabbed the briefcase in which he'd stashed the thin envelope Ler-montov had given him and opened the car door. The thickset Chechen who'd driven Frank's car blocked his way, waving his hands and speaking rapidly in Russian.

"Wait," said Lermontov. "Some mob has your embassy under attack."

Despite the warning, Frank made the turn onto Takht-e Jamshid. He'd driven less than a mile along the wide and now all but deserted avenue when he saw a car in flames at the embassy gate. The car exploded, spewing the street with a fountain of shrapnel and sparks. At the next side street, he turned left and took to the narrow alleyways. His instincts guided him well, and in less than a minute he pulled up to the embassy's back gate.

He shed his stocking cap, put the stick-shift Fiat in neutral, pulled on the hand brake, left the motor running, and very slowly eased his way out of the car. He approached the gate, arms extended to his sides, palms forward, and, he hoped, his American face visible despite the evening shadows. Three marines, each cradling a shotgun, emerged from the gloom, back-lit by the glow of the car still burning beyond the distant front gates. A fourth marine, holding a shot-gun with a finger on the trigger, stepped out of the guard house.

"Major Francis Sullivan. U.S. Air Force. Mr. Novak expects me. But your front gate looks a bit hot. I have ID I can show you."

"Sir, I recognize you, sir," one of the marines called out. Frank couldn't see his features, but he thought he knew the voice and the polite speech patterns of the poster-perfect marine he and Gus had met on their first trip to the embassy. "Please stand to, sir. We'll unchain the gates. Walk through, if you will, please, sir. One of us will drive your car in. Then we'll check your ID. And search you."

"I'm wearing a wire," said Frank. "Part of my job. Don't let it freak you."

"Thank you for telling us, sir."

"We'll leave your car back here with us," said the polite, nervous marine. "You'll be exiting by this venue."

He walkie-talkied to Rocky's office to get clearance for Frank, then drove him to the main embassy building in an open jeep. As they crossed the com-pound, Frank could see the smoke still reflecting the light of the fire from the front gates. He thought of his first view of Tehran, funnels of gray smoke stretching into banks of gray clouds. He remembered the day of their first Jayface meeting. He and Anwar had stood outside Supreme Commander's Headquarters, watching pillars of smoke twist into the sky.

"Something always seems to be smoking in Tehran," said Frank.

"Roger that, sir," said the marine as he pulled up to a rear entrance to the main building.


Lingering tear gas stung Frank's eyes. The young marine escorted him into the embassy, through various checkpoints and down to Rocky's office. "I'm afraid I have to leave you here," he said. "Mr. Novak is . . ."

"Busy," said Frank.

"Correct, sir. Very busy. Ask Mr. Novak to radio when you're ready to leave. Good to see you again."

After turning over the bug he wore to a technician, Frank sat by himself for nearly an hour in Rocky's office. He used the time to study the documents in the envelope Lermontov had given him. Lermontov had labeled the first "For You."

*I hope you soon have word on plans for my medical treatment.*

By now Lermontov would have read Frank's sanitized version of Henry James's approval of the plan. It included an update on Dr. Roth, now with Johns Hopkins and still considered the world's foremost expert on acromegaly. He had agreed to be the primary physician for a patient for whom James's counterintelli-gence shop had created a legend, including a new name, details of which Lermontov would learn at a later date. Merry Christmas, he thought.

"Merry fuckin' Christmas," said Rocky as he bulled his way into his office.

"I hope you didn't arrange this one," said Frank.

"What? Oh." Rocky smiled. "No. Sounds like a fuckin' accident, just about."

Frank shared Lermontov's "For You" note. Rocky grunted. "By now he knows we'll take care of him."

"I also got him to agree to a meet, Tuesday at seven, at our safe house, the one he knows. I let him know the main topic is the mole."

"Good," said Rocky. "You got any ideas to solve that little problem?"

Frank shook his head. "If you mean the mole, no silver bullets yet."

"Not good," said Rocky.

Frank quickly handed him the only other envelope Lermontov had provided. It was labeled "NIOC."

"Their take on the two Iranian Oil Company guys that got offed," said Rocky. "Nothin' we didn't have from Rushmore. Nothin' about your *homafar* buddy."

"Glad to hear that. What happened out front?"

"Another National fucking Iranian Oil Company story. The NIOC headquarters isn't but a couple of blocks from here. The ragheads had a demonstration out front this afternoon. Iranian oil for Iranians, shit like that. Peaceful demonstration, if you can believe it. Broke up around four. Crowd split in various directions, but a lot of them came this way, maybe just because Takht-e Jamshid is a main drag. Standard procedure, the radio dispatcher for embassy vehicles gets on the horn and tells all drivers to avoid the area until the crowd passes. But one I-ranian asshole of a driver only a couple of blocks away decides he can beat the crowd. He pulls up to the gates, but the marines already got the gates chained. He starts arguin', yellin', wavin' his arms, screamin'. By that time the crowd's on top of him. Somebody tossed a Coke bottle full 'a gasoline corked with a smokin' rag into his car. Pretty quick, the gas tank blew up, and the ragheads went nuts with their death-to-America shit and started tryin' t' pull down the gates, throwin' rocks, bricks, whatever they could find. A couple tried climbin' the fence, but the ambassador gave the word for the marines to let go with their tear gas. And a bunch of I-ranian army types posted at the gates to the residence came barrel-assin' up the block tryin' t'shoot the sky down with their M-fuckin'-14s. That about did it. Movie's over. The crowd went home."

"They'll be back," said Frank.

"I know," said Rocky. "You got somethin' else on your mind?"

"How'd you know?"

"Because I know you. Give."

"We'll, we've got another problem."

"Now what have you done?"

"Me? Nothing. But somebody tipped off the foreign journalists here, American and British, about who Bill Steele is, what he does, even his fucking phone numbers." He pronounced "fucking" very deliberately, making sure he didn't drop the final *g*. "Even his fucking home phone number."

"How come he tells you and doesn't tell me?"

"Because he knows he has an important job to do here. He wanted my advice. How to handle the journalists. How to let you know without getting himself sent home."

Rocky relaxed his hands and leaned back. "He's responsible for security at Dowshan Tappeh. Tell you the truth, I rely on him for other things, like security around here. But if his cover's blown, he's got a problem keepin' things secure."

"His cover didn't blow itself. Someone blew his cover. That's the real problem."

"I hear ya, Sully. He got any fuckin' idea who?"

"He's got some ideas. Including some of your communications guys he's had trouble with. He mentioned a guy name of Teasdale."

"Wouldn't surprise me. Tell Bill t' come see me. Tell you the truth, long as I'm here I want a guy like Bill Steele here t'watch my back. Get your ass back to Dowshan Tappeh. Tell Steele t' come see me soon's he can. Don't call. Just come. I'll be here. Tell him he stays."

"Good," said Frank.

"No," said Rocky. "It's not good. Just we don't have a whole lot of resources. That's why you're still here. Bunker, I could let go. Gus, if I had to, I could let go. You, Steele, even Belinsky with his hepatitis, sorry. You guys fuckin' stay."


Anwar blew the horn once, then, after a pause, twice. Frank cracked the front door. Despite the cold, far more intense than usual, *Allah-o akbar* echoed from neighboring rooftops. His eyes scanned the street and the building opposite. He saw no signs of danger. He waved in Anwar's direction and held up a hand. He hurried down the steps and driveway, undid the padlock, and grunted the garage door up. Anwar, as instructed, backed down the driveway, which Frank had salted. Earlier, Gus had driven their Fiat to Dowshan Tappeh, where he would watch another old Super Bowl video.

Anwar killed his lights and engine and climbed from the car.

"You're alone?"

"Yes," said Anwar. "I hope you don't mind. We have things to discuss, and my wife, sometimes, she can be . . . a bit, perhaps, distracting. Don't you agree?"

Frank hoped his smile didn't show in the dark garage.

"Perhaps," he said. "A bit."

He had put a sheet into service as a tablecloth, draped over the all-purpose folding table in their front room. Gus had hit the American commissary, well stocked for the holidays despite the revolution raging around it. Frank had laid out a spread that included a passable pâté, an array of excellent wheat and rye crackers, some of the caviar that remained from the carton Mina had given him, chilled vodka for himself and Anwar, and, in case she appeared, a pitcher of iced tea for Mina.

"I remembered that your wife doesn't drink," he said.

"That's very thoughtful of you," said Anwar.

Frank poured them each two fingers of vodka. They touched glasses and sipped but without much enthusiasm. They sat opposite each other at the table. Frank proffered caviar, then pâté, but Anwar shook his head.

"Hamid fed us before I left."

Frank realized that in Mina's absence the occasion would not be festive. Anwar seemed to want it that way.

Frank cut to business. "How are you doing with Belinsky?" he asked.

"Not yet with Belinsky," said Anwar. "With Mina's uncles in the bazaar. How we've done with them, that's the first question."

"Tell me."

"In truth, they've been quite wonderful," said Anwar. "Every kind of document. Wedding documents, birth certificates for our children, all showing that I am Baha'i. Old-looking letters where I tell my parents of my intention to convert. Your friend Mr. Belinsky seemed very impressed. And, most impressive of all, he expects within two weeks to have approval of his petition to grant me a visa."

Frank knew Belinsky had the authority to grant the visa without seeking approval. He suspected Rocky had intervened to delay the process, to keep Anwar in Iran as a productive agent in place for as long as possible. Productive, thought Frank, but not witting and never recruited. Frank studied his Persian friend, again wearing civilian clothes. He's done so much for us. We've done so little for him.

"That's good news," he said. "I hope it works out."

"It's good news," said Anwar. "But I am worried."

"What about?"

"Timing could be important," said Anwar. "Mina and the children could leave now, but for me, it would be difficult to leave with the Shah's government still in place. Even more difficult once Khomeini comes firmly to power."

"That may not leave you much of a crack to squeeze through," said Frank.

"I know. Plus, Mina has said she won't leave unless all four of us leave together."

Frank nodded, understanding why Anwar had left Mina at home. He had no ready solution to offer.

"What about your cousin?" he asked abruptly.

"My cousin? What about him?"

"Does he need to leave?"

"For now, he needs to stay in hiding. He may still have the uniform of *homafar,* but more and more he now wears the cloak of *Mojahedin.*"

"I don't see him in the gym anymore."

"The air force suffers. Many *homafaran* need to stay in hiding."

"I've heard a rumor . . ."

"I know the rumor."

"NIOC?"

Anwar nodded.

"What do you think?"

Anwar shook his head. "I have no knowledge."

"Perhaps, for now, at least, your cousin can stay in hiding. But you can't."

"Timing could be important," said Anwar.


When Gus returned, he and Frank shared a nightcap and the remains of the pâté and caviar. "This is a treat," said Gus. "Nothing quite like this over at the cafeteria. Which I had about all to myself, by the way. Except for a couple of sleepy Iranians behind the counter."

"Memories of the fat sergeant," said Frank.

"That plus it's Christmas," said Gus. "But I did run into one of our air force guard buddies. The blue-eyed one. Todd Waldbaum. He got on me about never comin' over, and to tell you the truth I think we ought to. Safety in numbers, plus they have guns. We ought to know where that place is and make sure they'll let us in. When we even got our neighbors up on their roof shoutin', 'God is great,' you and me would be sitting ducks if the shit ever really hit the fan around here."

"You're right," said Frank, but he worried more about Anwar being a sitting duck than he did about himself. He knew he had to find a way to get Anwar's visa okayed.

"You got an every-other-night deal with your Russian buddy, right?"

"Right," said Frank, only half aware of what Gus had asked him.

"Right," echoed Gus. "So I took a chance and told Todd we had a good shot, so far at least, to maybe get there Wednesday night. Okay?"

"Okay," said Frank. "At least, like you said, so far. I hope it works out. 'Cause you're right. We may need a safer safe house than this one."

"Meanwhile," said Gus, "I got the germ, just the germ, of an idea that might help your Russian buddy."

"Tell me."

"Okay. You know the job you're up for, the one I was up for for a while?"

"Yeah?"

"Well, they've got media outlets, places where they can place stuff pretty much all over the world. One of them's a rag called the *Near East Weekly Review,* published outta Qatar. My idea is to write somethin' about the Soviet Embassy operation here in Tehran. 'Inside a Soviet Embassy' kinda thing. A story that covers a lot of bases but also points a finger at a likely CIA agent inside the embassy. You need to talk to Lermontov to pick out a likely candidate, maybe use the target as an anonymous but recognizable source for the story. Also get Lermontov to provide lots of juicy details about KGB ops here. You write the story. Dean Lomax gets his shop to place it real quick. Maybe with a little push from Henry James."

"I told you I needed you," said Frank. "I'll try it on Lermontov next meet."


"It's a little late for a Christmas present," said Rocky. "But I've got good news for that air force buddy of yours."

"Fair exchange," said Frank. "I've got a good idea from Gus."

They sat alone in the bubble. Gus had elected to wait in Rocky's office.

"Oh? So why didn't Gus come up and tell it to me himself?" asked Rocky.

"Said he didn't want to take credit for it. Or get involved in the Lermontov–Henry James business.

"I don't blame him," said Rocky. "What's the idea?"

Frank outlined the concept of planting an article in the *Near East Weekly Review,* exposing KGB operations within the Soviet Embassy in Tehran and pointing to a possible CIA agent inside the embassy.

"Sounds far-fetched to me," said Rocky. "You try it on Lermontov?"

"Not yet. Not without your go-ahead."

"What the fuck. Covert Action crap always seems weird to me. Try it on him. We don't have much else to try. When's your next meet?"

"Tomorrow night."

"Okay. Bring your ass back here after the meet. Lemme know what happened. Meantime, Belinsky got clearance to go ahead on a six-month tourist visa. He's already got all the documentation he needs, including stuff from the wife's family guaranteeing financial support as needed for the six months. Once we get him there, we'll work on keeping him there."

"Thanks, Rocky."

"Don't thank me. Thank Belinsky. Besides, I don't think your buddy's gonna do us much good here. We'll see what him and maybe even his old lady can do for us back in the States."

"That's good news," said Frank. He'd wondered what he could do to get Anwar's visa approved. Rocky had found the answer for him. "Very good news."

"Oh, there's still one thing to work out on the visa. Belinsky can't issue it until your buddy gets an airline ticket. And that could be tricky."


"I have good news for you," said Frank as he and Anwar stood over the bathroom bunghole after their Jayface meeting broke up. He had chided Gus for always meeting Hamid in the bathroom. Now he realized how consistently he met here with Anwar. "Can you come by the place tonight?"

"I will," said Anwar.

"Nine o'clock," said Frank. "Same deal, except, can you bring Mina?"

"Of course."


With Gus again shunted off to Dowshan Tappeh, Frank settled into the front room by eight-thirty and waited for Anwar. The evening power outage had begun. He sat in the dark and sipped a chilled vodka. He wondered if he had made a mistake in telling Anwar he should bring Mina. He needed to talk to Anwar about his cousin and worried that Anwar might prefer not to say much in front of Mina, but he also needed to be sure Mina understood the importance of the airport arrangements they must make.

He lit a candle for the kitchen and two for the front room. He made sure the flashlight stood within reach and tasted another sip. Promptly at nine, a horn blew once and then twice.


"This is terrible," said Mina, once she'd molted out of her headscarf and furs and settled in. She wore a heavy red wool sweater and loose-fitting black slacks tucked into her boot tops.

"Well, thank you," said Frank. "We like to think of it as modest."

"How can you live like this? Do you live like this in America? Can I look around upstairs?"

She gave Frank no time to answer her questions. Anwar managed to answer her last.

"No, Mina. You cannot look around upstairs."

"Poof."

"Now you see why I didn't want to bring you. We have important things to talk to Major Sullivan about."

"I am sorry. I apologize to both of you. Sometimes I just get carried away. But you deserve better."

"To tell you the truth, I don't much think about it. The refrigerator works, except when the electricity is out. The stove works. I can cook. The shower works. I can wash. My mattress is firm. I can sleep. What else does a man need?"

"I could answer that, but Anwar would say I'm being forward."

"Even I can answer that," said Anwar. "Without, I hope, being forward, what a man needs, and what this place needs, is a woman."

"Exactly," said Mina. "Why don't you have your woman here?"

"Mina, please." He turned to Frank. "She is so very nosy."

"That's why CIA should hire me. I would find out everything."

You probably would, thought Frank. Including the fact that I don't know any woman who would want to be here.

"Anwar tells me there's good news," said Mina. "Tell me the good news."

"Chuck Belinsky's ready to issue Anwar's visa."

"Thank God," said Mina, suddenly very serious. "When?"

"We still have one problem."

"I knew it," said Mina. "I knew something would go wrong. What?"

"Nothing wrong," said Frank. "Just a problem we can work out. But it will take some work, some discretion, perhaps some risk. Before Mr. Belinsky can issue the visa, he'll have to see a round-trip airline ticket."

"We knew that," said Mina.

"But there may be some folks, like the Royal Iranian Air Force, who won't want Anwar to leave. And the other complication . . ." He hesitated, glancing toward Mina.

"You can speak freely in front of Mina."

"Anwar the Taller," said Frank.

"Poof," said Mina. "It's only a stupid *Savak* rumor."

"But *Savak,* the police, the air force . . . we understand everybody wants to find him." He turned back to Anwar. "And, since you both have the same name, if you try to buy an airline ticket, alarms go off."

"I understand the problem," said Anwar. "You said we could work it out."

"Listen very carefully," said Frank. The lights fluttered on, then out again. "It gets complicated and involves both of you. First step, bring me your passport tomorrow."

"I've got it now," said Anwar.

"I'll take it now." Anwar took his passport from his attaché case and gave it to Frank. "Good start. Second step, Mina gets tickets for her and the children."

"Without Anwar? I won't do it."

"Please, Mina. Just listen," said Anwar. "What else?"

"We'll help to make sure you get on a flight, but you'll have to take care of the arrangements yourself. We'll need three days' advance notice. Since Pan Am started up its flights again they have only one flight a day, so don't worry about time of departure or flight number. Just get us the date you'll be ready to leave."

"I feel like a spy already," said Mina.

"Please, Mina. Just listen," said Anwar again.

Please, just listen, thought Frank. "We'll make another reservation, two-way ticket, the same flight in a name you don't need to know. Day of the flight, Mr. Belinsky with his little consular officer's kit meets Anwar at the Pan Am ticket counter. Civilian clothes, Anwar, right?"

"That's all I wear these days. But I wonder if we have a week."

"We'll all move as fast as we can," said Frank. "But we also have to avoid panic. The whole exercise has to come off smoothly. If you act nervous at any step, try to rush things at customs or immigration or the ticket counter, attract attention, get somebody mad at you, that could be the end."

Anwar and Mina looked at each other and nodded. She reached out and took his hand.

"Let's decide now," said Mina. "Three days. Can you do it in three days?"

"If you can be ready in three days, we'll do it in three days," said Frank.

"Good," said Anwar and Mina together.

"When departure day comes," said Frank, "Mina and the kids get to the airport two hours early and board as soon as possible. Anwar, you should get there about an hour early, but don't approach the ticket counter until twenty minutes before flight time. Mr. Belinsky will talk to a ticket clerk who . . . well, who has an arrangement with us. Mr. Belinsky tells the clerk he has a reservation that he has to cancel. Instead, his Iranian assistant, Anwar Amini, will make the trip. The clerk cancels the reservation in the phony name and issues a ticket in your true name. You carry one suitcase and check it through. You and Mr. Belinsky get away from the ticket counter. He completes some form that already has your flight number, departure details, and destination and gives you back your passport with the visa already in it."

"What do I do all this time?" asked Mina.

"By this time you and the children have already boarded. And of course you're wearing a long cloth coat and a headscarf. No furs; no jewelry, makeup, or perfume. If you encounter each other, at no time do you look at Anwar, speak to him, or acknowledge him in any way. You've got to drill the kids to do the same. The flight goes through Rome. You can hug and kiss all you want when you get there."

"What about *Savak*?" said Anwar.

"They have people who work for all the airlines who also work for them, plus their own agents. They'll get your name sooner or later. But timed this way, and with the clerk misplacing whatever he has to misplace, you should clear Iranian airspace long before they figure out you're gone. Airport records of your passport show you're the one who left, not your cousin. You're not a fugitive. And we do, you know, have some influence with *Savak*. My boss will handle it."

"Why are you doing all this for us?" said Mina.

"Because Anwar's done a lot for me. And because I hope, after you settle the kids with Mina's parents in Los Angeles, you'll come to Washington and look up this friend of mine."

He gave Anwar a card with Dan Nitzke's name and a phone number.

"Is that the man who'll hire me for CIA?"

Frank shook his head. "Mina, you better start practicing not saying that name. In fact, you ought to practice not saying the first thing that pops into your head. For the job at hand, getting Anwar out of the country, you need to start practicing discretion."

"I understand."

"I hope so. Because Anwar's life may be at stake. Maybe even yours and the children's."

"I do understand," said Mina.

I hope so. This time Frank said it to himself. He turned to Anwar.

"What about your cousin?"

"He came to see us," answered Mina before Anwar could respond.

Discretion, thought Frank. I'm glad she understands. "That sounds risky."

"Not really," said Anwar. "Mina's uncle picked him up at his private garage in the bazaar, drove him to the compound in the back of his van."

"All my uncles have been very good," said Mina.

"What did he have to say?"

"I think . . . I think he felt lonely." Straining mightily, Frank suspected, Mina nodded and managed to say nothing. "Lonely for the family. He wanted to talk. To find out how everyone was. To let us know the *Mojahedin* had him well protected. He remains active, recruiting more *homafaran* for the *Mojahedin*. Without the *homafaran,* the air force grinds down. He told us he'd heard the rumor evidently spread by *Savak* that he and other *homafaran* had some involvement with the killing of the two NIOC officials. He wanted us to know they had not. He guessed you would have heard that story, and he wanted you to know it had no truth. And he wanted you to know he and the other *homafaran* from the gym admired what you did in the cafeteria with an army man named . . . Abbas?"

Frank nodded. "Sergeant Abbas."

"We did not know the story. He had to tell us about it."

"You were very brave," said Mina. "And clever."

"Which is what you must be," said Anwar.

Amen, thought Frank.

Soon after, Anwar and Mina made their long good-byes, expressed their thanks, apologized for leaving so early, and insisted they must get together again soon. In the garage, Frank opened the passenger door for Mina. She turned, wrapped a furred arm around his neck, kissed him, and said, "I bet your woman, whoever she is, I bet she's very beautiful."

He hoped Anwar did not suffer from jealousy. Devoted to her and confident in her love, he could let Mina be herself, the woman he adored. Lucky man, Frank thought.

Frank hadn't been in the safe house since the night six, maybe seven, weeks before, when Rocky had insisted on meeting Lermontov. Rocky had told him, it hadn't been used since but that Bill Steele's crew would clean it up and his technicians would check the listening devices. Frank laid his briefcase on the walnut-stained dining room table, stashed a bottle of Absolut and two glasses in the freezer, and settled into the blue Naugahyde armchair to wait for Lermontov.

He reached out to check the black telephone on the bookstand by the armchair. The dial tone reassured him. The phone had been dead when Lermontov checked it on their last visit. Frank heard the sound of a car braking and turning into the drive way, followed by the flash of headlights. He checked his Timex, seven-thirty-five. He pushed himself up out of the armchair and toward the stairs that led to the cellar garage. Each move echoed what had happened back in early November. Heave up the garage doors, step back as Lermontov's white Peugeot edged in next to Frank's blue Fiat. Lermontov wore the same bulky overcoat and lamb's-wool cap.

Frank pulled down the doors, and Lermontov said, "I hope this time there's no one waiting for me in the kitchen?"

"Not this time," said Frank.

"Let's get this over with," said Lermontov as he shed his cap and overcoat and tossed them onto the armchair. He set his soft leather briefcase next to Frank's on the dining room table. "Then we can talk."

The material Rocky had provided included assessments supposedly prepared by the ambassador on the probability of the Shah's departure and by Near East Division on the likelihood of a coup. Frank checked the labels on the envelopes Lermontov spread out on the table: a thick one on Afghanistan, another titled "Conflicts Among the Mullahs," then one each for Tehran, the Shah, Baku, and, most intriguing of all, Soviet embassy plans.

"Looks impressive," said Frank.

"Which is more than I can say for your material. Now, what about plans for my medical treatment?"

Frank explained the agency fear that the Soviets would only allow treatment by doctors approved by their Washington embassy. "That means the agency will accept your defection so it can provide the best possible treatment for you."

"Dr. Roth?"

"He's on board. Using the medical records you've given us, the agency will prepare a new patient identity for you. But all this won't happen until . . ."

"Until?"

"Until certain conditions are met. First and foremost, identifying the penetration agent."

"First and foremost," said Lermontov, "is getting Moscow Center off my back. Four Neanderthals from the counterintelligence line arrived yesterday. I've been shut up with them most of the day."

"Look, I've got an idea, but it's going to take . . . well, it's going take a lot of balls on your part. And a lot of work."

"Acromegaly makes my bones grow. Not my balls."

"What about . . . ?"

"No," said Lermontov, managing a smile. "It doesn't make that other part grow, either. Do you have any vodka?"

"Yeah. Sorry. I forgot about it." He hurried to the kitchen and returned with a tray that included the last tin of Mina's caviar.

"What kind of work? And balls?"

Frank pried open the caviar and poured them each a chilled vodka while he explained the idea of planting an article in a weekly news magazine that would point the finger of suspicion at someone else in the KGB's Tehran station.

"Moscow wouldn't take it seriously. A magazine you own."

"They might," said Frank. "The magazine has a good reputation. Accurate. Reliable. Considered left of center. Not an agency proprietary. Never identified as an agency front. Just one editor who's a witting agent."

Lermontov's smile reflected his skepticism. "Does this wonderful publication have a name?"

"Yes," said Frank. "It has a name. *Near East Weekly Review.*"

"Really?" The big man looked into his glass. "The station gets a subscription. It's quite good. I read it every week. I never knew it was yours."

"Good," said Frank.

Lermontov sipped his vodka. He studied Frank, shook his head, and drained the glass. "But I don't like getting one of our own sentenced to death."

"Even to save your own life?"

"Even to save my own life." He held out his glass, and Frank poured. "Why do you take so much trouble for me? Expose an important asset like this magazine. Put your own life at risk as you did at the university."

"Well," said Frank, hesitating. There's that wonderful word that gives you time to think. He remembered Ambassador Hempstone's effective use of it when delicately discussing the British interest in Lermontov. "Well," Frank repeated, "can I be honest with you?"

"That would spoil everything," said Lermontov.

"Well, maybe," said Frank, "but let me try. I need you."

"Really," said Lermontov, raising an eyebrow. "Perhaps you are being honest."

"Do you remember that day we met, that first meeting here, at the palace?"

"Of course I remember."

"You said your nursemaids, and the people who monitor me, must wonder about us."

Lermontov nodded, almost smiled, said nothing.

"Just before I came over here, after I'd been told you were here, I told a friend of mine that there were people in . . . in our organization who thought I must be a traitor."

"Because of me?"

"Yes. And my friend said the best way to put those rumors to rest would be to recruit you."

"So you need to turn me into a traitor to prove you are not a traitor."

Frank knew there was more to it than that. He wanted to prove to himself that he was more than just an outsider, that he could recruit and handle a high-ranking KGB officer. He wanted to prove he could play in the same league as people he admired, people like Pete Howard, and that he deserved the respect of people who had doubted him, people like Rocky.

"Well, I need you," he said, studying Lermontov, hoping he would understand.

Lermontov nodded and bolted down his vodka. "I know you need me. But I am not a traitor. Just a Soviet intelligence officer who needs medical treatment he cannot get in the Soviet Union."

"I know that," said Frank. "And I know that's why you take the risks that you do. And why you hesitate about using a *Near East Economic Review* article that would turn the accusations coming from our mole onto someone else in the KGB station."

"Yes, I'm reluctant to pinpoint one of our own." Lermontov took a spoon of Mina's caviar and let it melt in his mouth. "But why does it have to be KGB? Why not GRU? They have nearly as many people here as we do and they're even more incompetent and corrupt."

Frank pulled a chair up to the table and set down his glass. "But the note you gave me, didn't it say the penetration agent had alerted Moscow that the Americans in Tehran were attempting to recruit a KGB agent, identity unknown?"

"Read it again," said Lermontov. "The note said the Americans had targeted a Soviet intelligence agent in Tehran. Not necessarily KGB. We're the political line. As I would hope you know, GRU is the military line."

"Yeah, that much I do know." Frank drained his own vodka.

"But you may not know that we hate each other. Tomorrow the Neanderthals from Moscow spend their day with GRU. I already gave them some ideas of what to look for."

"Anybody in particular?"

"As a matter of fact, yes."

"Tell me."

"A GRU officer named Fedor Yevteshenko," said Lermontov, reaching out for the caviar. "Who is famously corrupt. And who has corrupted someone in your consular office."

"Oh?" said Frank, almost afraid to ask. "Does this someone have a name?"

"Yes," said Lermontov. "He has a name. His name is Charles Belinsky."


Sequestered in the bubble with Rocky, Frank explained the racket. "Aeroflot's the key. Because it's subsidized by the Soviets, Aeroflot can afford to be a lot cheaper than other airlines. Plus, a lot of foreigners, Brits, Europeans, and especially Americans, like to transit Russia on their way home. Consider it an exotic destination."

"God help us," said Rocky.

"Say a ticket from here to London costs a thousand dollars on British Airways. Aeroflot may only charge two hundred fifty. But the dumb tourist doesn't know that. So the GRU guy who has consulate cover and arranges the visa to transit Russia gets his Aeroflot buddy to charge five hundred. Cash only, right? That leaves a two-hundred-fifty-dollar profit for the Aeroflot guy and the GRU guy to split. According to Lermontov, until the troubles got real bad, they sold hundreds of tickets this way every year. And the tourists still think they're getting a bargain."

"But how's Belinsky supposed to fit into this?"

"His consulate job. Iranians and other foreigners come to the consulate for visas to go to America. Belinsky tells them about the great deals they can get from Aeroflot just by transiting the Soviet Union. Lermontov says Belinsky, least when he was up in Tabriz, was getting a cut from both the GRU crook and the Aeroflot crook."

"I don't believe it," said Rocky,

"Hear the rest of it. Remember the cable I did on how the Soviets here upgrade their imported cars, buy them without paying the two hundred percent customs tax, then sell them after four years on the open market? They get about double the price of a tax-free new car. Same GRU guy runs that operation and skims a personal cut off the top. And, 'cording to Lermontov, the guy gave Belinsky a new Mercedes for his wife when she was still here and Chuck was trying to convince her to stay. When she split anyway, she shipped the Mercedes back home."

"This Lermontov thug, you ask me, he's cooking all this up just to get Belin-sky blackballed and shipped outta here. KGB gets rid of the only American we got who speaks the languages, Russian and Farsi."

"I couldn't believe it, either," said Frank. "How 'bout we ask Chuck?"

# CHAPTER EIGHTEEN

Frank did not want to sit through another Jayface meeting or even to meet with the Shah or labor over another cable. He wanted only to confront Belinsky. But the next morning, in a way he hadn't expected, his day job imposed its demands.

The door to the Quonset hut that housed Tom Troy's offices swung open as Frank and Gus approached. Cantwell, in his corporal's uniform, held it for them.

"Good morning. Cold out there. Come on in. I have a message from downtown."

"I knew things had gotten too quiet," said Gus.

"Mr. Novak said he wants Major Sullivan to call him soon as you get here. I'll patch it through for you on the scramble phone from Bill's office. He's tied up with Colonel Troy."

"What's going on?" asked Frank.

"No idea, sir. I guess Mr. Novak will fill you in."

"Sully? Listen. His nibs got a call about ten minutes ago on the secure phone to the palace. Not from the Shah but from his latest majordomo. His Imperial Self wants to see you at ten. Don't ask what it's about, 'cause I don't know. Send Gus down to Jayface by himself. Have him tell the Jayfacers you got called to an urgent meeting at the embassy, which is about the truth 'cause I want your butt in here when you get done with the Shah. Okay?"

"I guess . . ." Frank began, but Rocky hung up before he could finish.

"Tomorrow, we will announce that Shapour Bakhtiar heads our new government."

The Shah stood behind his oak desk, looking trim in a gray wool suit that fit him well. "You knew it would happen, but now it happens. And we wanted to tell you something else because it will directly affect you."

The Shah's next words surprised Frank.

"Tell us about your newspaper." said the Shah.

"Well . . ." Frank fumbled for words. "*Armed Forces Times*. We've made good progress. Developed story ideas, done mockups for a twelve-page first edition. For sure we can make the January 7 target date."

"An interesting target date," said the Shah. "On that date a year ago, on the Islamic calendar, one of our Farsi newspapers, *Ittilaat,* published an article about Mr. Khomeini."

"I'd heard of that," said Frank.

"Did you also know the Grand Ayatollah has called for a day of mourning two days from now for some mosque students supposedly killed in Qom last year protesting that article?"

"Yes, sir."

"We may steal a bit of his thunder and lightning by instituting our new civilian government the day before. But the clergy will urge everyone to join in the Day of Mourning marches. This Day of Mourning, we fear, may begin a time of mourning for our throne."

He paused, pursed his lips, and said softly, "*Armed Forces Times*. But now, you see, by January 7, we will no longer have a military government. Your newspaper has existed, we hope you realize, only as a cover for you to continue to be here. We are the real reason for you to be here, and soon we will not be here. The time will never come for your *Armed Forces Times*. As part of the return to power of a civilian government, publication of all our newspapers will resume. Amusingly enough, the newspapers will begin appearing again on January 7. Perhaps *Ittilaat* can do another article for their first edition on Mr. Khomeini."

If I feel like this, thought Frank, how must he feel? I lost a newspaper. He lost an empire.

"When will you leave?" he asked.

"Soon," said the Shah, still standing, looking very much in control. "Very soon. A week. Perhaps two."

"Where will you go?"

"Ask your government. Perhaps we can fly together to America."

Frank smiled. "I don't have a plane."

"I do," said the Shah. He did not smile.


"It's true," said Belinsky. He huddled next to Frank in the confessional confines of the bubble. They both faced Rocky.

"It started up in Tabriz. My wife was pretty unhappy. I thought I could use the extra money to try and make . . . make things a little less grim for her. Financed a trip to London, Rome, Paris for her. Yeah, transiting Russia. Gave her a big wad of shopping money. And when she got back I had that red Mercedes waiting for her. She was pretty damn happy. For a while."

"I can't believe you'd do something like this," said Rocky.

"Neither can I," said Belinsky. "But it seemed . . . I mean, the way it worked, no one got hurt. The travelers still got a bargain. Aeroflot still made its money."

"And you made yours," said Rocky.

"Yes. Yes, I did," said Belinsky. "What happens now?"

"Sullivan here has an idea. He's been full of ideas lately. Can you arrange a meet with your Soviet consulate buddy?"

Chuck looked from Rocky to Frank and back to Rocky.

"What for?"

"Can you fucking do it?"

"Yeah. I guess. He still calls me once in a while. See if I've got any business for him."

"Can you call him?"

"Yeah. I guess. Professional courtesy. One consular officer to another."

Frank watched the verbal Ping-Pong, glad that Rocky required nothing of him, other than his presence. He did not want to torture Belinsky.

"Good," said Rocky. "I'm glad you can call him. What I'm about to tell you . . . what I'm about to tell you I want you to do, if you say you can handle it, I'm going to have to get an okay on it from the powers that be back home, or anyway one power. If we get the green light, and you pull it off, I'll do everything I can, move heaven and earth, to get you a deal that lets you resign, reasons of health, get whatever you got comin' in the way of pension, and everybody concerned keeps his mouth shut for ever and ever. Okay?"

"What . . . what do I have to do?"

"You call your fellow consular officer and say you need to urgently meet with him, some public place where maybe you met before, to discuss an important matter involving visas."

Belinsky nodded. "I can do that."

"You let us know when and where. I give you a big envelope. You tell your buddy your conscience bothers you about the money you took. You want to give it all back to him. You can't give it all back at once, but you want to give it all back to him. And you give him the envelope and get the hell out of there."

Belinsky glanced at Frank. "That's it?"

"That's it," said Frank.

"We figure your buddy's venal enough he'll take the fuckin' envelope with no questions asked."

"Can I ask what'll be in the envelope?"

"No," said Rocky. "Oh, and Chuck. You may get your picture taken."

"By *Savak?*" asked Belinsky.

No, thought Frank. By one of Lermontov's Iranian agents.

"*Savak?*" said Rocky. "Yeah. Somethin' like that."

"I'll do it," said Chuck. "And Frank, about the Aminis. Three days, four seats, counting the late switch for Anwar. It won't be easy. Some poor bastards will get bumped, but we'll do it. If they don't shut down the airports before then."


"This comes off," said Rocky, "you still think you're gonna need that stuff showin' up in *Near East Weekly?*"

"Lermontov does," said Frank. He and Rocky had remained in the bubble after a shaken Belinsky left. "He says otherwise the GRU will try to just sweep their boy's problem under the rug. That would leave the question of identifying the Soviet recruiting target still open. But if their boy gets nabbed taking an envelope of Ben Franklins from an American, and gets publicly identified in a news magazine, he's under arrest and Lermontov's off the hook."

"And Moscow figures the guy their mole fingered is the GRU thug."

"Right," said Frank.

"I hope James goes for all this shit," said Rocky.

"He has to."

"What's this magazine story gonna say?"

"Won't name the GRU guy, but Lermontov's given me enough details that everyone in his embassy, and in Moscow, will get the picture. And it'll quote an American consular officer who knows him well."

"When do I see it?" asked Rocky.

"I'll draft it tonight. Drop it off before I go to our Jayface meeting in the morning."

"Jayface? You still workin' that dog?"

"It's my day job."


The air force guards lived in a gated compound. Three taps on the horn, and a small panel in the metal gate opened. Several moments passed before unseen hands pulled one side of the gate open. A short, slender Iranian in pressed khakis crossed the open space. Frank noticed a walkie-talkie in his left hand. The other half of the gate gave way.

"No worries about your car being firebombed at the curb," said Gus, as they pulled in.

The sprawling, two-story stone house with a long open porch and metal shutters at all its windows looked as if it could shelter a small army. Frank counted four chimneys, all smoking.

Todd Waldbaum stood in the open front doorway and called out, "Welcome to our formidable abode." I feel safer already, thought Frank.

He also felt worried. Three uneventful days since the Christmas Eve attack on the embassy had convinced him something had to happen soon. Three smooth Jayface meetings; one meeting but no urgent news from Lermontov. And no new word about the still unknown and still dangerous penetration agent at Langley. Something has to go wrong, he thought, as he crossed the threshold of the air force bachelors' quarters.

At least for that evening, though, nothing did. The meal—meat loaf, mashed potatoes, carrots, and peas—had been pleasantly seasoned and decently cooked. The dessert, apple pie à la mode, would have pleased Anwar. Cans of Budweiser kept appearing, and young men came and went as the meal progressed in a spacious wood-paneled dining room warmed by a glowing fireplace. At various times, from twelve to fifteen men, not counting himself and Gus, sat around the table. Todd told him twenty-four air force guards, including three putative guards like Corporal Cantwell, lived there.

"But we're never all here at the same time," he said. They sat opposite each other at the now littered table. Gus and several young guards sitting nearby followed their conversation.

Frank had been introduced to so many he knew he would never remember all the names. "Cantwell, you never know when he'll get here."

"That's for sure," drawled Dwight. "Him and Bill Steele and Colonel Troy had to go down the embassy tonight. Don't know what's goin' on, but I got a hunch somethin's goin' on."

"Tell me," said Frank. "If anything messy does come down, Gus and I live on a block, kind of isolated halfway between here and Dowshan Tappeh. We're the only Americans around, and the neighbors have already taken to the rooftops at night shouting *Allah-o akbar*."

"We got some 'round here, too," said Dwight.

"But if it does get messy," said Todd, "you'd be a lot better off here. Just jump in your car and come on over. Hit the horn same way you did tonight. We'll let the guys on the gate know to keep an eye out for your Fiat."

"Any time, day or night," said another of the guards.

"Can't say the door's always open," added Dwight. "But we can sure as hell get it open right quick."

His next meeting with Lermontov, in their recent pattern of every-other-day sessions at KGB safe houses, moved quickly. The envelope Lermontov had stashed for Frank under the passenger's seat in his Peugeot was heavier than usual. In the quiet, concrete confines of Rocky's office, Frank opened the envelope labeled "For You."

*We must make plans for our final meeting. We will need a place where we can have an open discussion. Arrange to have your safe house available on short notice. I will come without a wire, and we may have to repeat some things at a later meeting at a Soviet facility.*

*My* rezident *believes Khomeini's return, which we expect within a few weeks, will mean the withdrawal of the entire American community. The Soviet Embassy will maintain its presence here. We will maintain and expand the good relations we have established with Khomeini's camp in Neauphle-le-Château and put the National Voice of Iran Radio in Baku at their disposal. (There are detailed reports for you on these topics.) Also pay particular attention to the report on Afghanistan. It includes information that could be of vital importance to your embassy there.*

"Whatcha got?" said Rocky, entering abruptly.

Frank indicated the stack of envelopes in his briefcase.

"Looks like quite a haul."

"And this." Frank handed him Lermontov's note.

"Interesting," said Rocky as he studied it. "Wonder what this is on Afghanistan? I'll check it. Meantime, we need t' talk about Belinsky."

"What's happening?" said Frank, fearing the worst.

"Lots. The Holy Ghost likes our scenario for gettin' Lermontov off the hook. I cabled him the story you drafted for *Near East Weekly Review,* and he said he'd handle it. I talked to Belinsky and told him to get in touch with the GRU crook. He said he'd do it."

"I don't believe it," said Frank. "It all sounds too good."

"Yeah, well, it all sounds too good t' me, too. I worry about Belinsky holdin' up his end."

"How so?"

"Dunno. Just Belinsky . . . well, he seems out of it. He says all the right things, but he's always lookin' off into space. Like his mind is someplace else."

"You ask him about it?"

"Yeah, but when I do he looks me right in the eye and says everything's fine."

"Want me to try talking to him?"

"Yeah," said Rocky. "I get kinda pissed when I think about the things people tell you they won't tell me. When you talk to him, see if you can figure out what ails him."

"He can't be feeling too good about himself right now," said Frank.

"He's still got a job to do," said Rocky.

Rocky set up a meeting for Frank and Belinsky in the bubble, then left them alone on the excuse that he had to attend to some urgent cables in the communications room.

"Be back in a few," he said.

"I have good news for you," said Belinsky.

"Oh?"

"It all went well for your friends, the Aminis. By the time I got to the airport, the wife, good as her word, had already cleared customs and immigration and boarded with the kids. Our guy at the Pan Am counter did his job. The switch from a ticket in my name to Anwar's went off just fine."

"Your name?" said Frank.

"Well, yeah," said Belinsky. "I had to use some name. Hey, don't look at me like that. I didn't plan to use the ticket."

"But maybe, if for some reason the Aminis didn't show . . ."

"I thought about it," said Belinsky. "I really didn't want to meet with that Yevteshenko bastard. But where could I go? So I waited till the plane took off. Waited a little longer to make sure the control tower didn't order it back."

He's a conniver, thought Frank. Till that moment, Belinsky's involvement in the Aeroflot racket had seemed out of character. Now Frank wondered. He felt empty, and his thoughts jumped from Belinsky to Anwar and Mina. He'd never said good-bye. He'd never embraced Anwar. He'd never kissed Mina, and then he remembered Mina had once kissed him.

"Anwar gave me this for you." Belinsky handed him a plain white letter-size envelope.

"Thank you," said Frank. "I'll read it later. To tell you the truth, I'm more concerned about your other assignment."

"What other assignment?" Belinsky's tone was sharp.

"Meeting with the GRU guy."

"I said I'd do it," said Belinsky, looking away.

"Have you tried calling him?"

"I just got the go-ahead this morning."

Frank noticed the jaundiced tone of his skin, the yellow rims circling his pale blue eyes. "You look like you haven't been following your doctor's orders."

"With all this on my mind, I need something to relax," said Belinsky.

"Not if the something may kill you."

"These days," said Belinsky, staring off, "all kinds of things may get me killed."

"Like what?"

"Meeting with students. Meeting with Shariat-Madari. Sticking my neck out for you and your air force buddy. Setting up a GRU agent, which I guess is what I'm supposed to be doing. It all seems so unnecessary. An envelope full of money. A photographer. Why not have me wear a cloak and carry a dagger?"

"Don't think about it," said Frank. "Maybe the best thing is to just do it."

"Why should I?" said Belinsky.

Because a KGB agent with acromegaly needs you to. Because a guy named Henry James wants you to. Because Rocky told you to. He wished he could tell Belinsky all the reasons.

"I guess maybe you should do it as a way to bail yourself out of the jam you're in."

"How'd you find out about it?"

"A source," said Frank.

"Couldn't you have kept it to yourself?" said Belinsky. "Or come to me about it?"

"I wish I could have," said Frank.

"How'd it go with Belinsky?" asked Rocky. He and Frank sat by themselves in the bubble. Belinsky had left before Rocky returned from the communications room.

"Not good."

"How come he didn't wait for me t' get back?"

"I think he felt pretty uncomfortable."

"You think he'll really try to find this GRU guy?"

Frank shrugged. "He says he just got the go-ahead on it this morning."

"True enough."

"But he also said he wonders why he should stick his neck out."

"He should stick his neck out so he doesn't get it chopped off."

"It might help if I could tell him about Lermontov, about what's at stake."

"No way," said Rocky. "I've got a lot of respect for Belinsky, but right now he's a loose cannon. The less he knows the better."

He read Anwar's letter that night. *I will never be able to thank you for all you have done for us and for all that your friendship has meant, not just for me and my family but also, I think, for Iran. You do your best to understand us, and if at times you fall short you have come much further than most. I hate leaving this way but this must be the way we leave. Perhaps in America one day we will all be together again, and then it won't matter that we did not say good-bye in Iran.*

Till that moment, he had not realized how much getting Anwar, and Mina, to America mattered to him. He'd been so focused on the importance of getting

Lermontov to America that he hadn't seen how much Anwar and Mina meant to him. I'm becoming my job, he said to himself. I can't let that happen.

Colonel Kasravi sat at the long table. "Welcome, Major Sullivan," said the colonel. "Please join me. Sorry about what's happening."

"Fortunes of war," said Frank, settling into a chair near the colonel.

"His Imperial Majesty summoned me to the palace early this morning, primarily to inform me of my new assignment. He also mentioned that yesterday he had let you know the return of a civilian government would also mean the return of the civilian newspapers."

He paused and Frank nodded.

"And that we would not publish *Armed Forces Times*."

"Yes, sir."

"My new assignment takes me out of the prime minister's office. I return to the Imperial Guard to work with General Abbas Ali Bardri, our new commander."

"Congratulations."

"Thank you. I was not cut out for the bureaucracy. Not even in a military government. When I saw him this morning, His Imperial Majesty also suggested I inform you that within a few days he will name General Abbas Karim Gharabaghi as armed forces chief of staff. One of my tasks will be as liaison between General Bardri and General Gharabaghi."

"Congratulations again," said Frank.

"You can report all this to your government, with the usual restrictions. Ah, yes. And also I am to become a brigadier general. No more the wings of a chicken colonel. Please tell that part to General Merid, but only that part."

Frank smiled. "I will, sir."

"General Gharabaghi and General Bardri will rank as the two most important men in our armed forces. If we can restore the monarchy . . . I think we all realize His Imperial Majesty must withdraw from Iran for a time, but, I can assure you, he will not abdicate his throne. Then, if the monarchy is to be fully restored it will be up to General Bardri and General Gharabaghi."

"Do you think that's possible?" said Frank.

Kasravi paused. He looked at Frank and slowly shook his head.

"As a military man, I believe we make our own possibilities," he said aloud. "And, in my new assignment, it occurred to me, I could benefit from having a direct contact with the American government. Can I do that through you?"

"I . . . I really don't know. It might be more appropriate through one of the . . . through the embassy's senior military attaché."

"I have limited respect for your attachés. General Bardri and General Gharabaghi will have official U.S. contact through General Weber, who is here again on a special mission. Through the ambassador and attachés as well. But His Imperial Majesty said you had been useful to him as what he termed a 'back door channel.' He recommended I use you in the same way."

Here we go again, thought Frank. "Perhaps we can work something out."

"How can I contact you?"

"Through Colonel Troy, the office of the U.S. Air Force Guards at Dowshan Tappeh."

"Good. I will return to your Jayface meeting with you and inform your colleagues of the changes that affect your group. I will also inform them His Imperial Majesty requires their presence at the palace at fifteen hundred hours tomorrow. He will bestow medals on them all and instruct them to continue their operations. At my suggestion and with His Imperial Majesty's agreement, Jayface will concentrate on civic action plans the military will initiate at a future date when the current troubles are behind us. Oh, you are to attend as well. You will receive the First Order of the Homayoon for your efforts as an adviser to the Imperial Armed Forces of Iran."

"I don't know what to say." But he knew what to think. Nobody in the good old boys' coven back at Langley loves an outsider who gets a medal, and Rocky would have another reason for resentment. Then he thought of another problem.

"What about Commander Simpson?"

"The Shah has no interest in Commander Simpson."

"Sir, I'm sure you can appreciate the . . . the situation. Commander Simpson has worked well as a member of the Jayface team. If everyone gets a medal and he doesn't . . ."

"Commander Simpson should feel grateful we did not expel him after his clumsy effort to recruit a waiter already recruited by *Savak* and J2. Explain it to him."

"I'll do my best," said Frank.

"And I hope you appreciate," said Kasravi, "that His Imperial Majesty takes these measures to make it difficult for your government to withdraw you. He believes Iran continues to benefit from your presence."

"I do appreciate that," said Frank. But I wish it hadn't happened.

"One other matter," said the colonel. "Your Jayface colleague Captain Irfani heard what you did to avoid what might have become an ugly incident at the American cafeteria at Dowshan Tappeh. It impressed him that you used a tape by Ayatollah Khomeini. And His Imperial Majesty has informed Admiral Hayati that the Americans are aware of his coup proposal. The Shah did not say so, but the admiral assumed that happened through you."

"I did manage to discuss it with the Shah."

"That is all we could ask. Munair, Captain Irfani, has begun to change his mind about you. He thinks perhaps you can be trusted, and he asked me to give you this." The colonel handed Frank a small package wrapped in brown paper and masking tape. "It is the latest cassette from Khomeini in Paris along with a summary Munair prepared for you in English."

"Thank you," said Frank. "Thank Captain Irfani for me."

"You may be able to do that yourself," said Kasravi. "He said he would join us."

Frank and General Kasravi did not have to wait long for Munair to make his appearance.

"Thank you for the tape from Paris," said Frank as he stood to greet Munair.

"The tape is important," said Munair, "but I have something much more urgent to discuss. May we sit down?"

"Of course," said Kasravi.

"Good." They drew up chairs at the head of Kasravi's long table. "I thought it important that General Kasravi should hear what I am about to tell you."

This does not sound good, thought Frank.

"What is it?" said Kasravi.

"This tape from Paris, perhaps, Mr. Sullivan, your embassy may already have it. A man from your embassy, his name is Charles Belinsky. Do you know him?"

"I've heard the name," said Frank.

"He seems very active. They say he speaks good Farsi. He seeks tapes made by the Imam in many quarters. If he is a good man, warn him. He is being watched. He may be killed. So may you."

"Me?"

Munair glanced at Kasravi. "It is no secret that I am a devout Muslim. I am loyal to Admiral Hayati and to my Shah. But I am devout, and I am in contact with others who are devout, including certain members of *Savak* who have formed a revolutionary *komiteh* that reports to Ayatollah Taleqani. They hope, in fact, to replace *Savak* with a new Islamic organization they call *Savama,* which hopes to take over the functions of *Savak* in behalf of the revolution."

"We are aware of them," said Kasravi.

But what the hell are you doing about them? wondered Frank.

Munair's dark eyes burned into Frank's. "These men kept watch on your friend Mr. Belinsky. They do not like his contacts with Shariat-Madari, a man as respected as the Imam among many believers, but a man seen by others as a rival to the Imam. *Savak* agents also saw this Belinsky at the airport with Major Anwar Amini and meeting with a Russian known to be a GRU agent. Your American friend Mr. Belinsky helped Major Amini get out of Iran with his wife and children. Right under the eyes of *Savak*. That embarrassed them, made them mad. One *Savak* agent in particular was angry. Someone you know, in fact."

"Someone I know?" Frank could not believe he knew any *Savak* agent.

"Your Mr. Belinsky's taxi driver. He drove you to the university."

Oh, God. Frank remembered what Rocky had told him about the *Savak* officer who had allowed Chuck to recruit him.

"He felt humiliated," said Munair, "because he also drove this Mr. Belinsky to the airport to help Major Amini escape. And of course he tied you and Belinsky together in that. He did his best to persuade other members of the *Savama* group that they should kill both you and your friend, but they feared they could not touch two official Americans until a certain clergyman, Hojatalislam Qomi Mohhammad, an influential man who hates Shariat-Madari, issued a *fatwa*."

"You lost me," said Frank, shaken but trying to pay attention.

"A command that puts all Muslims under obligation, in this case an obligation to carry out a death sentence."

"On me?"

"Yes, on you and on your Mr. Belinsky. But their real target, the real target of the *fatwa*, was not Mr. Belinsky or you. The real target was Ayatollah Shariat-Madari."

"I don't get it," said Frank.

"Of course not," said Kasravi. "You are not a Shi'a Muslim. This clergyman could not issue a *fatwa* to kill Shariat-Madari. That would have made a martyr of Shariat-Madari, a hero."

"Exactly," said Munair. "We would have seen a revolution within the revolution. This way the corrupt turban man has shown that he is more powerful than Ayatollah Shariat-Madari. People will say Hojatalislam Qomi issued his *fatwa* behalf of the Imam, and Shariat-Madari could not protect his American friend, your Mr. Belinsky."

"But why include me?" said Frank.

Munair shrugged. "I believe what you did for Major Amini and his family you did from the goodness of your heart, but you and your Mr. Belinsky play a dangerous game."


"Pretty impressive," said Rocky. "A medal from the Shah and a death warrant from some holy man. All in the same day."

"Right," said Frank. "I'm impressed as hell."

"Okay," said Rocky. "Here's what we do." He and Frank sat alone in the bubble. "We go downstairs. You plop your Irish butt down at a typewriter. Start with the easy part. The medals. Do a draft. Triple space it so I'll have lots of room for edits. This has to be finessed in ways you can only guess. Fritz Weber's gonna want your head on a fuckin' platter. If some *Savaki* doesn't put a bullet through you first. Fritz comes over with a special mandate from the President to get cozy with the military. And he finds you chewin' on his turf with Kasravi, who's just been named point man for a coup. And that's just the start. Then you get a fuckin' medal. You know how that'll play in Virginia."

"Maybe they'll forgive me if I get killed."

"The hell they will. You get killed, they'll just have t' give you another medal."

"You sure know how to make a guy feel good."

"Feel good is not my middle name. You talk t' Belinsky again?"

"I did. Belinsky told me Anwar and his family got outta here okay. Talked about his GRU job."

"And?"

"And he worries me. Drinking again. Real down on himself about what he did."

"He should be," said Rocky. "He should also get his ass in gear about a meet with his GRU guy. Let's go to work. You finish a draft on the medals. While I edit that, you do a draft on the death warrant."

"I can't do that," said Frank.

"Why the fuck not?"

"If we tell the folks back home there's a death warrant out for me and Belinsky, they'll pull us the hell out of here. And we've got a Soviet to recruit, remember?"

"I haven't forgotten," said Rocky. "But what's the difference? You get pulled out, we lose Lermontov. You get killed, you ain't gonna be much help recruitin' his ass anyway."

"There's a big difference," said Frank. "I get pulled out, it's all over. We don't recruit Lermontov. Period. I stay, and manage not to get killed, we've still got a chance."

"So don't get killed. And make sure Belinsky doesn't get killed. But what do you suggest we do meanwhile? Withhold vital information from Langley?"

"I wouldn't suggest anything like that," said Frank. "We can't hold back information about death threats. But we can wonder about how seriously those death threats should be taken."

"Okay. You draft. I'll edit. Don't tell Gus or Chuck or anyone else about your fuckin' death warrant."

Frank marveled at the way Rocky had massaged the final version of both cables. They had never worked so long and hard over any documents before. The bones of Frank's usual cable style remained, but puffed over with vague and convoluted phrasing. The Jayface team had been *summoned to the palace for a meeting with His Imperial Majesty at which each will be thanked appropriately. The relationship previously established between KUPEREGRINE and SDELECT-8 has at the request of SDFAM-1 been continued as SDELECT-8 relinquishes his duties with the SDG and resumes the military assignment under which he was originally in contact with KUPEREGRINE as a member in absentia of the SDJAYFACE team.*

"That should seem unimportant and confusing enough for the NE drones to turn their attention to something else," said Rocky.

"It confuses me," said Frank.

"Good. If some overinquisitive desk officer asks for clarification, I'll send back something even more confusing."

Frank's draft on the death threats attributed the information to a previously untried source of unknown reliability, an accurate description of Munair's classification. Rocky's editing made the threats sound vague. He sent the cable to James, eyes only.

Frank did a third cable on what Kasravi had told him about plans for a coup after the Shah's departure. Rocky took out Frank's description of Kasravi's silent, negative shake of the head when Frank asked if the military could restore the monarchy.

"Why leave that out?" asked Frank.

"He didn't say it. It's not on tape. You might've misread the guy just tryin' t' work a kink outta his neck."

"Rocky, you know it was Kasravi's way of telling us the military can't do it."

"Okay. So I know. But we leave it out because the folks back home ain't gonna like it, 'cause they still want a coup and Brzezinski for one keeps askin' the ambassador—and us—when they're gonna get one."

Same bind, thought Frank. I find out stuff, but if it's stuff they don't want to hear, I can't report it. "We didn't get a coup for Christmas," he said.

"No, but we did have a bunch of ragheads tryin' to slide down the embassy chimney on Christmas Eve. Look, can you square this medal business with Gus?" asked Rocky.

"I don't know," said Frank. "Like the rest of us, he does have feelings."

"Better let me do it," said Rocky. "He can't resent it comin' from me. Why don't the two 'a yiz come in before you have to trek up to the palace. Around two."

"Two should work."

"You got a meet with Lermontov tomorrow, right?"

"Right."

"You get stuck at the palace, which you can bet's gonna happen, same place next day?"

"Half hour earlier," said Frank.

"Fine, that gives me time to ask for Henry James's okay to give Lermontov a cleaned-up version of this latest coup d'état pipe dream. I can do it without

James's say-so, but this one's sensitive enough to make sure he's with us. Fact, even if you can get to tomorrow's meet on time, give it a pass. I want time to test the waters on this one, plus that gives us more time for Belinsky to track down his GRU buddy."

"Speaking of Belinsky, I've got something else," said Frank.

"Now what?"

"A package from Munair. Along with letting me know about the death threats. I took a quick look. A cassette from Khomeini with a note that says it just came by phone from Paris last night, but they've already started cranking out dupes by the dozens. Says it also indicates Khomeini has someone in the Shah's inner circle. Khomeini somehow knows the Shah has made plans to leave but has called on the military to stage a coup and bring him back to rule with a strong military government supported by the Great Satan, us."

"Jesus H. Christ," said Rocky. "You're more work than you're worth. Draft another cable on the summary. I'll go hunt down Belinsky. He may've been a stupid son of a bitch about this Aeroflot scam, but he's a smart son of a bitch about a lot of other shit."

Frank handed Rocky the cassette and Munair's summary. "He says Khomeini also calls on the religious leaders to get the people to form revolutionary committees in all parts of the country and prepare them to take over all government functions once the Shah leaves."

"Won't that be wonderful," said Rocky, "The Paris Tribunal comes to Tehran. Wonder if they got anybody knows how to build a guillotine. Kind of scary if Khomeini does have somebody inside the palace."

"Hey, since it looks like Lermontov's right and the Communistas have a mole in Langley, why can't the Khomeini-istas have a mole in the palace?"

"Fuck you," said Rocky. "That is not funny."

# CHAPTER NINETEEN

The Jayface team sat in a semicircle in the waiting room dominated by the bust of the Shah's father. Frank noticed that Munair again stared at him as intently as he had at their earliest meetings. Occasionally, he looked away and nodded. They'd waited nearly two hours before Kasravi, now wearing the star of a brigadier general, emerged from the Shah's office.

"Gentlemen, my apologies. The Supreme Commander . . . His Imperial Majesty will see you shortly. First, however, Major Sullivan, could you come with me?"

Frank stood, feeling the eyes of the others, and followed General Kasravi. The Shah sat slumped in his oak chair. For a moment his head seemed shrunken, grotesque and gray, peering up at Frank from behind the huge desk, like the head of a turtle poking out of its shell.

"Ah, Frank." He pushed himself up, took a deep breath, and straightened his shoulders. "Good of you to come. I have had a very difficult day. Please sit. General Kasravi, join us."

Frank and Kasravi pulled up two of the several oak chairs arrayed around the desk. The Shah took another moment to gather himself. He had looked so much better at their last meeting only three days before that Frank worried about his condition. His first remarks sounded as though recited by rote.

"I know General Kasravi has already informed you that our various military commanders have prevailed on me to leave the country for a time. During my absence they will stage a coup against the Bakhtiar government. Then, they shall call on us to return." Frank noticed the change from first person singular to the imperial "us." The Shah's voice took on strength and conviction and a tinge of bitterness. "All before the Great Ayatollah descends from the skies on the wings of his French angel. The military government our generals will install will have no direct ties to us or to any of our previous governments. When they have established firm control, they will invite our return."

"As happened," said Kasravi, "after Mosaddeq was overthrown."

Frank did not want to risk the Shah's anger, but he wondered how seriously he considered the possibility of a coup. "Do you think, sir, the Ayatollah's following compares to Mosaddeq's?"

"Neither ever had a following worthy of the name. Rabble. Street thugs. Some leftists. Russians backing both. Foreigners wanting a weak government so they could exploit our oil."

"The course of action we've plotted benefits from lessons learned during the Mosaddeq episode," said Kasravi.

"We hope your government understands our need for support," said the Shah.

"I share your hope, sir."

"Ambassador Zahedi, who is here for consultations, tells us we can count on Mr. Brzezinski to push for support, but that your President remains . . ."

The Shah looked to Kasravi for help, who in turn looked to Frank. "Wishy-washy?" said Kasravi. "Is there such a term?"

"Your ambassador's picked up well on American idiom," said Frank.

"It means indecisive?"

"Correct, general. And some of President Carter's critics say that about him. But I've also heard he's a very meticulous, careful man. He may want to make sure the Iranian military can initiate a successful coup before committing support."

"We recognize that we need American support to succeed," said the Shah. "By now even President Jimmy must recognize that."

"What kind of support will you need?" asked Frank. He realized he'd begun to tread on the territory of Americans far senior, including Ambassador O'Connor and the visiting General Weber. But he saw no way of avoiding the Shah's determination to involve him.

"Perhaps only symbolic," said the Shah. "Certainly not troops. Possibly no more than your country provided during the overthrow of the tyrant Mosaddeq."

"Covert support?" said Frank.

"That could be helpful," said the Shah. "*Savak*'s abilities in that line have . . . diminished."

"And perhaps symbolic support," said Kasravi. "A carrier task force in the Gulf. Flyovers by American planes, both from the carrier and from your base at Incirlik."

"The capacity of our air force . . ." The Shah hesitated.

"Also has diminished," said Kasravi.

"And you see, even though we may leave, we hope you will stay. Maintain contact with General Kasravi. He will work with our new chief of staff, General Gharabaghi, a man the Americans, including this General Weber, think highly of, and with General Bardri. We must maintain a difficult balance. The covert support must remain invisible. The symbolic support must be highly visible."

"Sir, Your Imperial Majesty, General Kasravi, all this goes way out of my league. My competence. You should be talking to others."

"You have proved effective in our effort to move your official representatives," said the Shah. "Since we have begun also to communicate through you, they pay much more attention to what we have to say. We do not want to lose that channel."

"I'll do my best," said Frank. Great, he thought. I get to stay and give some crazy *Savak* types more time to kill me. "Sir," he managed to say aloud, "when you leave, where will you go?"

The Shah smiled. "As you know, we had hoped to go to America. But in view of the plans of our military, we shall stay in the neighborhood. We will let you know where. General?"

"I think you have covered everything very well, Your Imperial Majesty."

"In that case, we can proceed to the other business at hand. As General Kasravi has told you, we plan to continue the mandate of the . . ." The Shah glanced at a sheet of paper on his desk. "The Joint Armed Forces Ad Hoc Committee on Enlightenment. Today we will present decorations to all its members. Including you."

"Thank you, sir."

General Kasravi again cleared his throat.

"Yes. General Kasravi brought up the delicate matter of . . ."

"Commander Simpson," said the general.

"Yes. We had not considered that question. After discussing the question with General Kasravi, and with our chief of protocol, we have a solution that differs from the plans General Kasravi outlined to you yesterday. Commander . . . ?"

"Simpson," interjected Kasravi.

"Yes. He, too, will receive a decoration. Which we will entrust you to bring to him."

"The Fourth Order of Homayoon," said General Kasravi. "The Royal Decoration."

Good, thought Frank. He hoped there might be less flak at home about his getting a medal if Gus got one, too.

"Accordingly," said the Shah, "rather than the Order of Homayoon, we have decided to award you the Third Order of Taj."

"The Decoration of the Crown," said Kasravi. "It is the highest honor His Imperial Majesty can bestow on a foreigner."

Not so good, thought Frank. He stood and bowed. "I'm deeply honored, Your Imperial Majesty."

"That's true," said Kasravi, looking up at him. "You truly are."

"We are not doing this purely out of the goodness of our heart," said the Shah, "or even out of our admiration for you. Please be seated." Frank sat. "In doing this, we also send another message to your government. The protocol officer at your embassy, we are certain, will explain the significance of what we have done to your ambassador. You need not tell anyone about it. Our press officer will make an official announcement, as we customarily do on the rare occasions when we bestow an award of this magnitude. Your government will realize the degree of respect and trust we have in you. They will have to honor accordingly all that you report to them."

As long, thought Frank, as my reporting doesn't contradict policy.

"We can't put all that shit in a cable," said Rocky. "Look, Sully, you draft like you did yesterday. I'll do a heavy edit. Concentrate on this cockamamie coup idea. Leave out you askin' the questions you did. Just report everything the Shah and his Bodyguard general had to say, includin' the Shah wantin' you to maintain contact with Kasravi when His Imperial Candy Ass leaves for wherever the hell he's goin'. Looks like you guys are gonna be here a while. Can't exactly ship you out if the Shah tells his key military leave-behind to stay in touch with you."

"You can ship me out," said Gus.

"No chance," said Rocky. "Sullivan's got me convinced he needs you. Sully, put in your cable what Kasravi said about U.S. planes out of Incirlik buzzin' Iran just so Washington can see how pipe-dreamy these guys are. No way in hell the Turks will sit still for us buzzin' Iran out of a base on their territory. Do a separate cable on the awards for everybody. They can find out about you gettin' anointed when the palace makes its announcement. We can act like it's no big thing, but they'll get the fuckin' message the Shah wanted them to get."

"Thank Allah for little things," said Gus, studying the medal Frank had brought to him.

"And gimme both the fuckin' medals. They get pouched back t' Langley." Gus and Frank surrendered their medals. "Maybe you'll get'm back someday." Rocky gave them no chance to protest. "Sully, I need to talk to you about your Lermontov meet. Gus, can you take care of a cable on the Jayface business?"

"Can do."

"I got a typewriter all set up for you, brand-new ribbon, in an empty office two doors down. Just be sure the ribbon—and the ball—get back in my safe."

"Aye, aye, sir." Gus grunted as he heaved himself up from his chair.

"You're gettin' old, Commander," said Rocky.

"Tell me about it," said Gus.

"I got some good news for you," said Rocky, as he and Frank settled into the bubble. "The Holy Ghost says you and Belinsky get to stay. Listen. Information in your previously cited cable notwithstanding, Ident A and Ident B, while observing all due precautions, should, in view of the importance of their current obligations, remain in place."

"I guess that's good news," said Frank. "If you consider staying here good news."

"You're the guy wants t' recruit Lermontov. Speaking of which, more good news. The Holy Ghost okayed giving Lermontov a sanitized version of your palace cable from the other day. Also, I drafted a note for Lermontov. About the stuff he gave you last time on Afghanistan."

"I still don't know what that was about." He realized he'd put more edge in his voice than he'd intended.

"Keep your pants on. I'm about to let you know. Scary shit. You know the Soviets installed a government in Afghanistan couple months back. But the puppets ain't dancin' so good. They've got a strong Islamic opposition, almost like here. The holy warriors want to attract some attention, and they figure the best way to do that is to go after some high-profile foreigners. KGB has some Dari-speakin' Soviet Muslims inside the opposition. They say American officials look like the target of choice. Moscow worries that America might start payin' attention t' Afghanistan if the Afghanis knock off a couple of high-level Americans. The Soviets would just as soon we didn't pay any attention and let them take over the country in peace."

"I have to admit," said Frank, "I'm more worried about the Iranians knocking off a couple of midlevel Americans."

"Hey, didn't the Holy Ghost himself just tell us not to worry about that?"

"Okay," said Frank. "I won't worry about that."

"Good," said Rocky. "Anyhow, my note to Lermontov, which you better read 'cause I tried to make it look like it came from you, asks him to keep those cards and letters comin' on Afghanistan, updates as often as possible. I figure we got a responsibility to warn our buddies in Kabul to lock their doors at night even though I know it won't do any fuckin' good. State will do a security check and find out that everything is hunky-dory, and next day the ragheads will park a ninety-ton truck bomb in front of the embassy."

"You truly do love the State Department, don't you?"

"Good and bad, like any shop," said Rocky, "but their security people strike me as all bad. If I were a betting man, I'd bet they've got more Americans killed than all the terrorists in the world put together. Meanwhile, the Holy Ghost's gettin' as antsy as I am about Belinsky settin' up this GRU meet. He better make it happen soon."

———

Rocky's harsh words about the State Department security apparatus had echoed in Frank's mind when Lermontov laid into him with his own harsh words about the recent take.

"You give us intelligence we already have. We know the Shah soon will leave. Because you talk to him about it doesn't make your information any more valuable."

"I thought you found the information I've provided useful," Frank had said weakly.

"Until recently. Moscow asks, seriously, if this relationship is worth continuing."

"I'll try to do better," Frank had said.

"You better."

Frank had returned to the embassy, fearful they might be on the verge of losing Lermontov. Now, as they sat in the bubble, Rocky let him know things he had never known before about how the superpowers played the Great Game at this level.

"They're pullin' your chain," said Rocky. "Classic agent handling. Give him some money. Get him salivating. Then tell him he ain't worth shit."

"What's the point?"

"What they want out of you is more product for less money."

"Like the capitalist robber barons," said Frank.

"Exactly," said Rocky, "'cause that's what they are. Exploiters of the proletariat. And you, my friend, in their eyes, are a fuckin' prol'. You came back in here with your tail between your legs and your head hangin', like you'd been whipped for not barkin' loud enough. Your Soviet buddy played you because he was playin' for the video cameras his *residenza* and Moscow will look at. They'll say, 'Attaboy, Vassily. You sure played that American boychik like a pro.' And you, you asshole, took it all for real."

"I guess I did," said Frank. "But I still think, for Moscow's sake, we ought to try to get him some hard stuff."

"I'll send a prayer up to the Holy Ghost," said Rocky, "see what he comes up with, but you better tighten up your asshole. The game gets rough around now. And we still don't know what games Lermontov may be playin'."

Lermontov had proffered no bonus, but the envelope under the passenger's seat weighed heavily in the briefcase Frank carried up to the bubble.

"Let's see what we've got," said Rocky.

Frank took little interest in the take. He worried about what games Lermontov, Henry James, and Rocky might be playing. I wanted to play with the big boys, he thought. I got what I wanted.

Rocky opened an envelope marked "Eyes Only" and handed Frank the single page it contained. On it was a one-word question.

*Belinsky?*

———

Ali dropped them at Dowshan Tappeh after their morning Jayface meeting. For a change, they found Stan Rushmore in his office.

"Well, hello, stranger," said Gus. "Who told you you could use our office?"

"These days," said Rushmore, "I gotta believe you guys see more of it than I do. Hey, Sullivan, you know the papers are back on the street?"

"January 7, right?" said Frank. "I knew today was the day, but I haven't seen any."

"I picked you up a copy of the one in English. Figured you might want to see it."

"I appreciate that," said Frank, though in truth the prospect of looking at it depressed him. Nice to see a local paper, he thought as he skimmed, but it wasn't the *Armed Forces Times*.


After another taxi ride with Lermontov's gofer, Frank emptied his false-bottom briefcase on the table in another nondescript safe house.

"I think you'll be happy with today's take. It includes special analyses on the probable local impact of a Khomeini takeover from our chiefs of station in Moscow, Kabul, Baghdad, and a dozen other Mideast capitals."

He hefted the huge envelope that had come by pouch onto the table. Rocky had told him James had the Near East Division working on it for weeks.

"You're serious," said Lermontov. He tore open the envelope and began glancing through the individual reports.

"It's meant for internal briefings with one set going to the National Security Council and from there maybe a précis to the White House." Frank guessed that James would have had it laced with a shrewd blend of actual but sanitized reporting and carefully calculated disinformation. "There's an overall executive summary and separate summaries for each country."

"If the reports turn out as good as they look, this will mean a special bonus for you. The mere fact you could get them says a lot for you."

"How big a bonus?" said Frank.

"That depends on a final evaluation," said Lermontov, his head buried in the reports. "Tripoli looks interesting. They say Qadaffi will shut down your station, and the embassy, within a month." He opened another report. "But Kabul seems to appreciate little of what's going on there."

"I didn't say all our stations were great. Just that this gives you an idea of the best they can come up with."

"The best," muttered Lermontov, " from the not very bright."

---

"I've got a virgin safe house on hold for any meets you have with Lermontov about his defection, or about Belinsky and our penetration agent," said Rocky, secure with Frank in the bubble. He handed Frank a sealed envelope. "It's all in there, location, two sets of directions. One for you. One for Lermontov. Set of keys. Never been used as a safe house before. The embassy took it over from the Germans when they closed down their Goethe Institute couple months ago. I talked the ambassador into lettin' us have it. He owes me, so he said yes. It's even got a phone that works. But the house isn't wired, so bring your trusty little tape recorder. Draft a note to Lermontov and slip him his stuff at your next meet."

"Will do," said Frank. "Thanks."


Lermontov himself picked up Frank for their next meeting at a prearranged street corner near the British Embassy. Heavy, wet snow had fallen earlier in the day, downing power lines, then turning to slush as rising temperatures turned the white flakes to gray rain.

"No need to bother with the glasses," said Lermontov. "Your people know where I live, and that's where I'm taking you. I have good news for you."

Lermontov broke out both vodka and caviar, plus a loaf of black Russian pumpernickel. "Baked fresh at the embassy," he said. "Just for you. I can't chew the pumpernickel, but my *rezident,* and Moscow, want me to toast you. *Na zdarovye.*"

*"Na zdarovye,"* Frank responded. They clinked glasses and, Russian fashion, bolted down the vodka.

"You're getting better," said Lermontov. "More Russian. The material you brought me from your various Near East stations strongly impressed everyone at our embassy who has looked at it, at least on a preliminary basis."

"Good," said Frank. "You had me thinking I let you down lately."

"You had. But you redeemed yourself. Here."

He tossed an envelope in Frank's direction. Frank ripped it open and began counting. Fifty twenties. Frank counted it again. "It's only a thousand."

"Interesting, how quickly traitors become greedy," said Lermontov, heaping caviar onto a spoon.

"I wish you wouldn't use that word."

"Traitor? You are too sensitive. But what is your expression? To call a spade a spade, no?"

"No," said Frank. "In polite circles we call a spade an implement for digging. And in polite circles we acknowledge that the material I gave you deserves much more than a thousand."

"Preliminary," said Lermontov. "I can assure you, if it stands up under analysis in Moscow, you will receive more."

"Good," said Frank. He hoped he sounded convincing, but he'd begun to hate playing the role of greedy traitor.

Frank wondered if the general had another first name, but he had never heard him referred to as anything other than Fritz Weber. When he met him the next afternoon, he saw why. The nickname fit like his well-tailored air force uniform. His brush-cut gray hair stood at attention, an extension of his ramrod posture. The soft folds in his leathery face contrasted with the cutting-edge creases in his trousers. Frank tried to determine the color of his hooded eyes. He could do no better than dark.

"So you're Sullivan. Heard about you."

Frank said nothing. They did not shake hands.

"Fritz and I had an interesting meeting with the Shah," said the ambassador. "He told us his plans for leaving. Which do not jibe with what he told you."

The ambassador had used the secure line from the palace to set up a meeting with Rocky and Frank in his office. Frank, who did not get the message until he returned to Dowshan Tappeh from his Jayface session, arrived last.

"What I don't understand," said the general, "is why Sullivan here meets with the Shah in the first place. Ambassador O'Connor's accredited to the Court of His Imperial Majesty, right?"

"Accredited, in fact, to the Peacock Throne," said O'Connor. "To the Shah himself, that is."

"Then why the hell is this CIA flunky meeting with him.?"

"At the Shah's request. They have . . ." The ambassador looked to Frank.

"We met many years ago," said Frank. "In another country. He remembered me. Heard I was here and sent word for me to come see him."

"We didn't like the idea at first," said the ambassador. "But it can sometimes get a little sticky saying no to a King of Kings."

"I still don't much like it," said Rocky.

"But I think Mr. Novak and I agree," said the ambassador, "that on balance it turned out to be a positive for us."

"Chain of command means chain of command," said the general. "Break it and you muddy the waters. Like the Shah telling this spook one thing and us another."

"The issue . . ." The ambassador got no further.

"The issue is this guy should not be talking to the Shah."

"The question, I should say, comes down to this. The Shah told us today he intends to leave not later than the seventeenth, only six days away, and that he plans to fly direct to the United States. But, Frank, he told you that when he leaves he plans to stay close to Iran, so he can return quickly after his generals stage a coup."

"He may have changed his mind," said Frank.

"Huh," snorted the general. "Who does he think he is? Jimmy Carter?"

"Sir," said Frank, turning to address the ambassador, "you know my reporting reflects doubt on the military's ability to bring off a coup."

"Not just your reporting," said the ambassador.

"That's the goddamn problem," thundered the general.

"Please," said Rocky. "You're upsetting my hearing aid." He adjusted the volume knob.

"Stuff your hearing aid," said the general. Frank suspected that Rocky no longer heard him.

"I'm over here on a mission assigned by our change-his-mind-a-minute President to encourage the Iranian military to get on with it. To take over with as little bloodshed as possible, hopefully with no bloodshed, before this holy man and his Commie supporters get a chance to move in. I know about your reporting, Sullivan, and it sucks. The same kind of pissing and moaning your outfit did in the early days about Vietnam. 'We can't win the war.' Now we got you saying we can't win this war, and I tell you we can."

"I'm a reporter," said Frank, finally able to see into the general's eyes, a blue so flat and dark they seemed purple. "I only report what various Iranians, including the Shah, have told me."

"Maybe, just maybe," said the general, "if you spent more time doing whatever the hell your outfit sent you over here for instead of sucking up to the Shah, we might have a better idea of what the hell is going on here. You're supposed to be in the air force, right?"

Frank wondered if he should salute. "Air force major," he said.

"I can tell you, you'd never be in any air force I had anything to do with." Weber turned to Rocky. "You better get some new cover for him. Or ship him the hell out of here."

"Fritz, you must allow me to say . . ." Again, the ambassador did not get a chance to complete his thought.

"Mr. Ambassador, allow me to say, chain of command, order of battle. You talk to the Shah. Your military attachés talk to their Iranian counterparts. I come over here with specific instructions to contact high-level Iranian military leaders, most of which I've known for a long time. I've met with them all, and I can tell you the Shah made a great choice in naming Gharabaghi his chief of staff. The man's a natural military leader, and he managed to open lines of communication to some of these raghead religious leaders. We will have a coup, and we will not have bloodshed, because General Gharabaghi has it covered on both ends. A military solidly with him and a religious leadership that won't oppose him."

"That sounds very optimistic," said the ambassador.

"If we had the gumption to be optimistic in Vietnam," said the general, "we'd still be there."

The ambassador closed his eyes. Rocky, hands folded on the table, looked blank. This guy's crazy, thought Frank.

"I'll report what the Shah told us," Weber continued. "Just what he told us, with no contradictions from the CIA. And there won't be any contradictions because Sullivan here won't be seeing the Shah anymore."

"We might agree that Frank won't seek a meeting with the Shah," said the ambassador, 'but that doesn't preclude the possibility the Shah will seek a meeting."

"Yeah, well, your chief of station here can preclude that possibility by shipping Sullivan out of here on the next plane."

That sounds like a great idea, thought Frank. Quick. Before someone kills me.

Rocky stared blankly at the general. "Do you read me?" shouted Weber. Rocky nodded, and Frank guessed Rocky did read the general, but only his lips.

The general spent close to an hour telling the ambassador how to conduct the business of his embassy and telling Rocky how to run his station.

"Thank you for your comments," said the ambassador.

Rocky, deaf to all Weber had said, read the ambassador's lips and echoed, "Thank you for your comments."

When the general finally left, Rocky led Frank up to the bubble. "Let's give it a minute to make sure that kraut got his ass the hell out of here. Then let's see if we can get his nibs up here. This shit with the Shah, we gotta work this out."

"You heard what Weber said about shipping me out?"

"No," said Rocky. "Anybody asks, my hearing aid must not have been working. But Langley's cleared him for access to our reporting. So we can't ask the ambassador to set up a meeting for you with the Shah or Weber will go ballistic. Can you talk to Kasravi?"

"That's what the Shah said I'm supposed to do. Stay in touch with Kasravi even after he goes on vacation."

"Good. Tell Kasravi you need to see the Shah A-SAP. If he asks why . . ."

"He won't," said Frank.

"You fucking assume he won't. But if he does, tell him the truth. In fact, even if he doesn't ask, tell him you need to clear up confusion in embassy reporting about the Shah's departure. He may offer somethin' interestin' himself, but you say you have to get it direct from the Shah. How soon can you get to him?"

"Tomorrow," said Frank. "It may mean blowing another meeting with Lermontov, but Kasravi should be able to get me in to see the Shah."

"Good," said Rocky. "Lermontov can wait. If the Shah does plan to go direct to the States, we may just say nothin'. No need to stir up General Fritz if we don't have to. But if the Shah doesn't plan to go to the States, we gotta let the boys back home know it real quick before someone in the White House or the NSC says or does somethin' dumb on the basis of what the ambassador and Weber file. What do you know about this General Gharabaghi?"

Frank shrugged. "Not much. Kasravi seems to think he's a good man."

"So does Washington," said Rocky. "He's our next hero on a white horse. Ever since George Washington, whenever we have a fuckin' political problem we start lookin' for a general on a white horse to solve it. Win a war. Stage a coup. Same way in Vietnam. Chile. Greece. If we can't get a general, we'll settle for a colonel. Give us a guy on a white horse we can put on a pedestal. Carved in stone. Anyway, this General fuckin' Gharabaghi is the latest."

"I kind of wonder about how great he is," said Frank, "if General Fritz is so high on him."

"Yeah, well, I wonder, too. But the word from Washington says Gharabaghi is supposed to be the one guy everybody respects. Mr. Clean. Religious, a man of honor, all that. Word is, and this comes out of National Security Council, Gharabaghi is supposed to be everybody's favorite candidate for the guy to ride back in on his white-ass horse and lead the coup. Force the Shah to bring his kid in as regent with a government of national unity with the National Front up front. So what NSC wants and flat-out asks for is reporting from here that verifies the speculation in Washington."

"Isn't that kind of ass-backwards?"

"Yeah," grumbled Rocky. "In the best of all possible worlds, policy oughta be based on intelligence. But back in Foggy Bottom, the EOB and the Oval fuckin' Office, they want it the other way round. Yeah, Langley, too. At least some of the time. They want field intelligence that's based on headquarters policy. Policy calls for a military coup. Fuckin' Gharabaghi on a white horse. So after you talk to the Shah your reporting better come up with good odds for a coup led by General Gharabaghi. And don't forget the white horse. Let's make your friend General Fritz happy."

"Does he have a real first name?" asked Frank.

"Weber? Yeah, first name, Charles. But nobody ever calls him that. He's a fuckin' Fritz."

Frank had enlisted Kasravi's aid in arranging a meeting with the Shah. At the scheduled time of five, the new majordomo ushered Frank into the Shah's office.

"We're glad you could come," said the Shah, seated at his vast oak desk. "In fact, we would have sent for you, but our time grows crowded, and short." His voice seemed assured; he sat tall, shoulders squared in his chair. Only his pale features betrayed the cancer. "Please sit."

Frank pulled a chair close to the desk.

"We had a most unsatisfactory meeting yesterday with your ambassador and this General Weber person. Since General Kasravi told us why you sought a meeting today, we assume you know some of what happened here yesterday."

"What was the problem?"

"The problem was General Weber. Your President sent him, it would seem, to pressure our military leaders to stage a coup, a coup that would preserve our government, but not, it would seem, our throne. So be it. But when our military men ask General Weber what support the United States would provide, the good general offers nothing. This lack of support offends us. We do not like or trust this general and will not confide our plans to him." The Shah indulged a rare smile. "We had, we must admit, another reason for saying our plans now include flying directly to the United States."

Frank replied with his own smile and waited for the Shah to continue.

"We wanted to see if we would be welcomed in the United States. Our visitors assured us your country would cooperate in every possible way."

"I'm glad to hear that."

"We were not. For we were not sure we could trust their words."

"I don't think they would try to deceive you," said Frank, but in truth he wondered.

"In any event, we do not want to deceive your country. We hope your report on this meeting will make it clear we will not go directly to the United States. In fact, you may report we confirmed our intention to leave for a vacation somewhere in the Middle East. Your government's capacity to leak sensitive information to the press makes us unwilling to say exactly where. We do not want to complicate our host's security arrangements."

"Sir, I believe we can take the proper measures to ensure confidentiality."

"What measures?"

Good question, thought Frank. "Emphasize the extreme sensitivity. Limit distribution."

"Eyes only and all of that?"

"Yes, sir."

"Not good enough, we fear."

Probably not, thought Frank.

"Today is what?" mused the Shah. "January twelfth?"

"Yes, sir."

"Come in two days. Sunday, the fourteenth. We have a lunch scheduled for the fifteenth with the British ambassador, who is leaving Iran, and with your ambassador. But you come the fourteenth. Here, in the morning. Can you arrange nine?"

"I will arrange it, sir."

"It will be, we are afraid, our farewell."

"I'm sorry to hear that, sir."

"We wish you could accompany us. But stay in close touch with General Kasravi. He will need you and he will be useful to you."

"I'd love to burn Weber's ass, but we can't put all that stuff the Shah said about him in a cable he's likely to read."

Rocky and Frank had cloistered themselves in the bubble.

"How 'bout the stuff about pressuring the Iranian military to stage a coup but offering no U.S. support?"

"Don't say 'pressuring.' Say 'discussing' a coup. You get anything about Gharabaghi?"

"I asked. He looked out the window and said discuss that with Kasravi."

"Better leave that out. Least till you talk to Kasravi again. All the other stuff goes in, including the bit about the British ambassador leaving. It'll get to James and let him know that may mean one less threat to our nailin' Lermontov. But no derogatory stuff about General Fritz."

"Got it," said Frank. "Can Lermontov have it?"

"Better wait till after your Sunday meet with the Shah. Give me time to cover my ass, clear the idea with James. By then, if we get the okay, maybe you can even tell him where Our Imperial Majesty will go."

"Sad," said Frank.

"Yeah," said Rocky. "I guess it is kinda sad."

Their Sunday morning meeting proved short. Both stood throughout. "President Sadat has invited us to stay in Egypt." The Shah stared at the Mercator projection on the far wall that showed Iran at the center of the world. "Egypt is not far. We leave in two days, with our Queen and a few others. We can go there and return quickly should we be called. If not, after a few days, we will proceed to the United States." He turned to Frank. "But we will give you our opinion. Our military, without American support, will not be able to manage a coup. And we believe America will render no such support." He looked back toward the wall. "I wonder what will happen to my map."

He turned again and, in a rare gesture, extended his hand to Frank. His eyes misted as their hands touched, and he said, "Good-bye, good friend."

"Good-bye," said Frank.

"Perhaps we will meet again," said the Shah. "Someday in America."

He had not expected to choke up saying good-bye to a man he knew bore responsibility for the deaths of thousands, including Major Nazih, at the hands of *Savak,* the police, and the military. My search for a father, he thought. My weakness for emperors.

"You visit the Shah often these days," said Ali, as he drove Frank back toward the embassy.

"I guess," said Frank.

Ali turned toward him briefly. "Does that mean he will soon be leaving?"

"No. But you know you shouldn't ask questions like that."

"Yes, sir. I know. But I have to think about my own leaving. And yours."

"I don't plan on going anywhere anytime soon."

"All the Americans will have to go when the Imam arrives." The Imam, thought Frank. Even to Ali. "I will stay with you for just now," said Ali. "You will need me. But I must soon leave Tehran and join my family."

"What about the army?" said Frank.

"There is no army," Ali responded.

Frank found Gus in Stan Rushmore's office, finishing up a cable on the Jayface meeting.

"Jayface worries me," said Gus.

"How so?"

"We miss your creative presence. You do a better job than the rest of us keeping up the pretense of a post-coup civic action program."

"Jayface still gives us a platform," said Frank.

"I know, but General Merid's wondering out loud if Jayface really has any function."

"Maybe you should recruit him," said Frank.

"What an outstanding idea," said Gus. "Like I said, we need your creative presence."

"Where were you yesterday?" said Lermontov harshly once he stood in the eye of the hidden video camera. He had again brought Frank to his home.

"At the palace," said Frank. "Sucking up to the Shah, as my favorite American general put it to me."

"What is this about?"

Frank described his confrontation with General Weber and the Shah's comments on the general. "Some of this is in a cable I've brought you, which also deals with the Shah's departure. He's going to Egypt. Leaving in two days."

"Interesting. Let me see it."

Frank pried the day's take from the false bottom of his briefcase. It included a thick but bland series of Near East situation updates prepared by the division.

Lermontov seemed interested only in the cable on the Shah. "This is a first-rate piece of intelligence. No matter what your stupid general says, you should suck up to the Shah more often."

"Not much chance of that," said Frank. "We said our good-byes."

"Wth him gone, how long can you hope to stay?"

"The Shah asked me to keep in touch with General Kasravi, Imperial Bodyguard. Liaison between General Bardri, who now heads both the Bodyguard and the army, and General Gharabaghi, the new chief of staff. Key people in plans for the coup. It's in the cable."

"Excellent. And you will stay?"

"Far as I know," said Frank. God help me.

"Excellent. We will make you a rich man before you leave Iran."

"Long as I leave alive."

"What's all this?" asked Lermontov, nodding to the rest of the material Frank had brought.

"Situation updates on reactions in various Near East countries to the situation here. It doesn't look as good as that last batch."

"Ah, yes. That last batch. You're going to use up all my vodka and caviar, but we do have cause to celebrate. Further evaluation of that last batch has made you a hero of the Soviet Union. Well, not quite. But Moscow has authorized a bonus of five thousand dollars. One thousand you already have. I have stuffed this fat envelope with four thousand more. I hope you don't insist on counting it." He spun a bulging nine-by-twelve manila envelope across the table to Frank.

Frank opened it and peered inside at five thick stacks of rubber-banded twenties. Since he couldn't keep them, the thought of counting all those bills depressed him. "I trust you," he said. "I guess."

"Then sign," said Lermontov.

Frank signed the receipt.


"Shame we have to turn all this in," said Rocky, counting out twenties in the bubble.

"Tell me about it."

"Hey, you're the one gets the caviar and vodka. All I get to do is count the damn money. Looks like it's all here. Four thousand. I can't believe you didn't count it."

"I was too busy with the caviar." Not to mention the vodka. He had a buzz on, a nice quiet buzz, and he wished he had another vodka to sip on, just to keep the buzz and to keep it nice and quiet. "Now that you've counted the money twice, do you want to take a look at the take?"

"First things first. A good bureaucrat always takes care of the administrative details first. Then he can play intelligence officer."

"I'll try to remember that," said Frank.

"You should. 'Specially when the administrative details equal two hundred Andrew Jacksons."

"That's too much paper to count," said Frank. "Don't the Russians ever have any hundreds?"

"Soviets," said Rocky. "Not Russians. The Soviets consider hundred-dollar bills a symbol of decadent capitalism. If your buddy is right and the Soviet Union collapses anytime soon, you'll see Russians willing to kill for American hundred-dollar bills. Let's see what else he has for us."

Rocky started with Lermontov's handwritten cover note. Frank could barely pick up his mumble.

" 'Thank you for the directions.' I guess he means directions to our new safe house. 'I ask you again. Belinsky? What has he done? You give me no answer. The four visitors from our counterintelligence line seem to have given up on GRU and are back questioning people in my office. If you are going to act, you must act soon.' "

"Your turn to talk to Belinsky," said Frank. "I've done what I can."

"I did talk to him," said Rocky. "What can I tell you? Said he'd let us know by tomorrow. When's your next meet with Lermontov?"

"He wants to meet again tomorrow," said Frank. "He's getting kind of anxious."

"Your Russian buddy doesn't seem like the worryin' kind," said Rocky. "But he sounds worried."

"You think the mole might've found out something more?"

"Possible," said Rocky. "I don't wanna stir up anything, but I'll get off a low-key cable t' the Holy Ghost. And you need a sit-down with Lermontov at your new safe house A-SAP."

"Will do. What else does he say?"

Rocky went back to Lermontov's notes. " 'Also, as you requested, an update on Afghanistan. Half Kabul under control of Islamic guerrillas . . . two-thirds of the countryside. Very detailed report. German military attaché kidnapped. Your embassy staff under tight surveillance. Expect trouble. Situation fluid. Intervention may become necessary sooner than anticipated. Separate, detailed report on Soviet troop and materiel buildup in border area north of the Salang Pass. From

Paris, report of effort by Bakhtiar to arrange a meeting with Khomeini in Neauphle-le-Château.'

"This motherfucker not only dots his *i*'s," said Rocky without looking up, "he puts his Frog accent marks in the right place. 'Sources say Khomeini will ignore Bakthiar overtures. From Tehran, report on Shah's departure, not later than three-one January. Destination, U.S.' Wrong on that. Holy shit. 'Plans for redeployment of Soviet Iran assets in anticipation of Khomeini takeover.'" Rocky looked up. "Good stuff, but at least the stuff you gave him shapes up."

"Agreed. But our people better keep on doin' better. Have you read Gus's cable?"

"Yeah. Good job," said Rocky. "Interesting the navy guy who told you about the death threats took Gus aside to tell him the top brass set up briefings for air force officers. Said the navy's about to do the same. I wonder about the army."

"We can ask General Merid."

"Gus said you suggested tryin' to pitch him. That worries me. We already got burned on one army fag. You sure you wanna risk another one?"

"He may be an army fag," said Frank, "but he's also an army general. Plus, I think he'd be flattered by the attention. The Iranians tend to leave him out of the loop, especially since the business with Nazih went down."

"Gus's hot for it," said Rocky.

"Let's do it," said Frank. "We probably don't have much time here anyway. Why not take some risks?"


Munair made no effort to hide the note he handed to Frank during their morning tea break. Feeling sheepish, aware that the eyes of the others had swung his way, he stuffed the note into a pants pocket.

"Excuse me," he muttered to no one in particular and, casually as he could, headed for the bathroom. The stench of stale urine and feces, stronger than usual, assaulted his senses. He scanned the empty room, squinted in its pale gray light, and read Munair's message.

*Please be so kind as to meet me in the lobby of the Sheraton Hotel at 1500 hours this afternoon. Failing that, 1530 hours tomorrow. Or 1600 hours the next day.*


He entered the hotel, relieved to see Munair already tucked into a corner of the large beige couch that stretched across the center of the marbled and tiled lobby. His head was bent over a book, but he looked up as Frank felt a swirl of cold air from the glass doors swinging shut behind him. Munair stood and approached Frank, giving him only a moment to survey the deserted lobby.

Munair tucked his book under his arm and bowed. "Come. Let us sit on the couch. It is best to be visible. We are being watched, but only by *Savak* and J2, our military intelligence. You are quite safe." Frank had never before seen him smile. "Safer than those perhaps who watch us."

They settled on the couch. Munair braced himself in a corner; Frank sat close enough that he could speak softly. To Frank's surprise, Munair made no effort to mask his words.

"For a long time, I avoided you," said Munair, his penetrating eyes fixed on Frank's. "I did not think you could be trusted."

"I understand," said Frank, forcing himself to meet Munair's stare.

"Do you? Even though so many others trust you? Even General Kasravi begins to trust you. But it is difficult for me because I do not trust myself."

"I guess I don't understand."

"You see, I do not trust myself in English." Munair looked down at the table. "I have never lived outside Iran. I know only the textbook. The classroom. If I speak to a man in our language, I know if he can be trusted. But you, of course, do not speak our language. You see, in English I can never tell if I can trust a man, a man who speaks only the language of the Great Satan."

Here we go, thought Frank. He feared he was in for an unproductive lecture.

"And of course," said Munair, again looking up at Frank, "English is the only language you Americans speak."

"It's true," said Frank. "We depend on other people speaking English." He fell back on his favorite analogy. "Like air traffic controllers. No matter what country, it's an unwritten law. All air traffic controllers for international flights have to speak English."

"It is not written here." Munair touched the book he'd been reading when Frank entered. "And all the laws we need are written here."

"The Koran?"

"No. It is the work of the Imam. *Hukumat-e Islami: Vilayat-e Faqih.* Of course, you do not know what that means. It is only in your arrogance that there is an unwritten law that other people must speak English. In these pages the law is written, and it is not in English."

Frank began a mental search for a polite way to escape, then remembered he hoped Munair could tell him what role the navy might play in an attempted coup.

"It is not because of this book, which describes how an Islamic government will come to power, it is because of your arrogance you will be driven from this country when the Imam comes."

"You think he will come?"

"He is already here. In effect. His will is done. He has told us America is the Great Satan and Satan must be driven from our country. And the people will obey him."

"Including the military? The navy?"

"Ah. That is why you are here."

"Yes," said Frank, deciding to be blunt. "I'm an intelligence officer. A spy."

"Yes. Perhaps General Kasravi is right," said Munair. "Perhaps you can be trusted."

"You can trust a spy?" asked Frank.

"Yes. A spy who says so. But for myself, I began to trust you when I heard what you did in the cafeteria at Dowshan Tappeh. Playing the Imam's tape."

"You know about Sergeant Abbas?"

"Of course," said Munair. "People who work in the cafeteria of course report to military intelligence. Word travels. You recognized the power of the Imam. You accepted that power and used it well. That made me trust you enough to warn you about the *fatwa* that calls for the death of you and Mr. Belinsky."

"Have you heard anything more about that?"

"Only that it is discussed. We will meet more often. I will keep you informed. But you and Mr. Belinsky must be cautious."

Frank and Munair met twice more during the week, once in a small room in an out-of-the-way stucco building given over to the navy on the grounds of Supreme Commander's Headquarters, and once at the Hilton Hotel.

"The orange drink is bad," said Munair, "but I have ordered for us both."

Two glasses with ice cubes and a cloudy liquid sat on their wrought-iron table in the Hilton's deserted marble lobby. Frank raised his and said, "Cheers," but did not risk a sip. Munair drank, scowled, and put his glass down.

"You need not drink," he said. "Merely listen. All over the country, including here in Tehran, *komiteh* form." He gave the English cognate its Persian pronunciation. "Very much on a local, neighborhood foundation. You followed my suggestion for coming?"

"I did." The complicated route had taken him east out of Dowshan Tappeh through the neighborhood called New Tehran, then north and west and north again along the far reaches of Pahlavi till he hit the Hilton.

"Good," said Munair. "That way you only go through neighborhoods where as yet they have not formed *komiteh*. But even in these neighborhoods soon opportunists will form *komiteh* when they realize the Shah will leave and not return."

"How do you know these things?" asked Frank.

"The *komiteh* are active," said Munair. "And now . . . I remain loyal to the navy and to Admiral Hayati, but now I also work with them, with the *komiteh*."

"And about the Shah?"

"I told you. I remain loyal to Admiral Hayati."

"I understand."

"Return the way you came. Not many safe passages remain."

"I understand."

Munair nodded and folded his hands together. He briefed Frank on the meeting at which Admiral Hayati told junior officers the role the navy would play if the military attempted a coup. Most of what he described had been spelled out in Admiral Hayati's proposal.

"Nothing was said about the role of the other military branches," said Munair. "In truth, what the generals and admirals say about a coup does not matter. But I have also brought you tapes that matter very much. The Imam's instructions on preparing for his return. Many people now believe he is in truth the Twelfth Imam, returning to us on a winged horse as the Prophet ascended to heaven. I think that is blasphemy, but, Hidden Imam become visible or not, he will come."

"I appreciate this," said Frank, "but I will need your guidance."

"Each tape is in a separate envelope with a summary in my schoolroom English of its message," said Munair. "The Imam talks about the *komiteh,* how they should be organized and function. I prepared charts to show you what *komiteh* exist now, what still need to be created. It is all in this shopping bag under the table. Simply take it when you leave. No one will bother you."

Frank had spotted the *Savak* black leather overcoats at the lobby's only other occupied table. He wondered if the men who wore them knew about the *fatwa* that condemned him. Their waiter chatted with a desk clerk, but both watched Frank and Munair. J2? wondered Frank. He suspected Munair's mission had been cleared.


"You know what you got here?" said Rocky. "You got the structure of the revolutionary committees within the military and fuckin' *Savak*. Plus the outline of what I guess must be most of the revolutionary committees in Tehran. And this Ayatollah Taleqani has made Munair his go-between with the military?"

"Right."

"And he'll keep meetin' with you and givin' you stuff?"

Frank nodded.

"It's gonna take you hours to put all this into a cable. What about Belinsky?"

Frank repeated what Munair had told him. "Chuck tells me he'll quit drinking," he added, "but he found another way to commit suicide. To get some Iranian to kill him. Maybe before he has to confront his GRU friend."

"How does Munair know about that?" asked Rocky.

"He won't spell it out," said Frank. "But he's let me know he has contacts with *Savak,* J2. Sounds like Chuck's been kind of careless."

"This Munair," said Rocky, "he wants to be helpful, right?"

Frank nodded. He'd spread the contents of his shopping bag on the glass table in Rocky's bubble.

"And he doesn't wanna go to the States."

"He's very devout," said Frank. "He wants to live in the Islamic Republic."

"The stuff he gave you on these revolutionary committees could turn out real heavy. We need more details. And keep after him about this *fatwa* business. Again, we need more details if we want to keep you and Belinsky alive. And functioning."

"We've got to get Belinsky functioning quick on this GRU guy," said Frank. "But I've got a hunch keeping Chuck alive and keeping him functioning may not both be possible."

"What is it with you? You got a death wish about Belinsky? First you worried about suicide. Now you worry about homicide."

"I worry about a lot of things," said Frank. "Including my own little death warrant."

"Don't worry," said Rocky. "Think. Think about Munair. Think about keeping Belinsky alive. And functioning. He does good work."

"I'll talk to Munair," said Frank.

"I want you to recruit him," said Rocky. "Not just for now. An agent in place. We'll need some leave-behinds when they ship us all outta here. And he's one guy who seems likely to survive once the holy ragheads take over."

"I doubt he'll go for it," said Frank. "But I'll do my best."


"It's a mission," said Belinsky.

"A suicide mission?" asked the ambassador.

They'd sequestered themselves in the bubble with Rocky and Frank.

"No, sir," said Belinsky. "Something I can do that has to be done."

"Munair told me that if you go to Qom again, you'll be killed there," said Frank. "At the airport where your chopper sets down."

"That means you get a chopper pilot killed, too," said Rocky. "You ready for that?"

"Ayatollah Shariat-Madari is the only ranking clergyman we have contact with."

"And that you have a good chance of being attacked, beaten up at the university or murdered in the bazaar."

"Look, I can exercise more caution. And Frank, I appreciate you letting me know the danger. But we all take risks, don't we?"

"Yeah, don't we?" said Rocky, staring hard at Belinsky. Belinsky looked away.

"Yes," said the ambassador, "we all take risks. But none of the rest of us have been warned that we might get killed. Warned by a man apparently in a position to know."

"That makes me safer than the rest of you. At least I know what to look out for."

"Chuck, let's lay down some guidelines," said the ambassador. "At least for a while, no more trips to Qom. Or the bazaar or the university. Get people to come to you, if you can. If not, stick to the embassy. We have a lot we need you for here. And you're no damn good to us dead."

Belinsky caught Frank's eye. "I have some obligations as a consular officer," he said.

"Turn them over to someone else in the consulate," said the ambassador.

"There's a couple he can't turn over," said Rocky.

"I don't want to know about it," said the ambassador.

"Matter of fact, sir, if you don't mind, there's a couple of . . . obligations Frank and myself need to talk to Chuck about."

"I understand," said the ambassador. "Gentlemen, I leave you to your sins." He pushed himself up from the table. "Chuck, be careful."

Rocky waited for the ambassador to pull the door to the bubble closed behind him.

"Okay, Chuck. You said you'd have something for us by today."

Belinky nodded. "I do. I meet with Yevteshenko tomorrow."

"Not much notice," said Frank.

"Best I could do. Anyways, you two have been acting like you're in a hurry."

"Where?" asked Frank.

"Naderi Hotel."

Frank remembered it. He and Lermontov had met there once. The Soviets used it often, which could be helpful.

"What time?"

He wrote it all down for Lermontov.

They met in the first safe house Lermontov had brought him to. He does a good job of mixing up his venues, thought Frank. But no vodka, no caviar, no envelope of twenties.

"My instructions from Moscow are to remain so long as you are here and useful to us."

"Good," said Frank.

"But we do not believe you Americans will be here for long."

"I've heard the embassy has contingency plans for evacuating nonessential Americans."

"Are you among the nonessential?"

"No."

"Excellent. We should have an interesting few weeks. What do you have for me?"

Rocky, on his own initiative, sanitized the cables reporting on the various armed services capabilities and gave Frank permission to pass them on to Lermontov. Frank added an envelope marked "open later" with the information on Belinsky's meeting at the Naderi.

"This is good," said Lermontov, studying the cables. "Stick close to this General Kasravi. Anything about a coup attempt. If you want another bonus, he could be your key to the money box."

"What about Gharabaghi saying he'd resign rather than participate in a military takeover? Doesn't that tell you something?"

"Something. But we never put as much stock in Gharabaghi as your General Weber did. I'll call attention to it in my cable, but don't count on a bonus."

"This General Weber makes the rest of the American establishment look good," said Frank.

"Really? How so?"

"He wanted the station to sit on our reports. Said they read too negative. Rocky, our chief of station, might have done just that. But Weber got him so mad he went ahead and filed everything."

"You are so naive," said Lermontov. "Your fight isn't with Rocky or the stupid general. Your fight is with the system. And what you don't understand, by fighting the system you make it stronger. You fight the system to get your reporting accepted, reporting the system doesn't want to hear. You succeed and the system is stronger, better informed, because you have fought it."

"Interesting," said Frank. "But I still don't think the system appreciates what I've done."

"Probably not," said Lermontov with a rare smile that turned into a grimace. It must hurt that jaw to smile, thought Frank.

"We should meet here again tomorrow evening," said Lermontov. "Things are changing rapidly."


Frank joined Rocky in the bubble after his meeting with Lermontov the next evening. He opened the eyes-only envelope among the material Lermontov had delivered. Rocky read the message aloud.

"'Meeting took place. Envelope with American currency delivered. Photo taken. Subject later taken back to our embassy.' Rocky handed it to Frank. "Done deal. Belinsky already told me. Seems kind of a . . . what's the expression? Anticlimax? Like there oughta be rollin' drums. Thunder and lightnin'.""

"You cable James?" asked Frank.

"On what Belinsky said. Yeah, I did. I'll do another on Lermontov's note. Looks like we got both those guys, Lermontov and Belinsky, off the hook. And put the fuckin' mole on ice. Moscow's gonna think their penetration agent nailed his man in Tehran. And he did. But it wasn't our man. Lermontov can relax. The Soviet spooks will quit lookin'."

"Let's hope so," said Frank. He felt a profound sense of relief. The mole had been foiled and Lermontov was safe. Belinsky would not be arrested or disgraced. He felt no pity for the doomed GRU officer but also no urge to celebrate. They were still in the midst of a civil war; a *fatwa* with his name still carried a promise of death; deep within the agency, the unidentified mole continued to dig.

# CHAPTER TWENTY

Frank and Gus sat in Stan Rushmore's office putting together the last of their cables assessing the capabilities of the various armed forces to carry out a coup. At first, they could hear only the sound of car horns and truck Klaxons pounding out an incessant beat—blaat-blaat, blaat-blaat, blaat-blaat. They exchanged a glance. Without speaking, they slipped into their parkas, pulled their stocking caps low over their foreheads, and, though heavy gray clouds hung low in the sky, put on dark glasses and went outside.

Taunting crowds had gathered outside the chained gates of the base. Frank and Gus, hands plunged deep in their pockets, their breath frosted, approached the guardhouse. Now Frank could pick out the words with the same incessant beat as the Klaxons—*Shah raft, Shah raft, Shah raft.*

Frank had no idea what *raft* meant in Farsi. The echo of the English word conjured up an image of the Shah swept away by turbulent waters on a wildly spinning raft.

"What are they saying?" Gus asked one of the Iranian air force guards on duty.

" '*Shah raft,*' sir. In English, 'The Shah has gone.' See, *Ayandegan,* one of our newspapers, has already put out a special edition. Only four pages. Someone pushed it through the fence."

He handed Gus a broadsheet on which two words in ornate Arabic script took up the entire front page. "*Shah raft?*" asked Gus.

"In Farsi, of course, sir. Also on radio. The Shah, himself at the controls of his 707, took off at fourteen hundred hours from Mehrabad Airport. But sir, we must ask you to retreat." Behind him, the other guards nodded in agreement. Bearded faces pressed against the chain-link fence, staring at them, and someone started a chant of *"Maag bargh Amrika."*

"Doesn't sound good," said Gus.

"No, sir. If they believe you are *Amrikazi,* it may incite them. We do not want them to attack the fence. Don't run. Just, if you would, walk slowly away."

"Can I keep this?" Gus indicated the newspaper.

"Oh, yes, sir. A souvenir."

Gus showed the paper to Frank, then held it up to the crowd with his left hand and began to chant, *"Shah raft, Shah raft, Shah raft,"* pumping his right fist in the air. Frank and the guards joined in, and soon cries of *"Shah raft, Shah raft, Shah raft,"* supported by the din of the Klaxons, drowned out "Death to America." Frank and Gus turned and walked back to Rushmore's office.

"The revolution in action," said Gus as they shed their caps and parkas.

Frank, still mute, looked at his watch. The hands blurred, but his mind registered. Sixteen January, 1979. Two in the afternoon. The Shah has gone. He pictured an hourglass with the sand rapidly running out.

They turned their completed cables over to Bill Steele.

"I'll haul them up to Rocky at the embassy for you," said Bill, "but it might be a while. Things being what they are out there."

"Understood," said Gus. With chained gates and a volatile mob out front, Frank decided against risking a run through one of the back gates to get to his designated pickup spot for his meeting with Lermontov, this time near the south end of Park-e Farah, opposite the Inter-Continental Hotel. The roundabout route he considered added up to about eight miles. Even if he made it out of the base, too much could happen on a day like this over a course of eight miles. The threat of being shot by a newly religious *Savak* agent was bad enough. The prospect of being torn apart by a hysterical mob seemed much worse.

Their cables presented a mixed picture. Frank had reported that, according to Kasravi, the *homafaran* almost to a man had taken an oath of allegiance to Khomeini. Many pilots had said they would fly no missions against people who supported the revolution. Shortages of spare parts, coupled with the *homafar* rebellion, made it likely few military planes would be airworthy.

Summing up Kasravi's view, Frank had written that the general considered the Bodyguard the only reliable unit. He thought the navy fairly reliable but also fairly unimportant; the air force he described as unreliable and the army as by and large disloyal. He said he could not comment on the police and *Savak*. Frank also reported that Kasravi had said that the Bodyguard would close down the airport should Khomeini attempt to fly in from France and that the Bodyguard had also prepared secret plans for confronting possible mutiny by any other element of the armed forces.

In a separate cable, Frank quoted Munair as relating the view of Admiral Hayati that the navy would be loyal but that logistics would limit its role. Frank cited the exact words Munair used. "Around the Caspian, we have little but a few patrol boats. Our strength lies far to the south, and the real test will come in the cities far from the Gulf."

General Merid, who had quickly proved himself the most eager of recruits, told Gus most enlisted men and junior officers would not oppose a popular revolution led by Khomeini. Gus's cable quoted him as saying, "I know what the people upstairs may say, the Gharabaghis, the Bardris, the Hayatis. In their hearts, they know the truth. But they will say with American help they can do this thing. I have many friends, not alone in the army, but in the other armed forces, the police, even *Savak*."

As he edited what Gus had written, Frank wondered if all General Merid' s friends came from Qazvin. "Forget the police," said the cable. "Not even *Savak* can be relied on. Perhaps if the Immortals and the navy help the Americans to invade, then our military can do this thing."

"You must understand," Frank reported Kasravi as saying, "our armed forces have no tradition of consulting with each other. The head of each branch reported directly to His Imperial Majesty. In times past, His Imperial Majesty felt it best to keep the various military branches from getting together. Politically, a good approach, perhaps, at the time. But now, how can we expect the army, the air force, the navy, and the Imperial Bodyguard all to work together to stage a coup when they have never worked together before?"

"Does General Bardri share these views?" Frank had asked.

"Yes," Kasravi had answered.

"General Gharabaghi?"

"I do not know what General Gharabaghi thinks. He has, however, in my presence, told General Bardri he would resign rather than be part of a military takeover. You can quote him as saying that."

General Fritz will love this, thought Frank as he typed it into his cable.

Warm rain and swirling fog shrouded the subdued city streets. The crowds' euphoria of the previous day washed away like the waste matter carried by the no longer frozen *jube*s. Ali drove with great care. "Thanks be," he said, "we won't have to drive up to the palace today. With this fog, and up there the rain may freeze, thanks be we won't have to drive up there."

"Thanks be," said Frank, sitting by his side as they headed to their morning Jayface meting.

Ali glanced in the rearview mirror and caught Gus's eye. "Commander Simpson, sir. Do you think you would like to drive this big Chevy?"

"Not I," said Gus. "Try Major Sullivan. I don't want to drive anything in this town."

"And you, sir?"

"Are you leaving us?" said Frank.

"The Shah has left us."

"Yes, he has."

"Already they form revolutionary committees, especially in the countryside. They have weapons from the military, the police. Even many soldiers desert and join the committees. Soon they will have roadblocks, checking identity papers, searching cars, trucks, buses. It could become difficult for me to get through to join my family."

"I understand," said Frank, thinking of his own family, thinking of Jake. Can I get through to join my family? Despite the risks, he'd managed to get Anwar and Mina and their kids out of Iran. He thought of the risk he put himself and Belinsky through in confronting Lermontov on the campus of the university and the even greater risk Belinsky faced in trying to entrap his GRU contact. Every trip through the city posed a danger. He thought of driving the Nova without Ali through a town he barely knew among people whose language he did not understand and realized that his palms had begun to sweat. All this and some holy man's *fatwa* hanging over my head like a sword.

"Without me, it would be better for you to drive this car than your little Fiat," said Ali. "Strong. Bulletproof. Do you think you could handle it, sir?"

"Last day?" asked Frank.

"I do not want to leave you, sir."

"Not much advance notice," said Gus from the back seat.

"Sir," said Ali, again glancing into the rearview mirror, "the Shah did not give his people advance notice."

"*Ali raft,*" said Frank.

"Yes," said Ali. "The Shah has gone, sir."


Frank felt they had carried the gloomy fog that prevailed outside into their meeting room. The radiators hissed as they often failed to do on colder days, casting a damp shroud of oppressive heat. Their Iranian colleagues sat mute, barely acknowledging their arrival. He and Gus shed their suit jackets as well as their parkas.

"Of course," said General Merid, stirring himself as they took their seats, "we knew this would happen. Still, so sudden."

"True, General," said Gus. "But still we have to soldier on."

"Ah, yes. We have much to do. A military takeover could . . . ah, take over at any time. We must be ready."

"Even if it never happens?" said Munair.

"We must be ready."

———

Frank drove the big Nova to the embassy, Gus at his side. "I hated to see ol' Ali go," said Gus. "Good man. Good driver. Not that you aren't a good driver, of course. And a reasonably good man, but I hated to see Ali go."

"Me, too," said Frank. "I just hope he makes it to where he wants to go."

"Rasht," said Gus. "I remember him saying his family has land, fruit trees, up near Rasht. Wherever that is. Sounds like a good place to get to right about now."

*Ali Zarakesh raft* Rasht, thought Frank. He wondered if the construction would make sense to an Iranian. *Shah raft* Egypt. *Ali raft* Rasht. Anwar and his family escaped. But not Lermontov. Not Belinsky. And not me.


"He still fooled us," said Rocky, as Frank and Gus settled into his office. "When he told you Egypt, we all figured Cairo. But I heard it on VOA this morning. He flew straight to Aswan. Landed the plane himself. Sadat there to greet him, red carpet, military band, twenty-one-gun salute. And no crowds. Pretty slick."

"He said he didn't want to complicate security arrangements for his host," said Frank.

"He already has," said Rocky. "Khomeini's been on CBS, BBC, everything that's loose, calling on Allah and all loyal followers of Islam to cut off the hands of anybody who takes in the evil Shah. And they've got an awful lot of Muslims in Egypt."

"Sadat's got balls," said Gus. "First Camp David. Now this."

"Look," said Rocky, "the job you guys did on those cables Bill Steele brought down here, you guys did a terrific job. Especially what Kasravi had to say. Great stuff. General Fritz, when he read 'em this morning, he didn't think so. What you had in there about his boy Gharabaghi really pissed him off. There goes another military hero. And the white horse he rode in on. Fritz didn't want me to file 'em, and if he hadn't been here bustin' my balls maybe I wouldn't file 'em. So you can thank him for the fact that your cables got sent. My *lantzman* back home, Mr. Brzezinski, he got on the horn to the ambassador asking him for a more balanced view."

"Balanced?" said Gus. "For godsake, we had Bodyguard and navy saying, 'Count on us'; army and air force saying, 'No way.' Two up, two down. What could be more balanced than that?"

"Four up," said Rocky. "All positive. 'Cause that's what they want to hear. The military will take over and bring the Shah back to power."

"Without American support?" said Frank.

"Suppose it turns out we did get it right?" said Gus.

"Shoot the messengers," said Rocky. " 'Cause if you guys got it right, they've got it wrong."

"I wish I'd gone into another line of work," said Gus.

A vacation aboard the royal yacht off the coast of Iran had turned into the flight into Egypt. That kept the Shah in the neighborhood, should the military recall him. Then, six days later, Frank learned at the embassy that the Shah, at the invitation of King Hassan, had left Egypt for Morocco. The Shah had added the whole of North Africa, Frank guessed two thousand miles, to the distance between himself and the Peacock Throne, He wondered if General Fritz still expected a coup.

A suspicious calm slithered through the city. Though they had little to do, the hours slipped by, unnoticed, and their days telescoped into each other. Frank had the gym to himself every afternoon. He met with Lermontov every other day. He sought out General Kasravi so often that Kasravi asked him not to seek him out.

"If anything of the least importance happens, or seems likely to happen, I will let you know at once. I promise you. I have not forgotten His Imperial Majesty's instructions, and I will carry them out. But these days, nothing happens."

"It's the awful calm before the dreadful storm," said Gus one morning as they inhaled caffeine steaming from coffee still too hot to sip.


"As you know," said Frank, "you've been most helpful to us,"

"Good," said Munair.

They met in the deserted dining room of the Damavand in midafternoon.

"It is better for you," Munair had said. "So near to your embassy. Not far from Supreme Commander's. Since you no longer have Sergeant Zarakesh to drive, I worry for you going very far in this city these days."

"I guess I have to agree," said Frank.

"I wish I could volunteer to drive you myself," said Munair. "Even I discussed with Admiral Hayati, but we agreed it would not be wise. Also, though he would like to, it would not be wise for him to meet with you."

"I understand," said Frank. "But we would like to continue working with you."

"I have brought more tapes," said Munair, indicating his briefcase. "But also what may be important information." Frank waited and Munair continued. "Some of the tapes are meant only for the *ulema,* for . . . select members of the highest ranks of the clergy. Ayatollah Shariat-Madari does not receive them."

"Why not?"

"Those closest to Ayatollah Khomeini's circle no longer consider him reliable.

In fact, they say he works with the CIA and point to Charles Belinsky. He lives in this hotel, does he not?"

Frank nodded.

"He should not," said Munair.

We've got to get him out of here, thought Frank. Maybe he should have flown out on Anwar's ticket.

"These tapes for the *ulema*," said Munair, nodding at the shopping bag he'd set on the floor close to Frank's chair, "they deal with specific plans for the return of the Imam and for the formation of an Islamic government. On one of them the Imam says soon after his return he will name Mahdi Bazargan to head a caretaker government."

Frank couldn't keep from glancing at the egg-shaped stigmata on Munair's forehead, a mark the devout Bazargan had also earned. "You told me that had been rumored before," he said.

"This confirms it," said Munair. "Also the Imam plans to return in time to lead Friday prayers at Behest-e Zahra cemetery south of the city."

"This Friday?"

Munair nodded. "Yes. This Friday."

Thank God, thought Frank, Anwar got out of here in time. But not Belinsky. Or me. "Why at the behest of . . . ?"

"Behest-e Zahra cemetery. Because many of the poorest martyrs of the revolution lie buried there. Passion will run high when the Imam returns. And that passion will turn against . . ."

"Against the Great Satan?"

"Yes," said Munair, "Against any Americans who remain."

Frank suspected that Munair, despite the tapes and the helpful guidance he provided, would as soon see the Great Satan be gone and be damned. Except for spare parts.

"I know that our new nation will be very lonely," said Munair. "We are Shi-ites, surrounded by Sunni. Our Islamic neighbors will fear the power of the Imam. On the other hand, the West will desert us, and our Russian neighbors will think that leaves us weak and alone."

He fell silent. Frank hesitated, trying to find a way to break through Munair's wall of resistance.

"You can trust in Allah," he ventured. "But you will need friends on the ground."

Munair smiled. "You are very clever, but where would we find such friends?"

"I think my country would to try to help," said Frank.

"Perhaps," said Munair. "But you see, even though we decided to trust you, we do not believe we can trust your country."

"Can my country trust . . . what will it be called?"

"The Islamic Republic," said Munair.

"Can my country trust the Islamic Republic?"

Munair fixed his dark, penetrating eyes on Frank but did not respond to his question.

"Then what can we do?" said Frank.

"There, I cannot guide you," said Munair. He hesitated. "But I must also tell you, perhaps you already know. Your Mr. Belinsky continues to be very active . . . so perhaps you already know two days ago Ayatollah Taleqani promised the people would wage *jihad* if the military attempted a coup. I told the Ayatollah he need not worry. The military can wage no coup."

"Would it . . . could you arrange a meeting with Ayatollah Taleqani for me?"

"No," said Munair. "He would not meet with a representative of the Great Satan. If he would, it would not be wise for you. These days, as I have told you, you should not, and Charles Belinsky should not, take risks. You should also know . . . You asked me the name of the Soviet your Mr. Belinsky meets with. His name is Fedor Yevteshenko. He is GRU military intelligence, with consulate work as his cover. He and your Mr. Belinsky met recently at the Naderi Hotel. Yevteshenko accepted an envelope from your Mr. Belinsky and was later escorted back to his embassy by KGB counterintelligence officers."

"You have such good information," said Frank. "You've done so much for us, we would like to return the favor."

"I understand what you are saying," said Munair. "But I need nothing."

"But we would like to continue working with you. My country and your country will need people who can keep communications open between us. Even when our governments may refuse to have official contact."

"No," said Munair. "I understand what you are saying, but I only wish faithfully to serve the Islamic Republic. Admiral Hayati wants to find a way to keep communications open, but there is no way. I want to help you now because I have come to respect you. But once you are gone, I cannot serve America."

"You would also serve Iran," said Frank. "We need people who can build a bridge."

Munair smiled. "Once, I could have served as your bridge to Iran, but you still do not understand," he said gently. "I will no longer serve Iran. I will serve only the Islamic Republic."

Frank studied him. He realized the importance of what Munair had said. There would be no Iran but a new nation, the Islamic Republic. He would file his cable, quoting Munair, but he wondered if America would ever understand.

He also wondered if Belinsky would understand how dangerous were the games he played. He thought of Fred Bunker, creating a medical emergency involving his wife to get out. He thought of the fate of Nazih, of the fears of General Merid. He thought of the Shah, extending his vacation from the Gulf to Egypt to Morocco. He wondered what he might do to escape Iran alive.

That afternoon tanks, armored personnel carriers, and thousands of army troops occupied Mehrabad Airport, shutting it down to prevent Khomeini from carrying out his plan to return in time to conduct Friday prayers. Anwar, Mina, and the kids beat the shutdown, thought Frank. When will the rest of us ever get out? And how?

"You've read your Marx," said Lermontov. "You know the forces of history determine what happens."

Frank had read Marx and had recognized the forces of history, but still he resisted. "I don't like having a guy I've never met, a guy named Ruhollah Khomeini, deciding when, and if, I get to leave Iran."

"After all," said Lermontov, "Khomeini decided when the Shah should leave Iran. If he can decide for the King of Kings, why not for an American spy?"

"Yeah, I guess," said Frank. "But I still don't like it."

"No doubt the Shah didn't like it either," said Lermontov, "but even he had to bow to the forces of history. And now he goes from Egypt, not to America, but to Morocco. I begin to wonder if he's no longer welcome in America."

"I hope he's still welcome," said Frank. Under the eye of the Russian safe-house camera, they exchanged a look, a look that said Lermontov wondered if he himself still would be welcome in America. "I'm sure the welcome mat is still out."

"Let's hope so," said Lermontov.

"You know I meet with the *komiteh* that operate within the armed forces."

Frank nodded. He and Munair had met at the Damavand, again empty and quiet as a mausoleum. He thought of Belinsky living upstairs. And the danger he was in.

"One group I coordinate with are *homafaran*. Many are *Mojahedin,* close to Ayatollah Taleqani. Some of them know you, from the gym at Dowshan Tappeh."

"Sometimes we worked out together."

"They mentioned you because they know I work with Jayface. But I did not tell them that we . . . discuss."

"Good," said Frank.

"Yes. Since they are *Mojahedin,* it could become dangerous for them to know. They plan to take over the airport, Mehrabad Airport, within a few days, force the Bakhtiar government to reopen it. They do not expect serious resistance from the army troops who occupied it on orders from Bakhtiar."

"What about the Bodyguard?" asked Frank.

"The *homafaran* believe the Bodyguard will not act. They have air force pilots who are with them who will fly over Mehrabad in F-4s and helicopters as the *homafaran* move in. Even General Gharabaghi, they believe, will not order the soldiers to fire."

"Are they right?"

"Yes," said Munair. "The *homafaran* are right."

"And they do this so the Imam can return?"

"They are good men. Of the left but faithful to Islam. They will make it possible for the Imam to return."

"When?"

"When the time comes the time will come swiftly. It is already too late for the Imam to lead tomorrow's prayer meeting as we—as the *komiteh*—had planned. But the plan now will bring him here in time to lead prayers next Friday."

"At the cemetery?"

"Yes. The *homafaran* will take over the airport on Tuesday. They will force the government to reopen it with air traffic controllers, full ground crews, and so forth by Wednesday in time for the Imam to leave France that evening and arrive here on Thursday."

"But none of the airlines have flights coming in. How will he get here?"

"That I do not know. But he will come, and soon you must go."

"I see."

"I hope you see. A few weeks ago gunmen murdered an American official at NIOC. For the first time we have undisciplined, angry people who now have guns to match their anger. We do not need the embarrassment of having an American diplomat murdered in the name of the revolution. You should leave as quickly as you can, but you must get Mr. Belinsky out of our country immediately. He is in great danger."


"Get back downstairs and get cranking on a cable on the airport takeover," said Rocky, alone with Frank in his plastic sanctuary on the third floor. "Quote what Munair said about the Islamic Republic. You're right. It is important, but no one will pay any fuckin' attention."

"That's what I was afraid of," said Frank.

"I better have a talk with Chuck," said Rocky.

"Can you get him out of here?" asked Frank.

"I'll ask the Holy Ghost t' authorize it. Maybe can get him on a military flight to Incirlik. If there are any military flights. Call it an emergency medevac. Which is about the fuckin' truth."

"Can we sanitize Munair's stuff for Lermontov?"

"Gimme a day or so to clear with the Holy Ghost. I'll tell him we need a quick okay so we can stay ahead of the curve with Lermontov on the airport takeover. Tell you the truth, right now I worry more about keepin' Belinsky alive than I do about keepin' Lermontov happy."

"Me, too," said Frank.

"Fact, soon's I finish up with you, think I'll mosey over to that hotel of his 'cross the street. Maybe try t' have dinner with'm."

Frank noticed Rocky had begun to run his words together even more than usual. Closer to the Bronx, thought Frank. He wondered if that also meant farther from Langley. The Rocky molded by Soviet Division would not cross Takht-e Jamshid to look after Belinsky.

"Okay if I come along?" he asked.

Rocky studied him. "I dunno. You worry me sometimes. You got a knack for drawin' trouble like shit draws flies."

"Gee, thanks."

"What the hell," said Rocky. "Come on. I can only get killed once."

# CHAPTER TWENTY-ONE

They found Belinsky already seated at a table in the Damavand's dining room. A tall, empty glass and a full pitcher of iced tea sat before him. He called out to them.

"Hey, guys. Having dinner?"

"We thought we might," said Rocky.

A sad-eyed waiter took their coats.

"Join me? I could use some company. Never thought I'd see you here, Mr. Novak."

"Slumming," said Rocky as he pulled out a chair and sat directly opposite Belinsky, facing the arched opening to the lobby.

Belinsky seemed nervous, but then, thought Frank, Rocky could affect people that way. He sat close to Belinsky so that both faced Rocky. Rocky studied each briefly, then raised his eyes to scan the archway behind them that opened on the lobby. He slipped his right hand inside his suit jacket, pulled out his Browning nine millimeter, and laid it on the table.

"There's a reason for that, Chuck."

"I was hoping there wasn't."

"There's a reason. Tell'm, Sully."

"Couple of reasons," said Frank. He wondered if Rocky had already primed a bullet into the chamber. "I have some new tapes, including one that goes only to select clergymen. Your friend Shariat-Madari doesn't get one."

"But . . . why not?"

"Because . . ." Frank heard a scuffle behind him. He turned to see their waiter pushed aside by a man in a ski mask with an Uzi. Frank saw two, three others, also armed.

"Duck," yelled Frank.

He and Rocky hit the floor. He tried to pull Belinsky down with him, but his arm bounced off Belinsky's back. Belinsky, his back to the gunmen, never moved till the bullets struck him. The force of the bullets thrust his body forward. He slithered against the table, slipped off his chair, and landed on Frank, pinning him to the floor. Face down, Frank could see nothing but the tiles of the floor. He had never noticed them before. The tiles were blue and white. And flecked with blood. Mine? Belinsky's? He heard the thud of feet, rapidly retreating, and the excited babble of Farsi voices. He managed to get his hands under him and struggled to free himself of the weight of Belinsky. Belinsky rolled over on his side. Frank looked into his staring blue eyes. His mouth hung open. "Scream," said Frank, half aloud. Scream.

He pushed Belinsky onto on his back, saw but barely registered the blood that covered them both. He wondered if he'd been shot or if Belinsky had taken all the bullets. You suicidal bastard. He tried pounding, pumping on Belinsky's heart. Blood spurted from one of the bullet holes against the palm of his hand. He leaned closer to press his mouth against Belinsky's.

"Give it up, Sullivan. He's dead as he's gonna get."

Frank straightened himself, aware of Belinsky's blood, aware of the hepatitis that had infected them both. Aware of how deadly it could be. Aware of suicide. Of bullets. Of death. Of the *fatwa,* wondering if the *fatwa* had claimed Belinsky's life and wondering what had spared his. He heard a voice and looked in the direction of the voice but couldn't bring Rocky into focus.

"You had your gun," he hollered. "Why didn't you stop it?"

"I've been tryin' to stop it," said Rocky. "For months. But you wouldn't listen. Both 'a yiz. Piss me off."

Rocky bent over Belinsky, two fingers of his left hand pressed to the carotid artery in his throat. He held the Browning in his right. He looked at Frank and shook his head.

"You could've used the gun," whispered Frank.

"Against four guys with Uzis? It wasn't even cocked. All's I wanted to do was put some fear of God into Chuck. How serious this shit is. You and him . . . you act like it's a game."

"Suicidal bastard," muttered Frank.

"Wadja say?"

"Nothing. Just talking to myself."


They sat, both silent, in Rocky's office, Frank still wearing the stains of Belinsky's drying blood. He studied the spots that freckled the backs of his hands and the dark circles and streaks against the dark blue sleeves of the suit jacket he wore.

"The ambassador took it pretty calm," he said at last.

Rocky did not respond. Still talking to myself, thought Frank. He knew he had to push himself up from his chair but could find no way to make his muscles react. He hoped Gus would be asleep but knew he would still be up, having one last glass of wine before tackling the dinner dishes. *What the hell happened to you?* He did not want to answer Gus's question. What the hell happened?

"You guessed it the other day, didn't you?" said Rocky. "Chuck was one of ours."

"Then why didn't you use that goddamn gun?"

"One Browning," sneered Rocky. "Four Uzis."

"Only three Uzis," said Frank. "One of those guys used something else."

"Wadda you talking about?"

"Maybe that Czech machine pistol you told me about. Guy with his left sleeve hanging loose. And a black hood pulled up over his ski mask."

"Belinsky's driver," said Rocky.

"*Savak,*" said Frank.

"We own those bastards," said Rocky.

"Maybe we don't own them anymore," said Frank.

"We own them," said Rocky, banging his fist down on his oak desk. "We own them and they gunned down one of ours," He glanced at Frank. "Not many people knew he was, you know."

Frank nodded.

"We kept it pretty tight."

"Even from me," said Frank.

"Especially from you. Even within our own shop, we kept it pretty tight. And you're a fuckin' agent, an outsider, remember?"

"You make it hard to forget."

"No need for you to know. I gotta live with that rest 'a my life. One of our own. On the analyst side. Got shifted over t' operations when the shit started gettin' real thick over here. Good Farsi, all that. Plus Russian. Lived his cover. Ambassador went along with the game real good. Best consular officer I ever saw. Always took care of his cover job first. Like you're 'sposed to."

Frank remembered how Pete Howard had drilled the same operational mantra into him long ago in Ethiopia. Always take care of your cover job first.

"Half the time Chuck even had me believin' that was his real job," said Rocky. "Never recruited anybody up in Tabriz but found out more about what was goin' on up there than we really wanted to know. We thought it was all Soviets up there, wantin' t' take over the rest of Azerbaijan. Chuck kept sayin' no. It was about national pride and Islam. Nobody wanted to listen."

"You think he was right?"

"I'm startin' t' wonder."

"It's a little late," said Frank.

———

The week bumped by, rattling like their now seldom-used Fiat over the potholes in their routine. General Merid announced to the Jayface team that an American CIA agent, Charles Belinsky, had been assassinated. He asked Frank and Gus if they knew anything about it.

"I was with him . . . having dinner with this Mr. Belinsky when he was shot," said Frank. "But I didn't know he was CIA." At least not for sure. Until a few minutes later. I could have saved him, he thought. How? I should have saved him. By not putting him in harm's way. He remembered Rocky's words. *One of ours. The rest of my life, I have to live with this.*

Thunder and lightning, he thought. Rocky had thought there should be drum rolls, thunder, and lightning when Belinsky brought off the entrapment of the GRU man Lermontov had targeted. Someone had delivered the thunder and lightning. But who? And why? Had it been *Savama* zealots executing the *fatwa*? Or had the gunmen wanted to kill Rocky? Or me?

Frank knew it was a long shot, but late that night, with no lights on behind him, he put a fresh chalk mark on his front door.

The next evening, at seven-thirty-five according to Frank's Timex, Lermontov's white Peugeot flashed its lights in the driveway of the American safe house they'd used before.

"I have no answers," said Lermontov once they'd settled themselves at the walnut-stained dining room table. "Your man did a good job setting up Yevteshenko. One of our Azerbaijani KGB men got the photograph, high-speed film and natural lighting, without being seen. From one of our agents at Iranian immigration I'd already gotten a copy of Belinsky's passport, with photo. Yevteshenko helped by making a great blunder. He told our interrogators Belinsky was just repaying a loan. Said they were friends and he'd loaned Belinsky some money. He thought he was covering up his Aeroflot ticket racket. He and his Aeroflot contact had done a good job of covering the paper trail on their swindle. When they changed their stories, they had no way to prove what they had been doing. It's almost amusing, isn't it?"

Frank noticed that Lermontov did not smile. Maybe not so amusing, he thought.

"Two crooks," continued Lermontov, "trying hard to prove they really are crooks. And not being able to do it. Now the Aeroflot man is also suspected of being an American agent."

"What happens next?" asked Frank.

"Both return to Moscow. For further questioning."

"Does that mean you're in the clear?"

"For now at least. In fact, in the language of capitalism, you might say my stock has gone up. I not only have recruited an American CIA agent, one Francis X. Sullivan, I have also uncovered a Soviet GRU traitor, one Fedor Yevteshenko. Since KGB hates GRU, that makes me quite a hero."

"Then why have Belinsky killed?"

"What do you mean?"

"Someone had him killed," said Frank. "And damned near had me killed."

"Don't be stupid. Every time a shot goes off in your neighborhood you want to blame me. First it was Beirut. Now here. Truly stupid. Killing you would be like killing myself. You are my only hope of getting to America."

"Not you," said Frank. "But maybe GRU."

"You know the rule. We don't kill each other. That can only lead to endless reprisal."

"Someone had him killed."

"Ask your Iranian friends," said Lermontov. "Who would benefit . . . who would want Belinsky dead? Or you? Or my good friend Mr. Novak?"


On schedule and without resistance from the army, the *homafaran* took over Mehrabad Airport on Tuesday. In a show of force, the Imperial Bodyguard paraded through Tehran, setting off fresh rumors of a military coup. But the Bodyguard did nothing but march. The Bakhtiar government capitulated and had the airport fully operational by Wednesday. That evening, aboard a chartered silver and blue Air France 747, Ayatollah Khomeini with a large following of aides and international journalists took off from Paris. The next morning, without incident, they landed at Mehrabad.

Once again, the possibility of violence confined Frank to watching history unfold on television. This time, Gus joined him.

"This isn't very Islamic of us, is it?" said Gus. "Sitting here with our skepticism hanging out, nursing our respective Scotch neat and vodka chilled. Mourning our own dead and watching the great unwashed greet their holy savior."

The night before, Frank thought, I witnessed more than just the possibility of violence. And escaped alive. If I were still a Catholic, I'd want to go to confession. To be absolved . . . for what? For being alive. If Belinsky were alive, he'd be watching Khomeini's descent from the heavens. Watching and understanding. I don't understand. Maybe that's why I'm guilty.

"Couple of chair potatoes," rambled Gus, testing words against the vacuum. "Butts in one chair. Feet propped on another. Staring at the flickering tube."

"Makes you wonder, doesn't it?" said Frank.

"Wonder what?"

"What kind of an intelligence agency we are. One of the most important days in the history of an important ally and we get our only information by watching television with audio in a language we don't understand."

"Better than being out there in that mess," said Gus.

"I wish we had Anwar," said Frank, "or someone, to tell us what the announcer has to say."

"I think I'd rather not know." The set's color balance had blinked out soon after Khomeini's plane set down. "I like it this way," said Gus, "History should be black and white. Color makes it propaganda. Like what announcers have to say."

"You may be right, except I'd like to know what the propaganda line looks like." Better yet, thought Frank, not Anwar. Munair with his egg-shaped, blood-flecked stigmata and true-believer's sensibility would make the ideal interpreter. But he knew Munair would be at the airport, as close to his Imam as possible. Anwar described himself as reasonably devout, and the reasonable part, the rational, skeptical part, kept breaking through. Munair would see the arrival of Khomeini with the eyes of a believer.

He'd been trying to keep Belinsky and the scene at the Damavand out of his mind. Now he wished neither Anwar nor Munair sat with them but Belinsky, alive, jaundiced skin but no bullet holes, understanding and explaining. Why did Christ die? He died for our sins. He felt some part of himself had died when Belinsky fell. His back muscles twitched. He thought of the blood of the flagellants on *Ashura,* the blood of the martyrs at Karbala. He had not been able to see the face of Ayatollah Khomeini in the full moon, but he saw his own image in the blood on the blue and white tiles of the Damavand's dining room floor. He stared at his glass of Absolut and thought of hepatitis and alcohol. In Lermontov's absence, he did not attempt to gulp his vodka but sipped it and held it in his mouth, hoping it would numb his mind.

He fixed his attention on a CBS camera crew among the crushed journalists trying to elbow their way closer to Khomeini. Before the day ended, somewhere in Los Angeles, with its eleven-and-a-half-hour time differential, Anwar and Mina would watch the scene he and Gus watched now. He wondered what they would think. He wondered if news of Belinsky's murder had appeared in American news media.

He decided Gus might be right. The black-and-white color scheme worked well, at least for Khomeini and his hold on history. Frank knew his voice, but, except for photographs and posters, he had never seen him before. His black turban sat like a crown above the full white beard that framed his wizened face and fierce dark eyes. The Shah has gone, thought Frank. Long live the Imam. But before his phalanx of armed bodyguards could get him from the plane to the airport lounge, the jostling of the crowd knocked the black turban from his head, revealing the bald pate beneath.

"He's not God," said Gus. "He's just a skinhead like me."

Somehow an Iranian cameraman must have managed to fight his way into the lounge, where a heated argument flared among the revolutionary guards. Frank caught the announcer's words, *"Maydan-e Shahyad,"* Shahyad Square, the towering monument in the vast traffic circle outside the airport on the main route into town. The television crews did an excellent job, cutting to a scene, evidently taken from a helicopter, of Shahyad Square, choked with people, then to shots of the mobs that clogged the roads, then to a Chevrolet Blazer surrounded by armed guards parked in front of the airport terminal. The announcer had to shout over the screams of the crowd. The camera next showed an armored personnel carrier bulling its way to the tarmac side of the airport lounge. A wedge of armed men opened the way for Khomeini to make his way into the military vehicle.

Revolutionary guards, aides in European-style suits and open-necked shirts, and one intrepid cameraman accompanied him. The personnel carrier made its way forward, carefully at first, then picking up speed at the edge of the crowd, heading to the far end of the field, where a helicopter waited, its blades slowly turning. They watched the Imam ascend again into the heavens.

The cameraman kept working, sweeping the interior of the helicopter. He focused on Khomeini, turban again in place, who chatted, amiably it seemed, with his aides. The camera switched to shots of the millions below as the chopper swung low over the city. They watched as the camera scanned what Frank later learned was the soccer field of a walled-in girls' high school in the eastern part of the city, not far from Dowshan Tappeh. A media-savvy aide evidently arranged for the lone cameraman to leave the helicopter first, so the Imam's arrival could be recorded live and, suddenly, in color, as the screen blipped in their front room.

"Propaganda," said Gus.

The next day they watched Khomeini's televised pilgrimage, again by helicopter, to Behest-e Zahra cemetery to lead a Friday prayer meeting in honor of the revolution's martyrs.

"He's got it," said Gus. "Even if he is a bald old man. In my day they called it pizzazz. Charisma, that's the word now. The old Ayatollah's got charisma."

He's got it, thought Frank. Though he could detect nothing in the Ayatollah's presence to account for it, the response of the multitude around him conferred it. The awed, uplifted faces. The screaming efforts to get close to him, to touch him. The cemetery appeared barren, graves dug in scrub desert. The wretched of the earth go to earth in this wretched landscape. How far from Nirvana? How far from Niavaran? What would happen to the Shah's palace now? he wondered. Another man who overthrew the despot would move into his citadel. Khomeini would not. Whatever it is he's got, thought Frank, he's got it. Then he saw it. Yes, he has the people. And they have anointed him.

On Saturday morning, the depleted Jayface team seemed spent.

"We confront a new situation," said the general, standing at the head of the table.

He cleared his throat, and Frank noticed for the first time that Munair worked a set of what Americans called worry beads.

"We must be prepared," said General Merid, "to . . . how shall I say it . . . shift gears? Yes. The armed forces remain loyal, as they should, to the legitimate government. At present represented by Prime Minister Shapour Bakhtiar. But, who knows, another government soon may be named. Headed, so some people say, by a very devout leader of the National Front, Mahdi Barzagan. Captain Irfani, can you perhaps enlighten us?"

Munair looked from his beads to the general, then back to his beads. "No," he said.

"Ah." The general did one of his brief up-and-down toe dances. "Perhaps we need to seek guidance from General Kasravi. Major Sullivan, could you help us in that regard?"

Someone's been priming him, thought Frank. General Merid seemed both better informed and more aggressive than Frank previously had known him.

"I could try to speak to General Kasravi," Frank said.

"Good," said General Merid. "Meanwhile, I should like each of us to begin to consider what role our group should play in whatever government the military supports. We will cut today's meeting short to give each of us a chance to prepare comments on this question by tomorrow. Informal, verbal comments, but, if you please, well-thought-out comments on our role in loyal-ity to the government likely to be in power."

The odd pronunciation struck Frank. "Loyal-ity." It sounds as if his loyalty is divided, he thought.

"Thank you," said the general. "That will be all for today."

"What the fuck is he up to?" said Gus as Frank turned the Nova through the gates of Supreme Commander's Headquarters for their return trip to Dowshan Tappeh.

"He's your agent," said Frank.

"God help me," said Gus. "I've got a safe house meet with him tonight. I'll see what he has to say about what he said."


They had abandoned the Damavand in favor of the Kayhan Hotel, also close to the embassy but less risky than the scene of Belinsky's murder. Frank asked Munair about his beads.

"No," said Munair. "We do not call them worry beads. *Tassbead*. Mine are of stone, though today plastic has become common. We use them to count out thirty-three repetitions of *Allah-o akbar*. Since *Ashura,* many people now add *Khomeini rakbar*. 'God is great. Khomeini is our leader.' I love the Imam, but that is blasphemy."

"Do you think the followers of the Imam go too far?"

"Yes."

Frank again probed for a way to recruit Munair. "Soon," he said, "we will have to leave. The Americans, the Israelis, possibly even the British will have to leave. We will have no ears and eyes. No bridge to the Islamic government. You could play a unique role."

"I understand what you seek. But do not ask me again. I will talk only to you. Only as long as you are here."

"That may not be for long," said Frank.

"It should not. I have tried to warn you. And I told you often to warn Mr. Belinsky."

"I warned him. Often. We were going to warn him again that night. But he wouldn't listen."

"Do you?"

"I'm listening" said Frank.

"Do you know what saved your life when the men in the ski masks shot Mr. Belinsky?"

He tried to respond. I hit the floor. I hid under the dead man. Maybe Belinsky saved my life. But a spasm of fear tightened his throat. His mouth turned dry, then tasted of bile. Finally, he managed to scratch out a mumbled "No."

"*Savak.*"

"*Savak?*" muttered Frank. "How could *Savak* save my life?"

"The last time we met, do you remember?"

Frank nodded and tried to remember.

"I told you certain members of *Savak* have formed a revolutionary *komiteh* called *Savama* and that some of these men kept watch on your Mr. Belinski."

"Is that who shot him?"

"No. If it had been *Savama* members, they would have killed you as well as Belinsky. What happened at the Damavand may have been the last gasp of the Shah's *Savak*. They were men angered by the way Belinsky embarrassed them by helping Major Amini escape and by collaborating with a Soviet GRU official, all without *Savak* being able to stop them. They thought that by killing Belinsky they could keep the *Savama* loyalists from killing you both as Hojatalislam Qomi Mohammad had ordered in his *fatwa*."

"But why?" said Frank. "What difference would it make?"

"It would mean that *Savak* officials loyal to the Shah were still in control."

Frank shook his head, wondering if *Savak* members who shared General Merid's strange notion of "loyal-ity" had saved his life.

"I'll never understand," he said.

"Of course not," said Merid. "You are not Persian."

Uniquely Persian. Frank remembered the phrase Anwar the Smarter had used.

"You're right," said Frank. "I guess I never will understand."

"As I told you," said Munair, "the real target of the *fatwa* was not Charles Belinsky but Ayatollah Shariat-Madari. And you did not meet with Shariat-Madari. Only Mr. Belinsky did. You were included in the *fatwa* only because of one man."

"He was there," said Frank. "The man with one arm."

"Mr. Belinsky's driver. He had driven Mr. Belinsky to the airport to help your friend Major Amini and his family to escape from Iran. He had driven Mr. Belinsky to meetings with the GRU agent he worked with. And after all that he drove Mr. Belinsky and you to the university. Only he had reason to see you both dead. And he prevailed with the Hojatalislam to name you both in his *fatwa*."

"But he's *Savak* agent," said Frank. "Correct?"

"That is correct. At least for the moment. He will, I suspect, soon become *Savama*."

"Then why do you say *Savak* saved my life?"

"The others who were with him, *Savak* officials still loyal, I believe, to the Shah. They reasoned that killing Mr. Belinsky would fulfill the Hojatalislam's aim of embarrassing Ayatollah Shariat-Madari. They saw no need to kill you, a man known to be close to the Shah."

"I can't believe I have reason to be grateful to *Savak*," said Frank.

"You do," said Munair. "But you must realize, sooner or later, perhaps much sooner, the *Savama* element within *Savak* will prevail. And the killing of Mr. Belinsky does not relieve you of the Hojatalislam's *fatwa*. That sentence of death is still an obligation for all Muslims who accept his authority. It will be with you, not only here, but, if you survive that long, it will be with you in America."


Frank had started to think of Rocky's bubble as a plastic mausoleum where the dead could communicate without fear of being overheard. Someday vandals would over-run the cemetery and collapse the mausoleum around their heads. And the dead would stop communicating. But now, knowing how close he had come, he felt like one of the dead. And he had come to let Rocky know that he had also come close.

"I knew about that *fatwa* crap, but I guess I didn't take it serious enough. I didn't think we for real coulda got our asses blown off because one holy man wants to make another look bad."

"Things like that happen when you stick your nose in other people's business," said Frank.

"We get paid to stick our nose in other people's business," said Rocky.

"I know," said Frank. He shivered and looked at his hands. "And Belinsky paid a hell of a price."

"I gotta give'm credit," said Rocky. "He put himself on the line."

"Again and again. All those trips to Qom. Taking me to the university to corner Lermontov. Setting up the GRU guy. I know he had his weaknesses, but it takes a lot to do what Chuck did."

"Yeah, it does. And you're right. He paid a hell of a price." Rocky didn't dwell on Belinsky's virtues for long. "Your buddy Munair, he give up any names?"

Funeral's over, thought Frank. Back to business. Munair had provided the names of the scheming clergyman and all four gunmen.

"He said the leader of the pack recognized you."

"Eagle-4," said Rocky, scanning the list. "Had a meet with'm just a couple weeks back. He was still talkin' a pretty good pro-Shah line."

"From what Munair said, maybe he is still pro-Shah. But another one was Chuck's taxi driver. According to Munair, that guy wanted to blow away all three of us. Argument, all in whispers, got pretty hot. Munair thinks another minute they might've started blasting away at each other till Eagle-4 pumped a couple into Chuck and everybody else turned and did the same."

"How's Munair know all this shit?"

"He coordinates the work of the *komiteh*. All the *komiteh*. Including *Savama*."

"Write it up," said Rocky.


After a street-corner pickup, Lermontov had him driven to a safe house new to Frank. He served Stolichnaya, but no caviar.

"Your material on the takeover of the airport proved both timely and accurate. Moscow approved a modest bonus, also for your cable on the penetration of *Savak*."

He handed Frank a letter-size envelope and poured them each a long draught of vodka. Frank hefted the envelope.

"A thousand?" he guessed.

"Correct," said Lermontov. "You're getting so used to your dirty pieces of silver, you don't even have to count them anymore. That's good." They clinked glasses. Lermontov swallowed his vodka in a Russian gulp. Frank took a deep breath and did the same.

"You still aren't a Russian," said Lermontov, "but at least you try."

Fearful of attracting attention anywhere in town, Frank and Munair met again at the navy's all but deserted building on the grounds of Supreme Commander's Headquarters.

"Representatives of the air force say they will meet with Ayatollah Khomeini after morning prayers at the Alawi Girls' School within two days and pledge their allegiance to him," Munair said. "If they go through with this, and I believe they will, representatives of the revolutionary *komiteh* in the army and navy will do the same."

"How representative are the committees?"

"At this stage, all but totally."

"There must be some who have doubts," ventured Frank.

"Always there will be some who harbor doubts," said Munair. "But fear will silence the doubters. Otherwise, the *komiteh* represent all. All but the most senior officers. And even some senior officers."

"How did you hear this?"

"Of course, through my contacts with the *komiteh*."

Frank thought of Anwar the Taller, the *Mojahedin,* and Anwar the Smarter, the doubter. Sorry, he thought. There's two the Islamic *komiteh* don't represent.

"Something else," Munair hesitated, then added softly, "I have not been authorized by my contacts on the *komiteh* to tell you. But now that the danger has passed, I can speak. The head of the air force, Amir-Hossein Rabii, proposed to the other generals that the air force should shoot down the plane bringing the Imam home, or at least force it to land in a remote area where troops on the ground could safely arrest him."

"Didn't the generals realize what would happen if they tried anything that dumb?"

"Of course," said Munair. "No one supported him. And the leaders of the military *komiteh* warned the Imam's people in Paris. They were very clever. They invited over a hundred journalists from all over the world, including many Americans, to fly with the Imam aboard his plane. And they let the world know it. In any event, by that time, General Rabii could not have found enough air force personnel to carry out his craziness."

"Thank God," said Frank.

*"Allah-o akbar,"* said Munair.

At their Jayface meeting General Merid told them that Ayatollah Khomeini, not more than an hour earlier, had named Mahdi Bazargan as head of the provisional Islamic government. Two weeks ago, Munair provided a tape on which Khomeini told religious leaders he would name Bazargan within days of his return. Now, four days after his jet set down at Meharabad, he had done so.

"I have no complaints about how soon you let me know what you know," said Frank.

"Thank you," said Munair.

"I only wish you would stay in touch after I leave."

"You do not give up, do you?" said Munair.

"Do you?"

"I am a Muslim. We can never give up our faith."


"How many of these places do you have?" asked Frank.

After another street-corner pickup, Lermontov had driven him to yet another safe house.

"An instructor in our training program once told a joke," said Lermontov. "He said there are four things there's no such thing as too many of. Too many mistresses for a Frenchman; too many drinks for an Irishman; too much money for a Jew; and too many safe houses for a KGB officer."

Frank did not respond.

"Are you sensitive about the Irishman? Or the Jew?" Frank shrugged. "Myself," said Lermontov, "I don't like the part about the Jew. We Russians are far too casual about our history in that regard."

"You aren't alone," said Frank.


Rocky and Frank sat opposite each other under the bubble. Rocky skimmed the material Lermontov had provided.

"Not much," said Rocky.

"No," agreed Frank. "Meeting every other day is more than we need to swap stories, but it could be less than we need if Lermontov suddenly gets the hook."

"Anything cookin' on that front?"

"Not since the GRU and Aeroflot guys got pulled out."

"Good," said Rocky. "At this point, no news may be the best news."

"That include no news from Henry James on the mole?"

"Not a peep. But that's his way. James expects everybody else to tell him everything they know. But he don't tell nobody nothin'."

"One other thing," said Frank. He related what Munair had told him about the plans for the air force and probably other military units to make a public avowal of loyalty to Khomeini and the aborted proposal to shoot down Khomeini's plane.

"Do a cable on the pledge of allegiance," said Rocky, "for what it's worth. The other's old news. The generals used their ambassador in Washington to try to get U.S. approval from Brzezinski. You really got no need to know this, but the way I get it the basic answer was . . . what's that guy in the Bible? Pontius Pilate, right? You wanna stage a coup? We wash our hands. You wanna shoot holy Khomeini's plane outta the sky? Pass the soap."

"Nothing I like better," said Frank, "than peddling old news."

"Don't sweat it," said Rocky, returning his attention to Lermontov's thin material. "Your KGB buddy also asks if you checked out our new safe house."

"Twice," said Frank. "Tried the keys. Checked the rooms. Looks good. Except I worry about the neighborhood."

"How come?"

"Well, it's so American." Frank had found the safe house on the same block as the U.S. Air Force guards' bachelor quarters.

"Yeah, well, let's face it. You're not gonna be havin' a whole lot of meets there. Maybe only one, and that one prob'ly after the shit hits the fan, so the less drivin' through town you gotta do the better. 'Sides, I shouldn't tell you this, 'cause the ambassador doesn't want folks to panic, but we've got some emergency plans to get all the Americans together in protected compounds where we can round them up in a hurry in case we have to evacuate in a hurry. And you and Gus and a bunch of others from that part of town have reservations at a compound on that block. So when the shit hits the fan, which it will real soon, you'll be livin' on the same block as your safe house."

"Sounds convenient for me," said Frank. "But it's a long way from Lermontov's place."

"Yeah, I know, but hell, he needs to get used to hangin' out in an American neighborhood. You have any problems with the safe house, Steele's in charge of it now. He's also got keys."

"Good," said Frank.

"Your buddy also says, 'If we can't meet at my place some day, let's try your new place for the next three days starting at four.' He says he won't be wired. But listen to this part. He says, 'Do not forget. I am still not in America. But our penetration agent is. He may still do us harm.'"

"He's right," said Frank. "We bought some time, but until we get Lermontov to the States safe and sound, we aren't out of the woods."

"Fuck Lermontov," said Rocky. "Until we get all of us back to the States, none of us are fucking safe."

Not even then, thought Frank, remembering what Munair had told him about the *fatwa* that would follow him even to America.


Realizing they had little to discuss, General Merid had decided the Jayface team would not meet on Thursday as well as Friday. Unexpectedly, Munair showed up at Dowshan Tappeh late Thursday morning.

"You must forgive me for coming here."

"Of course," said Frank. He knew something important must have prompted such a breach of normal procedures. "Did you have trouble getting through the gates?"

"General Kasravi paved the way with a call to the commander of the air force. This is about the air force, you see."

Stan Rushmore had abandoned his office to Frank on Munair's arrival.

"Early this morning," said Munair, "airmen in uniform demonstrated openly outside the Alawi Girls' School in support of the Ayatollah and the Bazargan government. I came all this way to tell you because . . . their defiance . . . General Kasravi, of course, is very well informed. He contacted me through Admiral Hayati."

"He expects trouble?"

"General Kasravi said the Bodyguard will not tolerate the defiance by the air force or by any other sector of the armed forces. He said he wanted you to know this and asked if I could contact you. I said I would try."

"Thank you," said Frank.

"We expect . . . we expect to see violence. Very soon. Military arsenals have been looted. The people, neighborhood *komiteh,* have sidearms. They have no training. But the *Mojahedin,* the *Feda'iyan,* they now have heavy weapons and they are well disciplined. And many defectors from the military now will defend the Islamic Republic."

"Where do you expect trouble?" asked Gus.

"Here," said Munair.

"Here?" echoed Frank.

"It could begin at the university. Bazargan speaks at the prayer meeting there tomorrow. It could be at Jaleh Square. It could be at any of the prisons or military installations. But we believe here. The *homafaran* are united, and they have won most of the air force to their side."

"How soon?" said Frank.

Munair shrugged. "*Inshallah,* never. But perhaps much sooner."

# PART IV

# CHAPTER TWENTY-TWO

Early winter dark had begun to settle in when they heard the first firing. "Is that the sound of shit hitting the fan?" said Gus, hunched over the IBM Selectric in Stan Rushmore's office.

Heavy feet thudded down the hallway, echoing the gunfire. Frank hurried to the door in time to see Cantwell and Steele rushing outside. The treble of rockets and the bass of flares stretched the scale that accompanied the unseen battle.

Frank's throat tightened. He took a deep breath and managed to say, "Let's go watch."

They stuffed papers and ribbons into the safe, locked it, and pulled on parkas and stocking caps. Outside in the frozen air, they could distinguish the crackle of automatic weapons from the thump of heavier equipment. Stuttering helicopter rotors drew their eyes to circling raptors that spat down rockets and heavy-caliber machine-gun fire. Whatever forces contended, the struggle crackled within the base's Iranian section. Bill Steele had driven Frank through that section and out a back gate on their way to Anwar's compound. It had seemed so tight, so disciplined, so secure then. Now chaos echoed from that quarter, and Frank wondered what direction the rebellion followed.

"Maybe we should go home," said Gus.

"Maybe we should try," said Frank. He checked the pocket of his parka and found the keys to the bulletproof Nova. They got no farther than the chained gates.

"Trouble," said the Iranian air force guard. "Trouble on Damavand. Trouble coming."

Frank backed the Nova away from the gate, U-turned, and pulled up outside their Quonset hut. "Looks like we're here for the duration," he said.

Bill Steele hurtled past them. "Don't ask," he said as he thumped inside. They followed him into Troy's office.

"Hold on a second," said Troy into his secure phone to Rocky's office. "Whatcha got?"

"Bodyguard," said Steele. "They've had a unit here watching over the air force types. They got into it with the *homafaran* and a bunch of civilian techies."

"Those guys don't have guns," said Troy.

"They do now," said Steele. "Must have raided the arsenal. They've got air force military police with them. Bodyguards let loose with rockets and flares, helicopter gunships, I guess just to scare the air force guys, but they didn't scare. Bunch of American advisers got trapped over there, and tell him we got a bunch of other Americans trapped here."

"Like us," muttered Gus.

Troy repeated it all to Rocky, then listened, grunted, and hung up.

"He'll get the ambassador on it," said Troy. "He's got special phone numbers for some of Khomeini's honchos. Maybe they can help, but meanwhile we better break out weapons."

Frank put in a bid for a Browning nine millimeter.

"You know you're not checked out on it," said Steele.

"I'm not checked out on anything," said Frank. "But I did learn how to use one."

"Unofficially?"

Frank nodded.

"Not good enough," said Steele. "Besides, for what we might be up against an automatic's not your best weapon." He unlocked and swung open the doors of a tall steel cabinet. Chain-locked gun racks and deep metal drawers, each with its own thick padlock, glared out at them. "Shotguns are what you guys need. If anything."

"Let's hope nothing," said Gus. "God willing and the creek don't rise."

"Take a couple of these," said Steele, undoing the chains on a rack of shotguns. "Winchester M97s. Twelve-gauge, buckshot. Designed for riot control. Pump action, five-shot magazines." He demonstrated the pump action and showed them how to release and insert the tubular magazine.

"We can count on the *homafaran* and the Bodyguard keeping their war to themselves, but word is some of these Islamic committees are on their way to help out the *homafaran*. Most likely, they'll come from the area around Jaleh Square, which means they'll hit the base from the other side. But others are out on Damavand, setting bonfires, burning tires, in case the Bodyguard tries to send in reinforcements from that direction."

"Basically," said Gus, "you just told us the hostiles have us surrounded."

"Basically," said Steele. "And if they try to come over or through our fences, we'll have you out there with some of the rest of us and some air force guards on a firing line. Shotguns and tear gas grenade launchers. I'll get gas masks for you. The idea is to stop the crowd, not shoot or kill anybody. What you do with the shotguns, you don't fire at the crowd. You fire at the ground in front of them.

That way, you turn the ground into shrapnel that skips into the crowd, low, along with your buckshot. Nobody gets killed, but it hurts like hell and can turn a crowd around in a hurry."

"Suppose they shoot back?" said Gus.

"If they're armed, heavily armed, we forget about it. Pull back in here and try to negotiate our way out. I'll give you guys an extra magazine each. If ten rounds of buckshot from each of a bunch of us, plus tear gas, doesn't turn them . . ." He left the sentence unfinished.

Cantwell, his face flushed from running through the cold, hurried into the office. "The Iranian guards supposed to be at the gates . . ." He caught his breath. "They disappeared."

Frank hadn't seen the cafeteria so crowded since Sergeant Abbas had frightened off its customers. Close to fifty Americans and a handful of Iranian workers huddled around a uniformed air force officer. He introduced himself as Captain William Petry.

"As you can see, some of us are bearing weapons, but we believe this sector will not, repeat, will not face any danger." Petry's face, new to Frank, belied his words. Heavy frown lines betrayed the effort he made to keep his eyes from shifting toward the gunfire beyond the walls. "Calm is what's required. Our chances of leaving the base anytime soon do not, repeat, do not look good. Food and refreshments will be free. We've got some movies and some Super Bowl tapes we'll be running. So let's keep our heads and make the best of it. We'll keep you informed."

Cradling the shotgun he'd been issued, Frank walked outside. Cantwell, standing in the walkway, turned at the sound of the door. "Prob'ly not a good idea to be out here, sir." Full dark surrounded them.

"You're here."

"I have to be."

"What's going on?" said Frank. To his left he could see and hear evidence of the fighting that continued on the base.

"Take a look back the other way," said Cantwell. Frank turned and saw the rosy glow illuminating dozens of swirling funnels of smoke. His ears followed the turn of his eyes, and he now realized the thud and crackle of weapons sounded equally ominous on both sides of the spot where they stood.

"Bodyguard reinforcements trying to fight their way down Damavand," said Cantwell. "But all kinds of crazies out there have them bottled up. Bodyguard has tanks, but tanks aren't very effective for a war on city streets."

Frank looked at the abandoned guardhouse and the chained gates of the fence and remembered the faces pressed against it a few days earlier, chanting *"Shah raft"* and "Death to America." It seems nice and calm standing here right now, he thought, like standing in the eye of a hurricane.

"I have to believe the Bodyguard's not gonna make it through. Then, the crazies'll either hit us or they won't. If they do, I don't think our shotguns and tear gas'll do much good."

Frank looked up Damavand toward the flaming sky to the east. Maybe Belinsky's lucky, he thought. He doesn't have to worry about getting killed.

"Better get inside," said Cantwell.

"What about you?" said Frank.

"Colonel Troy assigned me to keep an eye on things out here. Report back if the hostiles got closer."

Frank headed back toward the cafeteria, but the thought of being trapped in a room taken over by an ancient Super Bowl tape depressed him. Then he thought of the gym. He grabbed the shotgun, headed for Rushmore's office, and changed into his gym gear: jock, shorts, sweat socks, seriously smelly T-shirt. He grabbed the lined leather gloves he used on the heavy bag, then stopped. If anyone came looking for him and didn't find him in Troy's office, he might trigger a panic. But he also feared Steele wouldn't like the idea of him being in the gym alone. The seriousness of the situation around them made him decide to play by the rules. Bill Steele must have sensed him coming. He turned from the football huddle as Frank approached.

"What the hell are you dressed up for?"

"Could I talk to you for a minute?"

Bill left the circle. Other eyes, including Troy's, followed him.

"You planning on a beach party or something?"

"Just the gym, but I thought I better let you know. Can I give you the shotgun?"

"You are a pisser, but I guess it's okay. All the doors over that side that lead outside are locked, bolted, and chained. The air force, our air force, has some guards on patrol. I'll let them know you'll be over there."

"Thanks," said Frank.

"And hang on to the shotgun. The air force has some guys up on the roof of their admin building across the way. They can see pretty good up Damavand, where the Bodyguard's bogged down, and across most of Douche Bag Tapper, where the fighting looks to have tapered off a bit. But no tellin' what may happen next. So hang on to the shotgun."

"Thanks, Bill. Want to come shoot some hoops?"

"You really are a pisser."

Frank flipped the switch near the door, flooding the courts with light. He hoped the lights wouldn't draw bullets, like moths to a candle. He laid down the shotgun and walked to the ball rack. He looked up at the high arched windows set like parentheses in the brick wall. He decided to give the moths a minute or two. When none came, he dribbled onto the court. Thirty minutes and a good sweat later, he returned the ball to its rack, picked up the shotgun and his gloves, flipped out the lights, and headed for the gym.

He groped in the dark for the light switch, then realized someone stood in the deep shadow at the far end of the room.

"Do not be alarmed," said a familiar Iranian voice. "It is I, Sa'id, the *Mojahedin.*"

Sa'id, the juggler, thought Frank, too frightened to give voice to his thought.

"The light switch is more to your left."

Frank found it, blinked in the sudden glare, and saw Sa'id in his *homafar* uniform, a G3 automatic rifle in a sling over his shoulder, smiling at him from across the room.

"Welcome. We knew you might be here, and we worried for you. Then, from an advantage point we have on the roof of our hangar, we saw the lights come on. We knew only you would be on the basketball court at this hour with a war going on around you. So I came. And waited here. Knowing you would come here next."

"But how could you get in? Everything's locked, chained."

"We have our ways," said Sa'id, smiling again. "It is our base, after all." He stood next to the equipment cage, and, Frank noticed, the door to the cage stood ajar.

"But why? All that shooting going on out there. And we have guards, armed guards on patrol in here. Why would you take such a risk?"

"I take no risk. It is you who stand in danger. I come to take you to safety."

"Out there?"

"I must insist."

Frank dropped his gloves and changed his grip on the shotgun: one hand on the barrel; one on the trigger guard, but with the muzzle down.

"No, no. Not like that," said Sa'id. "Not by force. We insist only to protect you. Munair Irfani, the navy man, came to Anwar, our Anwar, yesterday after he spoke to you. He told us about the *fatwa* that calls for your death. He asked us to look after you."

"I appreciate that," said Frank. "More than I can tell you." It's good to know someone cares about my life, he thought. "But to protect myself," he said, "I insist on staying here. You've got a war going on out there. It's much safer in here. No war."

Sa'id shook his head and unslung his G3. "The revolution goes on everywhere. Even here. Out there we have surrounded the remainder of the Bodyguard unit. They can do nothing. We can keep you out of their line of fire. But out the other way, along Damavand . . ." He gestured with the muzzle of his gun. "Out there, a big war goes on. Islamic warriors who soon may come this way."

"Another reason I must stay here. With the other Americans." Frank hoped to sound as military as possible. He knew his voice sounded hollow, but he tried. "This is my post."

Not by force, Sa'id had said. But the muzzle of his G3 did not look peaceful.

"We have other Americans with us, about twenty. Air force men in a fortified bunker under the arsenal. We keep them safe."

Frank's curiosity had begun to wrestle with his fear. So far, fear showed the stronger grip. "Hiding out under an arsenal doesn't sound safe to me. Suppose a shell hits it?"

"No matter. The bunker is fortified, and the arsenal is empty. We have given guns to the people, and we have loaded two trucks that will go to the university at first light."

More good news, thought Frank. His throat tightened. He tried to inhale deeply but could draw only shallow intakes.

"Anwar would be angry if I had to shoot you," said Sa'id. "But I cannot leave without you."

"If I'm dead," Frank managed to say, "I won't be going anywhere."

"Oh, no. No. No. No. I could not shoot to kill. Or cripple you. A shoulder, perhaps."

Jesus, this is a war, thought Frank, remembering Belinsky's blood marking his clothes and his hands.

"Please, accompany with me." The barrel of the G3 edged up a notch. "You will be safer with us than to stay here."

I'd be safer here, thought Frank, but I should be there. Not because Sa'id, weapon in hand, insists. It's my job. We need to know what's going on out there. Curiosity outwrestled fear. Okay.

"I should be out there," he said. "Let's go."

They both reacted to a sound outside the gym, turning their heads toward the thump of a door closing. Booted feet and muffled voices moved closer. He glanced at Sa'id, who reached out his hand. Frank scooped his gloves up from the floor and moved quickly toward the equipment cage, leaving the lights on and following Sa'id into the cage.

Sa'id secured the gate with a strip of wire that hung from it. He led Frank into the shadows, and they crouched low behind a pile of exercise mats. They heard the door to the hallway open.

"Yo-ho. Anybody home?"

Feet shuffled, and a second disembodied voice said, "Lights on but nobody home."

"Steele said that major, Sullivan, whatever his name is, would be in here."

"Somebody the fuck was in here. The lights're on."

"Think he got kidnapped?"

"Hope so. I hate them fuckin' spooks."

A flashlight's beam cut through the wire cage and bounced off haphazard piles of equipment.

"Yo-ho. Anybody in there? If there is, fuck ya. Stay in there for all I care."

"I don't think he got kidnapped. I think the spook just finished his little workout and split. And left the lights on."

"Asshole."

The light switch flicked, and the room darkened, lit only by the glow spilling in from the hallway. Feet shuffled. The door closed, and the dark deepened. They waited till the muffled sounds from the hallway faded.

"Quiet," whispered Sa'id. He reached under the pile of mats and pulled up a trap door, wedging the mats against a wall. Dim light from an unseen source below enabled Frank to pick out the skeleton of a wooden ladder. "Quiet. Go."

Frank took a moment to put his gloves on, handed Sa'id his shotgun, and worked his way down the shaky ladder. Sa'id lowered first the shotgun, then his own rifle, to Frank and followed. He eased the trap door down after him. Frank heard the soft thump of the mats tumbling over it. Sa'id led the way through long, damp, shadowy tunnels. Frank could hear the scurrying of tiny clawed feet and felt grateful for the darkness that kept him from seeing the rats he knew scampered around them. They made their way up another rickety ladder and through another trap door into a tool shed that shook with the sounds of battle. They crept around the backs of several darkened buildings till they reached a spot where Sa'id raised a hand and told Frank to wait.

"I'm not dressed for the great outdoors," said Frank.

"I will fix. Wait me here."

Act in haste. What was the rest of it? Repent in something. No, he thought. No regrets. I wanted to do this. I'm here.

He waited, leaning against the brick wall of what he took to be a U.S. Air Force administrative building. He clung to the shotgun and shivered in his sweat-soaked gym shorts and T-shirt. What the fuck are we doing here? he'd said to himself months before as their plane circled above pillars of smoke spiraling up from the war-ravaged city. Now, as his teeth chattered, he knew he'd found the answer. This is why I'm here. To freeze my ass off and maybe find out what's going on this side of the war.

A low concrete wall sheltered him from the airstrip. Sa'id had disappeared around its far end. Above the wall Frank could see tracer bullets arcing through the air and flares bursting. For a moment, he wished he were in the cafeteria, watching a golden oldie of a Super Bowl. Uh-uh, he told himself. This is where I decided to go.

He cringed as a sack rolled over the top of the wall. It took him a moment to realize the sack was Anwar the Taller, carrying a greatcoat. Frank noticed the shoulder patch insignia of the spread-winged *homa*. He gratefully shivered into the coat.

"You are a *homafar* now," said Anwar.

No, I'm a peregrine, thought Frank. "I thought you were in hiding," he said aloud.

"I am. This is a good place to hide. Take this. My hat."

Frank pulled the blue cap low over his forehead.

"Now follow."

Anwar led him into the hangar. "We feel better knowing you are with us."

"I appreciate that," said Frank. "But I don't think my American friends will appreciate it."

"You can tell them we kidnapped you," said Anwar, smiling.

"I will," said Frank.

"At gunpoint." Sa'id twirled his G3.

They'd entered through a small side door. Facing the great doors leading to the runways, sleek planes crowded the hanger. Frank took them to be F-14s. Since the *homafaran* knew him as a U.S. Air Force major, he didn't want to expose his ignorance by asking.

"I'm afraid becoming a *homafar* means a demotion for a major," said Anwar.

"It beats freezing," said Frank.

"But I hope no one noticed your sneakers." Frank looked down at his scuffed, well-worn white sneakers. "Not exactly regulation," added Anwar. "We should be able to find you a pair of boots. Enough people have been killed here today. What size?"

"Eleven," said Frank. "But the thought of taking a dead man's boots . . . I'd rather not."

"That's my size," said Anwar. "The American equivalent of my size. We'll get you a pair of mine." He spoke to Sa'id in Farsi and handed him a set of keys. Grinning, Sa'id left them. Frank noticed bombs and missiles neatly stacked on either side of each plane.

Anwar saw his interest. "That's what started it," he said. "Top officers briefed the pilots this afternoon on targets they wanted strafed, groups of revolutionaries attacking prisons, arsenals, military sites. They ordered us to prepare these F-4s."

Okay, thought Frank. Not F-14s.

"But by then our pilots had let us know what they'd been told to do. Instead of preparing the planes, we disarmed them. Many pilots joined us, refusing to carry out their orders. We've had a Bodyguard unit based here for over a week.

They attacked us. Air force police refused to join them and instead came to support us. We had already taken over the arsenal. For a while, it was very bad. But we outnumber the Bodyguard, and they have suffered many casualties."

"What about the Americans?"

"We have them well protected, but we need to keep them."

"Why?"

"The Bodyguard has sent reinforcements, but they can't bombard the base as long as we have the Americans."

"Not to mention all this equipment."

"Yes, that, too. But they have to worry even more about American lives than about American hardware. If the Shah's military kill Americans, they fear it would turn your government against them. They sent in six helicopters earlier, gunships that pounded us hard. But we took one out with a Stinger missile. The others withdrew."

"What happens next?" said Frank.

"We have radio contact with Ibrahim Yazdi."

The name had a familiar echo, but Frank could not place it. "I don't know who that is."

"I thought you would. An aide to the Imam. American educated. The Imam's spokesman when they were in France. Your ambassador is with him. They want us to release the Americans. That is another reason we wanted you to come."

"Me?"

"We want the Americans to know what we have done here. To talk to someone the Americans can trust and we can trust."

So much for concern about my safety, thought Frank. "You've already got more than twenty Americans they can talk to."

Anwar hesitated. "We needed someone we can trust."

"Okay," said Frank. "Okay. Can I talk to the other Americans?"

"Of course. But not until we get you some boots. We can't take a chance on having those sneakers attract attention."

"Who are you worried about?"

"Islamic militants from the Jaleh Square area have joined us. They are . . . sometimes quick to shoot. In fact . . ."

Anwar's hesitation told Frank he might not want to hear what the *homafar* would say next.

"Because we want the world to know what we do here, we allowed a car full of journalists onto the base. Unfortunately, someone fired on the car. One journalist, an American, died."

Oh, shit, thought Frank. "Do you know his name?"

"I checked his papers. Charles Hughes. From Cleveland."

Frank closed his eyes. He'd worked with Chuck Hughes on the *Plain*

*Dealer.* They'd met again when Frank worked with the AFL-CIO and Chuck headed the *PD*'s Washington bureau.

"Did you know him?"

"No," said Frank, with no regrets about lying, "but killing journalists isn't a good idea. It attracts more attention than sneakers. What happened to the body?"

"We have it in the arsenal."

Great, thought Frank. And another twenty-odd Americans in the basement. "Are the militants still on the base?"

"Oh, yes. And truckloads more driving through to the east gates that lead into the New Tehran neighborhood where they go to support the forces attacking the Bodyguard reinforcements."

Sa'id still had not returned when another *homafar* Frank did not know approached Anwar and spoke to him in Farsi.

"I must see to something back there. If Sa'id comes, tell him to come find me."

"Find you where?"

"Tell him by the radio."

"Can I come with you and talk to the ambassador?"

"No, that is a different radio, in the arsenal. Wait, please, for Sa'id."

The sounds of the battle outside had become sporadic, punctuation points to the steady drone of what he now identified as truck engines. When Sa'id finally arrived, it was on the run through the side door. He carried a bulging duffel bag.

"Where is Anwar?"

"Have you got my boots?"

"Yes, but first I must see Anwar."

"Back there," said Frank. "By the radios."

"Good. Wait me here." He hurried off.

Judging by the heft of the duffel bag, it contained much more than a pair of boots. Frank wondered what would happen if he opened the door and, if the way looked clear, walked away. He could make his way back the way they had come, circling the concrete wall, through the tool shed, down into the tunnels. It could be done, but, God help me, I want to be here.

"Here are your boots." He turned to face Anwar, who held a boot in each hand. "There's a bench over there. By the door."

Frank took the boots and settled himself on the bench. He unlaced his sneakers and tugged them off. He'd expected the boots to reflect military spit and polish, but these looked like they'd been through a battle. "What are these spots?"

"Oh. Oil, perhaps. I wore them today when we worked on the planes."

Starting with his bigger, left foot, Frank tugged on a boot. The fit seemed good. He took an inner sole from his right sneaker, slipped into the second boot, and tried it on. Snug enough. He tried a few steps.

"That should work. Thanks. What can I do with the sneakers? I don't want to lose them."

"I will put them in a safe place for you. Also your shotgun." Frank tied the sneakers together and handed them to Anwar. He hesitated, studying the shotgun, then surrendered it.

"Good." said Anwar. "Wait here." He disappeared again into the hangar's shadowy interior.

Anwar returned quickly, with Sa'id but without the sneakers and shotgun. "Now we can safely cross the base and go to the arsenal. We have a jeep waiting. Mr. Yazdi wants to talk to us again. You can talk to the other Americans. And then to your ambassador."

That'll be fun, thought Frank.

Stripped of weapons, the arsenal's main floor had been turned into a headquarters for the *homafaran*. Frank saw no air force police, no civilian technicians or Islamic militants. The room bristled with communications equipment, typewriters, a copier.

"Are you in charge of all this?"

"No," said Anwar. "In fact, that is another problem. Earlier today, before they joined us, some air force police arrested our leaders and turned them over to the Bodyguard. The Bodyguard took them away. For now, we do without leaders. But we want our leaders released, returned to us."

"In exchange for the Americans?"

"No. Only as part of the conversation. That is why we wanted you. We thought you could understand the Persian way. Yazdi is with your ambassador. And of course Yazdi understands. We can talk to Yazdi. And you, with Yazdi's help, must make your ambassador understand."

"My ambassador will not be pleased to hear from me under these conditions."

"You must make him understand."

"Comrade Amini." A *homafar* in headphones spoke to Anwar in Farsi. Comrade, thought Frank. That's interesting.

"We have contact with Mr. Yazdi and your ambassador," said Anwar. "Come."

Frank sat before a microphone and slipped on the headphones Anwar handed him. Anwar sat beside him and spoke to Yazdi in Farsi. Frank picked out the word *inglissi* in Yazdi's reply.

"Is Ambassador O'Connor with you, sir?" said Anwar.

"Yes, he is," replied a voice that bore as much of an American accent as it did Iranian.

"We have an American with us, sir, who wishes to speak to his ambassador."

"Put him on." Frank recognized O'Connor's voice, and Anwar nodded at the mike.

"Mr. Ambassador, can you hear me?"

"Yes, yes. Who is this?"

"Sir, this is Frank Sullivan."

"God Jesus. Where the hell are you? And how in the hell did you get there?"

Frank told the ambassador more or less what had happened, embellishing his account with the idea he'd been kidnapped.

"Goddamn it, Sullivan. Rocky was right. We should have shipped you out of here the day you arrived."

"I'm still here, sir."

"Rocky got a call from Tom Troy." O'Connor's voice had softened. "You just disappeared."

"Correct, sir. If you get a chance, please let them know what happened and that I'm okay. The other Americans, all the American air force men, are all right, sir. They're in the same building I am, one floor below. In a fortified bunker, well protected by the *homafaran*."

"Protected? They're hostages, goddamn it."

"The *homafaran* say they're under no restraint. Except for the battle going on around us."

"Then why don't you and your Iranian friends just escort them the hell out of there?"

"Sir, there's no way the *homafaran* can get us out as long as the base is under attack by the Bodyguard."

"Who's in charge of these damn *homafaran?*"

"Sir, that's another problem . . . another part of the conversation. Earlier in the day, the Bodyguard took the leaders of the *homafaran* into custody. The men I'm with, they need to be back in touch with their leaders. They need direction."

"That may be a damn tall order."

"I understand, sir. But anything you can find out might be helpful. And sir, I do have one American casualty to report."

"I thought you said they were all okay."

"All the air force men are okay. But an American journalist, Charles Hughes, *Cleveland Plain Dealer,* has been killed."

"Good God. Any other casualties? American, I mean. Other journalists?"

Frank looked to Anwar, who shook his head.

"Apparently not, sir." An uneasy feeling stirred in his stomach. He looked at his boots. "But from what I can tell, hundreds of Iranian casualties."

"This Hughes interviewed me yesterday," said the ambassador. "Fine chap. What happened to the body?"

"Here, sir. Same room I'm in. On a table. Under a tarpaulin."

"Dear God . . . Look, Frank, I'm sorry I went off on you before. But you do have a nose for trouble. What else is going on?"

Frank relayed all the details Anwar had given him.

"Sounds like a mess," said the ambassador. "What can we do to help?"

"Can anyone find a way, maybe one of the military attachés, find a way to contact General Kasravi? General Hossein Kasravi. Imperial Bodyguard."

"If we could get in touch with General Kasravi," said the voice Frank now recognized as Yazdi's, "we would arrest him."

"We need someone who can help us further the conversation," said Frank. "I've worked with General Kasravi in the past. And we need to further the conversation."

"I understand," said Yazdi. "We will do what we can. Stay close to the radio. You've been helpful. We will be in touch."

"And Sullivan, for chrissake, stay out of trouble."

"I'll do my best, sir."

"That's what I'm afraid of."


A gray morning had replaced the thick night when they stepped through the arsenal doors, but the sounds of battle continued. Sa'id sat behind the wheel of an open jeep. Frank climbed into the back while Anwar took the passenger's seat and spoke to Sa'id in Farsi. Sa'id cut across the open area of the base and pulled up by an outside metal stairway at the far side of the hangar.

"I want to take you up to the roof. You'll be able to see the whole battle," said Anwar.

Despite his *homafar* greatcoat, cap, and boots, Frank felt like an exposed target as they clambered up the rattling stairway to the roof. A brisk north wind greeted them as they stepped over a low wall and onto the tar-topped roof. A dozen *homafaran,* all armed and several with field glasses, hunkered down at various positions around the roof.

"Stay low and come this way," said Anwar. They scuttled like crabs along the parapet to the closest *homafaran.* Anwar spoke briefly and listened long to the excited *homafaran,* who eyed Frank curiously as they spoke. Anwar took a pair of field glasses from one of the men and peered into the distance. He handed the glasses to Frank.

"Look, that way. Up along Damavand." Frank swung the glasses in the direction of the gunfire. "Have you ever seen tanks going backward?" asked Anwar.

Frank saw a tank he recognized as a Chieftain, backing up Damavand.

"It is a beautiful sight, isn't it?" said Anwar. "Look to your right, near the far end of the runways."

Frank picked up a long column of men, hands clasped behind their heads, marching toward the arsenal.

"What's left of the Bodyguard unit that had been based here has surrendered. It will soon be over, and the American air force men will be free to leave."

"What about your leaders, the men in Bodyguard custody?"

Anwar looked out over the base. "Who knows? Perhaps Mr. Yazdi or your ambassador will be able to do something. *Inshallah*. Perhaps not." He turned and studied Frank. "As you know, as Sa'id told you, Captain Irfani came to us yesterday."

"Yes," said Frank. "I know."

"We will do what we can to protect you. But this *fatwa* will follow you wherever you go."

"I realize."

"And we cannot be with you. Everywhere. Or all the time."

Wanting to worry about somebody else, Frank raised the glasses again to study the column marching under guard along the far runway. "What will happen to these men?" he asked.

"*Inshallah,* they may be all right. There is a stockade beyond the arsenal. They will be crowded, but for now they will be held there. Once the Americans can safely leave, the Bodyguard prisoners will be moved to the bunker under the arsenal."

"And then?" Frank wondered if he were asking about the Bodyguard prisoners or himself.

"I do not know. We will try to keep them safe from . . . from those who are quick to shoot. God willing, we will. But these days, Islamic justice can be . . . swift. Look over there."

Frank swung the glasses in the direction Anwar pointed. He spotted half a dozen U.S. Air Force officers on the roof of their admin building. All had field glasses trained on Damavand.

"We have a better view than they do. Come. I don't think we have to crouch anymore." He stood and led Frank to the far side of the roof. "See that section over there, beyond the armory. We call that the Farahabad base. *Homafaran* have their barracks there, and last night fighting was very heavy in that area. The television had shown Bazargan's speech at the prayer meeting at the university and followed that by replaying the Imam's arrival last week. Some of us began shouting, 'Long live Khomeini, death to Bakhtiar,' in the faces of the Bodyguard. They fired, over our heads at first, then at us. *Homafaran* broke into the armory. Word of the fighting spread, and Islamic militants, also *Mojahedin* and *Feda'iyan,* fought their way onto the base. Look that way. From here you can't see it, but over there is Jaleh Square. A year ago soldiers killed many people there. Now the

people control it. They have also seized the Parliament buildings—the Majles—
and the old Golestan Palace. As the Bodyguard tanks go backward, soon the
people will control all of east and south Tehran."

"Is that a power station?"

"Yes. Now in the hands of the people. Look beyond it."

Frank looked out over the far reaches of the city. Funnels of smoke stretched
up into low-hanging clouds. Like tornadoes, Anwar the Smarter had said.
Somewhere out there, beyond a horizon he could not see, Anwar, Mina, and the
children should by now be safe somewhere in America. And somewhere out
there, a mole lurked in the precincts of the CIA, still more of a threat than the
war that raged around him. And here, perhaps everywhere, a sword known as a
*fatwa* dangled, dancing on an unseen thread. As the dawn broke, he remembered his day job.

"How can I get through to Supreme Commander's Headquarters?"

"You forget," said Anwar the Taller. "There is no more Supreme Commander."

"I know. But we still have a meeting of our . . ."

"What my cousin called Jayface, correct?"

"Correct."

"I am very glad for what you did for my cousin. But if I were you, I wouldn't
even think about getting to *Padegan-e Bagh-e Shah* today."

"I must." He wondered why and thought of Belinsky, the perfect consular
officer. Always take care of your cover job first. Jayface had been the key to all he
had learned about Iran. He suspected this might be his last day on his cover job.
He couldn't ignore it now. He checked his watch. Five after seven. "Can you get
me back to my office?"

"I can." Anwar took the glasses and scanned the airstrip. "The Bodyguard
prisoners have passed the arsenal. We can release the Americans. We want you to
accompany them."

"But why?" said Frank.

"We want to send a message to America."

"What message?"

"For us to know. For the Americans to figure out."

Anwar left him in the hangar with Sa'id while he headed for the armory.
"Don't forget," said Sa'id. "Shotgun and sneakers."

"I'm glad one of us still has a working brain. I had forgotten."

"Come." Sa'id led him to the depths of the hangar. Frank looked down and
saw around the now empty duffel bag a scattered collection of boots of various
size. He stared at the boots he wore that matched the size of Anwar's. He studied
the putative oil stains and suddenly knew he stood in the boots of a dead man.

"These aren't your boots," said Frank when Anwar returned to the hangar.

"No," said Anwar. "They're yours."

"The oil stains look a lot like blood spots. Who had them on when he got killed?"

"I do not know," said Anwar. He shrugged and changed the subject. "But I managed to get through to your ambassador on the radio link. Mr. Yazdi was still with him. They had not been able to contact General Kasravi, but I told them we could now escort you and the American airmen back to the American section of the base. They said they would alert your people there."

"I still think this is a bad idea," said Frank.

"I think it would be a bad idea for you to return to the American base dressed as an Iranian *homafar*. I know you will be cold, but let us take the coat and cap."

"You can take the boots while you're at it."

"Do we have a blanket?" asked Anwar.

"No blanket, sir. But we have tarpaulin."

"The same tarpaulin you put over the American journalist?"

"Oh, no, Major Sullivan. Different tarpaulin," said Sa'id, very earnest.

Wrapped in the tarpaulin, Frank sat up front in the open jeep, next to Sa'id.

"Look behind you," called Anwar from the back seat.

Frank turned and saw the twenty-three American air force advisers clinging to the sides of an open truck.

"Major Sullivan's air force," yelled Anwar.

Munair, in scruffy civilian clothes and a checkered black and white headscarf, climbed out of the driver's side of an orange taxi as the jeep Frank rode in pulled up behind it. Bill Steele stood beside him.

"What are you doing in that outfit?" said Frank.

"Why are you covered with a tarpaulin?" responded Munair.

"I had to shoot the locks off the front gates to let your buddy in with his taxi-cab," said Steele. "No problem, once I figured out who he was. We got more locks. But what's with you and these *homafaran*?"

"Long story. Let me get some clothes on and get to our Jayface meeting. One quick take. In the equipment cage in the gym, back wall, under a pile of mats, there's a trap door. You might want to seal it up. That's how the *homafaran* got in. Okay I fill you in on the rest when I get back?"

"Yeah, okay. If you get back."

Munair had kept his motor running, steaming over the windows, Gus sat next to him. Frank eased himself into the back.

"What the hell have you been up to?" said Gus.

"Later," said Frank. "Munair, what are you doing here?"

The navy officer turned to him. "I told you I would help you as long as you are here." The headscarf obscured the stigmata on his forehead. "Today, this is how I can help, driving a taxi for you. You would never get through in your American car with your American face."

"Good," said Frank. "*Padegan-e Bagh-e Shah,* please."

"Good," said Munair. "My other passenger wants the same destination."

U.S. Air Force guards now stood by the open gates. Munair drove through and turned left.

"Munair thinks we should have an easy trip," said Gus, half turning toward Frank. "With that war still going on up the block behind us, Damavand is clear this way."

"No traffic at all," said Munair. "Everyone wants to be on the other side at Jaleh Square. I take you the way I came. No problems. Taking you back to Dowshan Tappeh, who knows?"

"Where did you get the taxi?" asked Frank.

"My wife's cousin. Also his Arafat headscarf. This Palestinian *kaffiyeh* look is very popular right now."

"I wish you had one for me," said Gus.

Their journey proved as uneventful as Munair had predicted. His elaborate precautions seemed unnecessary, but Frank appreciated them. He'd had more than enough excitement through the long night.

Munair removed his *kaffiyeh* as they approached the closed gate of the compound. Bodyguard troops had evidently replaced the army soldiers assigned to protect Supreme Commander's Headquarters. Hard-faced young men behind the gates leveled M-14s at Munair as he stepped from the taxi. Two Chieftain tanks, well back from the gates, flanked them. A Bodyguard officer with lieutenant's bars on his coat recognized Munair and began nodding. He spoke into his walkie-talkie and barked orders to the other troops, who quickly unchained the gates. Munair plunged back into the taxi as the lieutenant waved them through. Munair sped through the gates, then brought them to a squealing halt.

"I made this arrangement before I left," he said, "but now we must do ID. Let me have your papers." Frank and Gus handed Munair the plastic pouches that carried their passports, residency permits, and military ID. The lieutenant rapped a knuckle on Frank's window. Frank rolled it down. The lieutenant peered in, comparing Frank's features to the identity photos. He nodded, said, "Good," and handed Frank back his pouch, then repeated the process with Gus. He entered the guardhouse and emerged with the inevitable clipboard. He ran a finger down the list of names, looked up, and nodded. It had taken only seconds for the guards to wave them through the gates. The security check took almost ten minutes while soldiers ordered them out and searched inside and underneath the car.

"They must be very careful," said Munair as he again slid behind the wheel. "It is not very orthodox. A taxicab entering a military compound at a time like this. We could be a suicide bomb."

"Let's hope not," said Gus.

Munair pulled up by the stairway that led nowhere. "Let us go now. We are late."

Inside, he stopped and spoke in Farsi to a forlorn-looking civilian who sat on the marble steps under the crown-shaped chandelier with no bulbs. The man nodded and grunted in response to Munair's words. Munair handed him the keys to the taxi, started up the stairs, hesitated, reached into an overcoat pocket, pulled out the checkered *kaffiyeh,* and handed it over.

"My wife's cousin," he said. "He does not speak English." He shed his shabby coat as he climbed the stairs and dropped it outside the doors. Under it he wore his naval captain's uniform.

General Merid stood as they entered the meeting room. He pushed back the sleeve of his neatly pressed military overcoat and cocked his head to study his watch.

"Gentlemen, I know these are difficult times, but you are quite late."

"The fighting near Dowshan Tappeh delayed us," lied Munair.

Frank surveyed the assembled group, now reduced to four from the original eight. About like the Iranian military, thought Frank. Half what it used to be. Munair moved to the chair on the general's right. Gus and Frank moved to his left.

"Please be seated," said the general, who remained standing. Everyone except Munair still had coats on. Frank realized the building had neither heat nor light. "We must continue to be ready loyally to serve the official government and to assist the leaders of the armed forces to maintain the integrity of the military." Hands clasped behind his back, he bounced on his toes. His eyes darted from the tabletop to the door to the ceiling. "Though I have tried to reach Colonel, er, General Kasravi to press him on the subject, the air force has not yet appointed a successor to Major Amini, who has turned coat, deserted." He managed to catch Frank's eyes with a reproving look. "Lieutenant Colonel Bunker also has left us. We also continue to lack a representative from the Bodyguard and of course a replacement for my . . . for Major Nazih."

He hesitated before he could continue. "Events last night, which I am sure we are all aware of, show us exactly what we must bend our efforts toward preventing. Two branches of the armed forces fighting against each other. We cannot have that. Our group, the Joint Armed Forces Ad Hoc Committee on Enlightenment, is the only joint working group involving . . . ah, at least in theory, involving all branches of the armed forces. As such, we must act as the rallying point for all those who recognize the vital need for unified military action."

Good God, thought Frank, he's gone mad.

"Now, more than ever, the military needs enlightened leadership who can work together. We will, of course, involve other, more senior officers of all branches of our military in this effort. But I promise you this, gentlemen. We will have a military takeover, and the Joint Armed Forces Ad Hoc Committee on Enlightenment will be its focal point."

He again bounced on his toes. He scanned the room. And waited. Maybe this is why I had to be here, thought Frank. They'll love it back home. The latest plans for a military coup. Straight from General Merid.

Gus straightened himself in his chair, studied the others, and said, "What do we do first?"

"Excellent question. Jointly, we will formulate a plan for a military takeover, taking into account all aspects of the current situation. Each of us will make a verbal presentation at our meeting tomorrow morning, Sunday morning, at which everyone will arrive punctually on time. Major Sullivan, I assign you the task of preparing a written draft ready for review and finalization by Tuesday. By then I shall have contacted General Kasravi and will invite him to our meeting. He will serve as our liaison to other senior officers."

"You've talked to him about this?" said Gus.

"I shall do so as soon as possible," replied the general.

"Are there any others you've been in touch with on this?" said Gus. "Political leaders? Opposition groups? Followers of the Imam?"

"I am in touch with a wide range of people across the entire political spectrum."

"That's good," said Gus. "I can hardly wait to hear what General Kasravi will have to say."

Frank remained speechless. No waiter appeared at their usual tea time, but Munair suggested a break. Frank caught Gus's eye and moved toward the bathroom. He got to the hallway in time to see Munair heading upstairs to the third floor.

"I hope you got all that on tape," said Gus as he and Frank peed jointly into a bunghole.

"I did."

"Good. It should find a receptive audience at his sanity hearing."

When the meeting resumed, Munair turned to General Merid. "General," he said, "may I suggest, in view of your assigning us each to prepare ideas for a military takeover, that we might adjourn early today, adjourn now, so we may get to work on our assignments."

"Excellent suggestion. You see, we work well—jointly. Together. Gentlemen, in your thinking on this concept, I want you to be creative and . . . dynamic."

"Yes, sir," said Munair.

"Meeting adjourned," said General Merid. "We will meet tomorrow at zero eight hundred hours precisely."

Munair took Frank by the elbow, steering him toward the door. "Could you and Commander Simpson wait for me downstairs? I need to have a private word with General Merid."

Frank and Gus stood inside the glass doors. Frost had turned the glass opaque.

"I know you must have had an interesting night, which I'm dying to hear about," said Gus, "but you have to admit so far at least it's also been a pretty interesting morning."

"So far," said Frank.

"You got any good ideas for a military takeover?"

"Yeah. But Khomeini's already carried out all my best ideas."

They turned to see Munair hurrying down the stairs, dragging the shabby overcoat behind him. "Let us step outside."

The morning's clouds had dissipated. A cold, clear blue sky hung over them with a distant, white winter sun.

"See there," said Munair, nodding to the west. Funnels of black smoke curled northward, signals that the earlier morning quiet had not survived. "We think you should go now," said Munair. "General Kasravi has just now disbanded our committee."

"I'm surprised he found the time," said Frank.

"I knew how to reach him." He handed Frank the shabby overcoat he carried. "Please, I cannot drive you. I have things I must do here. Give this back to my wife's cousin. He will drive you. I contacted the guardhouse. They have gone to fetch him. He will pick you up soon here."

"Thank you," said Frank. "For everything. You've been a good friend . . . and teacher."

"I am proud to have been your teacher. Your trip back to Dowshan Tappeh may be more troublesome than our trip here. My cousin does not speak English, but he knows back alleys, other ways even I do not. He will get you there. Now, I must leave you." He extended his hand, first to Gus, then to Frank. For the last time, Frank glanced at the blood-flecked knot on Munair's forehead.

"Good-bye," said Frank.

"Farewell. And Major Sullivan, remember to be careful. Always."

Munair disappeared behind the frosted-over glass door.

As they waited in the shimmering cold, Frank studied the stone stairs that climbed into a blank wall. He counted the towers of dark smoke gyring skyward. Thirteen. Fourteen. He thought of the day he had stood on this spot with

Anwar the Smarter watching just four funnels of smoke. Watch the smoke signals, Anwar had told him, and maybe soon he could tell what would happen to Iran. Anwar had said he knew nothing about the stone stairs. Frank counted them. Sixteen, leading to a blank spot between second-floor windows. He wondered if the Shah, like Iran, had met the same fate as the stone stairway. He thought about the *Armed Forces Times* and the civic action program that had never happened and about his failure to recruit Munair.

"You're awful quiet," said Gus, as the orange taxi approached.

"I was just thinking," said Frank, "about all the things we never managed to get done. Like find out where that stairway was supposed to go."

The man he would never know other than as Munair's wife's cousin now wore the black-and-white *kaffiyeh*. Ignoring all who tried to flag him down, he drove with skill that reminded Frank of a combination of their army driver, Ali Zarakesh, and the old-time Jewish, Italian, and Irish cab drivers of New York, aware of every back street, pothole, shortcut, long loop around trouble, traffic light, and police threat. Like them, he talked without stopping, but Munair's wife's cousin, like the more recent clans of New York cab drivers, spoke a language Frank did not understand. He picked up the occasional word: Damavand, *Javand,* Dowshan Tappeh, *homafar, Maydan-e Jaleh,* and clung to the dashboard. Oh, wow, he thought with silent relief as the cab curled around a traffic circle and into a still-deserted Damavand toward the gates of Dowshan Tappeh. Farther up the wide street they could see the smoke and tracers of the continuing but dwindling battle.

After the long ordeal of getting through the gates, they pulled up outside Troy's office. Frank dug into a pocket and pulled out a handful of rials he proffered to Munair's wife's cousin. With all the voluble vocabulary at his command, he refused. Frank could pick out only two words. Munair Irfani. Frank tried again, with wagging hand gestures to accompany his words, but again he was rebuffed. Frank tried once more, and Munair's wife's cousin accepted, grabbed the rials, and gruffly kissed Frank on both cheeks, making a sharp impression with his stubbly beard.

He'd had to tell his what-happened-to-you-last-night story in detail, first to Gus, then to Bill Steele and Corporal Cantwell, and finally to Tom Troy.

"You're gonna have to run it all down again to Rocky and the ambassador," said Troy.

"There is no way in hell I'm going to try to get down to the embassy today," said Frank.

"Can't say I blame you," said Troy. "But Rocky may not see it that way. You had folks in a shit fit all the way from here to Langley."

Gus poked Frank's arm. "Do a cable on last night. I'll do our last stand at Jayface. Let someone else worry about getting them to the embassy. Standard operating procedure, right, Tom?"

"Okay by me," said Troy. "Bill's gotta get down there anyway, some-fuckin'-how. Gus, why don't you set yourself up in here with my typewriter? I got a meeting to go to with the air force brass over in their admin building. Sounds like they might want to pull out today before the hostiles take over the whole base."

"The better part of valor," said Gus.

Frank gave Gus his tape of their final Jayface meeting. He was glad they'd gotten there. General Merid's military takeover fantasy should make interesting reading back at Langley.

"It's not on the tape," he said, "but don't forget to get in what Merid said about Kasravi dissolving Jayface."

"It does kind of put things in perspective, doesn't it?" said Gus.


Frank settled down at Rushmore's typewriter, staring at the blank sheet of paper he'd rolled in. He'd told his kidnapping story so often he half believed it. The white paper looked so innocent. He could lie talking to people, particularly people who didn't need to know the detailed truth. But he'd been a reporter too long to lie to a typewriter.

He recounted the saga of his night as it had happened. How Sa'id had waited for him in the dark gym. What each of them said. He did not try to analyze his own motives for deciding to go with Sa'id. Just described what he'd done. Short, declarative sentences. Subject. Verb. Object. No atmospherics. No description. It took a while to get started, but then it flowed.

He found Gus in Troy's office, still pecking away at his Jayface cable. When Gus rolled his final page from the IBM Selectric, they edited each other's efforts.

"Doesn't sound like you got kidnapped," said Gus.

"I didn't get kidnapped."

"But that's what you told everybody."

"Not everybody. I didn't tell that to Rocky. I didn't tell that to Langley."

"Yeah, but Rocky heard it from Troy and by now probably from the ambassador, and Langley's heard it from Rocky."

"I guess."

"You may have dug yourself into some deep shit with this one."

"I guess."

"Why'd you make up the kidnap story?"

"I guess because when I decided to join the *homafaran* in the middle of their war against the Bodyguard I knew it would piss off a lot of people, from Rocky to Kasravi. I couldn't explain it, but I know I did the right thing."

"Think you can explain it now?"

"No. Not beyond what I say in the cable."

"You decided to do it?"

"Right."

"You didn't just let it happen?"

Frank studied him. "No. For a change." He thought about what he'd done, then added, "For a change I decided to make it happen."

"My advice?"

Frank nodded.

"Stick to the cable. Tell Rocky any talk about you getting kidnapped must have been some kind of misunderstanding. A story told secondhand, thirdhand. With everything else goin' on, people won't waste too much time nitpicking what happened to you. You may get away with it."

"Maybe," said Frank. Till someday Henry James has me put on the polygraph.

Troy, Steele, and Rushmore piled into Troy's office. Frank and Gus looked up.

"Cut-and-run time," said Troy.

"Shred and burn?" said Gus.

"You got it. If you guys are done with your cables, we could use some help."

They started by cleaning out Rushmore's safe, then put the cables they'd just finished into its yawning maw and locked it.

"Let's not forget to give those cables to Steele before we pull out," said Gus.

"We won't forget," said Frank.

"I'm pretty good on the shredder," said Gus. "Why don't I volunteer for that detail, and you can take those gym muscles of yours to give Big Bill a hand with the burn barrels."

"Barrels?"

"That's how it's done when you don't have access to the embassy's Auschwitz ovens."

Frank found Bill Steele and volunteered for the burn barrel detail. Cantwell and Rushmore joined them to roll out four heavy steel barrels from a storage room he hadn't known existed behind Troy's office. They positioned the barrels on the packed snow that covered the open area outside the Quonset hut and returned for four more. Frank noticed dozens of stacked boxes and several opendoored, empty safes.

"All this and more," said Rushmore. "We've been gettin' ready."

"I'll get some of these started," said Steele when they'd spaced out all eight barrels. "Why don't you guys start bringin' out the money."

"Money?" said Frank.

"Lots of money," said Rushmore. "Other stuff, too."

"But why burn good money?"

"We either burn it or the ragheads finance the rest of the their revolution with it."

By the time they'd lugged a dozen cartons outside, Steele had four barrels smoking. "My guess is you've never done this before."

"Here lately," said Frank, "I've done a lot of things I've never done before."

"Key thing is, is to be careful. We don't want anything droppin' or blowin' away. These are big mothers, fifty-five-gallon drums, fiber insulated so the heat stays in. Packed with sodium nitrate and topped with starter mix, kerosene thickened by napalm, some other stuff. Take a quick look in."

Frank bent and peered into the barrel long enough to see a wide-mesh screen licked by flames about halfway down. The smoke drove him back.

"Stuff'll burn as long as you don't pack it in too tight. And you gotta be careful gettin' stuff outta the boxes and into the barrel without you lose any. But you can't feed it in too slow or we'll be here forever. We're lucky there's not much wind. God forbid snow or rain."

He selected a box with a green X mark. "Rials," he said and slit it open with a box cutter.

Frank stuffed his winter mittens into his parka pockets and picked out a stack of thousand-*rial* notes emblazoned with the Shah's profile.

"Take the rubber bands off and drop 'em in low as you can without gettin' yourself burned."

Frank followed instructions and dropped in the first stack. The bills scattered as they fell and caught quickly, but one charred note swirled upward on a funnel of smoke. Frank caught it with his left hand, crumpled it, and dropped it back into the barrel.

"Good catch," said Steele. "You'll do just fine."

Four more towers of smoke spiraled into the blue winter sky. Before he'd emptied the last stacks from the carton, Frank went to Steele to borrow the box cutter and slash open another. Watching the others and following their lead, he tore apart the cartons as he emptied them and added them to the potlatch. Smoke now curled from all eight barrels. He had no problem burning rials, but then he slashed open a carton marked with a blue X and saw packs of American dollars in hundreds, fifties, and twenties. As he dropped in the first batch, he felt needles of regret pricking his fingertips.

He thought of all the twenties given to him by Lermontov that he'd turned over to Rocky. He thought of the money Belinsky had gleaned from his Aeroflot racket. He suspected it all added up to nothing compared to what he burned now. America, the magnificent. So powerful and rich, we have money to burn. He thought of stuffing a stack into his pocket and knew he couldn't. Why couldn't I? I might get caught. My often lapsed Catholic conscience would bother me. He stripped away another rubber band and fanned a stack of fifties into the tongues of flame that licked through the wire mesh. An afternoon in purgatory, burning away his sins.

They left the barrels outside to burn down and congregated in Troy's office. Frank had remembered their cables and given them to Steele. Cantwell and Rushmore had gone to check on the battle from the roof of the air force administration building. They weren't gone long.

"We didn't get to the roof," said Rushmore. "Air force guys had started to pull out and had the building locked up. Said last time they checked, the Bodyguard looked to be pullin' out. They'd backed up Damavand, and the head of the column had turned into some street that runs north."

"Maybe we should get out of here, too," said Gus.

"One last job," said Troy. "The weapons."

"Can we have our shotguns back?" said Gus.

"No way. Word is to surrender all weapons. The ambassador figures there's no way we can fight our way out of Iran. So we turn over weapons and try to talk our way out. He has great faith in this yardbird character. Yardi, or whatever his name is."

"We've got a lot of shit back there," said Steele. "Special weapons, explosives, more burn barrels. I could put a timer on some C-4 and blow it all."

"I like the idea," said Troy. "But there'd be hell to pay if some Iranians wandered in after we pull out and got themselves killed. Frank, I hate to ask, but think you could go back over there and talk to your *homafar* buddies?"

"What for?"

"Well, I'd feel a lot better if we surrender our weapons to air force types rather than have them wind up with some raggedy posse of ragheads. And those guys seem to trust you."

"I can do it if I have to," said Frank. "Except . . ."

"Except what?"

"Well, last night the *homafaran* emptied out their Dowshan Tappeh arsenal and gave weapons to the militants. They planned to take two truckloads of weapons to the university this morning."

"You get that in your cable?"

"Yes, sir."

"Good. Maybe when he reads it Rocky'll understand why I decided to just leave our weapons here. Time to go. No shotguns, Gus. If anybody wants to keep his personal sidearm, make sure I don't see it. And nobody's gonna see mine."

They could hear signs of the fading battle as Frank turned the Nova up Damavand. "Poor bastards," said Gus. "The Immortals don't look so immortal anymore."

"I can feel some hints of mortality myself," said Frank. "Watch out."

An open truck came barreling down Damavand toward them. Armed militants, firing their weapons in the air and shouting slogans, packed the back. The truck swerved around them.

"We go to the house, wash up, pack what we have to quick as we can, and head for the bachelors' compound, right?" said Gus.

"Sound like a good plan," said Frank, as he turned into their street. "Except . . ."

Clusters of armed teenagers in green headbands chatted among themselves along the street. They raised their rifles and chanted, *"Allah-o akbar."* Frank tapped the horn, blat-blat-blat, blat-blat, catching the rhythm of the chant. He kept his eyes straight ahead and drove past the young gunmen.


"Jesus, you look like hell," said Todd Waldbaum as he let them in the door of the air force guards' quarters. They told what had happened, and Todd offered showers and fresh clothes. "Major Sullivan, you're about my size. I can come up with a clean shirt and a pair of slacks. Commander Simpson, you're more Dwight's size. He's a toad, but I'll get him to give up some duds."

"'Preciate," said Gus. "Looks like you've got a crowd."

"More coming, most likely. Everybody's assigned to a compound they're supposed to hole up in." Bill Steele and Cantwell joined them.

"Looks like you guys didn't make it home."

"We tried," said Gus. "But we had unexpected company. Teenagers with M-14s."

Washed, shaved, and relaxed in clean clothes, Frank and Gus exchanged a glance.

"Vodka in the freezer," said Gus. "Scotch in the fridge."

"'Fraid not," said Frank.

"Surely these healthy young men must have something they'd let us have a drop of."

"I asked Todd about that. No booze at all. Embassy orders."

"No booze and no weapons," said Gus.

"They still have their weapons," said Frank. "But all stacked together in a closet, waiting for somebody to show up they can surrender them to."

"Let's grab a couple and go rob a liquor store."

"Good plan, except . . ." He realized he'd said that word often in the past hour.

"Except," echoed Gus. "I know. There's no liquor stores left to rob."

# CHAPTER TWENTY-THREE

He decided he would attract less attention by walking to the new safe house. He knew he might encounter an Islamic patrol or a band of marauding teenagers armed with AK-47s. He knew he might arouse the suspicions of the nervous Americans now crowded into the air force guards' bachelor quarters. He knew the risks, and he knew he had to take the risk. He knew he must do all he could to secure Lermontov as an agency recruit, to put to rest those rumors that Lermontov had already recruited him. Endgame. Checkmate. He understood little about chess, but those expressions seemed right.

Expecting Lermontov at four, he crossed the quiet street at three-thirty. He reminded himself that he'd grown up in New York, where crossing the street was always a risk. Piece of cake, he thought as he walked half a block east, climbed the stone steps, and let himself in. The decor showed signs of what Frank had identified as early Bill Steele. Drawn blinds, no curtains, a Formica-topped dinning room table, tubular framed chairs, and bare wooden floors. The refrigerator, turned to the lowest setting, gaped at him like a toothless mouth when he opened it. He turned the setting up, hoping Lermontov would bring Stolichnaya.

He extracted his tape recorder from his pocket and shed the parka. It still smelled of smoke and the acrid fumes of sodium nitrate, napalm, and cremated hundred-dollar bills. He edged his way down the narrow stairs that led from the hallway to the two-car garage he could unlock only from the inside. He undid the lock and tested the overhead door. It went up smoothly. He pulled it shut but left it unlocked. Upstairs, he sat by a front window. He lifted a corner of one blind and, with a wad of notebook paper, propped it open just enough to give him a view of the street.

At a few minutes after four, according to Frank's Timex, the lights of an approaching blue Fiat flashed on and off. He hurried down to the garage and heaved the door open in time to see the Fiat continue its way up the street. He caught only a glimpse but recognized the huge frame behind the wheel. He jerked the garage door down and locked it.

He repeated the ritual the next day, thirty minutes earlier. At three-thirty, the blue Fiat again appeared. This time the lights flashed on and off twice. The Fiat's front bumper nearly touched the garage door as Frank flung it up. Lermontov pulled in quickly and slammed on the brakes. The small car bounced as Frank lowered and locked the overhead door.

Lermontov put a hand on the roof of the car to pull himself out. In his great-coat and lamb's-wool hat, he seemed to fill the garage. "I'm getting old. Or fat. Or something." He reached into the back seat and lifted out his briefcase. "We should have met at my embassy. We seem to attract less attention from the Islamic neighborhood committees than you Americans."

"Considering what we have to talk about, that doesn't sound like a good idea."

"No, not a good idea. My apologies for running off on you yesterday. I was already a bit nervous by the time I got here. Fires everywhere. Many roadblocks. Then, as I turned into this street, in my rearview mirror I spotted several of our brave Islamic revolutionary allies walking up the block. With M-14s undoubt-edly provided to the Shah by his American benefactors. I suspected they might take too much interest in me, and in this house, if I pulled in."

"No need to apologize. Same thing happened when we tried to get home the other evening."

"I take it you now call the air force guards' house across the street your home."

"What makes you think that?"

"No car in the garage. In these times, I don't think you walked very far to get here."

"Someone might have driven me," said Frank.

"As a KGB asset, we will have to arrange some training for you in how to lie. You should have said, 'Someone drove me.' Not, 'Someone might have driven me.'"

"Gotta admit, I could use the training," said Frank. He often felt uncom-fortable about lying. "How 'bout we go upstairs?"

Lermontov got only as far as the foot of the stairs. "Wait. I think I'll leave my overcoat down here." He tossed his coat and hat into the car, then, moving sideways like a skier making his way up a slope, squeezed his way up the narrow stairway.

"I hope, when I leave my current employer, the apartment you provide for me in Washington won't have such a skinny staircase."

"I don't know what kind of apartment they'll provide," said Frank. "I've never worked with a traitor before."

"Touché," said Lermontov. "I didn't know if we would be congratulating each other or crying in our beer. But some instinct told me your cupboard might be bare. So I brought."

He opened his briefcase and pulled out the biggest bottle of vodka Frank had ever seen. "What is that?" he asked.

"Two liters. Export quality. I'll leave it with you."

"I appreciate that."

"It occurred to me you might need some reserves," said Lermontov. "You know they may pull you out of here any day. They can't, however, pull you out until the Iranians let them bring in some planes."

"It beats walking."

"Some people have gotten out by truck through Turkey, but I don't recommend it."

"What about getting Russians out?"

"No. Our embassy will stay. But once you're gone, Moscow will recall me and, *Inshallah,* reassign me to Washington. Normally, that would be a six-month process. But, given these circumstances, we can expect an accelerated transition."

"Let's hope so."

"We should meet at least once more at a Soviet safe house. It would be helpful, to keep Moscow interested, if you brought as much good material as you can get your hands on."

"That means I first have to find a way to get to the embassy. And right now we're under orders to sit tight where we are."

"I have great faith in your ability to make yourself an exception. But we must also prepare for the possibility this will be our last meeting. In Tehran, that is."

"I don't think it can happen that fast," said Frank.

"Who knows?" Lermontov's neck disappeared as he shrugged his enormous shoulders. "Knowing how our bureaucracy works, it will be at least a month before I return to Moscow. Another two to three months, at best, to work out my assignment to Washington. By then you will have been contacted by someone under the direction of our *rezidenza* in Washington. Someone working under deep cover, as an American under the name Howard King. He will take you to dinner and suggest you begin working with him. You will express dismay at such a clumsy effort at entrapment. Ask him if he works for your Counter Intelligence office or the FBI. At some point he will say this is only an interim arrangement until 'your friend' arrives. Leave abruptly. If we do meet again here, at a Soviet facility, no matter what I say then about your contact with Howard King, this is the way you will handle it."

"Understood," said Frank. Lermontov had again taken charge.

"And of course our station in Washington still has an active penetration agent in Langley. We must move forward, but with great caution."

"Any chance you can identify him before we're all out of here?"

Lermontov was slow to respond. "Perhaps. But only if he does something foolish that reveals himself. And he does not seem like a foolish person."

Neither are you, thought Frank. Giving him up from here might convince our Holy Ghost that he doesn't need you in America.

"In all probability," said Lermontov, "your second contact in Washington will come from me. But it will not come directly. You will receive a phone call at home from an Ethiopian. He will speak in Amharic, identifying himself as your old friend from Addis, using the name Hailu Gebre."

"I'm afraid my Amharic's pretty rusty."

"Understood. He will switch to English and arrange to meet you for dinner at an Ethiopian restaurant. But at the appointed time and place he will not meet you. I will."

"You've read too many spy novels."

"In fact," said Lermontov, "we use spy novels in our training programs. You should write one someday. I can guarantee you, KGB will buy hundreds of copies."


Frank sat in the quiet house after Lermontov had gone, wanting a moment alone. He sipped chilled Stolichnaya from a coffee cup and thought about Belinsky, about Nazih, Sergeant Abbas, about the GRU and Aeroflot agents he had probably sent to their deaths, and again about Belinsky and the *fatwa* that named them both. He knew he had put Belinsky at risk. With Mina and Anwar. With his need for translations. His quest for Khomeini's tapes. His scheme to entrap the GRU officer who could deflect Soviet counterintelligence attention away from Lermontov. Playing roulette, Russian roulette, with another man's life. And losing. He raised the coffee cup and sipped a silent toast.

He set the coffee cup aside. Belinsky put himself at risk. True enough, thought Frank, but he felt suffused by incredible, indelible guilt. His night would end in a sleeping bag on Todd Waldbaum's floor. He knew he should feel grateful. Instead, he felt resentment. He wanted to be alone, alone with the way he felt. He knew two of the upstairs rooms had beds. He longed to crash up there but knew he must preserve the sanctity of the safe house.

The phone rang. He stared at it. He reached out for the coffee cup and drained it. The phone went on ringing. His stomach knotted and the taste of bile rose in his throat. There was no reason for the phone to ring. And no reason to be afraid. He retrieved his smoke-scented parka and put it on. He slipped his tape recorder into a pocket and pulled on his black stocking cap and headed for the door. The phone still rang.


"Where the hell have you been?"

"I took a couple of days off," said Frank. "Cruised up the Caspian with

Lermontov. Spent some time in Baku. Checked out their National Voice of Iran Radio setup. Picked up some caviar."

"Very funny. I know where you've been. What I don't know is why the fuck you didn't get down here any sooner than this."

"Just one reason. I was scared shitless."

"After some 'a the shit you pulled off lately, I thought you were supposed to be Sullivan the fearless."

He remembered Rocky's words. *Feel good is not my middle name.* And fearless isn't mine, he thought.

"Not my name," he said aloud. Again he thought of Belinsky, overcoming weakness. And fear.

"You seen Lermontov?"

"Yesterday."

"What's up?"

"Contact instructions for Washington in case we don't hook up again here. He hopes we do see each other again with me bringing him a bushel of good stuff to keep Moscow wanting more."

"Put it in a cable. Moscow wants more, we'll get'm more. The Holy Ghost is hot to trot. I've got a cleaned-up version of your cable on the to-do at Dowshan Tap. You can pass it to Lermontov. I also got an okay to give him a wrap-up on the pullout, the burn barrels, all that."

"Good," said Frank.

"Nothing is good," said Rocky. "We just lost another war. The holy warriors took over just about everything, including your Supreme Commander's Headquarters, all the prisons, the armories, the palace, Lavizan, the works. They say some Bodyguard units are still hangin' tough. But yesterday Gharabaghi got together what's left of the generals, and they come up with a statement sayin' from here on out the military had declared neutrality and ordered the troops back to their barracks. Couple hours later the radio stopped playing John Philip Sousa. Some guy come on and said the revolutionary forces had taken over the station. He read Gharabaghi' s statement, and I wish I had a tape and a translation to send to your good friend Fritz Weber."

"So do I. What do we do next?"

"Nail Lermontov."


Frank fumbled with the keys while he chalked a thick line on the safe house door. He let himself in and locked the door. He listened and heard nothing but the quiet he wanted. He peeled off the parka, dropped it with his wool cap on a kitchen chair, and headed for the freezer. The phone rang. He'd told Bill Steele about the phone, and Bill had said, "You did right not to answer. If it happens again, don't answer." He told Rocky, and Rocky responded the same way. "Nobody's supposed to be there, so there's nobody there to answer the phone. If it happens again, let me know."

The phone kept ringing. Big brother, somebody's big brother is watching you. He wondered if the caller could be a one-armed Iranian with his head shrouded by the hood of his black wool jacket and a Czech machine pistol tucked in a shoulder holster. He went into the front room and glared at the jangling phone and did something he hadn't done since he was a teenager—the fuck you sign, left hand slapping into the crook of his right arm, closed fist directed at the phone. He went back to the kitchen, muttering, "Ring your ass off," and poured a deep wash of vodka into a coffee cup. He climbed the stairs to the second floor, headed for the back bedroom and slammed the door shut behind him, hoping to muffle the sound of the phone. He sat on the edge of the bed, sipping vodka and telling his mind to forget the phone. But his mind kept wondering what would happen if he picked up the receiver.

Nail Lermontov. He closed his eyes and saw the peregrine he'd watched one day as it nailed a pigeon in Central Park. How, he'd wondered, could an endangered species survive and make kills in midtown Manhattan? The world's biggest pigeon, Vassily Lermontov. Nail him. He'd circled his prey for years, and now his wings caught air, but still he only circled as their Pan Am plane had circled above Tehran the day he arrived so long ago. The peregrine studied the pillars of smoke that drifted skyward, still dimly aware of the distant, insisting phone.


At four the next day the orange taxi picked up Frank on Zarrabi Street. The Chechen behind the wheel nodded as Frank climbed in.

"No glasses. We go to Vassily's house."

Frank felt grateful. He wanted to see the city. Heavy traffic slowed their way. Long, peaceful lines waited at benzene stations. People shut up for days by the heavy fighting crowded the sidewalks under cloudy but mild skies.

"People think the war is over," said the Chechen.

I wonder, thought Frank, remembering a phrase he'd picked up in Angola. *La lutte continua.* The war continues. Always. Everywhere. All over the world.


"Well," said Lermontov, "it's been so long since I've seen you. You must tell me what you did during the war."

Sipping Lermontov's vodka, Frank related in detail all that had happened at Dowshan Tappeh. "I've got two cables on what happened, one about the battle, one about the American pullout. Also traffic the station filed over the past couple of days, plus some the ambassador filed."

"Just some?"

"I got all I could grab. Even some routine administrative stuff that may have some hints about the policy debate."

"Such as?"

"First, there's the big debate. Admit the Shah to the States. Keep him out. I brought you several cables on that."

"It looks like you Americans will betray another ally. The longer his trip to America gets delayed, the less it seems he will ever get there."

Frank suspected Lermontov worried more about his own prospects of getting to America than he did the Shah's.

"Then there's all the other debates," he said. "Make a deal with the mullahs or send in the marines. Impose sanctions. Seize Iranian assets in the States. Stay here or pull out. Shut the embassy down. Keep it open. They have clearance from the foreign ministry to bring in two Pan Am flights this weekend to fly out all the Americans in Tehran. That sounds like the close-the-embassy side won. At least for a while."

"All the Americans?"

"That's what they said."

"Even you?"

"Even me."

"It could be as soon as the weekend?"

Frank nodded. "And I heard they might haul us all down to the embassy Friday evening and make us camp there overnight to make sure no one's missing Saturday morning."

"Then we have much to do. I've arranged for your taxi to pick you up on a street called Behshid that runs parallel to Nezamabad. Thursday at four." He handed Frank a section of the city map. "If you don't make it, I'll see you in Washington."

"I'll drink to that," said Frank.

*"Bon voyage."*

They clicked their glasses. Lermontov drained his. Frank sipped.

"Now, what else do you have for me?" said Lermontov.

"Lots of stuff, including a summary the station received of a cable filed by one of our people who met with the Shah in Rabat. Says the Shah looked like a broken man but that he was proud of the fact he'd avoided a bloodbath. Said he has no contact with any of the military leaders in Iran. Makes no mention of him coming to the States."

"That doesn't surprise me. Let's take a look at all these wonderful documents."

Frank emptied the contents of his briefcase onto the table. He knew Rocky had doctored much of the material, particularly what purported to have come from the ambassador, but he thought the final product would impress Moscow. Lermontov agreed.

"This should bring you an excellent bonus, but it may have to wait till we meet in Washington. Meanwhile, I have a modest bonus, a thousand dollars, for the material you brought last time."

Frank counted the twenties, wondering if he would have to bum them himself. He signed the receipt.

"We need to spend some time on contact instructions in Washington," said Lermontov. He repeated the contact instructions he'd already given Frank, with alterations. This time, under the watchful eyes of the Russian eavesdropping equipment, he told Frank to extend "the greatest possible cooperation" to Howard King.

"You know how I feel about working with anyone but you," said Frank.

"You will extend complete cooperation, understood?"

"Understood," said Frank.

Lermontov made him repeat the instructions.

"Good. If we do meet again, I will have you repeat this scenario again. Do not attempt to assist your memory by committing any part of this to paper."

"Of course not," said Frank.


"He goes through all that," said Rocky, "knowing you're wired."

"He plays it to the video cameras."

"Yeah, he does. And he plays it by the book."

"I don't see why I keep wearing that damn wire. We never use it."

"We might need to check something someday. But the real deal is the tapes go to Henry James so he can convince himself you aren't playin' games."

"Great. And if I ever slip up and say something on one tape that contradicts what I say on another, he can hang me."

"Like that. So don't ever slip up. Lermontov's stuff includes a note for you. Says, 'If you have a problem getting to me on Thursday, put a chalk mark on your safe house door early as you can. I'll try to get to you that day. If not, I'll come Friday.'"

"Let's hope he doesn't wait till Friday," Rocky added. "You may be busy packing." He pushed the note aside. "Somethin' else we need to talk about. The *Wall Street* fucking *Journal*."

"Please," said Frank. "That's one of the world's great newspapers."

"Yeah, I know. Too fuckin' great. You heard what happened yesterday?"

"What?"

"Some guys tried to shoot up the Inter-Continental, where all the reporters hole up. Not once, twice. Bad news is they didn't kill anybody."

"Who were they?"

"Dunno. If I did I'd give 'em all medals for tryin' and a kick in the ass for not killing at least this *Wall Street Journal* bastard."

"What's he done?"

"Stuff about our ops here started showin' up. Accurate. No big stories, just stuff inside of the big stories they run on Iran these days. Nothing that could get anybody hurt. No names. Just . . . details. You got any ideas?"

"Only what I told you back in December, about someone giving Bill Steele's phone numbers out, not just to the *Journal* guy. BBC, *Washington Post,* I forget what all."

"Yeah, Bill and I talked. But what's showin' up isn't just about Dowshan Tappeh."

"Which means it's gotta be someone in your shop."

"Like who?"

"You must have a deputy who sees everything."

"Not everything. Not the way I work. Some things nobody, not my deputy, not the ambassador, nobody sees."

"Somebody does."

"Yeah," said Rocky, "the guy who gets it."

"Maybe they have a leak at that end," suggested Frank.

"But it shows up in stories filed from here, with this Arab guy's by-line on it."

"Doesn't matter," said Frank. "A paper like the *Journal* may feed material from its Washington bureau into a story filed from here. Or from any other source, for that matter."

"Like?"

"The wire services. AP, UPI, Reuters."

"Do me a favor," said Rocky. "Do me a cable. Langley's comin' down on my back to find the leak. Tell them what you just told me about how it could be comin' outta Washington. Don't overdo it. Maybe the problem is here. Say that. But at least give'm somethin' else t' think about."

"There's something else they should think about," said Frank.

"What?"

"The guy who sends it."

"Me?" Rocky's eyes narrowed.

"No," said Frank. "The guys in your communications room."

At a summons delivered by Bill Steele, Frank and Gus were back in Rocky's office the next morning.

"His nibs wants us up in his office," said Rocky. "I don't know what about.

He said ten-fifteen, but with everything goin' on around here, I got a hunch it's gonna be sit and wait a while."

Frank and Gus followed Rocky up the concrete steps to the ground floor. The marine they had first met at the back gates while a "Death to America" demonstration raged out front checked their IDs. "Good to see you gentlemen again."

"Thank you," said Frank. "Good to see you." The marine buzzed them through the gate to the marble staircase that led to the second floor.

"Sir," said the marine in an undertone to Rocky, "in view of the circumstances, perhaps you should know. Two newspapermen just went upstairs with Mr. Ross."

"Mister who?" said Rocky.

"Mr. Ross, sir. The press officer."

"With some newspapermen?"

"Yes, sir."

"Shit. Let's hope for the best." They climbed the stairs. "Lemme take a look in Belinsky's old office." Rocky cracked the door and peered inside. "It's clear. You guys park in here."

"Nice touch," said Frank.

"Don't be so fuckin' sensitive," said Rocky. "Belinsky wouldn't mind. Gets you outta the way of nosy reporters, is all."

Walking on a dead man's grave. Frank remembered the Shah's words. Americans, whistling in the dark as they walk by my cemetery. He thought of Khomeini at Behest-e Zahara. He thought about death, surrounding them. Like a shroud. He walked into the office that had been Belinsky's.

"I'll see what's up with Mr. Ambassador," said Rocky. He closed the door behind him.

"You seem wound a little tight, my friend," said Gus.

"A little," said Frank. He looked around the barren office. "Being in here doesn't help."

"It's a war," said Gus. "People get killed. Get over it."

"I will. Just . . . give me a minute."

"Sure," said Gus. "I wonder what those two reporters are after?"

"Hell, Iran's the hottest story in the world," said Frank. "Aren't you glad to be part of it?"

"No," said Gus. "And neither are you."

Frank moved around the metal desk and sat in the straight-backed chair Belinsky had used. Okay, he thought. I can do this. "Seems to me the ambassador would want to stay clear of reporters right now." I can think like a good covert action man should. "And you'd think his press secretary would help him steer clear." Get over it, he told himself. There's a war on.

"He says ten minutes," Rocky announced as he rejoined them. "He's in a snit about somethin'." He closed the door behind him, took a chair, and looked from one to the other.

"What's with your buddy?" he asked in Gus's direction. "You decide to move in here, Sully?"

"No," said Frank. "I don't much like embassies."

"Speaking of which, guess what happened in Kabul this morning."

"Islamic militants took over?" suggested Frank.

"Worse," said Rocky. "The ambassador, Spike Dubs, got kidnapped. You were right about what Lermontov gave you on the Islamic militants in Kabul. In fact, Sully, I hate to admit it, but you've been right about most of the shit you reported."

"Not reported," said Frank. "You mean tried to report."

"Come on. What have I stopped you from reportin'? Lately."

"You're funny," said Frank.

"Me? Funny?"

"Yeah, you." Frank felt his anger scratching. "Not too long ago, you son of a bitch, you wouldn't let me report much of anything."

"I am nobody's fucking son of a bitch," snarled Rocky.

"Yeah, you are, and now, all of a fucking sudden, you want me to report everything."

"Calm down," said Rocky. He seemed to try to take his own advice. "It took a while, you dumb bastard, but you made your fuckin' point. Like with that first atmospherics you did."

"That you fucking sat on."

"For a while I sat on. I finally sent it, didn't I?"

"If you guys are really going to go at it," said Gus, "you want me to hold your coats?"

"No."

"I was only kidding," said Gus.

"I wasn't," said Rocky. "But you and me don't need to be goin' at it, Sully."

"Why not?"

"I hate to admit it, but it took your fuckin' friend General Fritz to make me realize you and me been on the same side all along it."

"He's no friend of mine."

"Yeah, in a way he is. In his own ass-a-holic way. He was so down on you and the job you'd been tryin' t' do, he made me realize in my own way I'd been actin like a fuckin' Fritz. I'm a field man, always have been. But I learned t' play the headquarters game."

"Yeah, you did."

"Come on. I okayed your cable on what Lermontov told you was goin' on in Kabul, right?"

"Yeah. You did."

"If State had listened to what we filed, if the embassy in Kabul had paid attention, we wouldn't have a kidnapped ambassador. I wasn't your problem. Your problem was back in Langley and Foggy Bottom."

"And you played their game."

"You wanna survive in this business, you . . ."

The staccato thunder erupted from all sides. Windows smashed, and heavy-caliber bullets penetrated the brick walls. The three men spread-eagled on the floor. When the first wave eased, they crawled for desks and couches that offered some degree of cover. The intensity of the fire picked up, ebbed, crescendoed again. Frank looked across the rug toward Gus. Their eyes met. No wonder I'm wound up tight, he thought.

He knew high-rise buildings surrounded the embassy compound on three sides, but the heaviest fire seemed to be coming from across Takht-e Jamshid where two taller buildings flanked the six-story Damavand Hotel. The windows in the room where they'd flattened themselves looked out over the open space behind the embassy. He realized those windows had been smashed from the inside by bullets that had pierced at least two interior walls. In the front window, he thought. And out the back. With my bones in between. He thought of the blue and white floor tiles in the dining room of the Damavand and of the dead weight of Belinsky's body. He wished they were in the steel vault that surrounded the bubble upstairs. He wished he were back at their overcrowded bachelors' quarters. He wished he were home in Weehawken. Another loud wave of bullets raked the room. Then the firing slowed.

Stopped.

"Stay down," said Rocky.

Frank felt wedded to the floor, married to its Persian carpet. Stay down? Shit. I may never move again. I wonder if I'm dead. Dust, rising from the rug, tickled his nose. Guess not.

Automatic weapons thudded from outside the building.

"The fuckers must've come through the fences," said Rocky. The sound of metal shutters being pulled down clattered through the hallway. "Stay put till some marines show up and close those shutters for us."

Frank stifled a sneeze. He tried stretching his legs. They worked, and he felt a familiar pain in his right knee. He heard the door behind him open.

"Stay down," ordered a crisp voice. "We'll secure your window shutters." Frank heard the shutters rattling down followed by the clang of bullets cracking into them. He looked up and saw a tight pattern of dents in one of the shutters.

"G3s," said a marine. "Sooner or later they'll smash right through these damn shutters."

On cue, the sound of machine-gun fire and the clang of heavy metal bullets striking metal shutters rang like a chorus of anvils.

"There go the front shutters," yelled one of the marines as he dove to the floor. Still flattened, Frank, Gus, and Rocky did not have to move.

Again, the heavy-caliber firing eased.

"What've they got over there?" hollered Rocky.

"Fifty calibers, sir. Maybe some thirties mixed in."

"Ambassador wants everybody up on the third floor. Move it."

Frank looked up in time to see the chevrons of a marine sergeant turning away from the open door. He stood and looked to Rocky. Rocky nodded. Frank headed out the door and up the stairs to the vault that enclosed the steel-doored communications room and the bubble. He stood aside as Rocky punched in the code that unlocked the door to the bubble. "In." Frank and Gus edged into the bubble, and Rocky pulled the door shut behind them. The reassuring whoosh stirred a breeze. Rocky grabbed a walkie-talkie that sat on the plastic table. "Tom. Larry. Somebody. Over."

"Larry here. Over." The crackling voice sounded remarkably calm.

"Get everybody outta the basement. Now. Up to the third floor. Now. You got anything down there you wouldn't want your mother to know about, bring it with ya', because the mothers are on their way in."

"We got a demolition box we could use."

"No time. Grab and run. Now, or you'll be eating tear gas in a minute."

"Roger."

Not more than two minutes later, Rocky opened the bubble door to admit two middle-aged men in shirtsleeves. "No need for you guys to know each other. The drill is we surrender the lower floors, which is a good idea because those G3s'll cut through those metal doors sooner or later. The ambassador's had the marines stash their M-14s in the vault. They've got shotguns with nothin' but bird shot in them, tear gas canisters, and sidearms they can use only if they gotta t' stay alive."

"Sounds like we surrender again," said Gus.

"Yeah," said Rocky. "We surrender again."

"This surrender drill was planned?"

"Yeah, Gus. Planned and rehearsed."

Frank wondered if the kidnapping in Kabul and the attack under way around him could have happened on the same morning just by coincidence. He thought again of his cables on Lermontov's warning about the embassy in Kabul. Rocky had filed them. He wondered if a government that listened to its intelligence could have prevented the assaults. He thought of himself wearing the opaque glasses Lermontov gave him. Rocky with his hearing aid turned off. Back in Washington, an establishment blind and deaf.

"Rocky?"

"Yuh?"

Frank knew they would never come closer to understanding each other than they had a few minutes before, when Rocky confessed to having played the headquarters game, just before the .50-caliber bullets began to fly.

"Thanks."

"Yeah," said Rocky. "I'd been meanin' t' talk to ya about all that shit."

Through the thick translucent walls of their plastic bubble they could see the hazy outlines of ghostly human forms heading into the communications room, the embassy's skeleton crew filing into its mausoleum. I hope they come out alive, thought Frank.

"You can sniff it," said Rocky. "By now the first floor should be a blanket 'a tear gas. It won't stop 'em, but it'll slow the fuckers down. The ambassador, a military attaché who speaks some Farsi, and an Iranian interpreter who must have very big balls will meet the hostiles on the second floor. No marines. No weapons. The message is we want to surrender. Meantime, if we're lucky, the ambassador got through to Yazdi or some-fucking-body and maybe, just maybe, we'll get some fuckin' I-ranian help to get us outta this mess."

"*Inshallah,*" said Gus.

"We would've been better off in the communications room," said one of the middle-aged men, Tom or Larry. Frank guessed he would never know which.

"We're a whole lot better off here," said Rocky. "You won't get more than a whiff of gas through the bubble. And they're packed like dead sardines in there. Hot, sweaty, and panicked. Fact, I wish I coulda let some embassy creeps in here, but that's a no-no except for the ambassador, and he' s off bein' a general."

"General surrender," said Gus.

"Give him credit," said Rocky. "High command says keep the embassy open at all costs. In the face of that, it takes some brains to prepare for the worst, and then it takes some guts to surrender to try to save your troops from gettin' their ass shot off."

"You're right," said Gus. "I shouldn't be so snippy."

"O'Connor's a cut above the herd," said Rocky. "The other night, in the middle of all kinds of shit, General Gast and some MAAG guys trapped at Supreme Commander's Headquarters, the air force guys trapped at Dowshan Tappeh, and our fuckin' friend here gone missin', the ambassador gets a call from some gofer in Washington sayin' Brzezinski wants an update on the prob-ability of the Iranian military staging a coup to save the country from Khomeini. By that time there is no Iranian military. The ambassador tells the guy to tell Brzezinski to go fuck himself. Flat out. That's what he says. The guy says he doesn't think that would be an appropriate response. The ambassador tells the guy to ask Brzezinski if he wants him to translate it into Polish. And then he hangs up. Now, I don't like him sendin' a message like that to a countryman of mine, but I gotta give him credit."


As the day wore on, chaos and confusion seemed to Frank to play a larger role than the ambassador's courage. He guessed close to a hundred people huddled in the communications room. In the spacious and air-conditioned bubble, the five of them enjoyed relative comfort. He doubted more than a hint of tear gas rising from the first floor could seep into the air-tight bubble. He resumed normal breathing and felt normal. And then the electricity died.

"I don't hear something," said Gus.

"You don't hear what?" said Rocky.

"I don't hear the hum of the air conditioner." In a moment the lights flickered out. No one spoke. In the awful quiet, the muted sound of automatic weapons outside the building took on a new dimension. The firing seemed to come from two separate areas.

"That's not just G3s," said Tom or Larry. "One bunch has AK-47s."

"Maybe the civil war isn't over yet," said Gus.

The clang of heavy metal banging on metal changed the conversation. "They've got one of those doors shot to hell, and now they'll batter it open," said Rocky.

"Yeah, but who?" said Gus. "The G3s or the AK-47s?"

And which one's on our side? wondered Frank. If either.

The group armed primarily with German-made G3 automatic rifles battered its way in first. The group bearing mostly Russian AK-47s followed quickly. Pushing and shoving but not shooting, the two groups battled to be the first up the stairway to the second floor, where the ambassador, his military aide, and his interpreter waited. Even when he gleaned the details from the ambassador later, Frank remained confused.

"The group that attacked us, the *Feda'iyan,* obviously operate under the control of George Habash and the Popular Front for the Liberation of Palestine."

"Obviously?" said Gus.

"You can tell from the black-and-white headscarves they wear," said the ambassador.

Frank thought of Munair wearing a similar headscarf a few days before. He doubted that devout Munair and his cab-driving brother-in-law operated under the control of George Habash. He stood in the open air outside the bullet-racked embassy with the ambassador, Gus, and Rocky. A cold winter breeze thinned the lingering tear gas. He wanted to do a cable on the attack but realized he did not know enough about what really happened. And he wondered if Rocky would let him file it. Shit, Frank thought. I should give him more credit that that.

"Ibrahim Yazdi sent an Islamic group loyal to Khomeini to pull us out of it," the ambassador told them. "Yazdi was out here himself with a bullhorn telling everybody Khomeini wanted the Americans protected."

"And they listened?" said Gus.

"Eventually they did," answered the ambassador. "But I had trouble figuring out who was who. The first roughneck to get to the head of the stairs, he had one of those headscarves and an AK-47. Right after him comes this other bozo, bare-headed, but his only weapon is a bayonet. I thought he'd run me through. But I guess he was one of the people Yazdi brought in. Each of them starts tugging at one of my arms, like I was some kind of trophy they were fighting over. I guess they agreed to both walk out with me. Then Yazdi got ahold of them, and after a whole lot of palaver the *Feda'iyan* guy agreed to obey the Ayatollah and get his gang out of here."

"Now what?" said Rocky.

"Well, we're trying to get all the Americans over to the residence. It's shot up pretty bad, but at least it's not swamped with tear gas. And I didn't want people standing around out here in the open. Those machine guns are still up there on the rooftops across the street."

"The residence sounds like a very good idea to me," said Gus. "Let's go."

"Not me," said Rocky, "You guys go. I need to check my communications room."

"I believe everything's under control up there," said the ambassador.

"I'll check," said Rocky,

"Before you go, real quick," said the ambassador. "Reason I wanted to meet with you three. We have a hell of a problem with all these journalists. Fred Ross, my press officer, does a good job, but he can't handle them all. Today he let two walk in on me while I was on the phone with the foreign ministry. I could have killed him. I know Frank and Gus have experience working with journalists, and I wondered . . ."

"No way in hell," said Rocky. "These two guys, especially Sullivan, know too goddamn many newspapermen from too many different jobs with different cover in different countries. Last thing we need is some newshound recognizing one of them and getting nosy about what in hell they're doing here."

"Well, I'm afraid we have a bunch of them already over at the residence, interviewing embassy staff."

"In that case, hold your nose, guys. You're comin' upstairs with me." With Frank and Gus in his wake, Rocky turned from the ambassador and headed for the embassy's battered back door.

The tear gas had emptied the building all but totally. Frank's eyes watered, and he had trouble breathing. He could hear Gus gasping behind him, but Rocky bounded ahead. Frank heard his booming voice.

"What in the fucking hell do you mean, he isn't here?"

Frank followed the sound of Rocky's bellow past the bubble into the communications vault.

"He took the morning off, sir. Said he had some shopping to do. Wanted to get some gifts for the folks back home in case we got evacuated."

"I will fucking kill that fucking little shit. Why didn't he leave the fucking keys with you?"

"I don't know, sir."

Rocky came close to hitting the terrified radio technician but slammed his right fist into his left palm and turned his back. He saw Frank.

"Can you believe these assholes? We're supposed to shred, burn, or blow up every sensitive piece of paper and hunk of equipment in the place. We got just about everything except the fucking code boards that are locked up in that fucking steel closet over there. This asshole knows the combination, but you need keys and the combination to open the fucking thing, and the other asshole who went shopping walked off with the keys."

"Only one set?" asked Gus.

"No other set," said Rocky. "One of these idiots lost the other set couple days ago."

"It wasn't me," said the radio man.

"What's the other asshole's name?"

"Travis, sir. Travis Teasdale."

"That's a name?" said Gus.

"That's his name." He tried to smile but couldn't manage it. "Guys call him Travis T."

"Travesty," said Gus. "You're right. That's his name."

"You guys may know him," said Rocky. "He's holed up at that frat house you're livin' in."

"I know him," said Gus. "The one with the hair drier, right?"

"That's him," said the radio man.

"He spends more time primping than a woman," said Gus. "Hair drier, cologne, nail buffer, tweezers, cuticle scissors. Sleeps with a beauty mask over his ugly face and ties up the bathroom for days, in a house that's got maybe got one bathroom for every twenty people. He's not very popular with the rest of us. Travesty."

"He's gone shopping," said Rocky, his eyes tearing. "Let's get outta here, you two. Not you," he added, thumping the radio man on the chest. "You stay. Breathe deeply. I'll send a couple of marines up to try to keep any hostiles out. If Mr. Travis T. shows up, get the keys from him and have the marines shoot him."

---

"I'd rather take a chance on machine-gun bullets out here," said Rocky. "We've done a pretty good job of gettin' missed so far, but the fuckin' tear gas is a sure thing."

He looked back at the ravaged embassy. "Shame," he said. "Just before we shut everything down upstairs we got another message on Afghanistan. Afghan police raided the hotel where those holy warriors held Dubs. Poor bastard got killed. No one knows if the kidnappers killed him or if a police bullet got him. He probably got a hunky-dory security report just before he got kidnapped." He turned to Frank. "Your Russian buddy can gloat. He told us so."

"Yeah," said Frank. "He did."

"And we reported it," said Rocky. "For all the good it did poor Dubs. When do you see Lermontov again?"

"Tomorrow. His place. If I don't show, the next day at our place."

"After this shit here today I don't how much longer we'll be here, no matter what the hunky-dory team has to say. Look, I managed to get a call in to Bill Steele. He's on his way with an acetylene torch, HC-CH fuel tanks for the torch, oxygen tanks, sledgehammer, crowbar, whatever else he thinks he might need to get that fuckin' safe open upstairs. He was smart enough to stow some stuff in the basement of the frat house couple weeks back. We got a demolition trunk in the vault, so that's one thing he doesn't have to lug."

"You sure it works?" said Frank.

"Fuck you, Sully. It better work. We gotta get those code boards destroyed before the bad guys come back for another look. I told him to just bring one other guy. No need to stick out any more necks than we have to. Sully, think you can give 'em a hand?"

"Sure."

"Gus, do me a favor. Take a stroll over to the residency. Stick your nose in. See what's goin' on. Don't talk t' any reporters. Get back to me here. If you don't see me, that means I'm inside. Just wait for me here, outta the fog."

"Will do," said Gus. He moved off slowly.

"He's a good man," said Rocky. "But he doesn't deserve to be here."

"None of us do," said Frank.

They sat on the concrete steps, saying little, until Bill Steele and Cantwell pulled up in a battered gray truck with Farsi lettering on the door.

"Great-lookin' truck," said Rocky. "Where'd you get it?"

"Hot-wired it back of a grocery store. One of the servants told me it'd been sitting there." They started to unload. "How bad's the tear gas?"

"Like my hair," said Rocky. "Thinning out but still there."

"We may have to try to bust the damn safe open," said Steele. "The torch could set off an explosion if that gas is too heavy."

"Your call," said Rocky. "Me, I think I'd rather get blown up than try and knock that door open."

"We may as well peel off coats now," said Steele. "We'll work up a sweat no matter how cold it is in there. We'll get everything up there before we figure out how to work on the door. Gas masks first. Let me hook you up, Sully." He pulled the mask over Frank's face and head and tightened the straps behind his back that secured the oxygen container on his chest.

"Now all you have to do is breathe. The mask takes care of the rest."

Frank tried to ask what the oxygen tanks were for, but Bill waved his hands and tapped his ears. Frank read his lips.

"Don't waste your breath."

The tanks proved much heavier than they looked. Bill tipped one, put one hand under it, and grabbed the circular brass rim at the top and nodded at Frank. Frank latched on to the opposite side of the tank and together they hoisted it.

Holy shit, thought Frank, how many flights?

They struggled up the four outside steps and through the doorway. Bill nodded at Frank, and they set the tank down. Bill rolled it across the linoleum floor, tipped it, and nodded to Frank at the foot of the marble stairs that led to the second floor. They climbed the straight and broad stairway, but sweat drenched Frank's body. He felt short of breath, and his eyes began to tear by the time they reached the landing. They set the tank down, and Frank grabbed Bill by the shoulder, gesturing toward his mask. He had only a vague image of Bill slinging him over his shoulder and carrying him down the stairs and out of the building like a sack of flour.

Steele propped Frank against the side of the truck, ripped off his mask, and said, "Breathe."

He gulped cold air and heard Cantwell saying, "I'm about to put an oxygen mask over your face. Don't fight it. Just breathe through your nose and let the mask do the rest."

Where have I heard that before? thought Frank.

"I wondered what the oxygen tanks were for," he said.

"I hadn't figured on a gas mask not working," said Bill. "The oxygen's for the torch."

The blurry images around him came into focus. Steele, Cantwell, Rocky, Gus, two marines, and the frightened communications man.

Free of his mask, Frank asked, "Did Travesty get back?"

"Not yet, sir," said the technician. "But, but Mr. Novak, you didn't mean that about having the marines shoot Travis, did you?"

"Hell I didn't," said Rocky. "But I don't think they would."

Rocky assigned Frank and Gus guard duty at the truck while the others relayed the rest of the safecracking equipment upstairs. Frank told Gus about the old beat cops' technique of taking ten slow, deep breaths to raise the body temperature. They tried it and then tried flapping their arms and hopping up and down.

"Maybe we should just lug some of this leftover stuff upstairs," said Gus.

"Been there," said Frank, "Tried that. Rather not try again. What news from the residency?"

"War repeats itself," said Gus. "First as tragedy then many times as farce. The big concern over there is getting the generators back working. They're worried about all the food going bad."

"The care and feeding of diplomats," said Frank.

"You know what day this is?" Frank stared at him. "Valentine's Day. Last time they hit the embassy it was Christmas Eve."

"Remember Pearl Harbor," said Frank.

"I do," said Gus. "Sunday morning. That was a helluva little war you and Rocky had upstairs. Before the other war broke out. Couldn't have been easy for him. Ownin' up like that."

"No," said Frank. "Not easy at all."

"Motherfuckers." An angry Bill Steele vaulted over the iron railing at the top of the stairs. He lunged into the back of the truck and hauled out what looked like a footlocker. He dumped it on the ground. Frank and Gus jumped backward.

"Don't worry," said Bill. "It's not C4. A bump won't set it off. Just incendiary stuff. Thermite. TM4. Rocky told me not to bother to bring a burn box. Said he had one here. The one he's got has a tag on it says, 'Do not attempt to use after June 30, 1973.' Corroded wires. Dead batteries. Even a bunch of roaches crawling around. Mr. Novak says, 'Why hasn't this been replaced?' Pissed as I am, I say, 'Ask the chief of station. This is his shop.'"

"Not to worry," said Gus. "What can he do? Have you shot?"

"He would if he could. Sully, I'm gonna need two of these. Can you haul this one up? I'll grab another outta the truck."

Frank carried the surprisingly light trunk upstairs, struggling only on the narrow metal stairway with its tight turn halfway to the third floor.

"Put it in the bubble," said Steele. "Rocky wants to eighty-six that, too."

Frank placed his burden in the bubble and followed Bill into the communications vault. Steele plunged into the gaping closet safe with its torn hinges and came out with a stack of boards under each arm. Frank had no idea what code boards were but guessed they had something to do with the cryptographic dispatch of cables. Bill hunched over as he entered the bubble. He stacked the boards into the trunks, then knelt before each, like a priest administering last rites, closed the lids, and exited the bubble. He whooshed the door closed behind him and said, "Let's get out of here."

Frank lingered a moment as the others filed out, feeling an unexpected regret at the thought of the bubble being blown apart and burned.

# CHAPTER TWENTY-FOUR

That evening, after supper, Travis Teasdale showed off the Persian carpets he had bought. Several of the wives expressed admiration.

"You should take them down to the embassy tomorrow," said Gus. "I bet Mr. Novak would love to see them."

"To hell with him," said Teasdale.

Frank noticed his hair. Ash blond, full, straight. It shone in the light. Teasdale was short, slight, and stoop-shouldered, with a pointy nose and a pinched mouth; his hair stood out as his finest feature.

"Rocky kind of wondered where you were today," said Gus.

"While I was shopping, I heard the embassy had been attacked. I figured there was no point going back there, so I came back here. With my rugs."

Bill Steele, sitting on a couch across the room, glared at him. Frank sensed that he struggled to keep from saying anything. He turned toward Frank. Their eyes met. Bill nodded toward the kitchen and heaved himself up from the couch. Frank followed. Bill closed the kitchen door behind them and said, "Get him the fuck out of here before I kill him."

"Where should I take him? The Inter-Continental? I know a couple of journalists down there would love to interview him."

"Very funny. I wish the guys who shot up that place the other day had done a better job."

"So does Rocky. Other hand, we have to thank Allah the guys who shot up the embassy today didn't kill anybody either."

"Could be the same guys," said Bill.

"Maybe," said Frank. "And may all our enemies shoot crooked."

"Get Teasdale out of here."

"How?"

"Look, I've got keys to a house one of our guys who got rotated home lived in."

"Not my safe house."

"Uh-uh. Your safe house is sacred. Nothing else happens there. This one is up the block the other way. Overcrowded as this place is, I been thinkin' of givin' you, Gus, couple of other guys a chance to camp out there."

"With Teasdale?"

"I didn't think about that till today. But if I don't get him the fuck out of my sight, I swear I'll kill him."

"If walkin' up the block with him will make life easier for you, I'll do it," said Frank.

"Thanks, good buddy. I stoked up the heater, and there's hot water. We got two other guys up from our base in Isfahan that Rocky shut down a week ago. They lost the room they had to one of the families. Been sleepin' on the floor."

"Let's get them in here with Gus. You can lay the deal out to them and why you want Teasdale in on it."

"Poor guy's sleepin' on the floor. That's the only reason I want him in on it."

"Good. You lay it out that way to the four of us. Then I'll go talk to Teasdale."

"When you do, just tell him I gave you the keys. Teasdale knows I won't do him any favors. Just tell him I picked out two guys, told you to pick out two guys. Gus's your buddy. And you knew Teasdale was sleeping on the floor."

Bill introduced the men from the Isfahan base as Fred Savage and Tim McDonald. Savage had the worn look of a man who has seen too much, drunk too much, and hidden too much. His ashen features sagged, giving his lean face a jowly look. McDonald had the rosy cheeks and fresh-scrubbed enthusiasm of the innocent abroad.

"A bed," said McDonald. "What a beautiful thought."

Bill's instructions made clear the limits of their sanctuary, "Word is we're outta here Saturday. They may want all of us down to the embassy the night before. So what you've got is a house, not a home. All meals, here. All daylight hours, here. Anything happens at night I know right where you are and there's a phone. Incoming calls only. If I want you here, I'll say just one word, 'Now.' You got it?"

Grunts and nods told him they understood.

"You walk up the block, together, after dinner. You get back here for first breakfast. Together. You got a good chance of runnin' into neighborhood patrols between here and the house, so keep your cool. Don't panic. Don't run. Maybe they won't bother you. If they do, do whatever they want. Be sure you've got ID, not that they'll be able to read it, but they may want to look at it. The servants tell us they get real suspicious when they see anybody carryin' somethin', even if it's just groceries. They're nervous, and they have guns they don't know much about. They don't much like Americans, and most likely they don't speak English. So figure on sleepin' in your skivvies. Toothbrush, razor, whatever you think you need goes in your pockets or it doesn't go. Got that?"

Frank repeated Bill's instructions for Travis.

"I appreciate this, Major Sullivan. Sleepin' on that floor started really gettin' to my back."

"We meet by the front door in ten minutes," said Frank. "Got that?"

When the five men gathered at the front door ten minutes later, Travis T. carried a black leather bag.

"What's that?" said Frank.

"Just my ditty bag," said Travis. "I can carry it under my arm. No one will notice."

"Hey, I spelled it out for you. There are hostiles wandering around out there. With guns. They see that ditty bag, they'll sure as hell stop us."

"Keep it down," said Savage, and Frank realized they'd attracted attention from the others in the big front room.

"I have to take my bag," said Teasdale. "I shampoo my hair every day. If I don't, I get dandruff. I haven't shampooed today. I can't go to bed with wet hair. I need my hair drier."

"Let's get outta here," said Savage, "before we blow the deal. Let him keep his fuckin' bag."

"Ease up, Frank." Gus kept his voice low but emphatic. "And let's go."


The fifth house on the right, perhaps three hundred feet. The length of a football field, Frank told himself. The bracing night air quickened his senses. The street-lights flickered, casting a faint glow. He squinted to see as far ahead as possible and swiveled his head to look left, right, and over his shoulder. He spotted four armed men edging into the street from the shadows between two buildings.

"Company," he whispered. "Keep walking."

The patrol stopped and seemed content to watch them pass by. Then, one of the men called out, "*Be-bak-shid.*" How polite, thought Frank, hearing an expression he recognized. But a shot fired in the air punctuated "excuse me." He'd also learned to recognize the AK-47. Each of the men had one. Whoever fired the shot did not have his assault rifle set on automatic. He wondered about the others. The raggedly dressed crew formed a semicircle around them. One man stepped forward and poked the barrel of his assault rifle under Teasdale's arm.

"*On chi-ye?*"

"Just my ditty bag."

Frank could not pick out the sounds that followed, but he could read the motion of the gun barrel, jerked upward in short moves.

"I think he wants you to open it," said Frank. "Do it . . . real slow."

Frank watched the pantomime played out by the two men: Teasdale smiled and held out the bag. Frank noticed his crooked, overlapping teeth. The man with the gun nodded and grunted. Teasdale unzipped the bag. The man peered in. He handed his weapon to a companion, took the bag from Teasdale and began to rummage inside it. In a moment he pulled out a black hair drier with a pistol-grip handle.

"*In chi-ye?*" Whatever the words meant, the voice was loud and angry.

"He thinks it's a gun," said Frank.

"No, no," shouted Teasdale. "It's only my hair drier."

"Calm down," said Frank. He began talking slowly and earnestly to the man who held the hair drier, now pointed at Teasdale. He knew the man couldn't understand his words but he hoped the tone of his voice and his slow gestures would convey his message: The hair drier posed no threat.

But, as he spoke, one of the other men moved closer. He was short and elderly, with gray hair poking out from under his black skullcap. Frank felt the icy muzzle of an AK-47 against his left ear. He smiled, he shrugged, he moved the fingers of his right hand through his hair and made a circular motion with his left.

"He uses it to dry his hair. What can I tell you? He's very vain about his appearance."

Frank pointed to the ditty bag and gestured to indicate that something more should be pulled from it. The man with the hair drier and the bag caught his meaning and tugged out the drier's electric cord. Frank held out his hand and, after hesitating, the man dropped the cord into it. Frank hooked one end into the drier and went through the motions of inserting the plug into a socket made by his fist. He made a circular motion with the drier around his scalp, accompanied by a buzzing sound and a heavy exhale from his mouth. The men laughed, and he felt the icy prick of the AK-47 move away from his ear.

His peripheral vision caught a glimpse of the frightened, elderly man with a white beard and white hair sticking out from under a black wool skullcap. The index finger of his right hand cradled the trigger of his AK-47. My father, my executioner, he thought.

Smiling now, the men with the guns waved them on. They made their way to what Frank prayed was the right house. He climbed the eight stone steps and tried the key with the red mark on the top lock. It worked. He had just fit the unmarked key into the bottom lock when the rapid stutter of an AK-47 on automatic exploded behind him. He turned. The white-bearded man with the gun that had been in his ear a moment before now whirled in a circle. The weapon pointed skyward, spinning the old man like a top, his finger frozen by panic to the trigger. Safety off. Set for automatic fire. Frank tensed, cringed, tried to hold himself. But when the door swung open, his bladder betrayed him.

He'd found a washer and drier in the basement, tossed in a bar of soap from an upstairs bathroom, and, with a towel wrapped around him, dropped his shorts and pants into it. The smell of urine had already begun to make its presence felt in the gray winter-wool trousers. He thought of all the many ways he might kill Teasdale: with the AK-47 that had gone off moments after it had been in his ear; with Sergeant Abbas's .45. But nothing seemed as satisfactory as beating him to death with his knuckles protected by his thick, bloodstained winter mittens.

He pulled the pants from the drier. They'd shrunk. But, as he tugged them on, he realized he'd lost enough weight during his time in Iran to accommodate them. He could zip the fly almost all the way up. He couldn't button the top button, but he could pull his belt tight enough to cover the gap. At least they no longer smelled of urine, and he hoped they would soon get a chance to go back to their house for fresh clothes.

As the keeper of the keys, he claimed what he took to be the master bedroom. A double bed with a firm mattress. A private bath, where, for the first time in months, he soaked. He shaved. He brushed his teeth. Naked, he collapsed on the mattress, and he did not sleep.

A phone sat on the night table by the bed. The phone did not ring, but the phone bothered him. In his mind he could hear the phone ringing in the safe house, the phone he did not answer. Insistent. Someone knew he was there. He imagined a one-armed man dialing a phone, studying a scroll written in Farsi that might be his *fatwa,* firing a metallic machine pistol.

A *Wall Street Journal* reporter, or someone saying he was a *Wall Street Journal* reporter, had called Bill Steele at Dowshan Tappeh and at his home. And material about the agency's operations in Iran had appeared in the *Journal*. Including material Rocky said no one had access to but himself and whomever he'd sent it to at Langley. Information is power, Rocky had told him once. *The ambassador may have fancier rugs than I do, but I control information.* And the information flowed through the communications room. Frank began to think about radio men. He thought about Teasdale. He wondered about radio men in the communications center at Langley. He closed his eyes and saw the image of a telephone. At first he mistook it for the jangling phone in the safe house. But this phone sat quiet. On a windowsill. The second-floor hallway of the air force guards' bachelor quarters. Facing the street.


"He hates my guts," said Bill. "That's why he mighta done it." He looked down at the black rotary-dial phone on the windowsill. "The regular air force guys who live here all have a personal code they have to ring in to call home. Local calls, no problem. Just dial. This is the phone the guys mostly use. I've heard Teasdale spends a lot of time on the phone, like he does in the bathroom, and look, this window looks right across at the safe house."

"We may be jumpin'," said Frank. "How would he get the number? How would he get your home number?"

"Let me tell you somethin' about these communications guys. Some of them. Rocky gets them pumped up tellin' them information is power. He controls the flow of information out of the embassy, so he has the real power. But guys like Teasdale think, 'Fuck. We're the ones who really control the information. Without us Rocky can't cable shit.'"

"I don't know," said Frank. "Most of the communications guys I've gotten to know seem pretty decent,"

"Most are," said Bill, "Then there's the creeps like Teasdale. They get to thinkin' they're king of the hill, and it's not a big jump to start scratchin' around for other information like other people's phone numbers. God knows, it's not too tough to find. Phone numbers. Communications room. Emergency need to get in touch. They're all there."

Frank cautioned himself. "It seems to add up, but it doesn't mean he did all that."

"We can put him on the flutter box."

Frank considered himself a skeptic about the polygraph. "Right now," he said, "I think we, especially you, have too much else going on. Like getting our asses out of here."

"You may be right."

Soon after supper, Frank began to think the polygraph might be a good idea. The ringing phone barely intruded on his conversation with Gus until he heard Cantwell calling out, "Hey, Bill. It's for you. Some guy says he's from the *Wall Street Journal*."

Frank crossed the room to Bill's side, grabbed his elbow, and ushered him into the kitchen, where the receiver on a wall phone dangled on its cord.

"Take it," said Frank. "Keep him talking as long as you can. Your usual dumb act, but try to find out why he thinks you're here, how he got the number."

Bill picked up the phone and said, "Yuh?"


"Same guy," said Bill. "Yusef el Baz."

Frank and Bill stood alone in the kitchen. Cantwell stood on the other side of the closed door.

"Same voice?"

"Think so."

"What'd he say when you asked him how he got this number?"

"Said everybody in town knew about me."

"How?"

"Said word was around. Reporters talk to each other."

"That's for sure," said Frank. "How'd he call your name?"

"Mr. Steele."

"He ever say, 'Bill'?"

"I don't think so."

"William?"

"No."

"Anyone call you William these days?"

"Hell, no. And for sure no one ever calls me by my full name. William Oliver Steele."

"William Oliver?"

"Yeah. I hate it. Why you askin' me all this?"

"You're on a list somewhere. And I want to figure out how you're listed on that list."

"I don't give a shit how I'm listed," said Bill. "I want to find out how I got on the damn list. What do we do about this Teasdale prick?"

"We tell Rocky. We keep an eye on him. Beyond that, I don't think much. If he's the one who did it, the damage's he's done is done."

Bill stared at the kitchen phone. "He did it. I can feel it in my bones."


Frank had rechalked the safe house door that morning. He'd decided not to make his street-corner pickup with Lermontov and hoped the Russian would show up that afternoon rather than waiting for Friday. He'd asked Gus to sit in Todd Waldbaum's room, apparently reading. Through Todd's open door Gus had a clear view of the rotary phone on the second-floor windowsill.

"Three-thirty?" said Gus, checking his watch.

Frank adjusted his. "Three-thirty."


As he crossed the street to the safe house, he glanced up at the window that cradled the telephone. No one stood there. Don't look back again, he cautioned himself. He closed and locked the safe house door behind him and began his tour of the hushed rooms. Finding nothing out of order, he had just begun to pour himself a vodka when the phone rang. He checked his watch. Three-forty-two. He took a shallow sip of vodka and picked up the phone.

"Hello."

"Is this Frank Sullivan?"

"Who's calling?"

"Yusef el Baz. *Wall Street Journal.*"

"The hell you say. What made you think anybody was here?"

"You're one of several people on a list circulating among the reporters in town. Said to be knowledgeable about what's going on."

"Sure you didn't just get a call? From a guy letting you know someone would be here?"

"I've been trying to track you down for a couple of days. There's a story going around that there's a death warrant out on you, what Muslims call a *fatwa*."

Frank felt his throat tighten as though some unseen hand had wrapped the cord of the phone around his neck.

"Are you still there?" asked the voice on the phone.

"Yuh," croaked Frank.

"Supposed to be tied in with the CIA man, Charles Belinsky, they assassinated couple days back at the Damavand Hotel."

"Where did you hear all that?"

"Iranian sources."

"Bad sources," said Frank. "I'm not the guy,"

"Hey, level with me. Am I speaking to Frank Sullivan?"

"Someone's been misleading you, pal. I'm just a low-level embassy maintenance flunky checking on an unoccupied State Department residence. I mean, it would be a hell of a coincidence, you callin' an empty house just when somebody walks into it."

"Maybe I dialed a wrong number. Sorry for your trouble."

The phone went dead. He checked his watch. Three-forty-five. Now what, he wondered? Who else knows about this? Teasdale and even the *Wall Street Journal* had become unimportant. Only the scroll he'd imagined, the scroll on which his *fatwa* had been written, mattered now.

Lermontov arrived precisely at four in his blue Fiat. As he pulled into the garage, he raised a finger to his lips. He's wired, thought Frank. He waited for the big man to toss his overcoat and hat into the car before he spoke.

"Welcome," said Frank. "I'm glad you got the message and could get here today. God knows what tomorrow will be like."

"So, is Saturday definite for your departure?"

"As definite as these things get. I won't believe it for sure till the plane gets to its destination and I get off in one piece. But come on. Let's go upstairs. Good to see you."

They settled in the front room with glasses of chilled vodka on the table. "My *rezident* extends his compliments. He wants you to know, except for a few dry periods, your work on our behalf has proved excellent. Moscow has approved a large bonus which Howard King will have for you when you establish contact in Washington."

"How much?"

"Ten thousand."

"I'm impressed," said Frank. "But I'm afraid I don't have much for you today. After what we went through at the embassy yesterday."

"You were there?"

Frank nodded and told Lermontov all he knew about the attack. Lermontov took notes.

"You people can not read the handwriting on the wall."

I can read my *fatwa,* thought Frank.

"I understand you also lost an ambassador in Kabul," added Lermontov.

"So I heard," said Frank.

Lermontov let the sound of their voices and of Frank's replenishing their glasses cover the careful opening of his briefcase. He laid a sheet of paper on the table. Frank read as they talked.

*I have not brought you any material as you probably will not be able to get classified cables out before your departure. I will be here at least another month helping to rebuild our networks and getting my replacement established. After that I expect another two months in Moscow including some leave time before my assignment to Washington.*

"At least another month" bothered Frank, and he suspected it would bother Henry James. He looked up from the note.

"I would appreciate it now if you would repeat your contact instructions," said Lermontov.

Lermontov printed out another note as Frank recited his instructions, including his line about extending "the greatest possible cooperation to Howard King."

"Very good," said Lermontov.

*Don't look so glum,* said the newly printed note. *You have won.*

"I'm sure you and Mr. King will work well together," said Lermontov.

"I doubt it," said Frank. "Just get there as soon as you can."

"See you in America," said Lermontov.

Frank passed him a one-word note. *Mole?*

Lermontov's eyes narrowed. His lips tightened to a slash and his jaw tensed. Slowly, he shook his head. Worried? wondered Frank. Or pissed that I keep asking?

Their good-bye was perfunctory and businesslike, but as he watched the blue Fiat back out of the garage, Frank realized he would miss the oversize Russian behind the wheel. He looked again at Lermontov's final note. *You have won.* Three months before, when Lermontov had first expressed his willingness to defect, Frank would not have believed that. Now he did.

"You couldn't've been halfway out the door before our Travis T. comes up the stairs and real casual walks over to the phone on the windowsill. I guess he watches you walk into the house, then he picks up the phone and dials."

"What time?" said Frank.

"Three-thirty-three," said Gus. "That the time it started to ring across the street?"

"No," said Frank. "Three-forty-two."

"Tell you what," said Gus. "He was on quite a while, and I couldn't tell for sure with his back to me, but it looked like he was the one doin' most of the talkin'."

Talking to somebody named Yusef el Baz, thought Frank. They sat on the edge of the bed behind the closed door of Todd Waldbaum's room. Todd's radio played martial music broadcast by one of the local stations.

"Then what happened?" said Frank.

"He finally hung up and just stood there, lookin' out the window. I took a walk over and said, 'Mind if I use the phone?' He says he's expecting a call. I had no trouble gettin' real nasty with him about tyin' up the phone like he ties up the bathroom. He says he won't be long. I go off in a huff, back to the room. This time I don't care if he knows I'm watching him. Sure enough, a little after four, the phone doesn't ring but he picks it up and dials. Soon as he picks it up, I'm out the door. He isn't on long. I hear him sayin' a whole lot of 'okays' and then he hangs up. 'Done now?' I say, and he turns and nods and looks like he's seen a ghost."

"He had," said Frank. "His own."

Before the first supper shift, Frank, Gus, and Bill Steele met in the basement. Cantwell stood before the closed door at the top of the stairs. Between them Frank and Gus told Bill what happened: the call Frank had taken from Yusef el Baz at the safe house and Teasdale staring out the second-floor window and placing two calls.

"Soon after he makes the first call, the phone rings in the safe house and it's el Baz. Gus tells me that right after four when my Russian buddy pulls in, Teasdale makes another call. Maybe to tell el Baz that I got company. My guess is el Baz tells him about his conversation with me and Teasdale figures we may be onto him."

"It may not be enough to hang him," said Bill, "but I'd sure like to try."

"What's next?" said Gus.

"Tell Rocky," said Bill. "Cantwell, Petry, and me, we got a meeting with Rocky and the ambassador zero seven hundred tomorrow about the evacuation."

"Can I get in on that?" said Frank. He wanted to find a way to tell Rocky about the *Wall Street Journal* and the *fatwa*.

"No chance," said Bill. "Rocky would flip out, you showed up uninvited. 'Sides, I need both you guys to keep an eye on Teasdale."

"Forget Travis T.," said Gus. "Tell us about getting outta here."

"Looks like we catch a break," said Bill. "All the folks here, they figure they can rely on us to hang together, so we don't have to get to the embassy till Saturday morning. Vans and buses will pick us up. Gus, you're on the first flight. To Rome."

"Hallelujah."

"Frank, you and me got the second flight, along with three hundred and sixty something other people. To Frankfurt."

"Connecting flight to New York, I hope."

"That's the idea. For you, anyway. Stop in London. I'm headed for Boston, but the whole East Coast has had a shitpot of bad weather lately. And they expect an ice storm in Frankfurt."

"Out of the frying pan into the ice," said Gus. "What flight is Teasdale on?"

"I'll let you know on that when I get back from the embassy. Look, I know you guys have personal effects back at the other house. Get 'em tomorrow. I'd suggest right after noon. Midday prayer time. The patrols get a little lax around then. If you do run into one, just act normal, friendly, go on about your business. If they want to search the house, let 'em. Remember the ground rules. One suitcase that's light enough you can carry it yourself. One small carry-on that fits under the seat. Lotta people will have heavy winter coats to stow in the overheads. No weapons, of course, no knives, scissors, tape recorders. No official-lookin' papers except your ID. Large amounts of money, jewelry, big radios, even notebooks and maps may get confiscated. And get you interrogated."

"What about Teasdale while we're doin' that?" asked Gus.

"I'll have Savage and McDonald keep an eye on him. They don't have to know why. I'll find a way to get Rocky by himself in the morning. Break it down. See what he wants to do."

"You think he might run?" said Gus.

"Teasdale? He hasn't got the balls. Or the smarts. He's a good sneak, is all."

"He could try selling himself to the Russians," said Frank. "They'd love a defecting CIA radio man."

"You guys are his roommates. Keep an eye on him. Don't do or say anything to spook him any more than he's already spooked."

"He's been spending a lot of time in the bathroom," said Gus. "Flushin' the toilet a lot."

"Shittin' in his pants," said Bill.

"Or getting rid of phone numbers," said Frank.

Frank asked Bill to let him have a few minutes alone with the typewriter in his room. "If I can't go down to the embassy with you guys, I need to get an eyes-only message to Rocky."

"You type it," said Bill. "I'll deliver it."

He kept the message brief, dealing only with Yusef el Baz's knowledge of the *fatwa*. Since they were all leaving the next day, he knew Rocky could do nothing about it, but he didn't want Rocky to be sandbagged by the remote possibility that something might appear in the *Wall Street Journal*. He wanted to ask for a gun, but he knew there was no chance of his getting one and no chance of getting one through the airport.

A four-man patrol with what looked to Frank like G3s slung over their shoulders walked slowly in their direction as Frank pulled the Nova up to the house.

"Not again," said Gus.

"I'll get out and try and talk to them. Leave the motor running. If I can, I'll go down and open the garage door."

"I hope they all have those things on safety," said Gus.

Frank climbed out of the Nova, smiling and showing his open palms. He pointed to the house and said, *"Fardah Amrika . . . miram."* With the fingers of his right hand extended and his palm flat, he made a gesture he hoped would convey the idea of a plane taking off.

*"Forood?"* Frank had no idea what the man had asked. Intelligent, piercing dark eyes peered out from above his full beard. *"Mehrabad?"*

Frank recognized the name of the airport. *"Baleh,"* he said.

*"In towreh?"* said the man, casually unslinging his rifle. *"Sefarat-e Amrika?"* American Embassy. *"Baleh,"* said Frank.

"Pan Am," said the man with the gun. He nodded toward the house. "Okay."

Frank started to ask, *"Inglissi mi-danid?"* but decided to quit while he was ahead. He had permission to enter the house. He hoped. *"Mamnoon am."* He turned and walked toward the house. He unlocked the useless wrought-iron gate and climbed the concrete steps. He heard footsteps behind him as he undid the two locks. He glanced over his shoulder to see the four armed men coming up the steps. He held the door open for them and followed them in. They walked through the kitchen and into the front room. The man who had unslung his G3 turned and held the weapon up.

"Gun?" He made a sweeping gesture to indicate the house.

*"Nah,"* said Frank. *"Nah* gun."

"Good." The man pointed upstairs with his G3. Two of his companions headed up the stairs. The fourth man began poking around in the front room. Frank held up his house keys and pointed down. *"Otomobil,"* he said, grateful for the near cognate.

"Okay."

Frank made his way down the front stairs, unlocked and opened the garage door, and watched Gus back in.

"What's happening?" said Gus as he clambered from the car.

"They're searching the house. Mostly for guns, I guess."

"Leaving you alone?"

"I guess."

"Good sign. Shall we mosey on up?"

"I'm tempted to stay here."

"Let's mosey."

They entered the kitchen in time to see the man Frank had tried to communicate with open the refrigerator door. He bent to peer inside, closed the door, and started to turn away. He stopped and opened the door to the freezer. He reached in and pulled out a bottle of Absolut Frank had forgotten he'd left there. He feared he was about to see the remnants of his Absolut poured down the drain or smashed against the wall. The man studied the label.

*"A-be,"* said Frank, somehow remembering the word for water. He wished he knew the word for bottled. He wanted to say "bottled water".

*"A-be?""*

*"Baleh."*

The man unscrewed the cap and sniffed. "Baad *a-be."*

Frank pointed to the tap on the sink, nodded, and said, *"Baleh.* Bad *a-be."* He could make no sense of the torrent of Farsi that poured from the man. Then he picked up two words: Evian *a-be.* The man repeated, "Evian."

"Evian," echoed Frank, nodding. "Maybe that's how Iranians say "bottled water." The man screwed the cap back on the Absolut and returned it to the freezer.


They'd finished their swift packing and lugged their bags downstairs. Frank had changed pants, discarding the shrunken pair he'd had on the night an AK-47 had rested in his ear. The rest of what he'd decided to take he slung into the suitcase he would check through to Frankfurt. The carry-on held a change of socks and underwear and his toiletries. He suspected Gus had packed in much the same way.

"That's the lick-and-a-promise school of preparing for a long journey," said Gus. "Since our holy warrior friends didn't pour your vodka down the drain, how 'bout we pour some down us?"

"It isn't Scotch," said Frank.

"For a sailor on dry rations, any port in a storm."

They'd lingered over vodka, sipping and talking in fits and starts. Frank guessed that Gus's mind was on home, his wife, Rome. His own thoughts flitted from Lermontov to the still active KGB mole in the agency and back again and again to the *fatwa*. Somehow the fact that a reporter for a major American newspaper knew about it worried him as much as the death warrant itself, giving it a wider currency than he would have thought possible. Munair had told him the *fatwa* placed an obligation on all devout Muslims, but Frank had not really believed the threat could follow him to America. Now it seemed to be already there.

"Well," said Gus, "if we're gonna get outta here, I guess we better get goin'."

"Let's go," said Frank, pushing himself up from the Formica-topped table. They left the vodka behind.

# CHAPTER TWENTY-FIVE

Frank noticed a major change in the decor of the embassy cafeteria, the Caravansari. A huge photograph of Ayatollah Khomeini had replaced the full-color portrait of the Shah above the door.

Stripped of its liquor and luxury goods, the adjacent commissary served as a processing center. Lingering tear gas made the embassy uninhabitable for more than a few minutes at a time, and the consulate proved too small to handle the hundreds of Americans seeking exodus. He'd surrendered his passport, filled out emigration forms, and filed into the Caravansari. He and Gus soon discovered the extent of their luck in not having to arrive the night before.

Snipers had again attacked the embassy from rooftops across the street, but this time with nothing heavier than assault rifles. Islamic guards, assigned by Ibrahim Yazdi to protect the embassy, fired back from within the compound. Apparently, no bullets found flesh.

"The gangs that couldn't shoot straight," said Gus.

"They shot straight enough to take out the Bodyguard," said Frank.

"True, but from what I hear we might have faced more danger from the food. Hamburgers and canned corn."

"I'm glad we missed the bullets *and* the food."

"What's Rocky plan to do about Teasdale?"

Frank shrugged. "Bill Steele tells me Rocky's arranging for the FBI to pick him up in Rome, take him in for questioning, put him on a flutter box, work up some kind of revealing-classified-information charge, and ship him back to the States."

He realized he didn't care what happened to Teasdale. No more than he cared about what might happen to the GRU and Aeroflot hustlers Belinsky had worked with. Belinsky had already been killed, not for his sins, but for his courage. He did worry about what damage the still-active mole in Langley might cause. He worried about might happen to Lermontov. He worried about himself and the death warrant he carried back to the states as part of his baggage. He felt naked without his passport. He'd surrendered all his *rials* and several hundred dollars in large-denomination American currency to the station's administrative officer. A receipt gave him a good chance of getting the money back as expenses. He'd left many things behind: his tape recorder, erased tapes, notebooks, address book, scissors, anything that might cause problems when the Islamic militia searched luggage at the airport. He had no problem with anything he'd left, including the money he'd surrendered. But he kept checking his pockets to make sure he had his passport and then remembering he'd turned it over to an embassy employee he did not know in exchange for a Pan Am ticket to New York via Frankfurt and a bus assignment, number 8. He had his ticket home but felt he'd given up his identity.

A booming voice over a bullhorn startled him. "Bus number seven. All passengers on bus number seven, prepare to depart for the airport."

"That's me," said Gus. "I guess this is it."

"Yeah. I guess."

"All passengers for bus number seven, prepare to depart. Carry your own luggage on board. Stow it in the aisles."

"We'll have to have a class reunion in Washington someday," said Gus.

"Sounds good," said Frank, knowing it might never happen. They embraced. Gus hefted his suitcase and turned his back.


Still without his passport, Frank boarded the already crowded bus with a dozen or so people still on line behind him. He recognized it as a regular city bus and noted the large black-and-white photo of Khomeini taped to the front window. He scrambled over suitcases and several pet cages and caught an aisle seat next to a heavy-set man who already had fallen asleep. Lucky man, he thought. He soon realized his own luck as several latecomers found all the seats taken.

"Don't worry," hollered a male voice. "We'll stand all the way to America if we have to."

Subdued laughter underlined the tension of passengers fearful of snipers and mobs along the way. Frank knew the most direct route would take them by the gates of the university. He hoped for a detour. He heard a stir at the front of the bus. Three armed guards had boarded. Two remained by the front door. The third, tall, dark, and clean shaven, executed a difficult passage toward the back. Only when he leaned against a rail in the stairwell of the rear door and their eyes met did Frank recognize Anwar the Taller, carrying a G3 assault rifle, coatless in his blue *homafar* uniform but without the cap Frank had worn during the battle at Dowshan Tappeh. Very slightly, Anwar shook his head. Frank looked away.

The bus turned right, leaving the embassy gates, away from the direction of the military compound where for months a swaying, leaning building crane had teased his imagination with its defiance of gravity and its refusal to yield to the alternately frozen and muddy ground it stood on. He knew it must have toppled, yet a crazy hope lingered that it had somehow survived. But nothing had survived: not the military nor the government; not the friendships that had started to form; not the Shah. But the embassy still stands, he thought. A semblance of relations still exists between the United States and the government of Mahdi Bazargan. He glanced again at Anwar, remembering his warning of the civil war that might follow the takeover by Ayatollah Khomeini. He wondered if the embassy, or Bazargan, or Anwar the Taller would survive that. He tried to forget the crane as they turned left onto Pahlavi. The bus rolled across Shah Reza, which meant they would steer clear of the university. At the next major cross street, they turned, very slowly, to the right. He glimpsed an armored personnel carrier ahead of the bus. He noticed Anwar, finger on the trigger of his G3, checking the street through a glass partition on the door. As the bus picked up speed, he relaxed. His finger came off the trigger, and Frank saw him flick the safety.

"Excuse me," he said. "Do you know the name of this street?"

After a hesitation, Anwar said, "Shah Nader."

"Thank you." His question reflected only a minimal curiosity about their location. He had wanted to establish a final point of contact with Anwar. His question had been a way of saying, "Thank you. And good-bye." All his good-byes, even to Lermontov, had been perfunctory. Rocky had been absorbed by the problem of dealing with Teasdale. He'd enlisted the help of Cantwell and an American military doctor who prepared a hypodermic needle in a small room above the cafeteria. Teasdale seemed resigned to the idea of sedation. He appeared already numb, muttering again and again, "I understand. I understand. I understand."

"You understand shit," said Rocky. He turned to Frank. "Long flight home. Lotta time to think about a lotta shit." He adjusted his hearing aid. "I got a hunch your buddy will make it to the States. And hook up. Maybe catch a mouse. Who knows? You might even find out the truth about all that. Or somethin' like it. See ya around, boychik."

Frank said nothing, suspecting Rocky would not hear his parting words. Rocky shook a fist in Frank's direction, smiled, and popped a thumb straight up. A finger he might have expected, but Frank had never seen Rocky give anyone a thumbs-up. He returned the gesture. How sad, he thought, two grown men with so much unsaid between them and the best we can do is give each other a thumbs-up. A long flight home. A lot to think about.

Now he turned his attention back to their strange caravan. Leftist *Mojahedin* and Islamic revolutionaries protecting Americans from possible snipers who might or might not be *Feda'iyan*. Warm bodies and an overly protective heating system had made the bus stifling. Frank shrugged off his parka and removed his wool cap. The man next to him had begun to snore. He thought of Ali and the way he always had their Nova warmed and the windows steamed. The bus cut to the right, then made a dogleg left onto a street that soon would no longer be called Eisenhower. He caught a glimpse of the Shahyad Monument where millions gathered on *Ashura*. Armed revolutionaries ringed the otherwise empty square. He realized they'd encountered virtually no traffic. The revolution, he thought, has become a government. They had engineered the Americans' evacuation well. They may make the trains run on time.


He changed his mind as he fought his way into the airport terminal. The two Pan Am 747s would carry over seven hundred Americans, plus flight crew, but the mob in the terminal must have tripled that. Adding the Iranians with automatic weapons, Uzis, AK-47s, G3s, and M-14s, to the Iranians behind various counters with no visible weapons, Frank estimated a ground-crew to passenger ratio of three to one. But the service did not rate a gold star. Three men with AK-47s herded them toward a long table: Americans on one side; a motley knot of Iranians on the other, with suitcases gaping like open-jawed alligators and belongings spewed between them. As he approached, he realized competing groups of Iranians each insisted on searching every piece of luggage, arguing among themselves as they went. The largest group ranged in age from teenagers to elderly men and in facial hair from scraggly chin whiskers to full beards. All wore green-and-red headbands and photos of Khomeini pinned to their coats. A younger group, mostly clean shaven and hatless, had apparently come from the collapsed military. The third group seemed more random in age and appearance. Frank noticed a few uniformed *homafaran* among them and suspected they might be *Mojahedin*. He wondered what had become of Anwar the Taller. As the contending groups tugged at the contents of bulging luggage, he wondered, too, if the chaotic scene before him previewed the civil war to come.

Then he saw Anwar, off to his right. Sa'id, also armed with a G3, stood next to him. Anwar nodded, then looked away. In a moment, the crowd swallowed them.

Several feet in front of him, Frank saw a fur-coated woman struggling to hang on to a pet cage. Two Iranians pulled awkwardly at the metal grill. The woman clung to the handle. "No, no," she screamed in a piercing soprano. "You can't take my poopsie poodle. What would poor li'l Chatterbox do without his Momsie-pooh?"

"*Nah saag,*" cried an Iranian, again and again. "*Nah saag. Nah saag.*" The red-faced man standing with the woman began screaming at the Iranian so loudly and rapidly Frank could not distinguish his words. Despite his name and the battle raging around him, Chatterbox remained quiet, sedated, Frank suspected, like Teasdale. Frank wished he had a needle full of sodium Pentothol to jab into the poodle's barking owner.

While one Iranian held fast, the other let go of the pet cage, poked a stubby finger into the man's chest, and shouted over and over again, *"Saag. Saag. Saag."* He'd gone from telling the woman no dogs could go on the plane to telling the man he was a dog. The scene promised to turn even uglier. Several Iranians hefted their automatic weapons. Remembering Belinsky, he thought of hitting the floor but realized he would be trampled if shots were fired and panic broke out.

A young American with sharp features and a bouquet of papers clutched in his bony hand made his way through the circling crowd on the far side of the table. He inserted himself like a letter opener between the stubby-fingered Iranian and the irate Americans and their dog. He spoke to the Americans, nodding like a tightly wound-up doll. Whatever the young American said to his distraught countrymen, it had a calming effect. The woman even picked up his nods; her screams faded to weeping. Armed Iranians appeared behind them and gestured to the man to close their bags and pick them up. Loaded down with four overstuffed pieces of leather luggage, the man staggered behind an escort of Iranians. Cradling the pet cage to her, the woman followed. Two more Iranians trailed, gently poking with their weapons. They disappeared around the far end of the table.

Frank had his suitcase and carry-on bag on the table and opened before anyone noticed him. The man who had screamed at the woman with the pet cage poked into Frank's luggage. Fully bearded, he wore a green-and-red headband and displayed the Ayatollah's photo like a badge on his coat. He seemed to find nothing that interested him. He muttered a series of *nah*-somethings Frank took to mean no guns, no knives, no jewelry, no secret papers, no camera, no forbidden photos, or stash of hidden currency.

The Iranian looked up. Frank smiled and took a chance. *"Nah saag,"* he said.

The man looked puzzled, then grinned and started to laugh and repeat Frank's joke to others. *"Nah saag. Nah saag."* From the way the others joined in his laughter, he gathered the Iranians had not had much fun during their long day. The no-dog man motioned for Frank to close his suitcase. *"Farsi mi-danid?"*

If that means do I speak Farsi, thought Frank, the answer is no. *"Nah,"* he tried. He held thumb and forefinger close together in the universal sign for "very little." *"Kami,"* he said.

"Okay," answered the Iranian. *"Maash-allah. Safar be-kheyr."*

Except for hearing an *"Allah,"* Frank had no idea what the man had said. He hoped it meant something like "Go with God."

*"Mamnoon am."* Thank you. Thank you. Thank you. Now where the hell is my passport?

And then he saw him. The man in the unbuttoned black wool jacket with the hood pulled over his head and the empty left sleeve swinging loose as he moved toward Frank. His first thought, crazily, was to show the man his passport. Then he remembered he didn't have his passport. Or a gun. The man in black, who appeared to be alone, reached inside his jacket.

Frank had not noticed the *homafaran* closing in behind the *Savak* assassin. One of them, whom Frank recognized as the silent, heavy-set weight lifter from the gym, had grabbed the man in black from behind just as he reached into his open jacket. He and a second *homafar* pulled the jacket down over the hooded man's right arm and the stump that ended just above his left elbow. With the concealing hood pulled back, the man ducked his head. Frank still could not see his face.

Sa'id slid into position directly in front of the man. Holding his G3 in one hand, jutting it into the man's stomach, with the other he removed the metallic M61 machine pistol from its shoulder holster. It had happened very quickly, noticed by only a few people. The Americans who witnessed the scene stood openmouthed. The Iranians looked away and backed off.

The two *homafaran* who had grabbed the man kicked his legs out from under him. Sa'id yanked the man's hair and forced his head up till he looked directly at Frank. The man spat, and Frank studied his burning, bloodshot eyes, nose hooked like a scimitar, and dark, bearded face, sure that someday, somewhere he would see this man again. The arms of the two *homafaran* formed a yoke, wrapped through the man's armpits and around the back of his neck, where each man clasped the wrist of the other. It was only as they trundled him out of the waiting area through a side door, with Sa'id leading the way, that Frank noticed Anwar following, with his G3 leveled at the man's back.

No one turned to acknowledge Frank. No one had spoken to him.


Twenty minutes later, lugging his luggage, he approached the banshee backs of the howling mob at what he took to be the ticket counter. He thought of Teasdale. Not a bad way to travel. Sedated. Probably driven out onto the tarmac. Propped up in a first-class seat with a solicitous doctor at his side. Guardian angels like Rocky and Cantwell to watch over him. His luggage whisked through customs by someone else. His passport given a peremptory check. He even gets to fly to Rome and enjoy the mild weather. I fly to Frankfurt and a German winter.

A fatalistic instinct overtook him. He set his suitcase on its end and sat. The plane won't take off without you, he told himself. No need to kill a fellow American, one of our own. Or get killed. He'd just encountered death. And lived through it. The crowd will thin. I'll present my ticket and retrieve my passport. I hope.

"You owe me." He turned to see Stan Rushmore looming above him. He wore the tweed jacket he'd had on the day they'd met. Frank noticed Rushmore had managed to button it. I guess I'm not the only one who lost weight, he thought. He stood and shook Rushmore's hand.

"Now what have you done for me?"

"I got your passport." He reached into his jacket and pulled out several blue-bound American passports. He thumbed through them. "Here you go. Francis Xavier Sullivan. I love that Xavier. Good Jebbie military school on Sixteenth Street. Remember it?"

"Yeah, I do, but how'd you get this?"

"The usual way. I spread some dollars around. Rocky thought we oughta make good use of some of the station's excess, rather than just burnin' it all. I know a Pan Am guy helps us out."

"What about checking in?" said Frank, suddenly remembering the Aeroflot guy who helped out the GRU. And Belinsky.

"No problem," said Rushmore. "I'll take you around and my guy'll stamp your ticket. I took care of your buddy Simpson a while ago. Come on."

Frank followed him around the ticket counter. Rushmore nodded to two armed Iranians who stepped back and let them pass. "I spread some spare *rials* around, too. Gimme your ticket. Oh, and your suitcase. My buddy'll check it through. Wait here." Frank watched him disappear through a door behind the ticket counter. He returned in less than a minute.

"Everything should be so easy. Here you go. Passport. Exit visa. Luggage receipt. Ticket."

"Seat assignment?"

"Catch-as-catch-can. Except for us who got assigned to ridin' nursemaid on your friend the defective radio man."

"How's he doing?"

"Hasn't got a care in the world. Him and the doctor, Rocky, and Cantwell all got on board already. For all the good it'll do them. Look at that mob. Be hours before we get outta here."

Frank surveyed the terminal. The noise level had climbed and tempers had shortened.

"Try to get on board early if you can," said Rushmore. "But you still got passport controls and customs to go through."

"I've been through customs."

"That was just preliminary. Make sure you weren't carrying anything into the airport you shouldn't be. Like a bomb."

"Or a poodle?"

"Like that," said Rushmore. "Khomeini damn near shut down this whole operation last night when they found idiots on yesterday's flights tryin' to hide handguns and fancy knives in their carry-on kits. Couple of wives got pulled outta here today 'cause they had some fancy Iranian jewelry on them. Lot of folks just put just about everything they own in storage. Embassy's got lists of where they stored personal effects. Cars, too. Even pets. For all the good it'll do. Idea is, when things get back to normal, embassy'll have it all shipped back home. But I think what you see out there now is as normal as this country's gonna get for a long time to come."

"I got a hunch you're right," said Frank.

"I talked to another friend of yours," said Rushmore. "Back at the embassy. Navy officer named Munair Irfani. But in civvies. Showed up at Dowshan Tappeh couple of times there near the end. Said if I saw you to let you know you might have trouble here. Guy with one arm. Wears a black jacket with the hood pulled up."

"Yeah," said Frank. "I know who he means."

"Involved in the Belinsky mess."

Frank nodded.

"The navy guy said he also warned your *homafar* buddies from the gym. See any sign of 'em?"

"Yeah," said Frank. "They helped me out."

"Anything I can do?"

Frank shook his head. "They took care of it. For now, anyhow."


Armed men searched Frank's carry-on bag at three more checkpoints. No one frisked him, and he encountered no metal detectors. Only once did the search take more than a few minutes.

"Let me see your papers," asked one of the inspectors. Young and clean shaven, the Iranian spoke excellent English with a British accent.

Frank opened the plastic packet and handed over passport, air force ID, and Iranian residency permit.

"You will not need this anymore," said the Iranian. He tossed the residency permit into a box on the floor. "You are air force?"

"Yes," said Frank.

"I also. Formerly captain, Iranian Air Force. Now I am comrade in the Islamic Air Force."

"I hope good relations continue between our countries," said Frank.

"I agree," said the former captain in his clipped tone. "We need you for spare parts."


Frank could see the door to the tarmac beyond a booth where Iranians checked passports and argued among themselves. They appeared to check each passport against names on a list. At least one man spoke English. He questioned each passenger and several times, with passport in hand, disappeared through a door beyond the booth. Each time he returned Frank expected to see someone hauled off behind the mysterious door. Instead, the questioning resumed. The process continued and the line crept forward.

Through the day he'd made a conscious effort not to look at his watch. He knew the time would pass slowly enough without constant reminders of how slowly the time passed. Now he weakened. Five after one. He estimated they had arrived at the embassy about seven, at the airport by ten. The long day promised to get longer. The line crawled. He glanced down its length and at the far end saw Bill Steele. Big as he is, thought Frank, funny I didn't see him sooner.

Frank tucked his carry-on under his arm, turned, and pushed his way through the door to the tarmac. As he approached the plane, he turned back toward the terminal. The sign remained, just as he had seen it the day he arrived.

WELCOME TO TEHRAN.

Three hours later, the plane sat where it had sat when he boarded. Bill Steele had nodded but not spoken when he walked down the aisle past Frank. He'd seen no one else he knew. Twice, armed Iranians had come through, checking passports. After the surly stewards who had staffed their Pan Am flight from Rome, he noted with pleasure that attractive stewardesses now patrolled the aisles, offering soft drinks and sympathy.

"We're all volunteers," said one who managed to find a can of seltzer for him. "But I'll tell you, if we don't get out of here soon, we may not get out of here at all. Another half hour it'll be dark. The controllers are on strike again, and after dark we can't take off without air traffic control."

"Hey, push come to get stuck, we'll just make the best of it. I'll take you out, show you the town, all the bright bonfires, hit a few discos, drink some champagne."

"Yeah, right," said the stewardess, whose name tag read CAROL. "When we do get airborne," said Carol, "you get the first drink."

"Vodka rocks," said Frank.

"You got it."

A moment later, he wondered if they would ever get airborne. Another group of gun-wielding Iranians marched through, again checking passports. The man who looked at his passport held a slip of paper. Frank caught a glimpse and read "Bill Steele."

The man returned his passport, and Frank said, *"Be-bakh-shid. Dast shoo-ii kojast?"*

Politely, the man lowered his gun and pointed to the back of the plane, enunciating slowly in Farsi what Frank took to be instructions for finding the bathroom. He edged past the man with the gun and the even more dangerous piece of paper, relieved for a moment to see Bill in an aisle seat. He paused, touched Bill on the arm, and leaned close to his ear.

"These guys have your name, Bill Steele, on a piece of paper."

Bill nodded. "I know. Rushmore tipped me."

"Your passport read William Oliver Steele?"

"Yeah. Why?"

"William Oliver doesn't look like Bill Steele. Since they're lookin' for 'Bill,' if you're lucky they won't get any further than 'William.' If you can, show the passport with your thumb over Steele."

Bill nodded, and Frank continued to the back of the plane where he found one of the lavatories unoccupied. He hadn't known his bladder had gotten so full. He peed long, zipped himself up, washed and dried his hands, and eased himself out of the bathroom. He looked down the aisle. The men with the guns had moved beyond the row where Bill sat. They edged aside to let him pass. He tapped Bill on the shoulder as he walked by.

The passport check proved to be the last. Frank heard doors closing and, according to his Timex at five-twenty-five, heard the pilot saying, "Flight crew, please prepare for takeoff. All passengers should be in their seats; seat belts fastened; trays in the upright position."

Silence greeted the announcement, as though no one quite believed it. But soon the roar of the engines rattled the plane, and the 747 began to rock down the runway. The plane climbed swiftly to clear the foothills of the Elborz, then banked, heading west, still climbing as they arced above the Zagros Mountains that rose south of Tabriz. Though near dark had fallen over the tarmac at Mehrabad, at what Frank guessed might be twenty thousand feet a blazing sunset fired the sky.

"America, America, God shed his grace on thee." The soprano voice sounded strangely familiar. Frank turned and, one seat in, two rows behind him, he saw the woman whose hysterical screams had tried to defend her silent poodle. "And crown thy good with brotherhood, from sea to shining sea." Her voice rang like a bell . . . "America, America . . ." then quavered. "We're going home, everybody. We're going home."

True to her word, the stewardess named Carol served Frank the first drink. A tray with a tall plastic cup, a single ice cube, and five miniatures of Smirnoff vodka. "I know there aren't any discos in Tehran," she said, "but I bet I can find one for us in Frankfurt."

Frank poured two miniatures into the cup and said, politely, "I'll drink to that." But I don't think so, he said to himself. His mind was on death, not dancing. He felt uncomfortable with the feelings he harbored. He had wanted to beat Teasdale to a pulp the night his hair drier set off what could have become a deadly confrontation with the armed and nervous neighborhood *komiteh* members who had stopped them. Now he wondered if the *homafaran* would kill the killer in the black hood. He admitted to himself that he hoped so. Maybe that's why I carry a death warrant back to America, he thought. He wanted to forgive and be forgiven.

But I'm guilty. Against the fear of death, he confessed to knowing the urge to kill.

"Ladies and gentlemen, this is your pilot. Let me give you the bad news first. Earlier today Frankfurt got socked with an ice storm. Conditions still sound a bit uncertain up there, but once the I-ranians cleared us for takeoff, we weren't about to delay departure for any damn thing. But we will set down en route at the U.S. Air Force base at Incirlik, Turkey." A collective groan seemed to rise from the bowels of the plane. "Frankfurt doesn't know when they'll get a run-way clear. But our idea was to get you guys outta Tay-ran come hell, high water, freezing rain, sleet, ice storms, or snowballs. So we'll set down at Incirlik, refuel, take off when we get clearance from Frankfurt, but, just in case, we'll have enough fuel so we can circle or head for somewhere else if we have to."

Out of Tehran, thought Frank, but so far headed only as far as Turkey, a next-door neighbor.

"And now, just a bit more bad news," warned the pilot's voice. "In deference to local custom, we will not serve any liquor until we have left Iranian air space . . . Like hell. The stews will pour free booze from here to Frankfurt."

Frank had expected a cheer. His fellow passengers still seemed numb. The pilot sounded disappointed. "Anyway, I'm about to begin a countdown. Ten, nine, eight, seven, six, five, four, three, two, and one. Ladies and gentlemen, you may unfasten your seat belts. We have just left Iranian air space."

The plane rocked. The numbed, pent-up emotions exploded. Men and women cheered, shouted, struggled to their feet, yelled, clapped hands, kissed, embraced.

The soprano started another chorus of "America the Beautiful." A few passengers sitting near her joined in. The song spread. No one, except the soprano, knew all the words, but soon a confused rondo echoed up and down the aisles. "Oh purple mountains majesty and amber waves of grain . . ."

He listened to the lilting soprano and thought of the ugly scene in the terminal as the Americans battled the Iranians over the caged and sedated poodle. *Nah saag,* he thought. Then, *Shah saag.* The Shah as America's lap dog. "God shed his grace on thee," sang the soprano. The lyric seemed out of joint. He struggled to remember a seldom sung verse. "America. America. God mend thy every flaw. Confirm thy soul in self-control. Thy liberty in law." The soprano did not go beyond "sea to shining sea," and those cautionary notes would not sound.

He tried not to think of the lost Shah. Or of Chatterbox, the poodle that had vanished. He sipped his vodka and thought of Lermontov. Of the mole. The *fatwa.* The dark, bearded face of the *Savak* assassin with bloodshot eyes. Long flight home. See you in America.

*February 17, 1979*